THE CIRCLE

David Poyer

ORION

First published in Great Britain in 1992 by Orion
An imprint of Orion Books Ltd
Orion House, 5 Upper St Martin's Lane, London
WC2H 9EA

Typeset by Deltatype Ltd, Ellesmere Port
Printed in England by Clays Ltd, St Ives plc

ACKNOWLEDGMENTS

Ex nihilo nihil fit. For this book, I owe much to James Allen, David Bellamy, James R. Blandford, T. P. Cruser, Carol E. W. Edwards, Kelly Fisher, Frank and Amy Green, Paul Golubovs, Vince Goodrich, Lenore Hart, Milo Hyde, Robert Kelly, Robert Kerrigan, Lloyd Lighthart, Woody Miller, H. C. Mustin, Alan Poyer, Lin Poyer, Randy Wagner, George Witte, Patriots Point Naval and Maritime Museum, and many others who gave generously of their time to contribute or criticize. All errors and deficiencies are my own.

She was tired – that old ship. Her youth was where mine is – where yours is – you fellows who listen to this yarn; and what friend would throw your years and your weariness in your face? We didn't grumble at her ... All this time of course we saw no fire.

Joseph Conrad, *Youth*

ABOUT THE AUTHOR

David Poyer graduated from the US Naval Academy at Annapolis in 1971. After serving on various destroyer- and amphibious-type ships in the Atlantic, Mediterranean, Arctic and Caribbean, he transferred to the Reserves and began writing. *The Circle* is the third volume in his novel-cycle of the modern Navy, following *The Med* and *The Gulf*. Poyer is currently attached to the Surface Warfare Development Group at Little Creek, Virginia. He lives on Virginia's Eastern Shore.

Through forty years of twilight struggle
You balanced firmness with prudence
Readiness with restraint
And gave us, at last, victory
In America's longest and most dangerous conflict.
This book is dedicated to all who served during the Cold War,
1948–1989,
To the spouses and friends who supported them,
But especially to the crews of USS *Hobson*, USS *Evans*
USS *Thresher*, USS *Scorpion*, USS *Belknap*,
And all the others, from all the services,
Who gave their lives
For the defence of their country
And the triumph of democracy.

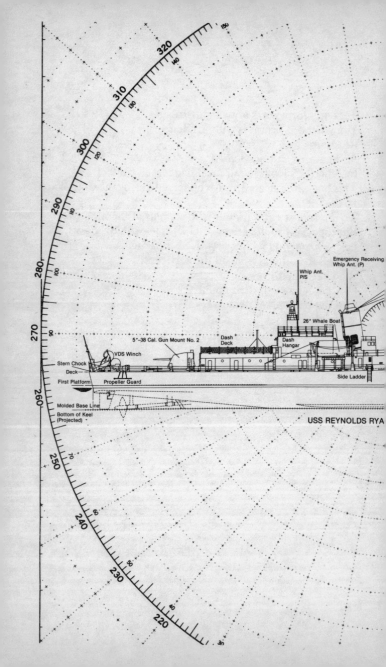

USS REYNOLDS RYA

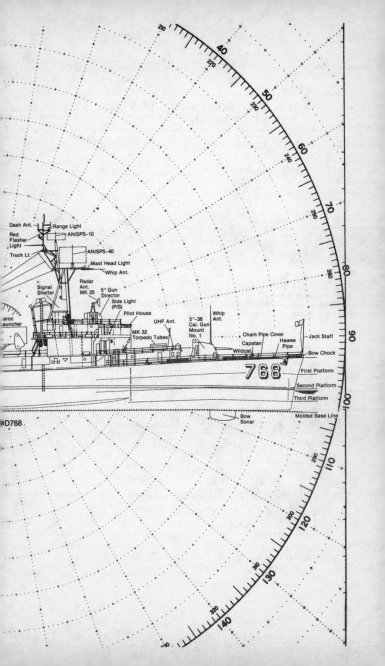

Dash Ant.
Range Light
Red Flasher Light
AN/SPS-10
Truck Lt.
AN/SPS-40
Mast Head Light
Whip Ant.
Signal Shelter
Radar Ant. MK 25
5" Gun Director
Side Light (P/S)
Pilot House
sroc auncher
MK 32 Torpedo Tubes
UHF Ant.
Whip Ant.
5"-38 Cal. Gun Mount No. 1
Chain Pipe Cover
Capstan
Jack Staff
Wildcat
Hawse Pipe
Bow Chock

768

First Platform
Second Platform
Third Platform

Bow Sonar
Molded Base Line

D768

20
40
30
50
230
60
240
70
250
80
260
90
200
110
300
120
30
130
320
140
30

THE NORTH ATLANTIC
AND NORWEGIAN SEA

GREENLAND

DAVIS STRAIT

ARCTIC CIRCLE

DENMA

HUDSON

BAY

NORTH

ATLANT

NEWFOUNDLAND

C A N A D A

50°

Gulf of
St. Lawrence

Brunswick

NOVA SCOTIA

UNITED

Newport

STATES

Norfolk

0   300   600
Nautical Miles
On 70°W between 40° and 50°N

0   300   600
Nautical Miles
On 30°W between 40° and 50°N

Prologue

The Pentagon, Washington, D.C.

Past the guard's rigid back, the buttoned holster and tailored uniform, Lenson looked down the corridor. Humming and empty, lighted so brightly the fluorescents mirrored themselves in freshly waxed green tile, it tapered into distance like a Renaissance perspective. Beyond the window at its end were thousands of white crosses. In the dying day, their shadows stretched across the snowy slopes of Arlington Cemetery.

When the court of inquiry had first convened, all the guards had looked alike to him. When it was in session, they stood at parade rest in the rear of the hearing room, motionless as monuments. When the survivors were sequestered, they posted themselves at their doors. But by now, the fourth and last day, Dan had learned to distinguish two types: big and hard-looking, and small and even harder.

The gleaming rows of tile ended at his door. The holding room was carpeted in a government gray green that would never reveal dirt, nor ever look completely clean. It held an end table and three chairs in oak and red leather. The other two were empty. The air smelled like a grove of artificial lemons. A brass clock, engraved with the name of a cruiser scrapped before he was born, clicked cadence to his heartbeat in a stillness he'd heard only once before in his life, deep in a limestone cave.

He examined his hands, twisting the heavy gold ring till the Academy crest faced him. His shoulder prickled beneath the dressings. The air was growing chill. Or am I, he thought, only imagining that it grows cold, as I watch the slow coming of night?

When he cleared his throat, the marine turned his head from the distant crosses. From the parade rest he came to attention. As he faced about, the doorway filled with six feet of service dress, garrison cap, precisely bent tie, three rows of ribbons, black Pentagon name tag, green fourragère. His eyes met the bulkhead three feet above Dan's head. They had no friendliness, no deference, no admission of relationship beyond an acknowledgment of rank so formalized it bordered on insolence. He'd met more welcoming looks from behind chain-link fences.

'Is the ensign comfortable. Sir.'

'I could use a drink of water, if you don't mind.'

The stare dropped, noted his arm, lifted again. 'The ensign knows the sergeant can't leave his post.'

'Look. The ensign has been burned. The ensign is on pain pills. The pain pills make the ensign thirsty.'

'Yes, sir,' said the marine. His face did not change. 'If the ensign is sick, or wishes to take a piss, the sergeant can accompany him to attend the men's can.'

'Never mind. I'll wait. You think – look. You people, the guards I mean, you must talk on your breaks. What's going on in there? Will they have a verdict tonight?'

'I can't say. Sir. Usually they hold court-martials over at the Annex. Or at CINC headquarters. Never seen one here before.'

When Dan said nothing more, the marine waited, then about-faced again. After 1.5 seconds at attention, he snapped back to parade rest.

Dan contemplated the rigid back until his attention wandered. He'd gulped one of the white pills at 1600 and found it hard to concentrate. He looked at the table. Three magazines lay squared across it. *Leatherneck. Proceedings of the Naval Institute. Annual Report of the Joint Chiefs of Staff.* He'd read them all twice. His cap lay cocked across the corner, its cover yellow in the artificial brilliance, the bill smudged where his fingers grasped it to take it off.

He crossed his legs again, the other way, and his eyes followed the crease of service dress blue trousers to the toe of his shoe. He'd polished them that morning at the Marriott, Susan still asleep. With one arm, it was a slow, painful process that he nevertheless cherished for its familiarity. For the achievement of a small perfection. As the layers smoothed under his blackened fingers, his image emerged as from a calming pool: long, pale face, short sandy hair, gray eyes. A wide mouth that smiled only reluctantly. When he was on the stand, he'd glanced down at them sometimes, reassuring himself.

He'd bought this pair the day he was commissioned. Now, contemplating them with the intense attention lent by a morphine derivative, he saw that beneath the gloss they were scuffed and cracked. They'd stood too many watches, absorbed too much saltwater, slammed into too many knee-knockers on *Ryan*.

Ryan. Always his thoughts came back to her. Relic of war, bride and harlot, first loved of so many in the strength of their youth; and he'd cursed her and loved her, too.

He closed his eyes, and shivered.

If only he could do it over. Climb her gangway for the first time, the future gleaming like his Academy-issue bars. Could cast off, clear of the land and its complications, ambiguities, encumbrances. Could cling to the starboard rail as a green comber boarded, as chunks of brash ice the size of scuttle-butts ground frozen paint off steel . . .

Above seventy degrees north everything had been so clear. Unequivocal as a wind like a snowman's fist, driving a man's breath back into his throat. Concrete as a fire-pump fitting, brass smooth and yellow as machined gold. Unquestionable as a hard right rudder, when a surfaced submarine looms from a midnight swirl of fog.

He'd boarded her like a boy going to his first woman. He'd gone to her in nervous eagerness, with secret dreams and secret doubt, and, like a woman, she'd fulfilled some and shattered others.

And then, outlined in fire, she'd abandoned them all.

His head sagged, and his good hand came up, shaking, to his face. From beneath the soothing of the drug, anger and regret rose like the slow loft of the ocean-dominating moon.

'What else could we have done?' he whispered.

The fading light crept across the tiles, retreating pace by pace as outside the day dimmed to night.

Alone in the ticking stillness, he stared down into a gray-green shimmer of tears.

It parted before his eyes, and became the sea.

1

THE SHIP

1

Newport, Rhode Island

Thirty feet below him the gray-green sea surged restlessly between splintered oak and painted steel. The water was murky, flecked with harbor scum. But at its surface, a thin slick of oil sliced the sunlight of a clear December morning into dancing rainbows.

Dan leaned forward, tranced by the mobile light. In that play of chance reflection, of ever-changing form, one might see suddenly and with total clarity anything, past or future, real or imagined. Might see his own face, as it would be at the hour of death.

But only for a moment, even as it, too, shattered again into that eternal dancing brilliance.

A diesel droned into life somewhere aft, and he came back to himself. Shivering in a raw wind off the Narragansett, he propped his elbows on the splinter shield, looking down the length of a *Gearing*-class destroyer, hull number 768, as she lay starboard side to Pier 2, U.S. Naval Base, Newport, Rhode Island.

It reminded him of backstage, the last minutes before the curtain rises. Sailors streamed up the gangway, some in dungarees, last-minute crates of frozen stores over their shoulders, a few still in liberty blues, toting suitcases and seabags. A forlorn-looking group of women and kids milled around at the foot of the pier. Three little girls waved to a petty officer, who blew a kiss from the stern. Engineers hauled cables and steam lines clear of the connection boxes. Seamen were unfrapping the mooring lines, triple strands of dirty nylon, as thick as a man's wrist.

'Excuse me, Ensign.'

He turned, then moved quickly aside for a middle-aged civilian in a windbreaker, a bullhorn under his arm. A slight

3

lieutenant behind him shot Dan a glance. He moved farther aft, conscious of his newness, of being in the way.

The pilot glanced down at the ruffled surface, the dancing light. His eyes narrowed. 'Wind's picking up,' he said. 'Will he want to take her out himself?'

'Always does,' said the lieutenant.

A tug coasted into position fifty yards off the port side. On the forecastle, seamen in ragged dungarees rearranged long rows of flemished line. Dan craned over the splinter shield. A heavy figure in blues was directing them, bare-headed, bald-headed, the points of his open collar fluttering in the wind. His shout floated above the rumble of the engines. 'Don't *stand* on it, Connolly, you shithead! You're gonna be screwed, blued, and tattooed, one of them fuckin' lines pulls you through a chock!'

A swarthy, broad officer with his cap tilted back strolled out of the pilothouse. Gold flashed above gray eyebrows. His eyes measured and then moved past Lenson, dismissing him in favor of the river, the tugs, the linehandlers. A different kind of chill came onto the wing with him, a crisp aura of business. An enlisted man in a peacoat followed him, adjusting a sound-powered telephone. The commander returned the lieutenant's salute.

'We ready to cast off, Mr. Norden?'

'Aye, Captain. All departments report ready to get under way.'

'Current?'

'Max ebb in an hour, sir.'

'Mr. Kerrigan, how are you this fine morning?'

'Fine, Captain. Taking her out yourself?'

'That's right, but it's nice to see you all the same. Grab some coffee and enjoy the show. Okay, Rich, let's go to sea.'

'Fo'c'sle and fantail, single up all lines. Engine room, bridge; ring up maneuvering, stand by to answer all bells,' said the lieutenant.

The talker dipped his mouth toward the phone, relaying the orders. Dan edged farther aft. Ahead, below, aft, forward, the ship was readying herself to move. The bridge was just filling with crewmen and officers, clamping on headsets,

4

adjusting binoculars, bending over charts and bearing circles. Maybe I should leave, he thought. But he didn't. He decided he'd stay till somebody ordered him below.

'Fo'c'sle and fantail report, all lines singled up, sir. Engine room answers, standing by to answer all bells.'

'Very well,' said the lieutenant. His voice was pitched just loudly enough to carry. He looked at the captain, who had clamped a pipe between his teeth. The older man nodded. 'Right hard rudder. Take in lines one through five.'

On decks below, seamen bent in unison. Six-inch samson braid slithered in through the bullnose, dripping where it had kissed the oily water.

'Stand by on six,' muttered the captain. 'You got wind, too. Ahead a touch on your port shaft.'

A narrow strip of dirty water appeared between the bow and pier. 'Port engine ahead one-third,' shouted the lieutenant into the pilothouse. Someone repeated it. A bell pinged. 'Engine room answers, port ahead one-third.'

'That's enough.'

'All stop,' shouted the lieutenant.

'All stop, aye! Engine room answers all stop.'

'Take in six.'

'Take in six. . . . Fo'c'sle, fantail report all lines taken in.'

'Very well. Rudder amidships, all ahead one-third. Bos'n, shift colors; give me one long blast.'

Through the window, he watched the helmsman flip the wheel into a blur of spokes. 'Rudder midships, aye . . . my rudder is amidships!'

The whistle let loose above them with a single note so vast thought ceased to exist. Dan had to cover his ears. No one else did. When it cut off, its echo came back from the hulls of ships and the walls of warehouses and barracks and then the hills rising beyond the piers. On the bow, a sailor hauled down the jack and tucked it under his arm.

The strip of dirty green widened between the steel sheer and the pilings, splintered and bent by generations of destroyermen. The pilot raised the bullhorn. 'Sixty-six, pick me up to starboard,' he said across the forecastle. Lenson caught the chief's face below, square, pallid, lifted to the

5

voice. He looked angry. The tug honked like a locomotive and dug her stern into the river, swung right, disappearing from sight behind the superstructure.

'All ahead two-thirds. Left ten.'

'Left ten!'

'Left ten, aye. Rudder is left ten degrees, no course given.'

Ping. Ping.. 'Engine room answers, all engines ahead two-thirds.'

Ryan began swinging, massively, like a huge, heavy, finely hinged door. Dan had a sense less of acceleration than of the parting drift of continents. A sudden burst of waving came from the pier, and thin, barely audible cries of farewell. He searched the receding faces, suddenly conscious of departure.

Susan had been incredulous when he called to tell her he was getting under way today. Incredulous, then instantly furious. He remembered anxiously how she'd said, in that level detached tone he knew meant the worst, that if he left her to have this baby alone, he'd regret it. But he'd explained, and apologized, and at last she'd said she'd try to make it down to see him off. But the pier was too distant to make anyone out now, and all the binoculars seemed to be in use. He lifted his arm self-consciously, and, after a moment, let it drop. 'Good-bye, Betts,' he whispered.

The lieutenant gave the helmsman his first course to steer. They moved past the gull gray citadels of tenders, the sleek black shark backs of submarines, the squat, chuffing tugs hove to off the piers like cops watching a parade. The channel out centered itself between the hills, flanked by rocky islets. Tug 66 came back into view, close aboard, edging in. Black smoke vomited suddenly from its stack. The hydrocarbon stink rasped his throat before the wind whipped it landward.

'Attention to port,' crackled the announcing system. A boatswain's pipe shrilled. From the corner of his eye, he gauged the men on the forecastle. They straightened wearily, formed a ragged line, hands thrust into the pockets of their jackets. Only two bothered to salute.

The pilot went below, escorted by the boatswain. The tug cast off and dropped astern as the destroyer gathered speed.

Her jack-staff bisected the circle of the world into equal halves, the sea, the hills. Then it wheeled slowly to face the channel out. 'All ahead standard,' the lieutenant shouted into the pilothouse. The lee helmsmen repeated it in a bored tone. Astern, the screw wash scummed upward in bubbling roils, lighter than the rest of the river. As *Ryan* surged forward, two wave trains formed behind her, sweeping outward toward the following shore. Her cutwater sliced the surface open with a hiss, shattering the glittering lay of morning sun into a mile-wide arrowhead of liquid topaz. A signal light clacked rapidly from the deck above.

And all at once, Dan Lenson found himself gripping the rail, sucking in icy air, wanting to shout aloud in glee and glory. He'd made it. He'd trained for four years for this. He'd pledged his youth, his ambition, and, if need be, his life.

And here you are, he thought. Graduation, commissioning, marriage, and now a kid on the way.

The exultation gave way instantly to anxiety.

It was the most enduring legacy of his childhood. When he was eight, his father had lost his place on the police force. Dan and his brothers had grown up dreading Vic Lenson's drunken anger. He'd escaped first into reading and sports, then discovered a more permanent deliverance: the Navy.

The knowledge that he had nothing else helped him endure Plebe Year and three more of the toughest engineering curriculum in the country. But even if he'd admitted his fear, he didn't know how to do anything about it. Or understand, as his roommate had told him once, that it lay at the root of his corrosive self-doubt.

The deck under his feet rose to the first long swell. He was afraid. At the same time, for the first time in his life, he felt he was where he belonged.

He'd reported aboard that same morning. Susan had needed the car, a get-acquainted visit to the Navy obstetrician, and she dropped him with his gear at Gate 17. From the hill, he could make out only a grey prickly mass, a leafless jungle of masts, booms, and antennas, and beyond it the river, fringed by ice. He showed his ID at the pass office and dragged his bags downhill, nodding to passing sailors; his hands were too full to salute back. Even when he reached the waterfront, sweating and feeling the strain in his arms, there were too many ships to tell which was his.

The pier guard directed him to an abused-looking structure of cracked concrete supported by tarred wood pilings. Ships lined it on either side. It smelled of oil, dead crabs, leaking steam, and garbage. He stared around as he picked his way past radar vans and generator carts, stumbling over vipers' nests of cables and hoses. Engines rumbled. Tractors grunted past him, towing dollies of crates and drums. Bells trilled and he watched a gun mount elevate. A mechanical arm lifted a missile canister like an offering.

He was examining a minesweeper when he noticed men looking down at him from its bridge. Faint laughter reached him over the clatter of an air-driven chipper. He flushed, dropping his eyes, and went on.

He had a sudden vision of himself from their perspective: an awkwardly tall, painfully thin young man in a new double-breasted blue bridge coat. He straightened a little. The single gold stripe and star on his shoulderboards were embarrassingly bright. To hell with them, he told himself.

When he saw the numbers 768 ahead, he stopped. The end of the pier, naturally. He settled the bags to the concrete and stretched, shaking fatigue from his shoulders. The wind from the river numbed his cheeks and ears. He followed the delicate balancing of a gull, narrowing his eyes against the winter sun.

He knew already he'd always remember this. Along with the moment of birth, so dimly recalled; the morning he reported to Annapolis; the first time he'd lifted his face from Susan's, and kissed away the painful tears. The times of beginning, which would define the way he knew and saw himself forever.

Trying to quell his nerves, he slid his eyes slowly along the length of his first ship.

USS *Reynolds Ryan* was one of four *Gearing*-class destroyers left in the Fleet. She'd had a hundred sisters, but their keels lay now on sea bottoms across the Pacific and

8

scrapyards across the world. She was built low and narrow, with a long sweep of main deck rising to a steep, slightly flared Atlantic bow. Next to the modern destroyers, she seemed small, old, and crammed with gear. But to his eyes, she still had the deadly grace of that most beautiful of all things hewn by man from the fabric of earth, a ship of war.

She was stern to him now and he saw with surprise that her main deck was barely five feet above the water. Her sides looked corrugated. The seas of decades had hammered in the thin shell plating between her ribs and stringers.

He wiped his palms on his coat and bent to dig out his orders. He took several deep breaths, staring at the river. He glanced at his hands again. The trembling had lessened, though the square knot in his stomach remained. He picked up his gear and forced himself into motion again.

As he covered the last few yards, his B-4 bag punching his legs, 768's warlike rakishness gave way to the signs of age and hard use. Rust streaked her side. Filthy water pulsed from a slime-encrusted overboard discharge. Her haze gray was patched with blue and orange primer. Steam leaked from the pierside connections in a hissing mist. He kneed his burdens ahead of him up the gangplank, into the fog.

For a moment he was alone, like a aviator in clouds. Icy droplets brushed his face. The steel grating was slick, and the hard leather soles of his new shoes suddenly went out from under him. He caught himself on the handrail, nearly losing the envelope into the scummy water.

Then he came out of the steam into clear air, stepped down, and was aboard. She was moving slightly, even alongside the pier. He dropped his gear with a grunt, lifted his arm to a wind-gnawed flag, then turned to salute the watch.

There was no one there. He held the salute, peering about. There was supposed to be someone on the quarterdeck. No one had ever told him what to do if there wasn't.

'Uh . . . anybody home?' It sounded silly, and he was instantly sorry he'd said it.

A face peered round the deckhouse, followed a moment later by the rest of a third-class petty officer in blues too big for him. He threw Lenson a casual salute, his mouth moving.

Dan dropped his hand, uncertain again. There was supposed to be an officer, a chief at least, in charge on deck.

'Permission to come aboard?'

'Sure thing. Help you, buddy?'

'I'm reporting aboard. Midshipman – I mean, Ensign Lenson.' He held out the envelope. 'My orders.'

'Just a minute.'

The petty officer disappeared. Dan stared round the quarter-deck, a narrow gap between the after five-inch mount, the lifelines, and the gangway. Steam blew between him and the shore. the wind skidded things past his new shoes. Cigarette butts. An Oh Henry wrapper. A Styrofoam cup with a peace symbol drawn on it. The nonskid decking curled under his feet, showing gray paint turning to chalk, salt stains, steel speckled with rust.

He was examining a ship's bell green as the Statue of Liberty when the sailor came back. 'Exec says for you to go on up to his stateroom.'

'Where's that?'

'Forward along the main deck, last door, around the handling room, port side.'

He hesitated. They'd told him that when an officer reported aboard, his bags should be carried for him. It was supposed to make the right impression. But the sailor was staring out across the bay. He made no move to help. In fact, it looked as if he'd forgotten Dan's existence.

'Say. How about taking care of my bags?'

'No problem,' said the petty officer. The motion of his mouth was gum, Dan saw. 'I'll keep an eye on 'em. You can come back for 'em after you see Commander Bryce. Shit! This wind's a mother, ain't it?' He went around the corner again, leaving Dan alone.

Okay, he thought, so the real Navy's not like what they told you at Annapolis. You knew that, anyway. Right? Right. He picked up his bags and struggled forward with them.

He undogged the door and found himself in darkness. His B-4 snagged on blackout curtains. When he got it free, the miniature maze led out onto a narrow passageway, hot, humid, grimy, and so low his cap scraped the pipes that covered the overhead. It smelled of fried food and oil and roach spray. The air grew even hotter as he battled his way forward, shoving his bags ahead of him.

When he came to the tarnished plaque that read XO, he set his bags down, wiped his forehead, and tucked his cap under his arm. He checked his uniform and knocked. Then opened the door, took two steps in, and came to attention. 'Ensign Daniel Lenson, sir, reporting for duty.'

'Lenson?' A heavy man in his midforties looked up from a foldout desk. He was in long-sleeved cotton khakis, not blues, and for a moment Dan wondered whether he himself was in the wrong uniform. But no, he'd seen men in blues on the other ships he'd passed. Gold oak leaves gleamed at the XO's opened collar. Dark patches showing at his neck and under his arms. He held out a damp, soft hand without rising. 'Commander Bryce, executive officer. Welcome aboard.'

'Thank you, sir.'

'Sit down. Take your coat off. Coffee?'

'Thank you, sir.'

'Help yourself. Pot's over there.'

Dan valved coffee from an urn and spooned sugar and cream substitute from battered silver cruets. The air in the tiny compartment was close and hot after the December dawn. His spoon rattled on the saucer. Take it *easy*, he told himself, breathing deeply again. He eased himself down on a leather settee, balancing the cup and saucer on his thigh.

Bryce had bent his head to the papers, smiling down at them as if they contained delicious secrets. Dan could see his scalp through the sparse veil combed over it. He sipped, letting his eyes wander. The stateroom was cramped to the point of claustrophobia. Steel desk, steel chair, wall locker, a door that must lead to a head. He guessed that the settee converted to a bunk. The bulkheads were green. The only things on them were a rack of pubs, a metal locked box, and Bryce's cap. His eyes came back to the XO, to find him smiling at him again. Dan smiled back uneasily.

'So, you're one of these Annapolis men, eh?'

'Yes, sir.'

'Worked my way up from a right-arm rate myself. No, up

from a red clay farm, studyin' the south end of a mule.' Bryce looked to the side, his jowls quivering around a chuckle. Then the eyes returned, small and black and suspicious. 'This where I'm supposed to ask you what sports you played, that so?'

'Uh – track and lacrosse, mostly, sir. A little tennis. Some fencing.'

'Uh-huh, real Joe College, eh? Understand you didn't have all smooth sailing down there, though.'

Dan set the cup carefully on its blue-rimmed saucer. Perspiration prickled his face. What was Bryce hinting at? He'd earned his share of demerits, sure. Caught out after taps, squeaked by on aptitude, bucketed a couple of semesters of calculus. He was no high greaser, but few of them went to destroyers; they flew, or joined Rickover's whiz-kid nuclear Navy. Could he mean Susan? Or that business with Davis, in 17th Company? Was that his Academy record Bryce was looking at?

'A little,' he said carefully. 'Nothing out of the ordinary, sir.'

'You went to damage-control and gunnery schools en route here, correct?'

'Yes, sir. They were good; I learned a lot.'

'Sounds like you from up north.'

'Pennsylvania, sir.'

'From Georgia myself. Biggest state in the Union east of the Mississippi. Know that?'

'No, sir.'

'So, just get into town?'

'Yes, sir, movers got here yesterday.'

'Married?'

'Yes, sir.'

'Long?'

'Six months, sir.'

'Oh my.' The exec's eyes sought the overhead. 'You'll be glad to get to sea, build up your strength again. Cigarette?'

'No thank you, sir.'

'Don't smoke?'

'Maybe a cigar once in a while, sir.'

'A cigar?' The eyebrows rose; the smile became intimate. 'Open that drawer. No, to the right. Push the button; it'll unlock.'

The box held a dozen black coronas. He didn't want one, but it seemed impolitic to refuse. He took one at random and bent it to the smoky flare of the XO's Zippo.

The first puff filled his mouth with dead mice, old socks, and gasoline. 'How you like that? Pretty good?' said Bryce, scorching the end of a Camel.

Through instantaneous nausea, Dan said, 'Is this Georgia tobacco, sir?'

The exec squinted at him. 'What? No! Jamaica. Nigger come aboard in Ocho Rios with a case of those for the wardroom. So, you know all the right forks to use, that right?'

'I guess so, sir. Just start from the outside and work in.'

'That the trick? Always wondered about that. They still handin' out that duty, honor, country stuff?'

'I guess so, sir,' he said again. He was trying not to inhale any more of the smoke. 'There's still an honor code, and all that.'

'Things aren't that cut-and-dried in real life, my friend. Get a few years on you, you'll realize that.'

'Well, it sounds good to me, sir,' he said. They looked at each other.

Bryce glanced at his watch, became brisk. 'Well, I'm going to have to cut this short. I see you brought your gear. That's good. We're getting under way at oh-nine hundred.'

'Today?' He sat up, dropping ash into his coffee.

'Yeah. At-sea trial for the VDS fish. Our playmate's out there waiting. Hope your wife's settled in. Might want to call her before we cast off.'

Dan stared at the cigar. It burned with little pops and sputters. Betts would be pissed. She was anything but 'settled in'; the duplex was three boxes deep in books, clothes, old furniture her parents had given them disassembled. And what were 'VDS fish' and 'playmates'? 'How long, uh, will we be out, sir?'

'Three weeks's my guess. Week up, a week operating, one week back. Slated to be back by Christmas. But it's elastic.'

Bryce waved away a month with his cigarette. 'Anyway, about your billet – you bring your orders?'

'Here, sir.'

'I know they assigned you as gunnery officer, but the CO and I talked it over, and we're going to break you in as first lieutenant instead. Deck gang, bo'sn's mates. We had a jaygee there, but he ran afoul of somebody's husband over in base housing and the legal beagles have got him deep-dished. Rather than move another man over, we'll leave Ohlmeyer as Guns and plug you into First Division. Any problems with that?'

'No, sir. Sir, I hoped I'd get some navigating experience, I – '

'All our junior officers navigate. You'll get enough time on the bridge, if that's that you want – Dick?'

'Dan, sir.'

'Dan. Daniel Lenson.' Bryce gave him an odd glance; it might have been suspicion, but then he seemed to dismiss it. 'We're standing one in three now. I'll tell Evlin to put you on tonight as jay-oh-dee. Jimmy John, that's Captain Packer, believes in shaking his ensigns down fast as they can take in slack. You're a Boat School type, I expect you to shine from day one. And if you don't, well, let's just say you won't be spending many evenings with that hot new wife. Understood?'

'Yes, sir. I'll do my best.'

Bryce nodded. He lifted his voice. 'Hey, 'Fredo!'

Steps sounded outside the door. 'Sah?'

'New boy here. Fix him up in Mr. Sullivan's bunk.'

'Mistah Sully, he be back?'

'No. If he's got any laundry, bring it here; I'll take care of it.'

'Sah.' The door banged shut at the same moment something squealed in the room, loud, like a small animal being hurt. Bryce's hand found a telephone under the desk. 'XO,' he said. 'Yes. Yes. Aye, sir. Be right up.'

When he hung up. Bryce sighed. He flicked the lighter open and closed. 'So. Followed Mabalacat. He'll show you your room and issue your linen. Report to the bridge when sea and anchor detail goes. Your department head's name's

Norden. He's a Yankee, too. And a . . . anyway, you'll see him on the bridge.'

'Thank you, sir.' He waited a moment, then stood. 'I'm glad to be aboard, sir.'

'Good to have you.' Bryce shook hands quickly and stubbed the cigarette out in a brass shell base. When he stood, his belly strained over his belt. He banged the door open and motioned Lenson out.

In the passageway, Dan slipped the cigar into a butt kit. He and his roommate had smoked a pack of Wolf Brothers once to kill the Severn mosquitoes, and gotten sick as dogs. This was worse. The back of his tongue tasted like sandpaper basted in creosote.

'Sah? This way to room.'

He stood beside his luggage, watching the steward's retreating back. Again he thought, They told me to insist on service. But they'd told him not to make threats to subordinates, too, and what Bryce had said sounded very much like a threat. Well, maybe he was being too sensitive his first day aboard.

He picked up the bags and followed the Filipino aft, into heat that, incredibly, kept increasing. Hell, he thought. Under way today. Under way *today!*

How was he going to break this to Susan?

And now past the moving destroyer slid the snow-coated rocks of The Dumplings, the low hills of Fort Adams, the bare prickle of trees above granite. The land was so close, it seemed he could spit to it. Somewhere to the east was fashionable Newport, the mansions of turn-of-the-century Vanderbilts and Oelrichs. But he couldn't see them from here. Ahead stretched the river, green-white and cold-looking, broken by a two-foot chop. The channel was broad as a thirty-lane highway, its edges marked by two lines of buoys – red to port, black to starboard. He watched one slide past. It was bigger than he'd thought, easily eight feet in diameter. Its steel side was hairy with barnacles.

Wedging himself into a corner, he listened to the litany of the piloting team.

'Navigator recommends steer two-two-zero.'

'Come left to two-two-zero.'

'Two-two-zero, aye! My rudder is left, coming to two-two-zero.'

'Very well. Quartermaster, got a set and drift yet?'

'Tide's behind us, sir. About a knot and a half.'

Ryan's bridge was thirty feet wide and ten deep. It was crammed with radar consoles, helm, engine-order telegraph, plotting table. Two leather chairs grew from pedestals to the left and right. Neither was occupied at the moment. In the space left over, a dozen men stood shoulder-to-shoulder or bent over gear. Officers in khakis or blues and foul-weather jackets. Enlisted men in dungarees, some neat and new, more shabby and faded. Most wore blue ball caps, though one had on the traditional white sailor hat. Two of the windows were latched up. The cold, bright wind blew steadily in through them. *Ryan* slid down the river like a Lincoln on a new highway. The steady vibration of her turbines tickled the soles of his feet. He leaned against a bulkhead, feeling raw tactile pleasure as knobs and levers dug into his back.

The lieutenant who'd given the course order – the officer of the deck, he assumed – stood in the center of the pilothouse, just ahead of the helm. Short blond hair stuck up around the edges of his cap. He was staring forward through a pair of heavy binoculars. His hands were deeply freckled, the deepest Dan had ever seen, giving the effect of countershading. Against it, a green stone sparkled in a silver-toned class ring. His slight shoulders were relaxed into the glasses, hips thrust forward. Dan had a moment of envy. He knew the basics of what was going on, but it was different from Tactics class, different from cruising around the Severn in Yard Patrol craft, making believe.

He was thinking this when the lieutenant turned to the man at the wheel. His pale blue eyes were overlaid with annoyance. 'Mind your helm, Coffey.'

'Am, sir. Seems sloppy.'

'Doesn't respond?'

'Some kind of give in it. Like it ain't hooking up right.'

'You on the port system?'

'Port pump, port synchro.'

'Shift to starboard.'

'Shift steering to starboard, aye.' The helmsman bent, flipped switches, straightened. He grasped the wheel again and a puzzled expression took his face. He moved it right, then left.

'Lost steering!'

The OOD had his glasses halfway to his face. 'Shift back to port system,' he said instantly. 'Fo'c'sle, prepare anchor for letting go. Jay-oh-dee, take a look astern, see if there's anybody coming up the channel. Chief, how much water to starboard, beyond the buoys? You' – he pointed to Dan, who flinched – 'crank twelve, get an auxiliaryman up here right now.'

The bridge exploded into activity. The captain came in from the wing, lips compressed. Dan found a sound-powered phone on the bulkhead behind him. As he spun the crank, three men began shouting at once.

'Fo'c'sle reports ready for letting go!'

'You have two hundred yards to shoal water to right of the channel, over a mile to the left.'

'Port pump on. Rudder still doesn't respond!'

'Freighter up channel, coming around the point. Maybe a mile back.'

The lieutenant reached above his head without looking. 'All engines stop,' he said, and pushed a button twice.

'After steering answers.'

'Engine room answers, all stop.'

'Sir,' said Dan, 'the auxiliaryman's on his way.'

'Very well,' said the lieutenant, speaking rapidly yet calmly, still looking ahead. The captain stood beside him, his pipe in his hand. 'After steering, steer by indicator. Helmsman, indicate left standard rudder.'

'Indicate left standard, aye.'

'Is she answering? We have a buoy ahead, Mr. Norden. Have you shifted the control aft?'

'Yes sir, just shifted.'

'You should have called me.'

'Yes, sir. Sorry, sir.'

Dan could see the buoy clearly. It was perhaps a quarter mile ahead. *Ryan* coasted toward it, driven through the water by momentum even though its screws were slowing. The bridge was so quiet, he could hear the gulls screaming as they rose from the black steel of their resting place.

'After steering says, she's not answering.'

The captain had his mouth open, but the lieutenant was already in speech. 'Port engine back full. Starboard engine ahead full.'

'Port engine back full, aye! Starboard engine ahead full,' aye! Engine room answers, port back, starboard ahead full!'

'Very well. What's the freighter doing?'

'Still bearing down on us, sir.'

Norden reached up again. The horn ripped through their ears. One long blast. Another short. Another short. He was talking on the intercom as the last blast died. 'Signal Bridge, OOD. Hoist "not under command" as soon as possible.'

'Signal Bridge, aye.'

The deck shuddered. The buoy disappeared beneath the rise of the bow. The ship began to pivot, twisted by her opposed screws, but very slowly. The bridge was silent. A ship's horn droned somewhere astern, three long blasts, the tone deeper than theirs. Dan tensed, waiting for the collision.

The buoy appeared to starboard and walked down the side of the ship about twenty yards off. Sea-gull scat stained the rusty sides. It moved heavily, thrusting itself in and out of the sea as it heaved on its submerged chain.

'Straighten her out now, damn it,' said the captain in a low voice.

'All engines, ahead one-third.'

The engine-order telegraph pinged as the lee helmsman racked the handles back and forward. 'All engines, ahead one-third. Engine room answers, ahead one-third.'

'Where's the goddamn freighter?'

'Coming up the port side, Captain.'

The merchant came into view, crowding the line of red buoys. It swept by them, an orange cliff of hull, stacks of containers, haze whipping off her stack. A tiny figure in a yellow windbreaker looked down on them. VERTICORE,

18

PANAMA CITY, read the stern. 'He didn't slow much,' said Lieutenant Norden.

'It'd cost him money,' said Captain Packer. 'I bet he never backed one rpm, the bastard.'

'Sir!'

'What?' said both men at once.

'I think – I have steering back, on the port pump.'

'Test it,' snapped Norden.

The sailor whipped the wheel left and right, arms bulging under rolled-up denim, studying the rudder indicator. 'Helm answers, sir.'

'Steer two-one-zero.'

'Two-one-zero, aye.'

The destroyer rolled to the freighter's bow wave. The men braced themselves against gear, some reaching up to a brass rail that ran the width of the bridge.

The captain ignored the motion, riding it out on wide-planted legs. Dan's first impression of him, on the wing, had been of imperturbability. He observed the captain closely now, from the side.

James Packer was of moderate height, no more than forty. Under crisply pressed khaki, his chest and shoulders were those of a stevedore or truck driver, one who earned bread by heavy work. Under the gold-crusted visor his face thrust forward from forehead to jaw, with prominent, almost Indian cheekbones, gray eyebrows above round ridges of brow, wide angry mouth. Dan saw now that the impassivity of his first impression was a mistake – or a mask. Something less indurate was showing now.

His teeth clamped on the stem of a short pipe, fists clenched, Packer was scowling after the receding stern of the freighter.

He turned his head a moment later, searching for some instrument on the bulkhead, and saw Dan watching him. Both men dropped their eyes. Dan felt embarrassed, as if he was watching a man wake from a sleep he had every right to think unobserved.

Packer stayed out on the wing the rest of the way out the channel. When the sea buoy fell astern, he went below.

Norden took off his hat the moment the skipper left the bridge. Most of the enlisted did the same. He blew out and grinned across the pilothouse at Dan. 'Almost put the fenders over for that one.'

'You did all right, I thought.'

'Like they say, as long as you remember port's left and starboard's right, it's not that hard to drive a ship. Something's wrong with that frigging steering. But the skipper says there's no way he's putting out a fail-to-sail report. . . . You our new ensign?'

'Yes, sir.'

'Come on up here, get acquainted. Mark, you ready to take her?' A black-bearded jaygee elbowed himelf off the radar console. 'Mr. Silver has the conn,' Norden announced.

The helmsman and lee helm carried on by rote, chanting out their course and speed. Norden stepped aside. Up close, Dan saw that his chin bristled with pale stubble. He was six inches shorter than Lenson. As they shook hands, he kept an eye on the sea. The slight-boned hand was strong. 'I'm Rich Norden. Weapons officer. You'll be working for me as first lieutenant.'

'Yes sir, that's what I understand from the XO.'

'You met him already?'

'Yes, sir, in his stateroom, just before we uh, cast off and got under way.'

It sounded a little too salty to Dan, but Norden just said, 'He sucker you into one of his cigars?'

'Oh . . . yeah. I can still taste it, in fact.'

'Those things are probably old as this ship. At least as old as the exec.'

'Yeah, they didn't seem too fresh.'

'Met the skipper?'

'Not officially.'

'You ought to pretty quick, not go wandering around his ship like the horse with no name.' Before Dan could reply, he had spun a crank; something squawked beneath their feet. 'Cap'n, Lieutenant Norden here. We got a new ensign waitin' to meet you.'

Pause. Dan looked out over the bow. Plowing steadily

20

ahead at fifteen knots, the destroyer was emerging from the embracing hills into a wide bay. At its far end, sparkling with sunlight off deep blue, the jagged rim of the open Atlantic underlined the sky.

Norden clanged the handset into its holder. 'He's got some kind of manual to read. Say's he'll catch you later today.' He craned his neck to check the gyrocompass, then relaxed again. Silver was by the chart table, muttering in his beard to the equally hirsute quartermaster chief.

'So, they told you much about this cruise?'

'Not much, sir.'

'Call me Rich. Except on watch, and in front of the enlisted. Well, we're out for three, four weeks, going to test the widget. You seen it? On the stern?'

'I didn't notice anything special.'

'Yeah, there's a lot of shit on deck first time you see us, I guess. It's new. Close-hold information: a towed body on eight hundred feet of cable. Gets down under the thermo layer, where the subs hide. We're going up north of the Arctic Circle, give it a workout under operating conditions. Know much about sonar?'

'Not much.'

'Better learn. We do a lot of antisub work.' His eyes tightened, the first crow tracks incongruous above the freckled cheeks of a boy. 'But it gets harder for her every year.'

'What do you mean?'

Norden's answer was to draw his lips back in a grimace. After a moment, he glanced at Silver, who had his head up again, and jerked his thumb toward the wing.

In the sun, it was almost warm. Norden pushed back his cap and rubbed his forehead. The freckles ended at his cheeks and nose; the cap band left a red line on fair skin. 'Look at that,' he said, lifting his chin at the horizon.

They were leaving the land behind. Its forested and rocky arms were flung wide, like a woman releasing a dove. Distance had softened pine green and earth brown to the hazy blue of a Turner. The old ship creaked, nodding to a ground swell. From time to time it rolled a few degrees, just enough to make their shadows lean on the wooden grid of the deck. The stacks breathed with a muffled roar, jetting a whiskey-colored haze. On the forecastle, chipping hammers clanged, slow, deliberate, like picks against stone. From aft came a warning bell, faint and trivial against the immensity of sea and sky.

'You supersititious?' Norden asked him.

'Me? I guess not.'

The weapons officer groped in his pocked, then leaned over the splinter shield. The coin spun free of his thumb, twinkling in the sun, and they watched the glint arc out and down. Dan watched it sink for a long time beneath clear blue, winking like a star, before the white roar of the bow wave swept over it.

'Sailors used to offer silver to Poseidon at the beginning of a voyage.'

'You believe in that?'

'Believe? Hell no, I'm a devout atheist.'

'I get it.' Lenson looked back at the land, thinking that those men, too, had left behind expectant wives, babies, and not for weeks. For years, in ships a quarter the length of this one. In his pocket, his fingers touched a milled edge. He took it out, drew back his arm, and threw.

Tradition ... yet he lived in an age of contempt for whatever had endured. The Academy had cast him in a mold honored by time. But sometimes he wondered whether the alloy had changed.

He saw the coin moved outward, and for a moment saw it simultaneously in four different ways. It was a gift to the gods, in whom he did not believe. It was a link to the men who'd blazed the road he traveled now. It was a remnant of primitive neurosis, a sop to forces that heeded no curse or prayer. And at the same time, he saw simply a moving mass losing its horizontal acceleration component as gravity took hold, bending its world line like a fishing rod.

It met the sea, and he could not tell which way of seeing was the truth, or even closest to it.

'What did you mean, Rich?'

'About what?'

'You started to say something about the ship.'

'Oh, that.' Norden shook his head. 'Let's talk about it later. There anything I can help you with personally, get you started off right?'

'Uh – how about uniforms? I notice they're kind of mixed – '

'That's because we were getting under way. In port, it's generally winter blue, the blue shirt and tie. Under way, we wear wash khakis, long sleeves, open collar. Where we're going, you might want to wear blues on watch just 'cause they're warmer. Is your stateroom okay? Where have they got you?'

'A little place back aft. Three other bunks in it.'

'That's Boy's Town. Junior officer bunkroom. Only seniority or death gets you out of there.'

Dan looked at him sidewise. His department head had lifted his closed eyes to the cold sun. He envied Norden's air of mastery. He remembered how swiftly and correctly he'd maneuvered when the steering went out, all the things he'd borne in mind and anticipated. Yet he was friendly, easy to talk to. He suddenly felt hopeful. Norden would take care of him.

'Norden – that sounds familiar. Isn't there a trophy at the Academy – '

'Yeah, the Norden Cup. Best essay on tactics.'

'And an Admiral Norden – '

'Been a couple of them. First one was my great-grandfather. Spanish-American War. None of that goes down too good with our worthy exec.'

'Commander Bryce doesn't seem to like Academy guys much.'

'You caught that?'

'He made it real easy to pick up on.'

'Fortunately, we're not alone. There's a sizable class of people in there with us. But I think this is what principally hacks him off at me.'

Dan studied the picture. A fair, rather aloof-looking young woman; Norden, grinning, in a sports jacket and tie; an older child, a boy, fair-haired like his parents; a baby. They were all smiling. The baby was brown. 'Lin and I just adopted her. Gabriela. She's Mexican. Cute, huh?'

'She's a sweetheart.'

'Never thought I'd sign up for two of 'em. But having a family changes a lot of things. Having someone else to live for, not just yourself.'

He was about to ask Norden what exactly it changed when the 1MC said, 'Now secure the special sea detail. Set the normal underway watch. On deck, Watch Section One.'

'About time.' Norden set his cap again. 'Let's get me relieved, then we'll give you the fifty-cent tour.'

With a last look at the receding shore, Dan followed him inside.

2

They clattered down the outside ladder from the pilothouse.

'What've you seen so far?' Norden called back.

'Just the XO's office, the bunkroom, and the bridge.'

'I'll give you a thorough look at her, then. Know much about this class?'

'Read about it in *Jane's*, World War Two construction.'

'Uh-huh.'

He was about to say more – he'd memorized it – but the blond lieutenant had begun opening doors and talking rapidly. Radio central. Radar equipment room. Crypto room. Teletypes clattered behind closed doors. They dropped another level into a passageway so narrow, men turned to slip past them. Dan braced himself against a bulkhead as it tilted slowly. From a nest walled by filing cabinets and pigeonholes, a monklike face blinked out over the platen of a gray Royal. 'Seaman Vogelpohl,' said Norden. 'Department yeoman. Vogel, this here's our new First Div-oh.'

'Good morning, sir.'

'Pleased to meet you.'

Norden continued down the passageway, talking over his shoulder. 'They built her in Seattle in '44. She's three hundred and ninety feet long. Forty feet, ten inches beam. Twenty-two hundred fifty tons nominal displacement, thirty-five hundred full load. Crew of two hundred eighty. Two General Electric geared turbines with sixty thousand shaft horsepower from four six-hundred-pound oil-fired Babcock and Wilcox boilers. Range, three thousand miles at cruising speed. Flank speed, thirty-two and a half knots. At least when she was new.

'We got the standard four-department breakdown aboard: operations, weapons, engineering, supply. I'll introduce you to the department heads at lunch.

'Okay, our department, weapons. They built her with six five-inch guns, torpedo tubes, forty and twenty-millimeter, but that's changed over the years. We got four five-inchers left, torpedoes, and the Asroc – antisubmarine rockets, that's the box launcher between the stacks. The pad aft was for these little radio-controlled helicopters they were playing with a few years ago, bu they didn't work out. Kept flying off over the horizon and nobody ever saw them again.'

'They must have been smaller then.'

'Helicopters?'

'The crew.' Dan looked at the overhead, noting the crust of cracked paint and painted dirt on the foot-thick bundles of cable that lined it. 'Everything's so cramped.'

'You get used to it. But you're right, it isn't as roomy as the new destroyers.'

'Was she in the Pacific?'

'Okinawa. Caught a kamikaze on the stern. It took the cap off the after stack and wiped out one of the quad forties. Killed six guys. They mothballed her when the war was over, then dragged her out again for Korea. She's been steaming ever since.'

They threaded their way past sailors lined up for haircuts, past the galley. As soon as Dan was sure he was lost, Norden hauled up a spring-loaded scuttle in the deck.

As it clamped shut above them, he caught his breath at the sudden crush of humid heat. It was like being wrapped in a blanket soaked in boiling water. Noise battered his ears. The handrail burned his palms. It led down and down, debouching at last on a slick steel grating. 'Forward fireroom,' Norden shouted over the din. 'Also known as Number One. Two boilers here, two more in the after fireroom, Number Two. You can cross-connect them to either set of turbines for split plant operations. You got all this at the Academy, right?'

Lenson had to cup his hands around his mouth. 'Some of it . . . yes, sir.'

'Then you recognize most of this.' Norden stabbed his finger rapidly around them. 'You're on what's called the boiler flat. Over there's reserve feed-water tank and fresh-water tank. On the boiler, steam drum, economizer elements, soot blower heads, safety valves, checkman's glass, et cetera. These are M-type boilers with separately fired superheaters. You'll want to memorize superheat and speed combinations: two boilers, twenty-two knots without, twenty-seven with; four boilers, twenty-eight without, thirty-two with, so on, so forth. Now for the lower level.'

Dan followed him along a shoulder-wide catwalk. He could see no relation between the diagrams he'd studied in Isherwood Hall and this roaring insanity. Some agoraphobic engineer had taken a thirty-by-forty sauna and crammed it with machinery, webbed it with dripping pipes, roofed it with I beams, and stuffed every remaining cubic inch with asbestos sheathing. The air burned his skin when he moved. Ahead of him, the lieutenant veronicaed around a steam-hissing valve stem and slid down a ladder, all one motion, his boots dangling in space until they slammed into the deck plates. He followed clumsily, feeling as if he was sinking through boiling liquid.

On either side, the boilers roared steadily, looming out of sight above. A tornado of white flame whirled behind a blue-tinted sight glass. Beneath his feet, through open steel grill-work, he could see oily wtaer eddying between deep frames as the ship rolled. A black fireman in a T-shirt cut off at armpit level twisted past, not looking at them, carrying a clipboard, flashlight, and rag. His face was closed, his knotted belly sheened with sweat.

Norden paused under a blower. The blast of air from topside was icy. Dan shivered at the sudden transition, tropical Brazil to New England winter. 'You'll qualify down here later,' the lieutenant shouted. 'Just wanted to show you Ed Talliaferro's sneak preview of hell.'

'He's the engineering officer?'

'Right. Now we're going to Number One engine room. To get there, you've got to go up to the main deck, aft in the passageway, and down again. There isn't any direct access from the other waterline spaces. That way, if she takes a hit, we might stay afloat long enough to get off a message.'

The engine room was almost as hot and even noisier. The air was murky with oil fumes and flaking insulation. Men glanced at them from a central control station, then returned their attention to gauges and handwheels. He ducked his head under pipes and barked his elbows on valves as Norden pointed out the main steam lines from the firerooms, the low- and high-pressure turbines, the main electrical switchboard, and the number-one turbogenerator, evaporator, deaerating feed tank, and main reduction gearing, along with assorted lube oil heaters, pumps, purifiers, and test stations. A spinning shaft sixteen inches thick, slick and gleaming under brilliant overheads, led out a weeping seal aft to its propeller. 'Twin screws,' he bawled into Lenson's ear over the tooth-chattering hum of gears and the *tappa-tappa* of air - compressors and the steady whispering drip of steamy water from taped-up couplings. 'And the engine rooms are com-pletely separate. They built two of everything into these. As long as we can float, we can probably limp back.'

Down another ladder, and he was lost now as he was introduced to the main condenser, two main feed pumps, and the auxiliary condenser. The lieutenant's arm traced a bronze casting like an oak growing up through the deck plates. 'This here's the main intake. Goes right through the bottom of the ship. Crack in this guy, engine room'd flood in about a minute.'

Dan stared. A rivulet wormed downward from what looked like a hasty solder job. He turned, checking the location of the ladder up, then, realizing Norden was watching him, jerked his eyes back. He searched a suddenly vacant skull for a question to ask. 'What's the, ah, operating pressure?'

'Of the steam plant? Standard. Six hundred pounds. Like I said.' Norden squinted at him.

'Oh. Sure.'

They climbed out of the engineering spaces, past the glances of pimpled messmen stirring soup, out onto the weather decks. He sucked cold air gratefully, looking around as Norden dogged the door behind them. He had to look hard to make out the land, now only a violet line astern. Shearwaters scaled across the waves on rigid dark wings. To the southeast, ahead, the sea was a mass of gold. *Ryan* had increased speed, slicing through light seas with a hissing burble.

The weapons officer led him forward, leaning into the wind. 'Forward five-inch mount,' he said. 'Got a new fiberglass shield on it, testing it out.'

'Right.'

The deck narrowed as they approached the bullnose. They stepped over massive chains toward the ground gear. He recognized some of it from the books. Pelican hooks, chain stoppers. The rest was just rusty iron to him.

'Okay, we get to your shit now,' Norden said. He crouched, putting the capstan between him and the wind. Dan bent, too. 'You'll be in charge up here during sea detail. You got two stockless anchors, five ton and seven ton. Five hundred fifty fathoms of chain, five-inch diameter, thirty tons breaking strain. . . . Don't you have a wheel book?'

'Uh, not yet.'

'Get one.' He pulled a green notebook from his back pocket and slapped it. 'Can't remember everything. You'll be responsible for a lot of gear. So write it down! Wildcat and brake. Electric drive, ten thousand foot-pounds of torque. . . .'

They finished the forecastle and headed aft. Dan, his head busy scrambling numbers, glanced up at the bridge as they passed beneath its windowed gaze. Someone was staring down at them. It was the captain. 'Torpedo tubes here, port and starboard,' said Norden, reclaiming his attention. 'And up there, aft of the stack, the Asroc launcher.'

'Yes, sir.'

'Boat deck to starboard. The whaleboat's yours, too.'

Dan nodded. They continued aft, under a portico formed by an overhang of the helicopter pad; Norden called it a 'Dash deck.' The weapons officer looked about with a critical eye as they passed kneeling men in dungarees and jackets. Hand irons clattered. The sailors glanced up, sweating despite the cold, then bent to work again. Norden stopped at each fire-fighting station and underway replenishment point. He pointed out corroded nozzles, frayed hoses, patches of bare primer, rusted scuppers, missing fittings. His voice edged toward reproach. It was as if, Dan thought, their condition was already his fault. His stomach tightened.

Two-thirds of the way aft, the lieutenant paused, looking over the lifeline into the sea. Then he put his foot on the scupper. Dan hesitated. You weren't supposed to lean on lifelines. After a moment, he put his hand on it, not trusting it with his weight.

'Now that you've seen her, what do you think?'

'Things look . . . worn.'

'Very diplomatic. She's a piece of junk.'

'Oh.'

'This is a wartime class. They built them to last five, ten years. They've been steaming for thirty. They put a lot of gear on the weather decks. It rusts. Even the interior spaces are going. Machinist's mate on *Ault* dropped a ball peen in the engine room and it went right through the bottom. Fortunately, they were in dry dock at the time. Everything aboard's been rebuilt fifteen, twenty times. Half the time when you order parts, the company that made them's out of business.'

'She seems to steam okay.'

'Oh, Ed does miracles down below. But she's wearing out. The main condensate pump casing cracked last year off Cape Henry. No spare for that – nobody expects a casing to crack. But metal fatigues.'

He nodded. Norden went on. 'On top of that – well, the war's been sucking cash and men to Westpac for six years. They keep saying withdrawal on the news, Vietnamization, but we're not seeing it yet. We're on a short string for operating funds. And we're undermanned – especially in the deck gang.

'I suppose the XO already told you this, but first lieutenant's no strawberry-pie billet. Not on *Ryan*. You're in charge of preservation and painting of everything topside, plus all the deck evolutions – anchoring, underway replenishment, mooring, towing, operating boats and winches. You can see the kind of shape the weather decks are in. We were supposed to get a complete blast to bare metal and repaint in the yard, but they pulled us out halfway through overhaul. Just ran out of money. The chief got a coat of red lead on the worst places, but basically we got to strip it and do the preservation ourselves before we get north of sixty.'

30

'Sixty?'

'Degrees latitude. It'll be too rough to paint after that.' Norden rubbed his chin, frowning.

'How much longer has she got?'

'What, in commission? I don't know what they're planning long-term. Squadron staff was saying when I came aboard that us and *Bordelon* – we're the only *Gearings* left on this coast – were slated for decommission and scrap. But that was two years ago.' Norden shrugged; his face darkened. 'She's like an old clunker nobody bothers to fix anymore or cares about. You just keep adding ten-weight till it craps out, then take the plates and leave it by the side of the road. Bloch, that's your boatswain's mate chief, he's good. But you're going to have to exercise leadership. We got some hard cases – guys been busted in rate, brig rats, that kind of shit. Anybody can't hack it in the other division, they shitcan them to you.'

'I see.'

'I don't mean to turn you off. We can use some youthful enthusiasm. But I want you to go in with your eyes open. You'll get a lot of sob stories from the deck apes. But our job's to keep this ship running somehow.'

'I'll do my best, sir.'

'I know that. Just wanted to give you the straight skinny.'

'I appreciate that – Rich.'

They walked aft, around the turn of the deckhouse, into a knot of shouting men. Dan caught one of the voices: '... don't got a fuckin' clue what's really going down – '

'Whoa,' said Norden into sudden silence. 'What's going on?'

'Nothing, sir,' said several voices. The shouters moved apart warily, then drifted aft. The one who remained put his fists on his hips and looked expectantly at Norden. He was the man Dan had watched on the forecastle.

'Ensign Dan Lenson, meet Boatswain's Mate Chief Harvey Bloch.'

'Pleased to meet you, Chief.'

'Welcome aboard, sir.'

Dan looked at him eye-to-eye, but height was the only dimension he matched this man in. Bloch seemed as thick as he was wide. His bare head was bald, whether naturally or shaved, Dan couldn't tell. His stomach bulged, turning the waistband of his trousers, and a nest of black hair showed at his neck. A knot of keys was clipped to his belt. He looked exhausted and angry.

'You our new division officer, sir?'

'That's what they tell me, Chief.'

'Mr. Sullivan's not coming back?'

'No, he's gone for good,' said Norden. 'He really stepped on his crank this time.'

'Too bad,' said Bloch, looking off to sea. 'I liked him.' His left hand slapped a chipping hammer into his right. It disappeared when he wrapped his fingers around it. His sleeves were rolled to his elbows. Dan stared at a blurred Betty Boop in a sailor cap, skirt lifted and bodice open, showing purple breasts larger than her head. On the other arm, a scroll – the letters too seeped and faded to read – disappeared under the sleeve.

'D'we come up with those anchor stoppers, Chief?'

'Yessir. Some dickhead storecreature sent 'em down to the snipes.'

'And did we get the pump covers, and the new garbage chute before we got under way?'

'Rousted 'em out of the tender last night.'

'Good. How about introducing Ensign Lenson here to some of his men?'

'No problem.' The chief bellowed downwind, 'First Division! Front and center! Yeah, you!'

The men he addressed the ones he'd been shouting with a few minutes before, dropped brushes into cans and ambled toward them. One straightened a paint-stained white hat; another slowly tucked in a ragged shirt. The others simply strolled up and stopped, swaying to the slow roll of the deck. 'This here's our new division officer,' said Bloch. 'Straighten up, Gonzales, for Christ's sake! That's Greenwald. Hardin. Jones. Williams. This here is Coffey. And this prize pupil is Seaman Recruit Lassard.'

The last named was older than the others. His face was handsome but spoiled by his hair. It was cut to the quick, boot camp-style. His pale hands were flecked with white paint. Seaman recruit, Dan thought. You couldn't get lower in the Navy. Most enlisted were third class, even second, at this man's age.

Lassard returned his stare with a faint, absent smile. His blue eyes were slightly bloodshot. He looked intelligent, but Dan had the feeling he wasn't really there with them, on the open fantail of USS *Ryan*, standing out to sea.

'Ay, four-oh to meet you, man,' he said softly. 'You can call him Slick. Everybody does. You Flamer's replacement?'

'Lassard, that fuckin' mouth of yours – '

'That's all right, Chief,' Dan said. It looked like a chance to establish quick rapport. He took a step forward and extended his hand. Lassard took it with the same dreamy look. Dan felt the callus, the hard muscle beneath.

The grip tightened, forcing his knuckles together. Dan hissed in surprise and pain before he remembered his father's old cop trick. When his left thumb found the paint-smeared web of Lassard's, the remote eyes widened, just a fraction, and then the seaman let go and stepped back.

'Ay, man, you got soft hands there.'

He felt something sticky on his palm, and stopped himself from wiping it on his uniform pants. His hand hurt now, but he ignored it and shook hands with the others, too, trying to match names with faces. Gonzales, short and dark, grinned and slid his feet around when he was introduced. Greenwald was thin, with a face like an accountant's unexpectedly but not without reason accused of fraud. Coffey's was rigid as carved teak, his hand dry and neutral. He wore a shoelace braided around his wrist.

'Okay, back to work,' said Bloch. The men ambled aft again. He turned to Lenson. 'The most useless set of cats' assholes in the division. No. In the ship. They call themselves the "kinnicks." '

' "Kinnicks?" '

'I don't know, and I don't care, sir. I just know I could get twice as much done around here without 'em.'

'Discipline problems? Or just lazy?'

Bloch uttered a fearsome blasphemy. 'This is the worse

division I seen in twenty-eight years in the Navy, sir. Half of 'em come in to dodge the draft. I got three new transfers – not these, these are the bright boys – Cat Five. That means IQ under eighty. You got to show them which end of a swab to hold on to. Every time. But they're not the ones give you trouble. Lieutenant here'll back me up – '

As he talked, Dan watched the men. Lassard was painting a white diamond around a pad eye. Each time he lifted his brush from the pot, he paused, staring out at the passing sea. As the paint drooled downward, the wind spun streamers of it out over the gray deck. 'Just pretend I'm not here, Chief,' said Norden. 'Give it to him straight.'

'All right.' Bloch rubbed his hand over his head. 'We got short-sheeted on the last overhaul. XO cut my budget again last month. We ain't even got enough paint – I had to cumshaw twenty gallons haze gray off a master chief on the *Sara*. I could make do if I had good men. But we're short a lot of hands, and like I say, there's major problems with the ones we got.'

'How about petty officers?'

'Two of 'em are okay. One just made third. My first-class . . .'

'What's the matter with him?'

Bloch looked at the deck but didn't answer.

'I'm just showing him around the ship now, Chief. You two can get together for record review later.'

'Well, nice meeting you, Chief.'

'Welcome aboard, sir.' Bloch hesitated. 'Don't get me wrong, sir. These old cans are the cat's nuts.'

'The what?'

'The best. We got problems, but I'd ten times rather be aboard here than the cookie tins they're building now. Aluminum! Single-screw! I done my whole career on these. When they go, that'll be time for me, too.' He turned away, leaving it unclear who had dismissed whom, and began shouting again.

Dan followed Norden forward again, catching up with him amidships. The whaleboat loomed above them, cradled in steel arms. 'He seems pretty much on top of things,' he said tentatively.

'Yeah. Bloch's good. Most of his twenty-eight's sea time, except for two years at Great Lakes pushing boots. Divorced. Lives aboard. Got a little marine surveying business he does part-time in port.'

'That about manning, and budget, that doesn't sound so good.'

'Well, don't let us gloom and doom you too much. We aren't the only ship in the fleet with problems these days. That reminds me, this is your first tour; you get to pick where you go. How come you aren't on your way to Nam?'

'We, uh, you know, choose according to class rank. When they got to me, it was this or a tanker.'

'Well, nice to know we're a notch above somebody.'

'How about you? How come you're not somebody's aide, or –'

'Or in some high-powered staff billet? My great-granddad started out on deck plates. I wanted to, too. I just told the detailer, send me where anybody of my rank and age would go if his name was Smith.' Norden grinned boyishly and slapped his shoulder. 'And they thought I was serious! Maybe next time I'll wise up! Ready for lunch?'

'Sure,' said Dan, grinning, too. Somehow he couldn't help it.

Ryan's wardroom was smaller than an average living room. It looked worn but clean. The only furniture was a threadbare couch, bolted to the deck through worn gray carpet, and a table. On the bulkhead hung an oil of a stern-looking man with high collar and rear admiral's stripes; in the background, a four-piper destroyer thrust its bow out of a malachite sea. A dozen men stood around the table, leaning on their chairs. They perked up as Norden introduced Lenson, reaching to shake his hand. 'Mark Silver you know . . . This is Ralph Weaver, the comm-oh; Ken Trachsler, damage control; Aaron Reed, sonar; Barry Ohlmeyer, guns, our bull ensign and duty bachelor; Ed Talliaferro, chief engineer; Al Evlin, operations and senior watch officer; Tom Cummings, disbursing and acting supply. You'll be relieving him as junior ensign, also known as George, also know as Shitty Little Jobs Officer. He'll get with you later about turning over the mess accounts. Right, Chow Hound?'

'Soon's we put down our forks.'

'I guess that does it except for Murphy and Johnson, and they'll be down after they're relieved.'

'Pleased to meet you all,' said Dan to the wardroom at large. Despite getting stuck with the mess treasury, a thankless job of nit-picking and bookkeeping, he felt warmed by their welcome.

'You married, Dan?'

'Yes, sir.'

'Kids?'

'First due in February.'

'Good grief.'

'She don't expect you back by then, I hope.'

'Like they say, you got to be there for laying the keel, but not for the launching.'

He grinned wordlessly and let it wash over him.

'Hey 'Fredo! Captain coming down?'

'He say he come down.'

The redheaded ensign, Dan had already lost his name, said, 'We'll give him five more minutes, then we'll – '

The forward door opened and Packer came in. The executive officer was behind him. Bryce was the only one in the room wearing a tie. Ohlmeyer ducked his head, glancing around in real or feigned embarrassment. The captain said nothing; either he hadn't heard the remark or he ignored it. He pulled out the chair at the head of the table and nodded to the assembled officers.

The table sat in a ripple movement, by seniority. Dan wedged himself into the chair at the foot, directly beneath the portrait. He had eight inches between the table and the bulkhead. When he looked up, the captain was staring at him over the silver. They were face-to-face, ten feet apart, with the others ranked on either side. 'Who's this?' asked Packer. 'Didn't I see him on the bridge?'

'This I the new man I called you about, sir. Daniel Lenson, Mr. Sullivan's replacement,' said Norden.

'Sully's not coming back?'

'No, I don't think the Flamer will rise again this time,' said Bryce, smiling.

36

'That so? Well, welcome aboard.'

'Thank you, sir.'

Packer lowered his attention to a bowl of mucky-looking stuff the steward slid in front of him. Mabalacat delivered along both sides, two plates at a time. Dan got his last. It was a spicy potato soup that tasted better than it looked. He sipped at it, glancing up furtively to observe the captain.

'Jimmy John,' Bryce called him, but Dan had a feeling no one called him that to his face. He was by no means the tallest at the table, but there was no question of his domination of it. It showed in the hushed tones the others used in the face of his silence. Now he was capless, Dan saw dark hair, but eyebrows the color of the silverware. He ate slowly, his attention on the soup. The tension he'd thought he saw on the bridge seemed to be gone.

The main course arrived. 'What's this called, 'Fredo?' said Bryce.

'Knockwurst, sah.'

'No. This.'

'Boiled cabbage, sah. You like?'

'Yes, it's tasty. Real down-home. Let me have some more of that, on the side.'

'So where you from, Dan?' said a man midway up the table. Lenson swallowed rapidly, groping for the name. Pock-marked cheeks, tired eyelids, a swatch of black hair plastered across his forehead. Talliaferro, pronounced *Tolliver*, the engineer. First names? He decided it would be okay over food. 'Pennsylvania, Ed.'

'Whereabouts? Out west? I'm from Bradford.'

'Uh, not really, it's near Philly.'

'Okay, hotshot check! You ready to take over my watch section, Lenson?' asked another man, a jaygee.

The others chuckled. He hesitated self-consciously. Should he act cocky? Confident but modest? While he was debating it, he lost his chance; the captain turned to the operations officer, Evlin. 'Al, you got the Gap Filler directive copied yet?'

The senior lieutenant dabbed at his lips with a napkin. 'It's in mimeo, Skipper. Distribute it right after lunch.'

'I want everybody familiar with it before we get to the exercise area. We can waste a lot of time up there if we screw up the runs. I want them to know it cold.'

'I'll see to that,' said Bryce, smiling around at the table.

'Was there anything else hot in that traffic they handed up before we got under way?'

'Nothing new, sir.'

'Ed, how's that port shaft sound now?'

Talliaferro shoved his plate aside. 'I think we got her in shape, sir.'

'The steering unit? And number-two generator?'

'Like I say, we got her running again. But once we clear coast-wise traffic, I'd like to kick her up to flank for an hour and get a stethoscope on a couple things.'

'Good idea. Let's combine a full-power run and crashback with a shakedown general quarters tomorrow, Ben, say around oh-nine hundred.'

'Will do, Captain,' said Bryce, looking alert and jovial.

Norden coughed into his fist. 'Could we possibly hold that till after lunch, sir? Deck division's putting fresh paint down aft. I'd like it to dry before people run through it.'

'Rope it off,' said Bryce, not waiting for Packer to answer.

'Aye, sir.' Norden glanced down the table at Dan, as if to say, I tried.

The steward raked in the empty dishes and dealt dessert: bread pudding. When the captain was done, he pushed the plate back and began packing his pipe from a leather pouch. That seemed to be a signal. The others folded their napkins and crossed silver on their plates. Mabalacat returned with coffee.

'Gentlemen, Mr. Evlin tells me he'll have the operation order for this little excursion available sometime this afternoon. Let me summarize it, just to put everybody in the picture – including our new ensign.' Packer's eyes lingered on him.

'We were pulled early from overhaul for this assignment. Squadron Ops says it was authorized at the Chief of Naval Operations level, via the type commander. *Morton*, that's the Pac-side test ship for the AN/SQS-thirty-five IVDS, reported performance degradation during cold-weather operations in the Chukchi Sea. Before COMCRUDE-SLANT signs off on a fleetwide buy, they want to check the figure of merit in heavy-sea, cold-weather operations.

'That's where we come in, as the prototype installation. We'll be heading up north of the Greenland-Iceland-UK gap to play convergence-zone ops with *Pargo*, a nuke attack boat. She'll be coming out of the Northern Fleet op area. She's up there now playing hide-and-seek with the Soviets around the Kola Peninsula. Estimated time out is three weeks, if all goes well. But I'll tell you now, much as I know everybody wants to get back to their families, doing this right has priority.

'The idea is to test the thirty-five B under the most demanding conditions any ship's likely to hit in wartime. So make sure you're ready for rough weather. If there's a storm up there, I intend to head for it, and I'll stay in it as long as I can.'

The men nodded. Packer paused. He lighted his pipe thoroughly, using a butane lighter set high, then went on. 'I had a talk with the commodore when we got these orders. He wanted to shift the fish to a newer ship. But operational demands in Southeast Asia mean the fleet's spread thin. *Dewey* and *Beary* were held over in the Med for that reason. I told him we could respond to the tasking.'

Some of the officers leaned their elbows on the table.

'So we're on line for it. It goes without saying that we aren't in the best shape for the North Atlantic in winter. However, this is the kind of mission that would be demanded of us in wartime, and I judge we can do it. If there's anyone here who disagrees, I'd like to know about it.'

No one moved. 'Well then,' said Packer, from behind a thickening smoke screen, 'we should have reasonable weather for the first few days. I want to get as much topside work done as we can. And be sure your gear's secured for sea. We can expect heavy weather and ice north of the Circle this time of year.

'Any questions?'

Men stirred, but no one spoke. Dan watched the engineering officer lift his coffee, his brows worried. He was kind of worried himself. He wasn't sure he understood what the captain was talking about. Then he thought, Well, I guess I'll find out.

'XO, anything to add?'

'Not much, sir,' said Bryce. 'So, this won't be a Caribbean cruise. But I've always said, there's nothing a crew can't overcome if they work hard and keep their cool. That shouldn't be too tough north of Iceland this time of year.'

He chuckled, but no one joined him. Mabalacat moved round the table, refreshing coffee from a battered silver server. One by one, the officers excused themselves; the captain acknowledged with a nod. Dan got up when Norden did, but on his way past, Evlin leaned his chair back to bar his passage. 'Say, Dan.'

'Yes, sir?' Some instinct warned him to be formal with the senior department head. Precise diction. Short brown hair and mustache. Wire-rimmed glasses.

'We'll be revamping the watch bill now you're here. You'll be standing junior officer of the deck. We're in three sections. You'll be in my section, which means – ' Evlin consulted his watch.

'First dog, mid,' said Norden.

'Right. You'll stand your first watch from sixteen hundred to eighteen hundred, then come on again at midnight to four.'

'Aye, sir,' he said, cheerily enough, but he felt his spirits sag. He'd been up since four; he was already tired, and it looked like a long afternoon ahead. Now what sleep he managed tonight would be broken. Disappointment struggled with eagerness and apprehension. His first underway watch. For a moment he imagined the OOD fallen, himself in charge, saving the ship.

As he followed Norden down the passageway, he stepped back, as he had on the pier, taking a moment in the midst of experience to reflect.

He'd seen *Ryan* from stem to stern, from keel to bridge. Had seen the crew in microcosm: the sailors, chief, wardroom; had been admitted for a moment into the mind of the captain. He'd felt her climates, from the roaring swelter of the engine room to the air-conditioned clatter of Radio Central, smelled fuel oil and insecticide, deck wax and electricity, men's sweat and paint. Almost three hundred men, crowded into a steel box the length of a football field but only a quarter as wide. In some eyes, he'd read dedication, competence, and respect. In others, barely repressed violence.

Ryan was not yet his. Only with work and time would he win his share in her, as crews in the old days won shares in prizes. He wasn't sure why this meant so much to him. But he knew what he wanted of USS *Reynolds Ryan*. He wanted to be tested, and to succeed. To be part of her. To belong.

'This swab locker's yours,' said Norden, banging open a door stenciled 1 DIV CLNG LKR. 'And it's a shithouse. The deck's rusting out. See that? Reason is, the spigot's busted. And it'll keep rusting till it's fixed. And it won't get fixed till somebody takes responsibility for making it happen.'

'Yes, sir,' he said, taking a deep breath. 'I'll get on it right away.'

Latitude 40°–51′ North, Longitude 66°–30′ West: 200 Miles East of Cape Cod

Shivering in a blast of freezing wind, Lenson stared open-mouthed into the immensity of space. Above the midnight sea, the Milky Way was a double rainbow of silver. A billion stars blazed down on him. They had no resemblance to the feeble candles seen from land. These were brilliant and unwinking, cold and close and terrifying as the eyes of God.

He stepped back, grunting as sore feet brought him back to the unyielding deck. After evening meal, Cummings had grabbed him to transfer the mess records. Then Norden kept him busy signing custody cards till it was time for watch. But the eagerness that had come now and again all that day closed his throat again as he leaned with Mark Silver over the glowing circle of the surface search radar.

The jaygee's finger traced the edge of a continent. They gazed like gods on the flaring brightness of mountains, the writhing shadows of bay and valley, the glowing masses of islands. Nantucket, Block Island, the cruel hook of Cape Cod leapt into fluorescent brilliance under the rotating beam, faded slowly, then leapt up anew, twenty times a minute.

Silver muttered into his beard. The rush of wind through the pilothouse, the hiss of radios drowned it. 'What's that?' Dan asked.

'I said, "contact 'Romeo.' " ' The offgoing junior officer of the deck's finger lifted, and Dan saw a separate luminescence, focused and hard compared to the inchoate sprawl of land. 'Range, eighteen thousand yards, past CPA 'n' opening. "Sierra's" up here, course two-six-zero, speed then, just about at CPA at thirteen thousand yards, time zero-five.'

The lieutenant (jg) rattled on, so fast he couldn't follow. Courses and speeds and times, radio frequencies, the status of engines and pumps and generators. When he asked for a repeat, Silver glanced up, the whites of his eyes gleaming weirdly in the phosphor flicker. 'What's the matter, Lenson? Haven't you read the night orders?'

'No, sir,' he mumbled.

'From now on, read them before you tell me you're ready to relieve. True wind's from one-two-five at twelve, sea state two – '

At last Silver handed over the bulky night glasses, the badge of office, with the reluctance of a priest blessing a dying mafioso. A shadowy figure stood beside the gyro, outlined against the stars. Silver told it, 'I've been properly relieved by Mr. Lenson, sir.'

'Very well.' The shadow's voice was even, clearly enunciated, as if he'd learned English from a book.

Dan swallowed. 'This is Ensign Lenson,' he began, saluting in the dark although he didn't have to, then realized he had it wrong. 'I mean, sir, I have the watch as JOD.'

'Very well,' said the shadow again. The bridge was so quiet he felt *Ryan* trembling as she drove over three-foot seas. 'Mr. Silver, you may lay below.'

Silver left the bridge, exhaling noisily. Someone, one of the enlisted men, chuckled in the darkness.

Dan was too anxious to notice. He lingered near the radar, wondering what to do. Lieutenant Evlin had both the 'deck,' the overall responsibility for, and the 'conn,' the actual control of the ship. He flipped the straps of the binoculars over his neck, felt the weight settle in. He paced a few feet to and fro, reviewing the layout of the bridge and its manning under way.

Steaming independently, a destroyer had ten men on watch topside. The officer of the deck, or OOD, was in charge. The junior OOD acted as his assistant and makee-learn. There were two senior enlisted men, or petty officers. Of these two, the quartermaster was a skilled navigator; he kept a log and plotted the ship's track. The boatswain's mate passed word, struck bells, and supervised six nonrated men.

Of these, one acted as helmsman, both steering and ringing up engine orders. Three were lookouts, to port, starboard, and aft, supplemented in fog by another in the bow. They stood watch in the open, scanning sea and sky. Another seaman manned a phone circuit, relaying reports from CIC. Finally, a messenger cleaned up and fetched coffee and did the hundred other chores nine people who outranked him could think up in the course of four dragging hours.

'Sir,' said the phone talker suddenly, 'CIC reports a new contact, "Tango," bearing zero-seven-zero, range twenty-five thousand, course one-nine-zero, speed ten; CPA three thousand yards at one-five-zero true, time four two.'

The shadow stirred. 'Have him on radar yet, Lenson?' said the even, precise voice.

Dan started, then fumbled with unfamiliar dials. The green world between his hands shrank and expanded, dimmed and flared. 'Uh, yes sir, I think this is him.'

'Mark it. Use the grease pencil on the string.'

'Aye aye, sir.'

'See if you can pick him up visually. No, the other wing, you won't see anything to starboard.'

'Yes, sir.'

The port wing was open to the sky. He tripped on a coaming as he came out. Then stood motionless, dazzled by the lavender afterimages the screen had printed on his retina. The wind found him as he waited and thrust icy fingers under the collar of his jacket. He shivered, fumbling the binoculars to his eyes.

He couldn't see a thing through them. Even the stars were blurry and distorted!

Then he realized Silver had set them for his nearsightedness. He calmed down and zeroed them while he did the math. Three hundred and sixty degrees in a circle, with due north at zero-zero-zero true. The radar bearing had been zero-seven-zero, which would be forty degrees left of *Ryan's* course. He steadied his elbows on the rail and searched slowly on either side of the bearing.

There: Two yellow sparks shimmered close together on the black curve of the sea. The right-hand one was lower.

The approaching ship's starboard side should be to him. He took a bearing with the port pelorus. According to CIC, she'd pass in front of *Ryan*, assuming both ships held course and speed. There should also be a colored side light – green for starboard, red for port. At twelve miles? He thought it through again, took another bearing, then went back inside.

'Got her?'

'Yes sir. Starboard bow aspect, slow right bearing drift. Too far for side lights yet.'

'Very well. Keep an eye on her.'

'Aye aye, sir.'

Dan checked the radar again. The two ships that had passed during Silver's watch were sliding aft, off the screen. He made a second mark on "Tango's" pip, grease-penciled a line to it from the first, and extended it. If they both held course, the pip should go down that trace.

'What's CPA look like?' came Evlin's voice.

CPA was closes point of approach, the least distance between them as two ships passed. He spun the dials and read off the range to the closest point of the extended line. The other ship would pass *Ryan* a mile and a half to starboard. A safe distance, but worth watching; if he altered course, they could be in trouble fast. 'Three thousand one hundred yards, one-five-zero, sir.'

Evlin said nothing. Dan looked about the darkened bridge, trying to fix the equipment locations. He could see the blue pilot lights of the radios, but that was all. Their steady frying crackle made him sweat. No, that wasn't it. He was sweating because he couldn't remember what Silver had told him about them. If a call came in, could he find the right handset? He resolved, if he made it though this watch without ignominy, to come up early next time and memorize them. He paced this way and that, checked the compass to see that they were on course, checked the barometer, though he was unsure what its reading meant.

How could Evlin be so calm? The motionless silhouette seemed to be waiting.

Waiting . . . oh. 'Keep an eye on her.' He went out on the wing again.

He could see the other ship with his naked eye now, twinkling in the distance, but through the glasses, at seven magnifications, she was all but on them. The fierce brilliance of the masthead and range, so bright that colored rays danced at the edges of the optical field; a line of smaller lights below them, shimmering on the onyx sea. Portholes. There, a green spark: the starboard sidelight.

He lowered the binoculars and leaned into the wind, trying to bleed anxiety into the night like body heat. So many stars! They seemed alike at first glance. Yet on examination, each had its own color, its own twinkle rate, its own inalienable position in the cosmos.

He gripped the heavy glasses in a sudden, inexplicable return of joy.

In high school, he hadn't dreamed of college. There was barely money for food. But he'd taken the test, afraid to hope – and been appointed. To the Naval Academy, still as prestigious in a small town as Harvard or Yale.

There'd been times at Annapolis, too, when he doubted he'd make it. After Plebe Year had come three more, night after night of calculus, engineering, hard science, tactics. Only once or twice a month could a mid hazard an illegal beer in Crabtown, usually followed by a mad dash back a few seconds ahead of the jimmy-legs.

But somehow he had. And here he was. Not aboard the smartest ship in the fleet, not the newest. But a destroyer, built to steam and fight.

Staring at the stars, he thought of how unused he was to contentment. It hadn't come often in twenty-one years. His stomach twisted when he recalled the prying self-righteous caseworkers, the contempt of neighbors for 'loafers,' 'reliefers.'

The politicians said welfare broke the spirit, made people shiftless. It had made him angry, ready to battle like an animal for accomplishment and respect.

And yet sometimes he still felt inferior, frightened, afraid he wasn't good enough.

He'd been proud when he married Susan, though he felt awkward around her parents. It wasn't that they were

Chinese. But their Washington home, their cars, even their diction intimidated him. His roommate had laughted when Dan told him that. He'd laughed, too, but bitterly. Only those who'd never been hungry believed class didn't matter in the United States of America.

The Navy was a ticket out of poverty, if he worked hard, if he succeeded.

If, he thought, leaning forward and sweeping the glasses through the great arc of darkness. But would he freeze or panic in the crunch, when it came? Was he as good as the others, the admirals' sons who were awarded stripes while he'd scraped along in the ranks?

'Mr. Lenson?'

'Yes?' He straightened, felt his heart accelerate.

'OOD wants you, sir.'

Crap, he thought. How long had he been daydreaming out here? A look at the other ship reassured him. He wiped his nose hastily and went inside, hearing as he came in the rattle of a headset returned to its holder.

'You wanted me, Lieutenant?'

'Yes. You don't want to linger on one side of the ship too long. Keep moving. Keep an eye on everything.'

'Sorry, sir.'

'What's your first name again?'

'Dan, sir.'

'Well, Dan, let's see. Did they teach you the three-minute rule?'

'Yes, sir, hundreds of yards traveled in three minutes equals the speed of the ship in knots.'

'Right. The radian rule?'

He didn't know it. The Academy response, then. 'I'll find out, sir.'

'Man overboard, port side. Orders?'

'Left standard rudder, life ring, smoke float, break Oscar flag, six short blasts, notify ships astern, execute Williamson turn.'

'What's the safe sector in a hurricane?'

He stumbled through that, remembering that it was the left hand in the northern hemisphere, but unable to explain why.

In five minutes, Evlin had picked him clean of what he knew about the sea. It didn't sound like much. He waited, fists clenched, then checked the radar. The merchant was nearing her closest point of approach. He told Evlin so.

'Very well. Tell me, Mr. Lenson, what would you do if you suddenly saw a red light on that ship?'

That would mean she'd altered course to starboard. He thought hard, trying to come up with the difference between the other ship's course and theirs; that would determine whether it was a meeting or crossing situation, and thus what the rules of the road required. 'Ah, I'd hold course. We're still privileged vessel, so – '

'Don't say *vessel*. Captain doesn't like it. No, Dan, take a look out there.'

He looked. The freighter had closed alarmingly, swelling out of the night into rows of portholes, light-limned masts and booms. Her lights blazed across the water. A curl of water shimmered at her stem.

'The minute we see him come right, we blow six short blasts, go to flank speed, and put the rudder hard right.'

'In spite of the rule, sir? It says we hold course till we're in extremis.'

'She's three miles away, Dan. Far as Captain Packer's concerned, that's in extremis. The way it was explained to me' – and the silhouette leaned across the stars toward him – 'is like this. A surgeon trains for years, because one slip of his knife means death. Well, down below, we've got three hundred men asleep. We slip up and they can all die. Quick, in a collision, or slow, one by one in the water. It won't matter what the rules said then. Do you know what existentialism is?'

For a moment, he thought he'd heard wrong. 'What was that, sir?'

'The belief that we're free in an amoral universe, and have to determine our own standards of right and wrong. That we make our own rules, and evaluate our lives according to how well we fulfill them.'

'Well, I saw *Waiting for Godot*,' he said, not sure he was following Evlin's drift. He looked out at the freighter. 'Are you . . . are you an existentialist, sir?'

48

Evlin laughed. 'Personally? No. But as a professional –
sure. There are sanctions against wrongdoing and incompetence, but in the end we do what's right because we choose
to. We build our lives around self-imposed intangibles like
duty and honor.'

Dan said cautiously, 'I think I see. But it seems to me you
could justify evil that way just as well as good. Also, I don't –
well, how does all this relate to the rules of the road?'

'Maybe it doesn't.' Evlin chuckled again, softly, and turned
his head. Beyond the open window, the freighter loomed
close, its lights paving tapered paths of yellow and white on
the sea. Dan could hear it now, a whooshing hum carried
down the wind. 'Or maybe it does. The old man's lying awake
down below. He's thinking, a mile and a half, thirty knots
closing speed, that gives Evlin and the new ensign three
minutes to act if something goes wrong. And not just us: the
helmsman, the engine-room throttleman, after steering; if
one man hesitates or screws up, that won't be enough. He's
waiting to hear that whistle. He's waiting for that phone to
buzz.'

The ship rode steadily by them. Now they could see it
through the wing hatch. The green light suddenly winked
out.

Evlin reached down, then held something out. 'Here.'

He took it. It was the phone. Before he had time to get
nervous, he heard the voice in his ear, alert, crisp, not the
voice of a man just awakened, though it was 1:00 A.M.
'Captain.'

'Uh, Lenson, sir, junior officer of the deck. Sir, contact
"Tango" is passing down our starboard side, range three
thousand, now opening.'

'Bearing drift?'

'Rapid right, sir.'

'Very well. Keep an eye on it. Any other contacts ahead?'

'No, sir.'

'You up there with Al?'

'Yes sir.'

'We're still in the coastal shipping lanes. Stay alert. Call me
if you're in doubt.'

'Aye, sir.' He waited, but there was only a rattle as the handset below found its holder. So he hung up, too.

'Okay?'

'He said, "Very well." '

'That wasn't too bad, was it? Remember: Stay alert, take action early, keep the captain informed. Those're rules one, two, and three on *Ryan*.'

'Thanks.' He hesitated. 'Look, sir – the captain, he – why's he so wired? He sounds like he's just waiting for someone to make a mistake.'

'It isn't what you think.'

'What did I think?'

'That he's a sundowner. He isn't. No, James John Packer – you didn't read about him in the papers? *Whipple*, off the DMZ two years ago?'

'I guess I missed that one, sir.'

'He put her in commission on the West Coast. A brand-new DE. Took her on her first deployment to Vietnam. Then he refused a fire mission. They pulled him off for the investigation. Apparently, he was right, because he got exonerated. There was press interest, so the Navy had to give him another ship. But they didn't have to give him a new one. Bottom line: He's walking a tightrope. So he watches everything real close.'

'Oh.'

'Now, we were talking about Sartre's central premise, that we are alone; that there are no absolute moral standards to guide us. . . .'

Dan grinned in the dark, and settled in to begin his military education.

When the boatswain's pipe drilled through the metal walls, he burrowed deeper into the bunk. But only for a moment. You learned the first week at Bancroft Hall to roll your unwilling body out no matter how much it craved sleep. He threw back his sheet – it was heavy with sweat – and dangled his bare feet over the edge, yawning and looking down.

The junior officers' stateroom was eight feet by seven. Four bunks were stacked vertically along the bulkhead. He blinked down from the topmost at a slowly slanting tile deck, a 1944–style steel washbasin, dented sheet-metal lockers. The overhead, at his eye level, was a dusty jumble of cable runs, piping, valves, and stuffing tubes. He wiped perspiration from his hair, recalling a shred of dream; he'd been wandering in a hell of dripping pipes and hissing valves, offering his soul for water. But there were no takers.

'Hey, Mark, Tom. Reveille. You guys getting up?'

'In a minute.'

'Uh.'

He contemplated caulking off for a few more seconds, too, then told himself sternly that he had a division to take over this morning. He groped for a handhold and swung himself out, hung for a moment, then dropped to the deck.

It seared his bare soles. He hopped about wildly. 'Ouch! Goddamn!'

'Use my slippers,' a sleepy voice muttered. 'By the shitcan. We're right over the fireroom here.'

He danced into the shower thongs, still cursing. Still, it was better than enlisted berthing. They bunked five deep, forty in a compartment. He shaved quickly and pulled on a set of wash khakis. He set the gold bars at the collar, considered, then added his midshipman-issue name tag. He checked himself in the mirror, rubbed the bill of his cap with his sleeve, and slid out into the corridor.

The wardroom was in full swing for breakfast, hot, crowded, noisy. He squeezed in between Talliaferro and a sleepy-looking Ken Trachsler, who'd been in CIC during the midwatch. Coffee came by and he sloshed a cup full, yawning so hard his jaw cracked. The wardroom began to tilt. Beside him, Trachsler balanced his mug; above him, Mabalacat steadied himself with a hand to the table as he set down hash and eggs. When Dan pricked the yellow hemispheres with a fork, an orange stream made for the edge of his dish.

'Where'd that one come from?'

'Getting 'em on the starboard bow now.'

'A love tap. Wait till we hit fifty-five, sixty, they get some fetch behind them.'

'How'd your watch go?' Talliaferro asked him.

51

'Not bad, uh, Ed.'

'What are you guys standing up there?'

'One in three. Four hours on, eight off.'

'That's what we've got down the hole, too. Be nice to get back to one in four someday.'

While he was wondering where 'the hole' was, Norden came in, small and blond and glittering, and sat across the table from him. He'd shaved this morning; he looked perky and inspection-ready. 'Bacon, eggs, grits,' he said to the steward.

'No bacon. Hash today.'

'That's what I said, hash. How'd it go, Dan?'

'Okay. It was real pretty last night.'

'Clouds?'

'Some light cover toward dawn.'

'You getting settled in?'

'Yes, sir. But I'm short on uniforms. I didn't figure on getting under way the day I reported in.'

'Stop by small stores,' said Cummings from along the table. Dan hadn't seen the acting supply officer come in. 'I can issue you some underwear and socks.'

'Thanks, uh, Tom. That'll help.'

'We need to get you into the divisional routine,' Norden said. 'Officers' call's at oh-seven hundred. Muster goes at oh-seven fifteen, forward on the main deck. I'll introduce you to the men.'

'I'll be there, sir.'

His department head transferred his attention to breakfast. Mabalacat threaded past with a covered tray. The captain's? Dan mopped up the last yolky trickle and excused himself. He stopped by his room again for the wheel book Vogelpohl had issued him, thrust his arms into a foul-weather jacket, and let himself out onto the main deck.

The morning was blue and chillier than the day before. Save for a few cotton wads of cumulus, their rounded tops shining in the sunlight, the ship was solitary in a vast curving saucer of ocean. *Ryan* centered herself in it flawlessly, hissing through four-foot seas the color of a drowned Norseman's eyes. Seabirds dipped along the crests. The deck gleamed with dew and spray, slick where the nonskid had worn away.

Officers' call was on the Asroc deck, between the stacks. He nodded to the others and leaned against the launcher.

For a few minutes, he gave himself up to contemplation. The sun glittered redly two points off the dipping bow. Every seven or eight rolls, the ship curtsied, making the men lean to keep their balance. He enjoyed the feeling of speed, the cold, clean breeze. The old destroyer's periodic inclinations were like the lurching stroll of an old salt. He'd worried about getting seasick, but so far he felt great.

Talliaferro, Evlin, and Cummings rattled up the ladder and fell in facing aft. Norden joined them. They chatted in low tones about something called a VDS hoist. The jaygees and ensigns fell in behind their department heads.

At 0700, a cap bobbed above the ladder. The exec's bulky body followed it. Evlin called, 'Attention on deck.' Lieutenant Commander Bryce adjusted his tie, aiming his little smile around at them.

'Carry on. Gentlemen, I believe you've all met Mr. Lenson. Say hello, Dan.'

'Hello, sir.'

'He's going to whip First Division back into shape, give us a red-hot new team out on deck. Or go the same way as his predecessor. Right, Dan?'

'Going to try, sir,' he said. He felt Bryce's eyes linger, and stared straight ahead.

'Lieutenant Norden, you'll be judged on that basis, too.'

'Yes, sir.'

'So. As the captain said yesterday, we won't have much good weather this trip. Items requiring clear skies or steady seas should be accomplished as early as possible. That means start today. We still have a lot of crap lying around from the yard, especially in engineering berthing and the shaft alleys. Clean it up! We'll have captain's inspection on Saturday, like we used to before the yard. Shakedown general quarters later this morning. Any questions? Very good. Carry out the plan of the day.'

That, apparently, was a dismissal. The officers saluted. Dan did, too. His mind was still on the threat. Had Bryce really said that?

Norden turned, waving in his division officers. He talked with Ohlmeyer and Murphy for a moment, then nodded to Lenson. 'Okay, Daniel, this is it.'

'Sir?'

'Let's go check out the lion's den. Ha! Get it?'

'Subtle, but I caught it, sir.'

He followed Norden down the ladder to the main deck and forward along the starboard side. The weapons officer pointed wordlessly at a fire station; he saw tools wedged behind hose, a blush of rust already creeping over them. At the turn of the deckhouse, he centerlined his belt buckle and tilted his cap forward.

They rounded the corner, into Bloch's hoarse 'Attention on deck!'

'Good morning, Chief. Have them stand at ease.'

'First Division, at ease.'

The triple line of sailors had straightened slightly at Bloch's bark. Now they slumped back into slouches. Lenson counted twenty-six, picking out the ones he knew. Coffey, Gonzales, Greenwald, Williams, Connolly, Lassard, Vogelpohl, Hardin, Jones. They swayed as the bow dipped, their jacket collars fluttering in the wind. A gull hovered behind them, as if uncertain whether to join the formation. He noted their ragged dungarees, the mix of dirty white hats and ball caps, the paint-stained boondockers. Here and there he caught an alert glance, a quirk of mouth or eyebrow. But most of the faces held only dullness, apathy, the slack lineaments of fatigue or despair. They looked like a chain gang.

He felt their examination, too, eyes flickering toward him, then away. He held himself straight, hands locked behind him, as Norden introduced him.

'Good morning,' he began, and stopped. His voice sounded high; he forced it louder, to overcome the wind. 'I'm Ensign Daniel Lenson. Captain Packer has asked me to take over as first lieutenant.

'This is my first assignment on active duty. There's a lot I have to learn, just as you all had to learn the ropes once. I hope you'll help me out and then later I can help you.

'Neither the chief nor the lieutenant here have told me

anything about you individually.' (Not precisely true, but . . .) 'As far as I'm concerned, we'll all start with a clean slate. I expect seamanlike work and a seamanlike attitude. If I get it, I'll do everything I can to get you the things you need. If I don't, then we'll have to talk.

'If you have problems, personal or Navy, feel free to come to me with them at any time.

'I'm glad to be aboard, and glad to be assigned to this division.' He waited, but could think of nothing else. 'I guess that's about all for now. Chief, go ahead with routine.'

Bloch nodded heavily. He removed his cap and wiped his baldness with a hairy arm. 'Welcome aboard, sir, from the division. Okay, today's our first workday at sea. We got ichi-ban weather this morning. We won't where we're going. You three petty officers, we got to lay some primer today. Assholes and elbows! No shortcuts, no holidays, no gundeck-ing. I want guys at the paint locker ten minutes after we break from quarters.'

The men regarded him stolidly, their bodies swaying toward him and then away. The moment of query had passed. Dan was part of their world now. Their faces were shut, hostile as a lee shore in a storm. For a moment he wished he'd spoken different words, something beyond the standard phrases, something ringing and electric. But when he tried to imagine what they would have been, he couldn't. The bow dipped and spray broke over it, blowing over them. The men flinched and cursed. 'Can't do no painting in salt spray,' a voice grumbled from the back rank.

Bloch ignored it. 'Isaacs, Rambaugh, Pettus, see me for a minute. Rest of you bastards' – he seemed to recall the officers' presence – 'of you *personnel*, atten-*hut*, dismissed.' He gave a salute as a man might throw dung.

The formation broke. The men straggled aft. Norden left, too. Bloch turned to Lenson. 'Sir, these here are the petty officers.'

Boatswain's Mate First Class Isaacs was big, graphite black, his movements slow and somehow tentative. BM2 Rambaugh was grizzled and wizened, with a tough jaw and tattoos like bad carbons of the chief's. Both were old enough to be Lenson's father. The third-class, Pettus, didn't look a clock tick over eighteen. His mouth worked like a cow's. Dan recognized him as the sailor on the quarterdeck when he'd arrived. 'For topside maintenance, I divvied the ship into three parts,' Bloch was explaining, picking at the wrapping of a King Edward. 'Put a PO in charge of each, with his own men. I've seen it work that way. But we're so goddamned undermanned – '

'Do you men feel you can make up what we missed in the yard?'

He saw the exchange of glances, saw them wait for the chief to speak. He decided to start with the junior. That encouraged honest opinions. 'Pettus?' he prompted.

'Uh, it's gonna be rough, but, uh, we'll try.'

'*Sir*,' Bloch said.

'Sir.'

'Petty Officer Rambaugh?'

The second-class squinted at the passing sea as he answered. 'Got a lot of gear midships, sir. Boats, unrep fittings. It's old. Keep it operating, takes a lot of work. We was just about keeping abreast before. Biggest problem is, we're short men. Division's allowance is forty. We got twenty-six.'

'How long has it been that low?'

Bloch turned back from a wind-cheating crouch, cigar lighted, flicking a smoking match to leeward. 'Since the war got hot, sir. They took a draft of ten men off her year before last. then we lost five more in the yard and got three recruits.'

'So it's not exactly news.'

'No, but that don't make it good.'

'Isaacs?'

The first-class lifted his shoulders and moved his feet. He was avoiding Dan's eyes; he realized Isaacs avoided all their eyes. At last his voice came up, deep and slow as a collapsing mine shaft. 'We catch up aft, sir. No problem there.'

He caught Bloch's lifted eyebrow, Rambaugh's glance away. Meaning? He didn't know. He didn't like the under-current here. Undertows could sweep you where you didn't want to go. But for the moment, he'd done what he had to do.

56

Met them. Asked for cooperation. He could fly by wire for a day or two, see how things went.

He felt them weighing him. There was resentment. There was also a grudging attempt at respect – or at least tolerance. All in all, he figured they'd try to get the job done. But these were the senior enlisted, career men.

'Thanks. I'll be seeing you all on deck later.' He half-lifted his hand. They saluted, together, and he completed his salute. He walked aft, leaving the four men standing in a circle, surrounded by the sea. Halfway down the length of the ship, he stopped, looking at the brass turnbuckles of the lifelines, at the green crud that covered them, and pulled out the notebook.

But before he wrote, he leaned over the lifeline, not resting his weight on it but leaning, and looked out over the heaving blue.

He had a brief daydream. *Ryan*, former rust bucket, become the pride of the Atlantic Fleet. A taut ship, clean, hard-working. That was happiness; knowing what you had to do, how to do it, and going to it with all your strength. The conversaton during the midwatch came back to him and he smiled, staring down into the hissing sea.

He lifted the notebook, feeling their eyes still on him, and began.

4

Latitude 57°–52′ North, Longitude 23°–21′ West: 300 Miles South of Iceland

Six days later he narrowed his eyes to a freezing wind beneath a charcoal dawn. 'Sir,' he said. 'Morning fix is plotted.'

Lieutenant (jg) Aaron Reed turned his head from his contemplation of the passing sea. The taciturn, somber West Virginian was *Ryan*'s antisubmarine officer, and stood OOD in Section III. 'We on track?' he grunted.

'A little ahead, by loran.' Bryce expected the JOD to do a morning fix. Ostensibly, it was for training, but Dan wondered sourly whether the XO, who was officially the navigator, bothered to do his own at all. He hadn't seen Bryce on the bridge yet this cruise.

'Loran. No star fix?'

'No, sir. I looked for a break, but no luck. Solid overcast. So I worked out a TD.'

'Okay.' Reed turned away. A moment later the wind banged the pilothouse hatch shut behind him.

Dan lingered on the wing, snugging the zipper of his foul-weather jacket. He felt disappointed. Reed hadn't asked him what he was doing still up, or complimented him on doing his first time-difference fix. He seemed to care more for his sonars than for the people around him. Stop whining, he told himself sternly. They're still paying you, no matter how they treat you.

He looked down on a changed sea. A week before, he'd lingered out here, enjoying the winter sunlight. Now, under a sky poured solid as concrete with low, dark, amorphous clouds, he clung to the splinter shield with gloved hands against a buffeting wind.

At fifty-seven degrees, the latitude of Scotland, the

Atlantic was not blue but gray-blue, the whitecapped rollers fifteen feet from crest to trough. *Ryan* cut her way through them like a huge, slow jigsaw. When the bullnose scooped a sea aboard, the solid water was smoky emerald for an instant, then suddenly white as spray exploded over the ground tackle. The wind, varying between twenty-four and twenty-seven knots, flapped the legs of his trousers and whistled in the taut lines and antennas on the signal bridge.

He'd watched the sea-change in fascination, standing above it eight to twelve hours out of twenty-four. Strange that water could present so many moods, that sky and sea together could mirror all the rages and softnesses of the human heart . . .

He caught his head drooping and shook himself. A shiver explored the backs of his legs. Yet he still lingered, relishing being free of duty, if only for a few minutes.

The days had passed like hours in continuous work. The beginning of the cruise already seemed distant, as if they'd been out for months. He was learning the ship in the traditional way. He'd memorized it from his stateroom to the bridge, bridge to the wardroom, wardroom to the head. He spent his time off watch reading equipment manuals, updating division records, and keeping his men at work. Four or five times a day, he'd stop by the office to get a form or a piece of advice from the eternally busy Vogelpohl, and he'd get called to Norden's room about as often.

A smoothly heaved hillock closed from ahead, crest ruffled like a child's hair by the driving wind. The old destroyer rose majestically, threatening the clouds with the stubby barrels of the forward mount. He felt his weight lessen as she hesitated at the peak of her bound. Then the bow dropped like a guillotine, tossing the sea up in two curved sheets the color of window glass seen end-on. He heard the crash through the hum of the rigging, felt the splinter shield tremble.

Jesus, he thought. This is getting to be serious weather. He found himself grinning.

His need for coffee became overwhelming, as did the related requirement for a leak. He turned and slid down the ladder to the 01 level. The aluminum handrails left black

59

semicircles on his palms. He headed aft, weaving as the ship pitched, glancing at the lashings of the life-raft containers.

In the shelter of the Asroc deck, one of the signalmen was lying on a coil of manila, spearing sardines out of mustard sauce with a marlinespike and drinking cola from a rusty can. Above them the wind whipped brown gas off the stack. To either side, Dan looked out over an immense heaving circle of empty ocean. Their last surface contact, the last ship they'd sighted, had been two days before, when they left the transatlantic latitudes. They were alone, and headed north.

His gaze traveled ahead to the whaleboat, and he paused, examining it with the critical eye he was developing under Norden's tutelage.

His scrutiny swept twenty-six feet of motorboat without the interruption of rust or dirt. The teak trim was smoothly varnished; the hull paint gleamed. A scarlet stripe separated gray from white. Even the brass letters on the bow had been polished. The releasing hooks at the bow and stern were slathered with fresh amber grease. When he bent, looking down the davit arm, the tint recurred to the turnbuckles, operating screw, and the hand crank used to lower away if power failed. The white paint, though, was a little dingy. Repaint? No, a scrub would do.

Even as he thought this, a man emerged from the half-cabin with a bucket in his hands. It was Greenwald. Unconscious of Lenson's gaze, he began scrubbing with a palmetto brush. Dan was about to speak, but just then someone inside started the boat's engine. It ran for thirty seconds, smooth and loud, then cut off.

Hard at work, and early, too, he thought. He thought of complimenting them but didn't. There was something about it he didn't like. It clashed too glaringly with the rest of *Ryan*. Instead, he shivered suddenly, and slid down the ladder to the main deck.

The narrow corridors were snug after the weather decks. He made his way to Boy's Town, tossed cap and flashlight into his desk, and looked around.

The anonymous cubicle was home now. He had a foldout desk, working surface two square feet, and a little safe with a broken lock. He was getting used to the speckled mirror, the dirty sink, the round-the-clock mess and jostle of four men working, dressing, coming off watch or getting ready to go on. The pipes and wireways made racks for his Gardner and Conrad, Dostoyevski, Wouk, Huxley, and Vonnegut.

And for her. Above his head, shielded so that only he could see it, he'd taped the photo of Susan he'd taken on the beach at Chincoteague early one morning. Two bands of white across a body that had spent the summer in a bikini. It was better not to think about her pale, small breasts, nipples erect with a want he'd satisfied between the dunes moments after laying the camera aside, wrapped in a beach towel against the blowing sand . . .

He pulled off jacket and shirt, and tried the faucet. One of the evaporators had gone down, and Bryce had set a quota for the crew and junior officers. He cupped the tepid trickle, lathered, and began to shave.

There were two things he hadn't gotten used to yet. The heat was one. It felt good when he came in from topside, but already sweat dotted his forehead in the mirror. Cummings had told him to tuck his socks under his pillow and put them on before jumping down. That gave him enough insulation to find his shoes. The second was the occasional visitor from the cable runs. He'd had no time to read, but his paperbacks came in handy as roach swatters.

He finished scraping and tried for a rinse. Too late. The faucet sucked air like an out-of-shape boxer punched in the gut. He wiped off lather and whiskers, pulled his shirt back on, and headed for the wardroom.

Most of the officers had eaten and the table was cleared. Some of them were still sitting at it, though, talking. They glanced up as he came in. 'Hey, it's Dirty Shirt Dan,' said one.

'Damn it, it's all I got. Nobody told me we were pulling out so soon.'

'See the XO; he's got some used ones he'll sell you.'

'Sailors belong on ships, and ships belong at sea.'

'I guess we're where we belong, then.'

'Not me, man. I belong in the Black Pearl, slamming down

brewskis till I fall on my sword,' said Cummings. 'You just get off watch?'

'No, I was trying for morning stars.'

'Good luck in this murk,' muttered Silver. 'If we see Rigel again this cruise, I'll eat it.'

'Mabalacat saved out oatmeal and toast for you.'

He got coffee and began to eat, sitting opposite Evlin. He was thinking about what he had to do that day, idly noticing the graceful curve of the lieutenant's wrist as he lifted a spoon, when laughter interrupted his thoughts. He glanced down the table, at the smiling, young, slightly empty faces.

'What could I do? I took my hand off her ass, flashed him my hazel eyes and boyish grin, and waddled off.'

'Risky shit, messing with another guy's wife. Look what happened to Sully.'

'He was drunk.'

'Him? The O club don't stock enough. That sucker can hold more than any three normal men.'

'He don't show it, either. I didn't know he drank till I saw him sober once.'

'What happened, anyway? I heard – '

'I got it from the duty officer. He was at the bar at the Sheraton over on Goat Island. He picked up this chick who swore her husband was in the Med. Anyway, she invites him home, base housing over on Girard. Next morning, he's in the kitchen pouring himself a wake-up when a key turns in the door and this huge marine gunny comes in. Sullivan freezes as the guy stalks toward him, then says, 'Glad you're here, buddy. That sonofabitch you're after is in there with her now,' and he points to the bedroom. The jarhead wheels, and Sully goes out the front door at the speed of sound.

'So now he's out in the bushes, wearing nothing but goose bumps. He works his way out to the street and waits till he sees a guy in uniform driving toward him. He runs out in the road, flags him down, and jumps in. 'Take me to Pier Two, please,' he says. Only the guy's a gung ho shore patrolman, and he takes him straight to the stockade.'

'Risky.'

'Maybe the variety's worth it. They got streets named after my wife.'

'No Entry?'

'One Way.'

'Like they say, sailors, whores, and officer's wives don't give a fuck.'

'Did you hear Lassard's latest? He and the rest of his bunch picked up some captain's daughter on Thames Street and set Circle William on her.'

'That guy's a BS artist. I don't believe anything from that quarter.'

Dan remembered that Circle William meant closing all accesses to open air. 'Hey,' he said. 'I thought you were supposed to keep the conversation light in here.'

'That's as light as we get, sex and drinking.'

'Light, but not obnoxious. That why you been keeping quiet, Dan?'

'I'm here trying to eat.'

'What is that shit, anyway? Looks like lamb barf.'

'It's Navy all-purpose breakfast!' said Johnson.

'It's used for breakfast, mucilage, damage-control compound, too.'

'Don't make fun. Supply Corps spent a lot of money developing APB,' said Cummings, blowing his nose on his napkin. 'You even get it in two colors, haze gray and khaki.'

'Didn't they just pass the word for you, Tom?'

'No, that was my rack calling me.'

'You spent all night there.'

'I rate eight hours a day, my man. What I get in the nighttime's gravy.'

Dan gave up. The disbursing officer had all the comebacks. He pushed away his plate. His stomach wasn't as enthusiastic as it had been on the bridge. Maybe it was the way the bulkheads tilted. He freshened his coffee and flipped open his notebook. The quarterdeck passageway had to be prepped for spray painting. The training schedule was due, maintenance chits had to be rewritten, and he had to review his men's records for dependency certificates.

The big item today, though, would be refueling. They'd

rendezvous with USS *Calloosahatchee* at 1400. He thought about it while the room dipped and swayed around him, then got up. ' 'Scuse me,' he said to Evlin. The lieutenant nodded absently.

The chief petty officers' quarters was one deck down. Three of the chiefs looked up from the mess table as he came in. The talking stopped. 'Morning,' he said. 'Chief Bloch here?'

'Try in back, Ensign. Through that door, hang a right.'

He found Bloch between two tiers of bunks, sitting at a wobbly card table in his undershirt. The chief's head gleamed like a freshy waxed car under the fluorescent lights. His big hands were paring a sliver of balsa from a three-inch-long boom with an X-Acto knife. He didn't look up as Dan pulled out a chair.

Lenson stared at him – the combination of muscle and delicacy was so incongruous – then at the model. Each plank had been riveted with minuscule copper nails. Gun ports were hinged up, suspended with tiny chains. A cannon muzzle poked out through one of them.

He felt angry that Bloch was down here during working hours, instead of on deck. But the boatswain's mind didn't seem to be on ship's business. He was intent on scooping a tiny gouge in the wood, humming under his breath in tune with the ventilation fans.

Dan examined the heavy, private face, the sag of chin, the leathery texture of Bloch's cheeks. In the harsh light, the corners of his nostrils were shot with broken veins. A thirty-year man, without much longer to go. Dan imagined a rented room ashore, more model ships, dishes in the sink. Not for him. When he got out Susan would be there, there'd be two more kids, they'd buy a place in the country. . . .

Bloch glanced up. 'Oh. Morning, sir. Thought you was Chief Ludtke, sittin' there.'

'What you building, Chief?'

Bloch leaned back as the compartment began to tilt. The knife started rolling and he flicked it point-first into the table. 'USS *Constitution*,' he said. 'Old Ironsides. You build models?'

'Used to, when I was little. It's a beauty. You do that carving on the stern yourself?'

Bloch said it wasn't much. He had a camphor-wood chest at home that'd knock your eyes out. 'Bought if off the Bund, trading with the sampans. Swapped a worn-out foul-weather jacket and two pair of boondockers for it.'

'The Bund. Germany?'

'Shanghai. I could tell you some stories . . . they used to sweep the harbor every morning, police up the bodies. They'd tie them to a buoy, string of 'em, like fish. If nobody claimed them in three days – cut 'em loose, bang, bang, down to the bottom. *Merrimack* was the last ship out of China in '49.'

'Is that right. Can we talk about the replenishment this afternoon?'

Bloch blinked. 'Sure,' he said. He slowly gathered the boom and a few spars, put them in a box, and got up. He pulled on a shirt and buttoned it outside his trousers. 'Let's go out in the lounge.'

They sat over heavy china mugs of coffee. 'All right,' said the chief. 'What you need, sir?'

'What's happening topside, Chief?'

'We mustered on station this morning. Ikey and Popeye are turning the guys to. Popeye, that's what we call Rambaugh. On account of he smokes that little pipe of his upside down, like the cartoon. And 'cause he's so runty, I guess.'

'How's painting progressing?'

'We're keeping at it, when we can.'

'Will we get it done before we're too far north to paint?'

'Well, sir – I don't think so.'

His stomach quivered. Bryce and Norden had been asking him this every day, and he'd been telling them it was on track. 'I thought it was going to be done before we hit sixty north.'

'We tried,' said Bloch. He looked regretful but not particularly upset as he lifted the white mug with the green stripe at the rim. 'The POs've had the guys at it from muster to dusk. We've been having these surprise general quarters, and you know we got to knock off in the squalls, too. You can tell the XO that, sir, if you're worried about him jumping your shit.'

'I'm not worried about what to tell the XO!'

Bloch pursed his lips. He took a King Edward out of his shirt pocket and began to pick apart the wrapper with his blunt, cracked nails.

Dan said reluctantly, 'Well, maybe I am. But if we don't get that primer covered, the rust'll be way ahead of us when we get back.'

The older man nodded thoughtfully, as if informed of the existence of corrosion for the first time, and recasting his life plans on that basis. He put the cigar in his mouth and popped flame from a kitchen match with his thumbnail.

'I want to get as much done as we can, Chief. If it means working after normal hours, setting up lights to work after dark, then that's what we got to do. They can have comp time – uh, rope yarn, when we get up where the bad weather lives.'

Dan felt uncomfortable. He felt stupid, giving orders to a man twice his age. But hell, he thought, that's how the Navy wants it. So that's the way it'll be. 'Refueling will go today at fourteen hundred. Are we set up for it?'

'We will be.'

'When?'

'I'll have Rambaugh get the gear laid out after lunch.'

'I'd feel better having it done earlier. Once the tanker comes in sight, we may go right alongside. Let's say eleven hundred.'

The cigar ceased its motion. Bloch's eyes left it to steady on Lenson. 'Look, sir. I know you want to start out makin' a good impression. But don't you think – '

The quiet of the lounge was shattered by a strident bonging. 'General quarters, general quarters,' stated the announcing system. 'This is a drill. All hands man your battle stations. Set material condition zebra thoughout the ship. Now general quarters.'

'Shit,' said Dan, jumping up. Bloch was already on his way out. Lenson tried to recall his route to his battle station, the gun director. But he couldn't remember how to get there from the chief's quarters. As he hesitated, running men pushed him aside. Hatches slammed as the ship subdivided itself into watertight sections. He hauled them open again, pushed through, dogged them behind him, sweating with the dreamlike desperation of lateness. At last he gained the weather decks and pounded up ladders. Cold wind tore at his clothes. Panting, he hauled himself up the face of the director, slid into the bucket seat, pulled on earphones, and dropped the heavy steel helmet over them. '. . . All stations manned, exception of director one,' he heard.

'Director one, manned and ready,' he shouted, mashing the intercom button. 'Mount fifty-one, fifty-two, Director: Stand by to put mount in automatic.'

The gunner's mates acknowledged in bored voices. He flicked switches and spun a handwheel. The director hummed and moved to the right. Below, on the forecastle, and aft, the guns began to train around, too, lifting, following his will. The seat was icy under his buttocks as he bent to roll his socks over his cuffs. Too late, he realized he'd left his jacket below.

'All stations manned and ready,' said Norden, on the battle circuit.

A moment later, Packer's voice boomed out over the shipwide speakers. 'This is the captain speaking. Time: five minutes, twenty seconds. We did a lot better than that before we went in the yard. We'll continue with daily drills until we're ready in under four minutes.

'We'll stay at GQ for a few minutes to check comms, then go to abandon-ship stations for drill. All hands use caution moving about the weather decks. I don't want anyone overboard out here.'

Dan bent to check out the sights. The seas were heavy. Through the magnification of the range finder, he could see them sawing at the horizon nine miles away. Nine miles . . . if this was for real, he could put four shells out there, two hundred pounds of steel and explosive, with one squeeze of the trigger that hung by his ear. He put his head out of the director and watched the ship climb a foothill of sea the hue of a blue shark's back.

'Mr. Lenson!'

He looked down and saw Bryce, hatless, looking up from the deck. The XO was bundled in a leather flight jacket. His face was flushed.

'Yes, sir?'

'Your men all at their stations?'

'Ah . . . I think so, sir.'

'So, are they all in battle dress?' the exec called up, smiling.

That sounded like one of those Brycean quandaries, the kind he already knew the answer to. 'They're supposed to be, sir. I don't know any of them who aren't.' God, he thought. That sounds so weak.

'I suggest you check, Mr. Lenson, instead of sea-lawyering me.'

'Director one, off the line to check battle dress aft,' he muttered into the mike.

'What's that?'

'Off the line, checking aft.'

'Hell you are – '

He hung the headset over the scope, cutting Norden off in mid-word, and wriggled out of the director.

The lookouts were crouched silent and miserable to port and starboard. Williams and Hardin, Hard-on the men called him. He ran an eye over them; socks rolled, collars buttoned, life jackets cinched, helmets buckled. He headed aft, clattered down the ladder to the Asroc deck. He was halfway across it when he saw the open window flaps on the whaleboat.

Aha, he thought. As he headed for it, smoke streamed out, edges shredded by the wind. He swung himself up and poked his head into the cuddy.

'Hey there, Ensign.'

Dan blinked. It was like peering into a cavern. Lassard was dimly visible far forward, his knees drawn up to his face. Coffey, Greenwald, and Gonzales sprawled beside him, boots propped on the thwarts. The troglodytic, feral impression was strengthened by a thick haze. All four seamen were smoking cigars, puffing out jets of smoke, their eyes fixed on his.

'What's going on in here?'

'We're at GQ, man.'

'Where're your helmets?'

'Boat crew don't wear helmets inside the boat.'

'Where does it say that?'

They exchanged glances. After a moment, Coffey said sullenly, 'We never did with Lieutenant Sullivan.'

'You do now. Get them on. And tie those life jackets properly, damn it.'

'Ain't no cause to swear at us, Ensign,' said Lassard. In the dimness of the cabin, his eyes were wide and blue. Like an optical illusion, they alternated from second to second between innocent and depraved. Dan found it hard to meet them. 'Navy regs say officers can't swear at enlisted.'

'Navy regs say you do as you're told, Lassard. That goes for all of you.' He turned away, then remembered something else and stuck his head back in. 'And put those cigars out. No smoking during general quarters.'

'Hey, whatever you say,' said Lassard slowly. The four of them regarded Dan with unblinking hate. 'Whatever you say, man, that's what us fuckin' peons got to do.'

As he was folding himself back into the director, the 1MC passed 'abandon ship.' A pessimistic sequence, Dan thought. He went to his station and waited, reading the directions on the raft placard as sailors trickled back. It was full of interesting advice. 'Attempt to swim underneath burning oil.' 'Take your shoes and cap along when you abandon ship.' 'Tie yourself to others; don't drift off alone.'

He was imagining himself breaststroking toward a palm-fringed atoll when one of the men asked, 'Sir, who's senior on this station?'

'Ah – I guess I am.'

'You're supposed to be mustering us, I think.'

'Oh. Thanks.'

The muster list was a plastic plate on the bulkhead, the names smeared, old, nearly obliterated. He began calling them out. Only a couple of men answered. He paused, halfway down it, with that feeling something was wrong.

'You got me on that, sir?'

'No.' He ran his finger down it. 'Hell, I'm not here, either. I wonder – '

The 1MC: 'Ensign Lenson, lay to the bridge.'

'Oh, crap.'

He stood beside the XO's chair for ten minutes while Bryce subjected him to a leisurely tongue-lashing on the importance of accurate abandon-ship lists. The raft placards, it seemed, had not been updated since before *Ryan* went into the yards. They were the first lieutenant's responsibility. Bryce expected more from an Academy man. Perhaps he was wrong to expect much of anything. Lenson had better start buckling down, or unpleasant things could happen. Packer smoked silently on the starboard side.

When at last they secured, he was at a slow boil. Half the morning was gone and he'd been reamed for something he didn't even know was his responsibility. Damn, he thought, clattering down the ladder to the main deck. Damn this excuse for a ship.

He found Bloch sitting on the forecastle, his legs crossed, like a guru spoiled by good eating. Rambaugh was flemishing down distance line, the soiled little flags fluttering in the breeze. Pettus sat between them, surrounded by colored hard hats, life jackets, signal paddles, spanner wrenches, coils of line and wire. Beyond the deck edge, the sea ran by swift and dark and close, bulging up occasionally to lick at the scuppers.

'Ax,' the chief was reading from a list as Dan came up.

'Check,' muttered Pettus.

'Pliers, side cutter.'

'Check.'

'Two marlinespikes, eight- and sixteen-inch.'

'Check, check.'

Neither of them seemed to notice Dan. 'Chief,' he said tightly, 'let's talk.'

'I'm listenin', sir. Sledgehammer, ten-pound.'

'Let's go aft.'

Bloch sighed, handed Rambaugh the list, and lumbered up. They strolled aft. 'Let me guess,' said the chief. 'The raft musters?'

'That's right. Damn it, who's in charge of those?'

'I guess we are, sir.'

'Sure we are, but who's supposed to *do* it? That's not our job, writing names on bulkheads with grease pencils.'

'Well, it was Ikey's, before we went in the yard. I guess over the summer, it just slipped his mind. And mine. So I'm responsible, too.'

The admission disarmed him. He's been in longer than I've been alive, Dan thought, looking at the age-faded tattoos. How many chewings out had Bloch endured? How many green ensigns had he broken in? 'Well, let's get them updated,' he said at last.

'You want that done before or after we refuel and paint, sir?'

'Now, goddamn it!'

'Sure thing, sir. Ikey's down gettin' a current muster from the XO's yeoman.'

'Good. Now, how about showing me how to set up for replenishment.'

'You're just in time,' said Bloch. His face was serious and respectful again, the face of a junior to a senior; but Dan thought he looked a bit, just a bit, tired.

5

At 1500, he broke off and went back up to the bridge. He found Packer nodding, his pipe in his hand, and Evlin bent over the radar. Dan was fidgeting, waiting for a chance to ask about the oiler, when the phone talker said suddenly, 'Sir! Starboard lookout reports a ship. Hull down.'

'Where away?' rapped out Evlin.

'Zero-eight-five relative, sir. Wait one ... says it's a big one. Four or five mast tops.'

'That's *Calloosahatchee*, all right.'

The captain woke and swiveled his chair, narrowing his eyes out along the bearing. He glanced around the bridge, saw Lenson, and waved him over with the pipe. Dan waited while Packer relighted it, studying the sagging flesh under the captain's eyes. The tobacco smelled heavy, like incense. He wondered why everyone in the Navy smoked.

'Mr. Lenson, what's the status of my underway replenishment detail? Is First Division ready to go alongside?'

'Uh, I can't say I really know, sir, but I think Chief Bloch's got it in hand.'

Packer frowned. 'You haven't been around here too long, so I'll let that one go by. But I don't want to hear that answer again, understand? I want you to take charge down there. You lead a deck gang, you can lead anybody anywhere. Besides, the chief won't be there forever.'

Dan wondered what that meant. But one of the many things they made plain at Annapolis was that you didn't ask somebody senior to you to explain himself. 'Aye, aye, sir,' he snapped, trying to look savvy and aggressive.

Packer relapsed into silence. After a minute or two, Dan drifted over toward Evlin. 'When do we rendezvous, sir?' he muttered.

'We just did.'

'I mean, when will we set the refueling detail?'

'Basically whenever the skipper says.'

'Okay, but how far in advance does he usually call us away?'

'Oh. If that's what you wanted to know, why didn't you ask? Forty, forty-five minutes.'

'Thanks.'

'Let's get on the horn, Al. Let's not keep these pump jockeys wondering who the hell we are.'

'Aye, Captain.' Evlin turned away, picking up the radio-telephone.

The 1MC called away refueling stations at 1538, when the oiler, now a low gray island, was still some miles distant. The early dusk of high latitudes was falling fast. Dan was already on station, pulling the life-jacket ties through the D-rings. He felt bulky and cumbered by the heavy kapok, the hard hat. He stood forward of Unrep Station Three, watching Bloch and Isaacs and Rambaugh chivvy the arriving seamen into position, rehearsing in his head what he had to remember.

Navy ships stayed at sea for months. Their appetites for fuel, food, spare parts, and mail were satisfied by oilers and ammunition ships. The transfer was the tricky part: moving cargo in bulk between two rolling and pitching platforms on a constantly moving element. Fuel was the hardest. Instead of winching across a few slings, the connection had to be maintained for as long as an hour, depending on the pumping rate.

It was the most challenging deck evolution there was, and the most dangerous. Green as he was, he knew it was one of the ways you rated a ship, a division – and a first lieutenant. Ships got names as fast fuelers or slow. Word of screwups or accidents got around the fleet fast. With names attached.

'Now bear a hand manning the refueling detail,' said the 1MC. Dan watched his refueling team gather forward of the fuel trunk, buckling their vests and bitching in resigned voices. Rambaugh had his pipe in his mouth bowl down. Pettus and Isaacs wore yellow cotton work gloves with the fingers cut off. Coffey was yawning, settling the sound-powered phones over his ears. They were all dressed warmly, foul-weather gear, black wool watch caps. He heard Bloch: 'Got 'em all, Ikey? Count 'em.'

'Ain't got but fifteen hands here. S'posed to have twenty?'

'Well, what you gonna do?'

'Send somebody up to the whaleboat,' Dan said. 'There'll probably be a couple guys caulking off in there.'

The oiler changed course as *Ryan* closed, steadying up into the oncoming seas. He watched them burst into spray against the gray hull, deep-laden, massive as an iceberg. As the two ships converged, the destroyer vibrated and began to turn.

Ryan curved round *Calloosahatchee*'s stern in a mile-wide circle, then steadied up on a parallel heading. Her motion changed to a pitch that from time to time rolled, too, throwing him against the lifelines. She slid gradually into position a thousand yards astern of the oiler, offset slightly to port. Despite the failing light, he could see the rounded stern clearly, the black letters of the oiler's name. He wondered what a calloosahatchee was, and who made up these crazy names. Along *Ryan*'s starboard side, the deeper ship's wake was a streak of foam over a gentled sea, as if she crushed down the waves as she passed.

A red and yellow flag snapped abruptly open at the oiler's yard-arm. The intakes whooshed and whined above him and *Ryan* leapt forward again. He saw Evlin and Packer leaning over the splinter shield. Evlin had his binoculars on the tanker. Packer turned aft, searched the deck, then saw him and cupped his hands. But what he called was lost on the wind.

'Say again, sir?' Dan shouted.

'. . . Word, you ready down there?'

'Ready, aye, Captain,' shouted Bloch.

Ryan closed and the tanker grew. Then, suddenly, they were no longer behind it but alongside. He stared across a rushing river of sea to her. He could see men moving about, could make out the expressions on their faces. The oiler's deck was a mass of piping, valves, hoses. It looked more like a refinery than a warship. She moved to the seas in a slow, majestic seven-second roll, showing twenty feet of her copper-colored bottom.

He glanced back at Bloch. Shouldn't they be doing something? But the chief stood with hands on hips, riding with the motion, the straps of his life jacket cutting grooves in his paunch.

The engines whined again. *Ryan* surged ahead, and the illusion of motionlessness was broken. He caught Packer's voice, followed by the engine bell. The destroyer drifted back slowly. The bell pinged again, and she stopped, settling in as if welded to the oiler by an invisible bar of steel.

Dan sucked air uneasily, chilling his tongue. He couldn't feel anything in his hands. He plunged them into his pockets. The wind was freezing.

Now he could tell the ranks of the men opposite. Hundreds of miles from land, the two ships were barreling along only a hundred steps apart. The seas roaring in from ahead were trapped between the parallel hulls. The bow waves, meeting, battered upward into concave peaks that were somehow familiar. Then he had it: a Japanese print, the kind with volcanic islands and monks on rafts. The sea had the same flamboyant elaborations as the wind shredded the crests in its teeth.

They were still too far apart. The book said 140 feet was best for the span-wire method, with 180 maximum. It looked like more than that to him.

'On the *Ryan*: Stand by for shot line forward,' crackled a bullhorn from the oiler, a whistle blew, and a man in a red helmet raised a rifle. Beside him, Isaacs slapped his pockets suddenly, found his whistle, and replied. The rifle recoiled; a faint *pop* floated past on the wind. The men around Dan ducked for cover. The dart detached itself from the sky and arched down, spinning out an orange spider thread.

It dropped across the forecastle, tangling itself in the lifelines. Pettus ran forward and came back holding it carefully aloft. Curved by gravity and wind, it hung in a long, fluttering arc back across the rushing sea to the oiler's midships station.

'On your feet! Get off those lifelines! Lazy, lay-down fuckheads!' shouted Rambaugh. His corncob hung empty. Dan smiled to himself. 'Popeye.' He even trailed his curses off into a mumble.

The men forward of the fuel trunk got up, rubbing their hands and clapping their arms. Pettus reeved the string through the snatch block on the bulkhead and passed it to the first linehandler, who began hauling in, passing the end to the next. At first, it looked comical, a dozen sailors gravely hauling in a piece of what looked like wrapping twine, but then he saw a heavier piece of line coming over.

A still-heavier rope followed; then, making the line-handlers show their teeth, a heavy steel span wire. The scarred metal gleamed dully as red work lights flickered on. Behind a shackle were taped three lighter lines, two of them insulated wire.

The men hauled in steadily, grunting at the weight. The shackle was almost to the ship when one of them slipped and knocked down a companion. The line ran through their hands with startling swiftness, and several men cried out in pain. The shackle dipped into the running sea. He started forward, but before he could think what to do, Pettus had belayed the line around a cleat. The runout stopped.

'Mr. Lenson!'

The captain on a bullhorn, depressingly loud. He raised his head over the grimaces and curses of the handling party. One man, gloveless, was leaving it, fighting his way back along the narrow deck. His face was pasty, eyes wide. The flesh of his out-thrust hand opened like a scarlet tulip.

'What's going on down there? Get that span wire inboard.'

'Sir, we – ' He stopped himself. 'Aye aye, sir.'

He turned to Rambaugh, but the second-class was already shouting the rest of the handlers back on the line. They stared glumly at the wire, which was skipping and slicing through the water, and rubbed their hands on their trouser legs. The gnomelike petty officer waited till they had a good grip and were taking a strain.

Then he flipped it free in one motion from the cleat. The weight of it took the ranked men aback. They skidded forward, boots grating over the deck in a grim tug-of-war with the sea. Then they recovered, setting their feet, and brought it in slowly again, hand over hand.

When the shackle came aboard, Rambaugh stepped in and

quickly stripped off the light lines and wires. There were phone lines from the oiler's bridge to *Ryan*'s, from the refueling station to theirs, and the manila remating line for hauling across the hose and for retrieval of the shackle when refueling was complete. Rambaugh gave the phone lines to Connolly and Gonzales, who made off with them at a run. The remating line he made fast to a three-horn cleat.

The shackle came to Isaacs's big hands. The black first-class's knife flashed as he cut it free from the rope messenger. He laid its open *O* in the pelican hook above the fuel trunk. Or tried to. But there was still strain on the line. *Ryan* was rolling now, away from the oiler, outboard. Isaacs fought to hold the open shackle, waiting for her to come back.

It happened too fast for Dan to say anything or even flinch. The men slacked off. The shackle wrenched loose and jerked out three feet, twisting so savagely it threw Isaacs's hands off. A glint of metal flew free, then vanished into the boiling green that bulged and sucked on the far side of the lifeline.

'Lay back, there, Goddamn it! Get your backs on that line!' shouted Rambaugh in his high voice. The party, looking scared now, hauled away at the same moment the destroyer rolled to starboard. The shackle leaped inboard and slammed into the bulkhead so hard it threw sparks. Isaacs jumped on it, wrestled it over the pelican hook, and flipped up the bill. He pushed up a keeper to lock it. At the same moment, Rambaugh was reeving the messenger rope, now become the remating line, through a pair of blocks below the shackle. The end of that line went forward through the hands of the hauling party.

Dan followed it intently, hands deep in his pockets to keep them from going from tingling to numb. Isaacs's face had tightened. He was still holding the keeper closed with one hand, gesturing urgently with the other. His voice came faintly over the roar of turbines, the whine and clatter of two ships now, the moan of the wind.

'Whassat, Ikey?'

'The pin, Baw. I lost the pin.'

Rambaugh whirled and stamped the deck. 'The keeper pin. He dropped it overboard.'

'Holy fuck,' said Pettus.

Isaacs was staring over his shoulder, watching the ships roll together. In a moment they would be rolling apart.

Rambaugh snatched at his belt, came up with a fid. It went an inch into the hole and stuck. Dan searched desperately through his own pockets: coins, a government-issue ballpoint, keys. He looked at Bloch. The chief stood still, his arms folded over his belly. He was watching the first-class, who stood frozen, still holding the hook closed with a big hand. 'Tool kit,' Rambaugh was shouting. 'Where's the gawdamned tool kit – '

Dan glanced at the bridge wing. Packer and Evlin were inside; apparently they thought the lines were mated.

When he looked back, Isaacs was still holding the keeper in place. But Pettus had the tool kit open. Rambaugh, working fast, hack-sawed the handle off a screwdriver, thrust it through the keeper, and seized it in place with wire.

He danced back, showing a fist to the rigging party. They staggered backward, slacking off, panting and blowing clouds of gray fog.

Now things were happening on the brightly lighted decks across from them. Four huge loops of black hose uncoiled downward along the catenary of wire. The refueling rig terminated in a steel penis seven inches in diameter and four feet long. The coupling crept out, paused, jerked forward a few more feet. Then it stopped, swaying violently beneath the line span.

Dan saw why. The span was too long, the wire was too slack. For the fitting to proceed farther, it would have to slide uphill. At least part of the time. Both ships were rolling, but when *Ryan* rolled to port, like as not, the oiler was rolling to starboard. When they went in opposite directions, the line leapt to a sudden dreadful tautness. When they rolled together, it dipped like a cheese slicer into the rushing sea.

He stared helplessly at the men opposite. Clustered together, they seemed to be discussing the situation. The oiler's phone talker nodded his head and bent to his mouthpiece.

A larger-than-usual wave, trapped by the parallel hulls,

swept in. It burst over the riggers and linehandlers in a head-high wall of spray and solid water. Dan grabbed for the lifeline just before it hit.

The sea was icy, breath-stopping, incredibly cold. It punched him casually back against the deckhouse, then swept aft, subsiding as it passed the Dash deck. Around him, men wiped ocean from their eyes, cursing hopelessly. A spark of anger ignited in him, like a welder putting flame to his torch. What the hell was Packer doing?

'We too far away, sir,' Isaacs bawled respectfully in his ear, making him wince. He nodded, agreeing, but not knowing what the first-class wanted him to do about it.

A few minutes passed during which nothing much changed. The night grew darker. The ships plunged on, the gunmetal waves swept by. Two more seas swept the starboard side. His teeth began chattering. The linehandlers talked angrily. One or two spat and swore in sudden outbursts. The petty officers stood looking toward the oiler, poised on the balls of their feet.

'Mr. Lenson.' That damned bullhorn!

'Yes, sir!' he howled.

'What's the holdup now? Get that hose across!'

He stood impotent, looking upward with his hands spread.

Bloch moved then. He shoved his helmet back and stepped up to the remating line. He put his hands on it and looked over his shoulder. 'Linehandlers.'

'Yo, Chief!'

'We got to haul that sumbitch uphill if we want a drink. Let's give it another try. Less you want to stay out here all night.'

The men knuckled saltwater from their eyes and adjusted their gloves and took determined hold of the line. Water flowed in vees around their boots as they pawed the steel deck. And not only water; Dan saw with a sick feeling that a skin of ice was forming, too.

'Haul!'

They laid back with little moans, with sucked gasps of breath. The line to the dangling probe lost its slack, then went taut. The metal phallus resisted, at the bottom of a dip, then came forward suddenly fifteen feet as the span wire assumed that frightening instantaneous straightness. Then it moved back five feet. The hauling party, cursing fearfully, their boots sliding on wet steel and foam, grunted and set their backs again.

They worked it ten feet closer, lost five, regained seven, lost four, regained three. As the probe moved out from the oiler, the heavy, stiff black hose unbent behind it in loops, like cold garden hose hanging from a wash line. Then it stuck again. It dangled, swaying above the rushing sea, its single aperture staring at them with thirty feet yet to go. It looked even more penislike from this angle.

He grabbed Isaacs's shoulder. The first-class's face was wet and glum. Under the sheen of water was unshaven beard. 'Ikey, what's the goddamned problem?'

'Can't get the probe inboard, sir.'

'I see that, but why not?'

'Told you, sir. Ships're too far apart.'

'Can't we put more men on the line party?'

'That'll get us another two feet maybe. No, sir, captain's just sheering off too far.'

'Well, what do we do?'

'Somebody got to tell him, sir.'

'*Tell* him? You mean Captain Packer?'

'Yessir.'

They stared at each other for a moment. Then, behind him, he felt a hand on his life jacket.

'Let me by you, there, Ensign.'

The heavy figure shoved crabwise past the linehandlers and disappeared up the bridge ladder. Bloch was gone no more than a minute. When he reappeared, he went directly to his post and stood there, face unreadable, watching *Ryan*'s bow.

It wavered, and drifted right.

Very slowly, they nudged closer to the gray wall across from them. The distance flags crept inboard, snapping like firecrackers: 240 feet, 200, 170, 150, 120.

'Holy hell,' muttered Pettus.

The sea increased its rage as iron walls closed on it. Dan

edged back, away from the lifeline, till his back bumped the cold steel of the deckhouse. The gray bulwark came nearer, towering over them. He could have tossed a baseball up to her deck. He could see the wrinkles around the men's eyes opposite him. Like a river in flood, lacking only dead trees, the sea between the racing hulls raged and foamed, here and there extruding itself in transparent lenslike bulges, like cast bottle glass.

He remembered suddenly that in close proximity the Bernouilli effect took over. The two hulls were sucked together, more violently the closer they approached. That was why Packer had held off, played wary.

If the steering gear went again, as it had coming out Newport channel, they'd be raked down the side of the larger ship before the helmsman could react.

Lenson rounded abruptly on the linehandlers. Their faces were pallid in the scarlet light. He caught Lassard's insolent smile at the end of the line. 'Haul now, *haul*, you bastards!' he screamed.

The gaping sailors bent to the line again. It glistened, and he realized it was glazed with ice. Their gloves scrabbled over it. But the oiler's winches had taken in on the span wire as *Ryan* closed. The connector came down it in a rush and clanged into its receiver like a bulldozer hitting a concrete wall. In an instant, Pettus and Rambaugh had lashed it with jigger tackles and riding lines. The engineers were guiding the couplings together and locking them.

When the operating lever was swung over, they stood back and looked at the completed connection, panting out steaming clouds that the wind snatched instantly away.

Dan turned to the bridge, and cupped his hands. 'Ready to pump,' he shouted.

The oiler's pumps thrust Navy standard fuel oil across at several hundred gallons a minute. The only sign of it was a drip from the coupling and a faintly obscene pulsing in the hose. At thirty-four minutes from start pumping, *Ryan*'s signalman circled his amber wand for blow-through.

Dan was freezing. Air temperature was forty degrees, but

the windchill had turned the outer layers of his wet clothes to sheet ice. He crackled when he moved. The linehandlers had taken shelter inside, but he stayed on deck.

Finally the command came to break away. He'd hoped the rest would go well. But something went wrong on the uncoupling – he couldn't see what – and a great gush of black oil burst out as the hose came free and flooded aft, running down the side of the ship. It ebbed after a moment. Rambaugh dashed sand on it from a bucket. The others continued the breakaway. The nozzle rolled back up the span wire, tensioned by the oiler's winches, still peeing a thin stream of fuel that the wind separated into drops. Rambaugh tripped the pelican hook and threaded an easing-out line through the shackle. Bloch and Pettus kicked it overboard, paid line till it was ten feet from the ship, then let go.

The span wire jerked evilly, lashed out left and right as the men jumped back, and slashed its way down into the sea.

'Now secure the underway replenishment detail. Set the normal underway watch.'

He was unlacing his life vest with numb claws, looking forward to hot coffee like the possibility of salvation, when Coffey said, the shade of a smile on his face, 'Ensign, they says that your presence is requested up to the bridge.'

6

When the chewing-out was over and they secured from replenishment, he stayed on the bridge for watch. He was frozen and exhausted, and two more hours on his feet didn't help. Near the end of it, Norden joined him on the wing. Together they stared into the darkness.

'Jeez, getting cold. Anything out there?'

'No, sir. Not a thing.'

'Where's the oiler?'

'Off the scope an hour ago. Headed south.'

'Uh-huh. Look, I wanted to ask you – you mind taking eight o'clock reports for me tonight?'

Dan said, 'Sure,' but he felt like a child who's had his birthday cake recalled. For two hours he'd been dreaming of his rack. After a moment, he added, 'What'd you think of the replenishment?'

'Not an inspiring performance.' *Ryan* rolled, and they both gripped the bulwark. The cold wind buzzed in a metal fitting like a trapped wasp. 'I was just talking to the XO about it. Or rather, listening. I understand he gave you an earful, too. All in all, I think it ranks as a fiasco.'

'It wasn't our fault. The captain was too far from the oiler.'

'Goddamn it, Dan, you don't snuggle up to twenty thousand tons of tanker in seas like this.'

'Well, I think my guys did all right.'

'You do? I don't. They lost two hundred gallons of oil, screwed up the whole starboard side. Hurt one of the storekeeper's hands. Cummings wants me to remind you, it's his man, but it happened during your evolution, so you get to write the accident report. And what was the big problem with the span wire?'

'Ikey lost the shackle. We had to jury-rig one.'

He saw a pale blur move; Norden had passed a hand over his face. 'Lost the *shackle*?'

'I mean, the shackle pin.'

'That's more like it, but it's still an awful clumsy performance for a first-class bos'n. I don't know. He's good with engines, he has a little spare-time business at home, but everything else, the things he's supposed to be able to do . . . his evaluation's going to be due pretty soon. I want you to start thinking about what it's going to say.'

He debated telling Norden about the lifeboat musters, that Isaacs had been in charge of those, too, but decided not to. He and Bloch shared responsibility for that.

'Isn't it turnover time? Where's your relief? You better go grab some chow.'

'Sure hungry. I missed lunch, checking out the gear.' Even to himself, his voice sounded whiny, a plea for sympathy.

Norden didn't answer.

He felt depressed and queasy through dinner, pork steaks and green beans in slimoid gravy. He cut up the meat, but the pinkish dripping edges disgusted him, Finally he abandoned it and sat playing with his fork.

He didn't like Norden's little remark about Isaacs's evaluation. I'm the division officer, Dan thought. I don't have to be told what to say about my men. Even if, as he undoubtedly did, Norden knew them better, as least so far.

Anyway, he'd already noticed that the first-class made mistakes, forgot things, often seemed at a loss for what to do. His trembling hands and reddened eyes reminded Lenson of his father. He closed his eyes, resisting the memories – but not the conclusion. There was something wrong with Isaacs, and he suspected it had to do with alcohol.

But he still didn't like the idea of grading him low. The guy made first class, he thought, crumbling a piece of bread between his fingers. For a black man with Ben Bryce in his chain of command, that couldn't have been easy. He deserved the benefit of the doubt. But the next minute, the other side of his mind said, But is that fair, to ask less of him because of his race? How would you treat a white guy who couldn't cut it?

The captain sat silently at the head of the table. Taking their cue, the junior officers finished hastily and dispersed. When Packer left at last, his dessert untouched, only Dan and Silver remained. When the door closed, he muttered, 'Say, Mark?'

'Say, Mark, what?' said the bearded jaygee suspiciously. 'No, I won't swap bunks with you.'

'I didn't want to swap bunks. I wanted to ask you what the deal is on the old man.'

'What deal? What old man?'

'The skipper. Why's he so uptight? So careful about everything?'

The electronics officer frowned. His eyes went to Mabalacat, who seemed to be counting the silver back by the pantry. Then he muttered, 'Get over here.'

When Lenson was sitting beside him, Silver leaned forward over his coffee. Dan watched it tilt toward the rim, hesitate there, then lean the other way. 'He's got personal problems.'

'Yeah? Oh, well, if it's personal – '

'But not secret. First off, his wife. Ginnie's a high school teacher. Just got tenure in San Diego when he got orders to *Ryan*. But there aren't any teaching jobs in Newport. So she doesn't do too much. Ken's wife, Gloria, said she saw her with a pilot last time we were underway . . . before the yards.

'Number two, his kid's fourteen. Been running away, giving him lip. Probably has something to do with Jimmy John being gone so much. He's worried about that, I guess.'

'Jesus.'

'Yeah. See, Packer had an XO billet in San Diego, then he went to Nam on the *Whipple*. Then after he got pulled off her, he gets orders way the hell up here. It's hard on a kid that age, losing all your friends.'

'What about *Whipple*? What exactly happened? I heard he refused a call for fire – '

'It's not that clear-cut. Barry's got some of the clippings out of the *Post*. Packer was actually kind of famous for a week or so. Seems like when he first got to Vietnam, he had a holding billet on one of the riverine squadrons, and got to know a little

85

about the coast. Found out how this one district chief would hold up the villages, ask for money. He didn't get it, the guy would either relocate them or declare them free-fire zones.

'Then later on, when Packer was CO of the *Whipple*, he was transitting south after a DMZ patrol when he got a call for fire on some village from the local ARVN commander. But his map showed the village as pacified. So he asked who originated the request, and it was this same official, the one who was shaking people down.

'So Packer turned it down, said he couldn't fire. Well, the Vietnamese Army guy went to his U.S. liaison, and *he* called Packer, and he still said no. Wouldn't fire, kept right on steaming.'

'Was the village really VC?'

'Nobody'll ever know. The liaison called the Air Force and they napalmed it that night. Blew 'em all away. Then he put Packer on report to COMNAVFORV. And the shit hit the fan.'

'Jesus,' Dan said again.

Silver scratched in his beard. 'It was the papers, TV saved him, I figure. They were just kicking up too much dog doo. But things haven't gone so good for him since then.'

After that, there was no use trying to lighten the atmosphere. He left a gummy-looking pudding untasted and headed for Boy's Town. Halfway there, he remembered eight o'clock reports.

In the thwartships passageway, he slid into line beside Lt. Talliaferro. 'Attention on deck,' said Evlin. Under roofs or overheads, the Navy didn't salute, but the line straightened as Bryce let himself down the ladder.

'Stand at ease,' said the XO, nodding around at them. He adjusted glasses and smirked down at a list. 'Engineering.'

'Here, sir. Fuel state, ninety-four percent. Potable water twenty percent, feed water seventy-two. Number-two evap still down. Main scoop injection temperature forty-two degrees and dropping.'

'What's that water percentage?'

'Twenty.'

'That's pretty low.'

86

'You're telling me,' said Talliaferro.

'So. Operations?'

'HF transmitter still down. Estimated time of repair, midnight.'

'Supply?'

'Nothing to report.'

'Mr. Cummings, you have that accident report done yet?'

'Mr. Lenson's doing it, sir.'

You bastard, Dan thought.

'What about that laundry? Where is it?'

'Can't do laundry without water, Commander.'

'You must have enough to do mine, at least. Why don't you just leave out the engineers? Since they can't seem to keep the fresh water coming.'

Neither department head said anything. After a moment the XO went on, 'Weapons?'

'Nothing to report, sir,' said Dan. 'Except for the accident report, and I'll do that before I turn in tonight.'

'You sure?' said Bryce smiling.

'Sir?'

'I thought you were painting tomorrow.'

'Down below, yes, sir.'

'That compartment's not set to paint,' said the exec, eyes gleaming over his glasses. 'It's not masked properly, there's dirt all over the cable runs, there's no papers or dropcloths to protect the deck. I don't like to hear sloppy jobs like that represented to me as ready to go. I expect you to keep on top of what goes on in your spaces. That's what we pay you for, Mr. Lenson. Are we payin' you too much?'

'No, sir.'

'Then turn to, Goddamn it! And you all better tour your spaces tonight before you turn in. That's part of your job, and if you're not doing it, gentlemen, I'm here to make sure you take the consequences. Understand me?'

'Yes, sir,' said Evlin. Apparently, as the senior lieutenant, he spoke for the rest.

When Bryce left and the department heads separated, Dan stood in place, frustrated, enraged. Know what's going on in my spaces, he thought. Watch, GQ, replenishment, reports, watch again. When was there time? What did Bryce expect? The anger glimmered brighter, warming his stomach.

At last he choked it down and zipped his jacket again. Tour, then write the report, that would get him to bed around 2200. He'd get an hour and a half sleep before watch again at midnight. If nothing else happened.

He started the topside tour aft of the bridge. When the hatch closed behind him, he hesitated, his hand seeking in the darkness. No stars. No moon. He could hear the sea rushing by, the steady shriek of wind, but he couldn't see a thing. The night, even after the dimmed lighting of the ship's interior, was opaque as blindness. His hand found icy steel and spidered out along it.

When he could sense the solidity of the superstructure on one side, the abyss on the other, he began groping his way aft. He found the pyrotechnic lockers and tested by feel that they were locked. Bracing himself against the wind, he went on, edging each foot out into blackness. Gradually he became aware of a faint rose light in the windows of the signal shack, and a pearly fog around the shielded masthead above.

Now that his eyes were adapting, he pulled his pencil flash and flicked it on. A disappearingly faint red oval appeared in front of him. Everything was in order on the Dash deck. He was headed aft, groping for the ladder down to the fantail, when he became conscious of something near him. He flicked the beam over it. It was the after lookout. He was seated on a roll of hose. He didn't respond to the light.

Dan reached out and shook him. The shoulder was slack under his hand for a second. Then it tensed, and the sailor came to his feet. 'Who's that?' Dan asked sharply.

'Ay, man, what's doing?'

'Are you supposed to be sitting down?'

Lassard's voice came slow and peaceful. 'Hey, old Slick was just relaxing for a minute.'

'Were you asleep?'

'Asleep? Hell, no.' The voice became intimate. 'I was just watching for it through these binocs, man.'

'Watching for what?'

'Uranus.'

He caught the whole double meaning. It was so gross an insubordination, he didn't know how to respond. 'Go to your post,' he said thickly. 'You keep fucking with me, Lassard, and you'll regret it.'

'Ay, Slick's *at* his post, Ensign.' The laugh floated on the freezing wind. 'What you gonna do, lifer? Draft him and send him to sea? Another thing. He hears you been bitching about the kinnicks you say loafin' in the whaleboat. They're workin' in that boat, man. They're like, the gig crew. Captain appreciates them keepin' it four-oh like they do.'

Dan stared into the darkness. Suddenly his chest tightened, and a prickle ran along his back. He started to speak, then turned away abruptly and slid down the ladder. Assholes, he thought blindly. Lassard, Bryce, Norden, Cummings. I'm surrounded by assholes.

The motion of the ship was worst on the fantail. The deck soared and then dropped away under his feet. The sense of falling through darkness was so nauseating, he welcomed the icy, bitter sting of spray. He paused at the stern, looking over the counter. Below him the wake boiled up white under the stern light. He leaned against the lifeline, looking down into the maelstrom.

I shouldn't have lost my temper, he thought. Shouldn't have threatened Lassard. I should either have chewed him out or else put him on report. Writing him up would be awkward, no witnesses on the dark and windy deck, a confession of his lack of personal force. No, I should have given him a good dressing-down, then made him stand an extra watch.

Why had he left so suddenly? Was it fear of the seaman? He didn't think so. Was it lack of self-confidence? He didn't think that was it, either.

It was fear of himself. He remember his father's drunken rages, his father's fists. He preferred control. If he hadn't turned away, he'd have hit the seaman.

He took a deep breath of lightless air, trying to quell his fear and rage. Beneath his clenched hands the lifeline was gritty with condensed salt. When the stern rose, some trick of the wind tainted the icy air with ship smell from the exhaust fans, with the warm stink of three hundred close-hived men. He glanced over his shoulder but saw only the black square of the after gun and above it a red spark: Lassard on the Dash deck, smoking. No, two sparks; someone had joined him.

After a time his rage lessened, and his thoughts went back to Susan. At least one thing in his life was true and lasting. He put his arms around his chest and hugged the bulk of his foul-weather jacket as if it were her shoulders. His skin remembered the softness of her hair.

He remembered the time they'd stayed at her parents' home in D.C., when they were dating. Mrs. Chan had put them in separate rooms and they'd said good night with a long kiss on the sofa. But later he'd come awake in the dark with her fingers against his lips. She was kneeling by his bed in her old-fashioned nightgown.

'This used to be my room when I was little,' she whispered.
'It's nice.'
'You like the bunnies on the walls?'
'Uh-huh.'
I used to lie here and wish I had someone to make love to me – when I was thirteen.'

He'd slipped his fingers then under the unbuttoned yoke and found two miniature erections on the incredible smoothness of her skin. Up till then, he hadn't thought she wanted it. All that evening she'd acted weird, almost hostile, reading magazines and responding in monosyllables.

But under the gown she was wet and ready. Grappling in the dark, whispering, she'd pulled him over the edge of the bed and he'd fallen a foot directly into her; no groping, no clumsy guiding with the fingers; like a zen arrow to the mark, he'd plunged between her parted legs. That was why he remembered that time beyond scores of others. That uncanny directness, exact and instantaneous, as if all causality led inexorably to their mutual transfixation.

And he believed that; that they were meant for each other; created for each other.

How mysterious it all was!

Through the thin fabric of his pocket, his fingers touched unyielding want. He'd read somewhere that a man's desire slacked off after eighteen. So far, it seemed to be getting worse. He wavered for a moment. He should turn in. No, he should write the accident report. But first he'd stop in the shower stalls. When he was this horny, release took only a moment. The most potent and precious fluid in the world, lost by thousands of gallons this night in silent cars, urinals, boys' bedrooms all over the planet . . .

He was walking past the gun when he realized several men were standing in its shelter. He couldn't make out how many, or what they were doing. Just vague forms, and the glow of cigarettes.

At the same moment he sensed them, the knot broke. A red glow flew over his head, shedding sparks, like a bottle rocket. Part of his mind waited for the burst, the flash, to illuminate their faces. Instead, it fell into the sea and died, and the dark remained.

'Who's there?' he said loudly, resolved this time to make his authority felt.

Without warning, a body slammed into him. He lost his foot as the stern twisted and dropped, and staggered back. He came up against the starboard deck edge and threw out an arm instinctively for the lifeline.

It wasn't there.

He sensed more than felt the dark rush of men, and dropped to his knees. Fingernails scrabbled down his jacket. His arm found a stanchion, tried to close on it. He was forced back instead. The deck edge bit into his leg.

His scream was instantly cut off as he hit something unyieldingly and terrifically hard, and rolled off it into the sea.

His arm, flung wide in the same gesture as a dropped baby's, struck something slick and salt-gritty and hooked into it with iron force. He twisted with the same reflex and wrapped his other arm around it. His legs and lower body hit something yielding at the same instant, yielding, fluid and so cold that his breath exploded from him in a paroxysmal exhalation.

He realized he was on the screw guard, a structure of steel pipe that kept the propellers clear of the piers. Somehow, he kept silent – partly because he had no breath. His fingers were tearing off. The sea sucked him down with incredible force. His legs trailed underwater. Voices gabbled above him. Then the sea rose and submerged him, freezing all thought in his brain.

He understood then that he was dead.

He felt the sea harden his fingers to metal, freeze his arms in their clutch around steel. Rusty steel. It needed chipping and painting. Make a note –

The wave receded, leaving him gasping, his eyes at the same moment burning and numbed. The screws, a few feet down, demanded his body with irresistible authority. His weakening hands scraped a few inches backward before his locked arms stopped against a support beam.

He saw the rest of it in that moment. The shock of cold as he let go. Fighting to the surface, only to see the stern light rising and falling, glimmering fainter, sinking at last beneath the waves. Drifting alone, the chill biting deeper each moment, a numb conquest cell by cell.

The sea would receive his body with the same silent equanimity as it received a bullet, a stone, a ship.

Then his imagination died and he had no thought at all. He knew simply and solely that he had only a few seconds left in which he could still try to regain the ship. And that he probably wouldn't make it.

As he realized this, understood it through the same instinct that had flung out his arm, the sea rose again and the ship dragged him through it with terrific force and instantly penetrating cold. The life was leaving his arms. His legs were already gone, weights tied to his waist, a dead burden dragging him down.

The sea receded. Through his blurred eyes rose light glowed from the signal shack high above. With unreasoning cunning, his body waited till the roll lifted him. Then it shifted one hand upward and pulled with such force that in that instant he feared he might tear the steel. Muscle strands snapped in his chest like strings.

His hand caught the next beam, but his fingers wouldn't close. He crooked his wrist around it instead, like a wooden hook, and, with another terrific and despairing lunge, pulled his chest up onto the guard.

The sea returned and he held, grimly, knowing his grip inadequate. But he was higher now, and when it receded, he got his knees up on the beam. Then he jumped. Too quickly, and his foot slipped. His chest slammed down across the deck edge. Lights exploded in his head. But at the same instant, his hand caught the base of a stanchion.

He pulled himself over and rolled desperately across the flat, cold steel, as far as he could get from the edge. Then he pushed himself to his feet, gasping, his lifeless hands raised, though he couldn't make them into fists.

He crouched there for long minutes, listening, peering into the wind and the dark. His heart was tring to fight free of his ribs.

There was no one else on the fantail.

When he could walk, he staggered forward and hooked his hand around the dogs of a hatchway. Shuddering, blinded by sudden light, he turned back from it to vomit into the darkness.

2

THE SEA

7

Latitude 63°–10′ North, Longitude 10°–33′ West: 116 Miles East of Iceland

From thirty thousand feet – the cruising altitude of the airliners, hurtling from Scandinavia toward Labrador, which were the only other evidence of human presence in this waste of water east of Iceland – the destroyer would have been invisible. Would have been impossible for the sharpest eye to discern, lost in an immense bowl of furry ocean, its wake indistinguishable in hundreds of thousands of square miles of whitecapped sea.

From much lower, from an altitude that would have made a pilot sweat, for forced down here there could be no rescue, he might have made her out, and seen that *Ryan* was making heavy weather. Her bullnose pointed doggedly northeast, into the teeth of the prevailing sea. Low and narrow, she did not so much ride as drill through, burrow under, penetrate the swells. Gray as slate, their tops frayed into spray by thirty knots of wind, they rolled inexorably in to burst with drumming booms over the forecastle. Swept aft in tattered streamers, lifted in curved veils over the forward mount, the white of spray contrasted with the dogfish gray of ocean, the sullen pewter sky. Rain mixed with blown seawater rattled in volleys against the sealed windows of the pilothouse.

Behind them, beside Al Evlin, Dan stared out on the combat of ship and sea. He held tightly to the overhead rail, fighting the endless stagger and plunge of the overheated space. He felt sick and weak, but alert. He winced as a vicious heel brought his weight against the cuts in his hands. The cuts he'd gotten going over the side the night before.

'It's not too bad on this course,' said Evlin. The operations officer was wedged between the radar and the helm. He took off his glasses and massaged his eyes. 'It'll be worse when we start quartering. These seas take us from the beam, we'll be doing some rolling then.'

This pitching's bad enough, Dan thought. Climbing a long swell, *Ryan* leaned backward like a runner taking a hill. The wind tore at her superstructure and whistled in her upperworks. Then, at the crest, as the spray clattered like hail on the windows and transparent sheets of water, mirroring the macrocosm in their own wind-roughened surface, surged for the scuppers, she staggered over like a drunk shoved from behind. Then down she went into the trough, leaving the men in the pilothouse staring into the sea, though their eyes were straight ahead.

'You know much about CZ ops?' Evlin was saying in his gentle voice.

'Ceasing what?' Dan jerked his eyes away from the belly of a comber. He'd been thinking about something else. About the moment he'd believed himself dead. He'd been imagining how Betts would take the news. It hadn't been a warm, fuzzy thought. He ought to stop by ship's office and look at his page two, make sure his next of kin, his GI insurance beneficiaries were up-to-date.

'Convergence zone operations. Why we're getting set to tow this fish all over the Arctic Ocean.'

He forced his mind back to the bridge of *Ryan*. 'It's sonar, right?' he said too loudly, then lowered his voice. 'We had the theory at school.'

'Well, you probably know more about it than I do, then.'

'No. Tell you the truth, we didn't get into tactical applications. That stuff was all secret.'

'Okay.' Evlin's eyes lighted up; he was, Dan reflected, never so happy as when he was explaining something. He finished burnishing his glasses with lens paper and put them on. 'You know how the conventional sonars work, like the one under our hull. Send out a pulse, detect the echo, then measure range and bearing and present it on a screen.'

'Yeah.'

'That works okay, but only out to a few thousand yards. Maybe five miles max, in good conditions. Now, that was enough when you were dealing with diesel subs. You could detect their scopes and snorkels with radar, move in and force them down; then localize them with the active sonar and drop your depth charges.'

'Active sonar?'

'Active, you ping and listen; passive, you just listen.'

'That's right; I remember that,' he said, feeling guilty and stupid. His knees hurt. He closed his eyes briefly to fatigue and nausea, then opened them again. The wipers whipped back and forth, shrieking on the downstroke as they slapped crystalline spray from the windows. At the edges it was freezing to a white crust. The steam pipes thudded and clanked, stuffing the closed pilothouse with oppressive heat.

'But the new Soviet subs go faster than *Ryan* can. Thirty knots, maybe more. And when the sea kicks up, it's worse: A surface ships's got to slow, but they don't. Down deep, they can hear better than us, too. Trying to find one of them with a standard sonar's hopeless. They hear you first, and move out of the way; or maybe just linger outside your active range, and send in a couple of torpedoes.'

'I get you.'

'The idea of the IVDS, independent variable depth sonar, is to get down where they hide. The winch gear astern reels out a towed body, with a specially designed sonar head inside, on a cable eight hundred feet long. That puts the transducers between two hundred and six hundred feet down, depending on the length of cable we deploy and the tow ship's speed. Now, you said you knew about convergence zones?'

'I think. Maybe.'

'I'll go over it quickly, then. Sound bends in the ocean. Usually upward, like a reverse rainbow. Depending on the temperature layers, it'll bend up from the source, hit the surface, and bounce. Then do it again. Or it'll scatter at the first bounce, if the surface is rough.

'The first convergence zone is generally around thirty miles from the radiating source and is diffused across a band three to five miles wide. If there's another bounce, it's sixty miles away, and the band's six miles wide. Sometimes you get a third one, ninety miles away, or even more. See how it extends the range? Once you can hear the sub – and Soviet subs are pretty noisy – you can send somebody out after it, like a helicopter, or another submarine.'

'Or use the Asroc.'

'Yeah. Only whatever you fire, it has to do the damage.'

'What's that mean?'

'You tell me. On the CZ detection – or if you see a periscope pop up on the radar, say – you have a location but not a course and speed. So the area where the sub could be expands with time. The formula's simple, pi R squared. In an hour, a sub traveling thirty knots can be anywhere in three thousand square miles. So if you want to fire on a detection and you can't do it immediately – ?'

'Then you expend more ordnance?'

'Or use a special weapon.'

He'd heard that euphemism before. 'We have nukes aboard?'

'There's a magazine back in what used to be the Dash hangar. But back to – what were we talking about? – convergence zones. You can get them sometimes with a hull-mounted sonar, but it's clearer if you get down below the surface layers and wave noise. Also you can do bottom-bounce and sound-channel operations better with a towed sonar. I read in *Navy Times* they're going to buy them for every destroyer in the fleet; that is, if they test out as good as they sound on paper.'

Dan was listening, but nausea was demanding most of his attention. He bent to fit his face into the rubber hood of the radar. Its smell of old sneakers didn't help.

The scope was flecked with random light. Wave clutter, so dense near the center that anything less than a mile away would be wiped out. He flicked a switch, varying the pulse length; no change. It had gone out completely for three hours on the midwatch, leaving them blind in utter darkness. Silver said it was the spray, water in the waveguides. There hadn't been any contacts since they'd refueled, so it probably hadn't been really dangerous, but he was glad to have it back.

'Okay, but what's the idea on testing it here? Up above the Circle, north of Iceland and all.'

'This is the killing ground. Half the subs in the Soviet Navy are based out of the Kola Peninsula. If the balloon goes up, they've got to get out into the Atlantic and cut off our resupply route to Europe. Only way out's through the Gap – between Greenland, Iceland, and the United Kingdom. We've got listening gear on the bottom and the P-threes flying out of Iceland. The surface fleet will be up here, and so will our subs. If we stop them here, and hold the line in Germany, that might finish the war without going nuclear – assuming mankind is so stupid as to let one start.'

Yes, Dan thought, of all the officers aboard *Ryan*, only Evlin would tack on that at the end. 'Okay, I get it now,' he said, wiping sweat off his forehead. 'Jesus Christ, it's hot in here. Can't we crack a hatch, sir? Just a little?'

'Boatswain's mate.'

'Aye, sir.' Pettus came out of the chart room, smoothing back his hair.

The wind hissed and clawed like a cat at the gap, blowing in white flakes that whirled in brief devils on the deck before they melted. He couldn't make out if it was snow or frozen spray.

The third-class stayed by the hatch, rubbing at the fogged glass and staring out. Dan watched him, feeling something corrosive and new gnaw at his heart. Had Pettus been on the fantail last night? He was the right age. So he was a petty officer. Did that make him proof against Lassard's influence? The sailor turned from the window to meet Dan's stare. He nodded, looking simply very young and tired and bored, then went back into the chart room. Dan stared after him. Christ, he thought. I'm starting to suspect people just because of their age. Just like Bryce.

'Captain's on the bridge,' drawled Coffey from behind the wheel.

'Carry on,' said Packer, looming into the pilothouse. Both the officers had turned at the helmsman's traditinal phrase. The captain, not looking at either of them, crossed the bridge with a heavy gait and hoisted himself into his chair. Evlin went over to stand beside him.

Dan bent to the scope again, more to hide his face than to

search for nonexistent contacts. Above the rattle of spray and the sizzle of the International Distress receivers, he heard them discussing the distance to the next course on the curved Great Circle route they were steaming to the operating area.

For some reason he had a sudden image of the submerged sensor, slipping silently through the dark sea hundreds of feet down, a metal fish, a submarine kite, an electronic ear tuned to the subtlest whispers of the deep.

The voices ceased. Dan heard the scratch of a lighter, smelled the captain's mixture. He lifted his eyes, examining him over the hood.

Packer's body was set into the chair like hardened concrete. He was staring out the window, jetting short puffs of smoke. The wiper cleared the windshield every two seconds, allowing half a second of clear sight of endless seas exploding one by one against the stem, before the spume froze again into opacity. Packer's swarthy face – tan? Skin tone? Looked hard, peasantlike, like a Soviet tractor driver's. The chair, elevated for a good view of the forecastle, vibrated as *Ryan* jarred into a trough like a harvester hitting a deep ditch.

Through nausea and fatigue, Dan felt a trickle of envy. Motion didn't bother the captain, nor lack of sleep. He never gave any indication of caring what his officers thought of him, or that he ever doubted himself. Part of him wanted to be like Packer. Another part wondered whether any man should be that silent, that self-assured, that . . . alone. Was Silver's scuttlebutt true – his wife, his son, his career. . . ?

Could he endure that? Losing everything, because he'd done what he thought was right? He tried to imagine losing Betts. He couldn't. To have love, then lose it . . . life wouldn't be worth the effort to breathe and eat after that.

'Captain,' said Evlin. Packer looked blindly at the officer of the deck, his face remote and a little astonished before it focused, like binoculars being adjusted to a closer view.

'What is it?'

'Noon weather, sir.'

'What's it say?'

'Force six in operating area Kilo right now. Poor visibility in spray and precipitation. Predict that will continue for the next three days. Possibility of storms after that.'

'Very well.'

The lieutenant retreated and Packer covered his eyes, propping hand-tooled western boots on a radio repeater. Dan watched him covertly as a roll leaned him against the armrest. The skipper grunted, stirred, then opened his eyes again. He drew his pouch and began the ritual of clearing and restuffing his pipe. His jaw bunched around the stem and he scowled forward, sucking blue flame into the bowl, as a squall broke on the windows and hammered on the steel just above their heads.

Again Dan tried to imagine what he was thinking about. The squall? The upcoming operation? His son? His mind retreated from the terrifying dilemmas of another soul. Then he remembered he had something to tell him.

'What are you smoking, Captain?' he asked before he had time to think about it.

Packer blinked and turned his head. 'Hullo, uh, Dan . . . what, this? Two-thirds latakia, one-third burley. Touch of cavendish for scent. You doing okay aboard?'

'Well, in general, yes, sir.'

'Getting enough rest?'

'Well, no sir, I'm pretty tired,' he said, then felt his face heat. Packer spent twice as much time on the bridge as any of the watch standers. He'd been in his chair all last night, smoking wordlessly in the dark and staring out the window the entire time the radar was down. 'I mean, I guess everybody is – '

'You get used to it,' said the captain, as if he understood what Lenson was thinking. He tapped the pipe against his teeth and slid his eyes sideways to Dan's, then beyond him. 'I never did get to welcome you aboard properly, did I? Understand you slipped last night, almost went overboard.'

'I *did* go overboard, sir. And it wasn't a slip. Has Commander Bryce talked to you about it?'

'He mentioned it briefly. What do you mean, it wasn't a slip?'

He lowered his voice. 'I mean I was pushed, sir. That's

what I told the exec, too. Sir, should we talk about this here? Or could we – '

The captain's face had altered subtly. He straightened, somewhat stiffly, and swung his legs down from the chair. 'Al, can you live without your JOD for a couple of minutes? I'll bring him right back.'

'Sure, sir. If you say so.'

The captain's sea cabin was just aft of the bridge. Dan followed him in, grabbing the jamb as *Ryan* screwed her way through a wave. 'Sit down,' grunted Packer.

The cabin was ten feet by seven, with a brown metal work desk, a round coffee table, thin green carpet with paths worn into it, and a porthole. Packer folded himself onto a leatherette settee. His legs stuck up awkwardly, showing calf above black socks. The coffee table was covered with message traffic and three-ring binders marked BUPERS and NAVORD and JAG. An inch-high pyramid of ash smoldered in a huge cobalt glass ashtray. Dan noted several Camel butts in the pile with the used pipe tobacco. Packer pointed at the other end of the settee.

'Thank you, sir.'

'Dan, I'm sorry if I've neglected a new officer. Getting under way on short notice, and I've had to spend a lot of time in the engineering spaces; Ed's got real problems down there. Maybe Ginnie and – ' He stopped. 'Maybe I'll have you over to the apartment when we get back, you and – Susan?'

'Susan. Her nickname's Betts. Yes, sir, that'd be great, sir.'

Packer leaned forward, cupping the pipe. 'Ben told me you had a close call, but he didn't mention being pushed. He says you're not clear what happened. That right?'

'Not perfectly clear, sir, it was dark. But clear enough to know there were other people out there with me, and more than one of them were trying to force me over the side.'

'Who?'

'I don't know, sir.'

'Any guesses?'

'I figure it's part of the deck gang.'

'Why?'

'Well, it just seems logical, sir. Rich – I mean, Lieutenant

Norden thought so, too.' He explained about discovering Lassard sitting down on watch, about catching them in the whaleboat at general quarters.

'You mean, after having a set-to with him a few minutes before, and so forth. Yeah, it's logical, but it's not the kind of thing you can do much with legally.' Packer shook his head angrily; arcs of smoke drifted up, then were shredded by the overhead blower. 'Why would Ben leave that part out?'

'I don't know, sir.'

'This isn't the first time something like this has happened. I knew a lieutenant was killed on the *Cony*. Medical officer. Guy in the air-conditioning gang picked up the clap in Turkey and made some kind of deal with him to leave it off his record so his wife wouldn't know. Then the guy got it in his head somehow that the doctor had *given* it to him, that people were talking about him, so on and so forth. Nut case. But he turned himself in – or maybe they caught him with the knife, I don't remember. Anyway, there was no question about whether it actually happened.'

'This happened, sir,' he said. It had been the same the night before with Bryce – only worse. The exec had all but accused him of making it up. He flushed at the memory. He'd thought officers told the truth and were assumed to have done so. Another fairy tale bites the dust. But something in Packer's manner reassured him. 'What do you recommend we do, sir?'

'Several possibilities,' said Packer, tamping tobacco with a little tool. 'One: I could send off a criminal investigation report. That would probably get us ordered to Reykjavik, have the Naval Investigations Service meet us at the pier. Or they might cancel the tests, send us back to Newport.

'That raises a problem. This is an important operation we're on. As you know. They're holding up purchase authorization on this gear till we get back. But CNO might figure the way things are going, fleet discipline requires it.

'But what'll really happen is, they'll do the investigation, do the interviews, and finally conclude they can't tell who was involved. And we can't punish on the basis of logic alone. So we lose all around.'

'I see,' said Dan. He recognized the captain didn't like that alternative. He couldn't see much in it, either. 'What are the other possibilities, sir?'

'Well, I have the power, according to the manual, to convene a board and investigate it here.' Packer's eyes flared into brilliance over the lighter. 'That would take time. Chew hell out of the wardroom. But what worries me is, it'd spread the story all over the ship. That could be bad. Considering how much longer we got to go out here. And I don't think they'd find anything, either.'

'Who would chair that, sir?'

'Probably the XO.'

'Yes, sir.'

'So, bottom line, my recommendation might well be to cool it. Play it close to our chest. Goes without saying don't repeat this, and it's a hard thing to say, but – I don't trust this crew. Their morale, their attitude. Nam's tearing the Navy apart. I don't know what's going to happen to the service.

'But that's beside the point, we've got to live with it. But we'll put the word out to the wardroom. And all of us will be more careful moving about the decks.'

Dan felt his mind searching cautiously along alternate paths. He recognized that the captain wanted his input. But the decision, like every decision made aboard this steel planet, was Packer's responsibility in the end. 'I don't know, sir. Seems to me we ought to do something. Otherwise, they might try it again.'

'You think I'm advocating the quietus. I'm not, or at least not for the reasons someone with a cynical mind might think.

'See, if there was no question it was attempted murder, there'd be no hesitation – we'd investigate. But the lifelines were down for repair – they may not have known that. Somebody might have gone back for a smoke and lost their balance on a roll and knocked you over when they didn't mean to. Could it have been that way? Think about it.'

Dan thought. For quite a while. Finally he said, 'I guess it's *possible*, sir. Being as truthful as I can. If they were still unused to the darkness, and I startled them doing something back there, it's conceivable they didn't mean to force me over the side. But I think they did.'

'I don't have to tell you, this doesn't make you look good, either. How long have you been with us now? Eight days? Have you made such red-hot enemies in that short a time?'

'Well, I didn't think so, sir.'

'And of course none from previous cruises in this case. . . . No, it's unlikely.' Packer glanced at the bulkhead. Dan saw he had a compass and rudder indicator there. 'I'd hate like hell to break this cruise. It's not the usual training crapola. You know, Dan, the commodore didn't think the squadron could sign up for it until I guaranteed him we'd come through. We worked three shifts welding everything back together. Despite what I said about the crew, some of them sweated blood to get us out here. Now, if there's one thing I've learned in the Navy, it's "don't overreact." I think an investigation would be overreacting on this one.

'Ben says he asked you to write out what happened, a statement.'

'Yes, sir.'

'Got it done?'

'Just about, sir.'

'Make it brief and factual. If it says basically what you just told me, I'll file it by message and tell the squadron staff what's going on. If they want to overrule me, so be it.'

'Aye, aye, sir.'

'But – *but* – only on the condition that you have no bellyache about it. Because if you're right, you're the one who's at risk.'

'I guess I'll sign up for that, Captain. If you think that's the best thing to do.'

'That's the spirit. Whatever, I agree with you on Lassard. I don't care how shorthanded we are, we've got to bottom-blow that bastard. He's off *Ryan* the minute we hit port. Administrative transfer, if nothing else. Christ, I'm glad we didn't lose you, though.'

'So am I, sir.'

Packer got up. 'Okay,' he said, slapping Dan's back. His hand was solid but his gaze was already long, as if he'd already dismissed him; as if he were looking through the steel into the sea. Turning his head, Dan saw that, yes, the captain was looking out the porthole at an approaching squall. 'You did right to come to me on this. Let me have that statement as soon as you get it fixed up, okay?'

'Yes, sir.'

Off watch. He paused inside the starboard breaker, looking out. Sixteen hundred, and already it had been dark for an hour. The foul-weather jacket Chow Hound Cummings had issued him was snug, his gloves warm, but his face was stiffening after only a few minutes in the open. According to the chart, they'd be crossing the Arctic Circle the next day.

CZ op area Kilo was even farther north, within the dotted line in the *Polar Atlas* that meant drifting ice.

Originally open to the weather, the breaker – the section of main deck to port and starboard below the pilothouse – had been half-walled with quarter-inch plate during one of *Ryan*'s past transmogrifications (Transmongrelifications, he thought). In bad weather it offered little more than shelter from the wind. He glanced around it, stamping his feet as the icy steel siphoned warmth from his toes.

It looked as if Pettus's guys had gotten to red lead, then stopped. The half-finished patches glowed faintly in the side wash of the port running light. Flicking on the flashlight he carried now around the clock, he glanced behind the stringers for tools or paintbrushes. Good, he thought, I'm getting through to them at last.

The ship rolled as he emerged from the breaker, going aft. The spray and the wind hit him at the same moment. He skidded in the darkness, the hard leather soles slick on pebbled ice, and grabbed wildly for the rail. Even through the glove, it was like grabbing a bar of solid cold. He stared downward at the faintly glowing sea, trying to master his fear.

Here, halfway down the length of the ship, the bow wave left at fifteen knots a five-foot boundary of smooth water, at least in troughs; when the sea crested, it climbed straight up the hull. He pointed the light down at it. Directly below him, a discharge spewed water in a steady arc. Where the hull met sea, the green churned into white. He couldn't see past the layer of bubbles. The sea was dark, and not only with night. It was murky, opaque. He raised his eyes to where the horizon ought to be. But there was only the Arctic night, the Arctic blackness, till the icy wind melted it and it ran across his vision mixed with salt tears.

What had it been like to explore these seas, not with the vibrating rail of a destroyer under one's hand, but the ice-crusted rope of a sailing ship? To an old frigatesman or whaler, *Ryan* would have been enormous, palatial. And they'd done it with no heating, poor food, no power but the wind; unable, under these impenetrable clouds, even to know their position within a hundred miles.

He flicked the light around suddenly, and lit an empty port side. Below it was the faint charcoal line of the propeller guard. Then the sea obliterated it. He looked away and pushed himself off the rail.

Usually in the evening, men stood along the lifelines, smoking, shooting the bull, or simply staring down at the passing sea. Tonight he was alone. Too frigging cold, he thought. Might be one or two in the lee. He thought of checking the Asroc deck but decided not to. Most of that was Reed's anyway. All that was his was the boat. And he knew who'd be there.

The kinnicks: Lassard, Gonzales, Greenwald, Coffey. Sometimes Lonnie 'Brute Boy' Connolly, one of the new draft of Cat Fives, obese and slow-witted. What the hell did kinnick mean? He'd figured out why they'd been smoking cigars at GQ. I ought to check the whaleboat, check they're not smoking it up there right now, he thought again, stopping short and looking once again down into the sea. But again he didn't.

Are you afraid to? he asked himself.

The stern was deserted in the gloom. He walked quickly round it, following the beam of his light, splashing through slush that had accumulated in the dented plates. The lifeline was up and taut. He checked that the pins were in and seized with wire. He kicked the lashed-down flagstaff, checked the chocks and bitts, then headed forward along the port side. He glanced up, to see a shadow looming over him. The flash showed him Vogelpohl, the lookouts' earphones clamped to his round head. The departmental yeoman blinked in the sudden light.

As he'd expected, a few men were loafing in the lee of the deckhouse, cigarettes glowing. They stopped talking as he approached, withdrawing, with the slow, ostentatious obedience of sailors complying with stupid orders, their arms from the upper lifeline and their feet from the lower. The sweep of his light showed him pallid, unfamiliar faces: snipes, boilermen or enginemen, from the chthonic regions where Talliaferro reigned. Jesus, he thought, looking at their soaked T-shirts. There must be a hundred degrees' difference between where they worked and this open deck, more if you counted windchill.

'Evening,' he said.

'H'lo,' said one of them. The others waited till he was past, then leaned back on the lines.

Fire station. Hose stowed, nozzle free of crud and ice, turns off and on by hand, spanner wrench in its bracket. Hatch to paint stowage, dogged and locked, gas flood lever sealed, pressure gauge in normal limits. His light waned to a ruby spark as the batteries chilled. A white figure approached, carrying something beneath its arm, like the ghost of Anne Boleyn. As it cleared the breaker a gust snatched away its hat. The cap blew free of the ship, settled, then was caught by the wind and whirled out into the darkness with dizzying speed. The messman ducked his head and continued aft, clutching the sack of garbage against the wind's claws.

His light died. God, he thought as he undogged a door, as ice fell crackling from the gaskets, how much colder will it get north of here? Will we see the sun at all?

His stateroom was hot and humid as saturated steam. He stripped off jacket and gloves in the sweltering dark and was unbuttoning his shirt when Cummings sneezed from what seemed to be his assigned station aboard ship, his bunk. 'God bless you,' Dan said.

'Uh. That you, Lenson?'

'Yeah.'

'Careful getting into your rack.'

'Huh?'

'You got a present. Look before you leap.'

He pulled himself up and banged the reading light. It buzzed and flickered and came on.

His bunk was filled with tools. Rusty scrapers, wire brushes, a ball peen, a two-foot length of wire rope, paintbrushes wrapped in paper towels but still bleeding red orange. He snatched them off the sheet, but they left a lurid stain. Beneath was a dustpan heaped with plain trash: cigar butts, Snickers wrappers, empty cigarette packages, a snuff tin.

'Where the fuck did all this shit come from?'

'Santa Claus.'

'I'm serious. Who put this crap in my rack?'

'Well, he's short, and blond, and wears two silver bars.'

'That bastard,' Dan muttered. His fartsack was covered with rust and oil. 'I got to sleep in this. Norden did this? That shitheel.'

So that was why there wasn't anything left in the breakers. He felt his face go wooden. Suddenly, decisively, he pulled a towel out of the nest of pipes and began tossing things into it.

The chiefs' lounge was full of men waiting for evening chow, but Bloch wasn't there. He went through it, heedless of their looks, into the bunkroom, expecting to find him whittling. He wasn't there, either, but his rack was. Dan unrolled the towel over it. The tools made an unholy clatter; the brushes smeared orange like a hunter's coat. There, he thought viciously. Shit flows downhill? I'm not on the bottom anymore.

'Mr Lenson? Lookin' for me, sir?'

Bloch stood behind him, bald head wet, belly bulging over a bath towel. His shoulders were blue with faded designs. His eye went past Lenson, and instantly registered understanding.

'Get that crap out of my rack, Ensign.'

'I told you about getting loose gear cleaned up after work.'

'Get it out of my rack! It doesn't belong there.'

'Put it in the petty officers'. Lieutenant Norden put it in mine.'

'No, that game stops here,' said Bloch. He stood without moving, an overweight, aging man with faded tattoos, in a towel. 'Move it. Sir. Now.'

He understood then that he was in the wrong, though he didn't know why. For Norden to do it to him was, apparently, all right. For him to do it to Bloch wasn't. And worse, he couldn't make Bloch accept his wrongness. His mind cast desperately for a compromise, but there was none.

'Fuck it,' he said to Bloch's hard eyes, his sagging cheeks. His voice began to tremble. 'Call Isaacs down to get it. I don't care. You clean it up.'

At the realization that he was shouting, a deadness clamped itself suddenly across the poles of emotion. He felt his mind separate; the rational observing part of it drew back and his body coasted free, weightless. His throat hurt. He turned and walked toward the door to the messroom, expecting, as he crossed the threshold into the waiting eyes, the clang of a thrown hammer; but from behind him, from all around him, there came no sound at all.

8

Latitude 67°–18′ North, Longitude 0°–31′ West: Operating Area Kilo, Norwegian Sea

'. . . And get the filters in early; filter-cleaning shop will close at noon.'

The line of bored and hostile faces swung toward him and away, greenish and ashen under the fluorescent light. He swallowed nausea, looking down again at his wheel book. 'The following is a message from the Captain.

'At dawn today, we will have steamed three thousand five hundred miles since passing Brenton Light. Despite bad weather and mechanical difficulties, *Ryan* continues to meet the demanding requirements of this special operation.

'Captain Packer asked the officers to pass his congratulations on to you, the crew. The number-one ship in the number-one Navy in the world can continue her long record of outstanding performance only as long as you perform with professionalism and excellence. He has every confidence that when we steam home past Point Judith, we'll do so with the good feeling that comes from having done our duty well and faithfully.'

Boredom and cynicism hung in the air like the smell of damp, unlaundered clothing on unwashed men. He turned to the silent figure beside him. 'Chief?'

'That's all.'

'Any questions? Okay. Carry out – ' A hand jiggled over the back row. 'Lassard.'

'Tomorrow's Sunday, Ensign. We doin' so outstanding, you gonna give us the day off?'

He glanced at Bloch, but the chief's face gave him nothing back. 'Well – I'll check. But I wouldn't expect it.'

'The other divisions got it off.'

'I said I'll get back to you on that.'

'Okay, then. See what you can do, Ensign.'

The men around Lassard snickered. Bastards, Dan thought. He said angrily, 'That's all. Carry out the plan of the day.'

The front rank returned his salute sloppily. The rest made tentative motions toward their caps, or simply broke into a drifting mass headed for the doors at either end of the passageway. The petty officers moved in like border collies, cutting them out and assigning the day's work.

The day's work, he thought. It wouldn't be dawn for hours, and some of them would be up past midnight. Anger struggled with pity as he watched them. The captain's gung ho pat on the back, passed on by Bryce at officers' call, might go down with the snipes, the signalmen, the electronic technicians – sailors with pride in themselves, their work, and their ship, old as she was. But the deckhands had listened with the glazed eyes of slaves commended by Pharaoh. The deck apes were at the bottom of the pay and pecking order. A recruit assigned to First Division tried to get out as fast as he could, striking for gunner, personnelman, quartermaster. The ones who failed stayed, scraping rust, putting their backs to a line, or standing for hours behind binoculars in sleet or rain. They had no illusions about 'professionalism.'

To make it worse, they were desperately overworked. They stood bridge and lookout watches, six to eight hours a day of wrestling the wheel or shivering on the main deck. In this constant spray, they had to grease the deck gear daily, wipe down bulkheads, check the securing lines rigged against the sea, lay sand and salt to keep the ice down. All of it was labor-intensive, on a ship built when labor was cheap. There was still more to do inside. Norden (direct from Bryce, Dan was sure) wanted the boatswain's locker and paint locker cleaned and painted out. The latest was an order to paint the bullnose blue, as tradition required north of the Arctic Circle. Dan shuddered. Half the time now, it was underwater.

If I had the assigned complement, he thought, forty instead of twenty-six, we might stay abreast. But his guys were putting in sixteen, eighteen hours a day, and the cramped berthing and unceasing motion were probably making what rest they got more like a dream-deprivation experiment.

He had no sympathy for the kinnicks. They were bad apples. But even the good men were being worn down to carelessness and apathy by chronic fatigue. He didn't need a leadership manual to tell him that was dangerous.

So why not give them a day off – rope-yarn Sunday, in sea lingo? They'd still stand watch, but they'd get a few more hours of sack time. He'd have said yes on the spot, but he knew Bryce would veto it. He'd heard the XO's philosophy before: 'There are no Sundays at sea.'

I should have just said no, he thought bitterly. Now that he'd waffled, the men would discuss it, hope for it, and the inevitable disappointment would embitter them even more. Another too-long-delayed understanding of the situation.

He was still cursing himself when Bloch said, 'Got anything more for me, sir?'

'Well, you know what we have to get done, Chief. Just keep them at it,' he said, frowning at a new scar on the toe of his shoe.

'That's what I told the POs before we formed up.'

'Well, carry on.'

'Aye, sir.'

He'd tried, the day after dumping the tools in his rack, to apologize to Bloch. The older man had said he understood, it wasn't easy coming aboard a ship like this fresh out of school. The words were right. But now there was a barrier, a reserve, that hadn't been there at first. And he'd caught looks from the other chiefs. I should have apologized in front of them, he thought. John Paul Jones's advice, memorized by every midshipman, was to commend in public and reprimand in private. To that, Dan thought, add apologize in public, too.

Couldn't he do *anything* right?

He came back from his thoughts to find himself alone in the passageway. He closed the notebook and climbed heavily toward the weather deck. He needed fresh air before his breakfast came out his ears.

Ryan had been on station since the day before. Packer had set them steaming in a rectangle thirty miles long and three wide, oriented with the long axis in the direction of the prevailing sea. At five knots, they spent almost seven hours beating upwind, taking the waves, which had increased gradually in size and fury, on the bow. The crosswind leg was angled ten degrees off the wind, making the rectangle a trapezoid.

That was the leg he dreaded. The seas came in on the beam and the old destroyer's rolls were brutal. During the night one rogue swell had boarded, tearing a davit from a rust-rotted socket at frame 55 and streaming a fire hose the length of the ship, the flailing nozzle smashing two portholes. He'd seen the clinometer swing to forty-five degrees, which meant it was as easy to walk on the bulkhead as on the deck. The instrument measured to seventy, but Evlin told him that if it ever hit sixty, there'd be nobody to read it but the fish; they'd be capsized and sinking.

The downwind leg was easiest, but with the wind astern, it was over in four or five hours. Packer had tried slowing, but below four knots the twin rudders lost bite in following seas. Then another crosswind, and finally around into the swell again, and endless battering and pitching that nonetheless was almost welcome, for when it came to an end, they'd have to sweat out those three crosswind miles once more.

Emerging onto the weather decks, he saw they were on that upwind leg now. The fantail was awash and shrouds of spray blew over it, trailing from the edge of the Dash deck like bridal veils. He caught at his cover just in time, then stuffed it into his jacket, making a lump. His hair and neck were soaked in a moment, the icy cold familiar now.

It looked as if half the crew was on the fantail. He joined them, studying the gray whalelike hulk that loomed, dripping spray, above the winch assembly. Norden, Rambaugh, Reed, all the sonarmen; a technician from Naval Sea Systems Command, installed aboard with the gear; the rest of the men from First Division. Bryce and the captain stood watching from the partial shelter of the deckhouse.

As experts on hoisting gear, or the closest thing the ship had, the boatswain's mates had been drafted into the VDS detail. The antisubmarine warfare officer was leaning over the lifeline, staring down. As Dan came up, he was shouting, 'Raising or lowering?' to Isaacs. The boatswain was standing off to the side, a cabled box cradled in his gloved hands.

'Lowerin', sir. Bitch is hung up again.'

Dan leaned to see what was wrong. The AN/SQS-35 towed body, the 'fish,' was ten feet long and four wide, and looked heavy as sin. The sonar was somewhere inside. It was raised and lowered on a complex arrangement of steel scissors driven by a hydraulic motor. Below hoisting gear and fish was an immense reel. The cable on it was fitted with thousands of tiny vanes, each independently swiveled, to streamline it and keep it from vibrating as it was dragged through the water. Cummings had said at breakfast it cost five hundred bucks a yard. The whole arrangement looked like a disaster from a maintenance point of view. Already he could see rust weeping from the bearings.

He moved back beside Norden. The weapons officer stood with folded arms, scowling up at a huge white bird that dipped over the passing crests. It seemed to be keeping station on *Ryan*. His cheeks were stubbled with blond beard and his eyes were red and puffy.

'Rich?'

'What?'

'The guys in First Div are asking for a rope-yarn Sunday. I'd like to give it to them. We can't do much topside in this weather –'

'You know the XO's got to authorize that. Besides, I want them on deck. We might need them fast if something else carries away.'

Dan pressed his lips together, tasting bitter sea. The wind slapped him, and he shivered and glanced around. Bloch had come up behind them.

'Try it now,' Reed shouted, leaning over the stern. Isaacs twisted a switch on the box. The motor whined. The steel levers edged down a few inches, but the fish stayed stubbornly aloft, swaying ponderously as the stern slammed into a trough.

'Is it moving?'

'Nossir.'

'Back it up, then forward,' suggested the technician. Isaacs twisted the switch. The motor groaned, levers jerked, but the fish didn't move, just shuddered a little each time *Ryan* rolled, its round belly and little fins swaying above the boil of gray-green sea.

Then Bloch was thrusting his way through the men at the rail. 'Cut that fuckin' motor off a minute, Ikey,' he said, handing Greenwald his cap. He looked down at the lowering gear, shielding his eyes from spray and wind, then threw a leg over the lifeline. Reed grabbed his arm. 'Chief – '

Bloch shrugged it off and disappeared below the turn of the deck. His voice came up, faint against the shriek of the wind and the creak of the suspended mass. 'Gimme a line, here, Popeye.'

Leaning down, Dan saw that Bloch had found footing on the lower arm of the assembly and was searching with his boots for the next step. Below him water foamed from the screws, swirling in violent dark green eddies laced with cream. For the first time he noticed ice, brownish chunks the size of dinner plates, rocking and spinning in the miniature maelstroms.

The chief's bare hands were white against gray-painted steel. He found the next foothold and swung himself down clumsily, hugging his stomach into the hull, and then reached to his belt. His hand came away with the combination knife and spike the boatswain's mates carried. He leaned into the drum, and a hollow clanging came up to the men on deck.

'Line, Chief!' shouted Rambaugh. When he tossed it, the wind caught the end and whipped it out and down into the wake. Dan thought at first he'd thrown it too far, but then he pulled it up. Soaked, heavy, it was less the plaything of the breeze. Still its knotted end whipped across Bloch's ass, making the chief flinch. He poked his head out of the drum.

'Line, Chief.'

'Okay. Okay. Slack off.'

Holding on with one hand, the seething sea surging to the soles of his boots, Bloch caught the line and pulled it round his paunch. His hand performed a quick flip and twist and Dan saw a bowline.

'Tie it off, Popeye,' said Norden.

'Naw, sir. Break his back if he slips. I'll just take a turn on this cleat.'

Bloch's bald head disappeared again. More clanging.

Finally he backed out. He swung back against the line. 'Gimme a hand up.'

Dan helped pull him back over the lifeline. The boatswain's face was red. He tugged his jacket down over where his shirttails had escaped. 'Awright, hit it now, Ikey.'

This time when the motor hummed, the swivel arms jerked and began to lower. The fish swayed, approached the water, plunged under as the stern sank. The tech showed his fist to Isaacs. The hum stopped. The fantail heaved up under their feet, water running forward past their boots, and the gray-black smoothness surged up, too, halfway back into the light. Water poured in through flood holes. The tech pointed downward, and Isaacs twisted the switch again.

Driven under by the arms, the fish submerged, air foaming and bubbling from its tail.

'Release it,' said Reed. Isaacs clicked over a toggle. A clank came from below them. The cable drum jerked, shedding a crackling cascade of thin, transparent ice, and began to rotate. The bubbles disappeared. The finned cable reeled steadily down, disappearing into the murky, turbulent water.

Bloch threw the coiled line to Greenwald and took back his hat. 'Toggle pin was fouled on the drum frame. Looks like it was put in backward. I'd say redesign it, make it yardbird-proof.'

'Thanks, Chief,' said the technician.

Bloch left, yelling at the seamen to come with him. The officers were left staring into the sea. 'How're the sonar readings going?' Dan asked the ASW officer.

'Okay. We've been getting background readings, mostly. Getting the sonarmen used to local conditions. Our playmate's supposed to show up today.'

'Great. Let's get this over with.'

'You aren't any more eager than I am,' said Reed.

He finished the last bite of a veal cutlet (an act of faith; he was still sick) and speared the last fry with his fork. It had been a long afternoon. Along with inventorying the forward gear locker, going over the Eldridge mooring method, and struggling with thirty overdue maintenance chits, he'd tried to get a first cut on Isaacs's fitness report. Now it would be a long evening, starting with the second dogwatch.

When he got to the bridge, it was dark. 'Any change?' he asked Silver.

'Wind's up, barometer's down. Twenty-nine point five and dropping. Quartermaster says there's a major low en route. Number-one generator's on the line. Fish is streamed at two hundred feet. You got a turn coming up at time twenty.'

He stepped behind the helmsman, checked the red glow of the gyrocompass, heading indicator, magnetic compass. Port pump and port synchro were on the line. 'We picked up the sub yet?'

'That should happen during your trick.'

'What do we do then?'

'Whatever Sonar tells us. Reed's down there; he'll give us our orders over the twenty-nine MC.'

'Uh – what's that?'

'The Sonar Control speaker. The intercom to the left of the XO's chair.'

'Who's got the conn?'

'I do. Hold on a sec while I give it to Al. Here, here's the binocs.'

He took his usual position beside the radar. Silver reported to Norden, who had his head down with Evlin over the chart table. Now that Reed was busy, the two lieutenants were standing port and starboard, six hours on, six off.

Silver came back. 'He says to give it to you.'

'To me? Great.' Dan grinned; this would be the first time he had control of the ship. 'I relieve you.'

They exchanged salutes. 'This is Mr. Silver,' shouted the jay-gee. 'Mr. Evlin has the deck; Mister Lenson has the conn.'

The seamen on the bridge acknowledged. Dan turned, to find Coffey's impassive face, lit red from below, regarding him across the helm console. 'How you hanging tonight, Clyde?' Dan asked him.

'No "Clydes" around here. Answer to Ali, or Seaman Coffey. When I answers at all.'

Dan grinned. 'How you hanging tonight, Ali?'

'Loose . . . sir.' Coffey grinned back, a little, warily.

'How's she handling?'

'Kind of rough in the pitches. I can hold it within about five degrees.'

'Good work. Keep it up. Boatswain's mate!'

'Sir,' piped up Pettus.

'We'll be starting the crosswind leg in twelve minutes. Make sure everything on the bridge is secured.'

'Aye, sir.'

Fingering the binoculars, Dan glanced around the bridge. Norden had left, but Evlin still had his head down over the chart. Through the windows, the sky, which had been solid with low nimbostratus during the short daylight, was solid dark. The wipers whined and clacked at blowing spray. He watched the bow rise to a dimly visible sea. Twenty feet, he estimated, trough to crest.

He turned and put the red spot of his flash on the wind gauge across the pilothouse. Forty knots. What had Silver said about a low?

'Got it under control?' asked Evlin.

'Yessir.'

'When you turn, remember you've got the fish astern.'

'Right.'

He fidgeted through the seconds. At nineteen after by the bulkhead chronometer, he crossed to the port side and searched the sea in that direction carefully. They were alone out here, but looking before a turn was a good habit to cultivate.

How much rudder? The turn would require a lot, since their speed was low. But too much could kink the cable, or cause a whipping action on the fish, hundreds of feet down. Forty knots of wind would have a sail effect once the bow started to swing. He peered into the phosphorescent dark, waiting for a long trough.

'Left twenty degrees rudder, steady course three-five-zero.'

'Left twenty, steady three-five-zero, aye. My rudder is left twenty, coming to three-five-zero.'

'Very well.' He waited, but Evlin said nothing. The helm hummed. The ship began to turn, slowly at first, then with gathering speed. A sea gathered itself a hundred yards ahead. Zero-three-zero ... zero-two-zero ... the swing of the compass accelerated.

'Meet her.'

'Meet her, aye.' Coffey spun the wheel back, checking her swing. The bow rose to the sea, but not fast enough. It crashed over the anchor chain, bludgeoning itself apart into glowing foam against wildcats, chocks, life rails, stoppers. Under the liquid water, ice gleamed faintly in the penumbra of the masthead light.

'Steady course three-five-zero.'

Three miles on this course, at five knots. They'd steadied up at twenty-two after. That would be thirty-six minutes to the next turn, or 1658. The downwind course would be two-four-zero. 'Watch the seas, now, Coffey. When you see one coming, give her about ten degrees right rudder.'

'No problem, sir.'

Beam on the swells looked immense. He'd read they came in patterns, but he couldn't make out any. There was also something new: a long cross swell under the wind-driven seas. He was peering out, trying to worm meaning from the boiling darkness, when the intercom said, 'Bridge, Sonar.'

He pressed the key. 'Bridge here.'

'This is Lieutenant Reed. Did we just turn?'

He could hear eerie whines and chimes in the background while the ASW officer was speaking. 'Affirmative. We're on three-five-zero now.'

'Mr. Lenson, the sonarmen would appreciate warning before a turn. *Pargo*'s moving into the second convergence zone band. We had a primary tonal, but you just pulled us off it.'

'Yes, sir. Sorry, sir.'

The intercom clicked twice and went dead. He risked a quick glance around the pilothouse. It was snug and stuffy-hot. Faint lights showed him instrument faces. A seaman sniffled behind him, just in from his turn as lookout. Evlin was reading message traffic now, apparently oblivious to what was going on.

He let himself sag against the repeater. he wished he was down in Sonar; what Reed was doing sounded interesting. More interesting than supervising spray-painting. That thought led him again to what had happened on the fantail. He wanted badly to talk to somebody about it. It was hard to keep your mind off coming so close to death.

But he couldn't. Packer had made that plain. So instead, he said to Evlin, 'How long you been aboard *Ryan* sir?'

'Almost two years.'

'What did you do before that?'

The operations officer's glasses caught the flicker of the radar as he glanced up. 'Usual stuff. Communications officer on an ammo ship, then put in for destroyers and got a *Mitscher*-class. A tour on *Bronstein*, department-head school – and here I am.'

'Two years – you're coming up on the end of your tour. What's next?'

Evlin hung up the clipboard. '*Ryan*'s my last ship, Dan.'

'What do you mean?'

'I've got my letter in. I'm leaving the Navy January twentieth.'

'Oh. I didn't know that.' The knowledge suddenly changed his perception of Evlin. He looked again, imagining more than seeing the clear, alert face, rimless glasses, lock of brown hair. Cold-looking at first, precise, demanding. Evlin grew on you. 'What are you gonna do?'

'Teach.'

'That sounds like it'd suit you. What are you going to teach?'

'Well, that depends. Deanne and I are going to go out to California and find out.'

'You're going all the way to California to find out what you're going to teach?'

Evlin chuckled and dug into his pocket. For a moment Dan thought he was going to show him his wife's picture. But when the flashlight came on, the face in the photo was gray-bearded, the eyes piercing yet good-humored. Dan looked up, puzzled.

'The Master.'

'Wait a minute.'

Evlin laughed again and put the photograph away. 'Ever heard of – ' He said something in a foreign language, too rapid to catch.

'Is it a place?'

'That's his name. Deanne met him in San Diego. I was upset over it at first. That some guru had something I couldn't give her. Then I got to know him. Once I'm out, we'll study at the Consciousness Center for a while. Then we'll be teachers – or whatever else he asks us to do.'

Dan checked the time. A while yet till the next turn. But – wait a minute! Evlin was no ordinary officer, but this was way out of bounds. 'What kind of things does this – guru – have that you and your wife need?'

'You don't strike me as a religious guy, Dan.'

'Well, I guess not anymore.'

'But you want me to explain a holy man to you, like explaining how a sonar works. Right? No, don't be embarrassed. I'd better get used to it.

'To start with, you probably figure me for crazy, going around with a picture like that in my wallet and calling him my "Master," as if I were a dog.'

'Oh, no,' he said guiltily. It was exactly what he'd been thinking. 'I just, you know, wondered. . . .'

'Why don't you go over there in that corner?'

'What?'

'There's something over there. I saw it earlier. By the intercom.'

Dan's flash picked out a black shape under Bryce's chair. 'You don't mean . . . a family-sized U.S. Navy-issue roach, somewhat lifeless?'

'That's it. I noticed it there last night.'

'You squashed it?'

'No. It was that way when I found it.'

'What about it?'

'As you noted, it's dead.'

'Well, everybody's got to go.'

'Correct and succinct. Now, what's the difference between the roach and you?'

Dan checked the clock again, checked the radar, rubbed the lenses of his binoculars across the blackness ahead. The conversation didn't seem out of the ordinary. At night, at sea, men grew close enough or bored enough to talk in subdued, casual voices about things they talked about ashore only with people they loved very much, or when they were very drunk. 'That I'm a thinking organism?'

'Oh, it *thought*. Not clearly. But that difference is in degree only. No, the difference is that the roach was as limited by its programming as our radar there. It couldn't choose what it was going to be or do. We can.'

'Suppose I buy that. Then what?'

'I think alternate paths, a degree of freedom, require the existence of a choice-maker. This implies consciousness: the awareness that we exist. That's our gift and our curse. That's what's really divine in us. But how many of us use that freedom?'

'Is it our business what other people do?'

'Point missed completely. Of course they're responsible for their choices, or at least it feels that way to you now. Later you realize most of that's an illusion, like the idea of self. But most people spend their lives plotting to get more freedom, which they conceive of as enough money and time to do what they – '

The intercom said in a gritty, hollow imitation of Aaron Reed's voice, 'Bridge, Sonar: Gained passive contact on submerged submarine, bearing zero-five-seven, range seventy-six thousand yards. Sounds like a U.S. nuclear attack running loud. Recommend classify friendly.'

'Stand by.' Evlin buzzed the captain, spoke briefly, listened, and hung up. 'Sonar, Bridge: Classification approved. Want us to do anything up here?'

'Just stay in the racetrack. He'll come to us.'

Evlin signed off. 'Now, what were we talking about? Oh yeah – that people will work and steal and lie to get money, and leisure, in order to do what they want.

'But I don't think the average guy spends ten hours of his life thinking seriously about what he really wants *and why*. Instead he desires what the local system, whatever it may be, wants him to desire. Liberty in Naples, or a sports car, or twenty years and a retirement check. Or four stripes, or his own command. But that's not freedom. That's programming. Just like the roach – only it never had another choice.'

'So where does that leave us?'

'It leaves us face-to-face with the tough one. That consciousness, does it survive after we die? Does it rejoin something greater? Or does it just stop?

'But even if the world's wholly material, as the Buddha thought, if we're going to live in it as conscious beings, we've got to turn away from the carnival. We've got to think about the important things. Such as: What are we going to do with however many years we have of thinking, acting life? That, by the way, is why I brought up Sartre before.'

'But you don't believe in existentialism, because you're not an atheist.'

'Oversimplified, but basically correct. Not secular existentialism, anyway.'

'Are you going to try to save me, Al?'

'Dan, I don't think being "saved" is all that hard. You don't have to have revelation, or starve yourself, or have some cracker in a polyester suit hit you on the forehead. A spiritual teacher helps, but I think compassion and good works will do it all by themselves. You don't have to believe in a thing.'

'In nothing?' He thought of Ivan Karamazov.

'Look. The basics are ridiculously simple – as if somebody laid it all out so clearly nobody could miss it. Every religion starts from the same rule: Don't hurt the other guy, unless you like being hurt yourself. But hell, you don't need threats to tell you that. Most people arrive at it more or less by instinct. Maybe not right away, but once they suffer a little, they do.'

'Not everybody has time.'

'We get all we need.' Evlin sounded certain in the dark. 'Most people get fifty, sixty years. How much do you need, if you're serious? The Master comes out of Hinduism, he says there are millions of cycles before we wise up. I suspect that's to justify their social system, with the Untouchables and all. There are times in everybody's life when he's close. When you know life's sacred, life's related, you're part of a whole. If you can break through to that on a full-time basis . . . or make it a habit . . .'

'What's our noble XO think about all this?'

'Bryce? He thinks I'm from another planet.' They both laughed. 'So it must not be as simple to him.'

'You don't think everybody really knows that, deep down, but they push the plate away?'

'What do you mean?'

'I'm not sure. Actually, I think I'm getting confused.'

'Well, maybe that's enough for one watch. But just look out there.'

Dan glanced through the starboard window just as spray wiped across it. The wipers flung it instantly away. As the ship rolled, he caught a glimpse of a comber. It moved in on them slowly out of the north, black on deeper black, a green phosphorescence rippling and flickering along its crest.

'There are things you can't say in words,' said Evlin. Dan heard the crackle of lens paper. 'Just look out there, and think about it. We can talk more later – if you want.'

The wave was almost on them. 'Get ready, Ali, here comes a big mother.'

'Got her clamped, sir.'

'Coffee, sir?' muttered Pettus, his face averted.

'Thanks.'

'Cream 'n' sugar?'

'Yes – no, just give it to me black.'

The sea hit square, so hard the old tin can's bones shook. The deck tilted and he grabbed for the steadying rail. Scalding liquid slopped over his fingers. He hissed, snatched a quick gulp, and burned his mouth, too.

When he was done cursing, he wedged the cup between two cables and bent to the radar. The white maculation of sea return covered the screen. Somewhere under this wind-lashed waste, a submarine was slipping quietly through the darkness toward them.

A hoarse seal-like barking startled him. His flashlight found Pettus, bent over a lashed-down wastebasket. His agonized face gleamed wetly in the pink light. Dan faced forward, breathing deeply. He'd been regretting the veal since he took his first bite of it, and hearing Pettus rapid-firing his cookies didn't help. He tried more coffee.

'Bridge, Sonar!'

'Bridge, aye.'

'Contact "Alfa" is now at first CZ zone, bearing zero-five-eight, range thirty-nine thousand yards. Course two-four-four, speed twenty-five. Tentative identification is U.S. nuclear attack, SSN-six thirty-seven-class.'

'I'll tell the captain.'

'I'll do it,' said Evlin, picking up the phone.

Dan nodded. He turned back to the window, and froze.

Another wave was on them. A huge one, special delivery for USS *Ryan* straight from the Arctic across a thousand miles of open sea. In the dim illumination of the masthead light, it curled its ragged mane toward him, hollow within.

He snapped his eyes down. The rudder-angle indicator glowed at right fifteen. Coffey, swearing softly at the wheel, had anticipated it. There was nothing for him to do but grab the overhead rail, and then, as the old ship heeled more, and more, listen to the clatter of gear leaving the chart-house shelves, the rumble of something shifting down deep in the hull. Spray battered over the windows, blurring the dark with a roar that continued for seconds. His feet left the deck. Mats and cups and logbooks leapt free as if thrown by a squad of poltergeists, rattling down smooth tile suddenly become the side of a cliff. His eye brushed the lighted arc of the clinometer, caught the bubble wavering to the left of fifty.

Could Evlin be right?

Because just then, suddenly, inexplicably, and just for a moment, he forgot his nausea; forgot the tension in his back; forgot the grit behind his eyeballs from lack of sleep, the ache in his legs from hours of watch. He laughed with the glee and glory of fighting the sea in a small ship, in a world where disaster and triumph were both possible and both exhilarating. But he knew even as he wondered, this wasn't the moment Evlin had described, the moment of insight, of revelation. This was visceral, not spiritual; a power and a glory that comes only a few times in each life. It wasn't epiphany. It was only youth.

The submarine came up as his watch was ending, and checked in on UHF from periscope depth. Evlin talked to him for a few minutes on the radio, working out ranges and bearings. Reassured, it broached its sail to provide a radar contact. *Ryan* was on the downwind leg, wallowing as she always did in stern seas. The two ships closed slowly, cautiously, like antique wineglasses too fragile to risk clinking. By the time Barry Ohlmeyer showed up to relieve Dan, they were close enough to make out *Pargo*'s sail and shears through the night glasses, a bladelike tower low to the sea. Below it in the troughs, a black cylinder showed from time to time. 'Ballasted down,' muttered Evlin, holding his binoculars with the tips of his fingers. 'And rolling like a sonofabitch. Guess we better get the captain up here.'

Packer, when he came, barely glanced at the sub. He went straight to the radio remote. A moment later the transmit light went on. Dan kept his binoculars on the sub as he listened to the conversation.

' "Playmate reporting," he says,' said the gunnery officer beside him. 'Casual, aren't they? Look at the way that pig rolls.'

' "Real destroyer weather." Got a sense of humor, too.' Dan lowered his glasses, wondering whether any of his classmates were over there. 'We'll be with them how long?'

'That's up to the captain. And Reed, and the sonar gang. Till they're satisfied they got enough data.'

The captain was still talking. Suddenly Dan realized he was wasting sleeping time. 'Damn,' he said. 'Barry, you ready to take it?'

'Hand it over, man. It won't be near as lonely with somebody to talk to now.'

He was almost to his stateroom, every nerve and muscle yearning for his rack, when he saw a small figure in khaki turn the corner ahead of him. He hesitated, then went on.

Norden was holding the door open, his head inside. 'Looking for me, sir?' Dan said.

'The commander wants to see us.'

'Now?'

'Right now.'

'Both of us?'

'Yeah, both of us. Why else would I be here? You just get off?'

'Right.'

'How's Al holding up? Never mind, he'll give me a buzz when he gets tired. Better change that shirt. What is that? Coffee?'

'I'll be right out.'

They knocked at the XO's door. 'Come in,' Bryce called. He sounded annoyed.

Lenson followed Norden in. The room was just as he'd seen it the first day he came aboard, except that the desk was bare now, and the silver urn had a shock cord clamping it to the bulkhead. Cigarette smoke hazed the hot air. 'Sit down,' said Bryce, nodding to the settee.

'Thank you, sir.'

'So,' said the XO, tilting back in his chair. 'Dan, you run into any more trouble out on deck?'

'No, sir.'

'How's everything with First Division, eh?'

'We're keeping them at work,' said Norden, a little shortly, Dan thought.

'Are you?'

No one said anything. At last, Bryce took out another Camel and charred the end with his Zippo. 'Cigar, Dan?'

'No thanks, sir, one of those was enough.'

Bryce chuckled, then stopped. 'You're keeping them at work. Doin' what? Ship looks like nigger heaven. It's rusty, it's dirty, I find butts in the corners. The forward head makes me sick to go in there.'

'We're above the Arctic Circle, sir,' said Norden, sounding tired. 'Have you been topside? We're taking spray on the signal bridge. It's too rough and too cold to paint and preserve.'

'I understand that, *Mr.* Norden. And I *have* been on deck today. I make a tour daily, you know! I'm talking about the internal spaces! What about them?'

Dan cleared his throat. 'Sir, we finished the paint-out on the transverse passageway, and cleaned out the flammable stowage locker. We've cleared and inventoried the bos'n's locker and we're catching up on interior maintenance. It's hard to keep things shipshape in weather like this.'

'Nonsense, Ensign. Rich, do you buy this no-can-do song and dance? It's not that hard to keep a destroyer clean and well preserved. I've done it. You all just got to attend to detail, detail, and don't let the men dope off so much. I was on the mess decks a few minutes ago and I counted four deck apes sitting there over coffee, Pettus and Coffey and two others, smoking and joking and scratching their asses, not one of them in the spaces doing a job of work.'

'They just got off watch, sir. They were probably warming up.'

'Sir, you've got a point, but Dan's right, too. I was on a new *Knox*-class my first tour. We managed with about the same number of men we have in First Division now. But you can't keep an old ship in the same shape unless you're pierside twenty-five days a month. Right now it may not look like much is going on. But when we get back into better weather, the men'll be topside again. Believe me, nobody's loafing.'

Bryce leaned back, sucking exhaled smoke back into his nostrils, then breathing it out in a rush. He took a comb from his pocket and drew it through his hair. He patted it down carefully. Then he leaned forward, wedged the cigarette firmly in the shell-base tray, and slid open his desk drawer. He came out with a wrinkled pack of Kools and a penknife. He tapped them out under their eyes. Then he unfolded the penknife and slit one of the cigarettes in half and shook the contents out onto the desk.

Dan leaned forward, examining the brownish green flakes. 'What is that there, Mr. Lenson?' Bryce asked him. 'What would you say that is, exactly?'

'I'm not sure, sir.'

'Don't play dumb with me! You know what marijuana is!'

'I've never seen any before, sir.'

'Where'd you find this, sir?' asked Norden.

'*I* didn't find it, goddamn it. Jimmy John did. In forward berthing, up in the overhead. I don't know what he was doing in there. My job, to do the messing and berthing inspections – '

'Lots of people bunk there, sir. Not just First Division.' Dan heard anger in his voice, but he couldn't erase it; he was too tired for circumspection. 'I don't think it's right just to assume – '

'Don't tell me what to "assume," Mr. Lenson. That highfalutin Canoe Club bullshit don't go with me! Rich, you'd better talk some sense into your bright boy here. Either he's not keeping proper tabs on his division or he's smoking rope right along with them.'

Dan leaned forward, his mouth open to speak, but suddenly the curtain came down. He was two people, one enraged, the other empty, a cold, detached onlooker. He pressed his trembling hands down on his legs. The silence endured, broken only by the hissing boom of a sea on the far side of a quarter inch of steel, a clicking scrape as the penknife skittered along the desktop, scattering grains over the gray-green carpet.

'You boys better find out who belongs to this. Hear me? Get me somebody to hang. Or else get real used to your rank, because after your next fitness report, you'll be in it till you retire. Remember, when push comes to shove, I got a jack in my pocket.' Bryce patted his flushed scalp again. 'That understood?'

'Yes, sir,' said Norden. 'I'll have Mr. Lenson begin the investigation immediately.' He stood, and after a moment, Dan did, too. Part of him didn't want to. It wanted to punch the grinning mouth across from him. But that part didn't have control. He couldn't afford to let it have control.

'Thanks, Rich.' A sneer edged Bryce's drawl. 'Glad you're seeing this my way.'

As the door swung closed, the last thing he saw was the executive officer, smiling down at the evidence with secretive delight.

9

Oh-five hundred. He lay with one arm wrapped around an angle iron, the other dangling over the bunk edge. Against his cheek, the pillow was damp and hot.

The sea and wind had risen steadily all night. Around him, the steel body born before his flesh screamed and banged as the sea racked it. The groans of twisting stringers and the pistol shots of riveted joints working mingled with the roar of water against thin plating.

There's something bad on its way, he thought, staring at the motionless hands of his clock, mysteriously luminous, like cats' eyes closed to slits.

During the midwatch, he'd pulled the *Sailing Directions for the Arctic Ocean* off the chart-room shelf. His mind was so accustomed to memorization that now he could recall it. 'The navigable waters of the Denmark Strait, the east Greenland, Norwegian and southern Barents sea are subjected to a barrage of NE-moving extra-tropical storms with their attendant problems of strong winds, high seas, poor visibilities and frequent precipitation. . . . Winter's arrival is heralded by increasing darkness, frequent and intense storms, and ice-choked waters . . . the Icelandic lows . . . raging, migratory storms that roam the periphery of the arctic regions.'

Yet how many waves, how many storms had *Ryan* endured? This was no easy weather, but he understood a hurricane, from a combination of Nathaniel Bowditch and Herman Wouk, to be much worse; and she must have lived through them, in the Western Pacific.

How many men had she carried away from their loved ones, and after long voyaging brought home again? Time had swept her sisters from the seas. Grounded, capsized, lost to enemy action. But *Ryan* had come through it all. She'd go quietly, as ships went, though her end in a wrecker's yard would be as noisy as her birth.

That end could not now be so many years off.

The old destroyer rolled like a stout woman doing the polka, then slammed so heavily the clock jumped free and clattered away into the dark. He slid sideways, fetching up against the line he'd rigged to hold himself in. How much margin had those wartime builders allowed in her frames and longitudinals? More to the point, how much was left after thirty years of rust, sandblasting, rust again? In the hot dark, a thread of light showed where the doorjamb had warped away from the bulkhead. His hand plucked restlessly across his chest through hair and sweat. He couldn't sleep, so he lay listening, and his mind moved relentlessly on.

He'd started his investigation the evening before in the berthing space. The men watched him sullenly from their racks as he prowled about with Chief Hopper, *Ryan*'s slow old master-at-arms. The beam in the overhead where the exec had found the marijuana was bare. He interviewed the men whose bunks were nearest it, fire controlmen from G Division. They shrugged and looked away as he questioned them. He checked the rest of the overhead, scrambling from top bunk to top bunk, probing cable runs and sheet-metal ductwork with a flashlight. He found dust, dead insects, and fuck books, curled yellow pages worn translucent by dozens of readers. He talked to the compartment cleaners, Higgins and Roseman. They were ignorant of where the grass had come from or whose it was. Or so they swore, and though there was no way to be sure, he believed them.

Screw this, he thought at last. Dirty, disgusted, he wondered for a moment whether Bryce had put the grass there himself. Then he scowled. That made a lot of sense, all right.

When he'd gotten back to the bridge at midnight. Silver told him the southerly swell was building and the barometer was dropping fast. The wind had veered easterly and was gusting to fifty knots, and twice the dark sky had opened for driving sleet that stuck to the wiper blades and did not melt.

Packer had adjusted the racetrack, but even two miles downwind felt like forever. The breaking rollers battered at the ship like karate experts breaking bricks. The southwest leg was getting rougher, too, as the southerly swells rose, and the two patterns merged at times to create seas Dan no longer enjoyed watching. At 0230, after steering reported taking water through the overhead, not serious, but not good news. Talliaferro had called the bridge at 0300 to report one of the bilge pumps out, but the machinists had gotten it back on-line before Dan went off at four.

And now it was 0500. Reveille in an hour, and it'd start all over again. Christ, he thought, if only I could sleep. But each time his consciousness began to unravel the ship slammed him into the bulkhead, or hung him, restrained only by the safety line, above a twelve-foot drop to the deck.

He hugged his pillow to the hot skin of his chest and imagined it was her. Without wanting to, he remembered her delicate yielding, a half-reluctant turning away of the head as he moved, delighting in the way her hips followed his, unable to resist. . . .

He struggled briefly with temptation, then yielded. He tried to call back her memory, her presence, her scent, as his hand moved beneath the sweaty sheet.

They'd left the Yard late on Friday, escaping on the weekend he'd earned from a cross-country second against Virginia Tech. The instant her scarab green VW left the gate, he tore off his cap, threw it back, and started unbuttoning his clothes.

'What are you doing?'

'Civvies! I'm a civilian!'

'Took you long enough.' But he was already pulling a knit shirt over his head, struggling to get his pants over his ankles. Shorts. Sandals! Miller time! He threw the sweaty uniform into the back, clawed an icy can out of the cooler, and dipped his head below the dashboard to drain half of it in one gulp.

'Let me have a sip. So, what's the surprise? Where are we going?'

'New Carrollton, on the Beltway. Keep going out this road, then we'll take Route Fifty. I got a reservation.'

'A motel? Dan –'

'Where'd you think we were going?' He stared at her. She drove with her lips pressed together, hair curled round her neck. He flipped it up and laid the bottom of the can against her nape.

'Jesus! Dan, stop it!' She pulled the car back onto the road.

'Sorry.' He kissed her shoulder blade. 'It'll be okay. As long as I'm out of uniform, they can't tell I'm a mid.'

'I'm not worried about that. Is it downtown? What if one of my teachers sees us?'

'Come off it, Betts. Moira knew what we were doing when you snuck me into your dorm.'

'Maybe I shouldn't have.'

'Well, what do you want? Separate rooms?'

She didn't answer, and he sighed, playing with her hair. Some instinct warned him to leave it alone. He hadn't known her long, but he suspected that under what he thought of as her Chinese-American submissiveness there lurked a temper.

After several miles of silence, she began talking about her physical anthropology class. She wanted to be an archaeologist. That disturbed him a little, at some level he could not articulate, but he said nothing. There was plenty of time.

When they reached New Carrollton, he went into the lobby while she parked. The man behind the counter wore a flesh-toned hearing aid clipped to his glasses.

'Hi. I reserved a double.'

'Name?'

'Lenson, Daniel.'

'Lenson with an *L*. Yep, got you right here. Mr. and Mrs.?'

He'd anticipated the question, and thought about what he'd answer. The problem was the honor code. This close to the end, two months before graduation, he wasn't taking any chances. 'No,' he said.

The old man examined him, gaze lingering around the ears. But he said only, 'Military rate?'

'No . . . well . . . okay, I guess so.'

'Here's your key. Pool's through the gate there, ice on the second floor. Checkout's at twelve.'

He was in, free and clear. He grinned at himself in a mirror when the clerk turned away. You monster, he told his reflection. You despoiler of women.

They found the room, unpacked, and went down to the pool. She'd brought a swim-team suit that covered everything he was interested in, but still she looked good. Slim as a branch of willow, fast as a porpoise. She showed off, doing somersaults and back twists off the board. Her parents had a pool.

When she backstroked to the ladder, he put his arm around her. Her flesh was smooth and cold. 'Tired yet?'

'What's the alternative?'

'Piña coladas.'

'I'm tired.'

'Me, too.' They laughed. Beneath the water his hand found her thighs, round and goose-bumped. They clung to each other, and he wondered whether she could feel him through his shorts.

In the room, he made a pitcher of drinks and they sipped them from hotel glasses, leafing through a guidebook. The rum cleared his head, unwound the tension that guarded speech and thought when he was in uniform.

It didn't take long to get undressed. He kissed her shoulders, still hard from the swim, her nipples, her belly. He wanted to do things he'd read about. She said no. But he was beginning to know, he thought, when she was being modest and when she meant it. When she spread her thighs at last, he gazed for a moment, curious. Not much hair there, brown rather than black; hardly any around the lips. They reminded him of the lining of a conch shell.

He took a breath and lowered his face to her, to the salty flower between her thighs. Her hair tickled his nose.

'Jesus. I feel drunk. I don't drink that much . . . Oh!'

He raised his head. 'You like?'

'I'm not sure. I don't think so. Let's do something else.'

'Okay. You do it to me.'

He didn't know the right way, but the way she did it didn't seem to be it. Maybe it took practice. At last he rolled over her. Her eyes slid closed, and she turned her head. He felt himself sharpening as he touched her there, wet, warm, opened.

'Dan . . . are you going to use something?'

'You want me to?'

'I really like you. You know that. But I don't want to get pregnant. Not right now.'

'I'll pull it out when I have to come.'

'Do they teach that at the Academy?' she murmured, but a little frown appeared at the corners of her eyes. 'I guess it'll be all right.'

He felt a great surge of tenderness at her trust. Wetness and warmth opened beneath his probing fingers. She gave a faint cry as he entered.

'Hurts?'

'Not anymore.'

She wasn't tight; he could feel no resistance; yet every centimeter of him was – *caressed*, was the only word he could fit to it. 'Pinch me, Betts?' he murmured, lost.

She tightened obediently. 'Nice?'

'Delicious.'

'You won't forget?'

He didn't answer, lost in the heat. At first she lay passive, absorbing his thrusts. Gradually her hips began to rock, too, and her hands came up, cupped his back, tightened around him. Her breathing matched his, short, fast, shorter, faster. She began thrusting against him, with him, in step, in rhythm. He clung to her shoulders, feeling it begin deep down in his belly.

He closed his lids on a blaze of light. Then pushed away, crying out as wave after wave burst free and ebbed out onto the sheets.

When he was done, she laid her cheek to his. She left little kisses on his neck, his chest, his stomach, and, after hesitating, on the slippery skin of his still-erect penis.

'Oh. Betts. That was tremendous.'

'I liked it too. I was almost . . . Why'd you stop?'

'I couldn't hold it in any longer. You were just too nice.' He stroked her back. His head felt light, as if he'd just finished a calculus final. It came to him suddenly that they hadn't had dinner. But she hadn't come yet. 'Do you want me to do it with my mouth, some more?'

'Hmmm . . . Is this worn-out? Still feels good to me.' Her tongue moved lightly along the shaft, tentatively, then her mouth engulfed him. When he looked down, her eyes were closed and her hair lay like a shining blanket over his thighs.

They made love twice more that night, and again between breakfast and a tour of the White House. By Sunday afternoon they were experts, and she was talking about seeing the school doctor for the pill.

But by then, he now thought, trembling spent in the hot dark of his upper bunk, it had been too late, though neither of them knew it.

He'd been speechless when she told him. They'd talked it over, her plans for graduate school, his going to sea, and cried together. It would be tough. She'd have to postpone her career. But he promised to help all he could, and put in for shore duty at the first opportunity.

The wind rose to a scream and the bunk dropped away and he seemed for a moment to float, free of the ship, free of sea and earth.

I love her so much, he thought. And it was as if she heard him, as if she were God, and he was praying to her. *I love you, Susan.*

He wanted it to be good and true and beautiful, and he wanted it to last for the rest of his life.

Mabalacat had set the fiddleboards and wet the tablecloth. Confined by the wooden grid, the dishes only stirred uneasily when *Ryan* took one of her savage leans. Dan and Evlin and Reed began without waiting for the captain, who'd called down for a covered plate.

'How the runs going, Aaron?' Evlin asked.

'Getting data.'

Dan said, 'Can you hold a submarine in this weather?'

'Sure. The surface return degrades the ducting, but we've got a thermocline at two hundred and a solid channel under that. Storms aren't all bad. You get a lot of surface mixing.'

'So you're getting what you need?'

'Oh sure. The idea's to wring it out. The rougher it gets, the better, far as we're concerned.'

'I'm still not sure I understand why,' he said, tentatively, because Reed never seemed to want to explain things, the way Evlin did.

'Why what?'

'Why, uh – why we need to test it way up here.'

'Well, see, the hull-mounted sonars, they were okay down south. But up here, this is just too freaking rough. You can use the twenty-four, our hull-mounted dome, maybe one day out of three. You can fly a helo maybe one day out of four. Unfortunately, this is where the war's gonna be fought. So the thirty-five, the new fish – it's a big deal, all right.'

Dan nodded, picking at his omelet. He felt sleepy and his arms and legs ached from bracing himself. He was hungry, but food appealed to him about as much as fried sawdust.

He planned to spend today, what there was left of it when he was off the bridge, interviewing his men one by one. Not just about the marijuana; it would be a chance to get acquainted. I've neglected that, he thought. But it was becoming more and more evident that there was something wrong in the division, and to fix it, he had to find out what it was.

'Thanks, sir, that clears it up. Excuse me, please.'

'See you later.'

Bloch was standing by the door of his stateroom. 'Morning, sir.'

'Hello, Chief. Come on in. How's the *Constitution* going?'

'Slow, sir.' Bloch sat, glancing around. He asked whether he could smoke.

'Those King Edwards?'

'Yessir. Good cigars for the price. Though the Tampa Nugget's nice, too.'

'Maybe I'll try one.'

They lighted up. Bloch hooked the trash can toward them with his foot. 'How you like this weather, Chief?' Dan asked him.

'Okay by me, sir. You roll like this for a while, it knocks your brains out. Then you're a real destroyerman.'

'How's work going?'

'Isn't. I had to pull the men off cleaning and send them up on the oh-two level with chippers. If we don't get some of this ice off, stability will go to hell. Traven says we've picked up a hundred tons already.'

'Who's he?'

'Leading damage controlman. Uh, sir, I understand the XO found some grass in number-one berthing.'

'How'd you know that?'

'Come on, sir. Hopper and me go back a ways.'

'Okay, you're right. Bryce – Commander Bryce – wants me to find out whose it is. What do you think? Is it someone in our division?'

Bloch trickled smoke like a broken steam line. 'Right off, I'd say Lassard, but then I'd think. It's easy to blame him for everything. Maybe too easy. Way I see it, there's always going to be troublemakers. Deck gang's not the best-behaved bunch aboard, or they wouldn't be where they are.

'But things have changed since I was a seaman. Specially the last couple years. I was their age, guys'd drink and fight and go UA, but there wasn't this anti-American shit. Burnin' the flag, sit-ins, riots . . . What I was going to say, suppose we caught Slick with it and fired him off the ship. After awhile, somebody else'd take over selling it. There's always the ten percent that fouls things up for everybody else aboard.'

'You're probably right. But we've got to try. How about performance? Have you noticed any of the men acting like they use drugs?'

'Hell, sir, how would I know? Brute Boy, he was born that way, I guess. Gonzales, Greenwald, Hardin, they're not real alert a lot of the time. They act fucked-up a lot. That mean they're using it? Or are they just naturally fucked-up? I don't know. They don't do it in front of me.'

It was the first time he'd seen Bloch on the defensive. 'Well, let's try it another way. If it was you, where would you go to smoke it?'

'Topside, probably. You couldn't smell it then.'

'On watch?'

'Christ, I hope not. That could screw us royal.'

'Ali X. did a good job of steering for me yesterday.'

'Who? Oh, Coffey. Yeah, he could be a good man, get him away from Lassard and them. There's good and bad, his color.'

'Which kind is Isaacs?'

'Lemond didn't do too great on the first-class test, sir. He got advanced on some special selection deal. Make the statistics look good, I guess. I been trying to train him. He knows what he's supposed to do.'

'That's not much of a recommendation, Chief.'

'Sorry, sir. He don't mean to screw up. It just happens.'

'How much do you think there is aboard? A lot, or do they just smoke it once in a while?'

'Like I say, sir, I could tell if they were drunk, but . . .'

'I see. Well, my idea's to have a one-on-one with the men, see if any of them want to talk in private.'

'I don't know, sir. Don't expect too much. The guys stick together when they talk to zeros – to officers. But you might get something out of the older ones.'

'Thanks, Chief. Let's start with Isaacs, okay?'

While he waited Dan worried it through again. The search had gotten him zip point nothing. If he didn't come up with something soon, he'd have to go back to Bryce empty-handed. That wouldn't be pleasant. 'Get me somebody to hang,' the XO had said. But then, just knowing the brass was on the alert might make people cool it. If he put the pressure on, maybe they'd ditch what they had, throw it overboard.

'Mr. Lenson?'

'Come in, Petty Officer Isaacs.'

The leading petty officer slid into the room and snatched off his hat. He had on a new set of dungarees and his inspection shoes, shined. Dan told him to sit down. They talked for a few minutes about the broken davit, then he said abruptly, 'Isaacs, you ever smoked grass?'

'Nossir, I never done none of that.' He looked frightened.

'Didn't think so. Don't worry, nobody's after you. Anybody you know in the division who does?'

'No, sir. Don't know no one that does. Sure not in my section. That stuff probably belong to them signalmen; they stay up all night smoking, playin' cards up in they shack.'

Dan studied the weathered, anxious face, the scarred fingers nervous on the white hat. What was going on?

'Ikey, I need your help. Do you have any problems with the men? Do they threaten you, or anything like that? If so, it's your duty to tell me.'

'Oh, it isn't nothing like that, sir. These boys is no angels. They bitch at me, sure, but they don't mean anything by it.'

'They shouldn't "bitch at you." Do they bitch at the chief?'

'No, sir.'

'You've got to come down hard on that. That's why you've got those stripes. You write up a man for disrespect, I'll take him to the captain. When they start losing pay and liberty, they'll come around fast.'

'Yes, sir, I sure will do that. I sure appreciate your advice.'

'You're sure no one's threatened you?'

'Nothin' like that, sir,' Isaacs repeated, looking at his cap.

Dan gave up and let him go. The next two interviews were no more helpful. Rambaugh had nothing. Pettus said he'd smoked pot in high school but stopped when he got to boot camp.

When the third-class was gone, he glanced at his watch. The odor of cigars, the continual motion of a confined frame of reference were suddenly too much. He decided to skip lunch, skip staring at Packer and Bryce and the others over greasy soup, and went up on deck.

He emerged into a blizzard. Snow clung to his eyelids, flicked by his instantly numbed cheeks without melting. It filled the air like fog, driven horizontally by the wind. Though it was near noon, the sky was almost dark, and between that and the snow he could barely see twenty yards. The bow was a white blur. So was the fantail. The snow whirled beneath the ladders. His bare palms stuck to the rails. He noted, climbing, that the sleet of the night before had frozen to it. He kicked at it, exposing layers, accretions, like a geological formation. There was more on the 01 level, inches thick on the deck, shoaled up in the corners.

A hundred tons . . . He crossed the Asroc deck, checked the boat. Empty. Ice sheathed the lowering cables like rock sugar on a string. He climbed to the signal shack, looked around the flying bridge, and, on impulse, began climbing the ladder leading up the mast.

Ryan's mast began as a tubular steel tripod aft of the bridge. The legs joined at the apex to support the air-search radar, a massive curved bedspring affair, the smaller surface-search antenna, and then the meteorological gear above that. Where the legs met was a little platform the electronics techs used to work on the radars. He approached it gradually. The air-search antenna loomed above him, sixteen feet across, sweeping around through the falling snow with a whooshing, whining hum. The rungs were icy and he climbed carefully, hugging them when the ship rolled.

He stopped at the platform and sat with his legs dangling, staring out into the snow. It came from one point, sweeping toward him and then opening out like, he thought, when you drove a car in a snowstorm. Beneath him *Ryan* plunged and rolled in the confused sea, and he clutched the skimpy guardrail.

Up here, when the wind dropped, he could hear all the sounds of the ship, muffled by the snowfall but clear, individual. Above him, gears ground coffee in the antenna motor. The wind plucked a tarantella in the signal lines and set off firecrackers in the ragged ensign. From behind and below came a breathy roar, and he turned, to see an inky cloud rolling out of the stacks. Talliaferro was blowing tubes. The snow whirled into it and disappeared, swallowed by steam-driven soot. He heard the clack of wipers, a hoarse shout aft, a steady clanging that must be the men chipping ice . . . all of it clear but faint, faint, as if he were Hans Pfaal, ascending in a balloon. Above him the mast sliced sweeping curves through billions of descending flakes. The motion was eerie. He couldn't see the sea. Yet its energy reached up through the steel framework, tossing him through the sky, whip-cracking his head on his neck and making him clutch the icy pierced steel with sudden primeval fear.

Below him, the door to the signal shack opened. The signalman stood at the rail for a while, peering around in the blowing snow. Dan watched him. Apparently satisfied he was alone, the sailor took a wad of money from his peacoat.

Dan started to pay attention.

When the signalman – Hedgecock, or was it Saufley? – finished counting it, he peered round again, then opened a box on the rail. He lifted binoculars out and stuffed the cash under the padding at the bottom.

He replaced the glasses, then stood for a moment more, shivering and pounding his hands together, peering about. He cast one glance upward, but Dan, not moving, must have merged with the upperworks.

The signalman went back inside. A poker stake, Dan guessed. He squatted, looking again into the wind. It drove steadily, endlessly out of the east, icy, pitiless. His whole face was numbed now, and he rubbed it with a numb hand, remembering the danger of frostbite. Why had he come up here? He wasn't sure. Maybe just to be alone for a few minutes.

I better get back on the job, he thought.

He had one boot on the ladder when he was almost startled off it by the foghorn, not twenty feet above. He cowered, kneeling on the slick steel. The sound vibrated in his lungs, battered his brain. When it stopped he listened, thinking of icebergs. An echo should return in fog, warning of white danger. But nothing came back but the rising scream of the wind.

He was getting up again when he saw someone below him. He blinked snow from his eyes and looked again. A bulky figure in a brown leather jacket. Gloves. Khaki.

Bryce.

The exec stood beside the binocular box, looking around the deck. Dan frowned. What was Bryce doing? If the exec looked up, there'd be hell to pay. He hadn't even thought about getting a mast chit.

A swirl of snow came down just then, hiding them from each other. When it parted again the XO was walking aft, hands thrusting into his pockets.

Dan waited till he was gone. Then he came down, fast but careful. He stood at the base of the mast, panting a little. He looked at the signal shack. He looked at the binocular box.

Then he opened it.

There was nothing under the padding but a few flakes of snow.

He had the twelve to sixteen hundred watch, noon to 4:00 P.M. This was the worst day on a three-section schedule, because he'd already stood the midwatch – midnight to four – and would stand the eight to midnight as well, for a total of twelve hours on the bridge out of twenty-four.

He stood it in a daze of fatigue, clinging to the console as *Ryan* pitched and shook. The captain sat belted into his chair, nodding over a tech manual. From time to time, he'd snap his head up, blink out the windows, and chew Norden out for a slow rudder order. He sounded tired and on edge.

For the first time, Dan heard the keel sonar. It came right up through the steel fabric of the hull, an eerie high note, like whale songs he'd heard on a National Geographic special. It went from tone to tone, *eee-EEEE-eee-ooo*, trailing off in a supersonic whine that sent a shiver up his back. He imagined it burrowing down from the storm-lashed surface, twisted by currents and inversions, reverberating down, down, down into two thousand fathoms of inky sea. Over and over, every thirty seconds, and always exactly the same.

He wondered what the whales thought of it.

A swell came out of the snow and swept over the foredeck, throwing spray thirty feet into the air as it exploded against the raked face of the gun mount. It rattled against the pilothouse like shrapnel, frozen before it hit.

He focused his binoculars on the chain stoppers. Bloch had lashed them down with six- thread, but he could see them shifting as the wave receded, banging off shell-shaped white carapaces. The swell left round chunks of ice big as garbage-can lids stranded in the scuppers. He shivered. Why was it so cold? He suddenly realized that the goddamn pilothouse was freezing.

'Mr. Lenson.'

'Yes sir.' He lowered the glasses, and went over to the captain's chair.

The skin under Packer's eyes was puffy and veins showed at the corners. His hands shook as he lighted his pipe. He was spending most of his time up here now, when he wasn't in Sonar. Dan wondered how long he could keep it up.

'Who's got the conn?'

'Mr. Norden, sir.'

'What leg are we on? Anybody keeping track?'

'Yes, sir, zero-six-zero, an hour yet to turn.'

Packer stared into the snow. 'How's your junior officer's journal coming, Mr. Lenson?'

'Uh, not too much done yet, sir.'

'You're required to complete one lesson a week.'

'Yes, sir. I'll get on it.'

'How's that investigation going?'

'I'm still interviewing, sir. Nothing concrete yet. You know, it might not belong to anybody in First Division.'

'I'm aware of that. If you don't find anything, we'll go on from there.'

He didn't know what the captain meant, but it didn't seem like a good time to ask for clarification. Packer looked like a dog about to bite. Damn it, he thought, brought up from fatigue by a slow anger. When have I had time to do lessons?

The sonar intercom light went on. 'Bridge, Sonar. Captain there?'

'He's listening.'

'Captain, we have *Pargo* calling us on the ULQ-six.'

'Hand me that mike.'

Dan turned up the speaker of the underwater telephone. A gurgling crackle filled the pilothouse, like a washing machine running very slowly. 'Bravo Delta, this is Alfa India. Over.'

'This is Bravo Delta. Go ahead. Over.'

The voice from the submarine wavered and bubbled, each word echoing for seconds before ebbing back into the crackle. 'This is Alfa India. Finex run one-four; I say again, finex run one-four; break; interrogative next run; break; how's the weather up there? Over.'

Packer said, glaring out the window, 'Alfa India, this is Bravo Delta. Weather is manageable. Break. Thank you for your services; you are released. Break. Request you open datum on corpen Juliet Lima, speed Mike, depth yellow plus five-zero. Break. We will track you outbound as far as we can. Have a good trip home. Over.'

'This is Alfa India. Roger all runs complete. Understand open datum on course two-three-five, speed one-five, depth four-five-zero feet. Is that confirmed by Charlie Oscar? Over.'

'This is Bravo Delta Charlie Oscar,' said the captain irritably. 'You have copied my transmission correctly. Goodbye and thank you for your services. Bravo Delta out.' He handed Dan the mike. 'Stupid bubblehead. Did you hear how he just gave away the code? The idea nukes are something special, it cracks me up.'

Packer stared out the window. At last he opened the manual again. Dan went back to the radar.

A shattering clang made him start. Ice showered past the windows, white, frangible. 'What the fuck's going on, Pettus?'

'I sent Hard-on up with a hammer to get some of that off, sir. It's really building up since the heaters went out.'

'That's why it's so cold in here. What's wrong with them? Are we getting them fixed? How long will they be off?'

The third-class cracked his gum. 'Prob'ly for a while. Went belly-up this morning. Snipes say they don't have the parts to fix 'em. Gonna bring up some of them electric space heaters, plug 'em in.'

'Oh, swell. Look, goddamn it, that's not a good idea. If we start – '

'Take it easy, Dan,' said Norden. The blond lieutenant looked tired too. 'I gave that order.'

'Oh. Sorry.'

'I know how you feel. But let's not take it out on the enlisted.'

He didn't answer. He knew if he said anything, he'd regret it. He contented himself with a mental obscenity.

Okay, check the radar. Nothing but sea return. He jerked his head out of it and went to the chart table and stood looking down at a 1:2,000,000 chart of the North Atlantic and Arctic oceans.

Their rectangular track, scuffed and dirty with erasures, was centered in an immense white vacancy. Three hundred miles to the east, the chart was bordered by tiny islands and then the solid mass of northern Norway. *Ryan* was at the latitude of Malstrom and the Vestfiord. To the south the chart was empty. Nothing in that direction but gray sea for hundreds of miles, till the Faeroes and the Shetlands, then, beyond that, Scotland. To the southwest, Iceland peeped from the corner. And to the north, the Arctic Sea stretched without hint of land till the sea grew solid and the sky reflected the creamy glow of pack ice.

The ship heaved, and he gripped the edges of the table, bending closer. The tiny numerals of soundings shaded from eighteen hundred fathoms at the south edge of their track to over two thousand. Well over two miles deep. Christ, he thought, staring at the tiny half circle that was their 1530 dead-reckoning position. What a godforsaken place.

Suddenly he felt as distant from Susan as if he were en route to another star. He'd thought of their separation in days, and it had seemed eternal. Now he thought of it in miles, and the sum staggered him.

He thought of the size of the earth, the pullulating billions of inhabitants, the rolling miles of ocean. Suddenly the bond between two people, a link insubstantial, immaterial, consisting only of remembered words and unverifiable yearnings, seemed tenuous and unreal. There were so many other men, better (he felt deep in his heart) than he; kinder, more handsome, more intelligent; more loving, and more lovable. How could he hope to hold her through weeks apart, months apart, years before they could be together simply, day to day, as wives and husbands were supposed to live?

Then he remembered that something real bound them now. Incipient, still only half-formed within her, was the supreme proof of love. No matter how long he pondered, there was something about it he didn't understand. Was it an accident, that as-yet-mindless burgeoning, that secret, silent self-assembling of matter into something capable of awareness? It hadn't been his intention. Or hers. But did that mean its creation was nothing more than chance, a ball popped at random from the bingo cage of biology?

Were there such things as accidents?

What was he doing here, so far from her?

'Dan,' said the captain irritably, 'buzz the wardroom. Tell 'Fredo to bring me up some joe.'

'Aye aye, sir,' he said, and pulled the phone savagely from the bulkhead.

10

At 1720 – five minutes late – the last man rapped at his door. Dan shuffled the records again and pulled one out. He took a deep breath.

'Come in,' he called.

Seaman Recruit William Lassard hadn't bothered to change for the interview. He wore his working uniform: heavy, battered boon-dockers, spattered red and gray and white; denim bell-bottoms, hems dragging at the back, paint-smeared and with one pocket torn half off; denim shirt; black web belt. A leather knife holster dangled from it, the kind the boatswains whipstitched from scrap leather. The letters AMIIGAF were picked out on it with white paint.

'Hey, Ensign.'

'Sit down, Slick.'

The others had looked uncomfortable. They'd sat upright, abashed by the summons to officers' country. The rigid caste system of the Navy divided four hundred feet of ship into a series of closed societies that interacted only in stylized ways, always with a clear understanding on both sides of which was senior.

Lassard slid into the chair and propped an ankle on his knee. He tossed his cap, not the dixie cup but the black wool watch cap, onto Cummings's desk. Freckles spattered the bridge of his nose liked dripped primer. His hair was shorter than regulation, no more than half an inch long. Though he was pale for a man who worked outside, again Dan was struck by his looks. He had the bone structure of a model or an actor, strong chin, high cheekbones, the symmetrical features that are the key to beauty.

But all was ruined by the eyes. Lassard brought with him into the room a sense both of innocence and barely suppressed violence, an impression that was, Dan thought, not entirely due to his own foreknowledge.

If he was right, this man had tried to kill him.

'Nice digs,' said the seaman, glancing around. 'Got your own sink and everything.'

'You could have had a room like this.' Dan opened the folder. 'Your combined GCT/ARI is one twenty. There are programs to send enlisted men to Officer Candidate School, the ones with leadership qualities.'

Lassard opened his eyes wide. Dan saw now that there was something wrong about their focus, as if the seaman was looking at something in the room only he could see. 'You think Slick Lassard's officer material?'

'I only said he – I said, you had the potential. Can I bum a cigarette?'

The request seemed to take Lassard by surprise. He blinked, then reached down to fish a pack out of his sock. They were Kools. Dan took one, could not stop himself from checking the end. Lassard looked amused. After a moment, he shook one out for himself.

'You made third-class twice. What happened?'

'You've got the record there, boss. Man with your education ought to be able to read.'

'I'd like to hear it from you.'

'Slick had a little run-in with Allen the Wrench. He was LPO then. Got transferred off last year. Then Nigger Baby moved up from second.'

Dan decided to ignore the racist language for now. 'What kind of run-in?'

'Allen was ridin' his shit, man, ridin' it into the ground. So one night outside the Acey-Deucey, Slick punches his face in. Busts his fuckin' nose. Then he goes over the hill for a couple months. Cops in Orlando caught him driving without a license. They sent him back under guard when they found Navy ID in his wallet. Then fuckin' Packer screws him to the wall at Captain's mast. Breaks him to recruit.'

'Don't call him "fucking Packer." He went light, Slick. You could have gotten a bad-conduct discharge for that.'

'What, the Big Chicken Dinner? Slick begged him for

it. Fucker said he wouldn't give him the pleasure.'

'I told you, don't refer to him that way in front of me.'

Lassard shrugged and looked around the cabin again.

'That's not the first time you've been to mast. What about this thing in Scotland?'

'Dry dock in Holy Loch. Slick's first duty. Went to mast four times there.'

'It only shows two in your record.'

'That's 'cause they tried him three times for the same offense.'

'I don't think they can do that, Slick.'

'Did it on *Los Alamos*, Ensign. Captain was a Mormon, XO was a rummy. Slick's shacked up with this chick in Glasgow, and he forgets to come back for three or four weeks. Captain gives him ninety days restriction and nine days bread and water. Then he goes on leave. Soon as he goes off the brow, the exec – he's Slick's good buddy – he reconvenes the mast and gives him a week restriction. Then the CO comes back, reconvenes, and gives him ninety and nine again. So Slick takes this shit over to base legal, and they say he don't have to serve any of it and take it off my page thirteen.'

'And number four?'

'Oh, the fuckin' – see, you used to could make your bird, then come back and pick up your paycheck, then go over the hill again. Then they started lockin' it up, so Slick gets a friend of his to steal it. Then this fucker starts tearing it up soon as it comes in. So Slick cops his fuckin' gig and goes to Glasgow in that. Finds a nice shallow spot and run it up on the beach. Skipper didn't mind that too much, but his fuckin' leather jacket was in it. You ever been in a English pawnshop? It's droll, man, they – '

'This is all very entertaining, Slick, but I wanted to talk about your future in the Navy. Can we do that?'

Lassard sighed. 'Ay, man, you – '

'That's "aye aye, sir." '

'Oh, go to hell,' Lassard said suddenly, sitting forward. 'What do you want, Ensign? Let's get to the fuckin' point. Or'd you just invite me up here for a two-man circle jerk?'

Dan controlled himself. 'I wanted to find out what makes

you tick, Seaman Lassard. From what I've seen, you don't give a rat's ass about *Ryan*, the Navy, or your shipmates. But apparently you were a good worker at one time. Somebody thought you rated a crow. I'd like to give you a chance to start over.'

'It's that routine? Got that from Sullivan, Norden, too. Fuckin' XO put it different. He told me to square my shit away or I'd spend the rest of my enlistment suckin' off the marines in the brig.'

'That sounds like Commander Bryce. Is that the only reason you're still with us?'

'That's it, man. Slick's got one year, three months, four days, and twelve hours – but who's countin' – before he torches his ID and blazes out of this chickenshit hole in the water. Uncle's a welder in Louisiana. He's making fifteen, twenty bucks an hour. Might do that. Or go to Mexico, see what's happening down there. Or back to Florida, if the bitch is still there. But none of that's important. The main thing's to get out.'

'Why did you join the Navy, Lassard?'

'The draft, man. That's the only – *fuckin'* – reason Junie Lassard's little Willie's here takin' tea with you.'

'There are other ways to avoid the army.'

'So he's stupid then.' Lassard laughed, a cold retrospection in his eyes; he could have been an old man talking of himself as a toddler. 'See, he grows up in Elkhart, Indiana. Corn-fed middle America. He figures he can make something out of himself. The fuckin' recruiter guarantees little Willie electronics school. Then right out of boot camp they change his orders – they need him in the fleet. Right on! They need him to chip paint on this fuckin' shithouse.'

'Most men start out in the deck gang. That doesn't mean they stay there. You could put in for a rate change.'

'Yeah, way he thought at first, but after a while old Slick gets to thinking. Like, what is this all about? And finally he gets it together in his head.

'It don't matter what kind of alphabet you got in front of your name. The enlisted man's still shit. It's work like a dog and then fuck you, keep a-smilin' like a Carolina nigger and yessir, yessir, salute and get out of my way. Slick, he sucked up to Bloch for a while, but then he says fuck it. He finally seen behind the bullshit.'

'What do you mean, Slick? What do you think's behind it?'

'Mean, you can be led on to believe in things, or you can lead your own self on, make shit up, happy shit, sad shit, you know. But that's just kidding yourself, because, man, there isn't anything worth a shit you can't just buy. Cash and pull – that's Amerika. If you don't got it, only a few things worth doing for the rush. Wake up, Ensign. More and more people seein' through the bullshit. Pretty soon everybody's going to.

'So warning you here and now, don't get on Slick's case. He don't give a flying fuck about that duty, honor, glory crappolini. He's just doing his time. He paints and cleans up, has a little fun now and then, so how about you just get out of his face. And that's the way it is.'

Dan looked at his hands. Again he had that strange mix of feelings. That he hated Lassard, that he was dangerous, and at the same time the suspicion there was something beneath the cynicism; the hope, or delusion, that somehow he could make contact. He had to find some common ground. He tried. 'The whaleboat looks good.'

'Fucking ay it looks good. That's the fastest, best-looking gig in the fleet. We won the squadron cup with her last year.'

'So you can still do good work. But I've seen you on deck, Lassard. You're sloppy, you get paint all over, you make more work for the other guys in the division. You're a bad influence on the new men. You want me to get off your case? Try putting out a little. Because right now, you're my number one problem child.'

'Is that it? He's fucking up your little kingdom for you? Hey, pardon me, man!' Lassard leaned forward, his eyes lighted, innocent and wronged. 'He begged Packer to let him go. Fuckin' Tricky Dick puts out all this crap about defending freedom. Who's defending Slick's fuckin' freedom? The fuckin' Navy's getting six years off his life. He'd rather be in prison, except once in a while we get some pussy. It's a motherfucking ripoff, man, they trick-fucked him into being here and they won't let him out. So Slick don't owe you or anybody else a fucking thing.'

'How about your shipmates? You owe them anything?'

'Why? They don't want to be here, either. We're all just dogs to you. It's simple, even a zero ought to get it. A free man can do what he wants, right? If you're not free, then you're somebody's slave. And you can't make a slave take responsibility. Anything Slick does wrong, it's your fuckin' problem, man, not his; it's the Navy's fault, not his, because he's here against his will. So don't lay that lifer "shipmate" chickenshit on me, man!'

Dan found himself staring at Lassard with an empty mind. For a moment he'd felt a curious identity. Without the single lucky break of the Academy, he might be sitting there himself in dirty dungarees.

But no matter what happened to him, he could never come to conclusions like Lassard's. This man radiated contempt and hatred like heat from a boiler.

And he had no idea how to answer. As far as he could see, Lassard was right, about the conditions aboard, at least. The wonder was that the men took the long hours and dirt and cold and cramped quarters as well as they did.

He decided to go on, get to the investigation. 'So what about the marijuana?'

'Mari*huana*, man, not mari-jawna. Jesus. You mean weed? What you talking about, Ensign?'

'You know what marijuana. The word's all over the ship. The stuff we found up forward.'

'What you want Slick to say? It's his dope? No way, man.'

Dan thought for a moment of saying one of the other enlisted had fingered him. But a lie didn't strike him as a good path to the truth. Instead he said, 'Well, let me put it this way. This guy Slick, does he smoke grass?'

'Hell no, man, the Navy puts you in jail for that.' Lassard smiled. 'What you want, a confession? Far out. Go for it, Richard Tracy.'

'It was in a pack of Kools. You smoke Kools.'

'Ship's store only carries three brands, Ensign. Don't have to be no rocket scientist to notice that.'

'Whose were they?'

Lassard just smiled. With the freckles and unlined face, he looked every day of eighteen.

'I think it's yours,' said Dan. The smile deepened. 'I think you and Greenwald and Coffey, Gonzales, too, maybe, smoke it in the gig. You were smoking it at GQ, and when you saw me coming, you all lit cigars to cover the smell.'

'Even if we did, Ace, so what? Shit ain't dangerous. Everybody uses it out in the world. It'll be legal in a couple years. The cigarette companies got the packs designed. Why's the Navy got this crazy hair up its ass about smoking a little herb?'

'We don't allow alcohol aboard ship, either. How would you like it if we were alongside an oiler and the helmsman was stoned?'

'Don't give me that shit. We got that lecture last month. You ever smoked a joint?'

'No.'

'Ever done any kind of shit? Speedballs? White crosses? Lemons? Black beauties? Blow? Ever tried any of that?'

'No.'

'Then don't make with the fuckin' lectures. You don't know what you're talking about. Slick knows people ashore never get straight, some of 'em drive trucks, one's a fuckin' ER nurse, she can't come without it. You gonna take that away from her?'

'We aren't talking about her or anybody else ashore. We're talking about you, here, aboard ship. I don't care what you do on the other side of the gangway. Do you smoke it ashore?'

'Already told you, Slick ain't admitting nothing. What he does's his own fuckin' business. You want to play games, we can do that all day. All it does is get this little E-One off cleanin' the forward head, man.'

Around them the ship slammed, hitting a sea. Dan looked around for an ashtray, saw one on Cummings's desk, and leaned across Lassard to put his half-burned cigarette out. The seaman had a strong smell, like a wet dog that's been into paint. 'Okay. You don't like games? Let's cut out the games. No more third person. How about off the record, Slick, just you and me.'

'One of those man-to-mans, huh?'

'Precisely.'

'What kind of silly dickhead you think Slick is, anyway?'

'Why not? You got nothing to lose. You'll be out of here in a year and three months.' He thought of Packer's intention to put Lassard ashore when they returned. 'Or less. Meanwhile, we'll be honest with each other. Maybe it would be good for you to be honest with somebody.'

'How does he know it's off the record?'

'I'll give you my word.'

Lassard nodded slowly, sticking out his lower lip. Dan saw that letters were tattooed inside it. FUCK YOU, they read. The seaman looked around the cabin, at the empty bunks. He lit another Kool.

'Okay,' he said. 'I'll play. Just between you and me.'

The anger, Dan saw, was suddenly gone. So was the craziness. A different Lassard sat in the chair. Calmer, without the grin and off-focus eyes.

And somehow, much more menacing.

'That grass we found. Yours?'

Lassard nodded once, eyes alert, drawing on his cigarette.

'Do you have more?'

'Enough for the cruise. It breaks up the monotony. You wouldn't know how monotonous it gets, being an enlisted boy.'

'Who else uses it?'

'I'll talk about me. That's all.'

'Do you sell it?'

'Sometimes. Sometimes I share. Want some?'

'What else do you sell?'

'Right now I'm holdin' 'ludes. And speed, for when a guy's out on his feet and has to stand watch.'

'What else?'

'What do you mean, what else? Whatever I got.'

'It's against the law. Doesn't that worry you?'

Lassard squinted in mock disbelief. 'It ain't the *law*, Ensign. It's just Navy Regs. Fun and zest? Better believe it. According to Article One-twelve, fucking Coca-Cola's illegal aboard ship.'

'Do you know who tried to put me overboard?'

'I was after lookout. I was tied to those phones, man.'

'Did you tell your kinnicks to do it?'

'I might have suggested they push you around some. Not put you overboard, though.'

'That's comforting.' Dan felt his hands tighten on the arms of his chair, tighten till his fingers hurt. Too late, he was realizing how Lassard had suckered him, turned the tables. 'You know something? I think you're the most dangerous man on this ship. I think you belong in the brig. Or a hospital. Yeah, a hospital. Because there's something wrong in your head.'

'Yeah, I'm Mister Psycho Bad Ass.' The cabin tilted, paused, tilted farther. Magazines shot out of Ohlmeyer's rack. Their chairs began to slide and both men half-rose, grabbing for handholds. 'Jesus. Why the hell are we out in this? Look, I'll give you some advice, Lenson. Don't fuck with me. All I want's to not get hassled. You leave me alone and we'll get along fine.'

'We could do that on one condition. Stop selling drugs. And throw what you've got left overboard.'

'I'll have to think about that one real hard, boss. Maybe for two or three weeks.'

'I'm also going to search the boat.'

'Go ahead. You'll never find anything, man. Not unless you got a cop dog or something.'

'Thanks. That's a good idea. I'll request one when we get back to Newport.'

'Oh, get off it,' said Lassard, scorn in his voice. 'We got you zeros figured out. You guys sit up there in your gold-braid underwear and quack-quack, "Left rudder, right rudder," and think you're running the show. There's so much shit happens on this ship you don't know about it isn't funny. You're living in a dream world.'

'What else goes on?'

'What, you want me to tell you? How about Bloch? He's got a half gallon of Dark Eyes in his rack right now. How 'bout Isaacs? The silly fucker's shitfaced half the time. I don't know how he can go around totally obliviated, breathing it right in your faces, and you just don't get it. Two of the officers, they buy shit from me all the time, get wasted ashore. And most of the machinists' mates are round-eye raiders.'

'They're what?'

'Asshole bandits, Ensign. Chocolate-divers. First-class caught two of them drillin' each other in after steering and didn't do a thing; he knew he'd never get replacements if he turned them in. Down in the hole, it's crazy down there, they strip the new recruits and string them up and cover them with grease. Talliaferro don't say nothing. There's a running poker game in the signal shack.'

'I know about that.'

'Whoa, I'm impressed. Do you know the gunners' mates rip off forty-five ammo and sell it ashore? And the shipfitters steal copper and lead, and the ETs take meters and stuff home? Did you know one of the torpedomen porked this asshole's old lady?' He pointed with the cigarette to Cummings's desk.

'I don't believe that. I don't believe half of that. It's just scuttlebutt.'

'Keep tellin' yourself that, man. Maybe life's easier with your eyes closed. You know the captain's getting a divorce?'

'No, I didn't.' Despite his revulsion, he was interested. It would explain Packer's subterranean tension. 'How do you know?'

'Duty driver's been taking him to the BOQ. June Cleaver told him to pack it in, he don't live with her and the Beav no more. Most of the lifers on this ship are divorced. How's your new frau like sitting at home alone?'

'Leave her out of it.' He decided it was time to wind up the conversation. 'Slick, this is all real interesting, but the bottom line is, you've got to cut out dealing. Aside from the fact it's illegal, it's dangerous as hell to have people use aboard ship. There's just too much can go wrong. So – either you stop, and get rid of it, or I'm going to find it. Or catch you using it. When I do, I'll do whatever's necessary to get you off *Ryan*.'

The seaman laughed out loud. 'Like that rabbit says, man, do it to my ass! Maybe I should turn myself in, huh? No, they'd slap me with a summary court, I'd pull twenty years. That's why I love the fucking Navy, 'cause it loves fucking me.

'No, I think I'll just go with the flow, try to enjoy myself a little when I can. Look, I got watch in half an hour. Was it good for you, Ensign? It sure was for me.'

'I think you can shove off now.'

'Sure.' Lassard sat a moment longer, still grinning, then got up. He picked up his hat. 'You know, I got nothing against you personally, man. See, I figure you for a straight arrow. That's why I talked to you. I trust you, you know?'

'That's good. If you want to talk again – '

'Plus, I figure if you keep hassling me, why, you might not be lucky enough to grab the screw guard next time.'

'Get the fuck out of my stateroom.'

'See you on deck, prick,' said Lassard, and slammed the door as Dan came out of the chair.

3

THE SUBMARINE

11

Latitude 67°–0′ North, Longitude 00°–0′ East: 330 Miles NNE of Iceland

Their first official warning of the storm arrived during the dark hours. It was coming in from the southwest, the midnight Fleet Weather advisory said, and would pass west of them, between *Ryan* and Iceland, over the course of the next three days. As it built they could expect seventy-knot winds, gusting to ninety or more, and thirty- to thirty-five-foot seas in the vicinity of the polar low.

Around ten the sky lightened. The sun was invisible, but enough light bled through a driving wrap of cloud for Dan to see the great swells that rolled now in confused patterns, random, jagged masses, but with the prevailing seas more and more evidently from the east. By 1800, when he came on again, it was long past the brief Arctic twilight, and pitch-dark once more.

Even so, he could tell immediately that the wind was rising. Even inside the pilothouse, enclosed by steel and glass, he could hear it. Not the eerie whistle they'd lived with for days past. This was a violent, vibrating scream. And it was still building. He watched the needle on the anemometer twitch upward, wavering with each laboring buck of the ship.

He looked down at the forecastle as a sea boarded, boiling across the gear, rising like a tide till it gleamed and bulged a few feet below the whipping wipers. The phosphorescent foam glowed feebly in the light of the forward range. Aside from that, the world was black. Pancake ice clattered against the hull. He clung to the overhead wire, wondering groggily what would happen if they hit something sizable. Destroyers were compartmented, but then so was the *Titanic*.

The 21MC crackled hollowly above the shriek. 'Bridge,

CIC,' it said under his hand. He pushed the lever twice, meaning, go ahead.

'Bridge, CIC: We have a high-altitude bogey on the air search. Racket shows Short Horn and Bee Hind radars.'

'Uh . . . can you translate that for me?'

'Those are Soviet airborne ASW and early-warning radars, Mr. Lenson. Assignment Ten in your JO Journal.'

The ship rolled, came back a bit, and stopped there, lying over uncertainly, like an aging dog wanting to obey but at the same time longing to curl up and rest. He pressed the lever. 'Bridge, aye. Lieutenant Evlin – '

'I heard him. Right rudder, quick,' said Evlin in a low voice.

That was right; he had the conn. He tore his attention back. 'Right full rudder,' he said loudly, pitching his voice against the unearthly scream.

The helmsman responded, his voice high. 'Right full rudder! My rudder is right full, sir, no course given.'

We can't stay on this leg, he thought. We've got to abandon the racetrack. Find a better course, and steady up on it. He turned his head to Evlin, an invisible presence beside him. 'What course, sir?'

Ryan was trembling like a live thing under the lash of the wind. She'd started to come back upright, but now sagged off even farther to port, driven over by uncountable tons of wind pressure on the superstructure. He twisted, searching the dark for Evlin's face. The lieutenant was watching the sea.

At last the OOD reached for the phone – the captain had gone aft a few minutes earlier, after spending all day in his chair – but just then Packer came through the weather door. Spray battered through it behind him. The dank-smelling wind battled with the overheated air, then was sliced off as the door sealed. The captain's foul-weather gear was soaked. Water ran off his face like rain off a mountain.

'Get her head around,' he said. 'Forget the wind. Head her into the swell.'

Dan steadied his voice before he said, 'Sir, I have my rudder right full. She's not responding.'

'That so? No sweat, Mr. Lenson. Use the engines. Wind direction?'

'Veered another ten degrees, sir.'

'Eye's getting closer. But it'll be a while. Bring her on around to the right. *Carefully*. Remember you got the fish down aft. Steady on one-one-zero, see how she rides there.'

'Aye, sir. I'll watch it, but Mr. Lenson seems to be doing pretty well.'

'That's good,' said Packer, looking at him, actually seeing him, Dan felt, for the first time since he'd come on the bridge. 'We can use another qualified OOD.'

'Sir, did you get the word about the high flyer?'

Packer turned to the radar, bent over it, began peeling off his soaked jacket. The boatswain helped him with the sleeves. 'Yeah. It's a Bear. The antisubmarine variant. Probably out of the Kola. He's got all his gear turned on and he's doing what looks like a grid search.'

'What's he doing out here?'

'Beats me.' Packer leaned into the intercom. 'Sonar, Bridge. I'm securing the racetrack due to worsening weather. Do you still hold that hundred-fifty hertz contact at zero-seven-five?'

'No sir, it faded about an hour ago.'

'Uh-huh. Well, are we wasting our time? Do you want to bring the VDS up?'

The voice of the 21MC changed, became Reed's. 'ASW Officer, Captain. Sir, this is what we came out here to find out: whether the AN/SQS-thirty-five will cut it in adverse conditions.'

'Goddamn it, I know what we're *doing* here, Aaron. Right now, I'm worried about losing the damned thing.'

'I don't see that as a problem, sir. The catenary should absorb our stern motion before it affects the fish.'

'What if it doesn't? I'm thinking about bringing it up.'

The metallic voice hesitated. 'Well, sir, actually we can't recover, not pitching like this. According to the technician, the cable'll snap. I recommend we lower it to six hundred feet and ride it out.'

Ryan seemed to draw a long breath, then launched herself into a tremendous roll. Things clattered downhill in the dark, then clattered back as she reared almost as far to starboard, shaking herself like a horse frenzied by flies.

The captain must have signed off, given Reed some final order, because now he swung on Dan. Lenson stepped back. In the darkness Packer's eyes were invisible, but something in his bent shadow, the waiting shapes around it, the still-increasing shrieking outside evoked unreality and horror.

'What's the anemometer say? Can't quite make it out.'

'Varies between fifty-five and sixty, sir, gusts to around sixty-five.'

'Sounds higher than that. May be reading low. Barometer?'

'Twenty-eight eight and falling, sir,' said Yardner, the quartermaster, through the porthole behind them.

'Steady on two-one-zero, sir,' cried the helmsman. 'No . . . swinging past it.'

'*Two*-one-zero?' said Evlin instantly.

'Sorry, sir, I mean one-one-zero, swinging left – '

'Hold her as close as you can,' said the captain. He sounded bored again, after that flicker of interest about the aircraft. 'Use as much rudder as you need.'

'Aye, sir.'

Dan clung to the cable as *Ryan* recovered. The sea streamed off her foredeck as she staggered upright. In the dim wash of the navigation lights, long streaks of foam burned with the cold luminosity of watch hands. His mind gave him two lines of Coleridge: 'About, about, in reel and rout/the death-fires danced at night.' Only that had been in a calm. . . . A swell high as a two-story house rolled toward them, a black monolith whose crest the wind peeled off even as it began to break, tore off and blew across the surface in a boiling pearly fog that froze the instant it hit glass and paint and steel. It kicked the bow upward, till he was looking at the boiling blackness of the night sky.

Then she toppled, like a woman executing a swan dive. He felt light, then abruptly heavy as she buried herself. The bullnose disappeared, black water closing over the anchor and wildcat. The wipers whined and grated at full speed, throwing spray off into the night.

'Sir, she's falling off again!'

'Mark your head,' said Dan.

'One-two-five – drifting right – my rudder's hard left – '

'Give her a full bell on the starboard shaft,' said Packer, face pressed to the window. 'We've got plenty of power. As long as the engines hold out and our stability's good, it'll punch us around, but it won't hurt us.'

'Starboard engine ahead full, indicate RPM for twenty knots,' said Dan, trying to keep his voice as even and casual as the captain's. Unfortunately, he was starting to feel sick again. The combination of violent motion and darkness was intensely nauseating.

'Keep the rudder out of the stops,' muttered Evlin. 'Or it'll jam.'

'Mind your rudder. Keep her out of the stops,' he said.

The engine-order telegraph pinged as the order went down. 'Mind my rudder, aye.' *Ping, ping.* 'Engine room answers, starboard ahead full.'

'Very well.' Sweat tickled his spine. God, he thought, we don't need a jammed rudder tonight. Without control, a ship would fall off, drift helplessly around till she fell into the troughs. Then she'd roll like death itself, gathering energy with each cycle, till she went far enough to capsize.

The red-lighted numerals of the compass were ticking slowly left when another bridge-high sea crashed over the bow, bludgeoning them bodily to starboard before the helmsman could bring her back. The old destroyer reeled, the pilothouse swinging through the sky in great sweeps. Dan clutched the radar as water sprang into his mouth. He thought briefly, for no particular reason, of *Pargo*. Hundreds of miles away by now, and hundreds of feet down. Storms didn't reach down there. They'd be eating ice cream and watching movies, no doubt, wondering why *Ryan* had stayed behind.

'She seems tender, sir,' Evlin was saying to Packer. His words were faint above the clanking clatter of gear aft. 'Last time we hit major seas, on the way back from the Med, she seemed to ride better than this.'

'It's the added weight aft. Long moment arm on that hoist. Just like a fat kid on a seesaw.'

'Should I call main control, get another boiler on the line?'

'No. I want to conserve fuel. We should be able to ride this out without going to full power. Have them stand by, though.'

'We haven't ballasted yet, have we, sir?'

He didn't hear the captain's answer to that. Something had broken free aft and was hammering on the hull, a dull, heavy thudding every time they pitched.

'Mr. Lenson,' said Evlin. 'Find out what that noise is.'

'Aye aye, sir.' He swallowed scorching bile as *Ryan* flung herself into the air, then fell away, floating his stomach free like the drop of a roller coaster. 'Bos'n, go see what that noise is.'

'I don't feel so good, sir.'

'Well, neither do I, Pettus! Do as you're told!'

His guts soared again as the old destroyer hesitated, halfway aloft, then aimed herself suddenly for the bottom two thousand fathoms down. For a moment it seemed she might make it. The sea rumbled like a herd of cattle stampeding below the pilothouse. He heard retching behind him, and turned, to see the quartermaster chief bury his face in the wastebasket.

That did it. He muttered thickly, 'Al, you got the conn,' and staggered toward Yardner. They vomited together, tottering back and forth across the deck, leaning into each other like sumo wrestlers, their hands gripping the slimy bucket and each other's clothes. When he came up, gasping, his face was a few feet from someone else's. He stared blearily. 'Who's that?'

'Pettus . . . sir.'

'I told you to check out that . . . banging. . . .' Then he doubled again as a fresh accession of nausea racked him. When he looked up, spitting and drooling, the boatswain's mate was gone. 'Pitch that overboard,' he said to the quartermaster, who had also straightened and was breathing heavily, his arms flung out against the aft bulkhead like a man crucified.

Wiping his mouth, he dragged himself behind the helmsman.

Coffey had taken over. The black seaman stood before the wheel with his legs straddled wide. The dim glow of the binnacle silhouetted him. He crouched, listening, as the ship debated with herself whether to roll or not. Then, as she decided, flung the wheel to port with all his strength. 'Coffey, you doing all right?' Dan asked hoarsely.

'Holdin' out, man.'

'Don't let her get away from you. Let me know if you get tired.'

'Ali X. don't get tired, sir.'

'You ready to take the conn back, Ensign?'

'Uh, yessir, Lieutenant. This is Ensign Lenson; I have the conn.'

A murmured chorus of moans and coughs answered him. Only Coffey's voice sounded strong.

Pettus came back a few minutes later, dripping wet. 'What was it?' Dan asked him.

'Whaleboat, sir. Shifting in the chocks. I got a couple of guys and tightened the gripes down.'

'Good work. Look – I'm sorry I yelled at you.'

'No problem, sir. I ain't feeling too good myself.'

Barfing made him feel weak but better. He pressed himself against the helm console and forced his consciousness out along the ship. The bow he could see. The lashings on the tackle were holding, but it looked like the range of motion of the chains was increasing. Still, as long as the brakes held on the wildcat, the stoppers could go and the anchors would still stay aboard. From what he'd overheard, the fish was in danger, and it was too late to hoist it. Well, at least no one would have to go out on the exposed fantail.

He wondered what it was like below. In the berthing compartments, shoehorned full of swaying men in the close, sickening darkness; in the offices – he'd seen publications a foot deep in the ops shack. It must be hell itself in the engine spaces. Worse; neither Dante nor Jonathan Edwards had thrown in fifty-degree rolls.

He gauged the angle of the deck and when it was downhill, let go and slid back to the radar. The screen was solid light, the whole scope face smeared with the sparkling acne of sea return.

The ship snapped back and he grabbed for the overhead. Packer, taken by surprise as he was climbing into his chair, almost fell. Dan caught his arm just in time. The captain settled himself without a word, but Lenson heard the seat belt click.

It was still black-dark when Ohlmeyer relieved him at 2000. He crept below, legs so shaky he had to stop halfway down the enclosed ladder and sit for a few minutes, hugging the handrail as the corridor spun around him in huge slow circles. He wondered where he was heading. His stateroom? Forget it. No point trying to sleep tonight.

The wardroom was a wilderness of tumbled chairs. The drawers had broken open on the sideboard and coffee and sugar and silverware lay scattered across the carpet. Salt-shakers and glasses patrolled the slanting deck with each roll, clattering over knives and salad forks like little trains going over switches. Silver, Norden, and Talliaferro sat in a stiff row on the sofa, as if posing for a daguerreotype, their arms gripping the back. Trachsler and Reed and Johnson had lashed chairs down in the corners with light line. 'Hello, Dan,' said someone as he came in. 'Help yourself to midrats.'

'Very funny.'

'No, 'Fredo made sandwiches. They're in the reefer.'

'Don't mention food, Rich. Ever again. Please.'

'Have some crackers. That'll settle your stomach,' said Talliaferro. The engineer had filled one black-nailed hand with a sandwich and the other with a glass of powdered milk. He looked exhausted, the pockets under his eyes matching the grease on his coveralls.

A roar of water came from outside and the ship staggered over to starboard. It took him by surprise. Their previous bad rolls had been to port. The chairs began to slide. The fiddleboards on the shelves gave way and magazines, books, and a chess set he'd never seen before cascaded out. The phone sprang free of its holder and extended rigidly on the end of its cord as if being pulled by a ghost. Talliaferro began to slide off the couch and had to decide what to let go of. The sandwich lost. It flew the length of the wardroom parallel to the deck, separating in midair into three separate projectiles. The ham hit Commodore Ryan's portrait, stuck for a moment, then dropped into a corner of the frame.

A splintering crash of crockery came from inside the

wardroom galley, followed by screaming in Filipino. Dan closed his eyes, remembering he was the mess treasurer.

'How's things topside, Dan?'

'Holding, sir. I made a tour before I went on and the captain made one around nineteen hundred. We regriped the whaleboat. The fo'c'sle looks okay but the stoppers are working loose.'

'We need to put somebody on it?'

'We've got line, pelican hooks, and the brake. I don't want to send anybody up there in this weather.'

'Not even if it means letting the anchor go?'

'Well, I don't know about that, sir,' he said rather weakly. 'I'll keep an eye on it.'

Norden shook his head. The weapons officer was clinging to the sofa with both hands, very pale. 'What the hell are we doing here, anyway? We ought to just run for it.'

'What's that mean?' said Talliaferro.

'Oh, nothing. I like to hang around in the dangerous semicircle of extratropical storms. Has he ballasted yet, Ed?'

'No,' said Talliaferro. He took a dainty sip at his milk. 'Shouldn't he?'

'I asked permission to. Service tanks are drawn down to zero. Lot of free surface down there. What's more, we got at least a hundred and fifty ton of ice topside by now.'

'What does that do to metacentric height?' Dan asked him.

'You don't want to hear it, kiddo.'

'It's up to him,' said Norden. 'But didn't they lose some of these cans in a typhoon because they weren't ballasted? Those were *Gearings*, weren't they?'

'Why don't you ask him, Rich, if it upsets you so much?'

'Because you're the engineering officer.'

'Then let me and him worry about it,' said Talliaferro.

'So. Everyone taking it easy, eh?'

Bryce had come in in his T-shirt, an unlighted cigarette in his mouth. He described a wavering walk across the deck as *Ryan* began another roll. Dan could tell by the way she gathered herself that this would be a bad one.

Trachsler half-rose. Apparently he meant to offer the XO a seat, but it was a misjudgment. The roll broke his grip on his chair. He staggered forward, lost his footing, and was catapulted onto the wardroom table. He slid down it on his stomach, too startled to brake himself, and went off headfirst into a tangle of chairs at the opposite end. The other officers jumped up, more cautiously, and slid and crawled across the floor toward him. 'Ken! You all right?'

'Watch his head.'

'You okay?'

'I think something's busted,' said the damage-control officer. His mouth was strained and uncertain. He held his right arm with his left.

'Can you move your hand?'

'Shit. Shit! I don't think so.'

'Get on the phone, call the bridge. And call sick bay. We need the corpsman here.'

The medic arrived quickly. He'd been up already, he said, a couple of guys had gotten whacked by bunk frames in M Division berthing, and a boilerman had burned himself on a boiler casing. A few minutes later, the 1MC came on.

'This is the captain speaking,' it said. 'For the next few hours, we'll be taking heavy rolls in cross seas. Exercise caution moving about the ship. Stay in your berthing compartments if at all possible.'

Dan upended his chair, which had fallen on its side, and took another turn around it with the line. 'Is it like this often?' he asked Reed.

'Well, we hit one coming back from the Med that was pretty hairy. We figured twenty-, twenty-five-foot seas max that time. But this here's already as rough as I've seen it, and as the eye approaches – '

Talliaferro got up, clinging to the back of the couch. 'I'm going up to the bridge. We got to ballast, right now.'

'Be careful, Ed.'

After the engineer left the conversation lagged. The ship continued pitching, varying it by flinging herself sharply to port and starboard and hanging there for endless seconds before staggering back. Spray or rain drummed on the hull. Dan wondered vaguely what was going on topside, but was too sick and weak to go find out. He clung to the chair with bruised arms and legs, far from sleep, but passing moment to moment from half dream to an exhausted semiconsciousness.

At 2330, the phone squealed. Then someone was calling his name. He coughed and rubbed his eyes, coming back from a confused, nauseated dream of Pennsylvania hills rolling in a heavy green sea.

'Dan! You hear me?'

'I'm coming, goddamn it,' he grunted, unwrapping his aching arms and legs, understanding at last through the groggy sick tiredness that once again it was his turn on watch.

12

Still half asleep, Dan hauled himself through the flickering, slanting corridors like a disoriented ape. A hundred feet aft through the port passageway, past the gunners' workshop and armory, past the department office and Norden's stateroom. Grab his gear, rub his face with a mildew-smelling towel, then forward again in the dim red light past Radio III and the Dash equipment room, Repair 3, the electrical workshop, all of them closed, the corridors of the sleeping ship empty, empty.

His mouth tasted like a used bedpan. He bent to a scuttlebutt, but the button brought forth only a hiss of air. A sudden rapid tattoo drummed above him like an automatic wash on the roof of a car. He realized with a shudder that it was coming down on the Asroc deck between the stacks. Seas that heavy on the 01 level . . .

Forward, staggering as the passageway rolled till he had to support himself with his arms . . . empty as the sewers of Paris, and as dark . . . the spray roared above him. Past ship's office and sick bay, the smells of electricity and disinfectant and steam were joined by the ghosts of departed donkey dicks, sauerkraut, two generations of stale cigarette smoke and rancid grease from the empty mess decks. *Ryan* dropped into a hole with a crash that quivered the steel under his feet. He reached the starboard side, grabbed the hand-smoothed dogging bar, and yanked it up.

And realized instantly he'd screwed up. He should've come up the port side. This way led to a ladder, but on the weather decks.

The heavy steel door blew open suddenly, driven by air pressure like a cork from a popgun.

It propelled him into blackness, and bitter cold. He clung

to the door as it slammed open, pinned by a gale that jackhammered his breath back down his throat. Pellets of semiliquid ice lashed his face. For a second he hung there. Go on, or retreat? The dark was an open maw, bellowing in his face. Above him the wind screamed and struggled, caught in the steel and lines and antennas above the signal bridge.

Well, no danger from the kinnicks out here tonight. Even the lookouts had been pulled inside. He fought the door, first angrily, then in near panic, knowing he had only seconds to get it closed and get up the ladder. Finally he got it far enough away from the hull that the wind grabbed it out of his hands. It sealed with a thump. He slammed the dogging bar home, ducked his head for a breath, then turned. Groped out in front of him in absolute blackness. Where the hell –

His hands closed on ice-encrusted, water-slick handrails. A bit of Plebe Year trivia surfaced into the heaving void of his conscious mind: 'What's the only ship in the Navy with water-cooled handrails, Mr. Lenson?' 'The USS *Nevada*, in Pearl Harbour, sir.' The rungs were crusted, too, with the Teflon-slick curves of wet ice. He scrabbled upward till his boots felt the flat. One deck gained, one to go.

Suddenly he sensed something behind him. Hair rose on the back of his neck. He gripped the handrail and half-turned, sucking black air through clenched teeth.

The sea hurtled in out of the dark, crests glowing and flickering with a running, velvety fire. It bulged over him as he crouched, frozen, staring up.

The thirty-foot wave exploded against dented steel in a roaring seconds-long welter of glowing green. He gripped the rails desperately. Cold air froze in his throat. Hard things clattered around him, rattled and grated. Ice clunked and rattled down along the ladder steps.

When the sea retreated, the ship staggered upright like a bloody, exhausted bull. He sucked black ice spray. Icy needles novocained his gums. The wind injected his neck and ears.

He grabbed steel and ice and surged upward a few more steps before he slipped. His knees slammed into unyielding metal. His bare hands scrabbled over the greasy ice. Only by hooking one arm around a riser did he catch himself from going back down. Then the stern rose, and rose, and for a moment the slanting ladder was nearly level.

He skidded, slid, and clawed the last few steps. His knees felt dull, the stunned sensation that meant when they woke up they'd hurt like hell. At the top of the ladder he hesitated. Then, deliberately, he turned to face it.

He stared out into the Arctic night, the mad storm sea in winter darkness, here at the top of the world. The ocean seethed below him. The gale whipped spray out of the dark, flash-froze it, and slashed it across his face like a shotgun blast of rock salt. He was scared and light-headed and his heart was hammering like an outboard motor. But he was grinning, too, grinning into the wind.

'Fuck you,' he said through teak lips.

When the pilothouse door slammed shut behind him he clung to it, panting in the sudden dark closeness, the steady warm pressure of bodies and electric heat.

'You ready to relieve me? About goddamn time.'

An unfamiliar voice, a taller than usual form. Then he remembered Trachsler was out of action. This was Carl Murphy, the sonar officer, a chief warrant the other officers called Super Goat. 'Yeah,' he said, swallowing the sour-bitter acid his stomach insisted he taste. 'What you got?'

They went over the usual things, course, speed, boiler status. Murphy said the wind was southerly now, and would probably veer even more as the storm neared. *Ryan* was headed 180 degrees true, with all four boilers on-line, but making only ten knots. 'Just keep her nose to the wind,' the warrant said. 'Go too fast in a head sea, you'll bash in the bow plating. Saw it happen on the *Ernest G. Small*, Sasebo to San Fran . . . you got military air distress, fleet common, international distress freqs on the bridge. Captain's in his sea cabin an' all's right with the *Ryan*. Any questions?'

'I relieve you. Oh, you got the conn?'

'No. You do, kid.' The slouching shadow returned his salute and a moment later was gone. He swung instantly to the bow, caught the white grin of a comber headed for his throat.

'Hard right rudder!'

And behind him, world without end, the tired, bored voice of Coffey again. 'Hard right rudder, aye.'

Two hours later, he was clinging to the repeater, head void of everything but cross swells and rudder orders and turn counts, when the sonar intercom light blinked on. It was Reed. He said they had a contact.

'A sonar contact?'

'Yeah, a sonar contact. That's mostly the kind we get down here in Sonar. You know what to do? I report it to you, you tell the OOD, and he tells the captain.'

He was too tired to resent the patronizing. He just hit the key twice, acknowledging. Evlin was bent over the bucket, so he groped around for the buzzer and flipped up the cover of the speaking tube.

'Yeah.' The brass pipe made Packer's voice hollow and metallic, as if he was talking into a spittoon.

'Captain, this is Ensign Lenson, on the bridge.'

'Yeah. How's it . . . how's it going out there?'

'Okay, sir. Sir, Sonar reports a contact at the first CZ range. It's got a . . .' He paused, trying to repeat it the way he'd heard it. 'It's a strong one hundred fifty-hertz source. Sonar thinks it could be a Soviet sub running noisy.'

For a moment he heard nothing but the wind. Some freak hole or poorly fitted flange made the hollow brass sigh and whistle, as if its diameter held a miniature cyclone of its own. Then Packer said, his voice more alert now, 'I'll be right there.'

He showed up a few minutes later. Dan was wrestling the ship around to starboard, trying to outguess the swells. He heard Packer and Evlin talking, then the click and rush of the intercom. Shielded flame clicked on, then off. He smelled tobacco. Packer straightened from a crouch.

'Boatswain!'

'Bos'n, aye, sir!'

'Call away the antisubmarine tracking team.'

'Now, sir? It's two in the morning – '

'Do it, Pettus,' Dan snapped.

The third-class hit the exterior speakers too, by mistake, and Dan heard the words wrestle with the wind out on the main deck; wrestle, and lose, tear, and fly away in tatters over the lightless waste of storm-racked sea. 'Now hear this. Set the ASW tracking team. That is: Set the ASW tracking team.'

He stopped thinking about it, concentrating on the next swell. Did they come in patterns out of the fog, out of the dark? He sensed a cross swell, maybe two, but he couldn't predict the seas. Right rudder, left rudder, right. Steady up. Steady as she goes . . . shift your rudder. His knees hurt now, and something clicked when he bent the left one. Sweat dripped under his jacket. Minutes eroded with excruciating slowness, but he had no consciousness of passing time.

The intercom, at his elbow. Silver. 'Hey, Bridge, you got Lenson up there?'

'Yeah.'

'Mr. Sullivan was our weapons liaison. You replace him, right? Get back here and get these phones on. Assist the evaluator.'

'I'm the JOOD right now.'

But when he looked around for Evlin, Dan saw he was handing the watch over to Rich Norden, and at that moment Barry Ohlmeyer, behind him, said, 'I'm your relief. Make it quick, they want you in CIC.'

The last time he'd been in the Combat Information Center, it would have made bats happy. Now, shielded lights were snapping on and screens were brightening into iconic life; petty officers were strapping themselves into seats; seamen were buckling on helmets and unspinning coils of phone cord. A second-class radarman rifled life vests to raised hands through slanting space with the skill of a quarterback. Lenson stood at the door, trying not to vomit again. Assist the evaluator . . . Evlin and Silver were adjusting headsets and helmets in a corner. He staggered toward them, fetching up against a waist-high table. Two enlisted men were covering it with what looked like white butcher paper from a roll, ripping it off, taping it down with masking tape.

Silver spoke into a rubber muzzle, then tucked one

earphone back. He said rapidly, 'Get those phones on. Plug in this socket. No, this one. Keep the wire clear, it's gonna get snarly around here. You got JC, five-JP, eight-JP – '

'Wait a minute, Mark! Help me out! What am I supposed to *do*?'

Silver leaned his beard forward and hissed, pissed off and disgusted. 'You're the ... *weapons* .. *liaison* ... *officer!* Understand? You follow the action on the plotting table here. Search, classification, then attack. You pass shit to the guys on the weapons, the Asroc and the torpedoes, see, and the guns. Then when the attack starts, you make sure there aren't any friendlies in the way, other ships or anything, and that the evaluator knows about any problems. *Jesus!* Okay?'

'We aren't really going to attack anybody, are we?'

'Course not. Use your fucking head! ... CIC, aye, go ahead, UB plot.'

Dan got the earphones on and the helmet buckled over them. He could hear people talking on the circuit, but he wasn't sure who they were, or whether he should make them stop. He stared around, trying to make sense of what he saw.

CIC was twenty feet wide by twenty feet long. The overhead was a foot above his helmet. He, Evlin, Silver, and three enlisted men were grouped in the forward right corner. Ahead was the radio desk, with a denimed back to them. On the far side of that bulkhead were the gun-director drives and the captain's sea cabin. To their right, at arm's length, was a folding partition that led to the electronic countermeasures room. Aft of that was a first-aid locker. Directly aft, again within arm's reach, was another folding door that led to underwater battery plot and sonar. This was half open, and through it he could see the circular glows of screens, the green-lighted faces of seated men. To their left was the rest of CIC, with twenty-two guys in it, and all their equipment and gear.

'Mark, datum,' said Silver, and Dan pulled his attention back to the plotting table. Across from him, Chief Pedersen grunted, 'Five hundred an inch, or a thousand?'

'Thousand yards an inch.'

Switches clicked. A light came on inside the table, shining up through the glass top, under the paper.

Dan leaned forward, over the little rayed circle that projected on the sheet. The rosette was graduated in hundreds of yards. As he watched, the two enlisted men moved in, keeping their bodies out from between Evlin and the circle of light. One swung a hinged ruler. Both writing at once, their hands curled round each other like circling carp, they placed a red line and a black dot, and penciled in the time: 0334. The black dot was at the center of the lighted circle. The red line, a line of bearing from it, was almost a yard away, at the far end of the table. Pedersen was spieling off numbers. As Dan watched, their eyes swung up to the bulkhead clock. Exactly sixty seconds later they bent again, and he saw that both new marks had moved, the lighted circle that was *Reynolds Ryan*, and the red line that was –

Suddenly, belatedly, he understood. Reed had detected a submarine. It wasn't a scheduled playmate, but Packer had decided to use it as a training target, exercising the VDS and the ASW team.

But now, in the middle of the night, in the midst of a storm? For a moment, he wondered whether that was wise.

Just then, Packer came through the curtain from Sonar. He was dressed now, khakis and bomber jacket. The light over the table etched shadowed eyes, tight lips, drawn cheeks. 'Al, how's that contact look? Got a course and speed yet?'

'It'll take a few minutes, sir; all passive gives us is bearings.'

'Okay, but I need data much scoche. Give me a ballpark soon as you can.'

'Permission to relax battle dress in CIC, sir?'

'Granted, Chief.'

Helmets rattled back into racks. Packer leaned against the radar repeater and patted his pockets. 'What've we got down there?' he asked, packing the pipe with vanilla-scented tobacco.

Evlin reached above his head to the intercom, even though, Dan thought, he could just as easily have turned and slid open the partition and talked to the sonarmen directly. He noticed other circuits and instruments above them, in easy reach from the plot. They were labeled SONAR RANGE INDICATOR, SONAR

182

CONTACT INDICATOR, TA/740 SECURE VOICE. There were also two more radio remotes, three barrel switches for phone circuits, and a battle lantern. 'Sonar, Evaluator. What's your classification on the goblin?'

'Hard to say, sir. He's so noisy, it's hard to get a discrete spectrum. A hundred and sixty, hundred and seventy decibels. It's a nuke for sure, twin screws, so it's Soviet. But I can't tell what type.'

'Why's he making so much noise?'

'Sounds like a glitch, sir. Could be lube oil, or reduction-gear casualty would make a wideband grinning like that.'

The captain asked whether they had a speed estimate. The sonarman said not from bearing rate, but from turn count he was probably making about fifteen knots.

The clock clicked over, and the plotters bent again, pencils poised like wasps depositing eggs. 'Got a range yet, South Plotter?' Packer asked the one with the red pencil. His dungaree shirt was stenciled M. A. MATT.

'No, sir. Bearings are steady.'

'He's coming right for us, sir,' said Pedersen.

Packer sucked his pipe, staring at the plot. 'Are you getting that from the IVDS or the twenty-three?'

The AN-/SQs-23, Dan remembered, was the ship's regular sonar, housed in a dome below the keel.

'From the fish, sir.'

'Can you get a bearing from the twenty-three, too? Triangulate?'

'Could if we were beam to him, sir.'

'Come left thirty degrees.'

Evlin relayed the order to the bridge, then glanced around. 'Hold on, everybody. This should be interesting.'

Dan watched the rudder-angle indicator swing, then the gyrocompass, spinning left like a green-lighted roulette wheel. The slamming slowed.

Suddenly *Ryan* reeled to port. Parallel rules clattered. A shock cord snapped and a shelf of publications assaulted one of the radarmen. She took several more rolls, each steeper and longer, before Matt cocked his head like a parrot, listening, and bent and drew another red line almost, but not quite, parallel to the first. As he moved back, Evlin leaned in with dividers to the point where they crossed.

'Twenty-eight thousand yards.'

'Chief Pedersen?'

Pedersen was working a plastic disc, a manual computer. He nodded. 'Concur.'

Packer said quietly, 'Okay, let's think about this a minute. Does he know we're here? I'm pretty sure he doesn't. Not making that much noise of his own. But where's he going?'

'He's holding the bearing, and getting louder, not fainter. That makes it something like two-four-zero,' said Evlin. He put his finger where the red rays of the passive sonar bearings converged. Dan saw suddenly how it revealed something moving, not a point, but an area of probability. 'That'll take him between Iceland and the Faeroes, and pop him out into the North Atlantic.'

'He's not a scheduled deployer.'

Evlin said nothing. Dan saw their eyes meet, the captain's and the operations officer. There was some meaning exchanged, but he couldn't guess what it was.

He suddenly wondered whether he should be doing something. He switched nervously from circuit to circuit, but heard only a hissing seethe, like the dream roar of the sea in a shell found on the beach.

'Tell Ed to go silent,' said Packer.

'Aye, sir. . . . Main Control, Evaluator: Shut down all nonessential machinery.'

The chief engineer's heavy voice rogered. Dan wondered what good that would do. What with the creak and strain of the hull as *Ryan* worked, anybody within a hundred miles ought to be able to hear them loud and clear. On the other hand, the sea was noisy, too. Maybe the storm would mask their presence.

'Put a track on him, sir?'

'Yeah.'

'Arm's length? Or close hold?'

'Let him get a little closer, then I'll decide. If he can't hear us, we can – '

The intercom said, 'Evaluator, Sonar. Goblin's turn count dropping.'

Packer reached instantly for the intercom. 'Main control, Captain. Ed, secure your pumps. We've got a Russki nuke transiting south, and he's slowing for a listen.'

'He'll hear our screws a lot farther away than our machinery, Captain.'

'Shit. You're right.' Packer punched buttons. 'Bridge, Captain; drop speed as much as you can, Rich. Bring her back to one-eight-zero, then use just enough power to keep her head to the seas. We got a bear sniffing the bait down here.'

As Norden acknowledged, Dan understood suddenly how it was. The transiting submarine slowed down from time to time to reduce its own noise and check for hunters. If *Ryan* could avoid detection during those periods, they could trail him for a long time without his suspecting it. Despite his fatigue, his bruises, and his soaked, itching feet, he felt a tingle of excitement.

Nothing much happened for the next half hour, though. The plotters plotted. Evlin rubbed his eyes. The captain's face flared yellow as he sucked flame into the bowl of his pipe. He muttered around the stem, 'Al, let's get a message off to Fleet reporting this guy. Classify "probable Soviet." Ask them to assign a track number. Make estimated course and speed two-four-zero at fifteen. Say we're holding contact and ask if there're any P-threes out of Iceland want to come out and play.'

As the lieutenant jotted on a message pad. Dan went over in his head everything he knew about antisubmarine work.

Sonar was nothing but sound in the water. Passive, you just listened. The ship's transducers, either hull-mounted or towed like the fish, turned sound into electricity, amplified it, and gave you its intensity, frequency, and bearing. Sometimes you could identify a contact by the noise of its screws, pumps, generators, and other rotating machinery. But the fact that you couldn't get a direct range made passive sonar less useful at short distances, and if the target was quiet enough, then of course it wouldn't give you any data at all.

Active sonar was what you heard in the movies pinging on the sub's hull. The echo gave you the target's bearing and the elapsed time gave you the range. Active sonar didn't give you much of an idea what you were pinging on, whether whale, bubble, or sub. It also had the disadvantage that the submarine could hear you pinging for it twice as far away as you could hear its echo.

He knew sound was affected by the temperature and salinity of the water, and that in shallow water, or when there were layers of different temperatures, sometimes you couldn't pick up a sub when it was right under your keel.

But he had a feeling that he was going to learn a lot more, and soon. From the way everybody was acting, you didn't get to play with a Soviet very often.

The intercom said, 'Evaluator, Sonar: Target's speeding up again.'

Packer: 'Okay. Watch him close now. Any sign of a turn?'

'Not yet, sir. Wait . . . wait . . . maybe a little to starboard.'

'Tell me when you're sure,' muttered Evlin. He stared at the lighted circle, his hand on the button of his mouthpiece.

'Datum's turning to starboard.'

The captain puffed rapidly. The smoke hung in hazy, slowly mixing layers above the flat white paper surface. 'Shit, he heard us,' muttered Silver.

'Come right, sir?'

'You're the evaluator, Al.'

'Bridge, Evaluator: Come right, increase speed to fifteen knots, steady up on – we'll give you the course in a minute.'

'Combat, Bridge: That'll put us beam to these seas as we're coming around.'

'She still turning?' Packer asked through the pulled-open curtain. Dan saw the pallid, startled faces of the sonarmen turned from the emerald cascades on their screens.

'Hard to tell, sir.'

'Al, let's come all the way around to two-seven-zero. That'll put the sea on the quarter.'

Evlin acknowledged. 'Mark, oh-four-thirty,' said Pedersen. Dan glanced at the clock, startled. They'd been here for an hour already. Five minutes on the bridge had seemed far longer.

'Now hear this. All hands stand by for heavy rolls while coming about,' said Pettus's voice, unnaturally strained and amplified over the general announcing system. If anyone was asleep down below, Dan thought, which was doubtful, that should interrupt their dreams.

'Hang on,' said Pedersen. He tucked the slipstick under his belt and reached up, gripping a voice tube with both hands. Dan wedged himself between the repeater and the plotter, eyeing the gyrocompass.

This time the deck slanted almost instantly, and kept going over. He saw too late that his position held him only fore and aft. His wet boots began sliding. Above him, the strained faces of the plotters looked down at him. Clinging by one arm, they were reaching out with the other to mark the 0434 positions. The north plotter added a little circle with a *K* inside it. Past Evlin, hanging from the overhead, he caught a glimpse of the sonarmen. Facing outboard, they stared almost straight up into their screens.

Ryan hesitated, then snapped back. 'Ger her *around*,' Packer was muttering. As if in answer, the rudder-angle indicator swung to right full. A bell pinged through the bulkhead. The engine-order needles jerked to ahead full on the port engine, back one-third on the starboard. The compass card, which had halted momentarily during the roll, gathered itself and spun right again, flickering as a sea crashed into the port side.

Reynolds Ryan rolled again, not quite as far, and the bell dinged again and the needles quivered and both went back to Standard.

'CIC, Bridge: Steady on two-seven-zero. Think we carried away something on the port side, though. Sending a man out to check it.'

'Negative,' snapped Packer. 'Everyone stays inside the skin of the ship. Whatever it is, it's not worth losing a guy.'

'Bridge, aye.'

The old destroyer seemed to ride better on a westerly heading. There wasn't much to prefer between the insane pitching and the crazy rolls. With the sea on the port quarter, though, she danced a stately minuet, lifting her stern like a dowager's skirts, skipping heavily to starboard; rolling back a few degrees as her nose dipped, then lifting her stern again.

'Evaluator, Sonar: Datum has increased speed,' said the intercom suddenly.

'Estimate course and speed.'

'Course, same as before. She's making a hell of a racket, though. Sounds like a fleet of dump trucks down there.'

'What is he doing?' muttered Packer. 'Al, any bright ideas about this son of a bitch? He's not on the Northern Fleet missile-boat deployment schedule. And nobody would go to sea in an attack boat that sounded like that. Obviously he's damaged. Why isn't he heading for home?'

'That sounds like good reasoning to me, sir.' Evlin's round lenses flashed as he turned from the clock to the plotting table. The white paper glowed under the light. 'Maybe it isn't Soviet. Maybe it's one of ours, a covert penetrator, coming back hurt.'

'You think so?'

'That'd explain the course.'

Packer bent, put a hand to the medical locker to steady himself, and disappeared through the curtain. Dan heard them talking back there. He took advantage of the break to ask Evlin, 'Sir, am I supposed to be doing anything on these circuits?'

'Didn't Mark tell you? You've got the weapons stations . . . torpedoes, antisubmarine rockets, and guns. You're supposed to feed them bearings and firing orders. Till then, just follow the action.'

He nodded, relieved. That cleared things up a little.

Packer came back from Sonar. 'Well, Orris's got me convinced it's got twin screws. Nobody else has a twin-screwed nuke. So it's Soviet. The noise spectra almost match for a *Yankee*-class missile boat. Anyway, it's hurting.'

'And going south.'

After a moment, Packer said, 'Yeah. Southwest, actually – maybe even west by southwest?'

'Evaluator, Sonar,' the intercom broke in. 'Datum increasing speed again.'

'Look at that,' said Pedersen, leaning forward.

Between the last two bearings, the red diamond Matt sketched at their intersection had jumped forward an inch.

'Oh, yeah,' muttered Packer.

'Chief, give me a speed,' said Evlin.

Pedersen slid dials on the computer. 'Twenty knots? And course looks like two-seven-zero, two-eight-zero now.'

'He's trying to outrun us, sir.'

'Beautiful,' said Packer. 'Can he tell what it's like up here?'

'Well, he'll hear wave noise. He'll know it's rough. But I don't see how he can tell what sea direction is.'

'And he's jogged west. The one direction I can run in as fast as he can.'

'It heads us closer to the track of the storm, though, sir.'

'I'll worry about that later. Okay, come right twenty degrees, get us a following sea, go to twenty.'

'We won't be able to hear him at that speed, Captain.'

'Not normally, Al, but I'm betting he's putting out so much racket, Reed can track through the ambient noise. If we can't we'll slow down once in a while to listen, just like he does.'

Evlin relayed the orders to the bridge. Dan hung on, expecting more rolling, but as *Ryan*'s head came around, the motion gentled even more. The room still rose and fell, making his headache worse, but the rolling all but stopped.

The seas were from dead astern.

'Combat, Bridge; I'm going to indicate twenty-two knots; keep us kind of in between these swell lines.'

'Evaluator, aye. Maneuver as necessary to minimize motion.'

The intercom clicked twice. Dan took a deep breath that turned into a yawn. He stretched and glanced at the clock, and was startled again: 0756.

'Sir, how about a ping?' said Evlin. He put his hands to the small of his back and stretched, too. 'He knows we're here now. Let's go active and get a solid range.'

'Does he?'

'He changed course. Slowed down to listen, then when he heard us, changed course.'

'He knows there's a ship here. He doesn't know *who* we are.'

'He's got us figured for a hostile. If he thought we were a merchant, he'd have gone right underneath us.'

'Maybe so,' said Packer. 'But hold off on pinging him. I got a funny feeling about this guy.'

'Coffee, captain?' asked one of the radarmen. Packer nodded thanks and grabbed the Styrofoam cup.

'Coffee, sir?' Dan took his gratefully. It burned his tongue, but he drank half at the first gulp. He adjusted his earphones, wishing the headache would quit. He wondered how much longer this would go on. It didn't seem as exciting as it had at first. The plotters muttered as they jotted down another round of bearings. Between the crash of waves and the creak of the superstructure, he could hear the grinding of the gears inside the plotting table, inching the lighted rosette that represented *Ryan* slowly but steadily west.

He came back from a waking dream some interminable time later. Hours had passed, but the faces were the same, the dim lights the same. The ship was still rising and falling. Then he remembered the words that had brought him back.

'Lost contact, eh?' repeated the captain. Evlin sucked his lip. His eyes moved to Dan.

'Mr. Lenson, see what's going on in Sonar.'

He shucked his earphones and hung them on a switch handle. His ears felt like a cut when you take a three-day-old Band-Aid off.

Past the curtains, the little sonar 'room,' actually a nook the size of three phone booths, was as good as dark. A blue overhead light had been taped over till only a faint radiance leaked out. Aaron Reed stood behind the two stack operators, looking over their shoulders. Behind him, dials glimmered with the shapes of ships, rows of switches marked MK 43 TORP INIT DEPTH SELECT and P/S 1, 2, 3. A pen traced a wavering line on a graphed scroll. A card beside it read, NO COFFEE ON THE SONAR STACK DESKS. VIOLATORS WILL LICK THE SPILLS OFF THE GEAR. SIGNED, THE CHIEF.

'Uh, captain wants to know what's the story, sir.'

Reed didn't answer. Instead one of the sonar techs turned his head. 'He's gone quiet. First the screws slowed down, then the circulation pumps in his reactors went off. All I get's a faint hum once in a while around five hundred hertz. There.'

He pointed to the screen. Dan had expected something like a radar picture, a sweep of light and a pip. But this looked like an emerald waterfall, speckled light, with here and there a faintly traced bar. He felt stupid again. It was getting to be a familiar feeling.

'I don't see anything.'

'Well, it comes and it goes, but it ain't the kind of thing I can give you a bearing on.'

'Okay.' He remembered the argument over identification. 'Do you know yet what kind of sub it is? What class?'

Reed reached forward, past Dan. The loose-leaf book was bound in red. When Dan took it, his hands sagged.

'There's a lead insert in the spine. That's identification spectra. Flip to page three-thirteen. That's a *Yankee*, a Russki boomer, a missile boat. Like our Poseidon submarines.'

He stared at the diagram. Along the ordinate was frequency. The abscissa was intensity, in decibels. Black lines of varying length stretched from the left side.

Meanwhile, the first sonarman screwed himself around in his seat and began pushing buttons. Two big tape reels whipped backward, slowed, then began turning forward. More buttons clicked, and one of the screens flickered. It was the same display shown in the book. He flipped the cover back. WARSAW PACT SUBMARINE IDENTIFICATION, it read. TOP SECRET.

'So it's a *Yankee?*'

'Look at the screen. That look like what you got in your hand?'

'Well, yeah.'

'Not exactly, it don't, Ensign. Look here, and here. A big spike at twelve hundred cycles a second. That's some kind of damage in his shaft, or his gears. And then these other machinery bands –'

'These two are the same.'

'That's his air-conditioning plant.'

'Oh. Well – do they always run their machinery the same? Can't they speed it up, slow it down, vary the tones that way?'

'Smart question, Ensign. Yeah, they do that, to throw us

off. But this one's different. But I'm just hairy-ass guessing, there.'

Dan thanked him and went back out through the curtain. CIC seemed very bright after Sonar. He told Evlin and Packer, 'He's slowed and gone silent, sir. The sonarmen think he's either a *Yankee* or some new kind of Soviet missile sub.'

'That so?' said Packer. 'Are they getting tapes?'

'Yes, sir, they showed me one.'

'Do they think they can regain track on him passive?'

'Doesn't sound like it, sir.'

'All right, Al. Ping his ass. Use the VDS; we're getting too much quenching on the twenty-three.'

'Sonar, Evaluator: Go active on the fish.'

They must have had their hand on the switch, because almost immediately he heard the deep, strong song of the sonar. It lasted for about two seconds, three falling notes, then trailed off. One of the sonarmen must have turned on a speaker, because behind the curtain he could hear it going on and on, echoing, reverberating, in an eerie ringing whine like a siren in a great cavern.

The Sonar Contact light went on. The little dials above his head spun and clicked. 'Zero-five-zero, eighty-five hundred yards,' said Pedersen. 'Close! He's quiet when he slows down.'

'This sea's making a lot of noise,' said Packer, but he, too, looked worried. 'Plot it, quick. Al, let's drop to five knots.'

When *Ryan* slowed, her motion changed, from a gentle tipping to a violent fore-and-aft slamming. The officers bent over the trace. 'She's slowed way down,' said Evlin. 'And turned toward us, looks like. If we'd waited a little longer to ping, he'd have been in our baffles astern, home free.'

'Well, now he knows what we are,' said Packer. 'Don't react to what he does; try to predict what he'll do next. Your bet?'

'Speed up again.'

'What do you do then?'

'Match speeds, turn to parallel him. If the seas let us.'

'What if he comes straight toward us?'

'Keep my bow toward him, track him in, then spin around and pick him up again as he passes underneath.'

'Sounds good,' said Packer. He passed his hand over his hair, seemed to remember his pipe, and looked into the bowl. He made as if to relight it, then said, 'I'll be in my sea cabin.'

'Aye, sir.'

As if waiting for him to return, the submarine did nothing for the next few minutes. Dan asked for permission to relieve himself.

When he came back, he knew right away something had changed. Chief Massioni, the leading radioman, was standing beside the captain, who had come back too. Packer wasn't watching the plot. He was putting his initials on a message board, looking grim. He handed it to Evlin with the pen.

Leaning forward as he put his phones back on, Dan couldn't avoid seeing it over the ops officer's shoulder.

FM: CINCLANTFLT

TO: USS REYNOLDS RYAN

INFO: JCS
      CINCLANT
      USAF SAC
      DEFENSE INTELLIGENCE AGENCY
      COMCRUDESLANT
      COMSECONDFLT
      COMSUBLANT
      VP-24 NAS REYKJAVIK ICELAND
      NAVSEASYSCOM, SEA-62L
      COMASWFORLANT
      MODUK
      UK SUBMARINE COMMAND

TOP SECRET

REF: USS RYAN 180534Z DEC (PASEP)
SUBJ: CONTACT REPORT (C)

1. (S) REF A ACKNOWLEDGED. NAVFAC NORWAY REPORTED TRANSIT OF SUSPECTED SOVIET NUCLEAR BALLISTIC MISSILE SUBMARINE 0230Z YESTERDAY. TRACK DESIGNATED B41.

2. (TS) OTHER NATIONAL INTELLIGENCE SOURCES INDICATE SOVIET NORTHERN FLEET BEING BROUGHT TO HIGHEST READINESS CONDITION. RADIO TRAFFIC IS 3 TIMES NORMAL. IT IS POSSIBLE THAT A SURGE OF SOVIET FORCES INTO NORTH ATLANTIC IS BEING CONTEMPLATED. NATIONAL COMMAND AUTHORITY IS INQUIRING THEIR INTENTIONS.

3. (S) COMSUBLANT IS SORTIING USS BATFISH, USS BARB, USS POGY. HMS CHURCHILL BEING MADE AVAILABLE FROM FASLANE. ABOVE SUBMARINE ASSETS ETA YOUR POSITION 48 HOURS. AIR SUPPORT WILL BE PROVIDED FROM VP-24 NAVAL AIR STATION REYKJAVIK WITH FIRST AIRCRAFT REPORTING ON TOP NO LATER THAN 1320Z.

4. (TS) IN VIEW OF UNCERTAINTIES OF SITUATION EXERCISE UTMOST EFFORT TO MAINTAIN CLOSE CONTACT WITH TRACK B41. FRUSTRATE ADVANCE BY ALL POSSIBLE MEANS. REPORT HOURLY. RULES OF ENGAGEMENT TO FOLLOW.

5. (TS) DESTROY B41 IMMEDIATELY IF SONAR INDICATES IMMINENT MISSILE LAUNCH.

DO NOT DECLASSIFY WITHOUT PERMISSION OF ORIGINATOR BT

They watched the red dots slowly materialize under the plotter's fingers. They made a straight line now, headed south by southwest at about four knots. 'He's on his battery,' murmured the captain. 'Or just barely simmering his reactors to drive some kind of backup propulsion. Yeah, that'd be smarter; he'd still have electrical power then. Did anyone log the last time we heard main machinery noise?'

Pedersen silently put his finger where it was marked on the trace.

Just then the sonarmen began cursing behind the screen. The contact light went out. Evlin straightened, pressing the phones to his ears. 'What is it?' asked Packer.

'Multiple contacts. Three . . . four, all around the last position.'

'Shift to passive. He'll eject decoys, then he'll run.'

But he didn't. Or if he did, the sonarmen couldn't hear him. When the false contacts disappeared, the sea was as empty as if there'd never been a submarine there. Four minutes passed. Six.

With reluctant deliberation, OS3 Matt drew a red diamond at the last position, and labeled it 1116.

'Shit! He's lost us somehow.'

'Go to all stop, sir? Shut everything down and listen?'

'We could barely hear him before. Now that we pinged him, he'll really be buttoned up soundwise.' Packer stretched, frowning. 'But he'll have to start up again sooner or later.'

'I figure, all we have to do is wait,' said Evlin. 'He can't run long without his air conditioning, and he shut that down, too. And if he's on battery, five hours, six, and he'll have to start his reactors, or he won't have enough juice left to put a bubble in them.'

Packer rubbed his chin. 'I hope you're right. Start a lost-contact search. Make that the search center, where he went sinker. Search axis, two-four-zero.'

Silver said, 'How long will we be at that, sir? I need to know, set up my watches in CIC –'

The captain cut him off with a raised hand. He said, closing his eyes, 'We'll be at it until we find him, Mark. And after that, until they call us off.'

An hour later they still had no contact. The captain was perched on a stool Pedersen had dragged over for him. Packer had attached himself to the bulkhead with the straps from a gas-mask pouch. From time to time, his head drooped, but he caught himself and dragged it up. Then it would loll again, till the next roll skidded the stool out from under him. Evlin asked him once whether he should report the lost contact. Packer grunted and shook his head.

At eleven-thirty, he stirred uneasily. He blinked at the clock, then glanced around. Dan straightened from his exhausted slump against the radar repeater, seeing Packer's eyes on him.

'Al.'

'Yessir.'

'Why don't you set up a watch rotation. Get Reed to spell you, get a few hours in the bag. We may be here for a while.'

'What about you, sir? Shall I get Commander – '

'No,' said Packer. He didn't add anything, and after a moment, Evlin said, 'Aye, sir. I'll do it port and starboard, six on, six off. Chief! Send somebody down after Mr. Weaver, to relieve Mr. Silver. Ask Ensign Cummings if he can spell Mr. Lenson. Tell them to get something to eat and be up at noon.'

As Pedersen left, Dan slumped back again. Now that a relief was on the way, he suddenly felt wrung out, feeble, as though all that kept him upright was the steel behind him.

At noon, a sullen-looking, sniffling Cummings poked him in the back. Dan explained what was going on. The sub was still lying low. They were pinging away for him, search plan RHUBARB. The disbursing officer grunted and took the headset.

When he was free, he staggered away from the plotting table. He'd been standing there for almost nine hours. And on the bridge for three hours before that. He'd be back on at 1800. He should sleep now. He should get something to eat.

Instead he went forward, into the pilothouse. Ed Talliaferro glanced at him from beside the binnacle. Rambaugh was there, and Shorty Williams. Lassard was at the wheel. Chief Yardner had the JOOD's binoculars. He felt an obscure pleasure in their unremarking, weary glances. Clinging to the overhead cable, he lifted his eyes and looked out – over the forward mount and antenna, crusted with an unfamiliar carapace, into a waste of wind and sea.

Suddenly his mouth began to water again. he had only a second to choose. Bridge urinal, corner bucket, or the wing. *Ryan* rolled, making the choice for him. He slid downhill to the door, and undogged it hastily.

The air was crystal ice, and ice coated the gratings under his boots. He fetched up against the splinter shield and clung to the rough, gritty steel, staring down into the sea.

The gratings soared upward, then dropped away. He was light and then heavy. When she slammed back down spray exploded around her stem. But she kept going down, and down. With horror, he saw her ice-coated chains and tackle wavering beneath many feet of clear green water. A second later the wave crashed into the gun mount, tearing itself apart into roaring tons of tormented, creamy foam that leapt upward like a pitted leopard, trying to claw him down into it. Then the gale whipped that away, too, as if enraged that its ally had failed in the assault.

Suddenly, all at once, his guts emptied like a squeezed sack. An instant too late, he realized he was facing the wind.

When it was over, he clung to the rail, gasping and shuddering. He ducked to the pool of mixed rain and seawater that rolled endlessly between the scuppers. He splashed his face and wiped it with his sleeve. But he couldn't do anything about his clothes. Through the porthole, he caught Lassard's smirk above the helm. It turned away, to Coffey, and then the other faces swung. Was that laughter? To hell with them. By the smell in there, they weren't doing so hot, either.

Weak, chilled, empty, he clung there, watching as the rising wind gilded another layer of ivory over the forecastle and o1 level. The gun mount was sheathed with white armor. Wind-slanted icicles bent from the tampioned muzzles. The whip antenna, the blast shield, range finders, all were cased with ice, shining with a dull, smooth internal light that echoed the opalescent sky. *Ryan* irritated the sea, and the sea had begun coating her, as an oyster coats a grain of sand to produce a pearl.

Beyond them, the gale heaved and roared in terrifying carelessness. Terrifying uninterest, and terrible power. He remembered what Talliaferro had said about ballasting, and Evlin's warning about the storm track.

He wanted to go below. He wanted to tie himself into his rack in the hot, stuffy compartment and sleep for a year.

But far beneath this rage, so many dark fathoms down that no motion of the storm could reach it, was something alien, something dangerous. Something they had to find again, and hold until help arrived.

Help . . . for the first time, it occurred to him that if U.S.

and British submarines were on their way, it stood to reason that more Soviets could be headed here, too.

When he got back to CIC Pedersen was still there, slumped in front of the unlighted air plot. A mug smoked in his twitching hand. He looked asleep, but the mug leveled itself automatically as *Ryan* began a fresh series of crashing pitches, kicking her heels to the sea.

'Chief, you got anything that'll tell me what I'm supposed to be doing up here? Something about ASW, about tracking subs?'

Pedersen opened his eyes. He looked surprised. Then he smiled.

'Sure, Ensign. We'll fix you up.'

He took the stack of pubs, braced himself grimly in a corner, and began to read.

13

Dan had never understood what made his father drink. When he was sober, Victor Lenson seemed subdued, but not unhappy. Dan remembered times they'd had fun together. How they'd rebuilt the old garage, Vic and the boys, small then, 'helping' their father with tack hammers and strips of broken lath.

Then one day, there'd be the bottle. And not long after the threats, the shouting, the accusations. The crash of glass, his mother's pleading, and finally her screams. Then at the last just the broken lost voice mumbling about Charlie Company, First Battalion, Seventh Marines, and the night the Chinese came through the perimeter at Yudamn-ni.

When he was little, he'd crawled behind his bed into a recess so small, he'd thought an adult couldn't reach him. But his father had, throwing the heavy bed aside in a terrifying display of strength, pulling him out and strapping him while he screamed and fought to escape. He never knew where he'd thought to go.

For a while after the hospital Vic seemed better. He didn't drink anymore, and they took him on again down at the station.

Then one day, Dan had been studying when he heard the front door slam. A little later, his mother's voice, with a catch in it, called to the boys to go upstairs.

He came out of the kitchen with his book in his hand, and saw Pat and Jimmy going up. Pat was crying silently, clutching his headless bear. Jimmy's face was waxen-pale and expressionless. He'd started to follow them. Then he stopped on the first step, hearing the crack of a palm against skin.

He told his brothers to go to their room and lock the door. He put the book down on the steps. Then turned around, there on the stair, and went back down.

The sweet whiskey smell filled the house. His father stood over his mother by the dining room table. Her face was in her hands and her hair hung down. Though he didn't look around, Vic must have sensed him in the doorway.

'Worthless bitch. All she ever gives me's trouble. God knows her family never did anything for us.'

He'd said, his voice breaking, 'Don't hit her anymore, Dad.'

His father, the cop, no longer towered to the ceiling. Dan was fifteen, as tall as Vic Lenson now.

There was a sudden clap of lightning in his head. He staggered, tried to stay on his feet, and his father slapped him again. This time he fell across his mother. She was crying. 'No, don't hit him again, darling, don't.' Shielding him with her body.

He'd always wanted to stand up for her. Sometimes he had, when he was small, and been beaten. He'd learned to stay out of it, or if he couldn't, to fall at the first blow the way she did, to cringe, cry, and feign surrender.

But this time, without warning, his mind shut off. He saw only a reddish blaze in place of thought. He got up, and his father knocked him down again.

He looked up from the rug at his father's revolver, hanging in its holster on the chair.

That was when the barrier came down, suddenly, like a fire curtain, cutting off the red blaze. From behind it, someone he'd never known he really was, someone as cold and remote as one of H. G. Wells's Martians, watched his parents and himself.

For the longest moment of his life, his father stared at him. The cold metal trembled in his hands, dragging them down. Then Vic Lenson had turned, snatched the bottle off the table, and disappeared into the kitchen. A moment later, the screen door banged.

Then his mother was screaming at him, hitting him with closed fists. How could he threaten his own father? He was *never* to do that again. From the upstairs landing, his brothers looked down on him, horrified and rapt.

Only this time, in his dream, his father didn't leave.

Instead, he came on, pulling the heavy leather belt out of its loops. And Dan had lifted the gun, to save them all.

The bang woke him. He groped beneath the desk for the fallen copy of *Allied Tactical Publication One, Volume I*. Search plan ARTICHOKE, PINEAPPLE, REDWOOD. MADVECs, sonobuoy barriers, containment patterns. His brain seethed, then clicked suddenly into fatigued alertness.

He rubbed his eyes and looked around. Pedersen had left. The crashing and groaning were the same, or maybe a little more violent than when he'd nodded off. He uncoiled his legs from the chair and signed himself off on the pub log. Swinging from handhold to handhold, he headed for the exit.

As he passed the plot, all he could see was backs. They were slumped but absorbed, like weary gamblers after an all-night game. Packer, Reed, Cummings, Weaver, two enlisted he didn't know. Their faces were gray-green in the buzzing light. The 29MC was saying, 'Up doppler, bearing three-one-two, range seven thousand three hundred.' They'd regained contact, then.

He suddenly remembered what they were doing here.

DESTROY B41 IMMEDIATELY IF SONAR INDICATES IMMINENT MISSILE LAUNCH.

Steel shrieked around him as the old destroyer reeled. He reeled too, groping through the red-lighted gloom of the ladderway. Now he knew why his legs hurt. Even unconscious, his body had been fighting the sea.

Beyond the door the pilothouse was black. Then lights appeared as his pupils expanded. The tiny planets of radio remotes, the restless needle of the anemometer, the melted-butter glow of the binnacle, occulted for a moment by an invisible arm. Last, he made out the circular cutouts of the windows. A little past 1600, and he'd missed the few hours of gray half-light that was Arctic day. The sounds were so familiar now he barely registered them: the ionosphere hiss of radios, the whining frenzy of wipers. Frozen spray rattled like marbles against glass. Then an irritated voice: 'Bos'n! Close that fucking door!'

Suddenly he realized he was ravenous.

The wardroom was empty. Someone had cleaned up the sugar and lashed down the chairs. The coffee light was on, but when he lifted the pot it was empty of everything but a scorched reek. He staggered to the ladder and slid down it destroyer-style, boots not touching the treads.

There were perhaps forty men on *Ryan*'s mess decks. Not quite a full house. You couldn't feed 280 in a sitting, but the white Formica-topped tables, the little swing-out bucket seats would take a fifth of them. Their faces were hollow, exhausted, nodding in nausea and fatigue.

He wondered for a moment whether he was wearing the wrong uniform. There was no money in his family; no gold braid-encrusted forebears, like Norden's. He should be one of these men, a radioman, a sonarman, a boiler tech. His senior year in high school, he'd already talked with the recruiter when the telegram arrived from the Academy.

Instead he was one of the ones in charge. The people who were supposed to know what to do. . . .

The steam tables were empty, but messmen were passing trays of bread, cheese, meat, pickles. Hands grabbed at them, throats washed them down with paper cups of purple fluid. When *Ryan* rolled, men grabbed the servers' belts, keeping them on their feet. Food and plastic forks slid across the dirty tile with each roll. The aroma of hot strong coffee radiated from the galley like lines of magnetic force. He saw khaki in a corner, and threaded his way over.

It was Al Evlin, alone. 'Couldn't sleep?' said the ops officer.

'Didn't really try, sir.'

'Once we go back, we'll be on till midnight. You can still get a couple hours in.'

Dan valved bug juice from a cooler. 'Anything happen since we got off?'

'Regained contact. That's all I know. We'll be back in it soon enough.'

'True.' He looked at Evlin's glasses for a moment. Then he sat down, and his voice came out guarded.

'So what did you mean, about the sea?'

'About the *sea*?'

'One night – before the storm – remember, we were having

a kind of philosophical discussion. You told me to look out at the sea, and think about it.'

'Oh. I remember now. And did you?'

The grin felt strange on his face. He'd wanted to ask Evlin this for a long time. 'I've done a lot of looking, but I've been too scared to think.'

A messman clattered down bread, peanut butter and jelly, butter in plastic tubs, sugar cookies. 'Soup in the galley. Drink it out of cups, you want some.'

'Thank you,' said Evlin.

'Anyway, what did you mean?'

'I'd rather have you tell me what you thought I meant.'

Dan said slowly. 'If I get you right – you were comparing our individual lives to the waves. Not as separate, but a – conceptual subset, like in Boolean algebra.' He paused, but Evlin kept silently impastoing bread with peanut butter. 'And . . . so that even though each wave looks different from the rest, and it seems sometimes they die and the sea's calm, really nothing's created, and nothing dies . . . it's just the sea, always changing, but always still the same.'

The ops officer took a bite. 'Chunky. I prefer smooth.'

'And that our existence is like that,' Dan said. He felt silly, but at the same time very clear, as if this was what he was supposed to be talking about right now, right here, in this crowded, careening space, with this man.

'I never said *that*. Nothing is *like* anything else. Language forces us to think in similes. It works when you're discussing things in terms of other things. But when you're talking about areas outside everyday experience – particle physics, for example – you can't use words at all, not and have it mean anything corresponding to reality.'

'But it makes sense, somehow. It's true in terms of matter and energy. They don't vanish. They just change forms.'

'But are the spiritual and physical worlds separate? The medieval Christians thought all of nature was a book revealing the intent of God.'

Dan said slowly, keeping his voice below the hum of other voices, 'But what good does it do you to believe that, Al?'

'What *good*. Well, how would people act if they really

thought everyone else was part of himself? That his neighbor's not only *like* him, the Golden Rule, but actually another, *separate* self, looking out through other eyes?'

'It would make you a lot more tolerant.' He thought about it. 'And maybe, kinder.'

'And if you believed you'd be back?'

'It would make you care more about a lot of things, stuff you just shrug about now, because you figure it'll be somebody else's problem.'

'It would change the world,' Evlin said.

Ryan gave a deep groan and rolled to her beam ends. The men grabbed the tables, letting go of food, cups, hats. The heavy steam tables shifted against their lashings, stirring above suddenly taut faces that turned to look uphill at them.

'It would change the world. And that's what the Master's trying to do. That's why I'm getting out, Dan. That's where I belong. At his side.'

Chief Bloch lurched out of the galley with BM1 Isaacs. The boatswain looked worried. Dan waved. They exchanged glances, then shoved their way through the men clinging to the tables.

Bloch hadn't shaved that day. The stubble was gray. 'What you doing down here, sir? Thought you was in CIC.'

'We're port and starboard up there, Chief. How are the guys doing? We getting anything done?'

'Not a damn thing, sir. Not in this shit. I had them turned to in the paint locker for a couple hours, but fumes got so bad and they got so sick, I told them to clear out. Most of 'em are in the compartment, seized down and flaked out.'

'How about maintenance? There's gear needs tearing down and rebuilding.'

'All our shit's out on deck, sir, 'cept the windlass and wildcat up in the peak.'

'Well, how about training? Any lessons we can give them, Rights and Responsibilities, or something?'

'I'll see, sir,' said Bloch without enthusiasm.

'How you doing, Ikey?' asked Evlin. Isaacs started, then looked at him with bleary, glazed eyes.

'All right. Lieutenant, sir. I'm doing okay.'

'What's going on up there, sir? We heard something about a Russki sub. Then we didn't hear nothing after that.'

Dan wasn't sure how to answer that. It was secret, part of it top secret, the first TS-classified stuff he'd ever seen. If you went by the regs, he didn't see that the deck division had any need to know. But who were they going to tell, three hundred miles northeast of Iceland? In the end, he bunted. 'I don't really know, Chief. It's so new to me, I'm not really sure what's going on.'

'How about you, Lieutenant? The guys ask us, we ought to have something to give out.'

'You're about up-to-date, Chief. We caught a Soviet submarine sneaking south, and we're trying to hang on to him.'

'Is that why they're keepin' us out here ... sir? Just to hassle some poor fucking Russian?' said a voice from the next table.

Dan turned, and found himself face-to-face with Lassard's flat, empty eyes, his detached smile. How long had the seaman been eavesdropping? 'We're out here because those're our orders, Seaman Lassard.'

Lassard got up. Into a little silence that had precipitated around them, he said loudly. 'We got no business out here, Ensign. *Loo*tenant. Listen to that, you guys! This fuckin' rust bucket ain't gonna take this forever. We hit a piece of ice, one wave too many, we're gonna feed the fish, all of us.'

Dan had thought about how to handle Lassard, and through him the other kinnicks. Since everyone expected it of him, the seaman had no choice but to act the rebel, the devil. And since he was a born leader, that made him more than just a pain in the ass. What you expected, they'd told him at the Academy, was what you got. If he treated Lassard like an adult, maybe he could reach him. Thinking this, he said with firm reasonableness, 'The old man's been at sea a lot longer than we have. What do you say we leave that up to him.'

'Hey, this is everybody's problem, Ensign. Look at these poor fuckers.' Lassard gestured around, at the pale faces, apathetic a moment before, interested now. 'They don't get off on hassling Russians. They're probably as sick and scared as we are, down there. What's the point, anyway?'

'I like that you're starting to care about your shipmates, Slick. But if the Soviets can get past us now, that means they can do it anytime it's rough. And if they know that, there's nothing stopping them from doing it for real.'

'Come off it! It's just another Navy mind job. You think these guys care about that World War Three bullshit?' His wave included the listening men. 'Hey, you raggedy-ass seasick motherfuckers, any you give a drizzly shit about that? Fuck, no! They just want to get home alive for Christmas.'

'You done eating, Slick?' said Bloch. 'Then quit shooting your mouth off. You talk more and work less than any sad sack of shit I ever seen. Get off your soapbox, there's guys waitin' in the mess line for a place to sit.'

'They want to see their kids again, too. You don't care about that, why worry about the mess line?'

'Slick –'

But instead of leaving, Lassard leaned in close. His pale eyes, the blue of a jay's wing, fixed on Dan's. 'I'm tellin' you: Things are changing. The Man doesn't take care of us, people gonna take care of theirselves. Going to take things into their own hands, people who know how to –'

Bloch jumped to his feet. 'Shut your fucking mouth!' he shouted. 'Go forward, or you're on report.'

The seaman shrugged. He gave Dan an innocent smile. 'Right. You're the boss, man. We just got to turn around, bend over, and let you drive. The fuckin' brass knows best for everybody. Even if they don't got the sense to puke to leeward.'

'*Lassard!*'

'Let's go,' he said. When he left three of four others got up with him.

Bloch looked after him, fists closed. 'You can't reason with that son of a whore, sir. That's the wrong approach. He'll just take advantage of you.'

'Maybe so, Chief. Maybe you're right.'

Bloch and Isaacs nodded and moved off, Isaacs settling at the edge of a knot of senior petty officers, Bloch headed forward toward the chiefs' quarters. Just before the doorway, he turned back. 'By the way, sir, the senior chief boilerbugger and me been talking. We're taking on a lot of ice. If the Skipper wants to find us a safe course, we can get some steam lines topside, blast some of it off.'

'Thanks, Chief. Good idea. I'll pass it on.'

Bloch left. Dan thought about that for a minute. Then he thought about taking a tour of his spaces before he went back on watch. Actually, he should have done that with the chief. But he'd better get something to eat while he could.

He was biting into white bread and processed cheese when the buzz of talking, eating men trailed off. He glanced up to see Commander Bryce by the serving line, tapping a pack of Camels against the back of his hand. His frown played over the ranked heads, coming at last to rest on the two officers. The frown deepened.

The men drew their legs out of his way quickly as the exec came toward them.

'Afternoon, XO,' said Evlin.

'Good afternoon, sir,' said Dan.

'Hello, boys. Taking it easy?'

'Having a sandwich before we go back on in CIC, sir,' said the ops officer. Dan noticed that he spoke differently to Bryce than he did to others. Formally, almost pendantically. The way he'd seemed to Dan at first: courteous, remote, intellectual.

'So, you made any progress on your investigation, Dan? I believe I asked for a report?'

He felt his toes curl inside his boondockers. 'Uh, no, sir. I mean, yes, you did, but I . . . I had my interviews complete yesterday, I mean day before yesterday. But I didn't get any leads. Then we went to Condition One. . . .'

'So bottom line is, you still don't know who belongs to that marijuana.'

'No, sir.'

'That's not the kind of performance I expected. In fact, it's pretty piss-poor. Still, maybe that's the best you could do . . . *is* it the best you could do?'

'Well, sir –' He struggled with that. 'No sir, I could have dug deeper. Maybe I could have found out who put it there. But there just hasn't been time.'

Bryce looked past them at the crew. They were eating and talking again, but eyes kept sideslipping their way. 'Well, maybe if there was less shooting the shit on the mess decks, there might be time to carry out orders, eh? If having the men use drugs really bothered you. But if you don't think it's important, we'll leave it at that.'

'It bothers me, sir.' Dan swallowed bitterness. 'I'll get right on it, sir.'

When Bryce left, Lenson stared at his bread and cheese without speaking. 'Don't take it so hard,' said Evlin. 'Don't let him get to you.'

'Just another wave, huh?'

'Something like that. And not such a big one, when you get it in perspective.' Evlin looked at his watch, tossed off his juice, and got up, all at once official again. 'Got to check the traffic. See you in CIC.'

'Yes, sir.'

Dan decided that he stank, and that he'd better do something about it.

The bunkroom was so hot he broke into instant sweat. Freezing cold outside, cooking within. As his eyes adapted, he made out Silver in his rack, arm over his eyes. Someone had thrown the shoes and pubs on the floor into the shitcan and wedged it under the sink. He stripped off khakis and skivvies, pawed his locker for soap, and closed the door softly.

The washroom was dark, too, and just as hot. He flipped on the light and stepped into the stall. A Navy shower, a quart to wet down, soap yourself, then a quart to rinse off. Even that would be nice. He twisted the knob. Nothing. He was so tired, he didn't even curse.

'All-officer meeting in the wardroom. That is, all officers not actually on watch, meet in the wardroom.'

He took a standing-room space by the sideboard, buttoning his last clean shirt over dirt and sweat. The chairs were still lashed down, so everyone else was standing, too, except for a few early birds on the sofa. Bryce gave him a look from the head of the table.

'Attention on deck.'

'At ease,' said Packer before anyone had a chance to come to attention. He stayed by the door, one hand braced against the sideboard, the other in his pocket. Dan, four feet away, saw the beard on his jaw and the veins in his eyes. There was a burn or callus, some kind of spot, on his lip, where he held the pipe. He didn't have it with him now, though. The captain said, a little hoarsely. 'Is 'Fredo here? I could use some coffee.'

'Mr. Cummings,' said Bryce. No one else moved.

'Okay. Thought I'd get you all together and tell you what's going on. I guess everybody knows we're holding close contact on a Soviet boomer. We lost him for a while, got him again, lost him again half an hour ago. He's running silent, and he's pretty canny. But we've got a P-three with us now, working barrier ops under my direction, and I think we'll snag him again, no matter how smart he is.

'Al, how about that last message.'

Evlin cleared his throat. He pulled a paper from his shirt pocket and adjusted his glasses.

'This is from JCS via CINCLANT. It came in Flash precedence half an hour ago. I'll summarize. The Joint Chiefs say that the Soviets have been in touch with them. This sub we got, track B forty-one, apparently has sortied on its own. It's a second flight *Yankee* boat, like our new Poseidons, with a full patrol loadout of SS-N-six mod threes.'

Evlin stopped for a moment to let that sink in, then went on. 'The Soviets say the boat's CO is a hot runner, one of the best they've got, but a hard-liner, a real old-style Communist. He was talking preventive war. This got the higher-ups nervous, apparently, and they sent the KGB in to shut him down.

'Unfortunately, they tried to relieve him aboard his ship, and that didn't go over too well with him. The Russians say he went over the edge. Told his crew that it was now or never for victory over the West, and got enough of them to go along to get under way. He evaded a Northern Fleet cruiser that tried to stop them, but sustained damage in the action.

'The Soviets have asked if we can help. They don't want the submarine sunk, but they very much want him stopped. So do we.

'The Russians have also notified NATO that they're sending eight to ten of their nuclear submarines into the Gap after him.

'Okay, that's basically what the message says, only it adds that there's a lot of VLF traffic out of the Northern Fleet, primarily to Soviet ballistic missile boats. Or maybe to this boat, the one we're holding down. We don't know.' Evlin paused. 'Captain?'

'Okay, that's the picture. Any questions?'

'That's the real story?' Bryce said. They all looked at him. The XO wasn't smiling now. 'What if it's a trick, to get their fleet out to sea, before we can get the cork in? That way, they get a great excuse to start a war – "They sank one of our boomers" – at the same time they get their subs into the chicken coop. That could end up lettin' them win.'

'I don't know, Ben. It's also possible that they're lying about what this guy's trying to do, that he's really trying to escape, or defect.'

'But if he was trying to escape, wouldn't he surface and give up, when he ran into us?' asked Norden.

'Maybe he doesn't trust us.'

'Sir,' said Dan. 'What about the directive – what about our orders to shoot, if we hear him getting ready to fire?'

'That's pretty clear, I think,' said Packer. He closed his eyes for a second, was about to speak when the pantry slider opened and a cup of coffee appeared. He took it and waited till the door closed again.

'It's a *Yankee*-class, flight two. Those are the Soviets' first-line ballistic missile boats. Some of those missiles probably have multiple warheads. The range is great enough that, if he makes it past us, gets another couple hundred miles south, he can hit New York. As it is, he can hit London, Paris, anyplace in Europe. JCS asked the Russians if he had codes, if he could fire. They didn't answer that one. So the assumption on this side is that he does.

'Now, *Ryan*'s the only Allied unit in the area, the only ship available to stop this guy. Nobody else patrols up here in the winter. So CINCLANT's leaving it to us. We have to hold contact for' – he paused, looking at the clock – 'roughly thirty-six more hours. Then we'll have four U.S. and British nukes here. They'll either hold this guy till the situation clarifies or else destroy him.'

'How long will the other Red boats take to get here?' said Bryce. 'Seems like we ought to finish up before then.'

'Finish up?'

'I mean kill him. Next time we get a solid contact, blow him out of the water.'

Faintly, Dan heard the keen of the gale outside. Packer straightened. 'I've been thinking about that. Any other questions?'

Dan looked around. Norden and the others were examining the table, absorbed in their thoughts. 'Captain –'

'Mr. Lenson?'

'About the ice topside, sir –'

'Yeah, I meant to say something about that. This storm will pass between us and Iceland in the next twenty-four hours. It's not going to be comfortable out here. Fleet Weather's giving us forty-foot sea, ninety-knot wind predictions now. I'll look for an opportunity to get people topside. Wanted to today but the courses we were on just wouldn't permit it.

'If we can't, and the weather gets worse –'

Packer didn't finish, as if he hadn't yet thought it through. 'Anyway, whatever we think, we have our orders. And I'm going to execute them. Ben, Al, let's get together in my sea cabin for a few minutes. Thank you, gentlemen. Let's go about our business.'

Dan came to attention automatically, though no one called it. He was trying to imagine forty-foot seas. Hurricane-force winds. How could they get men out to deice in that? And if they didn't, how would *Ryan* live?

When he looked at the clock, it was time to go back on watch.

14

Time, eighteen thirty-one. Standby – *shift*,' said Pedersen, swinging the rule clear. The officers stepped back, bracing themselves against repeaters and vertical plots as Matt and Lipson rolled the old plot up and off the table. The chief radarman stepped in with fresh paper. Dan swallowed hard, grabbed the edges, held it flat for taping. As their hands lifted, the plotting and evaluation team leaned forward again, Packer with them, part of the huddle around the smooth white field on which they were locked in the long game.

Lenson gripped the table, swallowing dry heaves. The closed cold air of the electronics spaces was supposed to be recycled through filters, but now it stank of cigarette smoke and barf and ozone. The compartment and the men sealed in it were progressing through space in slow gigantic bounds, like a bucking brontosaur. First pencils floated into the air, then everyone's head snapped down as they crashed into the sea. Then came the slow crawl upward again, his stomach contracting, anticipating that sickening descent. . . .

When they'd relieved, Reed had updated them on the action since noon. The first P-3B antisubmarine aircraft, call sign RD04, had reported in on the ASW tactical net at 1300. Later than they'd hoped, but doubly welcome, since *Ryan* still hadn't regained contact.

Reed explained that in 'creep mode' a nuclear sub was lucky to make three knots, little more than a brisk walk. Even so, after two hours the 'farthest on circle,' the area within which the sub had to be, covered 113 square miles. With each hour, that area increased geometrically, and the probability of reacquisition dropped accordingly.

Reed suspected B41 was trying to escape to the southwest. That had been its course at first intercept. So when the P-3 pilot placed himself under *Ryan*'s advisory control, Packer had ordered him to lay a Julie barrier twenty miles southwest of the 'datum,' the latitude and longitude of the last solid contact.

Dan listened intently. The pubs he'd read yesterday had defined a 'Julie barrier' as a miles-long line of sonobuoys – floating microphones with battery-powered radio transmitters – dropped in a carefully spaced sequence. On a second pass, the plane dropped small explosive charges. If the sonobuoys were laid properly, they'd pick up the echoes of the explosions from the sub's hull and transmit them to the aircraft. The P-3 plotted the results and radioed *Ryan* the target's position, course, and speed.

Reed had spread out the last two plotting sheets, pointing out where the plane had laid two successive barriers, then extended them to the west. Unfortunately, all they'd detected were faint echoes that the operators on the P-3, orbiting at 22,000 feet, evaluated as schools of fish.

At 1500, they'd had a break. A Flash message reported SOSUS contact from a naval facility in Norway.

Dan didn't know what that was, so he asked. Reed said SOSUS was a supersecret network of bottom-laid hydrophones, sensitive but not always dependable. In any case, it only gave a line of bearing, unless two stations could fix the same signal.

The message reported intermittent twin-screw tonals on a bearing that passed east and south of *Ryan*'s position. Packer had instantly ordered the plane to leave its barriers and drop another, using its last dozen sonobuoys, twenty miles to the east. The first pass had picked up a sizable echo *outside* the new pattern, twenty-eight miles southeast by east of *Ryan*.

Reed had leaned back wearily as he concluded. 'That's the good news: Romeo Delta's got him hooked, and he knows it. He's making runs this way and that, changing depth, trying to shake loose, but he's basically nailed. The bad news is that we can't get over to where he is because it'd put us beam-on to the prevailing sea. So for the moment, we're letting the airedales carry the ball. We're heading south, making eight to ten knots good. That's closing the range slowly. When we get to CZ range, twenty-one, twenty-two thousand yards, we'll try to pick him up again with the VDS.

'I guess the short version is, we still hold him, and it's thirty hours till the cavalry gets here. Now I'm gonna take fifteen minutes to eat and shit, then back to Sonar. Any questions?'

Evlin had asked him about how much longer the aircraft had on station. Reed said RD had fuel for four more hours before he had to return to Iceland, and another plane with full tanks and sonobuoy bays would be overhead before he left. 'Do you want to talk to him?'

'Later. Has he reported any channel-lock problems?'

'No, there's enough frequency separation that the barriers don't interfere with each other.'

Evlin turned to the captain, who had watched the turnover silently. 'Sir, I have the watch as evaluator.'

'Okay, Al. Thanks, Aaron, good work.'

When Reed was gone, Evlin said, 'Any instructions for me, sir?'

Packer blinked slowly and shifted on his stool. 'Not really. Just stay on his tail, and keep our powder dry. I'd rather hold contact myself, but second best's having the plane locked on. He's got Mark forty-sixes aboard. He can shit a torp, two seconds' notice. The idea of one-six-zero, that's as close as we can get to heading east without falling off into the trough.'

'My question is, why's he going east at all?'

Packer said, and his voice was patient and heavy, 'I figure, because he figures we're looking for him to go southwest. The SOSUS indication tells me he's pulling power off his reactor again, not full power, but enough to put machinery sound in the water. He's either running low on juice or trying to slip around our flank. If they hadn't tagged him, he'd have made it, too. This is a sharp bear. We've got to keep him on a short leash. Next time, we may not be so lucky.'

'Coffee, sir?' said one of the OSs. Packer took it without answering and sucked deeply, as if it were brewed with the water of eternal life.

'But he can't get anywhere if he goes east. There's nothing that way but the Norwegian coast.'

'That's a good place to hide, Al. Lots of cozy little fjords there he can duck into and nobody would ever find him. Not us, not the Norwegians, not the Soviets.'

'But isn't he trying to get south, into firing range?'

'Nobody knows.' Packer's face was rigid with fatigue, but behind the rising smoke from the pipe his eyes glittered. 'That's his *capability*. His *intentions*, who knows? If the Russians are telling the truth, then he's probably headed southwest. If they're lying, if he's really just out here to give them an excuse to surge their forces before we wake up to what's going on – then all he has to do is lose us, and the first inning of the war goes their way.'

Pedersen said, 'You don't think that's what's happening, do you, sir?'

'It doesn't matter what I think, Chief. But I'll bet anything you want that question's getting asked at the Joint Chiefs level, maybe higher. I'll guarantee you, the CINCs are recommending getting the fleet under way. Once that starts, the Reds are going to ask themselves. Do they jump the gun, follow up on B forty-one, crazy or not, or wait to be bottled up? We've always thought the big one would start in Central Europe, maybe just because the last two have. But it could be starting out here. Right now.'

Nobody said anything for a moment.

'Hammerhead, this is Romeo Delta Zero Four. Over.'

The voice came wrapped in static from one of the speakers above the plot. Evlin nodded to Silver. The CIC officer cradled the handset, waiting for the beep and green light that signaled the voice scrambler was engaged. When it came he said rapidly, 'Hammerhead. Over.'

Through the roar of interference and amplification, the distant voice said, 'This is Romeo Delta marking on top of trace at angels twenty-two. We hold contact proceeding one-zero-zero at nine knots, forty-eight thousand yards from you on a bearing of zero-nine-five. We made one low pass for ID and got a positive MAD contact. Man, it's rough down there. How do you skimmers stand it in that stuff?'

Dan knew now MAD meant a magnetic anomaly. The plane's instruments had detected something made of steel down there, a lot of steel. 'Plot that,' he muttered to Matt.

'Give him a roger, out,' said Evlin. 'No, wait. Ask him if he has contact with his follow-on yet.'

Silver asked the pilot about his relief. When the scrambler synced, they heard the drone of turboprops before he said, 'That's a charlie. I'll be handing off to Delta Delta three three. Right now, he's holding on Runway One waiting for visibility to clear. I told him it's heavy shit out here, make sure his deicers are checked out. Over.'

'Okay, sign off,' said Evlin. He reached up and hit the button on the 29MC. 'Sonar, Evaluator: Bearing to contact is zero-nine-five. Search on same freq bands as before.'

As Sonar rogered, Dan depressed the button on his mouthpiece. He had word to pass, too. 'Asroc Control, Torpedo Control, Director fifty-one: This is WLO. Target bears zero-nine-five true, range forty-eight thousand. An ASW aircraft is orbiting over it at twenty thousand feet.'

The petty officers at the various stations rogered indifferently. He pressed the button again. 'Look, you guys, stay on the ball. Make sure you're aimed out on these bearings.'

When the listless voices rogered again, one of them left his button down while he added a yawn. It was just another drill to them. Well, he could sympathize. He felt sick again, nauseated and weak. He'd tried to eat, but lost it, then given up trying. This time when he got off he was heading straight for his rack. He was so zonked he saw things moving in the corners of CIC. But when he looked, there was nothing there.

Evlin was studying the plot. Dan could see programs running behind his glasses. Every couple of seconds he frowned up at the silent intercom. Pedersen advised the plotters in a low tone how to record the MAD vector and extend the farthest-on circle from it.

He eased his phones and drifted over to the air scope. Silver stood over it, a grease pencil sticking out of his beard. They watched the sparkling wand of the trace sweep around. A bright pip flared to the southeast. Silver ratcheted the knobs and set the cursor on it. 'The bird,' he muttered. 'Got to keep track of it, case they lose an engine, or something.'

Dan nodded, but thought that if it went down in weather

like this, there wasn't much point in knowing its location. Even a four-engine wouldn't leave much but an oil slick, and from what Packer and Evlin were saying, *Ryan* wouldn't be able to get over there to rescue them. A destroyer didn't expose herself to forty-feet seas from the beam – especially when she was losing stability with every pound of ice.

'Sir, who shall I give this to?' asked someone behind them. When he turned, a shuddering petty officer in a wet pea coat was holding out a glass slide. Silver told him to take it in to the sonarmen.

For the next two hours, Dan stood as his legs went through pain into numbness. His feet felt as if they'd swollen to fill every seam in his shoes. The ship soared and plunged, hammered and rang like a hollow tube on a blacksmith's anvil. From time to time the lights flickered and the scopes contracted to tiny bright points, like electronic diamonds, then whirred back up to life. The P-3 held contact as if epoxied to the sub. Packer sat on his stool, blinking slowly as he tasted smoke, let it trickle out. The only conversation was the mutter of the plotters as they copied data from Romeo Delta. With dull curiosity Dan watched Packer struggle against going into the sonar shack. But every ten or fifteen minutes, he lost and disappeared behind the black curtain.

Once, when he was back there, Dan heard Evlin mutter something. He leaned to him. 'Sir?'

'Sorry. Talking to myself. I still don't understand why he's running east.'

'Like the captain said, because we expected him to go southwest.'

'I don't agree. He's *got* to go south. Otherwise, he'll be boxed up when our nukes get here. Time's running out on him. He's got to know that, that he won't be the only submarine out here for very long. And once our boats get their teeth in him, he's not going to get away.'

'Then what happens?'

'Then somebody's going to have to decide who fires the first shot.'

'Evaluator, Sonar: Still no contact. Continuing search.'

'Evaluator, aye.'

Around 2230, Packer lumbered to his feet again. He started for the sonar shack, but made a U-turn outside the curtain and went forward instead. He said he'd be in his cabin, to call him if anything happened.

When he disappeared, the ASW plotting team seemed to wilt. Evlin sighed, digging his fists into his back. Dan heard his spine pop. 'Didn't I see a jug of coffee? Thanks. Okay, school call. Might as well take advantage of this for training. Dan, Mark, you want to catch this.

'Okay, now ... where to start. Maybe with the sound-speed diagram. You guys know about thermoclines.'

'Layers of colder and warmer water,' said Dan.

'Right. But they aren't discontinuous; they're areas of gradual change. Normally you get warm water at the surface, then a band where temperature decreases rapidly with depth. Then an area of more gradual drop. Below say three hundred meters, you don't see much change even between winter and summer. The thermoclines move up and down in diurnal and seasonal cycles.

'Okay; why do we care? Because sound speed varies with temperature. Also with salinity, but in the open sea, temperature's what you most care about.

'Remember that slide Pelouze brought up here a while ago? That's a BT slide. BT means bathythermograph. It's a little instrument that goes down and comes up and gives us a plot of depth versus temperature. From that, with some charts, the sonar weenies –'

From behind the black curtain: 'Watch it, Mr. Evlin.'

'– like Petty Officer Orris, can predict sonar propagation. Give 'em the equation, Orris.'

A high voice from the inner sanctum chanted, 'C equals 1448.96 plus 4.951 T minus 5.304 times ten to the minus two T squared plus 2.374 times ten to the minus four T cubed plus 1.34 (S minus 35) plus 1.630 times ten to the minus two D plus 1.657 times ten to the minus seven D squared minus 1.025 times ten to the minus two T (S minus 35) minus 7.139 times ten to the minus thirteen T D cubed.'

'Thank you, Petty Officer Orris. The sea acts on sound like

glass on light. It can focus it or blur it; wrap it around corners, carry it hundreds of miles in channels, or bend it straight down to the bottom. The sub's figuring all this, too. He tried to hide; we try to guess where the best place to hide will be. Cat and mouse. Only he does this every day. Fortunately, the P-three evens things up. Everything clear as mud?'

'Where did he go when he disappeared this morning?' Dan asked. 'One minute he was there, the next minute – a ghost.'

'He read the water better than we did. He found a dicothermal layer that bent sound right around him.'

'Dicothermal,' said the high voice. 'From the Greek; meaning, cold as a dyke.'

'Crawl back into those earphones, Orris.'

'Wait a minute, Lootenant. There's women on that submarine.'

'What are you talking about?'

'Got to be. I hear screw noises.'

'We're getting tired, gentlemen,' Evlin announced.

Just then, the captain returned. He looked around at them. His face darkened.

'Knock it off,' James Packer said. 'This is no game.'

'Yes, sir. Mr. Silver, ask Romeo Delta for an update, please.'

For a while, he dreamed of food. Then he dreamed of sitting down. Finally he just dreamed of getting off watch. And at last, he dreamed, and prayed, that *Ryan* would steady herself just for one minute. That was all he wanted from life.

He clung to the table till his hands cramped like an old man's.

At 2300, Packer went forward again. The men watched the lighted rosette, the 'bug,' glumly while he was gone. When he came back, he stood over the air scope for a while. Dan heard a grasshopper clicking as he sucked on his empty pipe.

'We got a problem. Al.'

'What's that, sir?'

'This bow slamming kicks up a lot of spray. It's getting colder, too. I had one of the signalmen put the light on the top hamper. You can see it hit the stacks and freeze. It's over a foot thick on the mast platforms.'

'We ought to ballast, sir,' said Evlin. He rubbed his mouth. 'Mr. Talliaferro brought that up yesterday. Why don't we ballast?'

'Because it fouls the tanks. Once you get saltwater in there, you can pump all you want, but when you put fuel in again, you'll still have contamination.' Packer added heavily, 'That's why.'

'We'll have to sooner or later, sir. As we burn fuel, she gets lighter below. As the ice accumulates, she gets heavy above. You don't need an inclining experiment to tell you –'

'Yeah, that's what Ed was shouting at me about just before you came on watch.'

Dan studied the captain covertly. Were those shadows at the corners of his mouth a smile? He looked so exhausted, it was hard to tell. They disappeared as a flame flared, was sucked down into the bowl of his pipe, flared up again. 'You think I should, too, huh?'

'In your position, I would, sir. I understand the contamination problem, but it seems secondary.'

'It's not secondary to me. We lose the engines in these seas and we'll broach. Granted, if that happens and we're unstable, we won't come back, but given the choice, I'd rather not broach in the first place. That's why so far I've rated dependable power over ballast.'

'They lost some of this class in the war, didn't they, Captain? In a typhoon, from not ballasting?'

Packer shook his head sharply. 'I know what you mean, but that was different.' He glanced at the curtain, then pulled his eyes back. 'Those were prewar destroyers, not *Gearings*. During the war, they got loaded up with a lot of new stuff – radars, AA guns – and nobody kept track of their stability. Some of them ballasted, but it didn't save them. The court of inquiry concluded they lost power, fell off into the trough, started rolling, and capsized.'

The 29MC interrupted them with a monotone. 'This is the evening sonar-conditions summary. Sea suction intake is thirty-eight degrees Fahrenheit, salinity thirty-four parts per thousand. Predictions have been prepared for the following conditions: water depth sixteen hundred fathoms; own ship speed less than twenty knots; true wind speed, off the scale.

'BT drop and the deep history shows a sound-speed profile with good mixing down to four hundred feet and a faint thermocline at eight hundred. Beyond that, it's a straight fall down to a thousand five hundred. Best sensor is predicted to be passive VDS at five hundred feet. Target's best depth to listen is three hundred and his best depth to evade is below eight hundred. We have no best search speed due to heavy ambient noise. Active sonar prediction is poor due to sea return.

'Passive predictions: near surface, very poor; best depth, twelve thousand yards; convergence zone one, twenty-five thousand yards.'

Evlin reached up absently and hit the lever. 'Mark, what's range to the bird?'

The gears ground in the air-search repeater. 'Twenty-four thousand.'

'That's only twelve miles. According to that prediction, if he's over the sub, we ought to be picking him up, too.'

'With the SQS-thirty-five.'

'Right,' said Packer, and he sounded not tired anymore, but decisive. 'And we aren't. So he's not below the layer, where we expect him. He's shallow. Sonar, Captain: Bring the fish up to one hundred feet. Search on one hundred and fifty-hertz band.'

The 29MC acknowledged. Minutes dragged by. Then somebody shouted, 'Bingo!' behind the black curtain.

'Evaluator, Sonar: Passive contact against heavy background noise, bearing zero-nine-two true. No bearing drift. No doppler. Classification, *Yankee*-class submarine! We got her!' His jubilation was echoed around the plotting table. But the captain just snapped, 'Pass it to the aircraft. Tell your weapons crews, Lenson,' and the smiles froze and an instant later vanished, like gun smoke whipped away by a gale.

They held the submarine for the next hour and twenty minutes on passive VDS. The P-3 made two more low passes, two more MAD contacts, then lost it. It had used up all its sonobuoys, so now *Ryan* held on alone. They began passing range and bearing data the other way, to the plane.

The bearing remained steady. Since sonar could predict the width of the CZ band, they had a rough range, too. That also remained steady.

Dan wondered what was going on inside the captain's head. Since *Ryan* was moving generally south, albeit slowly, that meant the sub was moving south, too. But every time Orris reported, he mentioned ambient noise. The high voice sounded more worried as time dragged by. As midnight passed, he reported the noise was increasing, that they were losing the signal in it. Evlin ordered the fish winched in to fifty feet – so shallow, it started to broach. Sonar reported 'lost contact.' He dropped it back to two hundred. They picked it up again, but so faint, it dropped in and out of detectability.

'Captain,' said Evlin. He raised his voice. 'Captain!'

Packer jerked his head up from the radio desk. Evlin explained that they were losing contact.

While he was talking, Reed came out of the sonar shack and propped his leanness against the first-aid cabinet. His eyes glowed with fatigue. Dan thought, We've had a few hours off between watches; no sleep, but we could move around, relax a little. He's gone right from evaluator to sonar control and back. When Evlin finished, Reed told the captain, who had turned his face wordlessly to him, 'It's ice.'

'Ice? What ice?'

'Ask the bird if there's ice out there. Floes, or small bergs.'

But when Silver asked, the P-3 said he couldn't see the surface at all, it was too dark. He'd had to climb to get out of icing. He said he couldn't stay much longer, either.

'Where the hell did my pipe . . . ? Okay, but where's his relief? He was supposed to be here by now.'

'Wait one,' said the TACCO's voice. They knew Romeo Delta's copilot by name now: Lieutenant Wycoff. He was off the circuit for a while. When he came back on, he sounded apologetic. '*Ryan*, Romeo Delta.'

'Go ahead, Romeo Delta,' said Silver, speaking slowly and distinctly into the handset. If you spoke too soon after you keyed, it broke sync, and all the listener heard was a hissing rush like a faulty toilet.

'This is Romeo Delta. Keflavik advises they have Condition Charlie at present with fifty-knot winds.'

'Give me the set, Mark,' said Packer. The captain rubbed his forehead as he waited for the scrambler. 'This is Jim Packer, *Ryan* actual, Lieutenant. What's Condition Charlie?'

'Sir, that's a whiteout. When the wind gets above so high, it picks up loose snow, and it sort of hovers, and after a while you can't even see your props. They can't take off and we can't land. Commander Gephardt's talking to Bodo now; we'll probably have to divert to there or Kinloss, or maybe Machrahanish.'

'Are you telling me he can't take off?'

'That's about it, sir, not till the whiteout dies down. It's not the wind, a P-three can take off in just about anything, but you got to be able to see.'

'How much longer can you stay on station?' asked Packer, and his face looked like cast iron now.

'Headed south at this time, Captain. I gave you all the time on top I can. I'll have to shut down two engines to make Scotland. I'm sorry. Over.'

'I understand. Thanks for your support. *Ryan* out.'

He hung up the handset. No one spoke for a few seconds. Finally, Evlin looked back at Reed.

'Icebergs,' the ASW officer said again. 'He went east looking for them. I think he's found some. The ice changes the salinity, and the grinding of the floes covers his noise. If we can't close, we're going to lose him, sir.'

'I don't want to come left,' said the captain. 'I don't know if she'll take it, frankly.'

'Then shoot,' said a voice behind them.

Benjamin Bryce came into the circle of light around the plotting table. Evlin and Pedersen gave way as he leaned over the chicken tracks of hours of hide-and-seek. 'You got to do it this time, Jimmy John.'

'What are you doing up here, Ben?'

'I came up to see how it was going. And I'm glad I did, hearing the advice you're getting from your JOs.' Bryce put his knuckles on the glass. 'Word with you?'

'Will it take long?'

'You need to hear it.'

Bryce and Packer went back by the evaluator's desk, back on the port side of CIC. It put them around the corner from the men at the plot, but only ten feet from Dan. He couldn't hear everything. The wind howl and the slamming and the mutter of the plotters overlaid it. But he couldn't help hearing Bryce say, 'I wondered how much longer it was going to take you to figure out how this had to end.'

'What are you talking about?'

'I heard what Reed was saying. Only thing to do is put an Asroc out there, right now, while you still got contact. Don't ask permission. Just do it. Otherwise, you lose him. And you can't afford that. Can you?'

Their voices lowered then, and he saw Evlin's eye on him; he grabbed the mouthpiece and said, 'Uh, all stations, comm check.' They answered, drawling, jaded, and he lost the rest of the exchange behind him.

Packer came back a few minutes later. 'Any better?'

'Sonar reports still losing strength, sir. The SNR – signal-to-noise ratio –'

'I know what SNR is, Chief.'

'Yes, sir. Anyway, it's still dropping.'

Packer looked at the plot for another few seconds. 'Draft a message, Al,' he said at last.

Evlin grabbed the pad of blanks.

'Make it Flash precedence. Top Secret. USS *Ryan* to CINCLANTFLT. Subject: twenty-four hundred contact status.

'Para One. Due to weather degradation, P-three support no longer available. Sea state my posit is seven plus, wind eighty-five knots gusting to over one hundred.

'Para Two. Due to inability to conform to eastward movement B forty-one, anticipate losing contact in next half hour or hour time frame. Request instructions.'

The captain put his pipe in his mouth. His lips pursed around it, then flattened into a white line. 'Okay, that's all; get it out.'

When the pneumatic tube to Radio hissed, he turned to

Dan. 'Lenson, tell Asroc Control to prepare a two-round salvo of Mark forty-fours. Al, give him a bearing and range. Report when ready.'

Dan felt unreal. He stared for a moment too long, because Packer added angrily, 'You hear me?'

'Uh, aye aye, sir. Asroc Control, WLO: Prepare two Asrocs for launch.'

'Say again, there?' a lazy voice drawled in his ear. 'Doin' 'nother drill? We just did one last –'

'This is no drill.' He steadied his voice and took the slip of paper Pedersen handed him. 'Firing data follows. Target range is twenty-four thousand, five hundred yards. Bearing will be set from Sonar. Set Mark forty-four to circular search, five-hundred-foot floor, one-hundred-foot ceiling. Report when ready to launch.'

'Shit fire,' the voice said, and there was a hasty scramble of shouting, orders on the far end of the line. Dan licked his lips and glanced at Evlin. The operations officer was studying the trace, face sober behind the glasses.

'Sir, you're not really planning to –'

'I don't want to, Al, but I don't have the big picture. Keep updating the bearings and ranges. Make water entry point for the torpedoes about two thousand yards ahead of the last reported position. Dan, what are they giving you?'

'Uh, no word back yet, sir.'

At the same moment, an agitated voice in his headphones said, 'WLO, Asroc Control.'

He grabbed his mouthpiece. 'Go ahead.'

'Sir, we have a casualty on the launcher. The elevation motors – something about the elevation motors, Steffy says. Frozen, or something.'

Dan felt his hands go numb in horror and dismay. 'What are you telling me? We've been on station for ten hours now! You reported manned and ready!'

The voice became evasive. 'Yessir, we were manned, but nobody told us to train and elevate. We tried to do it just now and something's fucked. Stefanick's out there trying to find out what's wrong. There's a lot of ice all over the launcher.'

'You let *ice* accumulate on the Asroc launcher?'

'What's going on, Lenson?' Packer's voice, sharp as a whip crack.

For a quarter of a second, he was tempted to lie, buy time, hope it was something they could fix quickly. Instead he made himself say, 'Sir, there's some problem with the launcher.'

'What kind of problem?'

'They're trying to find out, sir, but it sounds like an elevation motor.'

'There's four elevation motors on that mount, and eight launch rails. One better work. Find out how long it'll be to fix it.'

'Is Stefanick back yet? Do you have any idea how long it'll take to repair?' he asked desperately. The voice on the other end said, hurt, 'Jeez, sir, he just went outside. Give him a couple minutes, all right?'

Evlin and Packer moved a few steps off. He heard them discussing torpedo run-out range, but his concentration was on his earphones. He wanted to tear them off and run aft, see what was going on himself. He wanted to strangle somebody. Every weapons station was supposed to check the gear when they manned up, and every hour thereafter while they were at GQ. He felt hot and ashamed. His hands shook as he pressed the button again. 'Asroc Control, CIC –'

'Wait one, here's Stefanick now.'

The captain came over and stood glaring at him, waiting. He couldn't meet Packer's eyes as he repeated what the voice told him. 'Sir, there's a glycol cooling and heating system in the launcher, that runs through a saltwater heat exchanger that also heats the hydraulic fluid. They say the heat exchanger must have ruptured. The saltwater mixed with the glycol and it's all frozen now. They're going to have to thaw it out and drain it, then flush it with fresh water and replace the –'

'Can they get a weapon off? I can turn the ship in bearing if they can't turn the mount.'

'Wait one, sir.' Sweat ran down his back as he repeated the captain's questions. 'Sir, Petty Officer Stefanick says it won't elevate, either, and none of the launcher doors will open. The whole hydraulic system's fucked, and he thinks the motors burned out while he was trying to move it.'

'Shit,' said Bryce. 'That's the kind of work Norden's been doing for you, I don't wonder all his people are smoking that – '

Packer said, in a voice of only slightly controlled rage, 'How about you, Ben? When's the last time you were up there, inspecting?'

'Now, Jimmy John, I don't see –'

'Al, is that Bear still around? The Soviet four-engine?'

'Haven't had him on the scope since yesterday, sir. My guess is, they recalled him when they realized the storm was coming through here. It's too rough and icy for him to do MAD sweeps down here.'

'Then we're alone. Us and him. For another' – he glanced at the clock – 'twenty-four, twenty-five hours.'

Evlin nodded.

There was a rumble over their heads, and a messenger tube farted itself into the padded cage. Simultaneously the 29MC lighted. 'CIC, Radio; Flash incoming, rabbit's in the hole.'

Packer got to it first. Dan watched as he scanned the message. As his shoulders sagged. When the captain looked up his face was no longer human. It was dark lava that had cooled and hardened into the shape of human features.

'What is it, sir?' asked Evlin.

'Maintain contact,' said Packer. He cleared his throat. 'Just that: "Maintain contact at all costs with B forty-one." '

'What did they say about preventing escape?'

'They didn't say anything about that.' He folded the message and buttoned it into his breast pocket.

'It's easy, then,' said Bryce. He lighted a cigarette with quick, nervous fingers. Sweat glittered on his scalp. 'It's there between the lines. They said it by not saying it. We just say we heard him open his tube doors. That covers our butts three ways to Sunday. I'll talk to the sonarmen, if you want.'

Utter quiet, broken only by the scream of the storm.

'Okay, that's it,' said the captain suddenly. They all looked at him. 'It's academic now; Asroc's crapped out and we're outside over-the-side torpedo range. I've got to go after him.

'Start coming around, Al. Tell Rich to come left gradually, ten degrees at a time, and steady on one-zero-zero.'

'We're going to roll like we've never rolled before, sir.'

'Pass the word, then. All hands stand by for violent motion. Do it, Mr. Evlin! And come up to twenty knots.'

Norden, from the bridge, acknowledged the order with misgiving in his tone. The radarmen grabbed handholds, set their feet wide, like sumo wrestlers readying themselves for an opponent's charge. The rudder-angle indicator quivered, then moved left reluctantly. A second later the gyro began moving, too: 175, 170.

Watching it, watching Packer's face watching it, Dan suddenly understood why the CO had buttoned the message into his pocket. It gave him authority for nuclear release. The six-digit code was right there in his pocket.

The key, if Captain James Packer miscalculated, to nuclear war.

The gyrocompass steadied at 170 for a few minutes. *Ryan* rolled, and it was bad, but not terrifying. They clung to the table, looking silently up as it began nudging left again.

At 160 the motion was worse. Packer's face was taut in the dim light. No one looked at him; no one looked at each other. They just stared down at the flat paper that represented the wild sea outside. Not even the plotters spoke now. There was nothing to plot.

One fifty. . . . One forty. 'Halfway there,' Pedersen muttered. Dan felt a surge of hope. No pitching, and even the roll wasn't that awful, though the gale screamed outside like a thousand gutshot horses.

'Hell, this ain't so bad,' muttered Lipson.

Ryan went over then, suddenly, with incredible force, as if the outraged sea had only now perceived the trick they were trying to play. She lurched to starboard, stopped with a crashing jolt that flickered the lights; then shifted to port bodily, and rose, pressing their weights against the deck, as if they stood watch for a moment on some more massive planet than Earth.

She hurtled over to port and kept going. Their feet shot out from under them. The captain's stool let go, slammed over and dumped him into Petty Officer Matt. The lights flickered again and went out. The battle lantern clicked on, projecting a weak yellow spot onto the suddenly dark plotting table. Dan tried to fight free of the phone cord, but it was too steep to regain his feet. From outside came the terrifyingly close crash of the sea hammering against the bulkhead just outside Combat. The 21MC, the command intercom, broke out in a series of half communications, cut off as others began shouting into the line.

'Chief. Chief –'

'She's not coming back!'

'Combat, Bridge –'

'Combat, Bridge, this is Main Control. We're taking water down the intakes to port. Is the captain up there? Securing blowers, securing boilers –'

'Negative!' Packer shouted. 'Somebody tell him – keep them on the line. Tell the bridge, come back to one-nine-zero. Damn it, Silver, get off me!'

Dan was first up, but only because he was on top of the heap. He got the wire off his legs, climbed over bodies to get to the intercom. He repeated the captain's orders.

'Bridge aye; I hear you.' Norden's voice, more strained than Dan had ever heard it before. Behind it was shouting and the crash of breaking glass.

Dan sniffed. Was that smoke? Probably just Bryce's cigarettes, Packer's pipe. Still, it smelled like paper burning, not –

The door to the bridge slammed open. Through it, he heard Norden shouting, 'Coming back to one-nine-zero. Main Control, give me emergency flank on the port shaft. Coffey! Right hard rudder!'

Through the shrieking and crashing came a sodden rumble from above them, a clattering, sullen roar like an anchor chain running out.

The smoke smell grew suddenly sharp. If they didn't smell it, he did. 'Fire!' he shouted. At that same moment, someone else shouted, 'Fire in the pilothouse!'

The captain's voice was unnaturally calm in the din. 'Get off me, whoever's on my legs. Lenson, see what's going on on the bridge.'

'Yessir.' He tore off the last of the wire and picked his way forward, climbing over men and shifting shoals of pubs, walking on the front panels of equipment as often as the deck.

On the bridge, flashlights licked about. He grabbed Pettus in midleap and asked where the fire was. The third-class said, 'Oh, we got it out already. Space heater tipped over into some of the charts. Ali, he hit it with an extinguisher. Hold on!'

He screamed that last into his ear, and Dan grabbed the lee helm instinctively, jerking his head around to where the boatswain was staring.

That was when the sea blindsided them, smashing not inward but downward on the now near-horizontal windows on the starboard side. The unbroken ones bulged inward under the impact of tons of water and ice. 'Right hard rudder!' Norden was shouting. And Coffey was shouting back, 'It all the way *over*! Won't go no farther!'

Dan clung to the helm, staring around. *Ryan* was pinned. Her rudder was over, her engines running all out, but the wind was lying on her, and every time she tried to rise, the sea smashed her back down. The waves hammered her like a street fighter stamping a fallen opponent to death. Another window bulged, then shattered, and the sea cascaded through, spraying him with icy water, broken Plexiglas, ice. He couldn't smell smoke anymore. All the windows on the starboard side were smashed.

Suddenly Packer was on the bridge. The captain shoved him aside and grabbed the brass handles of the engine-order telegraph. He racked them all the way back and all the way forward. 'Rich! Give her left rudder!'

Left rudder, sir? But –'

But Coffey was already bending. The wheel blurred as he spun it with one hand, clinging to the binnacle stand with the other. 'Left hard, my rudder's left hard.'

'Not hard, Coffey, full.'

'Ease to left full . . . rudder at left full!'

Packer's voice cut the darkness and confusion like a machete through tangled black yarn. 'Norden, by God, when I give an order, I want it obeyed, not questioned!'

'Yessir, I –'

'Never mind now. You have the conn back. Bring her stern through and steady on three-five-zero. Use full speed, twist her fucking tail. We can't hang around in these troughs.'

Past him, Dan saw Norden, face linen white, eyes fixed. His mouth moved but nothing emerged. 'D'you hear me?' Packer said sharply.

'Yeah . . . yes, sir. This is Lieutenant Norden, I have the conn! Come left, left full rudder, steady three-five-zero!'

But in that pause between Packer's order and the rudder's first leftward movement, the ship reeled and rose. Dan felt her lift as if to fly, like a sparrow trying to escape the bulletlike dive of a hawk. But even as she came up, he knew with numb, helpless terror that it wasn't going to be enough.

The wave hit them like a lead avalanche. The last windows blew inward. The black sea roared through the pilothouse, smashing men down as they struggled to stand on wet tile, sending hot fizzing sparks through radio remotes in the instant before they shorted and went dead. He hung from the EOT, numb with fear, unable to look away.

Ryan didn't come back.

She hung there, leaning far over to port, and the wind keened around her like a thousand jets going over on afterburner. She didn't move, and he realized suddenly how unnatural it was, how terrifying, when a ship *didn't move.*

Water rushed past him, icy black, pouring down through the shattered starboard windows, pouring down from above. For an eternity he knew he'd never come to the end of, he looked past his dangling, kicking boots through the windows to port. They were completely covered with the foamy darkness that had nothing beneath it but the bottom, two thousand fathoms down. If he let go, he'd drop straight down through them, straight into the sea.

Then, so slowly it seemed to take forever, the old destroyer staggered a few degrees back. Then Chief Yardner was between him and It, slamming and dogging the heavy armored ports of the inner pilothouse. He heard Packer shouting over the roar of countless tons of falling water: '. . . Circle William, set it now, everything but the main intakes. Ed, you got any free surface in the bilges?'

'Foot or so, sir, we're pumping down as fast as we can, but we're taking water somewhere.'

'Shit. Okay, ballast now. Ballast her down. You hear me? She's worse than I expected. That last roll, we were right on the edge.'

Talliaferro's voice acknowledged faintly, as if there wasn't enough power to get his voice from Main Control up to the bridge.

Ryan came back a little more, then suddenly lifted and swooped madly in a great crack-the-whip as the sea shoved her quarter up and around. Coffey slipped on the deck and went down, hard. The wheel spun unmanned for a moment before Dan grabbed it. He yanked it over to left full and then the black seaman was up again, saying, 'I got it, sir,' shoving back in front of him.

'Bridge, Main Control.'

'Captain here. Go ahead, Ed.'

'Sir, bad news. We're already ballasted.'

'What? Without orders? Christ, what –'

'No, sir.' The voice came louder now. 'I didn't give orders to. But when the oil king went to crack the valves to the fire main, they were already open. The wing tanks are full. It must have been a while ago, too, 'cause they're topped up, no free surface. I'm trying to find out how it happened now.'

'Find out later. Right now, look for what else we can flood. To starboard, preferably, that's windward up here. And *keep those boilers on the line.*'

Packer cut off, interrupting the chief engineer in mid-acknowledgement. He stared around, and saw Dan.

For a fraction of a second, so transient Dan wondered ever after whether it was just the shift of a flashlight, Packer smiled at him.

Then he turned away. 'Rich, you hear that?'

'Uh, yes, sir. Sir, we're steady on three-five-zero.'

'Okay, that's good for now. But I've got to go east, not north. Hear what I'm saying? I've got to go after this bastard or we'll lose him. He'll tiptoe away in that fucking ice, and we'll never see him again. Till we hear that launch impulse, when the missiles come out of the tubes. And unless we're sitting on top of him, right then, there won't be a goddamn thing we can do about it.'

'Yes, sir.'

'Now, we were ballasted, but we still went to sixty degrees on that roll. And she didn't want to come back. We're way more tender than we ought to be. We either got free surface somewhere, or a lot more ice than I thought. I can't come right again till we get rid of it . . . Mr. Sullivan!'

Dan got up from his half seat against the helmet stowage. 'Lenson, sir.'

'Yeah, Lenson. Get your division up on deck. Muster them in the Dash hangar. Sledgehammers, axes, pry bars, every man bring a tool. Rich, tell Main Control to get steam hoses rigged to the oh-two level. We've got to get some of this ice off.'

'Now, sir? It's pitch-dark –'

'Now, Rich, *now*. In half an hour, I'm coming right, and if we're not ready, we've got to roll, and if we don't come back, that's just tough titty. So get cracking! Dan, get your people moving; they won't have long to work. Make sure they wear foul-weather gear and life jackets.'

'Aye aye, sir.'

'And lines, lifelines. If anybody goes in the water, I won't be able to come about for them. Make sure they understand that. Move, Lenson!'

'Aye, sir,' he said without thinking, the way you responded at the Academy after a two-hour come-around, when your body screamed so loud your mind could no longer make itself heard. Then only something more kept you going. Something deeper. Discipline, and pride, and something that was neither of these, though it was part of them. Maybe it was only knowing it had to be done. Past Packer's squinted eyes, he caught the cracked face of a clock. It had stopped at five minutes past midnight.

15

He ran into Bloch on the ladder down. The boatswain had on a gray sweatshirt and a watch cap. His belly pressed out between the halves of his unlaced life jacket. He still hadn't shaved. 'You looking for me, sir?' he said.

'Yeah, Chief. We got to get our boys up on deck.'

'Up forward? Ikey's getting a party together now. We –'

'Forward? No, muster in the Dash hangar. We've got to get some of this ice off, fast.'

'Well, we're taking water up forward, sir. Somebody better be doing something about that right quick, too.'

He stopped halfway across the mess decks, swaying as the steel around him reeled to the stern seas. 'What are you talking about?'

Bloch took off his cap and wiped his forehead. Dan caught a faint whiff of something, after-shave or liniment. 'Talking about the handling room, sir, forward of chiefs' quarters. The gunner thinks we cracked the shield on the mount, running into these seas all night.'

Oh, Jesus, Dan thought, staring at the chief's bald spot. The ship was coming apart around them. And worse than that, the crew. He hadn't studied this at Annapolis. The tactics books took crews for granted, faceless and pliant material. Battles were duels between admirals, Scheer versus Jellicoe, Nagumo versus Spruance. But if you couldn't depend on the men, how could you take a ship into battle? How could you even stay at sea? He bit his lip, pulling his mind back as Bloch said, 'What you want us to tackle first?'

'Did the gunner report the flooding? Yeah? Let's get them on their feet, then see what we have to do when we get there.'

First Division berthing was a swaying, stinking cave. Men had slid off the mattresses, the mattresses had slid off the bunks, and the lockers had burst open, littering the deck with uniforms, boots, hats, books, magazines, toothpaste, condoms, letters, cans of Brasso and Kiwi. The locked-down air was yellow with sweat and grease and vomit. The men sat or lay between the bays, heads in their hands. A few looked up as he and Bloch staggered in. 'First Division,' Dan yelled. 'Petty officers and seamen. Grab foul-weather gear and muster on the mess decks. Right now!'

'What goin' on, sir?' said Rambaugh, getting up. His pipe was still in his mouth. Dan wondered whether he slept with it that way.

'Get your men on their feet. We're going up on deck, oh-two and oh-three levels. We got to deice to save the ship.'

'Williams! Gonzales! Coffey! Connolly! Jones! Lassard!' the second-class bawled out, turning to the compartment.

'Coffey's on watch, Baw.'

'I hear ya. Rest of you mugs, on your feet! Rain gear, Mae Wests, line-handlin' gloves!'

Ohlmeyer came in through the forward hatch just then. The gunnery officer carried a battle lantern. His red hair was plastered down wet above a white face. 'Cherry' Heering, the leading gunner's mate, was with him. 'Dan, can you give me some men?'

'I don't know, Barry. Captain wants my guys topside. What you got up there?'

'The seal's given way and the casing's cracking around it. We're taking water in the mount and handling room.'

'How much? A lot?'

'Couple hundred gallons so far,' said the gunner's mate. His eyes showed white around the irises. 'But more every minute, right in the electricals . . . few more seas and you can write this whole fuckin' mount off.'

'Can you stuff it from inside?'

'We tried. Nothing to hold it there,' said Ohlmeyer. 'No, we've got to do it from up on the fo'c'sle.'

Bloch turned to the second-class, who stood waiting, his old eyes alert. 'Popeye, take two guys and help him. Blankets and mattresses. Pick out the worn-out ones. I'll go topside with Mr. Lenson and get things set up.'

' 'Kay, Chief.'

'The rest of you meet us up on the Dash deck. Don't think to fuck off down here. If this bitch turns turtle, you'll never get out of this compartment. Where's Ikey?'

'Here he is, right behind,' said the first-class.

The men began struggling to their feet and pulling on gear. Dan and Isaacs followed Bloch out. Aft through the mess decks, up two ladders, aft again past the frozen Asroc launcher.

The hangar was dark and empty. From outside and below came the thunder of men running on thin metal, and a heavy, scraping clatter. It was a storeroom now, packed with the shadowy profiles of line spools, lashed-down boxes, athletic gear, the separate walled-in space of the torpedo magazine. The chief pointed to a crate of gloves and basketballs. 'Ikey, grab two, three your Louisville Sluggers out of there. Them bats is the best things to get ice off with.'

The door to the weather decks resisted them. Dan remembered this was aft, windward now. He got his shoulder to it beside Bloch and body-slammed it open.

The sea night was black as frozen tar. Frozen spray lashed them like a cat-o'-nine-tails. His foul-weather jacket was soaked instantly. It was icy, glacial, the cold of interstellar space sucked down into the sea and flung at them, riding a wind that flattened their ears and rippled their cheeks.

Bloch was shouting something. 'What?' Dan screamed.

The chief laid his head alongside his. 'Which side?'

'We're stern-on. It doesn't matter.'

'We may lose some men doing this, sir.'

Dan blinked, ducking as frozen spray needled his eyes. 'Get the lines ready,' he said, and turned forward, boondockers greasy under him, for the open area between the stacks.

Someone had turned on the lights on the 02 and 03 levels. Red and white working floods on the mast and over the unrep stations, bringing the beat decks and davits, lifelines and stacks out of the black with a weird pink glow. Looking forward, he saw for the first time what *Ryan* had been carrying on her bent back.

The ice on the decks was a foot thick, smooth and slick with new water, which slowed and congealed even as he watched into another suddenly translucent veneer. The lifelines were crusted six inches thick with white opaque ice, blown back and frozen like coconut Popsicle. The whaleboat was almost unidentifiable, a huge rounded mass solid with its davits and lowering tackle. Heat conduction had kept the stacks clear; they stood out black in contrast; but above them the top hamper, bracing and whips, the tripod mast and its trucks and lights and antennas was a thick frosted fretwork. Below it, the forward deckhouse, what he could see of it, was an ice palace. From beneath the translucent sheathing portholes and floodlights diffused a jewel-like luster, like an immense smoky diamond, plunging and leaning with drunken gravity as *Ryan* raised her stern to the overtaking surge.

Out of nowhere, he remembered looking through the microscope when he was choosing Susan's engagement diamond. The jeweler was having the little joke that Dan suspected he'd chuckled over to probably ten thousand other uncertain young men: 'Cut, color, and clarity are just as important as carat weight. Yes, that is a lovely stone, not as big as you might afford, but most women know that size is not all that counts, if you know what I mean. You'll never be unhappy with that stone.'

And looking into that crystalline microcosm of self-sufficient light, where not an atom had changed its position in 10 million years, he'd understood with sudden joy that their love would be like that. Fixed, never-changing, till death parted them, and maybe not even then.

Something black moved on the main deck. Men, dragging out long tubes. 'Give them a hand; that's the steam,' he shouted.

First Division ran forward, slipping on the ice, and hauled up the steam lances and hoses. Bloch and Isaacs moved among them, shouting and pushing, pointing to the thickest accumulations. Gradually, the men picked spots to stand, braced themselves, and began swinging axes and bats. Three sailors ranged themselves on one of the lances, a six-foot steel pipe, and suddenly even the wind was blotted out by a roar like someone had lifted the safety valves of hell; a billowing, opaque cloud obliterated them, then was shredded by the wind and whipped away. Dan skidded over. The live steam blasted and melted at the same time. When the nozzlemen undercut properly, whole sheets of white armor fell from bulkheads and stanchions, exploding into glistening curved chunks that kept, like castings, the shape of the steel to which they had clung.

When he was sure it was going well, he told Bloch to keep at it. The chief nodded, panting, and swung his baseball bat again.

Dan headed forward, pulling himself over the ice by the lifelines between the stacks. He'd only been topside for ten, fifteen minutes, and already his face felt as if it were made of cut glass. He wondered where Rich was. He was the only officer on deck. He didn't expect the XO, but Rich ought to be up here, too. He passed the Asroc launcher. Stefanick and two others he didn't know were jetting it with hand sprayers. He caught a sweet antifreeze whiff of chemical.

He was almost to the bridge when the ship began to roll again. He crouched instantly, grabbing the lifeline, praying it wouldn't be as bad as that last one. His heart pounded so hard he saw flashes behind his eyes. The old destroyer's recovery was sluggish, an overweight sea creature tiring of the fight.

When she staggered upright again, the terror released him, and he labored on the last few feet, panting out of a dry throat through dry lips. Below him, the wind was ripping the tops of the waves off and flinging them hundreds of yards downwind.

He wasn't looking forward to going down on the forecastle.

When the door clamped shut behind him, he saw Packer hanging by one arm from the overhead rail, shouting at the helmsman. He sucked desperately at the close warm air and looked around for Norden. Didn't see him. Then he did, bent over, face burrowed into the radar hood. He made his way toward him, but Packer saw him first. 'What are you doing here?'

'Sir, I came to – came to report. My men are at work on the oh-two level and oh-three level. I saw some Ops types turning to up on the signal bridge.'

'Good. A gang's getting steam hoses up to the –'

'They're back there, sir. The lances work pretty good –'

Packer kept right on talking, ignoring his interruption. 'They'll help you with the ice, but Bloch knows the drill. I want him in overall charge.'

'Aye, sir. Sir, did Mr. Ohlmeyer tell you about mount fifty-one?' Packer nodded. 'He asked for some of my men. I lent him three, and I'm going down there now to take them out on deck.'

'Very well,' the captain said. Dan swallowed and turned to go.

'Dan.'

He turned back instantly. 'Sir.'

The hand weighted his shoulder. 'But remember what I said. Make sure they wear life jackets. Rig your safety lines tight. I'll try to maintain this course, but if I have to alter while you're out, I'll sound the foghorn.'

'Yes, sir.'

'Go, Lenson!'

Just before the door closed, he heard the captain say, 'Rich, I relieve you. I have the deck. It sounds like they need you down there more.'

He didn't hear the weapons officer's reply.

He let himself out the starboard wing, and caught his breath.

The wind was lashing up a dark stampede. In the faint flashes and gleams the topside lights sent into the sea, he saw it heaving and bulging in terrifying splendor.

Looking out on it, like the world before land was created, tortured with the pangs of birth, he realized he might not see daylight again. Packer was determined to make easting. If they didn't get enough ice off her, she wouldn't recover from the next roll. She'd keep going on over. Capsize, and sink. What was the water temperature? Thirty-eight degrees. Sea water froze at 27.5.

If *Ryan* went over, he'd die long before dawn.

Drawing a shuddering breath that seared his mouth and nose, he pulled himself aft along the handrails. The ice was slick and wet and thick under his boots. He came to the Asroc deck and stopped, his head suddenly empty, looking at the men working between the stacks.

No, goddamn it, he wanted to go to the *forecastle*. He reversed direction, cursing his fatigued brain, and clattered down the ladders again and went forward.

On the main deck, Rambaugh and two seamen were uncoiling lines in the partial shelter of the port breaker. Dan didn't see Norden yet. He missed him. He needed somebody to tell him what to do. But now the men were looking at him expectantly. . . . 'Captain's going to hold this downwind course while we get the ice off,' he shouted over the din of the storm. 'We'll try to get that mount battened down, too. Popeye, where's these men's life jackets?'

'We don't need no life jackets, sir. It'll just hamper them hanging on.'

'I want life jackets on them.'

'Sir, I don't think –'

'Goddamn it, nobody goes out there without a jacket! Including you!'

'Get 'em, Rocky,' Rambaugh told Greenwald. Aside, as if to himself, he muttered, 'They go overboard in this sea, life jacket won't do them no damn bit of good.'

Dan ignored him. He let the wind flatten him against the bulkhead, and grabbed a coil of line and made one end fast to a stanchion. When the life jackets came up, he pulled one on, yanking the tie-ties so tight they hurt.

Norden pushed his way through the door and found himself a niche in the breaker. He made no move toward the jackets. 'Stand by for heavy rolls to port,' said the 1MC, but the words were blown away almost instantly.

The bow began to come around, slowly at first, then with great swiftness as the wind caught it. Dan stared into the night. With the spray and darkness, it would be hard to see an oncoming sea from the bridge.

The wind slackened, cut off by the deckhouse as they came around. 'Here she comes,' shouted Rambaugh in his ear, almost deafening him.

The sea towered above them and collapsed on the turning ship broadside. She faltered, tilted, and did not come back.

Dan stared down into the water. It glinted with shattered bits of red sidelight. It surged up over the deck edge like a vicious dog and snapped at his knees. One of the seamen screamed, then stopped; he looked shamefaced around at his fellows.

The ship crept back a few degrees, then reeled to another long sea. Again he felt horrified at her weakness, her sluggishness. Don't ever complain about a ship rolling again, somebody remote joked inside his head. The faster she rolls, the stabler she is.

Working lights came on on the deckhouse, making the flooded forecastle brilliant as a stage. Rambaugh swung a wrench and knocked two dogs off the breaker door with powerful underhand blows. 'Stand clear,' he shouted, the word almost inaudible in the roar of the sea.

Dan looked at Norden. The weapons officer was crouched in the corner, blinking in the sudden light, staring out at the water that boiled across the forward deck like scalded milk. His face was pallid as the icy foam.

'Sir, I'll go first,' bawled the second-class, right in his ear.

'No, hold it here till I get the safety line rigged,' shouted Dan. 'Crack the hatch, Popeye.'

When the last dog popped free the door slammed open in their faces, releasing a wall of spray and a freak wind that blew both men back a few steps. Rambaugh made as if to go through. Dan pulled him back. He bent, gathering the line behind him, and leapt.

The forecastles on *Gearing*-class destroyers were wet even in moderate seas. Now *Reynolds Ryan*'s was a welter of water over slick ice, slanted, at the moment, at about thirty degrees. He coasted forward a few steps, sliding helplessly on the glassy surface, then crashed into the outboard lifelines as she rolled sluggishly to starboard. She was yawing, too, as if it was harder to steer with the seas astern. When he looked back, hail stung his face like icy BBs. The wind was a frozen fist in his teeth. It pressed his eyeballs into his head. A hundred knots in gusts, he thought. He threw his arm over his face, sucked a breath, skated forward a few more feet.

The gun mount gave him a lee. He rested for a moment, feeling the cold like pincers on his cheeks, then gathered himself again and clawed his way on all fours across the slanted deck. Forward, all the way forward, as the deck surged upward and then sawed dizzyingly down. He had to grab the ground tackle to keep himself from floating off, like an astronaut on a space walk.

He was almost to his goal when a sea detonated over the gunwale, drenching him instantly to the skin. But this was the old easterly swell, dwarfed now by the storm surge from the south. It died, subsiding in a roar of blistering cold spume that crackled away aft, and he scrambled the last few feet to the mooring tackle. He lashed the line around a link of chain with wooden fingers. *Rig your safety lines tight*. He undid the knot and turned and hauled hard and made it fast again.

Greenwald and Rambaugh joined him, making their way out hand over hand along the line. A moment later, Lassard and one of the gunners followed, mattresses and blankets rolled under their arms.

He left the wildcat and slid aft to the mount again. It was stove in, all right. Below the barrels, holes gaped in the experimental fiberglass shield. Cross that bright idea off, he thought. Under the squatty BM2's whiplash voice, the men stuffed them first with blankets, then lashed the mattresses on top of them.

Dan looked around, noticing for the first time that Norden hadn't come out with them. *Ryan* was stern to the worst seas now and they had it gentler up forward, though the wind shrieked and howled around them, lashing their faces like a sandblaster as they worked.

When the mattresses were in place, Greenwald ran round and round the mount paying out line. Dan found himself beside Lassard, both of them hauling as hard as they could on the free end as Rambaugh and the gunner went to lash it in place.

He was standing there braced, the line icy in his hands, when he saw something gleam for a moment against the black waste ahead.

'What's that?' he screamed.

'What?'

The ship sagged to a trough. He flung out his arm. Lassard

242

looked along it. Dan narrowed his eyes to a crash of spray, peering out over the bullnose.

'Ain't nothing there –'

'Christ, help us,' Lenson muttered. He straightened, turning his back to it, lifting his head to the brilliant glare from the range light. Letting go of the line, waving his arms like a madman, he shouted up wildly to the bridge. His voice was a faint piping in the blast-furnace roar of the storm, whipped away instantly over the black waste between them and what lay ahead.

There were two men on the wing, but they weren't looking his way. The captain and Talliaferro. The chief engineer was pointing aloft, to where the huge SPS-40 air-search antenna was rotating. Their backs were to him. He screamed it again, despairingly, ripping his throat open.

'Ice! Ice! Dead ahead!'

The port lookout dipped his binoculars. Dan couldn't see his face. He had on a cold-weather mask. But he saw the glasses steady on him; saw them lift, and look beyond.

The lookout stiffened, and the next moment was grabbing clumsily for his mike. Dan turned forward again and stared.

The glowing mass lifted slowly, no more than a quarter mile ahead of the open oval of the bow chock. As the ship heaved he could see it plain, a huge patch of milky white. The seas seemed to slide around it, leaving it almost motionless, as if even its buoyancy were negated by its tremendous mass. As he watched, it rolled, with ponderous slowness, exposing a vast curved belly, then subsiding, covering its white teeth again beneath the lightless lips of the sea.

'Jesus,' Lassard said beside him.

The foghorn went off, a deep shout that underlay the polyphonic shriek of the gale. The men stared forward, as if gathering themselves, then scrambled slipping back over the ice-littered deck. Dan looked after them, then at the line he and Lassard gripped. Unsecured, it would whip away in a moment. He remembered the gaping cracked shield. Another few waves into that, more tons of water . . .

'Lenson! Slick!'

The ship was vibrating beneath them, beginning her turn.

He glanced back, to see Rambaugh and Greenwald waving them back to the shelter of the breaker.

He looked forward again. Too late to run now. He had time only for one swift turn of the line around himself and the seaman and another around the lowered barrel of the gun.

'We're staying,' he howled.

The prow turned away from the floe. It slid down the port side, rolling slowly in the confused sea. It glowed, giving back the light that fell on it. No monster, no more than a couple hundred feet across, but plenty big enough to gut a destroyer.

Ryan leaned slowly, coming beam to the seas now. She groaned and lay over as the first swell burst over her. He clung to the line desperately, his feet sliding as the lean increased.

Lassard was screaming in his ear. 'What?' he shouted.

'You're fucking crazy –'

'We'll be clear in another minute or two. Then the captain will come back –'

'Forget that shit,' screamed Lassard. 'Look out there.'

He wiped his arm across his streaming eyes and stared out into the darkness.

Ryan was listing to port, blotting out the sea to starboard with the upraised deck, but he saw a black line above it, beyond the lights.

Bowditch said it happens, some remote part of his mind whispered. Sometimes, when systems intersect, two seas will add, a freak wave the sum of their two heights. Fifteen plus thirty – but that would be forty-five feet –

Ryan rolled slowly back, and he saw it plainly. Blacker than the night, too huge to estimate or believe, it towered over the old destroyer like a falling building. It was higher than the 02 level. Staring up in horror, he realized it was higher than the *stacks*. Behind a beaded curtain of spray, its peak towered above him for an endless frozen second, a solid curved wall, its face glittering like an obsidian mirror that gave back for an instant the lighted windows of the bridge, weirdly curved, and the emerald glow of the starboard sidelight.

It collapsed, roaring onto the Asroc deck, staggering *Ryan*, and broke over the pilothouse and forecastle, submerging them. Squeezed down by tons of roaring water, pressed tight into steel, he felt the line cutting into his ribs, felt Lassard's body by his side. His open eyes stared into a swirling, airless blackness.

When it broke away, he still could not breathe or move. The cold seemed to have stopped his heart. He hung there, gasping, and then a fist thudded into his back and he coughed and caught a breath.

They took two more seas, smaller ones, before the ship labored clear of the floe and came left again and steadied up. Then he felt hands on his shoulders, arms pulling the lines free. He staggered back, panting through a face he could no longer feel.

Rambaugh yanked the last knot tight and grabbed his arm. 'You okay?' he shouted.

Dan nodded.

'Think she'll hold?'

He stared at the line. It was hard to move his eyeballs, as if they'd frozen in their sockets. He mumbled, 'If it doesn't, we'll do it again.'

'I don't want to come back out here, sir.'

'You got that right, Popeye.'

He waved weakly, gesturing the men forward. The foghorn boomed out once more. Bloch was shouting, his curses carried forward by the wind. They came out, carrying their tools and hoses, and in the next minute the clang of steel and the hollow roar of the steam hoses sounded again all over *Ryan*'s topsides.

He found himself next to Lassard. 'Good job, Slick,' he gasped. 'Thanks.'

The blue eyes were ferocious and brilliant. His mouth came close to Lenson's ear. 'Next time you decide to play hero, shithead, leave me the fuck out.'

Dan pushed himself away. Seeing a gap in a hose, he bent to add his strength to his men's.

Twenty minutes later, Packer passed the word for all hands to take shelter inside the skin of the ship. Dan was in the hangar, squatting with the exhausted, frozen seamen when the captain tried again to bring her around to the east.

Ryan didn't snap around this time. This time she oozed, as if the Arctic Sea had turned to oil. The men grew quiet as her pitching lessened, then grew into a long-period roll. Boxes and crates shifted uneasily in the near-dark. Coils of spare line and hose leaned out from their lashings in the overhead.

Dan squatted on a Yokohama fender next to Bloch and Isaacs. In the dim light of the spaced bulbs in their little glass jars, he saw that the chief's face was tattooed. When he looked again, it looked as if it had been stenciled in blood. 'It's the spray,' said Bloch. 'Busts the blood vessels under the skin. You got some of it, too.'

He touched his face.

'Captain, he going to try coming 'round again now, that it?' asked someone across from them. Gonzales, by his accent.

'Fucking-ay, Speedy,' said Lassard's voice from the creaking dim. 'Going to keep bashin' her head into the wall till he turns us the fuck over.'

'Put it back in the box, Slick,' said a dark voice. 'We heard 'nough out of you.'

'Ay, fuck you, man.'

'Fuck *you*, needledick! You fuckin' no-load shit-for-lunch!'

'Hey, you two silver tongues go fuck each other, aw right?'

'Who say that? Those be your dyin' words, man.'

'Don't let your mouth write any checks yo' ass can't cash, muh-fuh.'

'Put a lock on it, Lassard,' said the first voice again. 'You make me tired, you talking alla time. You fuckin' potheads is like turds. Ought to be forcin' you out, not forcin' you in.'

'What's I'm worried about is getting locked in these troughs,' Bloch muttered.

'Locked in? We just turn out of them. Like we did before.'

'You need power for that, too, sir. I knew a guy was on the *Dewey*, out in the Philippines in '44. They rolled so bad, they lost lube-oil suction and steering. They could only make five knots on one shaft. They were stuck in the trough for three hours, damn near went over.'

They fell silent again as the roll lengthened. Dan counted. Eleven thousand, twelve thousand, thirteen thousand. She rolled to the right, the wind howled, and she trundled slowly over to the left. He counted, feeling his heart shaking his chest. Thirteen thousand, fourteen thousand, fifteen thousand –

'She's not coming back,' a voice yelled in the sliding, banging dark.

Ryan toppled over, not all at once but with agonizing slowness.

Someone shouted to the dark, 'God, bring her back!'

A hatch or a door came open to starboard, and suddenly water was cascading in.

Dan thought, This is it. The waves knock her down and the wind holds her there till she dies. He'd never see the baby, never even know whether it was a boy or girl.

Isaacs said, 'If we goes over, there anybody around to get us, Mr. Lenson?'

He thought about telling him there was. Then he thought, better stick with the truth. He said quietly, 'Nobody I know of. But I don't think we'll any of us suffer too long.'

The ship shuddered under them. He felt the rumble of the screws racing at full power. It wouldn't help, not on this course. No amount of power would.

Then he felt her stern start to rise. They grew heavy and then light. The hangar seemed to spin.

Ryan sagged back two or three degrees to starboard. She gave a deep groan. The screws faltered, then raced suddenly, shaking her stern like an arrow held by the tail. The deck rose again and came back a few more degrees.

Ryan straightened up under them with a rumbling sigh, and the wind rose again to a terrifying whine.

'Thanks, Lord,' somebody said out loud, and there were mutters of agreement, some of it profane.

Dan wondered whether Packer had given up. Then he knew it was foolish even to wonder that. The phone behind him squealed. He picked it up. 'Lenson.'

'Dan? Rich. Get your guys out on deck again. We got to get more of this ice off.'

'Aye aye, sir.'

'Just to let you know, because it's your space: Captain's told DC Central to prepare to flood the chain locker.'

'Aye, sir.'

This time, Packer gave them half an hour. In thirty minutes of furious effort, the men got the last of the ice stripped off the 01 level, and started on the top of the hangar.

Dan was turning to with them, swinging one of the scarred-up bats, when he saw two men climbing the main-mast. Ohlmeyer and Heering were feeling their way up it with lines and chipping hammers like climbers up the face of a narrow glacier. The gunner's mate had an olive-drab haver-sack on his back. He realized after the second look that it must be one of the demolition charges.

He found out later that Packer had ordered the flooding then. The chain locker, forward powder magazine, all but one of the potable water tanks, and two deep storerooms aft.

At 0530, the captain brought her around again for the fourth try. But now when she took the first roll, there was a lightning crack aloft and a spurt of black smoke.

The bedspring framework of the air-search antenna toppled out of it. A corner of it smashed into the anemometer, wiping it off the mast. The little vane sailed away, its propeller windmilling, as the radar cartwheeled once and, trailing cables, plunged down into the slick-looking sea in the lee of the laboring ship.

The higher the weight, the worse its effect on stability. Dan, watching, multiplied the mass of the antenna, motor, and gear train by its height above the keel. As far as he could figure, it was better than taking fifteen tons of ice off the main deck.

Whether it was that or the flooding, or both, this time she rode better. She was logy but didn't seem to be rolling as far. She rode differently, no longer rising to the waves, but sliding her nose under them, like an old cat burrowing under the blankets on a winter night. He watched the seas sweep across the forecastle, so deep that he couldn't see the ground tackle for minutes on end. They swept over the mount, burying it, just the tip of the UHF antenna atop it sticking up like a periscope. Just as well we flooded the magazine, he thought.

For a moment, his swollen, wooden, blood-imprinted face tried to smile. It was as if *Ryan*, hunting a submarine, was determined to become one herself. Then his quivering lips stilled.

Only if she went down, she'd never come up.

He was thinking about coffee and dry clothes when the 1MC said, faint above the renewed howl of the wind, 'Now relieve the watch. On deck, Antisubmarine Condition One Alfa, Watch Section Two.'

16

Dawn arrived on schedule a little before 1100. Dan was topside when it came, making his way aft toward the head. He stopped for a moment in the lee of the bridge.

He stared out, shivering, as gray light seeped slowly back into the world of sixty-seven and some degrees north.

It showed him a universe conceived in monochrome. The sky was low and less gray than gray-black, as if slag heaps were smoldering just below the jagged horizon. Why did that edge seem closer, as if the world had shrunk overnight? As *Ryan* inclined sluggishly, he gripped the icy steel of the splinter shield and leaned out, looking down.

Yes. The black boot topping was two or three feet beneath the average waterline. The old destroyer was riding lower, like a gradually soaking log.

Beneath the growing light the sea steamed like a boiling kettle. White haze moved steadily past the laboring ship, pushed by the wind. Only dimly, in the last minute before they were on them, could he see the oncoming swells. He tried to count seconds between the crests. They were confused, hard to tell apart, but they seemed longer. They were still high, though. Thirty feet from crest to trough was his estimate. Their smooth gray faces drew closer and closer, solidifying gradually behind the sea smoke, then suddenly leaping from ghostliness into imminence, towering like black cliffs under the slaty sky. They collapsed with the roar of a gravel slide, shattering suddenly into white froth over new white ice.

The deck reeled back to port, flinging him downward through space. Clinging to the rail, he stared down into the smoky, roiling, gray-green surface. For a moment, in the smooth funneled surface of an eddy, his own blurred face peered back from beneath the sea.

From all this, he computed slowly that the prevailing swell was still from the starboard beam, or maybe a little abaft it. The wind had veered and was almost from astern. The storm center was still moving north, then. Good; about time they had a break. But then, if they had to steam southwest, they'd be beam-on again.

'There's no way you can win,' he said, then stopped himself. Not out loud! He *was* getting tired.

On the bright side, she was still afloat. Nine hours ago, you wouldn't have bet your paycheck on that, he thought. *Ryan* was wallowing, half submerged. She wasn't designed to ride this way. Old steel wouldn't take the strain forever. But at least she was coming back from the rolls. And for the last few hours, she'd been making twelve, sometimes fifteen knots as Packer ordered turns cranked on.

Then he remembered the floe. A shiver traced his spine under the foul-weather jacket. He squinted forward, scanning the hunch-backed sea. The lookouts had been doubled, and they'd maneuvered to avoid three more since sighting the first. Nothing now, though. He decided it was safe to take a leak.

The bridge urinal was aft of the pilothouse, tacked on as an afterthought next to the forward stack. A steel closet the size and shape of a coffin shielded it from wind and spray. Rock salt and broken glass grated under his boots as he set his legs apart, leaned against the bulkhead, and wearily hauled it out.

So far, this watch was a zero. They were making easting, but they had no contact. Reed and Orris kept talking about a front they expected to cross. They seemed to think that was hiding the sub from them. But whatever the reason, so far Sonar reported only the low-frequency rumble of ice floes grinding themselves to slush.

The only interruption of the hours of waiting and listening had been two messages. The one from CINCLANTFLT ordered Packer for about the eleventh time to make every effort to locate B41. The other, relayed from the British, was a heads-up on an AGI, a Soviet intelligence ship, headed in their direction from the vicinity of the Skagerrak. The original date time group of the contact was twelve hours old, which meant it might be anywhere by now. The surface radar showed nothing; electronic countermeasures, ditto.

He didn't like what it all pointed to – that they'd lost their quarry – but there wasn't much point denying it. They'd done their best. They'd held on to a nuke in a sea state 7 storm for almost twenty-four hours. Not too shabby! But they'd lost it at last. Sooner or later, even Packer would have to admit that.

Anyway, another hour and he'd be off watch and dead to the world. He sighed as used coffee hit stainless steel. The stack was right behind him, radiating heat. It was almost comfortable.

On the far side of the speckled peeling steel, the wind howled and hummed. He was used to it now. It was almost like silence, and silence would have shouted louder than any sound. Now it merged with the whine of the intake blowers and the hiss of spray. He slumped forward, letting his eyes close on gritty fatigue just for a moment.

The next thing he knew something cold and wet was pressing against his cheek and somebody was tugging on the collar of his jacket. 'Yeah, here he is,' Pettus was shouting. Then his voice came close. 'Jesus, Mr. Lenson, you want to crap out, I can show you better places than that. Get up, man, they want you back in Combat.'

When he got back to CIC, angry at himself, angry at Pettus, and angry at Evlin, the others were all still in the same places it seemed they had kept since the ship was commissioned. Pedersen, Matt, Lipson, Evlin, Silver, and Packer. He'd always remember them just like this, standing like the goddamn Dutch Masters around the plotting table. It was stenciled on his brain.

Now they were discussing where B41 might have gone in the hours since they'd lost track of her.

'She can't be moving very fast,' muttered Evlin. Beneath the fluorescent illumination, bluer than daylight, the flat sheet was blank save for the concentric glowing circle that represented *Ryan*'s eastward creep. 'After that first real noisy burst, she never made over fifteen knots the whole time we held contact. I think that's all she can make, and her CO'll hold that down because of the noise. Now she's on the far side of this front. She can't move fast through ice, either, unless she gets deep, and then she'll be in the sound channel and we'll pick her up. He knows that. So I'd look for her around two hundred feet, right about' – his hand hovered over a white emptiness a foot or so southeast of the rosette, then came down, fingers splayed – 'right about here.'

'He thinks he's lost us.'

'I'd agree with that, yes, sir.'

'Captain?'

Packer lifted his head slowly.

It was Trachsler. One of the damage-control officer's arms was strapped into a brace. His other hand held a large flat book. Dan wondered how he'd gotten up the ladders. 'Ken, you shouldn't be be walking around with that busted wing,' Packer said.

'That's all right, sir. Look, can I brief you on our counterflooding, on buoyancy –'

'Yeah, damn right. Let's get out of Al's way here.'

They moved off to the radio desk, and Dan heard Trachsler's whispery voice grave and low, going over cross curves of stability and free surface and loss of reserve buoyancy. He sounded like an undertaker discussing the cost of the obsequies. Dan breathed deeply, fighting a sudden access of fear. Every once in a while it reached in through the exhaustion and squeezed his gonads. Couldn't Packer just admit he'd lost? He reached out to brush gray paint with his fingertips. Solid steel. But only a quarter of an inch thick. How much longer could it keep out the sea?

How much longer would Packer expect it to?

At 1140, Cummings arrived to relieve him. Dan was taking off his phones when the Sonar Control intercom came on over their heads. 'Evaluator, Sonar,' it said. He tried to ignore it as it hissed for a moment. Then it said, 'There it is again. Must have just crossed the front. Evaluator, Sonar: active sonar on bearing one-one-zero true. I say again, active sonar, bearing one-one-zero degrees true!'

Evlin was hanging on the button only a second ahead of Packer. 'What kind of sonar?'

'We're trying to figure that out, sir; we'll tell you soon's we do,' said Orris's high voice. The leading sonarman sounded exhausted and anxious. 'Permission to lower VDS to four hundred feet, see if we can get a direct path.'

Packer leaned over Evlin's shoulder and said into the speaker, 'Granted.' Evlin snapped off. The captain said, 'Could that be him?'

'Could be, sir.'

'Going active to keep clear of the ice? Now that he figures he's lost us.'

'Could well be,' said the ops officer again, detaching his glasses. Under them his eyelids were inflamed. He massaged them delicately with the balls of his fingers, then fitted the glasses back on. Across from him, Matt and Lipson got up from their perches on the desk, pulled their pencils off where they were stuck to the overhead with tape, and checked the points with the grave expressions of infantrymen inspecting the bores of their rifles.

'Evaluator, Sonar: Contact at one-one-zero is not a Soviet submarine sonar.'

'Shit fire,' said Packer. He snapped the lever down. 'Orris, goddamn it – what the hell else can it be? Check it again! There's nobody out here but me and him.'

'I know my business, sir. It's a high-freq emission; could be a forward-looking underice rig ... but the frequency's wrong, the pulse repetition rate ...' The sonar tech stopped.

'What is it? Is Reed there? Put him on, please.'

'Yes, Captain. I was checking a pub. It's definitely not a standard signature. Another possibility is that he's operating in wartime reserve mode. If so, we won't have it in the book. Because the Soviets have never used it before.'

Packer and Evlin looked at each other. Chief Pedersen glanced at Dan, showing his teeth in a visual *uh-oh*.

The captain reached up. 'Assume it's him, Aaron. Get us a line of sound and a Warren range. Give me a course to intercept.' He snapped off viciously and looked around. 'Where's my fucking ...'

'On top of the first-aid cabinet, sir.'

'I got to stop smoking so much. My throat feels raw as hell.' But his fingers were packing the pipe as he said it, as if they weren't listening, Dan thought.

Bearings started to come in, and a little later, ranges. The plotting team began to plot. Packer sucked flame, then stood over the table, arms folded, staring into space as he puffed. Dan eased away. He was getting a headache. He figured it as part fatigue, part tension, but some of it and the runny nose for sure was from all the smoke he was breathing.

'Evaluator, Sonar. Bearing one-zero-eight. Estimated range thirteen to seventeen thousand yards.'

'That's pretty broad-brush, Orris. Can't you get me a sharper range than that?'

'No sir, not with this technique. We can ping if you want an exact range.'

'Negative. I don't want to ping yet. Can you get me a target angle?'

'From doppler, if it's a forward-looker, estimate starboard one forty, one thirty.'

'Coming up in his baffles?' mused Evlin.

'Could be. Could be here's where we get lucky for a change. Tell the bridge, stay alert for ice. He's looking for it, we better, too. Is our fathometer on?'

'No, sir, it's been secured since we went to Condition One A.'

'Good job . . . okay, quiet ship. Make sure Ed gets the word in Main Control.'

'Want me to take it?' asked Cummings, beside him. Dan started. He'd been standing there with his mouth open, trying to sort out what was going on. As far as he could make out, the submarine was running southeast, and *Ryan*, delayed by the storm, was emerging from the warm- /cold-water front astern of it, where every ship or submarine, because of its own screw noise, was deaf. He'd forgotten his relief. Now he hesitated, torn between his body's lust for rest and his own excitement. After so many hopeless hours, he didn't want to leave just when they'd regained contact.

Packer took the choice away from him. 'Mr. Lenson, I want

you to stay on the weapons circuit. No offense, Tom? Get yourself some sleep and come back up around four. . . . Al, get a message off to CINCLANTFLT. Flash. Para one: "Have regained contact with track B forty-one." Give our position, as near as you can figure. Para Two. "B forty-one emitting in war reserve mode. Sonar environment, scattered ice and confused propagation conditions. Cannot guarantee maintaining contact. Urgently need P-three assist. Urgently need guidance on engagement." That's all. Send it right away.'

The intercom said, 'CIC, Main Control: Quiet ship set in engineering spaces. Max speed available, fifteen knots.'

'Dan, can you get that? I'm writing this message –'

'Yessir.' He hit the button. 'Evaluator, aye.'

He suddenly realized he ought to get busy, too. Over the soundpowered phone, he told underwater battery fire control and the after five-inch – the only operable gun now – to reman stations, conduct movement checks, and train fifteen degrees to starboard. Just in case Packer wanted one, he asked Stefanick for a status on the Asroc. It was still down. All they had were torpedoes, then, the six trainable tubes forward of the bridge. And the gun, if the sub surfaced.

It probably wouldn't come to that. But if it did, he was ready.

So when Packer turned to him suddenly and said, 'Lenson, what have we got in the forward tubes?' he was able to say, 'Sir, they're full, three Mark forty-three war shots in the starboard mount, one war shot and two practice torpedoes in the port mount.'

'Are they ready? Free of ice, firing circuits checked? If we need them, I don't want another repeat of yesterday.'

'Yes, sir, I've been having the men go out and chip the ice off the muzzle doors every couple of hours.'

'Good thinking.'

They told you at the Academy never to say thanks when you were complimented. But that didn't mean the captain's offhand remark didn't make him stand a little straighter.

And suddenly there was Bryce again, looking rumpled, as if he'd just gotten out of bed. Must be nice, Dan thought. The XO leaned between the two plotters, getting in their way for a moment before their dance shifted to whirl on around him. 'Understand you got the cuffs on our Russki friend again. Least that's what I heard.'

Packer didn't respond. After a moment, Evlin said, 'That's right, Commander. We think it's him, anyway.'

'You *think*? Don't you know?'

The operations officer explained about the war reserve mode on Soviet sonars. Midway through, Bryce interrupted, 'I was born at night, Mr. Evlin, but not last night. I've spent a lot of years on destroyers; I know about war reserve frequencies. So, we in torpedo range yet?'

'Basically, yes, sir.'

'I don't see no torpedo danger circle on your plot. How about getting on the stick, Lieutenant? And we're coming up his tail? That's a dangerous position, Jimmy John.'

Evlin said, 'I don't think submarines have stern tubes anymore, Commander –'

'Shit they don't! Them Russians do, you can count on it! You better knock off that laid-back California attitude, Evlin. We could get a torpedo down our throat any second!'

'Excuse me, Captain,' Pedersen broke in. 'The contact's showing a right drift. We won't show it on the plot for a while yet, but I think he's in a slow starboard turn.'

Packer leaned over the table. In its upward-directed glow his eyes were black pits, his face a skull's. 'Al?'

'I concur. Recommend speeding up, then coming right, too, to stay in his baffles and continue closing the range.'

'Do it. Also, the commander has a point about torpedoes. Let's get the Nixie streamed and ready to turn on.'

'Aye, sir. Sonar, copy that last order?'

'Sonar aye, streaming antitorpedo noisemaker.'

'Bridge, Evaluator: Increase speed to fifteen knots; at plus ten, come right and steady course one-six-zero.'

Norden rogered from the pilothouse. He sounded exhausted, too. Again Dan watched the rudder indicator swing, the gyro creep around. *Ryan's* roll gentled, became a sway. A few seconds later, she began to pitch. It grew rapidly more violent. Suddenly she gave a great heave and corkscrewed downward. As her nose hit bottom, vibration tickled his feet through the deck plates and rubber matting. From outside, much louder, came a seconds-long roar, as if they were passing under Niagara Falls.

'Combat, Bridge. We're taking water in the pilothouse. It's above the ports now, green water, green water.'

He thought, Rich sounds calmer now. Good. It had worried him, the way his department head had acted last night, down on the forecastle.

A few seconds later word came up that the forward gun mount was taking water again. He had his mouth open to report it when the 21MC light came on. 'Combat, Main Control. Is the captain there? This is Mr. Talliaferro. After steering reports the tips of the screws are coming out of the water. Engine rooms report vibration in the shafts. Recommend either slow to five knots or come right or left to get us out of the swell.'

'Acknowledged,' said Packer. He said nothing more. Evlin looked at him, waiting, then said into the intercom, 'The captain heard you, Ed. We'll be staying on this course and speed. Operational necessity.'

'Okay, but if we shake these reduction gears loose, we aren't riding a ship anymore. It's going to be junk. Just twenty-two hundred tons of razor blades.'

Evlin clicked the lever twice.

Bryce said, 'You listening, Jimmy John? She won't take much more pounding. We could slide right on under one of these big lunkers. A bulkhead gives way down where you flooded, she'll keep right on going. Saw it happen in Korea. DE hit a mine going flank speed, the internal bulkheads went, and it was gone, fast as it takes to say that. Thing to do's a spread of Mark forty-threes in the water right now.'

'That's not the answer, XO,' said Evlin. Dan saw the tension in his back as he leaned over the table. 'This submarine has done nothing aggressive. It's done nothing to indicate it has any hostile intent. Just track it, that's all we need to –'

Bryce rounded on him, cutting him off with a shout. 'Don't give me any of that peacenik talk! You know, I'm slowly coming to grips with what's so shitty aboard this ship. You ought to relieve this – this *freak*, Cap'n. Calls himself a naval officer, but down in his office he's worshiping some swami –'

'That's enough,' said Packer. But he said nothing more. He just stared down at the plot, sucking his pipe. It was as if, Dan thought suddenly, he was keeping his options open – listening to them all, but not yet decided.

Or maybe he had, and only forebore to say.

'Are you going to shoot? Damn it – you listening to me? You feel all right, Jimmy John? Hey, he don't look that good. He's been on his feet for four days. Maybe we should call the corpsman –'

'That's enough, Ben,' the captain said sharply. 'Another word out of you on that subject and I'll order you below. We are going to hold on to this contact, we are going to hold him close this time, and we're staying on this course! Is that clear to everyone?'

Great, Dan thought. He's going to hold on. But how? USS *Reynolds Ryan* was pounding herself into scrap. Much as he hated Bryce, what the XO was urging made sense. Either give up, let the sub go, or strike first and kill her before she realized they were there.

If they didn't make a decision, do *something*, they might not live much longer.

Packer wanted to obey orders. But there was a line between obedience and madness. Was the captain sick? Not crazy, as in howling mad, but with the steady, fixed monomania of an Ahab?

Dan wondered for the first time how thin that line might be. So thin, one might never notice when he inched over it.

Ryan fell out from beneath them and crashed into what sounded like a bed of rocks. It was as if the ship had been dropped forty feet onto the floor of a quarry. For a few seconds she rode mushily, as if groggy from the impact; then shivered again as a wave raged against the starboard side, hammering like a drunken, angry father at a locked bedroom door.

Then it was pitching again. He clung to the radar repeater as *Ryan* reeled and wove and men stumbled across CIC. The closed, dim space soared and bounded through space like a box tied to a wheel. He'd thought his stomach seaproof by now, but now he bent, searching with sudden desperation for the bucket. The spasm buckled him over before he found it, but though his stomach kinked on itself like a wrung dishrag nothing came up. He gagged, eyes feeling as if they were being squeezed out onto the deck. Before he could stop himself, he moaned aloud in sheer nauseated agony. Christ, he thought, drooling and spitting. How would this end? How much longer before they went down?

Just then there was a cry from Sonar. 'Submarine close!' it sounded like. Then Reed was shouting, 'Come right! Come right!'

Beneath his feet the old destroyer seemed to hesitate, just for a moment, and sway backward, as if her stern was being dragged down. She surged up again, then floated free for long seconds before slamming down even more violently.

The lights flickered out, then on. Across the compartment, Pedersen was knocked to his knees. The lights flickered out. Packer's pipe fell, bouncing and rolling, spraying out red-hot sparks. Men were screaming below them, through the deck itself. The great girder of the hull hummed like a huge, slow tuning fork. The lights flickered on. Confused yells above his head, the 21MC and Sonar Control intercoms coming on together in a shrill gabble, voices blasting out into the swaying, dim air.

'What's going on up there?'

'No signal.'

'Combat, Sonar! No signal from the thirty-five!'

'Combat, Bridge: We've got to slow, hammering her to death –'

'Sounding and Security reports taking water in the mid-ships passageway, vicinity frame one thirty. Stand by – smoke in the passageway! Fire in the engine room!'

'Combat, VDS winch station: There's no strain on the cable back here. It's trailing loose in the wake.'

'Quiet down, goddamn it!' shouted Bryce above the din of the fire alarm going off.

Reed stood in the open curtain from Sonar. His haggard horselike face was gray. He said, across the slanting air, 'I think we hit it.'

Packer said quietly, 'Hit what, Lieutenant Reed?'

'Hit the submarine, sir. With the fish. The cable's gone slack and we show a short circuit.'

For a moment, Dan was glad. He tried to straighten, dragging his hand across his mouth. It came away gluey with drool and acid. His legs shook. Then he heard what Packer was saying, softly, as if to himself.

'We can't lose that gear. Now we'll have to track it till it surfaces. No, *force* it to surface. To make sure the fish isn't tangled in its shears, or in its prop.'

Evlin's voice, cool yet somehow disapproving: 'Stay on it, sir?'

And he heard with a chilling heart James John Packer's voice, tired and flat and yet hard as old hull plating, through the thunder of another sea smashing itself apart over their heads, over the bridge itself. 'Stay on it? Yeah. I'm not giving up now, Al. I'm not giving up, *ever*.'

17

Talliaferro was telling Packer about the flooding. 'It was Nobbs, one of the messmen. They're not cooking down there, so he didn't have anything to do. Guy goes to his locker, gets his Instamatic, and opens one of the doors on the main deck. He's gonna take a picture of the ocean, right? But he opens it just as we turn into the swell. That first big breaker smashes the door on him, mashes him like a bug. He's down in sick bay with broken ribs, bitching about how he lost his camera. But now the door's warped and won't dog, and every time a sea hits us, a hundred more gallons spray in through it.'

The captain was slumped against the first-aid cabinet. He muttered hoarsely, 'Get to it. What's the damage?'

'We got a foot of water in the fore-and-aft passageway. It's rolling up and down like one of those desk toys with the waves inside. Since we had ventilation buttoned up to keep out the spray, it gets real hot, over a hundred and forty in the hole. The guys had the engine-room scuttle open so they could breathe. The water rolls the deck pitches, all of a sudden it dumps down through the scuttle onto the switchboard. That's what's on fire. McElroy hit it with a CO_2 bottle, but that didn't cut it. Repair Four's fighting it. At the moment, we don't have any power aft.'

'The door?'

'Jacking it shut now, but it's a tender job to straighten it so it swings again.'

'You said no power aft. Does that mean to the Nixie?' asked Evlin, from the plotting table.

The engineering officer said, 'That's right, Alan. At the moment, we have no power to the towed noisemaker.'

'I want an emergency cable rigged. Right away. If they fire a homing torpedo – Make that your first priority after the fire's out.'

'Yes, sir. But we're still taking water forward, Captain. And we're still pitching too much. Every time the props come out of the water, the tachs wind off the scale. You can hear the shaft bearings working loose; you can see the reduction gear prying up the foundation bolts.' The engineer's pitted face was still, like barren ground waiting for rain. 'I got to tell you this in front of the others, sir. You know why. You're not gonna have the engines much longer if you treat 'em like this. How much longer are we going to hold this course?'

'I'll tell you how much longer,' Packer said. The mutter hardened. 'Till he gives up. Or one of us goes down.'

After a moment, Evlin said, 'That's . . . extreme, isn't it, sir?'

Packer didn't seem to be listening. He straightened jerkily, putting his hands to his kidneys. Staring at the overhead, he spoke in an inflectionless monotone, as if it was something he'd memorized years before and said so often that it had lost all emotional content.

'It's a wrestling match. Between me and him. The CO down there. He's doing the same thing I am. He's living on the conn. If he tried to turn in, they're waking him up four, five times every half hour, asking for decisions, asking him what to do. I've got to exhaust him. It's a test of stamina. His against mine.

'We're even, as far as equipment goes. He's damaged. So are we. We've got the storm to worry about; he's got us to worry about.

'How about his crew? How committed are they to whatever he'd trying to do? Has he lied to them, do they suspect? Even if they believe in him, can they go twenty-four, thirty, forty-eight hours without sleep?

'It's a game. A sniff here, a sniff there – a jab here, a jab there – looking for the advantage. He's got it when he goes slow. We can't hear him then; we've got to ping. We've got it when he speeds up. We can track him solid and cut him off.

'What determines the winner? Unless somebody's got a joker to play, it's going to be whoever gives out first, gets so

263

stressed and sleepy he screws up. Who can keep pushing longest – that's what determines who wins.'

He stopped for a moment but didn't look at them. Finally he added in a whisper, 'You've got to go till nobody can go any longer, and still have six hours in reserve.'

'Have you got six hours, Captain?' Evlin asked him.

Packer leaned back and closed his eyes. 'That's what we're gonna find out, Al. Ed, you belong back aft, holding those engines together. Get moving!'

The engineer stared at him. He seemed about to speak. Then his face closed, and he turned away.

When he was gone, Packer opened his eyes again. Dan saw that the whiskers on his cheeks were black, but those on his chin were gray, like ashes. He put both hands flat on the plotting table. 'What's he doing now?'

'I can't tell, sir.'

The captain got up and pushed his way through the curtain into Sonar. Dan could hear them talking, but he couldn't hear what they were saying. He braced his trembling knees against the repeater. He smelled smoke again. He hoped it was the switchboard, not some fresh disaster.

He'd felt this uncertainty, this pain, this endless fatigue before. Plebe Year. Shoving out, clamping on, the Green Bench. So scared to go out of your room into the free-fire zone of the corridors that you shit in your shower and hammered it down the drain with your shoes. Upperclassmen screaming in your face, one after another, for hours on end. Sweat and blood slicking the gray-green tile decks of Bancroft Hall. Bending over and waiting after you'd bet your ass and lost.

The upperclass said it built character. Prepared you to take stress and function. Taught you to play hurt and win.

Maybe they and Packer were talking about the same thing.

The sonar was active. It wasn't a ping; it was a song, seconds long and complexly pitched. Lipson sang softly, his head cocked, mimicking the sound of the outgoing pulse, 'Here-I, here-I, here-I, *am*.'

Dan thought, That's exactly what we're telling him. All he's got to do is squirt a couple of acoustic homers down our bearing. With the Nixie dead, even in rough seas one of them's bound to score. Damn, he had to piss. . . .

'He's pulling the plug,' said Pedersen suddenly, lifting the earpiece of his phones. 'Sonar estimates he's at eight hundred and still going down.'

'Very well,' said Evlin. 'How deep is it here, Chief?'

'Not sure, sir. We don't know where we are. Yardner says he hasn't seen the stars in a week, and loran's crappy up here. We got a dead-reckoning position, but you know how much that's worth.'

A chart appeared from somewhere and was laid out over the trace. Pedersen and Evlin sprawled over it with dividers. 'Could we be that far south?' the ops officer muttered.

'There's supposed to be a two-knot current, isn't there? Make it two point four over four days and we could be way down here.'

'Well, let's get a ping off the bottom. He knows we're here now.'

Dan thought, No one asked who he meant by 'he.' It meant the sub. Or, more specifically, the Soviet commander. Packer talked about 'him,' too. As if it was personal. Maybe it was. On land, the idea of dueling generals was faintly ludicrous. But at sea, it was different. A ship, at least as long as her crew obeyed, was far more purely an extension of her commander's will.

As long as her crew obeyed, and she stayed afloat. But *Ryan*'s meeting both qualifications was getting marginal.

He jumped when Packer spoke, right beside him. He could smell him, old sweat and sweet tobacco and the man himself. 'Anything more the torpedomen need to do? Impulse air verified, spin them up, anything?'

'Uh – I'll find out, sir.' The old Academy response. They'd taught him something useful, anyway.

'Do it, if there is. I want them on a hair trigger.'

'Aye aye, sir.' He waited for Packer to say something else, but he just stood there, sucking his pipe and watching Evlin and Pedersen.

'Permission to activate the fathometer, sir,' said Evlin.

The captain nodded and the ops officer called the bridge.

A few seconds later, Yardner called back. *Ryan* had 638 fathoms under her keel.

'No way,' Pedersen muttered. He smoothed the chart and bent closer.

Dan, looking over their backs, saw only a scattering of figures on blank space. The Navy was supposed to be mapping the Arctic bottom. But there was a lot of it and not many ships. Evlin and Pedersen fell to arguing whether they were east or south of the dead-reckoning position, or possibly over a seamount. He was wishing he had some coffee when he remembered with a start that he was supposed to be checking torpedo readiness. Goddamn, he'd better get on the stick.

The torpedoman said all they had to do to fire the Mark 43s was warm up the electronics and spin up the gyros. That would take eight minutes from the word *go*. After that, the tubes could be set and fired from underwater battery fire control, a panel back in Sonar.

'Combat, Main Control: Fire's out in after engine room. Permission to restow gear and set the reflash watch.'

Packer smiled as he gave permission. 'Okay, now what's he doing?' the CO asked, joining Evlin and Pedersen. 'You figured it out yet?'

'Not quite, sir.'

'He's not throwing some wild card down on us?'

'I don't know, sir.'

For some reason, Packer sounded more cheerful. 'Let's get Mr. Reed and Petty Officer Orris out here, get our heads together. I have a feeling whatever this is, it's his last gasp. We keep him pinned for another couple of hours, we could wrap this up.'

The tension relaxed a little. The knot of khaki and denim gathered around the plot – like a bunch of high rollers facing the last hand of the night money ahead, Dan thought. The sonar whined through the hull like an off-tune violin. Orris joined them last. 'He's still going deep, sir,' he said.

'How deep is deep?' Packer asked jovially.

'A thousand feet's getting there, sir.'

'Well, what's he doing down there? He can't launch missiles from there. Can he?'

'Our boomers can't. I think they have to be pretty close to the surface.'

'Okay, what does it do to us? Can the twenty-three still track him down there?'

'Yes,' said Reed; at the same moment, Orris said, 'Maybe.' Packer aimed his finger at the sonarman.

'It depends on two things, sir. Aside from all this surface noise, I mean. Tracking active, as the water gets shallower, you get insonification. Reverberations. That can muddy the picture. But it's not that shallow here, so I don't think that'll bother us. What I think he'll try is to hug the bottom. If he can get way down there in the acoustic basement our gear can't discriminate, the bottom sediment gives a kind of jelly-type blur. He'll, like, merge into it.'

'How close does he have to get?'

Orris turned his palms outward. 'All I can say is, depends.'

'What can we do about it?'

'There's some things I can do on the stack, sir. Tweak the freq up. That sharpens the picture some. I can't think of anything smart to pull on him from up here, if that's what you mean.'

'Okay, so we just try to hold him,' Packer said to them all. 'I think the fact he's trying to hide in the basement means it's his last card. He's either damaged or fouled in the fish or the cable somehow. So his back's to the wall. Like I said, we hold on for ten, twelve more hours and the cavalry'll be here. Soon as we turn over to our attack boats, I'm coming about and heading home. So let's get to it.'

Over the next hour, the red dot that was the submarine tracked very slowly south at between three or four knots. It formed a short trace under Matt's pencil.

Behind it, *Ryan*'s trail loitered back and forth. Packer had reduced speed. The pitching, though still violent, was less extreme, the assaults of the seas less frightening. Talliaferro called up to say the screws were staying in the water and that he had his snipes torquing down the foundation bolts on the gears and main shaft bearings.

B41 was still dropping. Orris's high voice reeled his

readings off with increasing disbelief. Pedersen sucked air through his teeth as he logged them. At 1420, Sonar reported contact depth at sixteen hundred feet. At 1440, it was two thousand.

At 1500, he reported the submarine was at 2,200 feet. The men at the plotting table eyed each other in doubt and something like fear. 'He's slowing,' said Evlin. His hand shook as he gulped coffee. It spotted the front of his shirt. 'Taking longer to go every hundred feet. He's got to be up against his crush depth.'

The captain looked from the red-backed book. 'For the original *Yankee*-class, intelligence estimates sixteen hundred feet operating depth. Figure rule of thumb, crush depth half that again, that's twenty-four hundred. He's almost there.'

'That's just an estimate, sir.'

'I don't know, Al, they probably base it on something hard, like how thick the hull is. It's probably a pretty good figure.'

Sonar broke in then to say that B41 was at 2,400 feet.

'God,' muttered Evlin. There were blots under the arms of his khakis. Dan was sweating, too, perspiration crawling like bugs down the backs of his legs. He still had to piss. He pushed the need away, as he had already several times in the last hour.

Packer hit the lever of the 29MC. 'How far above the bottom is he now, Orris?'

'We have the bottom tracing along at thirty-seven hundred here. He's still thirteen hundred feet above it.'

'Have you got a solid paint on him? He's not blending in yet, is he?'

'Not yet, sir. I'm using the twenty-three's highest frequency. There's some fuzzing but I can still pick him out of bottom contour. Wait a second . . . he's dropped again – twenty-five hundred feet.'

'Jesus Christ,' muttered Packer. 'Nobody knew they could go that deep. His crew's not going to go along with this much longer.'

Across his bent back, Dan caught Evlin's eye. He wondered whether they were thinking the same thing.

Crush depth . . . he knew what that was. Where the steel

cylinder of a submarine failed in lengthwise stability, first wrinkling between the hull stiffeners, then folding like an accordion. Then the sea crunched it like a boot on a beer can. Nobody knew how deep it was. You could estimate it, but there was no way to tell exactly, short of destroying a boat and killing all her crew.

The men down there knew that. They'd be hearing the hull squeal as it contracted. They could probably see it. The air would be getting hotter. Even before the hull collapsed, other systems – feed piping, sea chests, joints in the reactor coolant loop – would start to leak and break.

What would that do to her commander?

What would that do to his men?'

He found himself looking at the overhead, as if not a Soviet crew but *Ryan*'s was under a water column that weighed with eighty tons on every square foot. And hearing, every fifteen seconds, a hunting sonar drilling through it. When he pulled his eyes down, he saw Matt watching him. The radarman looked quickly away, at the deck.

'Twenty-*six* hundred feet.'

'Still got him, Orris?'

'Lot of quenching, but he comes through enough to – switching to passive . . . Christ! Listen to that.'

'Listen to what?' shouted Packer suddenly. 'Tell us, man! It doesn't do a damn bit of good unless I know about it!'

'I can hear something. Squeaks, or scrapes. Popping. Must be ring frames, bulkheads warping as the hull compresses. Going back to active . . . horizontal range, ten thousand five hundred yards, bearing two-two-zero true.'

The plotters bent. *Ryan* labored up a sea, labored down again. Dan sucked air in and out with mingled terror and gratitude. He had all of it he wanted. He could hear the wind. He could step outside right now and see, maybe not daylight, but at least the eerie glow of the wind-tortured sea.

He wasn't half a mile down, in endless cold and dark, wondering whether every inhalation would be his last.

'Evaluator, Sonar: Contact at twenty-eight hundred feet. Nine hundred feet from the bottom.'

Packer was rubbing his throat. Pedersen had gone pale, his

head cocked into his earphones as if he, too, could hear the sluggish scream of plastically yielding steel. Evlin's hands shook as he polished his glasses. Bryce was there, too, he realized. The XO must have come in very quietly. He leaned against the bulkhead, watching silently as a ghost.

'Seems to have stopped dropping,' said Reed into the waiting, harsh as a saw cut. 'Holding at twenty-eight hundred. Sounds like more pumps on the line.'

'Something gave,' whispered Packer. 'He took it down, and down, till something fucking let go. You still got him, Orris? Can you distinguish him from the bottom?'

'Yes, sir, he's almost in the jelly, but we can make him out. If he was two, three hundred feet lower . . . stand by . . . stand by . . . is that another pump?'

The 29MC cut off. They all stared at the little grille the voices came out of. With a sort of spasm, Bryce stuck a Camel into his mouth. The captain lighted it for him wordlessly, Bryce leaning into the yellow luminescent waver of flame.

Dan was leaning over the surface scope when he thought he saw something. A speckle, a sudden small bright point had flared up as the fan of light swept around. He frowned down at it. It painted once again, fainter, then didn't show for the next three sweeps. A small contact, or sea return? The bright pip in the center that was *Ryan* was surrounded by a seething green halo. He decided it was sea return. A freak wave, reflecting radar for a moment, then subsiding back into the confused maelstrom that surrounded them.

He forgot it as Reed's voice broke from the intercom, too loud. 'Machinery noise. Main reactor pumps on! Main shaft, reduction-gear tonals! He's blowing main ballast!'

'The son of a bitch's coming up,' said Bryce. His voice caught, and he coughed out smoke.

And Packer said, lifting his head, 'Go to general quarters now, Mr. Evlin, if you please.'

When the running and shouting had subsided, the rapid bong of the alarm had cut off, the compartment was crowded again. Dan found himself wedged between two petty officers. They smelled as rank as he knew he must himself. He finished buckling his helmet and put the headset back on.

The weapons stations had been trying to reach him. 'Torpedo control manned and ready.'

'Mount fifty-two, manned and ready.'

He acknowledged and said rapidly, looking over Evlin's shoulder, 'Torpedo Control, Mount fifty-two: Submarine is going to full power and rising rapidly. Train out on uh, on zero-four-zero relative.'

'We going to shoot, sir? What kind of ammunition you want us to load?'

'Captain, the gun wants to know what kind of –'

'Armor-piercing,' snapped Packer. He turned back to Evlin. As he was repeating the order to the mount, Dan heard the captain say, 'What's your plan, Al? Assuming he's surfacing?'

'I guess to hold contact, sir. Report it to CINCLANTFLT. And stand by to render assistance.'

'Not good enough. If he broaches, I want to be alongside in about four minutes. Let's go to full speed, get over where Orris thinks he's headed.'

The sonarman said over the intercom, 'B forty-one still blowing all tanks. Sounds like emergency blow. Now at one thousand feet. Very loud transients. All pumps are running at full speed. Stand by for a ping. . . . Mark, nine thousand seven hundred yards, bearing two-two-five, up doppler, repeat, *up doppler*. He's coming right! He's coming around toward us!'

'Keep calm, Orris. Al, keep your bow to him, follow him around.'

Dan calculated the new relative bearing and put it out over his circuit. The deck tilted as *Ryan*'s abused turbines shook the hull. The men snatched for handholds.

'Combat, Bridge: I need a course to steer.' Norden. Dan realized he hadn't been relieved, either. Well, it looked like Packer was right: This was the end of the game. Evlin gave him two-one-five and told him to get his lookouts alert, the target was trying for an emergency surface.

God, he had to *piss*. For a second he thought about handing the phones to Pedersen. But he couldn't. Not now. Not looking at Packer's face, set like granite.

'Mark, range eight thousand eight hundred yards, bearing two-three-zero, still up doppler, still in a right turn.'

'Very well.' Packer looked across the plot at him. 'Mr. Lenson, it's possible he'll broach, then lose the bubble in his tanks and sink. We might have to pick men out of the water. What's the status of the motor whaleboat?'

'Uh, I haven't checked it since last night, sir, but we got the falls and davits chipped free then, and Chief Bloch was going to spray some of that glycol on them. It would help to call away the kinnicks – I mean, the boat crew, get them warming the motor up and stuff.'

'Do it, Al,' said Packer. Evlin was reaching for the 21MC when a sudden bell blasted their ears. Heads snapped around. A red light was pulsing on the bulkhead to Sonar.

'Screamer, screamer! High-speed screws – torpedo in the water, bearing two-three-five! Torpedoes incoming! Nixie noisemaker switch on!'

Packer spun on his heel and bolted through the door to the bridge. A second later, the EOT pinged and *Ryan* heeled. Evlin whipped the protractor around to point away from the sub's last position. 'Bridge, Combat: Recommend continuing right at hard rudder, steady on zero-five-five.'

'Roger zero-five-five. Main Control, give me emergency flank power, now! If we don't have casualty power aft, we better get it on it the next four minutes, or our troubles are over, hear me?'

Dan didn't hear Talliaferro's answer. It was strange. He seemed to be frozen emotionally, but his eye had gone straight to the clock above the plot and his brain was making calculations in it seemed hundredths of a second. Eight thousand yards at fifty knots – his ballpark division was a fraction under five minutes from torpedo tube to their stern. No, they were at fifteen knots, accelerating to flank, say they'd be making twenty by the time the torps arrived – same calculation, but drop the overtaking speed by the average speed of the ship. Anyway, they didn't have over eight or nine minutes. He searched his mind for something he could do.

He couldn't think of anything. Turn tail and haul ass, turn on the noisemaker – that was about it. There weren't any defenses against an acoustic torpedo once somebody sicked it in your direction.

Just one of them usually sank a destroyer.

When he looked up from checking his life vest, the clock had advanced another minute. Beneath it Evlin frowned at the plot. Matt lifted his pencil from a red arrow, marking it with a neat circled *T*.

'I didn't think he'd shoot,' the operations officer said. 'But I guess I was wrong.'

Ryan swayed and hammered as a sea hoisted her tail. The deck plates buzzed. The whine of the blowers, thirty feet behind them, wound upward into a crazy howl. Over it, he heard Orris screaming. 'I hear it. I hear pinging! High-freq noise spoke bearing two-three-eight. Coming in louder. Two or three of them, can't tell –'

Evlin hit the 29MC. 'Better shut your sound gear down, Aaron. An explosion close aboard could knock it out.'

'Roger, out.' Curt and cold. Just like Reed, Dan thought. He suddenly remembered his own torpedoes. 'Sir, permission to spin up the gyros on the Mark forty-threes.'

'Do it,' said Evlin. 'We can't launch on this bearing, but if he misses with this salvo, we'll come around at flank and drop ours on his head.'

'You satisfied he's hostile now, Lieutenant?' asked Pedersen. Evlin nodded shortly.

From the corner of his eye, Dan saw the clock click over again. Another minute gone.

Out of nowhere, he was back in Bancroft Hall. Listening to the echoing clamor in the corridors as a hundred plebes shouted at once, 'Time tide and formation wait for no man, sir! Six minutes, *sir*!'

His earphones said, 'Gyros coming up on both SLTTs. Starting circuit warm-up. Sir, will they fire from Sonar or here?'

'I don't know yet. We may have to do an urgent attack. Be ready to fire local control on word from me.'

As they acknowledged, he glanced at the clock again.

Three more minutes. Till the machines streaking after them through the frigid black water overtook. Sometimes torpedoes broached in heavy seas. He wished he knew whether the noisemaker was working. Then he wished they had their own torpedoes in the water to distract *him* from a second attack. Unfortunately, the 43s were short-range weapons. If only the Asroc was working!

Ryan was moving now, still not at flank speed – steam plants took time to accelerate – but getting there, and rolling like a drunk running from cops as she charged through the following seas. But not nearly fast enough, he thought, to outdistance a fifty-knot torpedo.

'Main Control, Bridge: Did you ever get power to the Nixie?'

'Stand by, sir, checking on that now.'

The clock showed two minutes to go.

'Hold on to something,' said Pedersen. Dan grabbed a pipe in the overhead and bent his knees. The Soviets liked big warheads, the kind that broke legs when they went off.

He was braced when a faint thud came up from below, as if someone had dropped a paint can on the next deck down. 'What was that, sir?' asked Lipson.

'Damned if I know,' said Evlin.

Packer came back from the bridge, almost at a run. He shouted into Sonar, 'What you got, Orris?'

'High-speed screw passed us stern, circling to starboard now, sir.'

'Son of a bitch,' muttered the captain. He stood there, hand halfway to his mouth.

'Combat, Bridge: This is Main Control. We have some kind of problem in the after fireroom.'

Packer was on the intercom like a pouncing tiger. 'What kind of problem?'

'Don't know yet, Captain. All we got was a double growl on the two JV from the boiler face. Nobody on the line when we answered. Then steam pressure started to drop. Fast.'

Packer hung on the intercom, his face strained. Suddenly he pointed to Dan. 'You. After fireroom. Find out what's going on. Then back here, on the double; run all the way.

Chief, take his phones. Got it? Why are you still here? Go, go, go!'

He charged down ladders headfirst, nearly breaking his neck when his hand slipped on the rail. He slammed down into the inboard passageway and splashed aft into ankle-deep water. It wasn't much more than a hundred feet, but it felt as long as a cross-country course. A weird whine grew ahead as he ran. The passageway rolled around him, like the Crazy Hallway in a fun house. He caromed off a steel stiffener, but didn't stop. Halfway there the passageway went dark, lighted only sporadically by battle lanterns. Their batteries wouldn't last much longer –

In the dimness ahead, something black and wormlike uncoiled from the deck. His legs faltered, and he started to skid, trying futilely to brake on the wet tile.

The whine became the loudest sustained noise he'd ever heard, like a five-inch gun going off second after second. The black worm was men being vomited out of the after fireroom. They came up through the narrow scuttle as if propelled by compressed air. He screamed as loudly as he could, trying to ask what was happening below, but he couldn't even hear himself over the incredible sound. Anyway, they weren't looking at him. They were in panic flight.

He looked down into the hole. Then, before he could think about it, grabbed the handhold and dropped his legs in.

Somebody else was trying to come up. For a moment they fought in the darkness, in the mind-obliterating din. Dan stamped down, felt something snap. The other didn't even slow, climbing right over him as he hugged the slick steel rungs. When the man was past, he swung back on the ladder and descended as fast as he could.

Eleven feet down his boots dropped into ice-cold water, then hit a deck he couldn't see. Instantly, he clapped his hands over his ears.

The noise was like the worst earache he'd ever had, unbroken sound so great he couldn't interpret it except as pain. The air was impenetrable with steam or smoke. He spun blindly, searching for some clue. What were they fleeing? He took a step away from the ladder, and almost fell over it.

The torpedo danced on the grating between the boiler faces, jerking and howling as its propeller chewed a white-hot torrent of sparks off the solid steel of the boiler mounting. It was dark green and huge, fifteen or twenty feet long, two feet thick. Flame and smoke and the unbelievable sound blasted out of it from a hole in the propeller hub that was rapidly brightening through dull red to cherry-hot. The tail lashed about like a dying snake's, smashing a fin against a safety rail, prop clattering against the grating. Pieces from its tail shroud whanged around the space like grenade fragments.

A figure materialized out of the smoke and steam, bent as if trekking into a blizzard. A rag masked the lower half of his face. As he advanced, Dan saw he was dragging a hose over his shoulder.

Lenson took two steps and jumped over the vibrating torpedo. It jerked upward as if to get him, and he tripped. A scream ripped his throat as he thought he was falling into the prop. But his hand got the rail and yanked him forward.

The man saw him. WESSMAN was stenciled on his shirt. No words, they took their positions by drill, the boilerman on the nozzle, Dan behind him, hauling more hose off the reel, until Wessman got to the weapon's tail and pulled back the bail. A blast of mist hit the howling engine. He played it there for a few seconds. The water exploded into steam, joining the whirling cloud that filled the compartment like a sauna. Then he moved the jet forward, playing it back and forth, cooling the whole weapon from the tail to the bluntly curved, dented, scarred raw metal of the warhead.

The howling dropped in pitch, became a grating, shrieking clatter. The whole huge cylinder, thicker than a man's waist, lurched sideways and slammed against the boiler. The nubs of the prop screeched like two huge, hot, hollow blocks of rough steel being rubbed together, and stopped.

In the after silence, the roar of escaping steam sounded puny. Dan looked up to see the enlisted man shouting at him. 'Can't hear you,' he shouted back. Wessman stared at him, then shook his head, pointed to his ears. They both shrugged.

He suddenly noticed that water was pouring in behind him, not far from the scuttle he'd come down. A solid-looking torrent as wide as his chest. It bulged inward in a glassy stream, arched downward, and turned into white spray as it passed through the grating of the upper-level catwalk. When he pulled a battle lantern off the bulkhead and leaned over the rail, he saw water glimmering between the pumps and tanks and machinery down there. It surged sluggishly as the ship rolled. It didn't look very threatening. Just liquid blackness. But when it rolled back, it was higher, already licking over the lower-level catwalk.

He jerked his eyes up to see Wessman's teeth an inch from his face. Faintly, through the eerie chorus of the after deafness, words forced themselves. 'Came through over by the checkman's flat . . . first thing, fuel-oil valve, killed all the fires . . . told the guys evacuate, I'd secure steam and join 'em. We better get out of here.'

Dan howled back, 'We got to stay and plug that hole.'

'Fucking torp can go off any minute.'

'Hasn't gone off by now, it's not going to. You know we're going down anyway, this space floods.'

The boilerman gave him a look that combined disgust and reluctant agreement. 'Okay, sir, you gimme a hand and we'll try to get her slowed down a little. Just lemme secure this aux steam.'

Wessman disappeared into the fog. A few seconds later, the blasting hiss slackened. The cloud cleared, leaving a sinus-stinging smell of hot alcohol and fire, but the air was still so hot it scorched his tongue as he breathed.

The torpedo kept attracting his eyes. It lay like a dead slug across the width of the ship, inert yet ominous. The scars on its nose gleamed under the beam of his lantern.

He jerked the light away and centered it on the column of water. It pulsed, strengthening when the compartment leaned to port, slackening when it leaned to starboard. He moved in, stepping gingerly over the still-smoking debris of the tail shroud.

The blunt-nosed weapon had punched through the hull like a .22 bullet through a tin can, curling the plating inward in jagged points. The closer he got, the more he realized that there was a *lot* of water coming in. Jesus, he thought. I didn't know the hull was this thin.

Wessman came back. Now all he had to do was shout and Dan could hear him fine. 'That's the wall of the feed-water tank,' he howled. 'It come through the hull and then through the tank and then out here onto the checkman's flat. Would have got me, I hadn't gone to the ladder to tell Bluejay, quit scratching his balls and get that spare burner broke down. Now how you gonna plug that, sir?'

But Dan was remembering another time of sweating and cursing in the dark, a steel box with men inside that sank slowly in a huge tank of dank-smelling water: the damage-control trainer at Newport. For small round holes, the best thing was a wooden cone, hammered in and stuffed with rags. For *small* round holes. For this – 'Got any lumber down here?' he shouted. 'Any damage-control plugs, patching material?'

'Wait a minute,' shouted the boilerman. He ran forward, leaving Dan alone with the torpedo. It didn't feel good.

When Wessman came back, he was dragging a foam-rubber bunk pad. Dan propped his light on the workbench, shining it toward the bulkhead. They rolled the pad into a tight cylinder, then grabbed it like a battering ram. He caught the BT's eye. 'Let's do it.'

They got a yard from the hole before the water knocked them down and blew the pad back onto the torpedo. Dan picked himself up. He was soaked now, but the sea was so cold it didn't feel cold at all. It had numbed his flesh the instant it hit. He didn't want to have to try to swim in that. 'We got to keep this bitch floating,' he shouted. 'Come on, let's try it again. This time, wait till she rolls to starboard.'

The second time, he slipped on the grating as they had it halfway in. Wessman fell, too. For a moment, the black wet plastic foam covered his mouth and nose and he couldn't breathe. When he fought free, *Ryan* rolled and the light shot off the workbench and smashed into fizzing sparks.

They got up again grimly and groped about in the dark. They rolled the pad again, and lunged, feeling into the blast of icy water with their bare fingers. He felt jagged steel, sensed the incredible power of the black sea beyong, forcing its way into *Ryan* like a long denied lover.

278

Suddenly his body understood that he had to accomplish this or he would die. His muscles went rigid. For one moment, he knew he could lift the ship itself if he had a place to set his boots. Wessman grunted beside him like a man at the instant of climax.

When they staggered back, the bedroll uncoiled in the gap. It seemed to expand, to bulge inward. They watched it, swaying as the old destroyer rolled. Water streamed and bubbled in around it, weeping down the bulkhead. But the plug stayed put.

'Not too bad,' said the boilerman. 'That's cut it down a hell of a lot.'

Dan stepped back, panting, wiping his hands on his sodden trousers. 'Get the repair party down here, a sheet of plywood over it. Then brace it; that ought to do it.'

'That's not too bad, sir,' said the boilerman again. 'Better look at your hands, you cut them some.'

Suddenly he remembered he hadn't called the captain. 'Where's the phone? Or have you got an intercom?'

'No intercom, but there's a growler at the checkman's station; you can get Main Control on it.'

But when he picked it up, he heard Packer instead, shouting almost incoherently. From CIC, you could tap into any circuit on the ship. He broke in: 'Captain, this is Lenson, in the after fireroom –'

'Goddamn it, I told you to come right back! What the fuck's going on down there?'

'Sir, we had a hot-running torpedo come through the port side, about uh, frame one twenty. It's lying on the checkman's flat between the boilers. We got a quick patch on the entry hole, but there's still a lot of water coming in. We need a repair party down here soon as possible.'

'Is it still running?'

'No, sir, it ran for a few seconds and then sort of seized up, it sounded like.'

'But it's live?'

'Well, I don't know, sir. It doesn't seem to have gone off yet.'

Jesus, he thought, wasn't *that* a brilliant remark. But Packer only said, 'Christ. . . . Okay, get back up here. We still got this son of a bitch to worry about. Repair Five'll be there on the double. Ed, you listening?'

'They're on their way, sir. The other BTs just got here, told us about it.'

Dan gave Wessman the phone. He started to leave, then remembered something and turned back. 'Petty Officer Wessman.'

'Sir?'

'Good work on the patch. And on the hose, and securing the fires. I'll tell Mr. Talliaferro and the captain about it. Maybe we can do something for you.'

The boilerman stared at him. Finally, he said, 'Well – thank you, sir.' He had that funny look back again. Dan looked back once as he went up the ladder, and saw Wessman still staring after him, holding the phone in his hand.

'I don't think it's a dud,' Evlin was telling Packer when Dan got back to CIC.

'You're not making sense, Al. What else can it be?'

'It's a warning shot. We heard two torpedoes coming in. One passed astern, made two circles, and then the screw noises stopped. The other hit us. But neither of them went off.'

'So what's that mean?' Bryce's voice was heavy, sarcastic. 'The Nixie decoyed one, and the other did just what it was supposed to do, exceptin' it didn't go off. I say we get some of our own fish in the water.'

When they looked at him Dan became aware that he was dripping wet from head to foot. Actually, some remote part of his brain thought, it was just as well. Sometime in the last half hour, his overstrained and ignored bladder had let go. He hadn't even realized it till now.

Then he looked at the clock again. Not a half hour. Though it seemed like it. He'd been gone eight minutes.

'So what are you saying, Al? That they're, what, *deliberate* duds?'

The ops officer spoke with impassioned concentration, as if by intensity alone he could convince. 'It's one of two things, sir. One, it's a warning shot. Their CO doesn't mean to kill us, he just wants us to keep clear while he makes his repairs. Or, two, it means that the crew's divided. They were ordered to fire on us. Okay, they did, but somebody – torpedomen, junior officers, *somebody* – dudded them before they left the tubes.'

'So –'

'So, either way it means there are people down there who aren't trying to kill us. Therefore, I don't think we should be trying to kill them. That's all. Sir.'

'We're coming into Mark forty-three range, sir,' said Pedersen.

A new voice in Dan's earphones. No, it was Reed's, but he hadn't been on the Weapons Control circuit before. 'All stations, this is underwater battery fire control, taking control of forward torpedo mounts. Acknowledge.'

Reed was setting up to fire on the Mark 264. From the firing panel, in Sonar, he could set the search parameters into the weapons and fire all or any combination of them. The only thing he couldn't do by remote control was reload. Dan pressed the transmit button. 'Weps Control, aye. Do you have the readout on what we have in the tubes, sir?'

Reed said he had it on the board in UB Plot, but to give it to him again as a double check. The torpedoman passed him the data. Six Mark 43s, three war shots to starboard, a war shot and two practice rounds to port. 'Are those practice rounds or drill rounds?' Reed asked.

'Practice rounds, sir.'

When Dan focused on the plot again, Bryce was leaning over it, facing Evlin. 'You're telling us to just sit here and take the next salvo, too? Till they get one to work? Hell! These were just set too shallow, or too close. Next one hits us, we're dog meat! You've got to shoot, Jimmy John, and shoot now!'

They all stared at Packer. In that endless moment, Dan understood as he never had before the merciless weight of command. Building like the crushing pressure of the sea on a submarine's hull. . . .

On the plot the traces were only inches apart. Pedersen said quietly, 'We're in range now, sir.'

The captain said, 'Mr. Evlin, give me a three-round spread of Mark forty-threes, set to as shallow a ceiling as they'll run at and a floor of four hundred feet.'

Evlin said, 'No, sir.'

'What did you say?'

'He said "No," Jimmy John –'

'Shut up, Ben. Al, shoot the fucking torpedoes.'

'No, sir,' said the operations officer again. He sounded scared but calm, resigned. 'I can't, sir. I don't believe they're trying to kill us.'

'What kind of soft-headed –'

'Shut *up*, Bryce!' As if they were alone, instead of surrounded by men in a reeling, damaged ship, Packer and Evlin searched each other's eyes. The captain said, so softly Dan almost missed it, 'Lieutenant Evlin, I respect your moral misgivings, but *I am the captain.* I accept responsibility, and you obey. For the last time, goddamn it, *shoot.*'

Evlin looked at his hands. They were steady on the paper.

He said, 'I can't participate, sir.'

'Then you're relieved,' said Packer curtly, looking away. 'Get those phones off. Get out of here! Somebody get Reed out here –'

'He's on the firing panel, sir,' said Dan.

Packer spun. He was headed for the curtain to Sonar when Dan said, 'Captain!'

Packer hesitated, just for a moment, with his hand on the curtain. He didn't turn his body, but he glanced back over his shoulder.

'You, too, Lenson?' James Packer said softly.

Dan felt frightened, facing those eyes, as he hadn't been facing the sea. 'No, sir. I just wanted to tell you – you have another choice, Captain. If you want it. Remember, we have two practice shots in the port tubes. They'll run hot but there's no explosive –'

Packer looked into the space between them for a second. His mouth came open a little. Then it snapped shut, and set in a down-turned line. He jerked the curtain open and thrust his head inside.

'Fire the two practice rounds on line of sound, initial depth fifty feet, floor four hundred.'

Dan heard Reed acknowledge. He saw Bryce stiffen, and caught from the corner of his eye Evlin, at the door, looking back at him. Dan tried to smile at him. But the operations officer just looked back, his expression not changing. He looked sad yet understanding. Dan thought with a shiver that it was as if he was judging them.

Then Evlin wasn't with them anymore.

He was reminded what was going on by a shout from Sonar. Orris again: 'High-speed screws to port!'

Reed, in his earphones: 'Two shots in the water, running hot.'

'Torpedoes in the water, sir!'

'Theirs or ours?'

'Ours, sir. Sorry, sir.' His teeth were chattering; he was shivering. Packer said, 'Soon as this is over, Dan, get Cummings up here to relieve you. You need to get some dry clothes on. And get somebody to look at those hands. Chief, can we get you some coffee? I could do with some, too.'

'I'll call the mess decks, get some sent up, sir.'

Dan felt his eyes attracted again to the clock. Not long to wait this time. They'd been close when they fired, almost inside minimum range. The book said the Mark 43 went in at a steep down angle, reached·its initial search depth, then turned on its sonar and began circling. It spiraled downward, searching a great cylinder of sea as it slowly dropped to its floor depth. Then, if it still had juice in its batteries, it rose again. As soon as it detected a target, it broke off the search and homed in. The offset from the surface meant that the firing ship was safe.

'Orris, what have you got?'

'Still circling, sir – wait – there's a hit, I think. There's another one! Like a clang – no explosion –'

'Stand by on the starboard mount,' said Packer. Like the others, he had his head cocked, listening.

Nothing happened for the next few minutes. Dan's excitement ebbed, leaving him suddenly so weak that he could barely stand. Packer coughed and rubbed his throat.

Finally Orris reported a grinding noise. A new noise, at the same repetition rate as 41's screw.

'Could be we hit his prop,' said Bryce, emerging from the shadows again. Packer nodded shortly.

'Captain, Bridge,' Norden cut in on the intercom. The CO reached up wearily. 'I'm here, go ahead.'

'Sir, we have what looks like running lights off to port. Can't get an aspect yet, but appears to be a small surface vessel.'

'Be right out.'

'Want me to take over here?'

'Thanks, Ben, but I think Lenson's got the bubble.' Packer didn't look at either of them. He groped around for his pipe, then seemed to give up. He stumbled as he moved toward the door. Dan looked after him. Sudden pride fought with guilt. He should have reported that radar contact, momentary and doubtful as it had been. Next time, he would.

'So, somebody's got to keep ship's routine going,' Bryce announced. 'I'll be in my office, anyone needs me.'

'Aye aye, sir,' said Dan. His voice came out bland, just like he wanted it, though he really wanted to laugh in the exec's beefy face.

When both the XO and CO were gone, Pedersen held out the evaluator's headset. Dan slipped one earpiece of the WLO's set off and put one of the evaluator's on. That way he could monitor both circuits. Some part of him that was getting tired of being ignored said plaintively that his ears were getting sore. He ignored it again. 'Chief, hadn't we better start plotting that surface contact?'

'Uh, yes, sir.'

It had to be the intelligence ship the British had warned them about. Nobody else had any reason to be out here – not this time of year.

Suddenly he couldn't stand being inside, unable to see. He said, 'Chief, I'll be right back.' Hanging up the headset, he took ten steps forward and stuck his head into the pilothouse.

They were standing out on the wing. Packer, a shorter shadow that had to be Norden, and the third either Yardner or Lieutenant (jg) Johnson, the other Condition IIIA JOOD.

They all had their binoculars up. He leaned out, opening his eyes wide to the night. Beyond them were two distinct specks of light, aureoled with mist or fog but burning steady, and another that winked slowly.

He heard one phrase, torn from Packer's lips by the blast of wind: 'Where in the hell did he come from?'

Dan stared out, holding the door grimly against its attempts to compact him. Across the heaving darkness, the distant light tapped out, slow and distinct, so deliberately that he was able to make out the Morse: USSR SUBMARINES ARRIVE HERE SOON. YIELD AREA TO US TO MAKE CONTACT CAPTAIN OLFERIEV. FAILURE TO DO WILL LEAD TO USSR SUBMARINES TO ATTACK YOU.

'Mr. Lenson! Sonar, for you!'

He started and slammed the door. The other ship must be small, to paint so poorly on the radar. He hated to think how they were riding. But then, coming from the east, they'd missed the worst of the storm.

Two of the messmen had brought up coffee in a thermal jug and bread in a bucket. Some of the men were eating, gnawing it from their hands like squirrels. He grabbed a heel as the messman went by.

Only then did the meaning of the signal penetrate. The new arrival was ordering them to leave. Saving the Soviets would deal with this Captain – Olferiev. At last they could put a name to the man across the chessboard.

But as he put the headset back on, he realized with hollow apprehension that Packer wouldn't. He'd refused to before, when *Ryan* was close to sinking. Now, with part of the experimental IVDS wrapped around the sub below, after being fired at, he'd never leave, threats or no.

He listened to Orris's exhausted voice dragging out ranges and bearings. His heart felt sluggish and underpowered, like a four-cylinder Fury. His hands shook. Looking across the plot, he saw how ashen Pedersen's face was, how exhausted Lipson and Matt looked. Packer was older than any of them. How much more could he take? They'd been lucky so far. Torpedoes that hadn't exploded. A ship that hadn't capsized. How long could that kind of luck hold?

He suddenly noticed that there was bread in his hand and that he was hungry. He was tearing at it with his teeth, surprised his stomach accepted it, when Pedersen said, 'Check this out on the surface scope, sir. A small contact. Intermittent. Dead ahead.'

'Dead ahead? That's where B forty-one is.'

'Right, sir. I think he's surfacing.'

Only after he'd swallowed it did he notice that his torn fingers had left blood prints on the bread.

18

The working lights were on and Bloch and Isaacs were busy when Dan got back to the boat deck. The starter was grinding gravel. More First Division men were coming out of the hangar. They were olive-drab snowmen in a bulky assortment of rain gear, foul-weather jackets, hoods, caps, masks, and gloves. He noted Rocky, Speedy, Brute Boy, Ali X., Shorty. And Lassard, standing in the hangar lee with his hands in his pockets, smiling dreamily past it all at the sea. 'Where's Popeye?' Dan shouted over the baying of the wind. Nobody answered. Then he made out Rambaugh in the boat, bent over at the coxswain's station.

'How many you want in her, sir?'

'I'm not sure, Chief. How many we usually take?'

'Is it a boarding party, a rescue party, what?'

'I don't know. The skipper just told me – he just said to get our guys back here and get ready to put the boat in the water.'

'Well, we might not be able to. Not in seas like this. Hell, it's hard to board a sub in *good* weather. And plus, this fucking diesel's frozen or something. You people been starting it regular?'

'Every day, Chief man, you know we treat it right.'

'Ikey. Where's Ikey? He's good with – here, get up there, see what you can do with it.'

Dan looked at the sea. If he had to do this, he would. But he didn't want to think about putting out into that madness in a twenty-six-foot Mark Two motor whaleboat. The waves looked higher than the boat was long. Dark as hell's basement, too. Christ, he thought, what if we get lost? What if we get swamped, or capsize?

The engine puked blue smoke and began clattering. The black first-class, padded like a pugil-stick fighter with foul-

287

weather gear, life jacket, watch cap, straightened proudly, wiping his hands on a rag. Lassard howled, dancing like an Indian, fingers extended in peace signs. 'Cut it off, goddamn it!' Bloch shouted. 'We'll start it again when she lowers. Ikey, help Baw inventory her outfit.'

'Anchor.'

'Check.'

'Batteries, dry.'

'Check.'

'Bell 'n' bracket.'

'Gotcha, Ikey.'

'Thass Petty Officer Isaacs to you. Chain assembly.'

Dan studied the davits, the hoisting gear that would sway the boat up out of her chocks, swing her outboard, and lower her. Cranks and screws and lines and turnbuckles and gripes. He had no idea how they operated. He stood back, letting Bloch and Isaacs chivvy and push the hands into position on steadying lines and twofold tackles.

Finally, the chief called, 'Okay, crew.' Connolly, Coffey, and Vogelpohl pushed up to the metal ladder that led up to the still-chocked boat. Dan looked at the round-faced department yeoman. 'Pohl, what're you doing out here?'

'I'm boat crew, Ensign.'

'I didn't know that.'

'Grapnel line . . . bailin' pail . . . fenders . . . stern lines. Got it all, Chief.'

'Mr. Lenson, you boat officer?'

'Guess so, Chief.'

'Better board, sir. Bridge is sayin' we're starting our approach.'

'Have you got Mr. Norden on there?'

The phone talker nodded. Dan bawled, 'Ask him how many men we want in the boat, and what we're supposed to do.'

Out of nowhere, it began to rain. An icy, diagonal, freezing mix of rain and soft sleet that pelted down out of invisible clouds and soaked his foul-weather jacket in seconds. The men cursed and shoved around him, climbing up into the boat and settling on thwarts slick and sweet-smelling with glycol antifreeze. Loose ice slid around under the floor-boards. The sleet stung his eyes and trickled down his back. He wondered what they were supposed to be doing. If this was a boarding party, it seemed like they ought to be armed.

As if thought called them into being, there were two gunner's mates by the rail, handing over short shapes wrapped in tarp. The men started to unwrap them. 'Put them under the thwarts,' he shouted, standing up. 'Listen up! You, Heering – are these loaded?'

'Full magazines, empty chambers. Just work the operating rod to load the first round. This forty-five's yours, sir. Got fire axes here for you, too. Watch 'em, they're sharp.'

The pistol felt heavy and familiar. Plebe Summer, hot, dusty hours on the range at Greenbury Point. He checked it and stuffed it into his belt, under all the other gear.

'Mr. Lenson! Wanted on the circuit.'

He fought his way out of the boat and onto the ship again, stepping carefully across space to the boat deck. The headset was wet and cold on his ears. 'Lenson. That you, Rich?'

'This is the captain. You ready to lower away back there?'

He thought of the storm, the dark. The pistol was blue ice, sucking the warmth of his privates. He took a deep breath. 'Yes, sir.'

'Radar holds what we think's forty-one about a thousand yards ahead, on the surface. No lights, so she's running darkened. If she's running at all.'

'Yes, sir. What do you want us to –'

'I don't know what you'll hit over there. You're going to have to use your judgment. If there's nobody topside, or only a couple guys, board her and check out the sail and planes. Do it fast. Make sure there's nothing of ours fouled on her. If you see the cable, chop it free and either tow it back or let it sink. Got that?'

'Uh, yes, sir, but what about the sub itself? Do you want me to, uh – to capture it?'

A grim chuckle came over the circuit. 'With this guy to starboard looking on? That's how wars start, Dan. No dramatics. Just get aboard, check it out, and get back here. Fast.

'From what Sonar's telling me, they're in trouble. They're fighting major flooding. They're probably not going to have a hell of a lot of attention to spare for you. If it goes down while you're alongside, make sure all our guys get back aboard.'

'What about them, sir? What if they want off?'

'Good question, but you'll have to play that by ear. If he's sinking, and there's room in the boat, you can pick some of them up. I don't think I want them on the ship, though. Shuttle them over to the AGI. I'll be covering you with the guns in case anything goes wrong. Got it?'

He repeated it back. The captain snapped, 'Okay, go to it,' and left the line.

'What's the word, sir?'

'It's a boarding party, Chief.'

'Mind if I come? I don't think we've done one of those since – what – since the war –'

'No. I need you on the falls. Somebody's got to see we lower right, or we'll all end up in the water.'

Dan waddled up the ladder and pushed his way back toward the boat's helm. That answered one question, at least. He grabbed the monkey lines as *Ryan* rolled. Okay, he'd better make sure . . . 'Coxswain! Who's my coxswain?'

'Here, sir.' Rambaugh.

'We ready to lower, Popeye? Are the uh, are the plugs in?' The second-class nodded. 'Engineer?'

A voice, a face he didn't know. A snipe. Dan made sure he'd checked the fuel and oil.

'Bow hook?'

'Vogel's bow hook, Ensign.'

'Vogelpohl, you big enough for that?'

'Been doing it for two years, sir.'

'Okay, just checking. We got a light? Chief, I need a couple more battle lanterns. . . . Hey! You!' he shouted. 'Yeah, I'm talking to you! Put that under the seat, sailor!

'Now the rest of you listen up; here's the word on what we gotta do.'

When he was done, nobody seemed to have any questions. They stood and sat and shivered, muttering with the blaspheming patience of sailors in the rain and spray, clinging grimly to the knotted hand lines.

'Boat to the rail,' bawled the phone talker.

Dan couldn't follow everything that happened in the next minutes. Bloch shouted commands. The sleet fell harder than ever, driving down out of the night. The whips and steadying lines came taut.

The boat trembled under him, then lifted, swaying, from the cradle. The chief bawled, 'Release guys! Release gripes! Hoist away!' Dan grabbed for the gunwale, then remembered and shifted his clutch to the knotted hemp of the monkey line.

'Hold fast,' he shouted. The bent down-curving davits, like the hooks of two upright canes, pivoted outboard and aft. The boat swung aft, then out, then forward, weaving its way around them.

Then they were hanging out over the sea, the blocks and lines creaking taut above them, the ship's side a sea-stained wall in the rain-haloed work lights. The crew stood upright, swaying from the line. If the falls broke, dropping the boat, the men with good grips would be left dangling like a line of cured hams, to be swung back inboard. The others would plunge straight down. On the ship, Jones and Isaacs flipped fenders over opposite them. The steadying lines came taut fore and aft, and the men on them set their heels as *Ryan* rolled. Bloch was shouting something about a safety runner.

Lenson leaned over the gunwales and looked down at a sea like used motor oil. It rose dizzyingly swift, fell away, then surged back, its surface black and dull and somehow viscid, gruel-like, under the speckling impact of the rain, as if it were kept from solidity only by unending motion. And out beyond it, a swell and another swell and after that utter dark and dark and a thousand miles of dark till the coast of Norway.

Looking forward, he saw faces staring down from the bridge wing. Any minute, he thought. Away the motor whaleboat, away. Ten or eleven things had to happen at once when the keel slammed down. Cast off aft, cast off forward, trip the slings clear of the prop; take a strain on the sea painter; start the engine, put it in gear, meanwhile keeping clear of the side with the rudder, but not too far out, or the painter would haul the bow around and they'd crash into the gray wall of hull. And all the time soaring up and dropping, one moment opposite the helo deck, the next eye-to-eye with the copper red of bottom paint. They'd have to sheer away gradually, and watch every wave. Any of them could dump him and all these men out into the lightless, freezing sea.

Thinking this, he struggled to his feet, bracing himself on the shoulders of those beside him. Hands reached up, steadying him. He barely felt them. He was counting heads: twelve, including himself. 'When we going, sir?' somebody called. He didn't answer, counting them all again: twelve. Okay, he was as ready as he'd ever be. He shaded his eyes against a lashing of spray and looked to the bridge again.

But minute after minute went by, and still they swayed there, halfway between sea and sky, between ship and sea.

'Somebody closing, off to port,' said Rambaugh, touching his shoulder. He pointed between *Ryan*'s stacks. 'See him, sir?'

He screened his eyes again to see two small lights close together off to port. He watched incuriously for a few seconds. The lights grew brighter, farther apart, and sharper, but stayed in the same relative position between the stacks. The pistol was digging into his gut. Having the muzzle pointing at his balls made him nervous. He mined around under his jacket, trying to shift it, then glanced up again.

Then he was struggling back to his feet, shouting at the talker. *Ryan* loomed above the alien lights. In the rainy mist their halos lighted sea-swept decks, a shadowy array of masts and aerials, the hammer and sickle and star, painted on her stack.

Ryan's horn burst into a nasal drone. One, two, three, four, five short, rapid blasts.

The Soviet trawler swayed, and the distance between her lights shortened. All at once, he understood. *Ryan*, longer and heavier, was shouldering the smaller ship away, forcing her to sheer off to port.

His attention was jerked away by the talker's frantic gestures. He cupped his hand to his ear. ' . . . up forward,' was all he caught.

Dan leaned across empty space and shouted, 'Chief, what's he trying to tell me?'

Bloch grabbed the earphones. His bull-like bawl cut the rattle of rain and the blast of wind. 'Everybody out of the boat, to the fo'c'sle, on the double! Going to board over the lifesaving nets.'

'Shit fire,' Dan muttered. 'Goddamn it. . . . *On your feet*! Everybody out of the boat, to the fo'c'sle, on the double!'

The men slipped and stumbled, chilled through by sleet and wind. Heat loss tripled when you were wet. One seaman tripped on the rub rail, would have taken the long dive if Rambaugh hadn't caught his collar.

He tossed one backward glance. Abandoned, empty, the boat swung like a huge slow pendulum at the end of its whips, and the dangling monkey lines capered dripping in the wind.

Forward, forward. He ran in staggering, shambling exhaustion. Men caromed off him in fatigued slow motion, like padded ninepins. They fell and fought down the portside ladder, then splashed clumsily forward through sliding pools on the main deck. Saltwater jetted out of Coffey's boots, ahead of him, with each of the seaman's steps.

Pettus was on the forecastle when they got there, sawing frantically at the lashings of the life nets, broad mats of woven rope rigged along the sides. As Dan reached him, the starboard one fell away, unrolling down into the foaming sea like a venetian blind. He leaned out over the lifeline, blinking against the salt sting. His face felt like a cast in acrylic resin.

To port the lights of the AGI heaved up and down, reeled right and left. She was making heavy weather. He ignored her, running his eyes above his guess at horizon. Was there something there? Something blacker than blackness, out ahead? Or was it only his tired, obedient sight telling him what he expected to see? 'Got anything, sir?' Rambaugh shouted, at his shoulder. 'Not yet,' he shouted back. 'Should be just ahead, though, a few hundred yards now –'

'Flare!'

He snapped his eyes front. A green comet climbed for the black bellies of the clouds, a shooting star that slowed and faded even as he watched. Then spray wiped it out.

A sea smashed into the stern, and *Ryan* reeled so violently he staggerd into the lifeline. The breaker cascaded the length of the forecastle, spraying the men like a crowd of protesters being fire-hosed. They bent their heads under it, clinging to the lifelines with one hand, the other clutching their axes.

Another flare soared, and all at once he made out the submarine. It was blacker than he'd expected – a hole in the night sea. Then the squall parted, the sleet and rain swept on, and suddenly it was close, a great low shadow length. So dark, he couldn't tell whether it was bow-on, or stern to *Ryan*. He suddenly missed the battle lanterns. He cursed himself; he'd left them in the boat.

Suddenly the sun rose. No, three of them, behind and above him. Dazzled, he threw his arm up. Over their heads, *Reynolds Ryan*'s searchlights burned like white-hot swords thrust through a black curtain. Rain and spray blew through them, making them solid, like hot shafts of just-cast glass. He blinked away wind tears and squinted.

The submarine was enormous, much longer than *Ryan*. The seas broke over her like a black iceberg. Her conning tower – it was called a 'sail' now – was lower and longer than that of U.S. subs. Behind it was a squat squared-off fairing, part of the deck, but raised ten or twelve feet above the pressure hull. It sloped downward as it ran aft, till it merged with the tapered spindle of the tail. Along its upper surface were the outlines of huge hatches. A double raised line ran along it. It looked like a railroad track.

The submarine canted far over to starboard, then whip-lashed back. It was rolling violently, beam to the seas. *Ryan* wasn't rolling, but she was pitching hard. Each time she drove downward, she smashed the sea to cream under her forefoot. Not only were the two ships out of synchronization; they responded differently to the sea. The great swells swept over the submarine like a tide-scoured rock, but they lifted and tossed *Ryan* like a rubber duck in a child's tub.

He stared down the dangling breadth of the net, its bottom buoyed up by yellow kapok floats that bobbed in the churn. His mouth was metallic dry. They weren't going to make it down that. They'd be shaken like ants off a picnic blanket, dropped into the boiling sea, and crushed to pulp between the hammer of *Ryan*'s fore keel and the black anvil of the pressure hull.

'On the fo'c'sle,' an immense voice spoke through the blinding dark. He squinted up at the wing, a reluctant actor on a brightly lighted stage, and lifted his arm.

'On the fo'c'scle . . . Mr. Lenson. Down the nets, to port, make your preparations to board.'

At Annapolis, he remembered, the drill they sweated most was pier approaches in the YPs, hundred-foot diesel craft, like miniature destroyers. No one could teach you how to maneuver a ship. You had to discover it yourself. Had to anticipate the inertia of hundreds of tons of steel, the freakish and conflicting thrusts of wind, tide, current, rudder, engines, even the direction the screw turned. You couldn't do close-quarters maneuvering by rote. You had to integrate it all faster than any computer could do vector analysis, then apply power and direction to bring the ship alongside and stop, dead in the water, ten feet off the pier.

It was tricky and unforgiving, and the seawall's creosoted timbers and the reinforced bows of the YPs were dented and gouged. But you had to learn it. Because pretty soon, you'd be doing it at sea with ships ten or fifty times bigger, and far less maneuverable.

Now he watched openmouthed as *Ryan* came right slowly, smashed her way through a sea, came right again. Till she was beam-on, and fighting her way yard by yard closer to the reeling submarine.

It was an incredible demonstration of sheer shiphandling seamanship. As each swell approached, the bow swung right with just enough momentum to meet it, take the blow, and reel back still lined up for the approach. He's coming in upwind, Dan thought. The wind'll blow us down, pin us against the sub. But could Packer fight the old destroyer free again once she was alongside? What if one of the Soviet's planes or screw blades tore through her paper-thin, rusty sides?

'Stand by to port.'

'Stand by,' he screamed. He bent over the rail, looking down again.

The kapok floats, fat little yellow pillows at the foot of the net, streamed the mesh out ten or twenty feet from the destroyer's sheer, like a drapery hanging from a balcony. If Packer could lay her alongside gently enough, close enough, it might cover most of the distance between the ship and the sub.

Unfortunately, *Ryan* was picking up the period of the swell now. The incandescent rods of the searchlights swayed down, then up again, losing their quarry as they probed up into the squall.

Then they dropped again, and glided over the steel reef. He squinted. Something different, wrong about the hatches. But the lights moved aft, converging on the vertical stern plane, the rudder, that stuck up above the seas like a raked black tombstone. Then *Ryan* pendulumed to starboard and they swayed up again, canting crazily across the sky.

'Son of a bitch.'

'Popeye, you ever done this before?'

'Never, sir. Don't want to do it now, either.'

'Think the net'll reach?'

'It ain't that's what's bothering me, sir. It's going alongside that bitch. The captain screws up and we'll land on top of her. Bust our back. Snap the keel. Sink us all.'

'Well, it looks like he's –'

'Mr. Lenson! What you want us to do?'

He turned and screamed downwind, 'I want three guys with me, three guys with axes. Bring that grapnel, somebody. When we get there, claw it along the side, check there's nothing trailing underwater. If there is, fish it up and cut it. Understand?'

A light came on on the submarine, high on the sail, and swept around the sea like a two-handed sword. It steadied for a moment on the white blur to port that was AGI, then rotated round toward *Ryan*.

When it hit them, he shielded his eyes and peered down. The beam lighted the narrowing blackness between them. Solid steel, he thought, on both sides, and between them a little rope and a little flesh and bone. He didn't want to be the filling in this sandwich. His left hand fumbled across his life vest, checking that the straps were tight. His right reached under it to check the pistol. It was sliding down, and he hauled it up and wedged it in tighter under his belt, the spur hammer digging into his navel.

Under his breath he muttered, hardly aware of it, 'Bring her in, Captain, goddamn it!'

Ryan eased forward slowly, incredibly slowly. A sea burst over her starboard side, throwing spray high into the night. Her bow swung left, lifted by the impact of hundreds of tons of water. For a moment it looked as if she'd ride the submarine down. Then she came slowly, slowly, back to starboard.

She crept the last few yards and came to a crazily rolling, pitching halt, thirty yards upwind of the hulk and perfectly aligned fore and aft. The narrow strip of black water between them foamed. Then it began to narrow.

Ryan nosed forward a little more. She rose and fell, rolled and pitched madly; then for a moment lay almost still, like an exhausted whale tired of fighting rope and iron. A dragging clang came from aft.

'On the fo'c'sle. Away the boarding party, to port, away.'

Then despite himself he was cheering hoarsely, heard the men around him yelling too. He threw his leg over the lifeline, rolled over, and was starting down when he saw he wasn't the first. A round little figure was plucking its way down the net ahead of him.

The ship rolled, and his hands cramped on rough wet hemp as his boots brushed the sea. Then he was jerked upward, flying through the air. A kapok float danced about his legs like a puppy.

The net slammed down again. Above him the others clung grimly, heads bent. With sudden horror, he realized none of them had rifles. They'd forgotten them in the rush forward. He'd forgotten, too. Should he order them back . . . no, too late, they were committed.

Almost there. He wound one arm into the ropework, and twisted around to look.

A pudgy figure poised itself, stepped out, and disappeared from his line of sight, between the ship and the submarine.

'Vogel!' he yelled, letting himself down another foot or two, shielding his eyes against the insane glare of the searchlights.

The sub rolled away. Across from him, on rounded wave-washed steel, the departmental yeoman was running aft. He wasn't on the deck flat, but the curved pressure hull. The submarine rolled back, and he dropped to his knees, holding to some intake or protrusion Dan couldn't see. Then he was up again. He gained the stern and disappeared around the missile fairing.

It was too far now to leap after him. *Ryan*'s stern was being blown down against the submarine, but her bow was pivoting away. He was getting ready to try anyway when Vogelpohl reappeared, above them now, swinging the grapnel. He tucked it under his arm for a moment, coiling the line, then hurled the bitter end across the black gap of sea toward Dan.

It uncoiled in the air and lashed across his chest, wet and heavy. He snatched at it and almost lost. Then he had it. He whipped it through the net and bent it on with two half hitches, using his free hand and his teeth. When he looked up again, Volgepohl was doubled, hauling it taut, then stooping to make it fast to some cleat or grating on the deck.

'Follow me,' Dan screamed up at the other terrified faces. He waited for the roll, then made a clumsy half leap, half-pulling himself along the line.

His boots hit not painted steel but some sort of rubber coating. It gave for an inch or two, then went solid. He leaned into it, hauling himself hand over hand up the line.

Halfway across, the pistol slipped out of his belt and burrowed down his pants leg. There was nothing he could do about it. It made a thud like a handball as it hit the rubber, bounced, and disappeared into the sea.

'Fuck,' he muttered.

Then he was up, hauling himself the last couple of feet up onto the missile deck, and Vogelpohl was leaning down with his hand out. Lenson staggered upright, stumbling as his reflexes misjudged the roll.

He stood on a reeling rectangle twenty feet wide and

seventy long. At the forward end towered the sail. Two horizontal diving planes stretched out from it, the tips nearly touching the sea at the extremity of each roll. Aft of it, reaching toward him, two deep grooves ran along the top of the missile bay, then sloped behind him, disappearing into a welter of white water around the tail fin.

That was all – except for *Ryan* looming over them, flinging herself from side to side so desperately the sea surged out in great white billows over the even more desperately rolling sub.

Greenwald came off the net and scrambled toward him. Then Coffey. They both had axes, the handles stuffed down the backs of their jackets. He waited till Rambaugh got across, too, then waved them forward and aft.

Okay, first order of business . . . he ran ten steps forward, then came to a hopping, cursing halt as his toe caught the edge of one of the hatches. 'What the fuck!' he muttered, bending down.

It was opening, very slowly. He could hear grinding beneath him in the fairing.

He bent closer, wishing for a hand light. But in the flicker glare, black then brilliant, of the searchlights, he could still make out the foot-thick tapered steel plug of a missile hatch. It was hinged on the outboard edge. He could hear gears grinding somewhere, driving it slowly up. He couldn't see what was beneath it. But he could guess. A waterproof, frangible diaphragm, to keep out any stray leaks submerged.

Then the blunt ablative snout of a submarine-launched ballistic missile.

'Nothin' hung up aft, far as I can see. What you got there, sir?'

Greenwald. He looked up, and their eyes met. Then Dan's shifted to what the seaman carried over his shoulder.

When the ax head was down as far as he could reach in the gap of the massive hinge, he straightened. They watched as the hatch edge drove gradually back into it.

The inch-thick hardened steel ax head buckled slowly, like warm chocolate. The oak haft splintered with a crack like a pistol shot.

He spun to face the ship. Across fifty yards of black water, he stared into the triple suns of the searchlights. When he shaded his eyes, though, he could see them. The after five-inches.

Pointed right at him.

Destroy B41 immediately if sonar indicates imminent missile launch.

'What's next, man?'

'They're trying to launch these things, Rocky.'

'Yeah? We better –'

Rambaugh jogged up. He squinted at the hatch, then at Dan. 'What you want us to do, sir?'

They were all looking at him: Coffey and Greenwald, Vogelpohl and Rambaugh.

There was only one thing left, and it was probably useless. Whoever was up there would probably just shoot them. But do nothing, and they'd all die for sure.

They had to try to take the submarine.

He shouted 'Follow me,' and began running toward the sail. Boots thudded behind him, but he didn't look back to see how many.

Coming around the sail, he ran full tilt into a man in black foul-weather gear coming down ladder rungs welded on the outboard side. '*Kto eto?*' he said. For a second, they gaped at each other.

Then he was swinging a clumsy fist, missing Dan by a good six inches. Dan grabbed the Russian's jacket as he followed through, spun with him as his balance vanished, then let go, releasing him overboard as a sea roared over the rounded bow. It forced him and Rambaugh, behind him, to grab the ladder rungs and each other, clinging against the freezing seconds-long body slam of the Arctic sea.

When it dropped away, the man he'd shoved overboard was no longer there, but another was climbing down in his place. Dan punched him in the head before he could step away from the ladder. The crewman waggled his chin and dropped into a crouch, grabbing a handhold on the sail as they rolled violently. Dan tried to punch him in the face. This time the man parried the blow like a kitten batting away a dust ball. He was big as Isaacs, big as any man aboard *Ryan*. Dan fell back along the narrow deck, wishing more than he'd ever wished for anything before that he'd been more careful with the .45.

He couldn't just keep retreating. He had to get up that ladder, into the sail, interrupt the launch somehow. It didn't matter what happened to him then. He *had* to.

But more men were sliding down now behind the big one, jumping from above onto the diving plane, then sliding down the ladder to the rolling, heaving deck. On the narrow, wave-drenched catwalk between the sail and the sea, there was room for only one at a time.

The hulk growled. He let go of the cleat and came at Lenson, and Rambaugh shouted, 'Behind you, sir! The ax!'

Dan grabbed it and lunged into a roundhouse swing. The Soviet leaped back and the blade slammed into the sail, snapping off the haft. Dan gaped at it as someone shouted angrily above them, harsh peremptory barks of command.

The giant growled again and rushed him, and without thinking at all, Dan checked him Naval Academy lacrosse-style in the gut with the splintered end of the ax handle. He fell, but tore the haft from Lenson's hands as he went down. The others charged over him, shouting, and Dan turned and ran.

When he got back to the fairing, it was packed with Russians. Apparently there was a hatch astern, over the engine room. He was quickly surrounded. Fists and clubs hit him in the back and sides. His life jacket soaked up the first blows, but then he caught a seaboot in the crotch.

The flare of agony blotted out the night. He fell into the water that swirled around the staggering, battling men. He lay there unable to breathe, gagging, waiting for the kicks that would finish him.

They didn't come. He forced his eyes open at last, to see that his assailants, and the fight, had moved aft.

The rolling deck was covered with reeling, punching, splashing sailors, a despairing, drunken barroom brawl swept by thigh-deep seas. Greenwald ducked under a pale-faced Russian's swing, then literally waded into him, long arms flailing. Coffey had a half nelson on the one Dan had dropped, but who'd come back, apparently, for more; the seaman's arm pistoned as he rabbit-punched him. Vogelpohl was keeping two staggering crewmen at bay with the grapnel. Still the *Ryan* sailors were outnumbered. The Soviets were closing in on them, forcing them back toward the stern.

He jerked his attention back to the sail – to two men up there watching the melee. They had rifles. What were they doing? They could sweep this whole deck with fire.

Christ, he thought, I've got to do something. He sucked air into the vacuum in his belly and pried himself to his knees. He balanced there, gasping, in a weaving, uncertain stance.

Suddenly something small, and round, and dark arched upward from *Ryan's* deck. It arched and then dropped, falling directly for him. He froze. It seemed to slow, and he watched it fall, and his breath stopped in his throat.

He struggled to his feet, caught it, and spun. It splashed into the sea off the port side before he realized it wasn't what he thought it was.

More of them fell out of the searchlight glare, a volley of them. This time they were aimed at the Russians. The sub's crew fell back, shouting warnings to each other as the spheres hit, bounced across the deck, and rolled into the raging water. Some of them doubled abruptly, vomiting into the seas that rolled back and forth over the deck.

A ragged cheer came from aft.

When he turned, a second wave was leaping off the nets. Gunner's mates, quartermasters, messmen from *Ryan*, hastily dressed out in peacoats and foul-weather jackets, carrying baseball bats, chipping hammers, ball-peen hammers, dogging wrenches. They carried more of the round things, too. There was the windup; the peg – and another volley of Idaho potatoes mowed into the Soviet sailors, low and vicious this time, hardball pitches. He heard them thud home on chests and heads.

The line of seasick Russians wavered, bowed, then fell back under the onrush of shouting destroyermen.

Dan turned and sprinted forward, toward a suddenly empty section of deck below the great wings of the diving planes. Spray blew across the deck, isolating him briefly. When he came out of it, he was at the sail, and there, stretching upward, were welded steel rungs.

He grabbed them, not stopping to think, and began climbing as fast as he could.

It took longer than he expected. He was still weak from the groin shot. He was wheezing when he saw the turn of the sail outlined above him by a smear of light on wet metal. Someone was shouting on the far side.

For a moment he wondered: Is this smart? Then he remembered that there were no other options. He crouched for a second, listening, then poked his head over the coaming.

Black silhouettes. The vertical shafts of periscopes to his right. Confused shapes.

Then his eye made sense of them.

The men ranged by the periscope stands had guns, but they weren't firing. Someone between him and them was shouting at them. Instead of obeying, though, they were just looking down, their backs to him. One had slung his rifle and was clinging to the shears, gagging.

Dan grabbed the last rung and hauled himself with a convulsive shudder up and over the top of the sail.

Into a sort of wet steel cockpit, with folded-down windshields, and instruments, and loudspeakers bolted to the bulkheads. Gratings rattled faintly under his boots. And there was light, a round yellow circle of it just in front of him – leading down.

At that moment, one of *Ryan*'s searchlights licked up, right into his eyes. He flung his hand up, blinded. Then it flicked away, and he made out the man opposite him.

At the far side of the cockpit, a Soviet officer in a blue peaked cap leaned against the coaming. He was shouting at the men on the shears. His face was livid, enraged, his voice was cracking, but they didn't stir.

Then he bent to the open hatch, and the light from below glinted from the gold braid, from the red star.

He looked to be Packer's age. Under dark wet hair his rounded face was deathly white, with great bruises of fatigue. His mouth was a knife cut angled down, working angrily, screaming into the trunk. But again there was no response Dan could see.

The officer straightened, and looked out at *Ryan* again. His back was still to Dan. His profile moved against the glare of the searchlights, turning from the American destroyer to the smaller outline of the Soviet AGI, which was moving in now, Dan saw, to make up on the sub's leeward side.

The captain wheeled suddenly, and their gazes locked across the cockpit. The exhausted, swollen eyes widened, but only for an instant. Then he didn't look surprised anymore. He just looked . . . tired.

His right hand came up. Dan saw that it held a pistol.

'No!' Lenson shouted, and lunged forward. He was almost there when his boot hit ice, a slick patch on the grating, and his feet flew out from under him.

He hit with stunning force at the same moment that he heard the flat pop of a shot, faint even this close, and whipped away instantly by the freezing wind.

He woke into blackness and the sounds of a ship in a heavy seaway. He was flat on his back in the dark. His fingers crept across his chest like exploring roaches. They slid along rope. Was he a prisoner? Then they found the familiar switch of his own bunk light.

He fumbled the blanket back over him, checked the line that crossed his legs and chest, lashing him in against the rolls. Then he lay back, listening to the accustomed complaint of old steel, the rush of the sea, the steady keening howl of wind. Was it his imagination, or was it increasing again?

Then he remembered, all at once. His fingers found his head, and explored the back of it tentatively. It felt like wet cardboard.

Gradually he became aware of fatigue and chills that made his legs tremble. His clothes were damp, but he wasn't up to taking them off. He stared at the photograph, his eyes burning. *Susan, Betts, I love you.* . . . He couldn't remember the last time he'd slept. Four days, five? Bridge watch, CIC, endless motion, reek of barf, acid gut from endless cups of reboiled Navy coffee. When he retched now, that was all that came up. If he lived through this, he'd never drink coffee again. Under his sodden, dirty clothes his legs and arms ached with bruises.

What had happened, what had happened to his men? . . .

He was seized with a sudden uncontrollable rage at whoever had sent them here with such insane orders. Sent an obsolete ship, ready for the scrap heap, out chasing storms in the Arctic winter! In some plush, heated office, some gold-braided bureaucrat had shrugged and lifted a cheek to fart and staked them out like a rabbit in a dog pound. Then when it came time to stop a nuke, expected them to play goalie. . . . Lassard was right. They were idiots to acquiesce in this. Fools to carry out such orders. He lay under the humming light and trembled with fatigue and anger.

And they would *stay* out here. . . .

For how long? Till the last boiler gave out, or the rudder jammed, and *Ryan* toppled past the razor limit of stability? Till the submarines en route, hearing the tearing steel of a breaking ship, surfaced to search the roaring waste for corpses still clinging to life jackets with frozen arms?

Thinking of that, he swung his arm up. The hands stood vertical. 2400.

Midnight: the estimated time of arrival of the U.S. and British attack boats. And by inference, the Soviet subs would not be far behind.

He lay whispering mad curses till his rage failed and faded into darkness as the ship rumbled and groaned around him. His last thought was, Would they be at war when he awoke?

And his last clear image was of Packer, his gray face set relentlessly forward against the oncoming sea.

He knew then that if they were, *Ryan* would fire, and receive, the first deadly exchange.

4

THE INCIDENT

19

Latitude 64°–33′ North, Longitude 07°–53′ West: 120 Miles North of the Faeroe Islands

'Mr. Lenson.'

'G'way,' he muttered.

But the voice had penetrated into the country beneath the ice, a subterranean forest carpeted by gray-green moss that heaved and bucked under his feet. He'd been lost in it for days. Again and again, he'd had to choose between forks in the path, with no hint of which was right. At the end of some were monsters, but his .45 wasn't there when he reached for it. Once only the unexpected discovery that he could fly saved him. At first Susan had been beside him, and a child he didn't recognize. Then he was alone. Now at last he approached the central treasure. It lay across a black river on which floated a black swan. He pulled away toward the bulkhead, burrowing back into the dream.

He was wading into the black water when a hand shook a self he did not know existed, undeniably him but existing in a different reality. . . . He sat up suddenly and blinked down over the bunk edge into a hacked-off-looking face. 'What you want, Pettus?'

'Wake-up call, sir.'

He checked his watch, rubbed his eyes, and looked again. The hands didn't make sense. Evening or morning? Then in a rush, he remembered the submarine, the eyes of the Soviet captain, the shot. . . . He touched his head gingerly. How had he gotten back to *Ryan*?

'It's oh-seven hundred. You up? I got to get back to the bridge. They want you up there.'

'You mean in CIC – '

'We're not in Condition Three anymore. There's been

some changes. Lieutenant Evlin swapped the bill around during the night to give the regular guys some sleep.'

Changes, he thought. He could feel that *Ryan* was riding differently. She was rising and falling to quartering seas, but compared to the creative violence of the last week, it was almost gentle. 'Thanks,' he said, and tried to roll out before he remembered the safety line. 'Tell them I'll be up in fifteen.'

After he washed his face, surprised that fresh water came from the tap, he stuck his head into the wardroom. It had been swept, the chairs were upright, and a tray of sticky buns was lashed down on the table with shock cords. The light was on on the coffee warmer. He grabbed buns in a napkin and found a Styrofoam cup. He alternated quick hungry bites with gulps of scalding brew on the way up to the bridge.

The sky was inky and the pilothouse was dark except for one bulb forward where three men were replacing the windows. The foghorn droned as he groped his way to the single officer on watch. He was surprised to recognize Evlin. Where was the JOD? Where was the captain? The ops officer returned his 'Good morning' wearily.

'You don't sound good, Al.'

'I'm all right. Look, I told Pettus I didn't want you if you don't feel up to it. A crack on the head, that can have delayed effects – '

'I think I'm okay. But I don't know how I got here.'

'Where, on the ship? Rambaugh brought you back.'

'Oh. Well, I think I'm fit for duty, sir. I needed the sleep more than anything.'

'Okay, here's what let's do: Rich'll be up in a few minutes to relieve me. I'll give you the gouge now and turn over the conn. It's not the regular watch rotation, but we should be back on that by tonight.'

He wondered briefly about Packer's order to Evlin to lay below. What was the ops officer's status? But he didn't want to ask. So he just said, 'Roger, sir.'

'We're on one-eight-five, speed fifteen – '

'One-eight-five?'

'Here's the situation. After Olferiev . . . shot himself, the captain reported it and asked for instructions. CIN-CLANTFLT told him to return the sub over to the AGI and to render assistance if necessary. The trawler put some guys aboard with pumps and they got the flooding stopped. She's escorting it north on the surface, restored to Soviet command. Back to Murmansk, is my guess.

'*Ryan* has been recalled due to low fuel state and successful mission accomplishment. We've been heading south since oh-two hundred. Seas and wind have continued to drop. Number-two switchboard's back up and we have power restored aft. The damage controlmen are welding a hard patch in the fireroom. Dewatering's started forward. Evaporator's back on the line and we have fresh water from oh-six hundred to oh-eight hundred. Am I going too fast?'

'No, hell no, sir.' He swallowed, staring out at a blackness that looked both exactly the same and yet somehow much friendlier than it had last night. 'It sounds great.'

'Wind's from three-one-zero, twenty-five knots. Nothing on the radar. Weather is fog and fine drizzle, visibility one to two miles. Sounding fog signals in accordance with the international rules of the road. Guarding air-distress and marine frequencies. One and two boilers on the line while drying out three and four in the after fireroom. Eight hundred and fifty degrees superheat. Plant is cross-connected. Number-two turbogenerator providing electical power.'

'Got it. Where's the captain?'

'Sea cabin. I don't think he's feeling well, so I haven't been bothering him, but he said be sure and call him if anything happens. He was awake last time I called him, about the fog.'

'I relieve you, sir.'

'This is Lieutenant Evlin; Ensign Lenson has the conn.'

Dan looked around, trying to think whether there was anything else he should do. His fingers set the binoculars. They still felt numb. The quartermaster was changing the charts, unrolling the paper tube and holding it down with his elbows while he applied masking tape. Coffey's hands lay asleep on the wheel, his binnacle-lighted face somnolent. The ash on his cigarette trembled an inch long. Dan couldn't imagine him on the deck of a submarine, swinging an ax.

Pettus chewed gum beside the ship's bell, humming 'Light My Fire' and switching his hips to the beat as he wrote in a logbook.

'That's the last window, sir,' said the leading damage controlman. 'It's tight. Just give that monkey shit couple hours to set before you can lean on it.'

'Thanks. That looks good, Traven.'

He looked out through the new Plexiglas. In the false dawn the sea was dark as shattered slate under a fine drizzle. He could make out whitecaps close in, white as boiling milk but without curl or spray. Coming from astern, they took a long time to catch up. When they did, the old destroyer seemed to hold her breath, traveling for seconds tilted slightly forward. A 2,250-ton surfboard, he thought. Farther out was nothing but the glow of fog reflecting the ship's lights, green or red or white depending on which point of the compass you looked out along.

Thinking of that, he checked the centerline gyro. Coffey was dead on one-eight-five. The clock ticked. The anemometer needle oscillated around twenty-five. The barometer was up. He realized that he was standing on the deck without holding the overhead brace, without having to wedge himself into a corner.

'Well, I'll be darned,' he said out loud.

Norden came up a few minutes later. He looked around the bridge. 'What's going on?'

'Heading south. Al says we got a recall message.'

'He say where to?'

'Who cares? As long as it's not north again.'

'Good point. Where is he? Where's Al?'

'In the chartroom, I think.'

'You're not supposed to have it alone, Dan. You're not a qualified OOD yet.'

'Well, he's the senior watch officer, Rich. I figured if he trusts me, it's okay.'

'Keep your voice down. Don't argue with me. And don't call me Rich on the bridge.'

When Evlin went below, Norden wanted the conn. Dan went through the turnover, keeping resentment from his voice with difficulty. Something was eating the weapons officer.

But he decided he didn't mind. He felt like a man who's just been told his surgery won't be necessary, after all. Maybe they were going back to Newport! The thought made his heart leap. When he finished the turnover, he drifted over to the chart table, whistling under his breath the same Doors song Pettus had been humming.

Their new track extended south for four hundred miles, past the Faeroes, then bent west to take them along the coast of Scotland. Past that, it ended off the Rockall Bank, west of the Hebrides. His elation yielded to a penknife twist of alarm.

'You know where we're going, Chief Yardner?'

'I don't know, Mr. Lenson. What did Lieutenant Evlin say?'

'He didn't. Just that we were going south.'

Norden came over. He said wearily, 'Goddamn it, you're supposed to read the message board before you relieve. Here it is . . . "proceed to rendezvous point Lima, such and such a latitude and longitude, for rendezvous with CTG twenty-one point one aboard USS *Kennedy*. Refuel as conditions permit with USS *Carloosahatchee*. Thence accompany *Kennedy* Carrier Battle Group for operations in the eastern Atlantic."' He let the sheaf of messages fall to the end of its cord. 'Shit.'

'What's that mean, Rich – I mean, Lieutenant?'

'There goes Christmas.'

'But I thought . . . Al said our operation was over. Doesn't that mean we get to go home? I – '

'That was the original plan, do the tests and then zip back to home port. This's new. Probably what happened, some other can had to drop out, and we're already out here, so we get moved over two squares to plug the donkey. *Kennedy*'s an aircraft carrier. Be good for you, you need experience working in a formation.'

'Yes, sir. But they can't keep us out here much longer, can they? Do you think we'll get any repairs before we head back?'

'That's possible. England or Spain would be my guess.'

England . . . he'd always wanted to go bicycling there, to see the Strand, Baker Street, all the places he'd read about.

Spain would be fun, too. If only Susan could join him there. Still, he felt better. It was amazing what rack time and a course change could do. His hand found one of the pastries in his pocket. 'D'you get any sleep, sir?' he asked around a mouthful.

Norden propped a foot against the binnacle. 'Couple hours. You?'

'Don't know how much, but I was out like a dead dog.'

'Good.' Norden looked out at the sea, checked his watch. 'Pretty quiet right now. . . . I'll give you the conn back after a while.'

Dan understood that as an apology for snapping at him. He checked the radar, swallowed the last of the bun, and after a time thought of the division. He went to the window and looked down on the fo'c'sle in the pewter light. The safety lines were still rigged, but the life nets had been triced up again. A tatter of blanket flapped at the corner of the gun mount. There was no one in sight, though. He went out on the wing and looked aft. The breeze was fresh but already seemed less frigid. No one there, either, not at the swung-in whaleboat, not in the breakers, no one at work on deck at all as far as he could see. He went back inside.

'Pettus, what did we do for quarters today?'

'Exec said muster on station, Mr. Lenson.'

'Thanks.' Great, he thought; if the guys were getting their heads down without Bryce objecting, he was damned if he would. 'You catch up some on your sleep last night?'

'Yeah. Mr. Evlin got some of the signalmen down here, said there wasn't anybody for them to wave their skivvies at, anyway. They spelled the lookouts some. We broke guys off to go crap out.'

They pitched steadily southward through the morning watch. At noon, Ohlmeyer relieved him. Dan went below to find a hot lunch waiting: bean soup, swiss steak, collard greens, peach pie. The wardroom was crowded for the first time in days. Weaver, the comm officer, had the latest poop. *Ryan* would be steaming with the task group for two weeks, screening the carrier during an exercise west of Ireland.

Then they'd put into Rota, Spain, for five days alongside the tender before heading home.

'Do you know why they diverted us, Ralph?' Dan asked him.

'Boiler explosion on *Jonas Ingram*, DD-nine thirty-eight. Burned a couple guys pretty bad.'

'Do they know about our damage?'

'I don't see everything that goes out, but I think so, yeah. We were putting out two reports a day during the *Pargo* play, and then every couple of hours while we were tracking the Russian. The captain reported all the equipment casualties and gave the weather data. But he always finished up by saying we could continue the mission. I guess they needed us more here than they did in Newport.'

'Won't we need an air-search radar to play with the carrier?'

'You're thinking again, George. Leave that to people with more than one stripe, okay? They got a cruiser with a lot better air picture than we'd ever get. Usually, we just plane guard, tag around after the flattop in case one of the fly-boys has to punch out.' Weaver returned his attention to his pie.

Dan was back in his room, torn between another nap and a long-overdue start on a letter to Susan, when the phone squealed. 'Lenson,' he snapped.

'Dan? This is Commander Bryce.'

'Uh – yes, sir.'

'I can't seem to locate Mr. Norden. Could you find him and come down to my stateroom, please?'

He suddenly remembered the search of the compartment, the interviews, his confrontation with Lassard. It seemed like months ago. But it had only been days. The executive officer wouldn't have forgotten. He hadn't been standing watch, or missing sleep.

'Aye, aye, sir,' he said, hearing wariness and hostility edge his voice. 'We'll be right down.'

He knocked at the exec's door with the same fatalistic dread he remembered from Plebe Year. When the drawl soaked through the aluminum he took a breath and pushed it open.

'Ensign Lenson, sir.' God, how he hated that rhyme.

'Come in, Dan. So, hear you played Charge of the Light Brigade out there last night.'

Last night? Had it only been last night? He sat on the sofa and looked at the XO with a strange mix of feelings. He still hated him, but the fat lieutenant commander looked less intimidating now. Compared to forty feet of oncoming sea, or a live torpedo, or an armed Soviet sailor.

'Popeye and the other men did most of it, sir. I just sort of supervised.'

'That so? I heard different. Heard you did us proud.'

He didn't know how to respond to a compliment from Bryce, so he didn't say anything. There'd probably be something less pleasant along pretty soon, anyway.

Bryce didn't offer him a cigar this time. Instead he pulled out a file. The XO looked rested and chipper as he studied it, then laid it aside. He light a Camel, then leaned back, smiling. It wasn't the same smile at all – it wasn't dreamy or remote – but it still made Dan think of Lassard.

'I think we have something to talk about. That is, you – you and Norden – I know a lot's been going on, but I believe y'all still owe me a report on that there investigation. That right?'

'Yes, sir.'

'Well? You got one?'

'Yes sir.'

'Where's the lieutenant?'

'Up forward, sir. He asked me to send his respects and report that he had to supervise the dewatering of the powder magazine at present.'

'Oh?' Bryce frowned. 'I guess we'll have to make do with you, then. Okay, proceed.'

'Sir, an exhaustive investigation was conducted over a period of two days,' Dan began, slipping into the official passive of Navy correspondence. 'The bunkroom was searched from deck to overhead, and compartment cleaners and personnel who bunked near the site of the cache were interviewed. I then proceeded to interview every member of First Division. That process was completed, uh – two days before yesterday? Anyway, just after *Pargo* left. Sir.'

'So good; I was afraid the two of you would slough it off, try to pass off some phony gun-deck job on me. Did you find out whose it was?'

He felt dismay. The way the exec had phrased it made it impossible to wriggle out of the question. He said slowly, 'Yes, sir. I found out – whose it was.'

'Good! I'll teach him to possess unauthorized drugs on my ship. Who is he?'

'Sir, I have to say this carefully. The guilty man is in my division. But I gave him my word that what we had discussed, including his name, was between the two of us.'

Bryce looked at him for a moment without really having an expression on his face. He tapped the file folder on his desk. It gaped open for a moment, and Dan saw that it was empty. After a moment, the XO shook out another cigarette. He measured the end slowly with flame.

'I'm not real sure I understand what you're trying to tell me here, Lenson.'

'Well, sir, it went this way. I interviewed every man, from senior to junior. I kept the one I suspected most till last. I had no leads. Nobody knew anything. When he, too admitted nothing, I was faced with failure of the investigation.'

'Go on.'

'To avoid that, I tried as a last resort to get him to talk to me man to man, off the record. He laughed and agreed. He then admitted that the marijuana was his, that he had more, and that he sold it among the crew along with other drugs.'

He had thought about this up till the Soviets had diverted his and everyone else's attention. It was a fine question: his reponsibility to the ship against his word to Lassard. He knew it wouldn't go over well. He wasn't even sure it was right. But it was what he'd done.

'Okay.' The XO leaned back again, blowing a smoky circle in the direction of the ventilator. 'Now I hear you. I like quick thinking in a junior officer. So, who was this trusting lamb?'

'I can't tell you, sir.'

'Lassard, right? Just nod.'

He didn't nod. 'I can't tell you who it was, sir.'

'I know, he told you in confidence. That's fine. I like to see a sense of honor, too – as long as it's balanced against efficiency and safety.

'Now, I'm sure you can understand my position here. The safety and welfare of the crew, that's my bailiwick, Dan. Jimmy John deals with the relations of the command with outside security. But he leaves the day-to-day management to the exec. As he should. As long as he shows he can handle it, that is. And that means solving knotty little issues like this.

'Now, you know you just gave the game away. You said you went from senior to junior and the guilty man was last, and Slick, course he's a seaman recruit – can't get any more junior than that. So let's just say it's understood. Now we've got that out of the way, where do you think we should put the nails?'

Dan stared at Bryce's little eyes. The XO had trumped him. He tried to keep his tone neutral. It came out stubborn instead. 'No, sir, that's an incorrect inference. The rank order was not that rigid.'

'Do you *deny* it was Lassard?'

'I'm not *denying* it, sir, I just can't answer that question.'

'Can't, or won't?'

'Can't, sir.'

Bryce examined the overhead. 'Mr. Lenson, without some kind of backup in the way of proof – such as this here confession you got – I can't do squat to Mr. Dope Pusher. Those goddamn shore-side sea lawyers would tear me up one side and down the other. This is all well and good, but what use is it to us if we can't bend your damn scruples a little, like we all have to once in a while, so we can get anything done? Will you tell me that?'

'What did you plan to do, sir?'

'God*damn* it!' The exec threw down his cigarette, which bounced off the ashtray, throwing sparks. He retrieved it hastily from the carpet, but the accident seemed to irritate him further. He started to stub it out, then changed his mind and lighted another from it. 'This is too much,' he muttered. 'Okay. The book says, confine the suspect till we get back to Newport, then turn him over to the Naval Investigative Service. But I don't see no point in doing that till we give him a chance to straighten out and fly right from now on.

'So what I *planned*, Ensign, if you don't *mind*, is to confine the goddamn suspect in the supply locker, then have him up to mast in front of the captain and bust – well, we can't bust a seaman recruit, but we can sure as hell make sure he doesn't draw a collar of pay or walk on grass again till his enlistment expires, that's for damn sure. Does that satisfy you? He's selling drugs through the ship. Isn't he?'

'Yes, sir.'

'You condone that shit?'

'No, sir,' said Dan miserably.

'Look here, boy. I understand your problem. Honor, honesty, they're important. But discipline is, too. I don't believe you've got the right perspective on this business. That Annapolis stuff may be all right when you're dealing officer to officer. But his here's the real world. You can't have people working on engines, and guns, and such as that with their heads in a cloud of dope.'

'I'm sorry, sir. I guess I screwed up, telling him that.'

'No, goddamn it, I already said you handled that part right. Look.' The exec hitched his chair forward. 'I've had a bellyful of this crap! There's other people trying to stop me establishing naval discipline aboard this ship. You know who I mean.'

'Well – no, sir, I don't.'

'I mean my laid back, liberal, let-the-animals-pee-on-the-carpet department heads. People like them are handing out a load of hokum all over the country, and I don't need to tell you who's behind it all. You can see the sorry results of that, goddamn sandals on the steps of the White House! You can see it on *Ryan*, too. And how they turn yellow when the chips are down.' The avuncular tone was gone; as Dan was wearily becoming aware, it was only another tactic. 'So, let's just cut through the bullshit. Give me his name and everything goes smooth. You don't, then far as I'm concerned, you're making yourself a party to it. And once I start hoeing that row, I'm telling you now, I go all the way to the end.'

He wanted to apologize, to explain, but he'd done that already. He stared at the exec helplessly.

'For the last time: You won't tell me?'

'Sir – believe me, I'd like to, but – '

'Hold it right there,' said Bryce. He lifted his chin a little and suddenly looked shrewd. 'Yeah . . . tell you what. Seems to me maybe that crack on the head got you a little confused. Maybe you need time to think about this. Considering how important it's going to be when it comes time for me to write your first fitness report.' He picked up the folder again. In a dry, uninterested voice, he added, 'We'll talk about this later, Ensign. Dismissed.'

Outside the door, Dan paused. He looked at his hands. They were shaking. Thoughts bounced around his mind like scared rabbits. Bryce didn't seem so harmless now. He'd rather face the forty-foot sea. At least if it got him, Susan would be taken care of. But if Bryce shafted him, he'd never get promoted, and if he didn't get promoted, he'd be out, with a wife and infant on his hands.

He thought very clearly: Maybe I should tell him. USS *Reynolds Ryan* wasn't the Naval Academy, Bryce was sure as hell right about that. Did you have to keep your word with scum like Lassard? He'd laugh if you expected him to keep his. If someone else, if the captain had asked him . . . anyone other than Bryce . . .

But what was this business about giving Slick a chance to 'straighten out'? Something didn't sound right about that. It didn't sound like the way Bryce operated, to give anybody a second chance once he had them on the deck looking up.

He wanted to go back inside so much, he made himself turn and walk aft. Away from the gray door. No, he thought. I made a mistake promising Lassard confidentially. I shouldn't have given him the opening. I screwed up again trying to waffle with Bryce. Breaking his word would just be another wrong move. He'd never get to whatever made Slick Lassard run then.

He had the feeling he was making a lot of mistakes, even for an ensign. But sooner or later, Slick would foul up, too. He'd just have to be on his ass steady from now on. He thought of Lassard's words on the forecastle. And when I catch him off base, Dan thought grimly, I've got to ax the bastard.

Before he axes all of us.

*

Late that afternoon the 1MC announced that both evaporators were fixed and water hours were lifted until further notice. He luxuriated in a two-quart shower and his first shave in days.

Second dog, he thought, planting one foot ahead of the other up the bridge ladderwell. Two hours, then seven hours in the bag till the next watch. He wondered what it would be like operating with a carrier. He decided to break out the tactical publications over the next couple of days and bone up on stationkeeping before they rendezvoused.

The daylight had lasted longer today, but when he got topside it was dark again. The seas had dropped even more and the drizzle had cleared. The pilothouse seemed quieter than usual. After a moment, he realized that for the first time in a week the wipers were quiet. The captain was in his chair, head back on the leather headrest at an uncomfortable-looking angle. He was snoring, something Dan hadn't heard him do before.

Silver was standing by the chart table, digging wax out of his ears with the eraser end of a pencil. They discussed the turnover in low tones. Course and speed were unchanged. Dan glanced at Packer. 'The old man's still tired,' he muttered.

'He was up writing the after-action report. Then he went down to watch them welding up the feed-water tank. Then he had to answer some more messages. I think he's caught your roommate's cold, too.'

'How could Chow Hound give him a cold? Guy's never on the bridge.'

Silver shrugged. They reported to Evlin, then the jaygee went below.

Dan studied the captain. Packer's mouth gaped. He sounded congested, as if it was hard for him to breathe. His hands twitched on the armrests. Into Dan's mind came a picture of him at the height of the storm: cool, deliberate, unaffected by fear or fatigue. Some things James Packer did puzzled him. Some seemed foolhardy. But he had to admit he was a hell of a seaman.

During his musing, Evlin had drifted to the starboard side of the bridge. The lieutenant reached now to the speaker that monitored the distress frequencies. When he turned it up a hissing roar, like a rain shower on a tin roof, filled the bridge. He turned it down. The captain didn't stir. He turned it up again. The snore faltered. Evlin turned the static down again. After a moment Packer's hands twitched. They crept to his waist, groped for the seat belt. He opened his eyes suddenly.

'What's going on?'

'Sorry, sir, just checking the circuits.'

Packer's eyelids sank again.

'Sir, you had dinner yet? Spaghetti and ice cream tonight.'

A grunt. 'What time is it?'

'Eighteen fifteen, sir, second sitting. Mr. Lenson and I have the watch. The scope's clear, visibility's good. Why don't you grab some chow, maybe get your head down in your cabin.'

The captain stretched. He coughed into his handkerchief and blew his nose. Then he searched out his pipe, tucked it in his mouth, and got up. He prowled about the bridge, peered at the barometer, the radarscope, the chart, and then disappeared.

'Captain's off the bridge,' Pettus announced.

'Pretty clever. You do that often?'

'No. You get to know how a CO'll react after a while.'

Dan thought how weary Packer had looked. At his age, fighting a ship through a storm must be ten times as exhausting as it was at twenty-one. He thought then about the captain's family, about what Lassard had told him. Maybe Evlin knew something. But he decided not to ask. The man was entitled to his privacy.

'I wish I could figure out the XO that easy.'

'Our fearless second in command been raking the coals over you?'

'You could say that.' He thought about it for a minute, then sauntered to the radio and tweaked it up again. 'Look, I maybe need some advice, sir.'

'I'm listening.'

'I can't seem to get a track on the guy. He doesn't trust anybody. And every time he talks to me, he threatens me at the end, like that's the only thing that'll keep me in line.'

'He doesn't trust me, either. In fact, he thinks I'm crazy. But whatever happens on this other business, I'll be out of the Navy pretty soon. And his fulminations will just be history.

'As far as getting along with him – I just try to remind myself that even Bryce thinks he's on the side of the angels. As long as they're white conservative angels in the proper uniform. And as long as he gets a cut of the poker games in heaven.'

Dan remembered a snowy night, a wad of money, a binocular box on the signal bridge. 'I had the feeling something like that was going on. He gets a chunk of the pot?'

'And other things. The anchor pool. Sometimes a man will need extra leave. Cash down helps it along.'

It made a lot of things clearer. Like *Ryan*'s lousy morale, and the cynical way the men talked. It made other things less clear, though. 'It doesn't seem to bother you very much.'

'I try not to judge him, Dan. He's overage. Passed over for promotion. He'll never make full commander, or have his own ship. He's looking at retirement, and he doesn't know how to do anything but shuffle Navy paper. Here, he's a big deal. On the outside, he'll be nobody. Most evil is motivated by fear.'

'You'd defend anybody, Al.'

'Sure I would. Not their actions, necessarily, but them-selves – sure.'

'What's the difference?'

'That goes back to Plato and Paul.' Evlin settled his foot in a nest of cables and Dan grinned, recognizing the start of another session of Metaphysics 101. 'Difference between flesh and spirit. You can't deny the influence of early experience, or blood chemistry But neither can you deny that something in people shines through everything that ought by rights to crush them.

'Deanne works with multiple sclerosis patients. Some of them kids, a lot more old folks – people think MS is a kids' disease, but it gets you more often between thirty and fifty. She manhandles them into the pool. They try to swim. They can hardly move without the water to hold them up. But some of them, she says, have clear, untroubled, liberated souls. The light inside shines through the sickness and age.

'So there's an element of choice involved too. But deep down, people are better than we realize. Than *they* realize.'

'You're an idealist, Al.'

'Guilty.'

'A mystic.'

Evlin chuckled. 'I think I'm a realist. I just define reality in broader terms.' He glanced at the radar, then out the window. 'Did you check the running lights when you came on?'

Dan went out on the wings, checked the sidelights, looked up at the masthead and range. He went back inside. 'All lights bright lights.'

'Very well.'

'Do you remember what we were talking about before? About how people would act if they believed what you do, that they're not really separate, but all part of the same thing?'

'Yes.'

'That it would be a different world, a better one?'

'You'd hope so,' said Evlin. He set his binoculars for a slow sweep of the sea to starboard. 'But in my less sanguine moments, I can also see it interpreted in the sense that since no one's irreplaceable, you could destroy this one or that without really losing anything.

'I think belief has to go beyond dogma. Doctrine's a dead end; it's just accepting metaphors somebody else thought up. It has to be either revealed truth, direct access, or else a conscious, consistent model you arrive at yourself and believe in enough to live by.'

'Have you got this direct access?'

'No.'

'Have you got a model?'

'It's not consistent yet. Or maybe it is, and my mind's too limited to run the program. But I know a few people who have it. I'm going to see if I can get it, too.'

'Even though you'll never be able to prove it exists.'

'Right.'

'Or explain it to me . . . because you can't communicate

that kind of stuff with words, right? So it's still a matter of my accepting your metaphor. On faith.'

'I'm afraid so.'

'Do you believe there's a God?'

'I feel something greater than myself. I don't know if it's 'alive,' or has a personality. But there's something there.'

'What does it feel like?'

Evlin didn't say anything for a while. In the chartroom the fathometer began chattering as it ran out of paper. Dan could barely hear him as he murmured, 'I guess the closest I can come is, evil and good have no meaning to this . . . power. We can cooperate with it. Or we can fight it. But either way, it's going to win. Because everything's the way it's supposed to be. And everything's going to turn out all right.'

Dan studied the lambent circle of the radar. The beam swept around smoothly, prickled by pinpoints of sea return that were gone when it came round again. But there were always more.

What Evlin was saying had a certain logic. But there was nothing he could see that tied it to the world he knew, a world of conflict and scarcity, of betrayal and pain and loss. It was too easy. No commandments, no judgment after death, no punishment – how could God punish part of Himself? It was unsatisfying. But he didn't want to say this to Evlin. If his weird faith helped him through a court-martial, he had every right to it. He sighed and finished the last of his cold coffee. 'Well, two more days, we'll be steaming with *Kennedy*.'

'That's right. They'll probably transfer me off as soon as we join up, then fly me out to the States. There'll be a trial later, probably when you get back to Newport. Officially, I'm restricted to my stateroom, but the captain said I could stand watches if I wanted. Seeing as how we're so short on qualified OODs.'

There it was, the subject he'd so carefully avoided: Evlin's refusal to fire. He didn't know what to say about it. He respected him, but if Evlin wasn't going to obey orders, what was he doing in the Navy? He said, just to say something, 'That's what the captain decided?'

'It's not like he has a choice. I refused a direct order in front

325

of witnesses, in a combat situation. He can't let anybody do that and walk.'

'I guess I understand why you did it,' he said carefully. 'But, Al – you joined the service. Why? If you felt like that?'

'I didn't then. But that was six years ago. Before I met Deanne and, through her, the Master. I've done a lot of thinking since. I had to get used to the idea that what I thought was important was worthless. I had to replace the idea of success with the idea of usefulness. Finally I concluded I had no place in an organization that exists, when you get down to it, to do violence in the service of the state. That's why I decided to resign.'

'Maybe they'll take that into account. If it's a religious issue, and you – you really thought you were right.' He didn't believe it, though, and he was afraid Evlin could hear it.

When the lieutenant spoke again, his voice had turned brisk, but it was touched, or perhaps Dan only imagined it, with regret. 'Well, I did it. I guess I've got to take what comes after.

'Okay, break out the maneuvering boards. Let's see what you know about repositioning bent-line screens.'

Latitude 53°–32′ North, Longitude 13°–50′ West: 200 Miles Due West of Ireland

'Pull!'

The disk flicked upward and dwindled swiftly. Quicker than thought, he threw the barrel up and squeezed as the bead steadied. The crack of the twelve-gauge made his ears ring.

The skeet drifted down like a feather from pillows of cumulus scattered across a sky like a blue wool blanket, and settled whole and untouched into the broad road of *Ryan*'s wake. 'Well, three out of ten, that ain't bad first time out with a scattergun,' said the potbellied gunner's mate. 'Want to try her again? Twenty rounds each training allowance.'

'Thanks, Cherry, my shoulder's starting to hurt.'

Dan handed back the riot gun and strolled forward. Inside his head tiny sirens rang only to him. Should have worn earplugs, he thought. As he reached the grills the messmen had set up on the Dash deck, his appetite wavered between the conflicting odors of roasting meat and stack gas. Gulls whirled overhead. He took a paper plate and stood in line past catsup, relish, buns, the stale, tasteless Navy potato chips. He wondered whether they specified them that way, so they'd taste the same after months at sea, like hardtack.

'What you be havin', Mr. L?'

'Double burger, cheese, I guess.'

'Coming right up.'

'Hey there, Ensign.'

When he turned, the seaman recruit was standing right behind him. 'Hello, Lassard.'

'Going for that hamburger? Or one of them officers' steaks?'

'Those steaks are for anybody who wants one. You know that.'

'Far-out. Slick'll maybe have one, then. If you're sure nobody'll mind.' Lassard kept grinning. 'Got to hand it to you. You really faked him out.'

'What are you talking about?'

'Making Slick spill his guts, thinking you'd keep the lid on. Yeah, the XO had him in last night about that. Thanks a lot, man.'

He stared at the red-rimmed eyes. 'Wait a minute, Slick – I mean, Seaman Recruit Lassard. I didn't tell him anything. You mean Bryce said that I – '

'Slick had you figured for a straight arrow. Well, he just got himself to blame. Hell, Brute Boy could of told him better than to trust the fucking brass.' Lassard hawked noisily and spat on the deck. He pushed past and sauntered toward the grills.

Dan looked after him. He hadn't expected this. But it made absolute sense. All his worry, his agonizing over doing the right thing –

Goddamn Benjamin Bryce. God *damn* him.

He settled in the deck-edge nets with the loaded plate and bug juice. He didn't want any now, but still he took a bite. Greasy low-bid hamburger, frozen for months and scorched by a messman with a day of training. Self-preservation won. He tipped it over the side and concentrated on the pickles. It was hard for the supply department to ruin pickles.

The sea gulls whirled down after the floating bread. He watched them dip and wheel over a gray-green restless sea, choppy, but welcoming compared to the Arctic. The air was still cold, though in the last two days they'd made nine hundred miles southing. It felt strange to see blue again above the slowly leaning mast.

Norden came by and he moved over on the net. The lieutenant had a New York strip. Dan looked at it, trying to decide whether to go back.

'How's it going?'

'Oh . . . so-so, Rich. So-so.'

'You getting much done up forward?'

'Well, we got all that chipped and red-leaded where the chains were knocking around.'

'Good. How are . . . other things going with the division?'

Dan looked down at the fantail. The kinnicks were queued up to shoot skeet. He wouldn't have trusted any of them with a loaded shotgun. The trap twanged and the report drifted up. A fragment separated from the clay disk. It wobbled, canted, spun down, and sliced edge-on into the face of a wave. The gulls whirled down at it, crying bitterly at being forestalled by the bottomless appetite of the sea.

'Oh, about the usual, I guess.'

'Any more evidence of drug use?'

'I don't think so. Maybe they're playing it smart.'

Norden sawed at the steak with the plastic knife. 'About that night we had to go up on the forecastle. During the storm.'

'Yes, sir?'

'You probably think I should have gone first.'

He'd thought about it. But not as much, he suspected, as Norden had. 'I didn't notice it at the time,' he said, at least half truthfully. 'You looked pretty seasick.'

'I wasn't seasick. I was scared.'

Dan examined his pickles.

'Let me tell you something. Last year during refresher training, when we were firing off Culebra, we had a hot gun. A live round jammed in the breech. It could have cooked off any time. I went out there with the gunner's mates while they cooled it down with the hoses. I didn't want to. I made myself do it.

'But this last time . . . I should have been out there with you. But I couldn't make myself go.'

'You don't have to tell me this, Rich.'

'I know,' said Norden. He rubbed his mouth with the back of his hand. 'I just wanted to let you know I'm not happy about it.'

'You don't have to take a risk just because it's there. You got a family to think of.'

'Maybe that's it.' He seemed to turn that over, then put it aside for later consideration. 'Anyway, I'll be out there with you and the guys next time.'

'Okay,' said Dan.

He decided to try a steak, and got the last one. Then it was time to go. He took the outside ladder two steps at a time, noticing as he climbed the direction of the swells and calculating the relative wind in his head.

'Ready to relieve, Mark.'

Silver had shaved his beard off, complaining that saltwater made it itch. Without it he looked like a naïve boy. He stroked his chin as he briefed on the rendezvous. 'You should have *Kennedy* and the rest of the task group in sight on your watch. The captain wants to be called as soon as we make visual contact. When we join up, we'll take station on the oiler. They'll let us know when we can come alongside to refuel.'

'Roger. Who's got the conn?'

'I do.'

'I'll take it. Al wants me to get as much experience as I can. He wants us both to be qualified OODs before he leaves.'

'Good luck.' Silver raised his voice to the helmsmen and boatswain and quartermaster. 'This is Mr. Silver: Mr. Lenson has the conn.'

Dan kept checking the radar. At 1300 he had a collection of pips ahead that looked like the task group. He went out on the wing. Lassard was standing there, binoculars dangling on his chest, staring down at the water. Dan studied the horizon. Nothing yet.

'Whatcha looking for, Ensign?'

'Ships. We should have them showing soon about zero-one-zero relative. Keep a sharp eye out and report as soon as you see them.'

'Sure.' Lassard yawned. 'That cookout was a blast. How many of them sea gulls you hit, man?'

He didn't see any point in responding. Bryce had put paid to any hope of reaching the head of the kinnicks. He was suddenly filled with a cold anger. 'Quit fucking off, Lassard. Get those binoculars up.'

'Cheery aye aye,' the seaman sneered. Dan waited till he raised them, then went back inside. When he glanced back, Lassard was staring into the water again.

At 1400 the other lookout reported masts ahead. Dan laid

his glasses against the window and caught them, half hidden by the waves that jagged the horizon, three pinpricks spaced across five degrees of ocean. A few minutes later, Packer came up. He settled into his chair with a grunt. 'What's formation course?' he asked the bridge at large in a hoarse voice.

'Don't know, sir,' said Evlin. 'The rendezvous message didn't say, and they're steaming in radio silence except for primary tactical.'

'We'll pick it up when we get closer. You say they're using pritac?'

'Yes, sir, it's short range only.'

'And radar silence?'

'That's right, sir.'

'Go ahead and shut down, then.'

Evlin bent to the intercom. A moment later, the radar picture shrank to a bright point and disappeared.

The captain said nothing more. Presently he nodded off.

The formation gradually took shape ahead. When they were close enough to make out the carrier, a tiny gray V seen end-on, Dan began taking bearings with the centerline alidade. Over several minutes, they showed a slow drift right. 'I think we're coming up astern of them,' he said to Evlin.

'Sounds good. Keep taking those bearings. We'll be depending on that, without the radar.'

He centered the alidade on the carrier and noted the bearing carefully. Tactical maneuvering was done by relative motion. You could do some by eye, but most were solved on polar coordinate paper, maneuvering boards. It could get complicated with several ships in a formation. He was nervous about it, but he'd studied up.

He could make out the oiler now. There were three other ships that through the binoculars looked to be destroyers or maybe frigates. Or maybe one of them, a bit larger, was a light cruiser. It was too far to tell.

'Okay, JOD, give me a recommendation.'

'I figure head right for the oiler, sir. Slide up her port side, outside of the formation, then drop speed to match whatever they're making.'

'Sounds good,' said Evlin, who was studying the operation order. He reached for the intercom. 'Signals, Bridge: Be alert for flag hoist or flashing light from ships ahead.'

'Sigs, aye.'

The exchange woke the captain. He stretched and sniffled and asked the boatswain to call up a cup of coffee for him. He blinked around the horizon, squinted over the bow. Then he sat up suddenly.

'Mr. Evlin. What are you doing?'

'Sir, we're going to port of the carrier and slide up outboard of the oiler.'

'Like hell we are! Which way's *Kennedy* going?'

Evlin frowned for a moment at the formation, still some eight miles distant, then lifted his binoculars. A second later, he snapped, 'All engines stop.'

'All stop, aye. Engine room answers, all engines stop, sir.'

'That bird farm's headed right down our throat, Al! Are you watching her?'

'Sir' – he glanced at Lenson – 'no, sir.'

'Get on the stick, Lieutenant! You're at all stop with superheaters lighted! Kick her in the ass, left full rudder, get the hell out of their way.'

'Ahead full. Left full rudder, steady course one-three-zero.'

'Zero-nine-zero; show them you mean it.'

'Steady course zero-nine-zero.'

The helmsman answered. The bow swung rapidly as the screws dug in again. Packer shaded a stare out the window with one hand. 'Okay. Now plot a course to station a thousand yards abeam of the oiler. Assume formation course as three-five-zero, speed ten.'

Evlin grabbed the pad of maneuvering paper, not looking at Dan. Lenson bit his lips and stared at the alidade. He could think of nothing to do but read off another bearing. He saw now that the carrier's island, her superstructure, was on the left, his right. That meant she was coming at them, not going away.

He started to sweat.

'Damn it,' said Evlin under his breath.

'I'm sorry. It's hard to tell – '

'Not if you look at them.'

Packer interrupted. 'Lenson. You understand your screw-up?'

'Yes sir. I'm sorry. I thought – '

'*Sorry* doesn't fix a goddamn thing. If you don't know what's going on, ask somebody. Al, you're letting him conn during incompany maneuvering?'

Evlin took the conn back. Dan stood rigid, waiting for Greenwald to snicker. There were mutters behind him. Greenwald snickered.

'Silence on the bridge,' said Evlin.

The gray pinpricks burgeoned rapidly into oncoming warships, flung miles apart across the gray-green sea. *Ryan* described a sweeping turn around them and fell in a mile behind the tubby silhouette of *Calloosahatchee*. Halfway through the maneuver a light began blinking from the carrier. When the signalman brought the message down, Packer scowled as he read it. He crumpled it and stared out the window.

The light began winking again, a steady chatter that went on with only an occasional bang of shutters as *Ryan*'s signalmen receipted. When this came down, Packer studied it, then held it up. 'Plot this, please.'

It was the screening plan. Dan took it back to the chartroom and pulled dividers and parallel rule from the rack. The carrier was the guide, the hub around which the other ships took station. There were four screening stations spaced around the perimeter. The destroyers would spend most of their time there, providing antisub and antiair coverage. The tanker trailed astern, within the circle but some thousands of yards behind *Kennedy*. There were also two plane guard stations, astern of the carrier to port and starboard. When aircraft were being launched or recovered, one of the destroyers would stand by there to recover the pilot should an aircraft ditch.

He diagrammed it quickly but carefully, placing a small flag in the middle to symbolize the carrier, then drawing in each screen sector. He didn't plot a course and speed. This would change as the carrier steamed hither and yon during the exercise, seeking the wind and trying to evade 'enemy' attack. When he was done it looked more like a dartboard than anything else, round, with curved numbered segments circling the bull's-eye that was *Kennedy*. He checked it against the message one last time, resolved not to screw up again, and took it out. 'Done, sir.'

Packer told him to tape it up on the bulkhead. The signalman came down with another message. The captain coughed as he read this one, then waved it at Evlin without comment. The lieutenant taped it up too. Dan went out on the wing, checked the bearing of the oiler, and came back in. 'Slow right drift, now bears zero-eight-three.'

'Where are you measuring to?'

'Her bridge.'

'Know how to use a stadimeter?'

'Yes, sir.' He got the manual range finder from its walnut box, examined it, then took it out on the wing.

'Twenty-two hundred yards, sir.'

'Indicate rpm for eleven knots. Left, steer course three-four-seven.'

'Left three-four-seven, aye ... engine room answers, eleven knots.'

Evlin kept him busy for the next few minutes. Without the radar, maneuvering was a complex combination of trigonometry, vectors, and seaman's eye. When they were exactly two thousand yards away and abeam of the oiler, Evlin came back to formation course and speed and reported to the captain that *Ryan* was on station.

'Okay, I'm going below. Call me if we get any orders or course changes.'

Things relaxed when Packer disappeared. Dan leaned against the bulkhead and read the message. It was from the task-group commander.

FM: CTG 21.1
TO: TU 21.1.2
FORWARD TO USS *RYAN* ON RENDEZVOUS
SUBJ: MANEUVERING

THIS EXERCISE WILL TEST AND HONE OUR PERFORMANCE OF SCREENING AND CLOSE-IN MANEUVERING X AT 2000Z ALL UNITS WILL SET AND ADHERE TO WARTIME CONDITIONS INCLUDING RADAR SILENCE AND DIMMED LIGHTING X ALL COMMANDING OFFICERS BEAR IN MIND THAT WHEN UNITS ARE NOT ACTUALLY ON STATION THEY ARE NOT CONTRIBUTING TO FIGHTING EFFECTIVENESS OF TASK GROUP X THEY WILL ACCORDINGLY ESCHEW SLUGGISH MANEUVERING AND CHANGE STATIONS IN THE MOST EXPEDITIOUS MANNER X IN WAR AS IN LOVE TIMING IS EVERYTHING X PROMPT AND RESOLUTE ACTION EVEN AT THE EXPENSE OF AN OCCASIONAL MISTAKE IS A HALLMARK OF SMART DESTROYER OUTFITS X ADMIRAL HOELSCHER SENDS

He was thinking this over when Evlin clipped another message to the board. Information was coming in steadily. They had to play catch-up, and quick, before the exericise started.

'Say, Dan – '

'Sir?'

'Don't get down in the mouth about misreading the situation. Everybody screws up once in a while. That's how human beings learn.'

'It was just a stupid mistake.'

'Well, you won't make it again. See this, from the oiler? We'll be refueling at seventeen thirty. Station Two.'

'I'd better get on that. Can I get a relief? I need to get my guys ready.'

'Sure. Call Trachsler, why don't you. He can shoot an approach even with a busted arm.'

He found Bloch, as he'd expected, in the chiefs' quarters. He was sitting in a sweat-stained T-shirt, a cup of coffee in front of him, a cigar sputtering smoke into the air from a stamped aluminum tray. Dan was opening his mouth to ask him what happened to working hours when he saw what he was doing.

Enlisted evaluations, scribbled and lined through and erased, covered the table. Bloch glanced up. 'H'lo, sir,' he said, his pouchy eyes dull as old sea glass.

'Chief. Look, we just got a message topside – '

'Refueling at seventeen thirty. Station Two. The boys are on it.'

'Well, okay.' Bloch seemed always to be either ahead of or behind him, but never quite with him. He glanced at his watch. They had an hour yet before fueling would be called away.

'Siddown, sir. Care for a King Edward?'

'No, thanks.'

'Coffee? Hey! Gigolo! Pump the ensign some java.'

The messman slid Dan a cup of joe. He nutated it in the mug, noting the film it left behind, like bunker fuel. It tasted like Bloch had been putting out his cigars in it. He watched the chief work for a few minutes. He finished one of the evaluations, sighed heavily, and reached for the next.

'When are you going to check the rig, Chief?'

Bloch glanced at him under his brows. He sighed again, shuffled the papers together, and rose. He stuck the cigar in his mouth and pulled on his shirt. Together, they went up on deck.

The formation had turned west while he was below. *Ryan* had dropped behind the oiler and was following its broad stern around in the turn. They stood on the 01 level and watched the replenishment team lay out the gear on the forecastle. Rambaugh went from point to point along the distance line, attaching little flashlights. He tested each one, replacing a battery or a bulb here and there.

'Calmer today than 'twas last time we did this,' said Bloch, waving the butt of the stogie at five-foot swells.

'I hope it goes better than last time.'

The chief leaned aginst the rail and puffed smoke into the wind. Dan caught a whiff of it, rank as smoldering rope. 'You know, sir – '

'What's that?'

'You don't need me on deck. Popeye's been refueling damn near as long as I have. He knows the business. So does Ikey. Least, he should.'

336

'Well, I guess that's relative, Chief. They don't seem to need me around, either, a lot of the time, but here I am.'

Bloch stared at him. 'Hey,' he said. 'Good comeback.' He slapped Dan on the shoulder. He felt as if he'd been knighted. 'Well, what do you say we both just stand around and enjoy the scenery, long as they're paying us to. Better than that fuckin' paperwork. Remember when I was a seaman, on the Unholy *Toledo*, I don't think the division chief could even write. Now it's more like recruiting duty every year. I guess they'll end up makin' us all titless Waves.'

Replenishment stations went as the sky edged toward sunset. The sun hurled its dying brilliance along a vast corridor of scarlet cloud, carpeting the sea with rose like a triumphal avenue. High above arched streaks of thin golden cirrus. The men trooped aft for life jackets. Bloch threw his on, buckled the top snap hook, but let the bottom dangle. He saw Lenson's look and sighed. He buckled the bottom and pulled his belly up with both hands and tucked the loose tie-tie ends into his pants.

They closed slowly on the oiler. Dan, glancing aft, saw that the line handlers were on station, passing jokes and farts, cuffings and shoving each other. Pettus stalked by them and the grab-assing stopped.

'That Pettus, he'll make a good petty officer, he gets some time in.'

'He's kind of got a chip on his shoulder, seems to me.'

'It's not easy, being a new third. You got to leave your pals behind. Maynard's going to do all right.'

'Maynard?'

'Yeah, he goes by Martin, but that's his middle name. Maynard Martin Pettus.'

As *Ryan* closed, the rounded stern of the oiler, outlined black against red sky, looked familiar, like the corner gas station. The gunner's mates waited, line guns lowered. Dan glanced up at the bridge. Trachsler was standing beside the alidade, calling out rudder and engine commands. He felt a twinge of jealousy. It would be a long time before he got to shoot an approach.

When *Ryan* slid into the notch, the guns popped and two

337

lines came sailing across. One plunged incontinently down-ward and was swept off in the wake. The other dropped across the signal bridge. Greenwald came running back with it. Isaacs passed it through the block and the line handlers hauled away. In a few minutes, the span wire was across and fast and the hose was creeping down it toward them. The line handlers chantied out in rhythm, hauling it down. They didn't sound depressed. Well, a couple weeks exercise, a week in Spain, and they'd be headed home. He felt better, too, thinking about it.

'Start pumping,' Isaacs shouted. The talker muttered into his mouthpiece. The hose began throbbing, the ship sucking black oil like a whale calf at its mother's teat. Dan imagined her sinking under his feet. This would be a long replenish-ment. They'd burned a lot of fuel screwing around up north.

He stood in the sea wind and thought about home, about Susan, about holding her again. For a little while, he was almost happy.

They were still fueling after dark dropped a sable curtain over the sea. The stars gleamed steady and cold between the clouds. Below them the distance line was a swaying catenary of lights, glittering between the mated ships. Dan bent his wrist under the working floods. They had to have the ship darkened by eight, when the exercise began.

At that moment, the phone talker cried, 'Cease pumping. Refueling complete.'

The signalman gestured with lighted wands. The throbbing ceased. Men ran about the decks opposite. Dan leaned over the rail, looking aft toward the rig. As the retrieving wire tightened, Isaacs separated the hose. A few gallons of oil splashed out on the deck, then cut off. Hardin bent with a rag and swabbed busily as the hose retreated up the span wire.

'Going nice,' he said to the chief. Bloch nodded, Roosevelting an unlighted stogie between his teeth.

The span was now the only connection between the ships. Above them Trachsler shouted into the pilothouse. Isaacs stepped up to the wire and pulled at the cotter pin.

A vibrating roar came from the stacks and *Ryan* began to gather speed. Isaacs yanked at the pin again, then stepped back and looked at it uncertainly.

Dan stiffened and glanced at the bridge. The conning officer was no longer in sight.

'Go tell 'em,' said Bloch. He was already swinging his heavy body over the rail.

Dan was halfway up the ladder when Evlin came out. He shouted, 'Swing back in, Al! It's hung up; it's still attached!'

Evlin eyes widened. He turned and yelled into the bridge. Dan reversed himself and almost fell down the ladder. The ship began to heel.

Below, at the station, he saw Bloch at the pelican hook. The chief boatswain waved the others back, then stepped forward of the rigid span wire. He lifted a hammer and brought it down, once, twice.

At the third blow, the heavy steel bail flicked open. Dan couldn't see how it happened, but suddenly Bloch was staggering back, clawing at his head. The hammer clanged against the bulkhead. The span wire leapt out into space, coiled itself, and ripped down into the sea.

For a frozen moment, they all – he from the ladder, the men from the deck, Trachsler and Packer and Evlin from the bridge – stared down at the fallen figure in dirty khakis.

He knew the bloody hammer back into the toolbox with a clatter and looked around at the men. The corpsman had taken Bloch below. His skull was fractured. He was dead. Dan looked away from Isaacs's wet eyes, his trembling hands.

'Petty Officer Rambaugh, you're acting chief as of now.'

'Aye aye, sir.'

'Secure from unrep detail. Get this all policed up.'

The men saluted. He saluted back. There was something final in the gesture.

The weapons officer and the exec were waiting for him in the breaker. 'Everything secured?' asked Norden.

'Yes, sir.'

'Let's go below,' said Bryce grimly. 'In my cabin.'

'Gentlemen, I was not present at this latest fiasco. This time, it wasn't just the usual substandard performance. This time we lost a man. Mr. Lenson. In your opinion, was Chief Bloch in full command of himself this evening?'

The question took him by surprise. He stammered, 'Bloch, sir? He was cold sober.'

'Sober, eh?' said Bryce. He lighted a cigarette deliberately. ' "Cold sober." Why did that pop into your head, Dan? That you assumed I meant he was drunk?'

'Sir, I didn't mean that the way it came out. I meant only that he was in full command of himself.'

'What about your first-class? The Negro boy, Isaacs?'

'He was . . . acting kind of slow, sir, but I have no reason to believe that he was under any undue influence.'

'Then why'd you give Popeye the division?' asked Norden, speaking for the first time. 'Rather than Ikey? He's next senior.'

'Sir, I can only . . . I can only say I don't have full confidence in Petty Officer Isaacs's professional ability. That's not to say I think he's intoxicated or drugged, or in any other way . . . or anything else. Or that he was responsible for the accident. Rambaugh just seems to have more on the ball.'

Bryce squinted thoughtfully, fiddling with a pencil. When Dan stopped he grunted, 'Rich, you agree with that?'

'I'll back up my division officer, yes, sir.'

'I see. Well, the Navy doesn't work that way, gentlemen. Can't have a second-class bossing a first. Only one way to clear this up. Get Isaacs up here.'

'Now, sir?'

Bryce nodded curtly. After a moment, Norden reached for the phone.

When Isaacs came in, he was plainly terrified. Tears gleamed on his cheeks. His hands twisted his work gloves. 'Stand over there,' said Bryce, distaste in his voice. 'You've got oil on your boots, boy, it's getting on my carpet.'

'Sorry, sir.'

'What happened on Station Two, Isaacs?'

'Sir, the ship, she tried to pull away too soon. Got a strain on the span wire. The cotter pin bound up. I couldn't get it free with the pliers. Chief Bloch, he come down and pushed me off, started hammering on it to free it up. That's what I was going to do, sir. When it let go, the bail snapped up and knocked the hammer into his face.'

'Isaacs, are you drunk?'

The petty officer gaped at him. 'No, sir, no sir, haven't had nothing to drink for a long time.'

'Smell his breath,' said Bryce. Dan sat still. Norden, his eyes on the exec, got up slowly.

'I don't smell anything, Commander.'

'Get out of the way.' Bryce put his face close to the black man's. 'Bend down here. I smell it! I smell whiskey. This man is drunk.'

Dan began to tremble, too. They were destroying Isaacs. And he'd started it, by doubting his fitness to take over the division. He got up and stood next to the XO. His nostrils caught the reek of fuel and sweat. That was all. 'Sir, I don't smell anything.'

'Well, I do,' said Bryce. He picked up the phone. 'Bridge? XO here. Send the master-at-arms to my cabin. With the keys to the supply locker.'

Lenson opened his mouth to protest, but Norden was already speaking. 'Sir, wait a minute. I think you're jumping to –'

'That's enough out of you,' said Bryce. Suddenly he was shouting. 'You understand me? Enough! I'm sick of coddling drunks and hopheads in your department. I've been through this with Lenson and I've had a bellyful. You're holding a shipwide search tonight. All the weapons spaces. Berthing compartments, heads, mess decks, every-where. I told you we were riding for a fall when you wanted me to recommend Isaacs for first class. And I was right. Yes! Come in!'

Chief Hopper slid in, a fat, overage clerk with a fistful of keys. 'Lock this man up,' said Bryce. Hopper peered around at the officers. 'Him! Isaacs! Get him out of my sight.'

'Aye aye, sir. Come on, Ikey.'

The first-class lifted a shaking hand. For a moment it

seemed he might beg, or protest. Then Dan saw his eyes drop, his shoulders wilt.

When he staggered out, Bryce collapsed into his chair. 'Okay, that's taken care of. Now, this search. I want all petty officers in the search party. Fore and aft. Open every locker. Use flashlights in the overheads.'

Norden's face was pallid. 'Sir, I have to say, I think – '

'Do me a favor, Rich. Shut up, get out, and do as you're told. Forget your great-grandfather's brilliant career. Start worrying about yours. You and Evlin've fucked up my ship pretty goddamn thoroughly. Now we're gonna do it my way. I want a report by midnight.'

'Come on, Dan,' said Norden. He pulled at Lenson's arm. 'It's no good. Come *on*.'

Dan felt it, but he couldn't move. He was straining forward, his mind blank, staring at the executive officer. So this is the way it is in the Navy, a voice in his head sneered. Lassard's voice. This is how it is on *Ryan*, man. Somebody dies, somebody has to be crucified. You gonna change that, Ensign?

He wasn't sure what he wanted to do. No, that was wrong. He wanted to kill Bryce. 'Wait,' he said. He felt as if he was choking. 'This isn't right.'

'Get out, Lenson. Take him out, Lieutenant!'

Only the last shred of self-control, and Norden's fingers digging into his shoulder, let him turn away at last.

The search party reassembled at ten minutes to midnight in the wardroom. Seven chiefs and petty officers, the four officers in the department, and the chief corpsman.

The master-at-arms, a pistol awkward on his hip, stood guarding the table. On it were three opened packs of cigarettes, two sandwich bags of marijuana, a half-empty pint of Seagram's Seven Crown, two wads of bills with rubber bands around them, two switchblade knives, a pot-metal starting pistol, and an assortment of pills and capsules in plastic bottles. Each item had a tag on it. Where it was found, whose locker, whose space.

The funny thing is, Dan thought in the frozen, waiting

silence, not one tag had William T. Lassard's name on it. Not one had the name of any of the kinnicks.

They stood waiting uneasily, their bodies moving slightly with the sway of the deck.

At midnight, the door opened and the captain came in.

21

'Well,' said the sarcastic voice in the darkness. 'Here he is at last, the late Dan Lenson.'

'Lay off, Mark. I got enough trouble without you in my face.'

'Tough shit. I've had it up to here standing my watches and yours, too.'

Dan stared around, trying to conjure some hint of outline out of blackness. The bridge was darker than he'd ever seen it before. He was exhausted. But the familiar weariness of missed sleep bothered him less than the sick feeling he'd taken away from the wardroom.

James Packer hadn't ranted. His face didn't give much away. But they could see how terribly disappointed he was in them. And that hurt more.

Silver clicked on the light over the chart table. Dim at best, it had now been covered with paper till only a pink glow penetrated. Dan's formation diagram was taped onto the chart. He struggled to concentrate as the jaygee said, 'Formation's on course zero-one-zero, making twenty knots. *Kennedy*'s the guide, bearing zero-six-five degrees true, range three thousand yards. I'm on station, near as we can tell without radar. The sea's three to four feet. Wind's variable from the west. Radar silence and dimmed lighting in effect.'

'What have we been doing?'

'Mostly just maintaining screen station. *Kennedy* launched aircraft around twenty-three hundred. We were ordered to plane guard. I expect when she recovers, they'll want us back. The launch course was two-five-zero. Internal to the ship, we have three boilers on the line, one, two, and four. The plant's split; superheat temperature's eight hundred and fifty; both generators are on the line. Max speed is thirty knots. OOD has the deck and the conn. The captain's in his sea cabin. Any questions?'

'Did you write up the log?'

'A-firma-titty. Oh, and allow some extra time on speed changes. Main control's got some glitch they're checking out.'

'Okay, shit, I got it.'

He sipped at the coffee he'd brought up with him as he groped toward the radar. The all-revealing circle was dark. He brought his head back up, feeling stupid, and set his binoculars by feel. The carrier should be to starboard. He groped till he felt cold Plexiglas smoothness. The darkness was so solid, it made no difference whether his eyes were open or closed.

'Dan? That you?'

'Yes, sir.'

'You oriented yet?'

'Uh, almost.' His penlight cast a russet oval over two square feet of deck. 'What you want me to do?'

'Well, principally stay alert for bearing changes. Have you picked up the guide yet?'

'No. Where is she?'

'Mark should have showed you before he left. Look about zero-five-five relative. You can see it easier without the window in the way.'

He went out on the starboard wing and tipped up the alidade, then remembered it was fogged. Also that was degrees true, and Evlin had given him relative. He steadied his binoculars on the rail. A gelid breeze streamed past from straight ahead. Its invisible pressure felt eerie against his cheek. He could see nothing of the sea, and the sky was so lightless his retina formed inchoate coruscating patches that floated downward as he blinked. Being buried must be like this, he thought. Like being stuffed into a coffin and covered with cold powdered carbon.

Deprived of sight, his imagination supplied images. Bloch's bloody head against the oily deck. Isaacs's terrified tears. The expressionless tightness of the captain's mouth. One by one, they flashed up, then vanished, sucked back into the dark.

He shuddered. He'd never wanted to kill before. But Bryce deserved it. He threatened. He lied. Used helpless men as scapegoats.

But ... they'd found the whiskey in Isaac's locker. And they'd found drugs, a lot of them, in a lot of lockers, though the individual caches were small. The only thing he still didn't understand was how Lassard had come off clean.

I don't care, he said to himself. I won't condone it. Not the way he does it. I won't condone and I won't forgive and I'll never be the way he is.

He shivered then and recollected and searched around what he figured to be zero-five-five relative. At last he made out a blue pinprick haloed by mist, or moisture in the old binoculars. Without the glasses he couldn't see it at all. He went back in. 'That's the carrier?'

'Yeah. Dimmed stern light. Need bearings on it every ten minutes. Can do?'

'Can do, sir.'

He sensed the unseen existences of Coffey, Connolly, Yardner, and Pettus as he crossed to the centerline gyro. A red spark on the wing caught his eye. 'Bos'n.'

'Sir.'

'No smoking under blackout conditions. Make the lookouts ditch their cigarettes. Don't let them light up again.'

'Aye, sir.'

'Stay on them tonight; we're depending on them, with the radar off.'

'Aye aye,' said the third-class resentfully.

He decided to use the centerline alidade; it was warmer inside the pilothouse. He focused it on the faint luminosity Evlin had said was *Kennedy*. 'Zero-six-six, Lieutenant.'

'Very well. Keep an eye on her.'

He marked the time on his watch with a grease pencil. He felt groggy and disoriented. He slapped his face, then the other cheek. It helped. He went to the chart table and shielded his flash over it.

The task group was in the same formation he'd plotted yesterday. The carrier was in the center. *Talbot* was due north of her at six thousand yards. *Calloosahatchee* was northwest,

346

tucked inside the screen at four thousand. He picked up a dim glow that might be her stern light. *Dewey*, with the best antiair armament, was to the east, seven thousand yards out in the direction of the enemy threat. *Garcia* was to the southeast at five thousand yards. He went outside again and tried to pick each of them up. He caught an intermittent twinkle far out to starboard but couldn't tell whether it was *Dewey* or the frigate.

Christ, he thought, how are we going to maintain station like this? It was like asking blind men to juggle. But they'd done it in World War II, and before. No radar then. He thought about that. Then went back inside and got another bearing.

'Guide's dropping aft, sir.'

'How much?'

'Two degrees in ten minutes.'

'Engines ahead standard, indicate ninety rpm.'

He studied the diagram again, rubbing his mouth. Evlin was slowing. That should make them drift back onto station. But how had he figured out how much to slow, and converted that to rotations per minute of the screws?

The lieutenant muttered, 'Making out okay?'

'Yeah. Just trying to figure out what we're doing.'

'It'll make sense after a couple of nights. Just keep those bearings coming.'

He stood uncertainly for some minutes, musing over his problems. At last his mind switched off and let the anxiety gnaw at his guts without putting words to it.

'You're quiet tonight.'

'Yeah, guess so.'

'Too bad about Bloch.'

'I should have been down there with him.'

'Blaming yourself doesn't do any good.'

'I guess not. But I still feel guilty. Then all the shit they found. . . . Bryce's got us where he wants us now.'

Evlin was silent. Then he said abruptly, 'Come out on the wing.'

They leaned against the shield, and out of habit, Dan screwed the glasses into his eyes. Nothing showed. Not even a star. The overcast must have closed in again, he thought. Well, we had blue sky for a day.

'You're taking this pretty hard.'

'What do you mean, sir? My chief's dead, leading PO's in the brig, my whole division's under suspicion. How would you take it?'

'Are you responsible for any of that?'

'Damn it, they're my men. Of course I'm responsible.'

'In a legal sense. In a real sense – what any reasonable man would take into account – you've only been aboard for two weeks.'

'You think my fitness report will included that little fact?'

'You're not really worrying about that, are you?'

'Well . . . no.'

'I hope not. Isaacs was on the sauce long before you got here. Those drugs came aboard before you did. From what I've seen, you've been trying your best to recoup a difficult situation. And maybe even making some headway.'

'Thanks, Al. But I still feel I could have prevented Bloch's death . . . and what they're going to do to Isaacs. . . .'

'How? It was a combination of a green conning officer and a piece of metal that didn't do what it was supposed to. An accident.

'Look, I've been watching you work. You make errors, but you don't make the same one twice. When you're not actually conning, you've got some pub out studying. You're capable and conscientious, and you'll do fine, no matter what your first fit rep says. And Isaacs – you're right, that's a travesty, but it goes on Bryce's account, not yours.'

'Yeah, but – '

'Stop arguing and listen. The one thing I see wrong with you is that whenever something goes wrong, you condemn yourself. You talk about Bryce suspecting everybody? You suspect Dan Lenson.'

'I just think – '

'I said listen. Keep your ideals. But don't be too tough on yourself. You're as good as the next man. If you act like you're not, you'll end up convincing everybody you're right.

'You can't control the world, Dan. Sometimes I think that's what the captain's trying to do. He's trying so hard to make everything right, trying so hard not to make a mistake, that he gets tired, he misses things – '

'Somebody's got to be responsible.'

'Of course. But we're only human, Dan. You've just got to do your best, and after that, let go. The *Gita* says we have the right to labor; but we have no right to the fruits of our labor. That's what it means. Doing our best, then – letting go.'

Dan felt like punching the bulkhead. He should have relieved Isaacs from the refueling detail after the first screwup. He'd failed leading the division, failed with Lassard, failed with Bryce. He'd dicked up all along the line, from the moment he'd stepped aboard.

He saw now where Evlin was wrong. Men weren't fundamentally good. Maybe in an ashram, with a bunch of saints. Not aboard ship. They were greedy, vicious, lazy, incompetent. They needed discipline and punishment. If they kept screwing up, they had to be purged. Bryce's methods were questionable, but you couldn't argue with his goals.

Tears stung his eyes, welling up from some vast reservoir of pain and anger and guilt. He'd wanted to succeed on *Ryan* – to accomplish something, to *be* someone. But he'd failed.

Who could he blame for that? Somebody else, like the XO did?

'Do you understand me, Dan?'

'Yeah,' he said. His throat ached. There were tears on the eyepieces of the 7 × 50s. 'I hear you, sir.'

At a little past two A.M. the pritac came on, a soft mutter. He reached for the message log. 'Angelcake, this is Beacon. Message follows. Turn niner. Execute to follow. Over.'

The screen ships answered one after the other. When *Ryan*'s turn came, Evlin said briefly into the handset, 'Snowflake, roger, out.' The transmit light died. Dan heard him fumbling in the dark. 'Captain, Bridge.'

Silence. Then, 'Sir, message from force commander, changing course ninety degrees to starboard, execute to follow.'

Pause. 'New course will be one-zero-zero, sir. Figure they're getting ready to recover the air strike.

'Roger, sir. Aye aye, sir.' The phone holder rattled.

'Angelcake, this is Beacon. Turn niner. I say again, turn niner. Standby. Execute.'

'Right standard rudder, steady one-zero-zero,' said Evlin to the helmsman. Then, into the transmitter, 'This is Snowflake, roger, out.'

Packer came up after they steadied. He bumped into Dan, sneezed, and muttered, 'Sorry.' He and Evlin huddled over the chart table. Parallel rules clicked. At one point, Dan heard them arguing. He was on the wing and caught the tones rather than what they said. The captain sounded tired.

He felt sad again, then angry. Over a pound of marijuana in bags, and more in cigarettes. Plus pills. That fucking Lassard. It *had* to be Lassard's. He could be wrong, but he couldn't be *that* wrong.

At the thought, he glanced around. Where was the port lookout? He found him at last curled into a corner away from the wind. 'Lookout,' he said.

'Ay.'

'Slick. What the hell are you doing?'

'Nothing, man. Nothing. *Nada, rien, nyetu. . . .*'

'Goddamn it, Lassard, you're on watch! I've warned you before. What good are you doing down there?'

'Who you puttin' on? It's pitch-dark, man. There's nothing to see.'

'Do you know what's going on here? We're steaming in close formation. There's no radar. Do you know where the carrier is?'

'Sure, man.' The slouched figure gestured vaguely. 'Out there.'

'Okay, Dan said. The dragging, vague voice told him clearly enough what Lassard had been smoking. 'That's it, that's enough. I'm through screwing around. You're on report.'

The slow voice became drugged with contempt. 'Yeah? You scare me, Lenson. Know that? You really do. Really do . . . you haven't got a thing on Slick Lassard, man. You're clueless what's going down on this ship. Everybody, they all laugh at you, man. Call you Cadet Cuboid, call you Milk

Duds, call you Ensign Fuzz, call you Dudley Dickhead. You're one sorry, lost, lying motherfucker.'

'That's it, Slick. I don't know how you got through that search clean. But this time I'm writing you up myself. I – '

'Go fuck yourself, Officer Pig.'

Dan grabbed a handful of foul-weather jacket and jerked the seaman upright. He shoved him toward the shield and heard binoculars clang against steel. 'Do your fucking job!' he shouted.

'You're dead, Lenson. For that, you're a dead man. Slick's friends'll see to that. They'll find you driftin', man. Then we'll all go fuck your slant-eye bitch wife – '

Dan cut him off. He had to leave or he'd hit him, beat his face in, kill him. 'We'll talk at captain's mast. Shut your face and stand your watch!'

'Yeah, you and the XO, we'll see you later.'

He was shaking with rage when he got back inside. Evlin was by the radio and the captain had settled into his chair. He listened to them with half his attention. The other half was occupied with Lassard's threat. How had he known about Susan?

'Darn. I forgot my pipe.'

'Why don't you go below and get it, sir?'

'Al, you know as soon as I leave, they'll put a signal in the air for us to take plane guard.'

'Then I'll take us there, sir.'

'Suppose they come around to two-five-zero, two-six-zero, like they did to launch. What'll you do?'

'Same as last time. Come around with ten degrees right rudder. That'll give us a turning circle of twelve hundred yards. Steady on two-six-zero, slow to fifteen knots. I'll wait for *Kennedy* to pass us, then come right and fall in astern.'

'No, damn it. It'll – wait a minute.' Dan heard Packer coughing. 'It takes forever that way. No, when she comes around this time I want you to come right to one-three-zero, kick us up to flank, and down the bird farm's port side. Once you're past, swing hard left and you'll be in the slot.'

'Sir, that'll be faster, but it'll put us a lot closer to the carrier. She'll be turning into us. And we'll be crossing her bow at some point.'

'It's too slow your way. Bring that board over here.'

They conferred for a while. At last Packer swung down. 'Captain's off the bridge,' Pettus announced.

'What was all that about?' asked Dan.

'Oh, changing station. I'll go over it with you after we've executed.'

They stood in the dark for some minutes. Then the pritac began muttering again. 'Angelcake, this is Beacon. Signal follows, execute to follow. Foxtrot corpen two-six-zero. Foxtrot speed twenty-seven. Over.'

'Well, he called that one,' said Evlin. 'Soon as he goes below, things happen. *Kennedy*'ll execute in a minute. But he didn't – ' Dan heard the rattle of the handset. The transmit light glowed. 'Beacon, this is Snowflake. Do you desire us to take Station Two? Over.'

'This is Beacon,' said the speaker faintly. 'That is affirmative. Break. All units, turn two-six-zero, speed twenty-seven. I say again, turn two-six-zero, speed twenty-seven. Standby. Execute. Over.'

'Right standard rudder, steady course one-three-zero, engines ahead flank for twenty-seven knots,' said Evlin.

The enlisted men repeated it in bored tones. The telegraph pinged. Dan took a bearing on the carrier. The stern light had disappeared and new ones, a pattern of them, prickled the night. All were fuzzed as if by mist. 'She's coming around,' he reported. 'Now bears zero-six-three.'

'Very well,' said Evlin. 'Bos'n, we're going to plane guard again. Get the boat crew up. Have them make preparations to lower at three minutes' notice.'

'Steady on one-three-zero, sir,' said Coffey from the wheel.

'Very well. Mr. Lenson, bearing to the guide?'

'One-six-five again, sir.'

'One-six-five?'

'I mean, zero-six-five. Sorry, sir.'

'Keep them coming.'

The door opened and someone came on the bridge. Dan

could tell by the cavendish scent who it was. He felt a twinge of annoyance. A pipe didn't break blackout, he supposed. But he'd just told the men not to smoke.

'You start the turn, Al?'

'Yes, sir.'

'Where's *Kennedy*? I can't see her.'

'Off the port bow now, Captain.'

Packer crossed the bridge with heavy, dragging steps, and went out onto the wing. Dan saw his face lighted momentarily by the alidade, heard muttered speech. Actually, he thought, there's a little light. He could see better now than when he'd come on. Could see silhouettes, at least.

The captain's bulky shadow came back in and stood looking forward. 'Damn it, Al,' he said, sounding irritated. 'What are we doing? Come left. Left standard rudder, come to course zero-nine-zero.'

'Left standard rudder, zero-nine-zero,' repeated Coffey in a slightly less bored tone.

'Captain, have you taken the conn?'

'Yeah, I've got the goddamn conn, nobody else up here seems to know what to do with it. What speed are we at?'

'Twenty-seven knots, sir.'

'Let's kick her up. Give me ahead flank, twenty-nine.'

Connolly, the lee helmsman, repeated the order as he racked the handles ahead.

Dan went out on the wing. The alidade was slightly off and he centered it on the carrier. it was dead now and the lights had changed from a line to a cluster. Some were white, some red, some green or greenish white, low in the water. They seemed to be closing; he could see them plainly now without magnification. He couldn't tell what angle he was seeing the other ship from. He went back inside. 'Bearing zero-eight-zero,' he said.

'To what?' said the captain. Evlin was bent over the chart table.

'To *Kennedy*, sir.'

'Sir,' said Evlin, 'this course puts us only four hundred yards from the carrier's track.'

Packer peered forward. Dan went out on the wing again.

The lights ahead were getting brighter. A few seconds went by. He heard Evlin say something else. Almost at once then the captain called out, quite loudly and clearly, 'Increase your rudder to left full.'

'Left full, aye,' said Coffey. He sounded alert now.

Dan realized suddenly the carrier was much closer than he'd thought. The small lights were not in her superstructure but at the leading edge of the flight deck. He went inside in time to hear Evlin say, 'Sir, we're closing way too fast.'

'Increase rudder to left hard. All engines ahead emergency flank!' shouted the captain. Evlin left the chart table and ran to starboard. Dan followed him.

The lights were bright now, imminent, moving from dead ahead to starboard as the destroyer heeled. Bells rang as Pettus, shoving Connolly aside, cranked the engine-order handles from ahead flank to back full and forward again. Evlin hung in the wing door for a moment, muttered, 'My God,' and ran back to the helm.

Dan, left alone on the wing, stood frozen as the silhouette of an aircraft carrier suddenly took shape out of what had a moment before been empty night. Seventy feet high, filling the sky. The lights were steady along the deck edge. The cream of bow wave glowed a lighter black. It could not be more than a hundred yards away, and it was coming directly at him. He gripped the splinter shield, unable to move or breathe. Behind him a cry of 'Stand by for collision!' was followed instantly by the electric clang of the alarm.

The carrier's bow tore into them a hundred feet behind the bridge. *Ryan* heeled bodily, knocking him off his feet onto the gratings. A long, terrifyingly loud shriek of tearing steel succeeded the blow. The ship whipped and shuddered under him. He hugged the deck mindlessly, binoculars biting into his stomach. The lights, penumbraed by mist, slid by high above. A scream of rending metal, a roar of escaping steam struggled against the drone of a horn. Something exploded aft, jolting the deck against his cheek and lighting the bridge like instantaneous daylight.

He scrambled up and was propelled by the lean of the deck into the pilothouse, his legs buckling under him.

He blinked flash from his eyes, to find its snug familiarity transformed into something new and terrible. Coffey was still at the wheel. Pettus was shouting into the 1MC, but nothing was audible above the din. The chart table light flickered and went out, as did the binnacle and the pilots on all the radios. Packer was clinging to his chair, staring out to starboard. Dan didn't see Evlin.

He fetched up against the helm and clung to it, looking out. The deck-edge lights were still sliding by above them, like a train on a high trestle. Then they were gone. The deck shuddered. Another explosion came from aft, a deep boom that rattled the windows. The ship swayed back to vertical, then reeled to starboard with sickening ease. The deck took on a backward slant.

'Abandon ship,' Pettus was yelling into the mike. But it was dead.

'Knock that off,' said Dan.

'Sir, we got to get off her – '

He ran to the port side. The carrier loomed abeam of them, a black cliff higher than *Ryan*'s mast tops, studded with dim lights. It was moving away. He craned aft over the splinter shield. Kerosene reeked the air. Flames were shooting up, with crackling rapid bangs, all along the Asroc deck and down to the waterline. A black mass loomed astern, not burning, but illuminated by the flames. It took a few seconds before he understood that it was the aft section of the ship.

A door slammed open on the 02 level and men spilled out. Some of them stopped at the life-jacket lockers and began to pull gear from them.

He turned back into the bridge. Packer was on the starboard wing, still looking aft. His pipe was still in his mouth. Evlin was with him, standing straight, hands white on his binoculars. 'She's cut in two, sir!' Dan shouted above the rising roar of the fire. The deck lurched again, rising under them, and the slant aft steepened.

'She never responded to the emergency bell,' said Packer hoarsely. His face was bleak and still in the growing firelight.

'She's cut in two aft. Should we pass "abandon ship," sir?'

'Al, what do you think?'

'I'm afraid she's going, sir.'

'All right,' said the captain. 'No power to signal with . . . but I guess the fire'll show everybody where we are. Pass "abandon ship" by word of mouth. Try to keep her afloat, and get as many off as we can.'

He found himself at the bottom of the ladder on the main deck. He didn't recall the process of getting there. He felt disoriented, remote, as if watching a film. His mouth tasted strange, as if he'd been sucking on a knife. Men shoved past him. He saw their faces clearly now in the glare. A man in trousers but naked from there up threw his legs over the lines and dropped, running in the air. 'Abandon ship,' Dan shouted, fighting his way aft, in the direction of the fire. He heard them repeating it behind him.

The flames were coming up from the after deckhouse, from what was left of the Dash deck, licking swiftly forward. Their tips fluttered in the wind like bright pennants. They danced on the surface of the hull, and he thought for a confused moment that the metal itself was burning. The smoke was choking and the heat grew as he fought his way aft.

He got abreast of the Asroc launcher before the smoke and heat forced him back. he suddenly realized he was still carrying the binoculars. He tore them off and wedged them carefully behind a standpipe.

He had to think, had to think what to do. Boy's Town was forward of the break. He wanted his books, Susan's picture. He fought his way inside, past the sailors coming out. The stream pushed him back.

One of the men coming out was Norden. His skivvy shirt was torn and he was barefoot. He clutched Dan's arm. 'Lenson! What happened? I was below, in my rack, all of a sudden – '

'*Kennedy* hit us.'

'Christ. Christ! And the captain – '

'He said to abandon, Rich. Get as many guys off as we can before she goes.'

The weapons officer stared past him. For an infinitely long, suspended space of time that could have been instants or

356

years, Dan saw the fire reflected in his wide-open eyes, two miniature cones of vivid flame, as if the burning was within him, not around him.

Then Norden was gone, running, headed aft.

Suddenly his disorientation, his remoteness, was replaced by fear. Forget the picture. He had to get a life jacket, get to his raft, get *off*. He was going to die here if he didn't get off. He lurched into a clumsy run, slamming into other men. The deck slanted farther and he dropped to all fours, scrabbling on hands and knees. An animal moan rose in his throat.

Then someone was gripping his arm, calling his name over the growing hissing roar. He tried to pull away. But the hand held fast.

He came back to himself with a rush of shame, straightening and turning, shielding his eyes against the light.

Chief Pedersen and three others were hauling gear out of one of the fire stations. One of them, mustached, thin, grime-faced, let go of Dan's shoulder. He bent, straightened, and his glasses flashed as he tossed the end of a roll of hose over the side.

Dan saw that it was Alan Evlin. His uniform shirt was torn and dirty and his khaki trousers were wet to the knees.

'Better get to your station, Dan; get your men taken care of. We probably don't have much longer.'

'What about you, Al? Why are you still here?'

The others staggered out of the locker like pallbearers around a coffin. They set their burden down and the firelight played over the bright machined brass fittings of a portable pump. Evlin grimaced but didn't answer. He bent and began priming it.

'Did you all get the word? Captain said to abandon ship.'

'Yeah, we all heard, Mr. Lenson.' Coffey pulled at a cord. The pump started with a whine. The black seaman had to shout his next words. 'Gonna try some water on it, anyway. Might hold it back a few minutes, let more guys get topside.'

Pedersen hefted the nozzle. The motor increased speed. A stream gushed out, faltered, then reached out toward the fire.

'You need help?' shouted Dan.

357

Evlin answered this time. 'No, think we got it covered. Thanks.'

The operations officer glanced behind him. Pedersen and Matt and Coffey were walking the nozzle slowly aft, shielding their faces from the heat. The water went into the fire and disappeared. 'Doesn't look good, does it? Well, we'll try this for five minutes, then pack it up.'

'Don't stay too long.'

'No problem,' Evlin grinned suddenly, teeth white against his smudged face. 'See you later.'

'See you, Al.'

Evlin turned away. He shielded his forehead with an arm and went to join his men, kicking a kink out of the hose.

Dan left them and went on along the slanted deck. The iron taste was still in his mouth. His stomach was jumping and he knew without looking that his hands were shaking. But somehow, now, he wasn't so afraid. Seeing them go about their business so calmly had steadied him. Men below, he thought. He hoped none of his guys were down there in the dark –

He halted, struck by a sudden horrifying thought. Isaacs was below. *Locked* below. Had anyone thought of, remembered, cared enough about him to go back?

He reversed direction and fought his way down a leaning ladder past frantic, cursing men in skivvies who were trying to come up. The part of his head promoting self-preservation was still trying to argue him out of it. He belonged topside, organizing the survivors. She could go any minute. He'd be trapped –

But something about the way a soot-streaked face had grinned at him kept him going down.

He reached the foot of the ladder and crouched, glancing around swiftly. The interior of the ship was dim, more shadowed than lighted by the sallow gleams of emergency lanterns. The green tile decks by the mess line slanted upward, shining faintly with the satin smoothness of fresh-buffed wax. The tables glowed too, clean and ready for an

358

early chow that now would never come. White smoke eddied along the overhead, feeling its way like a rising tide in the expectant, waiting silence.

He gathered his courage and ran forward, past the chiefs' mess, then down another ladder and forward again into the narrowing forepeak, deep below the waterline, parts of the ship where, even normally, few people went. Behind him the shouting and din died away. No running feet drummed here. He jerked open rusty scuttles, scrambled down canted empty ladders, possessed by the same feeling he had in dreams, when everyone else had left for formation and he alone searched for some item of uniform, something without which he didn't dare go back.

A hammering and howling gradually grew below and ahead as he scrambled panting forward through the shadowed, humid, paint-smelling dark.

The supply locker had a thin metal door secured from the outside by a brass Navy padlock. He could hear Isaacs hammering and screaming on the far side. He tried the hasp. It was locked, all right.

A dogging wrench offered itself on the bulkhead, a seven-inch length of heavy pipe. He jerked it free and began hammering at the hasp. Sobs burst from his throat. The club dented the mental, dented the door. He thought, Slow down. Think, goddamn it! He caught his breath and aimed the next blow. Hard to see now. Eyes smarting, filling with tears. A flicker showed at the far end of the corridor.

The lock snapped off and clattered to the deck. He forced the door inward. Isaacs was just inside. Blood covered his hands like red gloves. They stared at each other. 'Mr. Lenson,' Isaacs whispered.

'Get out, Ikey,' he gasped. 'We're abandoning. Get topside, get out.'

The petty officer bolted out and disappeared up the corridor without another word or backward look. Dan followed him, his feet sliding and splashing. He realized suddenly that the deck was covered with running water. He passed the open door of one of the supply storerooms and halted. Cummings was squatting by a safe, hunched forward, coughing in the thickening haze as he set the dials a millimeter at a time.

'Chow Hound! Tom!'

'Yo.'

'D'you get the word? We're abandoning.'

'Just a minute.' The disbursing officer cursed and struck the steel with his fist, then bent forward again to the dial. Dan left him and ran on, downhill now, planting his feet in the corner formed by the deck and bulkhead. He had only one idea now, to get out.

At the next level, there was less smoke but more water. It was a foot deep in the corners. Two chiefs were coming out of the lounge. One was swinging a gym bag. The other was pulling on a foul-weather jacket. In the amber dim of the battle lanterns, the deck with littered with chairs and dishes and clothing. Floating on its side in the rising water was Bloch's model ship, masts snapped and rigging snarled by someone's boot.

Sailors pushed by him, going the wrong way. He shouted and grabbed their clothes, got them turned around and headed aft and upward. When no more came out of the dark he followed them. At the next ladder, he caught up to the chiefs. They climbed with maddening slowness. A wave of hot air and bitter whitish smoke overtook them, scorching his throat, and he coughed until his feet slipped on the canted treads.

He finally emerged at the top into a transverse corridor. At the same moment, he realized he was lost. He scrambled instinctively uphill into darkness and came to a dead end. He clawed at metal, and suddenly, unexpectedly, it opened over him. He grabbed the edge of the hatch and pulled himself up into the open air, sobbing and retching out the smoke that coated his lungs.

Life jackets littered the deck, soft, yielding beneath his feet like lifeless bodies. The deck was bright as noon, lighted by an immense roaring pyre that soared above the masthead, shedding sparks at its apex, slanted by the wind. The sea was burning around it.

He hauled himself up by the lifeline and looked for the after section of the ship. Couldn't see it. Maybe it was already gone. The engine rooms were the largest spaces on *Ryan*, and the carrier's bow had ripped right through them.

He turned and looked up at the bridge, expecting to see the captain still there. But the wing was empty.

Almost helplessly, he turned again, like a moth, toward the mountain of flame. Within the burning light, shadows moved. He picked his way slowly toward them, shielding his face from the radiated heat.

The shadows became men, clustered around the whaleboat. They were on the far side of the flames from him, too surrounded and suffused by roaring, wavering brightness for him to recognize individuals. The inferno had spread, cutting them off. It looked as if they were having trouble lowering the boat. *Ryan*'s increasing list wouldn't make it any easier. For a moment, he thought one might be Lassard. Another gesticulated lankily, like Greenwald. But who was that heavy man climbing over the gunwale? And behind him, that one in a blackened T-shirt? Then the curtain of flame shifted, thickened, scorching his face, and he had to fall back and turn away.

It occurred to him that it was time he thought of abandoning. Should he go to his assigned raft? No, it was in the heart of the fire. He picked up a life jacket and began strapping it on. His hands shook ludicrously; he heard a short bark of laughter; it was his. And after everything, his cap was still on his head. He thought for a moment of keeping it. Then he ripped it off and threw it over the side.

Seeing it disappear reminded him, as he knotted the last tie, that you shouldn't go over the high side. Barnacles, ripped steel could shred you like cheese in a grater. He thumbed the waterproof light pinned to the vest. It didn't work. Fortunately, there were plenty of Mae Wests lying around. He pulled lights off two and stuck them into his pockets.

A group of men came running up the deck. One of them was Lipson, who stopped. 'You all right, sir?'

'Yeah, thanks.'

'You got blood on your trou, there.'

His fingers found a sticky tear in one thigh. 'Must have caught an edge someplace. It's all right.'

'Well, okay, sir. Don't hang around too long.'

'Gotcha. You, too.'

The radarman ran aft. Dan went forward, limping a little.

When he came out of the breaker onto the forecastle, he was surprised to find a group of sailors standing by the mount, looking out into the dark. 'What's going on?' he asked them.

'Ship out there, sah,' said one. He recognized Mabalacat, the wardroom steward.

The bow was rising slowly. Which meant that the stern was going down. 'You guys better get in the water.'

'It's gonna be awful cold in there, sir.'

'I hear you, but if she goes down sudden she may suck us under. Jump in and swim clear.'

'Aye aye, sir.'

They didn't act frightened, but neither did they move. He picked up a life jacket and threw it at a man without one. 'Get over the side,' he said again.

'Hey, you first, sir.'

'It's a deal, Cherry.' He threw his legs over the lifeline and looked down.

The sea was black, with sparkling highlights of fire. Heads bobbed here and there, faces bright, looking strangely tranquil. His hands gripped the line. He tried to make them let go, but they wouldn't.

'Jesus,' he said out loud, 'we got to get off this thing.'

The ship didn't seem unstable, though it was still listing, and pitching a little in the seas. He cast a wild glance aft. More men, lightless cutouts against the intense white brilliance, were leaping from the o2 level. He saw one hit on his stomach and disappear. He didn't come back up. The fire sound was enormous but bizarrely cheerful, like a bonfire at a pep rally. He remembered a brush blaze he'd fought as a teenager. The boys were bussed out and given Little Indians to strap on their backs. The nozzles gave out a thin stream, like a man pissing. There'd been lots of joking about that.

'Goddamn it,' he said. 'I've got to jump.'

The lifeline was biting his flesh, but still his hands wouldn't let go. A cook in a white apron climbed over the line next to him and went headfirst into the glittering water. He came up on his back, looking up at the ship, and began to backstroke clumsily away. His face glowed like the moon in a dark sky.

Dan pleaded silently with his rigid fingers and suddenly, unexpectedly, they released. He teetered for a moment vertical on the deck edge and then kicked away weakly and plunged feetfirst, bent forward, into the sea.

The impact slammed the breath from him and water filled his mouth. He clawed at the darkness, but it was the life jacket that brought him up with a rush.

He bobbed limply on the surface, wheezing at the sudden intense cold. The side of the ship was an arm's length away. There was slimy growth along the boot topping. A man hurtled over him and hit within spitting distance, sending water over his head.

He began swimming then, starting instinctively with a dog paddle, then turning on his stomach for a crawl. The life jacket dragged maddeningly. He swam as hard as he could for fifty strokes and then was exhausted. He turned on his back and let the life jacket hold him up and looked back at the ship.

The forward half of USS *Ryan* floated bow high, her deck tilted toward him. She had moved in the water and he realized she still had a little way left on her. From the forward stack aft, a solid pyramid of white flame ran down along the sides and spilled into the sea. Patches of inky darkness showed between the fires on the water. Light glowed from the windows of the bridge, ruddy and warm, welcoming, like farmhouses passed by night. He remembered the decades-deep accumulation of paint, the crowded cable runs full of flammable insulation. The light wavered on the black water. A few men were still jumping. A black man in white trousers and life jacket stood calmly at the rail, looking out.

He lifted his arm and turned the face of his watch to the flame. Thirteen minutes had passed since the collision.

He wondered then what had happened to the others. He hadn't seen the captain since he left the bridge. He hoped Al and Chief Pedersen and Ali X. had left their pump. All his men forward in berthing . . . he wished now he'd stayed aboard longer. At least he'd remembered Isaacs in time. The makeshift brig must be underwater by now.

363

He became conscious then of the men around him in the water. Some were still shouting, but most were quiet now, tossed up and down by the four-foot seas. Some had turned on their lights. One he did not recognize with hair plastered over his forehead called out, 'Think she'll float, Mr. Lenson?'

'Not much longer,' he shouted back. The words came out slurred. He couldn't feel his lips anymore.

'She looks pretty buoyant. Fire'll get her first.'

'Maybe,' he shouted.

'Five bucks says she's still there tomorrow morning.'

'I guess I'll take that,' he shouted.

He was still peering at the man, trying to recall who he was when beyond him, forward of what remained of *Ryan*, he noticed the lights of a ship. They were bright, masthead and range and the red sidelight all bright and a lot of little lights also. They looked like the Pleiades. He dropped to a sea and lost it and then caught it again when he rose on a crest. It was a big ship. He dropped to a trough and it disappeared again.

When he rose again, it was much closer. Bearing down fast, he thought. Good, get in here and pick us up. Already he couldn't feel his legs, or his balls. He kicked his feet but the numbness didn't retreat. God, the sea was cold. He was glad he had clothes and shoes. Some of the men had gone over naked.

When he came up again the ship was almost on top of them. In the firelight he saw that it was the carrier. The bow rose like a lee cliff, broadening from the knife edge of the cutwater to a bulbous swelling beneath the flat line of the flight deck. Fans of light reached out from the island, probing the black sea. Then a sea broke over his head and he sputtered, clawed saltwater that burned like cold acid from his eyes with cupped fingers.

The carrier struck the forward half of *Ryan* just aft of the stack. The destroyer rolled toward him, scattering a burst of burning wreckage and sparks, and went over. The carrier, immense, ploughed over it, not lifting or slowing at all, shoving it down into the sea to a crunching scream of buckling plates and tearing ribs. The larger ship's side lighted suddenly in a smear of flame, and the concussion kicked him in the testicles. The old destroyer's underwater hull showed for a moment amid the drifting fire, red as blood, curved, rolling slowly.

The carrier moved past, blotting out *Ryan*. Flame followed it toward him, scattering in gouts of yellow that flared up again into white as it hit the water. The cliff heeled slightly, and the burning sea broke into patches, rolling out on the bow wave. A sheet of burning fuel swept toward him, leaping and guttering along the jostling crests as it ignited first blue and then glaring yellow and then an intense incandescent white. He screamed as it seared his shoulder and arm before he finished ripping the jacket off.

As the sea closed over him the immense beat of the carrier's screw filled his head. He frog-kicked desperately through the icy dark, eyes cramped closed, and came up into a stink of kerosene and smoke that seared his lungs. He dived again and swam and came up again in a patch of oil that for some reason was not yet burning.

He was in a shimmering tunnel of flame. It roared up on both sides, choking him. He couldn't breathe. His eyes and mouth burned. When he raised his hands, he saw that they were black with oil.

A strange thing happened to him then. He was drifting in a sea of fire, but at the same time he was above it. He could see the whole bright circle on the sea, the forward half of the old destroyer capsized and drifting amid fire, the aft section dark and almost gone. Around them bobbed the tiny dots of heads. But he saw it all from above, as if he were back in the dream, flying over it all.

He was Dan Lensn and at the same time he was someone who had no name; he was all the men drifting and crying out and the men trapped inside, hammering without hope at steel in the dark. He saw at the end of the tunnel of flame a place cool but intensely luminous, brighter than the fire, so bright that the fire was dark around it like a dark halo. He moved faster and faster upward through the flame and it did not burn, and the brightness grew, and before he had time to be startled or afraid, he hurtled through the incandescent oblivion into a place of clean, cool wind.

When he came to, the sea was in his face and someone was hitting him on the neck. For a moment he was bitterly disappointed. Then he jerked his head out of the water.

'You alive, buddy?'

'Yeah. Yes.'

'Good. I can't hold you up any longer. Swim over there; there's some shit floatin' there you can grab.'

The hand left his collar and gave him a shove. He went under for a moment and panicked; struggled up again and swam weakly, blindly, feeling nothing in his hands and legs. The sea tossed him up and down. It was very dark and his chest hurt and his eyes burned too fiercely to bear. He coughed into a wave, retched, gagged, then kept coughing. He stopped only when he was too weak to continue. Then he could breathe. The sea seemed warmer now. This first reassured and then frightened him. From time to time, he could see lights. One blinking set of them moved in the sky. Helicopter, he thought. The idea of help gave him a little energy and he told himself firmly that he had to stay afloat.

He breaststroked slowly into a jostle of men and flotsam. When light licked across them, he saw boards and cushions and paint drums and life jackets, it seemed dozens of them. There was also a life raft, but it was full of silent bodies. He grabbed a Mae West and put it between his legs and another around his neck. He couldn't feel the straps, but he got one under his crotch and into the wrong D-ring. It held him up. One of the men bumped into him and they grabbed each other and held on, neither of them speaking.

The light licked out of the darkness again and swept over them. They waved and screamed hoarsely. Then he saw a green light, very close to the water. They shouted and screamed.

A boat grumbled out of the night, lifted on a wave, and slammed down beside them. Dan and his friend shouted and hands came over the side and pulled them up and over the gunwale and tumbled them into a heap of other oily, sodden bodies.

He lay there for a few minutes, thinking with regret of the

windy place, and then tried feebly to get up. He was terribly cold. He wished he was back in the water and not out in the air. He was too weak to move. But he was alive.

He tried to laugh, needed to cry at the same time. Then the dark keel smashed him under.

When he came up again, the gig was alongside a ship and he was being rolled into a stretcher. He waved a hand and tried to say he didn't need to be carried, but something was wrong with his voice and the men just kept lashing him on. 'This one's burned, too,' he heard one them say. A little later, he felt a needle in his arm. Then he felt nothing at all. Except the cold. It seemed that that would stay forever.

5

THE COURT

Section 910, Article 110. Improper hazarding of vessel

(a) Any person subject to this chapter who willfully and wrongfully hazards or suffers to be hazarded any vessel of the armed forces shall suffer death or such other punishment as a court-martial shall direct.

(b) Any person subject to this chapter who negligently hazards or suffers to be hazarded any vessel of the armed forces shall be punished as a court-martial shall direct.

—Uniform Code of Military Justice

SECRET
IMMEDIATE

From: USS Kennedy CV–67

To: Secretary of the Navy

Info: Chief of Naval Operations
Commander in Chief, Atlantic Fleet
Bureau of Personnel
COMCRUDESLANT
Destroyer Squadron 22

Subject: Loss of Ship

1. In accordance with Naval Regulations Article 0778, LCDR Benjamin W. BRYCE, Jr. USN, senior survivor USS Reynolds Ryan (DD–768), reports loss of ship.

2. USS Ryan was assigned to screen of USS Kennedy early morning 25 December. Reduced lighting and radar silence were observed in accordance with operation order for exercise WESTERN VIGIL. At 0210 Zulu time the formation executed turn into wind to recover aircraft. Ryan was ordered to leave the screen station and take plane guard station on Kennedy.

3. At approximately 0215 Kennedy and Ryan collided approximate position 54 degrees 26 minutes north, 16 degrees 10 minutes west. Kennedy hit Ryan starboard side amidships, cutting Ryan in two. After section sank in approximately twenty minutes, forward section fourteen minutes after collision. Search by Kennedy, Talbot, Dewey, Garcia continuing, but recovery of additional survivors unlikely. Muster shows 239 officers and men in complement, 61 survivors recovered, 178 dead or missing presumed dead.

4. All survivors and recovered bodies currently aboard USS Kennedy. CV–67 will dock Gravesend 0700 27 December for repairs/debarkation. Request instructions as to disposition of bodies and survivors USS Ryan and notification of next of kin.

BT

SECRET
Do Not Declassify Without Approval Of Addressee

UNITED STATES ATLANTIC FLEET
HEADQUARTERS OF THE
COMMANDER IN CHIEF

From: Commander in Chief, U.S. Atlantic Fleet
To: Vice Admiral Charles R. Ausura, USN

Subj: Court of Inquiry to inquire into the circumstances surrounding the recent collision of USS John F. Kennedy (CV–67) and USS Reynolds Ryan (DD–768).

1. A Court of Inquiry consisting of yourself as president and of two other flag officers to be named is hereby ordered to convene in the OPNAV Conference Room, Pentagon, at 1100 5 January, for the purpose of inquiring into all the circumstances surrounding the collision between Kennedy and Reynolds Ryan. Lieutenant Commander Stanley Fox Johnstone, U.S. Naval Reserve, is hereby detailed to you as counsel for the Court.

2. The Court shall make a thorough investigation into all the circumstances connected with and surrounding the collision and the subsequent loss of USS Ryan. The Court shall report its findings of fact, opinions, and recommendations as to the cause of the collision, damage resulting therefrom, deaths of and injuries to naval personnel, and the responsibility for the collision and subsequent loss, including recommended disciplinary action.

3. All Proceedings of the Court will be closed. All testimony, including the subject of such court, will be classified SECRET and witnesses and members of the Court will be so notified in writing. The courtroom will be guarded. A copy of the transript will be forwarded daily to the Secretary of the Navy.

J.W. Richardson,
Admiral, US Navy
Commander in Chief, U.S. Atlantic Fleet

22

Washington, D.C.

Behind the fluttering gauze of a January flurry, the largest office building on earth loomed lightless and forbidding, surrounded by the endless acres of icy oaks and ranked white stones of Arlington Cemetery. Its five huge entrances were pillared by unadorned slabs of granite.

To Lenson, shivering as he let himself down from the shuttle bus from the bachelor officers' quarters, the Pentagon looked like a citadel. He stared up at it as the snow whirled down, then whirled away on a biting wind.

Only a few days, he told himself. It'll only be a few days, and then you'll know. And in the evenings – well, Susan would arrive today.

The surviving officers and men from USS *Reynolds Ryan* had been flown in to Andrews the night before. He saw the ones who'd come over on the bus's first trip up ahead, huddled in front of the river entrance.

He bent, and began struggling up what seemed like endless steps.

When they had all assembled, a guard took them in through corridors and turnings so complex and endless and identical each to the other that within seconds he was lost.

They sat now around a World War II-era library table in a small room in the B ring. Exhausted from the climb and dizzy from the 0800 pill, he slumped back, staring at Lieutenant Commander Stan Johnstone. The counsel for the Court had a chisel-pointed chin, half-erased hair, horn-rims, and a nervous habit of easing his neck within the collar of his service dress blue.

'I want to emphasize, gentlemen, that a court of inquiry is not a court-martial. There are similarities, but also important legal differences. Judges will preside, but they're called 'members.' There'll be attorneys, witnesses, and testimony. At the close, there'll be preliminary findings of responsibility – '

'Sounds like a court-martial to me,' said Bryce, smiling.

'– but findings of guilt and subsequent sentencing will be determined by a duly constituted court. Now I'll try to anticipate your other questions. First, I can't tell you when you will be called. That'll be up to the president of the Court, Vice Admiral Ausura.

'Second, although you have the right to private counsel, I would not at this point necessarily advise you to exercise it. This is an extremely sensitive case. That's why it's being heard here, instead of at the Annex or the Yard. I advise you to answer the questions you will be asked over the next several days truthfully and fully. Evasion, withholding information, or lying may lead to charges being laid against you.

'Finally, the proceedings will be secret. I have here a document stating that you understand this.' He opened a black leather portfolio. 'Pass these around, please. One copy each. Read and sign. . . . Everyone got a pen?'

When Dan jerked awake some moments later, Johnstone was putting the papers back into the briefcase. He couldn't remember signing one. He pushed himself upright, rubbing his face with his good hand. Get a grip, he thought. Can't be signing things you don't remember reading.

'Have any of you discussed what happened among yourselves – especially with the other officers?'

'We've shot the breeze, sure,' said Bryce.

'I advise you not to "shoot the breeze" anymore, Commander. If you become a party, it could be misconstrued as undue influence on witnesses.

'You have separate rooms at various area enlisted quarters, BOQs, and hotels, is that correct? You're free to move about town between Court hours, but keep to yourselves. Don't discuss this case with each other or members of the public – not even family. Everything you have to say will be heard. The Court will consider it and make a fair decision. Should you not think so, there will be procedures for appeal. Is that understood?'

They all nodded. Johnstone looked at Lenson next. 'Ensign, I see you have an arm injury, and apparently some difficulty remaining awake. I understand you suffered burns during the abandonment of *Ryan* – '

'Actually, afterward, sir. In the water.'

'Just so. My question is, Will you be able to take the stand? Will you require special attention?'

He tried to look alert. 'I'm under medication, sir, but I can testify.'

'Very well. Are there any other questions?'

'Do you think we'll be called today?'

'I can't say, Lieutenant. I can't predict how long each witness will take on the stand.'

'Will we be able to get copies of the transcript?'

'I can't answer that right now, Chief. Who here wants one?' Dan put his hand up. 'One, two . . . six. I'll raise that with the convening authority and get back to you with an answer, hopefully before the proceedings are over.'

A marine stuck his head into the room. 'Sir, we're ready to convene.'

Johnstone turned his neck in his collar, cleared his throat, and reached for the portfolio. 'Any further questions? Thank you for your attention, gentlemen, and the sergeant will show you to the courtroom.'

The codeine made small things large, enlarged details into worlds, made important things like the future insignificant. His mouth was dry and his shoulder burned. Sometimes his attention wandered. But the crystalline lens of the drug focused the senses intensely, almost photographically. He smelled the leathery tang of the hearing room, the hot closeness of steam heat and inadequate ventilation, the starched-cotton smell of new uniforms. He could close his eyes and still see wainscoted plaster, a gray-green carpet leading up to a flag-flanked table covered in green baize. As they took their seats in front of it he looked around at the other survivors. Their pale, shocked visages reflected his own bizarre amalgam of anger, pain, dizziness, and, somewhere below the drugged, furry apathy, fear.

'All rise,' called a guard. As he struggled to his feet, three men in late middle age, gold solid on the sleeves of their blues, filed in. He scrutinized their faces. One was short, heavy, white-haired. The second was wiry, with deeply lined, tanned cheeks. The third was tall, with a gray mustache. What were they feeling? Mercy? Vengefulness? He couldn't tell. They all looked the same: dispassionate, reserved, and grim.

The heavy one, apparently the president, nodded to a chief Dan hadn't noticed. He sat at a table, with a little transcribing machine. 'Is our recorder ready?'

'Here, Admiral.'

'Very well.' He sat, and the room echoed with the scrape of chairs. He examined something in front of him, then glanced up at Johnstone.

'Commander, you may begin.'

EXCERPT FROM TRANSCRIPT
OF USS *RYAN/KENNEDY*
COURT OF INQUIRY: DAY ONE

The Court convened at 1000.

Present: Vice Admiral Ausura, U.S. Navy, president; Rear Admiral Morehead, USN, member; Rear Admiral Dennison, USN, member. Lieutenant Commander Stanley F. Johnstone, U.S. Naval Reserve, counsel for the Court.

The counsel for the Court read the appointing order.

All matters preliminary to the inquiry having been determined and the members having viewed photographs of the damage to USS *KENNEDY*, the Court was opened in the presence of witnesses and survivors of USS *RYAN*.

COURT: Good morning, gentlemen. The Court has decided to admit the witnesses to most of the testimony in this case. This should aid us in reaching a speedy conclusion to a matter as troubling to us as it is to you. I would like to remind all hands that we will be discussing classified matter. We are dealing with an accident that occurred while the forces involved were operating under simulated wartime conditions, in conformity with wartime doctrine. I trust to your discretion. However, when we discuss matters secret and above, I will clear the Court of all but witnesses and members.

Are there any parties to the inquiry who have not already been introduced, Commander Johnstone?

COUNSEL FOR THE COURT: For the record, Admiral, it would be best if I were addressed as 'Counsel.'

The Court indicated acquiescence.

Captain Ronald Javits, USN, Captain of *KENNEDY*, then entered as a party to the inquiry. He was informed of his rights.

COUNSEL FOR THE COURT: In accordance with a request of the father of *RYAN*'s deceased captain, Commander James J. Packer, the judge advocate has provided a legal officer to represent him at this inquiry. The counsel will be permitted to cross-examine witnesses as necessary in his interests. I introduce Lieutenant Robert Hauck, U.S. Naval Reserve.

COUNSEL FOR CDR PACKER: Sir, if it please the Court, I understood I was to be accorded all the rights of a party. You have mentioned only the right to cross-examine.

COUNSEL FOR THE COURT: The Court will extend to you all the rights of a party.

COUNSEL FOR CDR PACKER: Thank you, sir.

COUNSEL FOR THE COURT: I refer now to section 0309 of the naval supplement to the *Manual for Courts Martial*, referring to the right of any party to challenge the Court. Do any of the parties desire to challenge?

CAPTAIN JAVITS: I do not.

COUNSEL FOR CDR PACKER: I desire to examine Rear Admiral Morehead on the grounds of lack of impartiality.

The challenged member took the stand, was properly sworn and examined as follows.

Q. Admiral, I present here a copy of your official biography. Would you read over it, sir, and tell us if it is an accurate history of your naval service?

A. [Witness read the document.] It is substantially correct, yes.

Q. Substantially correct. I offer into evidence as Defense Exhibit A this summary of Admiral Morehead's naval career.

COUNSEL FOR THE COURT: That is court-martial

terminology. I think you should offer it as Exhibit A. Not as Defense Exhibit.

There being no objection, the document was received as Exhibit A.

Q. Admiral, if I may summarize, this document states that you served aboard aircraft carriers in the Pacific as a reserve flier during World War Two. You were recalled to duty during the Korean Conflict as a flight officer in attack squadrons. You applied for reinstatement in the Regular Navy and after service at the Bureau of Aeronautics served on seagoing staffs with the Seventh Fleet. You were executive officer and then commanding officer of USS *MAUNA LOA*, following which you commanded *HORNET*, an aircraft carrier. You are now serving on the staff of the Supreme Allied Commander, Atlantic. Is this substantially correct?

A. You left out the fact that I commanded an attack squadron. After I was with the Seventh Fleet.

Q. Thank you, sir. Admiral, do you think, in the light of your long experience in the naval aviation community, that it is better for an aviator to command a carrier, rather than a surface line officer?

A. Well, that's Navy policy. There are certain special knowledges aviators have that surface officers don't get in the line of their experience.

Q. And you agree with that policy?

A. Yes, I do.

Q. Admiral, should the facts tend to show that Captain Javits, commanding USS *KENNEDY*, was at fault in the loss of *RYAN*, would not such a finding conflict with a vested interest of yours – namely, your opinion that carriers should be commanded by naval aviators?

COUNSEL FOR THE COURT: I object. This line of questioning is irrelevant.

The Court replied that the objection was not sustained. The witness was instructed to reply.

A. It would not prejudice me in any way.

Q. Do you know Captain Javits? Have you ever met?

A. Possibly at parties. I do not know him well.

Q. What is your opinion of his professional reputation?

A. I assume it is good or he would not have command of *KENNEDY*.

Q. Would that bias you in favor of his decisions?

A. No, I don't believe it would.

COUNSEL FOR CDR PACKER: I have no further questions for this witness, sir.

COUNSEL FOR THE COURT: Admiral Morehead, have you formed any opinion whatsoever yet as to who is at fault?

A. No, I have not.

Q. Is there any reason you cannot approach this inquiry impartially, with an open mind?

A. None whatsoever.

COUNSEL FOR THE COURT: No further questions.

The Court was cleared, the challenged member withdrawing.

The Court was opened. All parties reentered. The Court announced that the challenge of counsel representing Commander Packer was not sustained.

COUNSEL FOR THE COURT: The Court is now duly constituted. I will now read for the benefit of the witness the relevant portion of the naval supplement to the *Manual for Courts-Martial*.

'Whenever inquiry is made into the loss of a ship, the Court shall call for the official report of the commanding officer of the ship, containing the narrative of the disaster, and this report shall be read in the presence of the commanding officer and of such of the surviving officers and crew as can be assembled, and shall be appended to the record.

'After the survivors have been sworn as witnesses, the following questions shall be put to them by the Court: (1) to the commanding officer: Is the narrative just read to the Court a true statement of the loss of USS *REYNOLDS RYAN*? (2) Have you any complaint to make against any of the surviving officers and crew of the said ship on that occasion? (3) to the surviving officers and crew: Have you any objections to make in regard to the narrative just read to the Court, or anything to lay to the charge of any officer or man with regard to the loss?'

I will now read the dispatch sent by the senior surviving officer.

Dan straightened, blinking what felt like balls of dust from his eyes. He took several deep breaths and looked at his watch. The steady tapping of the yeoman's machine was hypnotic. Another hour and a half before he could have another pill. Maybe the pain would help him stay alert.

He stared forward, taking another deep breath as Johnstone said, 'Lieutenant Commander Benjamin Bryce.'

Lieutenant Commander Benjamin W. Bryce, Jr., USN, was called as the first witness. He was reminded of his rights and was advised that any statement made by him might be used as evidence against him in any subsequent court-martial. He then took the oath.

Examined by the counsel for the Court.

Q. State your name, rank, and present duty station.

A. Lieutenant Commander Benjamin Bryce, executive officer of . . . [the witness paused].

Q. You are still attached to the crew of USS *RYAN*.

A. Thank you. So, executive officer of *RYAN*.

Q. Were you attached to that ship on the night of this last December 24?

A. Yes, sir.

Q. On the morning of the 25th, was *RYAN* lost as the result of a collision?

A. Yes, sir.

Q. Are you the senior surviving officer?

A. I am. The captain did not survive.

Q. Do you have a list of the men believed to have died?

A. Yes, I do.

Q. And a list of the survivors?

A. It is the same list. What I did was, I got our sailing muster from squadron staff and drew lines through the names of the men who were not picked up alive.

Q. Have you mustered the survivors?

A. I did that on *KENNEDY* the evening of the 25th.

Q. Are there any who are unaccounted for in any way? That is, who were aboard *RYAN* when she sailed, and are not accounted for?

A. There is one man who might fall in that category. We had a boatswain's mate chief who was killed in an accident the day before.

Q. His name?

A. Harvey Bloch.

Q. He was dead before the collision?

A. Yes, sir, his body was in sick bay. I assume that it went down with the ship.

Q. Would you give to the Court, in the presence of the surviving officers and crew here assembled, your estimation of the events leading to the collision between USS *KENNEDY* and USS *RYAN*, and the subsequent loss of *RYAN*?

A. To the best of my ability, I will. As executive officer, I did not stand watches, although I kept my hand in by maneuvering her from time to time. So a lot of what I have won't be as, you might say, an eyewitness. I was in my stateroom at the time of the collision, working on ship's correspondence. I understand that we were in a sector formation – '

Q. Let us have only what you personally witnessed. We will take testimony from those actually on the bridge later.

A. All right. My cabin was forward of the collision area but not by much. When I heard the impact, I immediately went out on deck. I then began organizing the fire party. But cut in two, there wasn't anything I could do at that point to save her. After some minutes, I was told that the captain had passed the word to abandon ship. So, I then abandoned in the ship's motor whaleboat, and attempted to save as many as possible of the crew. I also saw – I then saw *KENNEDY*, or it might have been the oiler, come back.

Q. Come back?

A. It came back and rammed the forward section of *RYAN*.

A. Go on.

A. Well, on the whaleboat, we had lowered away and were in the water searching for survivors when the engine conked out. The wind and seas carried us away east of where she went down. Eventually, we got the motor running again. We then resumed the search and took those we found to nearby ships for treatment. The boat itself was picked up by USS *TALBOT* about 0400.

Q. Go on.

A. We were given medical treatment and a shot of brandy. At dawn a helo took us to the carrier. That is about all I have to say.

Q. Commander Bryce, what was *RYAN*'s last port of call before the collision?

A. It was our home port, Newport, Rhode Island.

Q. How long had she been at sea?

A. Sixteen days. We operated in the North Atlantic and Arctic, then west of Ireland.

Q. Is the dispatch which you sent to the Secretary of the Navy a true statement of the loss of *RYAN*?

A. As far as it goes, but of course it's not complete. There are many facts that this Court will have to uncover, and I hope to assist it in that.

Q. Have you any complaint to make against any of the surviving officers and crew of *RYAN*?

A. As I said, I was not on the bridge at the time. I do know many relevant facts, some of which relate to individuals who were on watch during the collision. I would like to hear their versions of what happened before I make a formal complaint.

COUNSEL FOR THE COURT: I will have further detailed questions to ask this witness. However, in order to expedite the hearing, I ask that he be excused from the stand at the present time without cross-examination.

Neither the counsel for the Court, the Court, nor the other parties desired further to examine this witness, and he resumed his seat.

Lieutenant (jg) Aaron Reed was then called as a witness. He was sworn and examined as follows.

Q. State your name, rank, branch of service, and duty station.

A. Aaron Reed, lieutenant junior grade, antisubmarine officer on *RYAN*.

Q. What was your duty station on the morning of 25 December?

A. I was off watch. I had turned over the deck to my relief, Lieutenant Norden, who I understand turned it over again shortly thereafter to Lieutenant Evlin.

Q. You have heard the narrative by the senior survivor read. Have you any objection with regard to it?

A. No.

Q. Lieutenant, what was Commander Packer's condition the last time you saw him on the bridge?

A. He seemed fatigued. He had been sick, he had a cold, and between us waking him up to ask about course change and so on, he would nap in his chair.

COUNSEL FOR CDR PACKER: I object. I believe that the bridge was dark at the time. The captain may have merely been silent.

THE COURT: Does the witness have any grounds for saying that *RYAN*'s commanding officer was sleeping, other than that he was silent?

A. He snored.

THE COURT: The counsel for the Court will continue.

Q. Aside from his 'naps,' did the captain seem alert when you woke him?

A. Yes, sir, he would come awake and listen to you and then give a response or an order.

Q. Were the responses consecutive and logical?

A. I would say so.

Q. Yet you said that he was, and I use your words, 'fatigued' and 'sick.' You must have based that conclusion on some evidence. What was it?

COUNSEL FOR CDR PACKER: Sir, the counsel for the Court is attempting to lead the witness to conclusions rather than elicting evidence.

COUNSEL FOR THE COURT: It is obvious, I think, that establishing Commander Packer's physical and mental condition are vitally important in this investigation. I am trying only to get the witness to elaborate on a matter he does not seem too helpful with.

LIEUTENANT (jg) REED: I am trying to be helpful, sir.

THE COURT: Commander Johnstone will continue.

385

Q. To return to the captain's condition: What led you to believe he was fatigued and sick?

A. As I said, he had a cold.

Q. And had become fatigued, I assume, by being on call or on deck almost continuously for many days?

A. Yes, sir. During the whole time we were involved with the sonar trials, the storm, then during the – subsequent events, with the –

THE COURT: We will not go into certain events occurring before the night of the collision. They are irrelevant. Do you understand?

A. Yes, sir.

COUNSEL FOR THE COURT: Go on, please.

A. As I was saying, he had been on deck essentially nonstop for a period of four or five days, and hadn't had much sleep before then, either.

A. You have heard the senior survivor's narrative. Have you any objection with regard to it?

A. No, sir.

Q. Have you anything to lay to the charge of any officer or man with regard to the loss of USS *RYAN*?

A. No. I was proud to serve with Commander Packer. He was a fine seaman and a fine commanding officer. Whatever happened that night, I'm sure he wasn't to blame.

Neither counsel for the Court, the Court, nor the parties desired further to examine the witness. He resumed his seat.

Lieutenant (jg) Marcus R. Silver was then called. He was sworn and examined as follows:

Q. State your name, rank, branch of service, and duty station.

A. Lieutenant Junior Grade Marcus Roland Silver, USNR, CIC officer on *RYAN*.

Q. Where were you on the morning of the collision?

A. On the bridge. I was in Lieutenant Norden's section from 1945 till midnight, but since my relief was late, I stayed there until 0115.

Q. Do you know why your relief was late?

A. There was some kind of shakedown going on in the

weapons department. For that reason, Lieutenant Evlin was standing part of Mr. Norden's OOD watch also.

Q. So you stood several hours of watch with Evlin, ending about an hour before the collision?

A. That is right.

Q. What was Lieutenant Evlin's condition at the time?

A. Condition?

Q. Was he in proper condition to stand watch? Not tired, upset, or sick?

A. I'm sure he was tired – we all were – but not so tired he couldn't stand watch. He seemed okay to me.

Q. Was Commander Packer on the bridge during your watch?

A. Yes, sir, he was on deck in my first watch – I mean before midnight – when we took station in the screen, and when we went to plane guard, and then when we went from plane guard back to screen.

Q. We will return to that maneuver, but first, I am going to follow the same line of questioning with you as I just have with Lieutenant Reed. Do you agree with his evaluation of the captain's condition as 'fatigued' and 'sick'?

A. In general, yes.

Q. In general?

A. I agree with what he said.

Q. What was your opinion of Commander Packer?

A. He was a hard-driving man, pushing himself hardest. He may have driven himself too hard in regard to staying on the bridge essentially on a 24-hour basis. I thought he was maybe too tired to immediately grasp everything we said to him. And as Aaron – Lieutenant Reed, said, he had flu or a cold.

Q. Mr. Silver, you mentioned *RYAN*'s taking plane guard station aft of *KENNEDY* in the watch previous to the collision, effectively prefiguring the maneuver that later – during which the disaster occurred. We are now going to go over that in detail with you, to add to our understanding of that situation.

A. I'm ready.'

Q. Can you describe how the ship maneuvered at that time?

A. Yes, sir. The formation was on a southerly heading, about one-eight-zero. The carrier corpened around – changed her course – to two-six-zero and ordered us to take station astern of her. We calculated a solution in two legs, two-five-zero at fifteen knots for eight minutes, then right to I think it was three-zero-zero at twenty knots; but by then, we could steer by eye on her stern light.

Q. How close did you come to *KENNEDY* in this maneuver?

A. I can't answer that, sir. We had no means of determining range.

Q. Can you give us an estimate?

A. On the board, we figured we would pass her outside 1,000 yards. That's about what it looked like by eye, too.

Q. Commander Packer approved this maneuver?

A. He didn't say anything either for or against it that I know of.

Q. Did you consider it an unorthodox or dangerous maneuver?

A. I've been taught that any operation close to a carrier is dangerous, sir. But this one seemed safe to me. It took us quite a while before we reported to the KENNEDY we were in position, though. The captain asked once how much longer it would be. I think this was in view of the message.

Q. What message was that?

A. The one that said to take station as quickly as possible.

Q. To your recollection, what did the message say?

A. As I recall, it said that screen units were taking too long to get to station – it must have meant the others; we hadn't done any yet – and that from now on to proceed to station in the fastest way possible.

Q. You saw this message, or heard about it?

A. I read it. It was taped to the bulkhead on the bridge. I'm sure it's in the group commander's outgoing message log.

Q. Let me ask this again, because it's an important point: Did Commander Packer express any reservations or impatience when Lieutenant Evlin executed this maneuver on your watch?

A. No, sir. Not that I heard or can recall of. Just asking that once how much longer it would be.

When Dan hauled himself upright, sweat poured down his ribs beneath his blouse. The Court seemed to be proceeding chronologically, calling first Bryce for an overview, then establishing conditions on Reed's watch, then Norden's. Rich Norden should be up next, then. He saw the lieutenant's fresh blond crew cut in the front row, beside Bryce.

But if that was how they were going, he'd be about the last man called. If he could hold out that long. Would there be a break for lunch? He wormed his wrist around to see his watch, gasping a little as the pain, which had been growing slowly beneath it, suddenly tore through the Saran Wrap coating of the opiate.

And when were they going to get to the important questions – why it had happened, why *Ryan* had been rammed, why so many had died and so few been saved? When would they ask what had happened in *Ryan*'s whaleboat after she cast off? Norden and Bryce hadn't mentioned it. The remaining officers hadn't talked at all about it while they were in Newport, just done the routine things, getting clothes and places to sleep for the men, writing the letters to the next of kin.

He sat sweating, tasting metal again, as he had on the deck of a burning destroyer.

Were they going to leave it all up to him?

Lieutenant Richard Norden was then called as a witness by the counsel for the Court. He was sworn and examined as follows.

Q. State your name, rank, branch of service, and duty station.

A. I am Richard N. Norden, lieutenant, U.S. Navy, weapons officer of *RYAN*.

Q. What was your duty station on the morning of 25 December?

A. I had been called off watch to deal with matters internal to the ship, at the request of the executive officer. I notified the senior watch officer that I might be late relieving him. This was Lieutenant Evlin. He proposed that we swap watches, that I get some sleep and relieve him at 0400.

Q. Have you any objection with regard to the narrative read by the senior survivor?

A. No.

Q. Have you anything to lay to the charge of any officer or man with regard to the loss of *RYAN*?

A. [Witness hesitated]. No.

Q. Do you have any objections to the narrative submitted by the senior survivor, or any charges to lay to the account of any of the officers or men of *RYAN*?

A. No, sir.

COUNSEL FOR CDR PACKER: I would like to ask one question of this witness before he steps down.

Permission was granted. Cross-examination took place as follows.

Q. Mr. Norden, what was your opinion of Commander Packer's professional competence?

A. Sir, he handled the ship well, and he was always in possession of himself, though at times he would get angry when we made what he felt was a mistake. But he was fatigued and sick and quite possibly in that condition, could have made an error.

Neither the counsel for the Court, the Court, nor the parties desired further to question this witness. He took his seat.

The Court decided unanimously to adjourn till 1230, resume questioning until 1500, and then adjourn for the day.

The yeoman's clatter ceased. Dan went past his table on the way to the door. He was telling some of the others where to eat. There were satellite cafeterias nearby where you could get fast food, sandwiches, burgers, and drinks. There was a main cafeteria, with steam tables and a buffet. Then there was the executive dining room. He didn't feel like going far.

'Where you headed, Mark?'

'Grab a sandwich.'

'That's all I want. That and a glass of water. Wait up, damn it.'

'We're not supposed to talk.'

'We don't have to *talk*, I just want somebody around in case I fall down.'

Silver relented, or at least didn't say anything else. Dan limped after him along the endless receding corridors. Floors, rings, bays . . . he'd better figure out how things were laid out, or if he took a wrong turn, he'd be doomed. He had a ham and cheese on white cardboard, a Sprite, and, washed down with it, the noon pill. Silver sat at the same table but looked away, out into the corridor, crunching the ice out of his drink. 'Nice ass,' he said.

'Say what?'

'The one in pink. You see her?'

'Oh. No, I missed her.'

'Your eyes are like zonked. You done? We better get back. We only got half an hour.'

He felt a little better now. He chugged the rest of the Sprite and got up. In the corridor he saw a phone booth and stopped suddenly. 'I got to make a call.'

'Suit yourself. Just go down this corridor till you see the flag display, remember that? Then turn right and you're there.'

The desk at the Marriott said no Susan Lenson had checked in yet. He left a message, that he'd be waiting at the river entrance of the Pentagon a little after three.

He had just time for a pit stop on the way back to the conference room.

The Court reconvened at 1240.

The counsel for the Court then called Chief Petty Officer John Yardner. He was sworn and examined as follows.

Q. State your name, rank, branch of service, and duty station, please.

A. John Yardner, quartermaster chief, U.S. Navy.

Q. Duty station?

A. Leading QM on *RYAN*, duty QM for Watch Section Three, sir.

Q. What was your duty station on 25 December of this year?

A. I was on the bridge.

Q. You have heard the narrative read by the senior survivor and the subsequent testimony. Have you any objection to these narratives?

A. Well, they seemed sketchy, sir. A lot was happening on the bridge.

Q. Everything that happened there will be closely reviewed. Do you have any other objections at this time?

A. No, sir.

Q. Have you anything to add?

A. I would like to apologize for the loss of the quartermaster's log.

Q. The record of course and speed changes, and so forth?

A. Yes, sir. What happened was, when 'abandon ship' went, I took it down with me like I was supposed to. I had it buttoned inside my shirt. It must have slipped out somehow after that, when I was in the water, and I didn't feel it.

Q. Your explanation has been recorded. Have you anything to lay to the charge of any officer or man with regard to the loss of USS *RYAN*?

A. No, sir.

Neither counsel for the Court, the Court, nor the parties desired further to examine the witness. He resumed his seat.

The counsel for the Court called Ensign Daniel Lenson. He was sworn and examined as follows.

'I swear that the evidence I shall give in the case now in hearing shall be the truth, the whole truth, and nothing but the truth. So help me God.' He lowered his hand slowly.

'State your name, rank, branch of service, and duty station,' said Johnstone. He stood beside the witness chair, but he didn't look at Dan when he said it.

He took a breath so deep it hurt. 'Daniel Lenson, ensign, U.S. Navy. I was first lieutenant on *Ryan*.'

'What was your duty station at the time of the collision?'

'I was the junior officer of the deck.'

Johnstone turned away, addressing the admirals, and Dan let his breath ease out, trying to relax. 'Neither the captain nor the officer of the deck having survived, Mr. Lenson is the senior remaining officer from the bridge team. Would you give the

Court if you can, in the presence of the surviving officers and crew, a detailed narrative of events leading to the collision between *Ryan* and *Kennedy*?'

Eyes swung back to him, refastened. This time he felt them on his skin. Sweat slid down his back. He groped into his blouse, forcing himself to speak slowly and distinctly, trying to ignore the katydid clatter of the stenographic machine.

'Sir, I have written out a narrative that I would like to read.'

'Proceed.'

'On the morning of 25 December, I relieved Lieutenant (jg) Silver as JOOD at about oh-one hundred. The OOD was Lieutenant Evlin. Seas were moderate. The night was overcast with no moon. The wind was westerly. *Ryan* was steaming in company with *Kennedy, Talbot, Garcia, Dewey,* and *Calloosahatchee.*

'When I relieved our course was zero-one-zero, twenty knots. The ship was darkened, running lights were dimmed, and the radar was secured. *Kennedy* was bearing zero-six-five true. It was difficult to estimate the range, though, without radar. At a little after oh-two hundred, *Kennedy* signaled "Turn Niner." Mr. Evlin informed the captain, and he gave permission to make the turn. We then came right to one-zero-zero.'

He wanted to wipe his forehead, but he had only one hand available. And it held the paper. 'Shortly thereafter, the captain came on the bridge. He discussed with Mr. Evlin the maneuver we would make when *Kennedy* came to recovery course. Then he went below. A few minutes later, the OTC, the officer in tactical command, signaled "Flight course two-six-zero, speed twenty-seven." We rogered, then asked whether he wanted us to take plane guard station again. They replied in the affirmative, then executed the turn.' He paused. 'Am I going too fast?'

'You're doing fine, Ensign,' said one of the admirals. 'Go on, please.'

'Yes, sir . . . Mr. Evlin then began heading for station as directed by the captain, coming right smartly to one-three-zero and increasing speed to twenty-seven knots.

'The captain came back a few seconds later. He must have

felt us heel to the rudder. He asked if we'd started the maneuver. Mr. Evlin said we had. He then went out on the port wing for a little while. When he came in, he suddenly ordered, "Come left to zero-nine-zero," and increased our speed to flank.

'Mr. Evlin asked if he had taken the conn, since the helmsman was executing the order. The captain said he had. I went out to the wing to check on the carrier. Mr. Evlin apparently also had misgivings, because he went to see what zero-nine-zero would do on the maneuvering board. All this time, I had been taking bearings on the carrier. I took another now and reported, "Guide bears zero-eight-zero." The captain expressed surprise.

'Mr. Evlin had finished plotting the course change and he now told the captain it would take us too close to the carrier. Commander Packer seemed to make a decision, and instructed the helmsman to put his rudder to left full.

'Just as Coffey reported his rudder was there, the captain ordered "left hard" and "ahead emergency flank." We ran out on the wing and saw the carrier bearing down on us. Mr. Evlin called out, "stand by for collision." Pettus passed that over the 1MC and hit the alarm.'

Sweat weas streaming down his face. A picture was forming between him and the shaking paper. He felt the night wind again, smelled vanilla-scented tobacco. No one said anything. He could feel all their eyes on him, like some penetrating radiation.

He swallowed, blotted his face with the side of his sleeve, and went on hoarsely, blinking down at the words.

'*Kennedy* hit us at a ninety-degree angle at about the location of the after engine room. We were thrown around the bridge. When she steadied up, the carrier was already through her – had cut right through her and went on – and a fire had started aft. I think a fuel line or aviation gas line on the carrier must have been sheared by our mast and dumped fuel on us as she went through.'

'Please go on,' said Johnstone.

'Yes, sir. The captain and I and Mr. Evlin assembled on the starboard wing. We asked Commander Packer if we should abandon. He said, "We never got the flank bell" – I think those are his exact words. He seemed calm. After a short discussion, he said the fire would show the other units where we were, and to abandon ship. He said to make sure all hands got the word.

'I then left the bridge, went along the main deck, and told everyone I met to abandon ship immediately. It had to be passed by word of mouth since power was out. The ship was down by the stern and I felt it might go any minute. I wanted to leave. Lieutenant Evlin, whom I met on the main deck just then, restrained me. I then recovered myself, went below, and released one of my men who was in the brig. I stayed below to direct more survivors topside for several minutes, then returned to the main deck. After that I went forward and abandoned ship from the forecastle.'

He wiped his sleeve over his face again. His mouth was so dry. He ran his tongue around his lips and went on. 'Shortly thereafter, *Kennedy* came in a second time, as previous witnesses have said. It struck the forward section of the ship, capsizing it, and it sank. This action puzzled me as it undoubtedly contributed to the heavy loss of life. The only reason I can think of is that the collision may have jammed her rudder.

'After that in the water, we were just trying to stay afloat and stay out of the burning oil. I never saw the ship's whaleboat. I was picked up fifteen or twenty minutes after the capsizing by *Garcia*'s gig.

'That is my narrative of the collision and loss.'

'Thank you, Mr. Lenson,' said Johnstone. 'It will be appended to the record. Have you any objection to the dispatch sent by Commander Bryce to the Secretary of the Navy?'

He sat rigid for a moment. 'Not to the dispatch.'

'Or anything to lay to the charge of any officer or man with regard to the loss of *Ryan*?'

'Yes, sir. I believe the loss was due to – '

'We will address that question in detail later. For the moment, I need to know if you feel anyone acted in a negligent or criminal manner.'

He licked his lips again. Why did Johnstone keep inter-rupting him? 'Yes,' he said again, looking at the men in the front row. Bryce. Norden. Lassard. They stared back at him. 'You do so feel?'

'Yes, sir.'

Johnstone faced the Court again. 'I have further questions to ask of this witness, too. He is obviously one of the keys to the causality of the accident. But it seems best to defer this line of inquiry, which will require detailed exposition and cross-examination, until the remaining witnesses have been heard.'

Dan gaped at him. 'But, sir – '

'Thank you, you may step down.'

He sat with his chin propped on his fist as Johnstone called the next witness. What was going on? They hadn't let him speak, said he'd be called back. But when?

Johnstone was calling the remaining survivors assembly line-fashion now, going through the regulation questions with each man. Only two made Dan sit up and listen. The first was Pettus.

The counsel for the Court called Boatswain's Mate Third Class M. Martin Pettus. He was sworn and examined as follows.

Q. State your name, rank, branch of service, and duty station.

A. Martin Pettus, sir, boatswain third, U.S. Navy.

Q. What was your station on the morning of 25 December?

A. I was boatswain's mate of the watch, sir.

Q. You have heard the testimony of the senior survivor and of other survivors from the bridge team. Have you any objection with regard to these narratives?

A. No, sir.

Q. Have you anything to add?

A. If it is all right, I would like to add something to what Mr. Lenson just gave.

Q. You may.

A. He mentioned that the captain said, after the collision,

that we never got the flank bell, or words to that effect. It's part of my job to watch the lee helmsman, make sure he rings up the right speed and the engine room answers properly. From where I stand, I can see the little indicator that tells how many turns the screws are actually making. The rpm indicator, yeah. Anyway, Popeye, I mean BM2 Rambaugh, he had the watch before me; he told me the engines was answering slow. So I was watching that, and I noticed that after the captain came to flank, it just hung back where it had been when he had twenty- seven rung up. And then when he went to emergency flank, there at the end, it didn't move at all. I don't think the snipes even got around to answering that one.

I was about to bring this to somebody's attention, but everything went to [expletive deleted] before I got a chance. Anyway, I think that's what he had in mind, and if he thought he was getting twenty-nine or thirty knots when he was only getting twenty-seven, it might have made the difference between making it or not. See, if we'd gone another couple hundred feet before she hit us, we'd have been okay.

Q. Do you have anything more?

A. No, sir.

Q. Have you anything to lay to the charge of any officer or man with regard to the loss of USS *RYAN*?

A. No sir, I think all the guys were doing their jobs, we just got our [expletive deleted] caught in a crack.

THE COURT: This is not a reprimand. I would however like to remind all present that we are dealing with matters of observed fact. Witnesses will refrain from uttering personal opinions.

A. Yes, sir, I'm sorry if I was out of line.

Neither counsel for the Court, the Court, nor the parties desired further to examine the witness.

Q. State your name, rank, branch of service, and duty station.

A. DC1 Xavier Traven, USN. In charge of Repair Two, midships.

Q. What was your station at the time of the collision of USS *KENNEDY* and USS *RYAN*?

397

A. I was up on the mess decks when the alarm went. Lucky I was, because very few of the men in engineering berthing got out alive. When I heard it, I got up and ran for my DC locker.

Q. Why were you on the mess decks?

A. I was eating pudding they had there. I couldn't sleep because of some physical problems.

Q. You have heard the narrative of the senior survivor. Have you any objection with regard to it?

A. No, sir.

Q. Have you anything to lay to the charge of any officer or man with regard to the loss of USS *RYAN*?

A. No, sir. All my guys arrived on station within about four minutes and we all tried our best to save the ship.

THE COURT: Are you the senior surviving damage controlman?

A. Yes, sir, I was the senior DC man on *RYAN*.

THE COURT: It would be of interest to hear your estimate of the damage and the measures taken to keep her afloat.

A. Well sir, when we got hit we were at condition Zebra, which means most of the watertight scuttles and doors were dogged. The hatches were not in good condition. We had bad gaskets, loose dogging mechanisms. We had put in a work order in the yard but they never got to it.

THE COURT: That is apposite, but we are more interested in what happened after the collision.

A. Sir, we got up on the sound-powered phones right away. We made contact with the forward repair locker, but the after one didn't answer up. We had battle lanterns, so we could see. Since there was smoke, I made the men put on oxygen breathing apparatus. We tested pressure in the fire mains, but it was zero. I didn't know it then, but that was because the engine rooms and firerooms were gone.

Anyway, I sent out investigators. They came back saying there was nothing but water beyond frame 110 and the superstructure was burning above that. Well, I heard at that time from the forward locker that we had been cut in two. I figured then we had to try to make the forward half float and fight the fire. We were taking water by then and the smoke

398

was getting thick. It didn't bother us because we had the OBAs, but I was getting worried because I didn't have contact with nobody but the forward locker.

Well, then I moved the party forward along the 2 level and sent men back to try to establish a watertight boundary. I sent men topside through a scuttle and we rigged two Handy Billies, that's a gas-powered pump. Some of the operations guys had another one going and we all got water on the fire. The guys reported back, though, it was a fuel fire, and water wasn't doing much good. Also they were afraid the magazines might go.

But anyway, we couldn't get a boundary set – the hatches were buckled; you couldn't dog them. We didn't have no steel-bending gear. I was still on the circuit, but now the forward station didn't answer, either. Then the captain came on the line.

THE COURT: Commander Packer?

A. Yes, sir. There's a phone on the bridge, by his chair; you can tap into any circuit on the ship. He asked me were we still down at Repair Two. I said, 'Yes, sir,' but that we were getting kind of discouraged. He told me to get out of there. I said, 'Sir, we might could stop the flooding forward of frame one ten, and that fuel fire's gonna burn itself out if it doesn't get into the cable runs.' He said it was already on the bridge and the ship was done. He said that was an order, for us to get out and abandon.

Q. At what time did the captain call you?

A. I can't say, sir. Anyway, I passed that word and got the guys out haiko, I mean pronto. I was climbing the ladder myself when everything went to hell. There was this terrific crash, and she just went right on over. I fell down through the scuttle and lost my OBA mask.

When then. I knew we had to get out the main deck, what was then underwater. I knew capsized with all the flooding she already had, she'd go bow-up in a couple seconds and slide on down to Davy Jones's in box. One of the guys had a light that still worked and we found the main deck scuttle. There was water just shooting in. I made them go down into it and told them to swim for it. But a lot of them I never saw again after that.

After we come up outside, the guys that made it, we saw her go down. She didn't last but about fifteen seconds after we got out. We swam around a while. We found a raft, but there wasn't room for everybody. Some of us hung to the sides. We gradually sort of moved away from things. The wind pushed us I guess faster than the men in the water. We saw lights, but we didn't have no paddles to get over to them. Later a boat went by. We waved and shouted, but they never stopped. It was after that a couple other guys slipped under. It was awful cold in that water.

Q. What kind of boat?

A. Like a ship's boat, but it wasn't showing any lights; we couldn't tell whose it was.

Anyway after dawn, about eight, a helicopter come over and saw us and then *CALLOOSAHATCHEE* come picked us up.

Dan sat rigid. So that was what had happened to Packer. To Evlin. To Coffey and Ohlmeyer and Popeye Rambaugh and OS3 Matt. To all those brave enough to stay. Brave, as he hadn't been. Unto death.

The next time he was called, no one would cut him off. He owed it to them to see that the truth was told.

The Court adjourned at 1510, to reconvene at 0900 the following day.

23

As Susan Lenson piloted her father's MG through the tangle of access roads east of the Pentagon, the Potomac opened before them, edged with ice under a winter sky, the center, broad as a ship channel, the dull, dark, burnished hue of antique bronze.

Dan slumped on the passenger side, his tie loosened. He was watching his wife.

She drove fast and skillfully. As she often did when driving, or writing, or studying her archaeology monographs, she'd tucked a twist of hair like black glistening rope between small, even teeth. She'd perched sunglasses on her nose, but they rested instead, as they often do with Asians, on her cheeks.

He dropped his eyes to small, fine wrists. She didn't look third trimester in the loose overcoat. Her perfume brought back memories of watching her put it on, touching the stopper to her body here and here and here before the mirror. In winter she grew almost sallow; in summer she tanned in a day. Her neck was delicate as glass. He touched it lightly, stroking downward, and after a little while she turned her head, rubbing his hand with her cheek as she reached down to shift.

The last time they'd been in this car, she'd been straddling him, moonlight glowing on her sweaty breasts. He half-closed his eyes. All at once the image was more vivid than the oiled walnut dash, her wool coat, the snow hissing in the wheel wells. He remembered her whispered cautions, and his clumsy fumbling toward something unknown and frightening and incredibly desirable. An erection stirred beneath the codeine buzz, then subsided as he realized she was not nude, it was not summer, that the seat belt all but disappeared beneath the swell of her belly.

'Crap,' she muttered, jerking the wheel. The car skidded

for a few feet before the tires caught again. Blown snow broke over them like a wave as a cement truck rocketed by, on its way to the complex springing up at Hyman Rickover's fiat in Crystal City. He flinched before he realized it was only that, snow. The sun glared down on the inch-thick film of white that covered the city.

He closed his eyes, letting the 1600 pill wash him to and fro like a starfish in surf. What a winter. Endless. Still only January. He wanted to hack his way sweating through green jungle. Then suddenly he could *see* the jungle, smell dank vegetable rot, hear in the verdant distance the echoing harsh judgments of mynahs. . . . He forced his eyes open, blinking as the little car whined up onto the George Washington Parkway. Weird, he thought. Things happen in your mind when you take this stuff. Good thing I'm not driving. But I'm here. Back with Susan. A hell of a lot of guys off *Ryan* won't ever hold their wives again. So knock off the crazy visions, or whatever they are, Mr. Mind.

'Boy,' she said. 'That hurts.'

'What hurts?'

'My belly button. Nobody told me my belly button would hurt.'

'Is that right?' Dan said. 'Does it hurt bad?'

'I'll live. Say, I read an interesting fact. Something you might like.'

'What that, Babe?'

'It's about seals. They can dive fifteen hundred feet down, then surface rapidly. They can collapse their lungs. They can stay under for more than an hour.'

Thinking of diving seals made him thirsty. 'Uh, that's interesting. Where'd you pick that up?'

'Mom and I went over to the Mall last week. Museum of Natural History.'

The Chans, her mother and father, living northwest of Washington, in Rockville, Maryland. She'd taken leave from school for the last month of her pregnancy, staying with them. The Navy hadn't been able to find her with the news about the sinking. When he finally figured out where she was, and called from Newport, they'd decided it would be just as well for her to stay in Rockville till he came down, then join up at a hotel in town.

So that this, having her pick him up today, was the first he'd seen of her since she'd dropped him off at the pier in Newport. He'd recognized her dad's car as it pulled up to the west face. They'd hugged, kissed, but there'd been something perfunctory and tentative about it.

He'd looked forward to this so much. There'd been times he thought he'd never see her again. But now that they were back together, it wasn't what he'd expected. It's physical, he told himself. Her pregnancy, his injuries made it awkward. A few hours and everything would be fine.

'I've never been there,' he said.

'It's worth a trip. They have a big exhibition from South America – Craig Morris's work. He's been excavating on the Inca.'

'I'm glad you enjoyed yourself.'

She caught the exit for the Key Bridge and rode the car's momentum up the hill into Rosslyn. When they pulled into the Marriott she slowed suddenly, snatching a parking space as a cab pulled out from in front of it. A businessman who had been waiting behind the taxi gave her a dirty look. He half-raised his hand, then saw Dan and lowered it and put his car back into gear, looking for another space.

The lobby hit them in the face with warm air. He blinked, dragging himself across clean, unworn carpet. He'd forgotten how elegant the civilian world could be.

'Dinner? It's early yet, but – '

'I'm ready. All I had was a sandwich.'

'Here? Or do you want to go out?'

'Oh, let's eat here.'

'Are you feeling all right, Dan? You look tired.'

'It's this goddamn shoulder. I haven't done anything all day but sit and listen to people testify.'

'Weren't you on the stand?'

'Yeah, once, but not for long. I think tomorrow's Dan's big day.'

'How is it going?'

'I'm not supposed to discuss it.'

She glanced at him. 'Even with me?'

'Even with you.'

'Okay, fine,' she said. They went down the corridor. There was a line, but after a look at them both, the maître d' seated them right away.

Facing each other, they seemed to have nothing to talk about. He played with a fork. Anger pushed dully against the protective membrane of fatigue and apathy as he followed her glance out into the night. In the early darkness traffic choked the parkway and the Roosevelt Bridge. On their way home, he thought, to wives, husbands, families they saw every day. One thing about the Navy, it taught you not to take anything for granted. Beyond the shimmering lines of stalled traffic, Washington was a scattered, twinkling hurly-burly of light, like a distant carnival. The floodlighted Memorial was a white finger flipping off the world.

'What's wrong, Betts?' he said at last.

'Nothing. I'm tired, too. My back hurts.'

He was considering pressing it, getting it out in the open, when someone said from beside their table, 'Excuse me. You're from *Ryan*, aren't you?'

The woman was stocky, with shoulder-length brown hair. Her voluminous green dress looked odd, though he couldn't have said how. Her face was round, not chubby, but broad. It was hard to guess how old she was.

'I'm sorry to interrupt your dinner. I'm Deanne Evlin.'

It took a second before the name registered. By the time he'd stammered something Susan had asked her to sit. He pulled another chair over. Even close up, she could be twenty or forty; she had an air of immunity to time that, when he thought of it, Evlin had sort of had, too.

'I'm glad to meet you. Sorry I didn't understand right away – '

'You're hurt.' She had a soft voice, soft and clear.

'Not too badly. Look, Mrs. Evlin.'

'Deanne, please.'

'Deanne, I had no idea you were in town. I'd have looked you up. I had a lot of – a lot of respect for Alan.'

His words seemed to release some inner tension. She

404

dropped her eyes, and he thought for a moment she'd weep. But she didn't. Instead she smiled up again, a slow, sad smile with peace woven into it. 'I'm glad to hear that.'

'It's the truth. Al and I – we got to talk some. On the bridge, at night. I wish we'd had time for more. He was quite a man. A good officer, but . . . in a different way from the others.'

'Did he show you the picture of the Master?'

Dan grinned.

'He shows that to everybody. I think he uses it – used it – as a test. The Master heard of it, and laughed! He thought it was amusing. There's power, you see, even in a photograph of him.'

'Well, I don't know about that. Al told me about you, and your MS work, and your – plans together. I'm sorry. Did you come here for the court of inquiry? I guess that's a stupid question.'

'Not so stupid. I guess no one expected me. They won't even let me in.'

'That's right, it's closed except to survivors. I was trying to think where you would have been sitting. But still – '

'That's terrible!' said Susan, putting her hand on Deanne's.

'Yes, you'd think they'd let me know something. But all they say is that it's in progress and I'll be informed of the outcome. But how can I just wait? It's as if he's on trial, isn't it? Even though he's already rejoined?'

'Rejoined – yes. Yes, it is.'

'I wish – not that it hadn't happened, everything that happens is right – but that he'd had just a little more time. He was thinking of leaving the Navy, you know. It wasn't my will, or the Master's. But we discussed it, his participation, and whether it was appropriate for his stage of development. He was close to a decision.'

'He'd made it.'

'I'm sorry?' The calm eyes turned to him.

'He'd made that decision, Deanne. On this cruise.'

'And what did he decide?'

He said awkwardly, 'He told me he'd decided to get out. And when it came to, to when he had to act on what he believed – I don't know if I agree with what he did. But I think it was the decision you'd have wanted from him. It would have made you proud.'

'I think I see. Will you be able to tell me more later? It would mean a lot to me, to know more.'

'If I can.' He caught Susan's look. 'I mean – yes. After the trial.'

'And now they're trying to find him guilty of crashing his ship into the other one, is that right?'

'It's not that simple – well, maybe it is, when you get right down to it. There're two easy goats. The captain, and Alan. I don't think either of them deserves the blame, but Packer was the commanding officer, and Al had the deck when *Kennedy* hit us.'

'Is there a lawyer? Someone to represent him?'

'I don't think so. Captain Packer's family had someone there. A Lieutenant Hauck. But he had to go through some kind of appointment process.'

'Then I want to ask your advice, as someone who knew and loved Alan.' In the candlelight her face shone like an icon. 'Our society has a branch here in Washington. Perhaps they could arrange for someone to represent him. Do you think Alan ought to have someone there?'

He struggled briefly with an unwillingness to drag civilians into the struggle he saw shaping up. But the way Johnstone was hammering away, with only Hauck against him, seemed unfair. 'That might not be a bad idea. If you really care – '

'Of course she cares,' said Susan hotly.

'I only meant – '

'I know what you meant,' said Deanne. 'Thank you for your advice. I hope you are both happy, Dan and Susan, and find peace.'

When she had left he sat staring into his coffee. Then he looked at his watch, and shook a tablet out of the envelope. 'That was funny, running into her.'

'Not that funny. There're only two hotels this close to the Pentagon.'

'But how did she know who we were?'

'That's not hard, either. There's nobody else here in uniform.'

'You're probably right. Dessert?'

'God, no. Maybe a glass of wine. A little one.'

'Is that okay for the – for the baby?'

'I gave up smoking for her. I'm not giving up my whole life.'

He shook his head when the waiter asked what he wanted. It didn't seem like a good idea to mix alcohol and pills.

'Well, I guess it's time to go up,' Susan said at last. He thought she didn't sound very eager.

In the room, he drew the curtains, then shrugged slowly out of his service dress blouse. He hung it carefully on a chair, leaning against the wall for a moment, fighting vertigo. The wall itself seemed to tilt, as if the solid ground were rolling. She was in the bathroom, teling him about some friend of hers she'd had lunch with. 'Moira Liberman. Remember her? We were roommates. She was with me when I met you. At that dance, in Smoke Hall.'

'Uh-huh.'

'Don't say "Uh-huh." Do you remember her or not?'

'The heavy girl, right? Long dark hair?'

'She's not heavy. Just solid. And it's short now. She's doing her master's in North American Prehistory with Robert Kelly. I wish they had something like that in Newport. But of course they don't. . . .'

He was only half-listening. The bed yielded softly, unlike a bunk. Despite the drug he was getting excited. 'I thought you were in the program at Salve Regina.'

'That's an evening class, and it's not very good. I'm just going to get farther and farther behind. . . .'

She came out in a shapeless gray sweatshirt and pants. Beneath the Naval Academy crest her stomach thrust out at him, round as a mooring buoy. 'I recognize those,' he said.

'They're the only things that fit me now. They keep me warm at night.'

'I can take over that job again.'

When he put his arm around her she stood still, letting him

hug her. 'Don't squeeze me too tight,' she muttered into his neck.

'Sorry.'

'Want to feel it?'

'What?'

'The baby, stupid. Put your hand here. Feel it? She's kicking.'

Beneath his hand he felt a faint movement, slow yet violent, somehow unsettling.

'How do you know it's a she?'

'Just a feeling. I talk to her sometimes. Sometimes she answers. That reminds me, we have to talk about names soon. We were going to, and then you – left us.'

He let her move his hand over her belly, intimidated at its taut convexity. It seemed unnaturally hard. He couldn't imagine how it must feel, having something growing inside you. Then pushing its way out. . . . He shuddered a little.

'Ow,' she said. 'Right in my *bladder*. Ouch.'

He had to lie on his right side, or his back. When they were in bed he groped out for her. She was a foot distant, facing away. He rubbed her shoulder. She felt very warm. 'Betts,' he whispered.

'What?'

'In your dad's car . . . I was remembering the time we made love. By the lake. Remember?'

'Uh-huh.'

'I know we can't do it the regular way. But do you think. . . ?'

She rolled over. 'I thought you were hurt.'

'That doesn't mean I don't want you.'

'And it doesn't mean I feel like it. I thought you'd be a little more considerate.'

'Well, I missed you. Can't you just use, you know, your hand?'

'You're burned. You need to rest.'

'Susan, what's wrong? You don't sound like you're glad I'm back at all.'

'Don't say that! Of course I'm glad. And I'm glad you made it off the ship, when so many people didn't.'

The words were right, but her tone didn't match them. He lay rigid, staring in the dim light at a vague hump that must be her shoulder. She'd turned away again, then. Was this what he'd waited for? Dreamed of? He said, trying not to get emotional, 'You don't sound glad. You sound like you hate me.'

'I don't really feel like discussing it right now.'

He touched himself gingerly. Like an oak shovel handle. 'Now's the only time we have. Didn't you miss me?'

'When did I have time? I had to get our furniture moved in, I had to make up all my lesson plans for school, I had night classes, I had to go to Lamaze. *Alone*. I didn't like being left alone, Dan. And you didn't do anything about your pay; I had to ask for an advance. That's not a good way to start off with the administration.'

'What about deployments? It'll be six months before we see each other then.'

'That's part of what's wrong, I guess. I didn't really understand that when I said I'd marry you.'

He felt cold. He listened to her breathing: regular, slow, immeasurably distant across ten thousand miles of empty bed. 'I told you there'd be separations.'

'I guess it didn't register then.'

'What are you trying to say?'

'Nothing. I told you, I don't want to talk about it now. I've sort of tied myself in, anyway, with the baby.' The bed creaked reluctantly; her tone softened, her voice closer now. 'I guess it's a lot of things. I'm glad you're here. Just not . . . it's complicated. Maybe I'll feel differently tomorrow. Will you be able to see me tomorrow? Should I keep the room?'

'I think so. The other guys are staying over at Fort – I forget the name; the army post behind the Pentagon. We'll be off every night of the court-martial – I mean, the court of inquiry.'

'What happens then? Will you go back to Newport?'

'I guess it depends on the verdict.'

'Well, maybe I'll feel different tomorrow,' she said again. He heard her yawn; her fingertips patted his cheek twice. 'We both need sleep. Let's just give it a little time. Not rush it. Okay?'

He felt disappointed and angry. Still, he kissed her palm, telling himself, She's right; she's not in the mood; give it time. He was soft now anyway. 'I love you, Babe.'

'Love you. G'night.'

But a little later, he found himself awake again. Something had just occurred to him. Floated up, from the place in his mind that kept on working, kept on thinking, whether he was aware of it or not; and let him know what it had concluded only when it was ready.

If Packer and Evlin were both defended successfully, there was only one officer left who'd been on *Ryan*'s bridge the night of the collision. Only one man left to blame.

That one man was himself.

24

From Transcript of *Kennedy/Ryan*
Court of Inquiry: Day Two

The Court met at 0912. Present: Vice Admiral Ausura, U.S. Navy, President; Rear Admiral Morehead, USN, member; Rear Admiral Dennison, USN, member.

Lieutenant Commander Stanley F. Johnstone, U.S. Naval Reserve, counsel for the Court.

Lieutenant Robert Hauck, USNR, representing Commander Packer.

MR. CHARLES BARRETT: Sir, if it please the Court, I have been retained by the widow and friends of Lieutenant Alan Evlin as his counsel and request the rights of a party.

COUNSEL FOR THE COURT: Mr. Barrett has appeared before military courts many times and is well known in Washington. He has been granted clearance up to the secret level.

THE COURT: We regret the necessity for admitting additional individuals to this investigation. However, it is true that Lieutenant Evlin has the rights of a party. You are recognized as his counsel.

COUNSEL FOR LT EVLIN: Thank you, sir.

COUNSEL FOR THE COURT: This morning I will begin by recalling our primary witness of the events on *RYAN*'s bridge just before the collision. He will provide us with a detailed reconstruction of the maneuvers leading to the incident. I would like to defer cross-examination until we have completed this reconstruction. Then I will turn him over to Lieutenant Hauck and Mr. Barrett.

At this time, the counsel for the Court recalled Ensign Daniel Lenson. He resumed his seat as a witness and was reminded that his oath was still binding.

*

He sat in the same hard chair, in the same dull light. His body felt numb and bloated, as if it were made of plastic foam.

'You are the same Ensign Lenson, the senior surviving member of *Ryan*'s bridge team, who previously presented a written narrative of events leading up to the collision between *Ryan* and *Kennedy?*'

He told Johnstone that he was.

'Do you feel up to testifying? It may become somewhat stressful.'

'I will cope with it to the best of my ability, sir.'

'Do you feel that your recollection as to these events is trustworthy?'

To hell with *you*, Dan thought. Aloud, he said carefully, 'I believe so. I may be off by a minute or two, but I remember what happened.'

'Were any of the records such as the deck log or engineering bell book saved after the collision?'

He resigned himself to the grinding of Johnstone's mill. 'No,' he muttered, settling himself for a long siege.

Q. You know of no documentation whatsoever that was saved?

A. No, sir.

Q. Now, on the night you had watch, what was the command situation?

A. We were under Captain Packer's command.

Q. I mean external to the ship.

A. We were under the tactical command of the flag on *KENNEDY*, CTG 21.1.

Q. Was there a screen commander?

A. The captain of *DEWEY* was screen commander.

Q. What was the condition of the ship at the time she joined this task group?

A. We had undergone heavy storms in the Arctic and sustained damage. Pumps and evaporators were down. The forward mount was smashed in and we had taken water forward and aft.

Q. In your opinion, did any mechanical failure or material

deficiency on USS *RYAN* contribute to the collision and subsequent loss of life?

A. They may have contributed, yes.

Q. What is your opinion of the general state of training and morale aboard?

A. I think the state of training was okay. We had some good men. But they were overworked and morale was poor.

Q. Did the helmsmen and lookouts perform properly?

A. The helmsmen did. I had to ride BM3 Pettus about the lookouts.

Q. Why?

A. They – one in particular – did not stand proper watches. I had caught him sleeping on watch before and found him flaked out again a few minutes before the collision.

Q. Please define 'flaked out.'

A. Asleep on watch.

Q. Did you place him on report for this, or take other action?

A. I told him I was placing him on report.

Q. Who was this man?

A. Seaman Recruit William Lassard. I believe he was one of the causes of the accident.

Q. How so?

A. It was a complicated situation that goes to the root of what was wrong on *RYAN*. I believe he used drugs and sold them to the rest of the crew. Earlier in the cruise, someone, several men, one of whom I believe to be Lassard, shoved me around on the fantail at night and I almost went overboard. In fact, I did go overboard, but caught the propeller guard and pulled myself up after they left. I reported this to the XO and to the captain and they instructed me to keep it under my hat until we returned to Newport, and Lassard would be taken care of there.

Q. This is the man who was port lookout?

A. Yes.

Q. How do you relate him to the collision?

A. I have thought this over for some time. I believe what might have happened is that the captain went out on the wing to pick up *KENNEDY*. He may have asked the lookout where

413

the carrier was. If Lassard gave him the wrong bearing, he would have been looking at *CALLOOSAHATCHEE*, quite a few degrees to the left. If he thought that was the carrier, he might have concluded we were too far to the right.

Q. Did this man survive the sinking?

A. He is present in this room.

Q. We will examine him this afternoon. Now, Mr. Lenson, would you go through the sequence of signals before the collision once more?

A. We were on zero-one-zero, twenty knots, heading almost due north. The first signal brought the formation course right to one-zero-zero, a little south of due east. Then we had a flight course order to two-six-zero, almost due west, and increased speed.

Q. Why were two course orders given? Why didn't the carrier simply come all the way around to two-six-zero?

A. My understanding of the matter – according to the maneuvering instructions, you can't make a course change of greater than 180 degrees in one signal. You have to do it in steps to make sure everyone turns the same way.

Q. Those were the only signals before the collision?

A. As far as I heard.

Q. It is possible you did not hear a signal?

A. I suppose so, especially as the time of collision neared.

Q. Were all the alidades on the bridge working?

A. Yes – no, they were not. The starboard alidade was fogged.

Q. Did you report this?

A. No. It had been fogged up since we got to the Arctic. We used the centerline and port alidades instead.

Q. Did the captain know this?

A. I think – no, I don't know if he did or not.

Q. Did he use the starboard alidade?

A. Not to my knowledge.

Q. Did *RYAN* or *KENNEDY* sound any signals prior to the collision?

A. *RYAN* did not. I recall a whistle from *KENNEDY*, but that was during or just seconds prior to colliding.

Q. Did either ship turn on its navigation lights full?'

A. I don't think so.

Q. Now, Mr. Lenson, we have brought into court a chalkboard, a pad of maneuvering-board paper, parallel rules, and dividers. I ask you to illustrate the position of the two ships, the maneuver in which they engaged, and the sequence of events leading up to collision. We will photograph the results and offer them in evidence.

A. Yes, sir.

COUNSEL FOR THE COURT: Let the record show the witness is drawing on the blackboard.

WITNESS: [indicating chalkboard] At 0100, we were steaming on course zero-one-zero degrees, speed twenty knots. *KENNEDY* was in the center of the formation. The first signal changed formation course to one-zero-zero, about here. This was the first indication we had of her coming around. The second signal, turn two-six-zero, speed twenty-seven, brought her around to point almost directly at us. We had to maneuver such that we would end up astern of her and a little to port.

The maneuver the captain planned was to come right to one-three-zero until *KENNEDY* was somewhere along this line [indicating]. After we passed her, we were to come left with hard rudder. That would slide us into position astern. We were to start the maneuver as soon as the turn was executed and time the last part of it by watching *KENNEDY*'s lights.

What actually happened was that we came to one-three-zero as planned and held that course for about a minute and a half or two minutes. The captain then took the conn and came left to zero-nine-zero. We held that course for a minute or two, then in here some place [indicating] for some reason the captain gave a left hard rudder. The effect of this was to cut across the bow of the carrier, and she hit us.

COUNSEL FOR THE COURT: Now, you say this was all diagrammed on a maneuvering board. Did you see this diagram?

A. No, sir, I base my reconstruction on what I heard. The carrier had headed west to launch her planes on the previous watch and everyone assumed that they'd recover on the same course, or close to it, since the wind was the same.

Q. And *RYAN* had been assigned plane guard then, is that correct?

A. Yes, sir.

Q. And what is that station?

A. It is, 1,000 yards astern of the carrier offset twenty degrees.

Q. And Mr. Evlin had discussed the maneuver with Commander Packer?

A. Yes, sir.

Q. Will you relate that conversation to the court?

A. I heard only part of it. It started out that the captain had forgotten his pipe and Mr. Evlin asked him why not go and get it. Then he said, 'Well, you know about the time I leave they'll put a signal in the air.' The lieutenant said he could handle it. The captain asked him what he would do if they came to two-six-zero. Mr. Evlin told him he would do the maneuver the same way he had before – come around to the right with ten degrees rudder, slow down, wait for *KENNEDY* to pass, then fall in behind her.

But as Mr. Silver testified, we had received that signal when we joined, saying that when a destroyer wasn't on station, it wasn't doing any good; that there wouldn't be any more sluggishness, something about love being dependent on timing, and that from now on ships would get to station by the fastest means possible even if they made a mistake. So when Alan – Lieutenant Evlin – said that, the captain blew up and said no, that would take forever. He then outlined the maneuver he wanted.

Q. After Mr. Evlin had recommended a more conservative maneuver?

A. Yes, sir; as I said, they had words over it.

Q. What did Mr. Evlin say, as precisely as you can recall?

A. He admitted the captain's solution would be faster, but he said it would take us too close to the carrier, and that she would be pointing right at us at some point.

Q. This message you refer to was from Rear Admiral Hoelscher?

A. Yes, sir.

Q. And who assigned you to plane guard station?

A. Beacon – that would be him. Or his staff, I guess.

Q. Who receipted for that order?

A. Lieutenant Evlin made the call on the pritac. As I said yesterday, they forgot to assign a plane guard, and he wanted to clarify that it would be us again. That was logical, since she was turning toward us. It was easier for us to fall in astern than for another destroyer to try to catch up.

Q. That question was raised subsequent to the execution of the signal to turn two-six-zero?

A. It was answered in the same transmission as the execute signal.

Q. All right. Now the carrier has turned toward you. *RYAN* is on course one-three-zero, heading for her new station astern of her. At what point did the captain take the conn?

A. About a minute and a half after we had steadied up on two-three-zero. I mean, one-three-zero.

Q. Take your time. Who had the conn at the moment of collision?

A. Commander Packer.

Q. How long did he have it before the collision?

A. It is hard to say, but I would guess – I would estimate, no longer than two or three minutes.

Q. Let us return to the moment when he ordered a course change forty degrees to the left. Did either you or Mr. Evlin raise any objection to that order?

[Witness requested a glass of water. When he was refreshed, the question was repeated.]

A. Not immediately. Mr. Evlin went to the chart table to check what it would do. I went out to the wing for another bearing on *KENNEDY*. I recall now that when I went to use the alidade, it was set a few degrees off to the left. That might have been where the captain left it when he had gone out a moment before to do the same thing.

Q. But no one made any verbal objection?

A. Yes, we did. A minute or so later, I came back and told the captain the bearing to the guide was zero-eight-zero. At the same time, Mr. Evlin said that the new course put us only 400 yards from the carrier.

Q. When you took this last bearing, did you observe *KENNEDY*'s sidelights?

A. I have the impression of having seen green lights, more than one. I am almost sure I saw them, but things were happening so fast, I couldn't swear to that.

Q. How long before the collision was it that you saw the green lights?

A. Not more than a minute.

Q. And you did not report them?

A. I was not sure they were running lights. They were dim and there were all kinds of deck-edge lights and others. I think they were turned on for aircraft recovery.

Q. You are positive that the maneuver the commanding officer had in mind ended with a left turn rather than a right?

A. Yes, sir.

Q. And your explanation of the reason Commander Packer decided to depart from his plan was that he mistook the lights of *CALLOOSAHATCHEE* for those of *KENNEDY*?

A. As I have said, I believe he was misinformed by Lassard and focused his attention on the wrong lights.

Q. Had any maneuvering-board solution been done that included a course of zero-nine-zero?

A. Not to my knowledge.

Q. Now, when the captain received these two pieces of information – your bearing and Evlin's estimate of how close *RYAN* would pass *KENNEDY* – what was his response?

A. He hesitated, then increased his rudder.

Q. To the left?

A. Yes, sir. I had gone out on the wing again by then. I realized that the carrier was almost on us, and went back inside. The captain then increased his rudder to hard left and ordered all engines ahead emergency flank.

Q. Which would give what speed?

A. We had boiler power for thirty knots.

Q. And then you collided.

A. Yes, sir. Another 200 feet and we would have made it. Or if the captain had given a right rudder instead of a left, we might have shaved down *KENNEDY*'s side but not hit her.

Q. Did you see the commanding officer after the collision?

A. We spoke on the wing, as I described yesterday.

Q. At what point did you leave the ship?

A. As I said, after leaving the bridge, I went about the ship, down to the second deck to release a man from the brig. I helped others find their way topside. Then I went over the side.

Q. Would you describe the situation after the collision?

A. It was chaotic. Because of the fire and the fact we were cut in half, there was no opportunity to muster at life-boat stations. Each man went over on his own. Fortunately, there were plenty of life jackets. But they didn't protect us against the cold. That was why the absence of the ship's boat is disturbing.

Q. Have you any criticism to make of the search-and-rescue effort?

A. Of the search-and-rescue, no. I have two questions, though, one concerning the return of the carrier; the other concerning where *RYAN*'s boat went after the ship went down. If this is the place to raise them.

Q. It is.

A. My first question concerns *KENNEDY*'s return. Lieutenant Evlin and others were still fighting the fire when the carrier hit us again. There were still men aboard and many in the water nearby. Then, after that, the ship's boat disappeared. The combination of these two events is why there were so few survivors. Most of the men who died did so after the initial collision. I hope we will find out why.

The witness requested a short break. A fifteen-minute recess was granted.

Examination recommenced.

Q. You have referred to a message directing *RYAN* and other screening units to expedite getting on station?

A. Yes, sir.

The counsel for the Court requested the reporter to mark a message Exhibit B. It was so marked and submitted to the parties and to the Court.

Q. I hand you a message marked Exhibit B. Would you read it, please?

A. 'From: CTG 21.1. Action: TU 21.1.2 Subject: Maneuvering. This exercise will test and hone our performance of screening and close-in maneuvering. At 200Z all units will set and adhere to wartime conditions including radar silence and dimmed lighting. All commanding officers bear in mind that when units are not actually on station they are not contributing to fighting effectiveness of task group. They will accordingly eschew sluggish maneuvering and change stations in the most expeditious manner. In war as in love timing is everything. Prompt and resolute action even at the expense of an occasional mistake is a hallmark of smart destroyer outfits. Admiral Hoelscher sends.'

Q. That is the message to which you were referring?

A. Yes. I think this was the reason Commander Packer decided on a risky maneuver rather than the safer one Lieutenant Evlin recommended.

Q. Can you explain why, feeling as you do, you did not object?

A. Well, Mr. Evlin already had, and the captain overruled him pretty strenuously. Maybe I should have spoken up, too, but I was not confident enough in my understanding of the matter to do so.

Q. After Commander Packer gave his order to come left, then increased his rudder to left full, did it not occur to you to warn him that it would bring him into the path of *KENNEDY*?

A. I should have. I did not. I thought he knew better than I did what was going on.

COUNSEL FOR THE COURT: This concludes my re-examination of this witness. Do the other counsels desire to cross-examine?

COUNSEL FOR CDR PACKER: I so desire, yes.

Cross-examined by counsel for Commander Packer.

Q. Mr. Lenson, when *RYAN* came left to course zero-nine-zero, you left the pilothouse to check the captain's solution, is that correct?

A. No, sir. I crossed the bridge to use the alidade on the port wing. It was Lieutenant Evlin who checked the course at the chart table.

Q. And your conclusion was that he would pass close to the *KENNEDY*?

420

A. Again, that was what Lieutenant Evlin said. His solution showed us passing her within 400 yards, which at night, at sea, without radar, is too close.

Q. In which direction?

A. On *KENNEDY*'S port side.

Q. Is that why you intimated in your previous testimony that you were surprised that the captain turned left?

A. Yes, sir. If he had just held his course, there would have been a close passage, but we would have all been safe.

Q. Now, when you were out on the wing: Could you see the running lights of the *KENNEDY*?

A. I could see lights.

Q. 'Lights'?

A. Yes, sir. As I testified, there were many small dim lights on the carrier's bearing. I could not distinguish the running lights among the others.

Q. During the time *RYAN* was on zero-nine-zero, did you get any reports from the lookouts?

A. No, sir.

Q. Did you have any reports from your lookouts at all between the turn to one-three-zero and the collision?

A. Not that I recall.

Counsel for Commander Packer had no further questions of this witness.

Cross-examined by counsel for Lieutenant Evlin.

Q. Mr. Lenson, I am coming in in the middle of this case and we will perhaps go over some material already covered. I would appreciate your correction if I err. Now, during the period you were on watch, you said the captain was off and on the bridge. How often was he off?

A. He was on the bridge from about – from when I came on at 0100; he went to his sea cabin for awhile, till Lieutenant Evlin called him about the turn; then he came back up at 0200 or 0205. He was on the bridge from then on, except for the short time when he went aft to get his pipe, about 0210.

Q. So that while you were in the screen, steaming in close proximity to other ships, the captain was off the bridge more than he was on it, during the period of your watch?

A. That is misleading on two points, sir. First, we were not 'in close proximity' when we were in our screen station. Second, although he wasn't there every minute, he was in phone contact and came back immediately when we began our course change.

Q. Was the executive officer on the bridge at any time during your watch?

A. No, sir. Occasionally he came to CIC, but I have never seen him on the bridge.

Q. What kind of information were you getting from CIC?

A. None. CIC was secured because the radars were not operating.

Q. Mr. Lenson, are you are a qualified conning officer?

A. No, sir.

Q. You have had extensive training, then?

A. At the Academy, but this was my first time in actual fleet steaming.

Q. How long had you been on *RYAN*?

A. About two and a half weeks.

Q. *RYAN* was your first afloat duty?

A. Yes, sir.

Q. So that about two and a half weeks is the sum total of your Navy experience?

A. Well, yes.

Q. Isn't it a little odd that you would be assigned to such an important watch with no training?

A. I did – that is, I had some training.

Q. Was *RYAN* shorthanded?

A. Not in terms of number of officers. But the captain wanted Lieutenant Talliaferro, the chief engineer, off the watch bill. The plant was old and needed attention. So he did not stand bridge watches.

Q. How long had Mr. Evlin been aboard?

A. He said to me once he had been aboard for almost two years.

Q. Did you have confidence in him?

A. Yes, sir, he was a very good officer.

Q. Can you tell us how much experience the bridge team in general had in formation maneuvering?

A. Well, that calls for a comparison I'm not – I can't answer that. I had not been in formations before. I suppose Mr. Evlin had. I'm sure the captain had.

Q. But he was only on the bridge sporadically. Would it be fair to say, Mr. Lenson, that in terms of any assistance or backup whatsoever, Lieutenant Evlin was essentially alone on the bridge of USS *RYAN* that night?

COURT: You have just established that your witness is incapable of answering that question intelligently, Mr. Barrett.

COUNSEL FOR LT EVLIN: I withdraw the question. Would you describe the lights burning on *RYAN* on the night of the collision?

A. Dimmed navigation lights.

Q. Please describe them.

A. It would be masthead and range, and port and starboard and stern lights.

Q. But that is the normal lighting for a ship under way.

A. Well, dimmed I guess would be cutting down the illumination from them. There's a switch on the light panel that you throw to turn on the navigation lights, and it has a Dimmed position.

Q. Did you check them when you came on watch?

A. The boatswain's mate did that. He reported to me that the lights were burning.

Q. Did you verify that?

A. No, sir.

Q. So in fact, one or more of the lights might have been out?

A. It is possible, if Pettus did not bother to check them. But I'm sure he did.

Q. Correct me if I am wrong, but is it not one of the duties of the junior officer of the deck to check the running lights personally when he comes on watch?

A. [witness paused.] I believe it is.

Q. And you did not?

A. No, sir. I was late relieving and I did not check the lights.

Q. Let's go on. What was *RYAN*'s turning radius?

A. I think – I think about 1,200 yards.

Q. At what speed?

A. At standard – at fifteen knots.

Q. And how fast was the ship traveling when Mr. Evlin and the captain were doing their calculations?

A. Twenty-seven knots.

Q. What is the turning radius at that speed?

A. I'm not sure. Probably less than 1,200 yards.

Q. But you're not sure?

COUNSEL FOR THE COURT: Mr. Barrett, the ensign has said clearly that he was not.

COUNSEL FOR LT EVLIN: Thank you, sir. I withdraw that question, as well.

Let us go on now to the maneuver that Evlin recommended versus the one Packer ordered. Can you reproduce from memory the maneuvering-board solution that he and Commander Packer discussed, as you said in your testimony?

A. Yes, sir, I think I can. [Witness illustrates.] Commander Packer asked him what he would do if the carrier came to a recovery course around two-six-zero. He told him he had worked it out and that he –

Q. Who?

A. Lieutenant Evlin. He intended to slow to fifteen knots and turn right, away from *KENNEDY*, all the way around to two-six-zero; wait for her to pass us; then fall in astern. The captain said that was too slow. He wanted him to come only slightly right instead and head down the carrier's port side at flank speed, making a hard left turn into station when he was past her. They had a disagreement about it, and the captain told him to do the maneuver his way.

Q. Did you hear Lieutenant Evlin object to the solution?

A. Yes, sir. That's what I meant by a disagreement.

Q. Did you feel that the maneuver the captain ordered was dangerous?

A. Well, not exactly. But it sounded riskier than the solution Mr. Evlin wanted.

Q. But you didn't make your misgivings known to anyone.

A. As I said, it was the first time I'd been in this situation.

Q. In other words, you had not been adequately trained?

A. I don't know.

Q. But you said nothing?

A. I said nothing.

Q. Let's go on. If you had been watching *KENNEDY*, could you have seen her at all times?

A. That's an unfair question, sir. Mr. Evlin wanted a bearing on her every ten minutes. I did that. I also had other things to do on the bridge.

Q. I stand corrected. Now, do you recall what Mr. Evlin, your OOD, did after the captain relieved him of the conn?

A. He went to check the new course on the maneuvering board.

Q. He no longer was in charge of the ship?

A. No, sir, the captain had taken the conn.

Q. What precisely does that mean?

A. That Commander Packer was responsible for subsequent maneuvers.

Q. And you heard him, the captain, take the conn?

A. Yes, sir, distinctly.

Q. And he legally took control of the ship from that moment on.

A. That is the way I understand it.

Q. What was your status as a result of this?

A. Mine?

Q. That is correct. How did your status change as a result of the captain's taking the conn?

A. I'm not sure. I suppose I was still the JOD.

Q. And your duty then would be to assist whom?

A. The captain?

Q. Please answer.

A. I suppose it would be to assist the captain, since he had become the conning officer.

Q. And did you then assist him?

A. I was confused. I went out on the wing to try to clarify the situation in my mind.

Q. Mr. Lenson, in your opinion, was there anything that could have saved *RYAN* after the collision took place?

A. I don't think so, sir. I heard DC1 Traven's testimony and it seems to me –

Q. Personal knowledge, please.

A. I don't think she could have been saved.

Q. Even the forward section of a ship has considerable buoyancy. Did you consider staying aboard to try to save her, as Lieutenant Evlin apparently did?

A. I trusted the judgment of the captain and followed his order to abandon ship. When I thought all of the crew had that word I went into the water, too.

Q. Mr. Lenson, since the collision have you had any duties in regard to the survivors of *RYAN*?

A. Well, I spent the first few days after we got back to the States in the hospital. After that, in conjunction with the other officers, I've had to try to reconstruct the men's pay records. I helped the XO in getting them clothes and gear and so forth, and I helped write the letters to the next of kin. He signed those, but we wrote them.

COUNSEL FOR LT EVLIN: Thank you, Ensign.

If I may make a brief summary of this cross-examination: The points I have established are, first, that Mr. Evlin was not properly assisted by Mr. Lenson or anyone else normally required to provide such assistance; second, that he had warned the captain in advance against this maneuver; third, that in the midst of a maneuver that he had executed safely only hours before, he was relieved of his post; and finally, that the last orders before the collision proper, which in fact rendered it inevitable, were given by the captain after he had relieved said officer.

I have no further questions of the witness at this time.

Lieutenant Commander Benjamin Bryce, USN, was recalled as a witness. He was warned that his oath was still binding.

Examined by the counsel for the Court.

Q. Commander, you have listened to the testimony given this morning. I know that you were not present on the bridge, but do you have any comments on it?

A. It seems to me that we have here a case of people doing their best to evade responsibility.

Q. Please elaborate.

A. I'm a little old-fashioned in these matters. I was taught that when you had a watch, you were responsible for what went on during that watch. Now, on duty that night we had Lieutenant Evlin and Ensign Lenson. So, the argument that Mr Evlin's lawyer here seems to be using is that once Captain Packer got up there on the bridge, all Evlin's accountability just vanished away.

Now you have to have known this officer, Evlin I mean, to know that even at the best of times he was not the kind of man to actively seek responsibility. In fact, he was just the opposite.

COUNSEL FOR LT EVLIN: I must ask the witness to refrain from personal opinion and stick to facts.

COUNSEL FOR CDR PACKER: Certainly the judgment of his immediate superior as to Lieutenant Evlin's capacity to stand a watch is of interest.

COUNSEL FOR LT EVLIN: But Commander Bryce has stated earlier that he himself did not stand watches, and that therefore –

THE COURT: The examination will continue.

COUNSEL FOR THE COURT: What do you mean, Commander, when you say Evlin did not actively seek responsibility?

A. He had a lax approach to duty and a tendency to let the men get away with things. We've heard Lenson testify to the same attitude in his action when he found a man supposedly sleeping on watch. I had hopes for Lenson when he joined us, but found that he had, through association with Mr Evlin, who he stood watch with, he soon took on this same coloration.

Q. Do you feel Lieutenant Evlin was lax on the bridge?

A. I can easily believe it. That would account for the casual attitudes of the lookouts, the slow response by the lee helmsman, the way everyone seemed to freeze or panic when collision was imminent. I don't know about this other maneuver he is supposed to have recommended, but I think what likely happened was Captain Packer arrived on the bridge, found a dangerous situation, and had to take charge cold.

I say this with reluctance, but the Court has to take into account the possibility that things are not exactly as Lenson described them. That is, in his eagerness to clear his friend, and of course himself, he has altered the sequence of events.

Q. Go on.

A. Let's say, for example, that the course to zero-nine-zero was ordered before Commander Packer reached the bridge. Then the Captain, arriving, realized that the ship was standing into danger. He summarily relieved Lieutenant Evlin, and ordered increasing amounts of left rudder in an attempt to save *RYAN*. Ultimately, he was unable to rectify the situation and the collision occurred. If events happened this way, you could hardly lay the blame on James Packer.

Q. What evidence have you for such a scenario?

A. That he was trying to straighten things out? Just that I know, knew, Commander Packer, and I knew Evlin, and that sounds a lot more likely than that he made the mistake and Evlin didn't. Not to put too fine a point on it, let's call a spade a spade. Evlin was a coward. He had refused orders in a very difficult situation, and at the time of the collision he was on restriction, scheduled to be flown back to the States for court-martial.

COUNSEL FOR LT EVLIN: I must object. All this is mere personal vilification.

CDR BRYCE: All this is a matter of record. Message traffic from *RYAN* dated 21 or 22 December will support me.

COUNSEL FOR THE COURT: Why was such a man permitted to continue standing bridge watch?

A. James Packer was too forgiving. I warned him not to, but he allowed Evlin to stand watches until he left the ship. This was the result.

Q. The testimony of the enlisted men – the quartermaster and the boatswain's mate – support Mr. Lenson's version of events.

A. I don't know about the QM. But Pettus, let me point out that he was in Lenson's division.

I think it's time to let a little light into the air here. So far in this investigation, it's been soft-pedaled that Lenson's division was the worst in the ship, that we had recently completed a search of its spaces – the night before, in fact – and found a large amount of marijuana, pills, drug paraphernalia, even weapons. By great good luck, I had in my pocket when I left *RYAN* the master-at-arms's list of these materials. Lenson wants to blame this collision on a seaman recruit. In fact, this man came up clean in the search. My attempts to break up this ring, and that's what it was, were resisted by Lenson and others. He even admitted at one point that he knew who the ringleader was, but refused to tell me.

Q. May I have that list?

The list was submitted to the parties and the Court, and marked Exhibit C for identification.

Examination by the counsel for the Court continued.

Q. Yesterday you intimated that you had serious accusations to make. Are these the accusations you were referring to?

A. Yes.

Q. Are you implying also that Lieutenant Evlin was involved in drugs?

A. It's not impossible. He had a sluggish, doped-up attitude about him that in my view – though I'm no expert by a long shot – it could have been something like that.

Cross-examined by counsel for Commander Packer.

Q. Commander, let us return to your idea that the commanding officer of *RYAN*, far from making an error, was trying to correct one previously made. You have served in the Navy how long?

A. Twenty-eight years, starting as a seaman recruit.

Q. In that time, you have served under many commanding officers. How would you rank James Packer among them?

A. As one of the very finest.

Q. As a ship handler?

A. Flawless. A very good seaman, cool under pressure.

Q. Did he take chances with the ship?

A. No. But he didn't pussyfoot around, either. He was a decstroyerman.

Q. We have heard testimony that he was ill and exhausted the night of the collision. How would you respond to that?

A. He may have had a sniffle. That's all.

Cross-examined by counsel for Lieutenant Evlin.

Q. Commander Bryce, it's evident that you had a low

regard for Alan Evlin. Let us go back to your grounds for this attitude. What were they? We are looking for facts, not suspicions or hearsay.

A. Well, it's hard to – you're a civilian. It would be easier to explain to a military man.

Q. Please explain to the Court, then.

A. Evlin and I disagreed over many things. Basically, he had a disinclination to exercise discipline, either over himself or his men. Since he was the senior department head, this had a bad effect through the whole ship.

Q. Could you be more specific?

A. He had weird ideas.

Q. What ideas?

A. I don't know. I couldn't make any sense out of them.

Q. Were those ideas spiritually based?

A. Spiritual?

Q. Yes.

A. I wouldn't know. I never hold a man's religion against him. I'm pretty broad-minded that way. I don't even know what religion he was, if any.

Q. I see. Let's examine your theory, or story, about what might have happened. What evidence can you offer for it?

A. I said I had no evidence. It's just my interpretation, you might say, of what might have happened.

Q. Unfortunately, Lieutenant Evlin is not here to defend himself. Because of that, Commander, I must ask you again what concrete evidence you have for this frivolous theory.

COUNSEL FOR THE COURT: Mr. Barrett, your implication of frivolity is out of place.

COUNSEL FOR LT EVLIN: Sir, it is the only word I can find for this kind of speculation by a witness who was not present and who, in fact, as other witnesses have testified, hardly ever appeared on the bridge.

THE COURT: Proceed, but refrain from commenting on the witness's testimony.

COUNSEL FOR LT EVLIN: No further questions of this witness.

THE COURT: We wish to point out at this time that a court of inquiry is not bound by the strict rules governing objections that prevail in courts-martial. It is our desire to afford the widest possible latitude for examination.

The Court informed Commander Bryce that he was privileged to make any further statement covering anything related to the inquiry that he thought should be a matter of record in connection therewith, which had not been fully brought out in the previous questioning.

The witness stated that he had nothing further to say.

The Court then adjourned until 1400.

'Can I help you with that, sir?'

Dan looked up from salad and coffee. He didn't know the man in line behind him. 'No thanks,' he said. 'I think I can handle it.'

He glanced cautiously around the cafeteria. It was almost empty; perhaps by design, the court had recessed after the normal lunch hour this time. He saw a corner table and aimed his tray toward it.

'Hey,' said a familiar voice. 'It's the ensign.'

Lassard, Gonzales, and Isaacs were sitting at a table with paper cups in front of them. They looked like new men. Fresh haircuts, regulation shaves, the new uniforms the survivors had been issued in Newport.

'Swell testimony this morning, Ensign.'

He didn't look at Lassard. 'What are you doing with these two, Isaacs?'

The first-class dropped his eyes without answering. Lassard said, 'Talking to you, Ensign. Or didn't you hear him?'

'I have nothing to say to you, Slick.'

'Got plenty to say *about* him, sounds like.'

'Only the truth.'

'Only *shit*, man. Get over here.'

Dan went on, ignoring them. For a moment it looked as if Lassard would get up. Then he glanced around and settled back. He took a pull at his drink and bent his head toward the others, all three men looking after Lenson.

At the corner table, Dan tapped a tablet from the green-edged pharmacy envelope and gulped it. He'd skipped one to be clear-headed for his testimony and his shoulder seared as if the burning oil still clung to it. He thought about taking two. Then he forced himself to put the envelope away.

He stared at the salad. He wasn't hungry. The long session with Johnstone and Hauck and Barrett had wrung him out like wet laundry. His hands had trembled at the board; everyone had heard the clatter of chalk. And then Bryce . . . that bastard! Now he and Evlin were both on record as incompetent, worse, of being tied in with drugs and permissiveness. While the ones who were really responsible –

He looked up to find Lassard leaning on his table.

'Got a message for you, Lenberg. From the Man. Anything else, have a ball, but lay off me, lay off him, lay off the boat. Hear?'

'What's he got on you, Slick? I still don't get what put you two together.'

'Negatory, man, no way. Nobody "got anything" on Slick Lassard. He just got on the winning team. His ass is covered. Yours ain't. You're out in the wide blue open, my man. You're in the nutcracker, and we're gonna crack your nuts.'

'Tell Bryce to fuck himself, Slick. That goes for you, too.'

'Okay, man. The kinnicks just wanted to cut some slack for a shipmate. Give you one last chance to get in the boat. But you just stepped in it, man. The Man and me, we're gonna waste you.'

Lenson sat there for some time, picking at the food. In the middle of the Pentagon, he was alone.

The Court reconvened at 1400. Present: All members, counsel for the Court, the parties, and counsels.

Lieutenant Edson D. Talliaferro, USN, was called as a witness by the counsel for the Court. He was duly sworn and examined as follows.

Q. Mr. Talliaferro, you were attached to *RYAN* as engineering officer. Is that correct?

A. Yes.

Q. How long had you been so assigned?

A. About a year and a half.

Q. I will pose to you the same question I posed to Mr.

Lenson this morning. What was the material condition of *RYAN* when she joined TG 21.1?

A. As he said, we'd sustained damage during storms and action in the Arctic, but by the 24th most of these were repaired. All evaporators, generators, and pumps were operational. Flooded spaces had been dewatered and accesses to the sea patched.

Q. In your opinion, did any mechanical failure or material deficiency contribute in any way to the collision and subsequent loss of life?

A. No sir.

Q. What is your opinion of the state of training and morale aboard *RYAN*?

A. In my department, engineering, they were good. As to the rest of the ship, I can't say.

Q. On the evening of 24 December and morning of 25 December of last year, where were you stationed?

A. I was holding down Main Control.

Q. In the engine room?

A. Yes, in Main Control there.

Q. State the sequence of commands you received after 0200, please.

A. From memory, we had twenty knots rung up; then a flank bell for twenty-seven. A few minutes later, we got an increase to twenty-eight and then an emergency ahead flank.

Q. You were on the throttle at that time?

A. No. I was supervising the throttleman and other members of the watch.

Q. But you were in a position to observe the throttle and so on?

A. That's right.

Q. Did you answer the engine orders you received?

A. Yes, sir.

Q. All of them? Promptly?

A. Yes, immediately.

Cross-examined by counsel for Commander Packer.

Q. What were the conditions of your engines at that time?

A. We had three boilers on the line, the superheater fires were lighted and the plant was split.

433

Q. You stated that all orders were answered immediately. Will you clarify for me what that means?

A. We indicated on the engine-order telegraph that we had received the order.

Q. But did this mean that it had been carried out? Correct me if I am wrong, but changing speed on a destroyer is not as simple as, say, pressing a gas pedal on a car, is it?

A. No. On receipt of an engine order, the watch has to evaluate power available, decide routing, then set the valves. On major changes like a backing bell, it gets complicated. The engines have to be stopped, steam has to be shifted to the reverse turbines, and so on. The speed changes we are discussing here, all we have to do is use more burners on the boilers. But it does take time to accelerate.

Q. So answering and responding are two different things. And there is a delay in response, even in normal operation, is there not?

A. Yes.

Q. How long is this delay?

A. It can take as long as three minutes or just a few seconds to set up the plant. But then the ship has to gather momentum. From twenty to twenty-seven knots ahead, say, it can easily take ten minutes before she is actually at that speed.

Q. That is when everything is working perfectly.

A. Yes.

Q. But we have heard testimony to the effect that everything on *RYAN* was not working perfectly.

A. She was an old ship. The overhaul was cut short. There were lines I had to hold together with radiator clamps and wire. And we had problems left over from the Arctic.

Q. Please elaborate.

A. I think what you are getting at is the remark Lieutenant (jg) Silver, or maybe it was the boatswain's mate, made about a problem with engine response. The reason for that was that we had water in the fuel.

Q. How did water come to be in the fuel?

A. When we were in a severe storm, some days previous, Commander Packer ordered me to ballast.

Q. Which means?

A. Pumping seawater into the empty spaces of the fuel tanks to give us more stability.

Q. Did you think this was a reasonable order?

A. Yes, given the ice we had accumulated. I thought at the time he had even delayed doing it too long.

Q. But he had not?

A. That's hard to say, sir. According to the stability diagrams, ballasting was the right thing to do. But it's risky, because later on when you refuel, you may have contaminated tanks, which is exactly what we got.

Q. What was the effect of this water?

A. It's almost impossible to get all the seawater out of the tanks after you ballast. It settles to the bottom, but when the ship rolls, it mixes a little. Not much, but once in a while we were getting a slug of water in the fuel lines. This makes the boiler fires sputter, and, as a worst case, can put them out.

Q. And you had this problem that night.

A. Once in a while, yes.

Q. Yet you said that you answered all bells immediately.

A. What I meant was that the ship might not respond.

Q. When you got the captain's emergency flank order, did the ship respond promptly?

A. That's hard to say.

Q. Why?

A. I was not in Main Control at the moment we got that order.

Q. Where were you?

A. I had gone forward to use the head.

Q. But weren't you on watch?

A. I didn't say I was on watch. I was exempted from bridge watches to spend most of my time below, but there was no requirement that I be in a specific space at a specific time. I went where problems required my attention. Those members of the Court who have served in engineering billets will understand this arrangement. My chief was a qualified engineering officer of the watch. He was on watch, and he was there.

Q. So you were in the head when the collision occurred?

A. Yes, sir. It knocked me off the throne onto the deck.

Q. Were you in Main Control before that, when the order for twenty-seven knots came down?

A. Yes.

Q. Was that responded to?

A. The response seemed sluggish. I went foward, intending to go back to the boilers and check them out as soon as I was done. But there were good men on the controls and the throttle. I'm sure they did all they could to increase speed. Down in the hole, you don't have much idea what's going on topside, but when you get an emergency bell you jam every ounce of steam you got into the lines.

Cross-examined by counsel for Lieutenant Evlin.

Q. Mr. Talliaferro, do you think *RYAN* was ever traveling at twenty-seven knots through the water before the collision?

A. I think we may have done that, yes.

Q. But never at flank emergency, which was what –

A. About twenty-nine knots would be all we would get out of three boilers, even all out. Calm water, downhill, maybe twenty-nine point five.

Q. So the difference was about two knots. How far would a ship go in two minutes in that two-knot difference?

A. What do you mean?

Q. Perhaps I am expressing it clumsily. How far ahead of its position at collision would it have been if it had been traveling at twenty-nine knots instead of twenty-seven?

A. I don't know. Too many variables in that.

Q. In fact, in two minutes, would it not have been almost 150 yards farther on, and cleared the carrier by almost 100 feet?

A. You seem to know more about it than you let on, Mr. Barrett.

Q. I served in destroyers during the war. The point is, had not whoever was in charge on the bridge given an order that would have carried the ship clear if the engines had responded as they should?

A. I wasn't up there and can't tell you that.

Recross-examined by counsel for Commander Packer.

Q. Let us return to the order to ballast. You assert that this was justified by weather and stability conditions?

A. It was the right decision.

Q. What would have happened had you not ballasted?

A. We would have capsized.

There was no further questions for this witness, and he resumed his seat.

Richard N. Norden Lieutenant, USN, was recalled as a witness. He was reminded that his oath was still binding and was examined as follows.

COUNSEL FOR THE COURT: Mr. Norden, go over again for us where you were at the time of the collision.

A. I was in my stateroom, in bed. I explained earlier that Mr. Evlin and I had exchanged watches, so I expected to be called around 0330 to take the morning watch.

Q. But in fact, you were awakened by the collison.

A. That's right.

Q. Then what happened?

A. I don't remember much about it. Everything was confused. I remember talking at one point to Mr. Lenson. He told me *KENNEDY* had run us down, and said 'abandon ship' had been passed.

Q. Continue.

A. I then abandoned ship.

Q. That's all?

A. Apparently I went aft, got into the whaleboat, and abandoned ship.

Q. Did you not have any duties, in the event of a collision?

A. Not after the order to abandon ship had been given. My recollection of this is not the best, because I sustained a head injury at some point during the events of that night.

Q. But you remember talking to Lenson?

A. Yes.

Q. Let us return to the allegations Lieutenant Commander Bryce has made about conditions in Mr Lenson's division, in fact throughout *RYAN* to some extent, if I understand him correctly. Were you aware of these conditions?

A. I had taken part in the search the evening before. I knew what had been found, yes.

Q. Did you know there were problems before that time?

A. No.

Q. Are you acquainted with Seaman Recruit William T. Lassard?

A. He was in my department. I did not know him well.

Q. What is your evaluation of his performance?

A. As far as I know, he is a typically effective seaman.

Q. You have heard the questions raised as to the movements of the ship's motor whaleboat after *RYAN* went down. What can you tell us about such movements?

A. I don't remember anything that happened between talking to Mr. Lenson and coming back to consciousness aboard USS *TALBOT*. Shortly thereafter, we were transferred by helicopter to *KENNEDY*.

Cross-examined by counsel for Lieutenant Evlin.

Q. Mr. Norden, as a watch stander and a department head, how well did you know Lieutenant Evlin?

A. Pretty well.

Q. What is your evaluation of him? As an officer and a watch stander?

A. I agree with Commander Bryce's description of him.

Q. Please elaborate.

A. He was not dependable.

Q. Do you believe he was ever under the influence of drugs?

A. [Witness paused.] It's not impossible.

Neither the counsel for the Court, the Court, nor the parties desired further to examine this witness. He resumed his seat.

William Theodore Lassard, seaman recruit, USN, was called as a witness. He was duly sworn and was examined as follows.

Examined by the counsel for the Court.

Q. State your name, rank, and branch of service.

A. William Lassard, seaman recruit, U.S. Navy.

Q. How long have you been on active duty?

A. A little over six years, sir.

Q. How long have you been attached to *RYAN*?

A. Four years.

Q. State your duty station at 0200 on 25 December.

A. On the bridge.

Q. Port lookout?

A. We swapped around. Believe he was the lookout then.

Q. Who was the lookout?

A. I was.

Q. Please state to the best of your recollection the location of the ships around *RYAN* at that time.

A. The lookouts don't know the position of the ships. That's the officers' job.

Q. Is it not your duty as lookout to keep abreast of the situation?

A. Lookouts just report what they see. It's up to the officers to figure out what it is.

Q. Please state what you saw, then.

A. It was dark. There weren't any ships on my side. There was one almost dead ahead, way off; you could only pick it up once in a while. There was some others off on the other lookouts' sides. To starboard.

Q. The one ahead would be the *CALLOOSAHATCHEE*, and the ones to starboard *KENNEDY* and *GARCIA*?

A. Told you, we didn't know what they were. Just lights.

Q. You have heard Ensign Lenson's testimony that he found you asleep on the wing shortly before the collision. Is that true?

A. I wasn't asleep or anything like that. I was standing a proper watch.

Q. Did he make any remarks to you?

A. Yes.

Q. What did he say?

A. Mr. Lenson made remarks every time he saw me. Didn't matter what he – what I was doing at the time, he would jump me. I tried to shrug it off and just do my job.

Q. What in fact did he say this time?

A. Said something about putting me on report.

Q. Why?

A. Like I said, he had this idea that I was [expletive deleted].

Q. To what do you attribute his attitude?

439

A. Don't know. Slick – I mean, I never did anything to him.

Q. He has testified that you used drugs and were furnishing them to other members of the crew.

A. That's not true, sir.

Q. Is it true that you were previously rated to third-class boatswain's mate on *RYAN*, and broken for unauthorized absence and fighting?

A. Yeah, but I was never busted for drugs. You can check my record. Or you can ask the XO.

Q. Let us go on to when the captain came out onto the bridge, apparently just a few minutes after Mr. Lenson talked with you. Please recount what happened then.

A. The captain came out and leaned over the alidade. Then he went back in.

Q. Did he say anything to you?

A. No, nothing.

Q. Did he notice that you were there? Nod, or acknowledge you at all?

A. No, sir, I don't think he was thinking about me; I don't think he even noticed me.

Q. He did not ask you, for instance, where the carrier was?

A. No sir.

Q. Where was the carrier at that time?

A. We were coming around, I think, and you could see it around the corner of the deckhouse.

Q. Think back carefully. When the captain looked through the alidade, was he looking in fact at the carrier? Or somewhere off to the left?

A. His back was to me. I couldn't see the alidade.

Q. Could you tell by the position of his head what he was looking at?

A. No. I was scanning with my binoculars, like I was supposed to.

The Court then informed the witness that he was privileged to make statements covering anything he thought related to the subject of the inquiry that had not been brought out in previous questioning.

The witness stated that he had and the Court instructed him to proceed.

WITNESS: I wanted to talk about after the collision – what happened after that.

COUNSEL FOR THE COURT: Go ahead.

WITNESS: After it hit us, the officers was freaking out, running around the bridge and shouting. I stayed put on the wing. When things quietened down, I went into the pilot-house. There was nobody there, so after a while I went out on the starboard wing. The captain was there alone.

COUNSEL FOR THE COURT: Go on.

WITNESS: Well, he looked at me, sort of not seeing me, and I stood there beside him for a while. He kept looking aft at the fire. Finally, to make conversation like, I said, 'Ay, what happened, Captain?' And he said, after a minute, 'Somebody [expletive deleted] up, Slick.'

So I stood there with him for a couple of minutes and we watched the fire, and the men jumping overboard.

Then I was thinking I better get back to my boat and get her in the water. I asked the captain, 'Sir, we better get off this bucket.' And he shook his head and he said, 'You go ahead and abandon.'

She was listing bad then, so Slick, he decided to go. So he was going down the ladder when the old man leans over and calls him back. He goes up a couple steps, and he hands him something and says give it to his son. So Slick sticks it in his pocket and here it is.

COUNSEL FOR THE COURT: Let the record show the court has received a gold ring for transfer to Commander Packer's son.

WITNESS: That all I got.

Neither the counsel for the Court, the Court, nor the parties desired further to examine this witness. He resumed his seat.

The Court then, at 1653, took a recess until the next day at 0900.

Lenson followed the afternoon of testimony with close attention. He felt supercharged, unaffected by the codeine. When the court broke for the day, he hoisted himself to his feet and followed the others out to the E-ring and down the ramp into the mall. It would be nice to get Susan something. Perfume? Candy? He glanced in the window of Dart Drug and saw Norden standing in front of the greeting cards

'Rich. Hey, Rich!'

Norden flinched, raising startled eyes. He looked pale, thin, like smoke from a hot fire. Rusty freckles stood out on white skin. 'We're not supposed to talk.'

'To hell with that. What is this bullshit you're giving them about Al? He never used drugs. He didn't even smoke! You're the one told me about Lassard, what a fuckup he was. Where are you going? What happened in that boat, Rich?'

But Norden was walking away, then jogging, too fast for Dan to follow. The clerk called after him. He wheeled, threw the card back at her. It fluttered to the floor. Then he was gone, sucked into the crowd of Army and Marine green, Air Force and Navy blue, and civilian employees pushing toward the Metro entrance.

Dan stared after him like a man overboard watching his ship disappear over the horizon of the sea.

The little toy MG was waiting, idling in a handicapped space. Susan had on a violet tam today. It looked familiar. Then he recognized it. She used to wear it when he visited her at Georgetown. 'How'd it go?' she asked as he eased himself in, hissing as his shoulder brushed the corner of the door.

'Not so good.'

'You had the stand again?'

'All morning. Then they had Bryce on, Norden, some of the other guys. What'd you do?'

'Went to a lecture at American U, then got tired and came back. I read a little. Then I just thought.'

'This is for you. You like pecans, right?'

'Thanks. . . . What's happening down there, Dan? You look mad as hell. Or scared as hell.'

'They were on me hard today.'

'Who?'

'The lawyers. Bryce. It's not going real well.'

'Tell me what happened. I want to know. I *ought* to know.'

'I told you, I can't discuss it, Susan.'

'You could tell me something.'

He turned his face to the window and watched the Potomac speed by, gray and sullen under its white mantle. 'Okay, Mr. Spock,' she muttered, flooring the gas. 'Warp speed to the hotel.'

He had two drinks while they were waiting to order. He was too angry to care about mixing them with the pills. After dinner they took the elevator to the sixth floor. She fumbled in her purse for the key. He knew she was angry, too, but he pretended not to notice. He didn't want a scene. He hated scenes. They reminded him of his parents' all-night-long screaming arguments.

As soon as the door closed, she began speaking to the wall. 'You know, it's not exactly fun for me, being alone all day, worrying about you. I'd like to know what's going on. It affects my life, too.'

'Maybe later.' He fell on the bed. The scotch made his head vibrate. 'Can you get me a drink of water, please?'

He held the glass and watched as she undressed, facing the mirror. Her hair came free and swung down, tangling in the catch of her bra. Her back was crossed by a white line, though summer was long gone. She undressed quickly, without looking at him, and went into the bathroom. A moment later the shower roared.

He pulled himself up and peeled off his blouse. His shoulder burned, but the drug held it separate from him. He took off his shirt and trousers and underwear. They were soaked.

In the bathroom her body glowed behind translucent plastic. The water roared like flames. He shouted, 'Want company, Babe?'

'Come in if you need help.'

When he stepped in she was soaped up, hair lathered, her body slick with foam like waves in a gale. She helped him wash briskly and efficiently, keeping the dressings dry, not touching him unnecessarily. When they were done, she stepped out and helped him towel. Her face in the mirror was blank as she dried his back. It was like being bathed by a nurse.

He sat on the bed and watched her sort through her clothes. There was a faint, high whistling in his head. He watched the sway of her breasts, large-nippled, heavier than they'd been when he last saw her; funny how they changed color month to month, like a slide show. The outward curve of her belly; her legs, strong and tapered, still brown. Then he considered himself. He was thinner, white, bruised the color of cheap wine. His arm dragged like a dug-in anchor. Part of him wanted to sleep, to check out of this fucking planet for a few hours. Another wanted not so much to make love as to possess, to reassert his ownership over her. It seemed like centuries since he'd seen her naked.

'Feeling better tonight?' he muttered hopefully.

She came out of the closet, holding her old-fashioned blue flannel nightdress. 'What?'

'Want to make love?'

'I thought we went over this last night.'

'This is tonight.'

'Well, I'm still tired,' she said, spreading out her nightdress and bending over the bed. 'Exhausted, in fact.' Her breasts swayed forward, half-covered by her damp hair. Her scent flowed out from her, lavender and lemon and some musky spice he didn't have words for. He caught the dismissal but refused to accept it; in fact, it determined him. He took her shoulder with his good arm and pulled her down gently.

She lay quietly on her side as he kissed her nipple, feeling it erect under his tongue. A little fluid seeped out, thin and insipid.

She didn't resist when he slipped his hand between her thighs Nor did she cooperate. Apprehension touched him. At another time he would have felt himself, made sure he was ready, but supporting his weight on one arm this was impossible. Her pubic hair grated dryly against him.

He came halfway to attention, and wedged it in quickly, before it could reconsider. There seemed to be no sensation in him, as if he were covered with a huge condom. He ground away for several minutes, lying half above her, half beside.

Gradually, in the motion, he lost track of himself.

He thought suddenly of the dead. They'd never touch a

woman again. Never return to the ones they'd loved. Guilt and terror gripped him like a cat gripping a mole. Guilt, at living. Terror, at the unimaginable endlessness of absence, of ending, of termination.

He remembered how they'd screamed, out beyond the firelight, how neither he nor anyone else could help them. . . .

The memory opened out then, suddenly, and he was no longer remembering but *there* in the water, gripped by the icy pincers, watching floating flame close in on him. Trying to swim in the blackness without air. The sea choked him, battered him, numbed him, then caught fire. His hands when he raised them were black with oil. A man screamed beyond the wall of flame, and his throat closed. The screaming man was himself; he was still screaming, and he would never stop.

When, sweating and rigid, he forced his eyes open, hers were closed. 'Do you have to put all your weight on me?' she said.

He shuddered, unable to speak through a throat soldered shut with horror. His erection had died inside her. Her vagina expelled him. He rolled away, desperate for air.

'Dan, what is it? Are you all right?'

'Nothing,' he gasped.

He heard her getting up. The soft, heavy pad of her feet. Her nightdress whispered.

He lay rigid, listening. He knew now what he'd wanted. Not sex, but reassurance he was still alive. The bed creaked and he glanced over. She lay motionless, staring away from him at the clock on the nightstand.

'What's eating you? Are you mad at me?'

'I'm just tired of this.' She stared at the clock. 'I'm tired of not knowing, tired of Navy secrets, just tired. And yes, I'm mad at you. I'm very angry.'

'What for? Do you think the collision was my fault?'

'Fuck the *collision*, Dan! I'm glad you got out. I said that! But it was – when you went away like that, just a phone call and you were gone, I was all alone in Newport. I didn't know anybody, not one person I could call for help. I know it's not your fault. But God knows the Navy doesn't care, so I'm mad at you. It may not be logical, but damn it, that's how I feel.'

He did not see at all. 'Yes,' he said.

'And other thing, I've been thinking about it now, I don't like being fucked when I'm not ready. I don't like it at all.'

'I didn't hear any major objections.'

'I thought I might want to once you started. Anyway, I said I wasn't interested. What am I supposed to do, scream?' Her voice rose. 'Don't ever do that again. I'm your wife, not a goddamned piece of meat with a convenient hole in it!'

'I see,' he said. The need for sympathy slid away and something cold as the sea took its place. 'I don't think that's a very constructive attitude. My friends died, I almost died, and I wanted you. You've treated me like a crippled stranger since I got back. You don't know what we went through.'

She stared at the clock silently.

'Being left alone like that, like you say – You knew what being a Navy wife meant. We discussed it before we got married. You said, as I recall, that you wouldn't mind being by yourself from time to time. That it would give you time to work on your degree.'

'It's different doing it. Maybe it's different after years of it. I haven't . . . we haven't spent a week in the same house. I'm eight months pregnant, but I don't feel married yet. I feel closer to Moira than I do to you.'

Moira, he remembered with an effort, was her ex-roommate. 'That's a great thing to say.'

'It's true. You bottle everything up, I wouldn't be surprised to hear your brains fizzing. That rigid Academy bullshit . . . I don't know if I can go on with you if you're so . . . so cold. With the baby coming . . . Jesus, I feel so alone.'

'You know,' he said slowly, 'when I was in the water, when I thought I was doing to die, I was praying. But I wasn't praying to God. Maybe it sounds blasphemous, but I was praying to you, that you would help me. And when that guy held me up, and I thought I might live another few minutes, I thought you had answered me.'

She put her hand over her eyes. 'Jesus,' she whispered.

'I'm sorry, Susan. I do love you, so much.'

The wrenching sound of her breathing told him she was crying. He groped to his blouse and handed her his handkerchief.

In the dim light from the window, from the city, she got up from the bed. She stumbled away. Then she turned, awkward and huge and swollen, and came back to him. He held her tightly, ignoring the scream from his burned shoulder. They clung to each other angrily, despairingly, hopelessly, like castaways in a stormswept sea, not knowing whether there is rescue ahead or only the last and final darkness.

25

When he left the lobby the next morning, six inches of snow covered the ground. Not a taxi was stirring in the District of Columbia. By the time he found a Checker he was already late. At the Pentagon he limped up the ramp hurriedly, flashing his pass at the security guard. It was tougher persuading the marines to let him in the courtroom.

But finally they did. As he took a seat in back, realizing belatedly that he'd forgotten his morning pill, a tall, balding, slightly stooped man in service dress blue was being sworn in. 'State your name, rank, branch of service, and present duty station,' Johnstone was droning.

'Leonard. A. Hoelscher,' the tall man said quietly to the three members of the Court. Dan saw that the broad gold on his sleeves matched theirs. Only Ausura, the president, outranked him. 'Rear admiral, USN. President duty station, commander, Carrier Division 42.'

Q. state your duty station on 25 December, sir.

A. I was Commander Task Group 21.1 in the eastern Atlantic, aboard USS *KENNEDY*.

Q. Under whose control were you operating?

A. I was under operational control of Commander, Second Fleet, for operation WESTERN VIGIL, an exercise to test the defenses of a carrier strike group.

At this point the Court sat with closed doors. Witnesses not party to the proceedings withdrew from the courtroom.

Q. I show you this document. Is it the plan under which you and the ships under your command were operating?

A. Yes, it is.

The document was submitted to the parties and the Court

as evidence. There being no objection, it was admitted as Exhibit D.

Q. Now, on the day in question, who was in tactical command of USS *RYAN*?

A. Commanding officer, *KENNEDY* was in tactical command of all the accompanying units.

Q. Under your orders?

A. That is correct.

Q. Where were you, sir, in the ship, from about 2200 the night before to the time of the collision?

A. I was in flag plot most of that time, though I went to the bridge once to speak to Captain Javits.

Q. Will you please recount the events of the early morning of the 25th, up to the moment of the collision with *RYAN*, with particular attention to the orders you gave?

A. As I said, I was directing the air battle from flag plot. I was in contact with *KENNEDY*'s bridge, and we had a remote pritac speaker in the plot. We launched an air strike about 2200 on the 24th. The first wave reported inbound at about 0145. Jake, Captain Javits, got that word at the same time from Air Control. As I recall, there were no specific orders given to him as to course to recover and so forth. There are standard operating procedures for this sort of thing, and he was following them.

Q. Were you kept informed of his movements?

A. That is standard procedure.

Q. By what means?

A. Intercom from the bridge.

Q. Did you concur with his intentions and movements?

A. Yes, I did.

Q. Do you feel in retrospect that he acted correctly?

A. I have to say I do.

Q. Would you have given different orders in his position?

A. In retrospect, perhaps. But in retrospect we are all a lot wiser.

Q. Please go on. Will you tell the court what signals you heard before the collision?

A. I heard the corpen – the new course – signal go out. I heard the units receipt for it and I believe I recall *RYAN* coming back and asking about taking plane guard. I recall that because it was sloppy of *KENNEDY*'s conning officer to overlook it. But I thought no more about it. Then I heard the change left to two-five-zero.

Q. What signal was that?

A. *KENNEDY* modified her recovery course to two-five-zero instead of two-six-zero, her original intention. The wind had shifted slightly.

Q. This has not been brought out in previous testimony. At what time did this signal go out?

A. I'm not sure.

Q. Did the ships in company acknowledge this signal?

A. I believe I heard acknowledgments, but I can't recall which units responded.

Q. Is there a radio log that would have these transmissions and the responses to them?

A. Ther is a log, but as to completeness you would have to examine it.

Q. All right, sir. Go on.

A. Well, things happened pretty quickly after that. I heard the whistle go and called the bridge immediately; at the same time, they were calling me, and we got a little fouled up for a minute on the intercom. Then a shudder went through the ship. By that time, we had got comms straightened out and Jake told me what was happening. I went out and saw that we had run over *RYAN*.

Q. Go on.

A. Well, our first thought was of rescue, and I put out orders to the screen to break off exercise play and pick up survivors. I checked on the remaining time our planes had – I had to think of them – and they still had about twenty minutes or half an hour of fuel; so I ordered them to orbit till further word.

Next priority was damage to the carrier. Jake had been getting reports and it sounded like we had come through okay except for a sheared fuel line. No shaft damage, which was what had me worried, though I feel she was Newport News – built and pretty hard to hurt.

At that time we were turning, and Jake and I were

discussing the situation, and it occurred to us that we had a dangerous situation. The forward part of the destroyer was on fire. Now, I knew her loadout.

Q. Please elaborate.

A. *RYAN* had an operational combat loadout with both conventional torpedoes and nuclear depth bombs for her Asroc. I believe from her reporting-in data that she had five of them aboard. The nukes on that class of destroyer are stored in a locked magazine in what used to be a hangar. We could see that area was a mass of fire.

Well, this was a difficult decision. I knew three things. First, there were men in the water and on the ship. Second, these weapons are vulnerable to fire. Not exceptionally so, but if they're roasted for a while, they'll react.

Q. The nuclear weapons?

A. Yes. We wouldn't have had a nuclear explosion per se, but if the conventional explosive in the triggers went off, or if the torpedoes stored with them detonated, we'd have had a big plume of material in the air. The wind, as I have said, was from the west. We were only a couple of hundred miles off Ireland. I was scared we'd get that explosion, that plume, and it would of course be carried straight off to the east.

I had to make a command decision. I tried to call *RYAN* but got no response. I had no way of knowing whether they had flooded that magazine, and it sounds now as if they hadn't. My decision, and I knew at the time it would cost lives, was to bring *KENNEDY* around and push the burning section underwater quickly as I could. That would put out the fire, and once under water, those warheads would be safe.

I discussed this briefly with Javits. He too was reluctant, but he agreed. We sealed the ship up in case the nukes went off around us, and went around at full speed and got it over with.

I've spent a lot of time since thinking about it, second-guessing myself. I still think it was a single-solution problem. I couldn't take the risk, politically or, you might say, in a humanitarian way, of putting a fallout plume over Donegal and Belfast.

Q. Please continue.

A. Well, after that we vectored the small boys in to pick up survivors. *KENNEDY* went on west and recovered her strike. Then I launched search-and-rescue helos. We continued area search until noon the next day, when I got orders to discontinue the exercise and put the survivors ashore.

Q. Admiral Hoelscher, what in your opinion caused the collision?

A. I have not heard all the testimony before this Court. However, from my understanding of events, I think the captain or conning officer of *RYAN* made a mistake in maneuvering that niether *RYAN* nor *KENNEDY* had time to rectify.

Cross-examined by counsel for Commander Packer.

Q. Sir, I have two points I'd like to explore. The first is whether or not you were in operational command of the formation.

A. As I said, Captain Javits was in tactical command.

Q. I understand, but on a carrier, it is common for flag and commanding officers to work closely together. You have testified that you were in almost continuous communication with the bridge.

A. That's so, but at the same time I was responsible for many other things. The maneuvering of units of the task group was specifically delegated to Javits.

Q. But you remained responsible and exercised close supervision.

A. That is true, Lieutenant.

Q. Second, you were located in flag plot. That is a space within the skin of the ship?

A. Yes.

Q. Could you see *RYAN*?

A. No.

Q. Were you maintaining a radar plot of the formation?

A. No. We were in radar silence.

Q. Yes, sir, that slipped my mind. Let us now turn to your message of the day before, the order you sent to screen units over your signature. Do you recall that order?

A. The directive to expedite maneuvering. *TALBOT* and *GARCIA* had been imprecise and sluggish occasionally. I wanted that tightened up. That was the intent of the message.

Q. We have heard testimony to the effect that message was the driving force behind Commander Packer's using a risky maneuver in preference to a safe one to reach his plane guard station. Would you respond to that?

A. That's [expletive deleted]. U.S. Navy destroyers are built for fast maneuvering. We're trained for it. It's a combat necessity and we're out there preparing for combat. You don't do that by creeping up on station like a bunch of maiden aunts. I have served in ships like *RYAN* and such a maneuver was well within her capability, if the bridge team was properly trained and alert.

Q. You were knowledgeable, were you not, of *RYAN*'s material condition?

A. Yes, that she had sustained some damage during her operations in the Gap, but the report Packer sent me when she joined said she was C-1 in maneuvering – fully capable, no degradation worth mentioning. I took him at his word and expected RYAN to perform like the other units of my screen.

Cross-examination by counsel for Lieutenant Evlin.

Q. Admiral, let us talk for a moment about your decision to ram *RYAN*. I may have to have some of the background on this explained to me.

Witness asked whether Mr. Barrett was cleared to the proper level. He was assured that such was the case.

Q. How much experience have you had with nuclear weapons, sir?

A. I went to school on them.

Q. When? How long ago?

A. I don't recall the exact year. When I was a lieutenant commander.

Q. Have they not been upgraded to be much more resistant to fire and shock than they used to be?

A. I think so. But they'll still cook off eventually in the middle of a conflagration.

Q. Are you certain of that?

A. [Witness paused.] Pretty sure.

Q. How long had the fire been going when you sent *RYAN* to the bottom?

A. I don't know. Ten or twelve minutes.

Q. How long does a Mark Five warhead take to cook off in a JP-5 fire?

A. You'd have to get an expert to answer that one for you.

Q. What is being done about these weapons now?

A. The ones on *RYAN*?

Q. Yes.

A. Well, I'm out of the picture on that. Water depth where she went down is over 1,000 fathoms. It would be hard to get to them, if that's what you mean. If we can't, I don't think anyone else will be able to.

Q. What was your state of mind when yu ordered Captain Javits to ram *RYAN*?

A. Upset, of course – reluctant – it wasn't an easy decision. But as I said, I still think it was the right one. I've forwarded my report on it. There hasn't been any response yet.

Q. Let us return, to Lieutenant Hauck's question about your hurry-up message. Was your task group engaged in combat at the time?

A. Of course not. We were simulating such operations.

Q. Do you feel, Admiral, that in peacetime we need to take exactly the same risks we would in war?

A. You're trying to trap me into giving a yes or no answer. I will reiterate that the only way to prepare for war is to train realistically, and if we don't, we aren't doing our jobs right. Obviously, I was not ordering people to take foolish chances. I was asking them to do things the way they're supposed to be done.

Q. If you were sent out again to command a task force, would you reissue that same order? Specifically, sir, would you order them to maneuver at high speed, in the dark, without radar, 'even at the expense of an occasional mistake'? – As your original message put it?

A. [Witness did not answer.]

THE COURT: Please respond to that, Admiral Hoelscher.

A. I was going to. I would say that I would, if my ships were moseying around and going too slow.

Q. Then you have learned nothing from this incident?

COUNSEL FOR THE COURT: Mr. Barrett, I must caution you –

THE WITNESS [interrupting]: No, I will respond to that. Sir, I have drawn no conclusions that would reduce what I expect from a Navy destroyer skipper.

Neither counsel for the Court, the Court, nor the parties desired further to examine this witness.

The Court informed the witness that he was priviledged to make any further statement covering anything he thought should be a matter of record that had not been brought out by previous questioning.

WITNESS: I would like to say that I did not mean to imply, as I may have seemed to, that occasional accidents like this are inevitable. I don't think anything's inevitable. But I don't think the solution lies in reducing what we expect from our commanding officers. I hope we can find out what happened to *RYAN* and find some way of fixing it. It's hard to see a ship go down and go back to sea as if nothing had happend.

The witness stated that he had nothing further to say.

He was duly warned and withdrew.

At this point the Court sat with open doors. The survivors reentered.

Captain Roland Javits, U.S. Navy, a party, was called as a witness, and was sworn. He was reminded of his rights under Article 31, Uniform Code of Military Justice, and advised that any testimony given by him might be used as evidence against him in any subsequent trial by court-martial.

Examined by the counsel for the Court.

Q. State your name, rank, branch of service, and present duty station.

A. Captain Roland J. Javits, USN. I am captain of USS *KENNEDY*, CV-67.

Q. Will you please briefly describe your naval and aviation experience?

A. I graduated from the Naval Academy and served in the Air Force for a time before requesting transfer back to the Navy. I did the standard things Navy fliers do, including a spell flying F-9s in combat. I was CO of VF-114. Then I attended the Industrial College of the Armed Forces. After that I served with the Chief of Naval Operations staff.

Following that, I was commanding officer of *DENEBOLA*. Following that, I put *KENNEDY* in commission.

Q. And you are still her commanding officer?

A. So far.

Q. Will you state to the court your recollection of the events leading up to the collision of *KENNEDY* with USS *REYNOLDS RYAN*, DD-768?

A. Yes. I have made some notes here and I will refer to those.

Q. Would you like to submit that as a narrative?

A. No, they're rough. I haven't had time to ... I'll just make remarks, if that's all right.

Q. Go ahead.

A. On December 24 I was the OTC of a carrier strike formation off the Irish coast. Exercise WESTERN VIGIL was in progress. I had assumed tactical command, since CTG 21.1 was engaged with the developing threat picture. At 2000, in accordance with the operation order, all ships were darkened. The weather conditions were favorable for night flying operations. It was clear, extremely dark, middle overcast around 8,000 feet; visibility 10 miles, wind west southwest, fourteen to fifteen knots; sea smooth, wave height 4 feet, period 6 seconds, direction 270 degrees. There was no visible horizon, and from the height of *KENNEDY*'s bridge the hulls of the escorts merged with the water. Due to the tactical conditions, all our orders were sent by short-range tactical radio rather than signal light.

About 2230, the admiral ordered me to launch our first strike on the RED fleet. I'd anticipated this, and at 2245 I put out a signal to stand by for a simultaneous left turn to launch course and designated *RYAN* plane guard. All units acknowledged. Meanwhile lead fighters were being placed on the catapults and pilots briefed. I executed the signal at 2250. We steadied up on two-six-zero, the screen steadied up, and *RYAN* reported in position. I then manned and launched ten F-4Bs with drop tanks on a vector of one-nine-zero toward the simulated enemy forces.

The purpose of this exercise was to familiarize the pilots with night launches and strikes under dimmed conditions and

456

radar silence; second, to exercise the deck crew, flight crews, and small boys in night carrier operations.

At 2316, with the last off the deck, I signaled a new course and came right to zero-one-zero true, the course Admiral Hoelscher had directed. All ships rogered and *RYAN* returned to her position in the screen.

We had some electronic intercepts around 2400, but the enemy attack we expected didn't materialize. At midnight, we conducted a radio check with all the screen ships, and comms were satisfactory, though *RYAN*'s response was weak. At 0055, the strike leader reported 'attack complete' and that the force was returning.

In accordance with my instructions, preparations for night recovery commenced at 0157. This included a voice radio message giving my course and speed intentions. All ships receipted for this signal. *RYAN* again came through weak and asked about plane guard. My OOD, Lieutenant Commander Garner, had neglected to do this, and I spoke to him about it. At 0221, we commenced a simultaneous turn to the right, first to one-zero-zero, then on around to two-six-zero. I also increased speed to twenty-seven knots. At the beginning of this maneuver *RYAN* was on our starboard quarter, bearing two-four-five, range 3,000 yards. His new position for night recovery was to be 1,000 yards off my port quarter.

As we neared recovery course, I noticed that *RYAN*'s lights were slightly to the right of my bow, but that the relative bearing was changing slowly to the left. I noticed that the actual wind was slightly to port of the anticipated wind, and so I directed a course modification to steady at two-five-zero vice two-six-zero. This message went out and was receipted for.

The next time I looked out, *RYAN*'s lights had suddenly become much brighter and closer. I immediately ordered all back emergency. *RYAN*'s lights closed rapidly. She passed under my bow so close she disappeared from sight under the overhang of the flight deck. The bow and forward stack reappeared on my starboard side. I thought for a moment he had cleared us. However, almost immediately *KENNEDY* struck *RYAN* midships on her starboard side. I stopped all engines as soon as it was evident we had hit.

Practically simultaneous with the collision, I ordered 'light ship' and sounded collision quarters. I had already passed 'man overboard' and called away fire and rescue parties when Admiral Hoelscher got to my bridge.

We then had a short conversation while *KENNEDY* coasted forward in the water. Meanwhile I was receiving damage reports. We were basically unhurt, but a JP-5 line under the starboard forward sponson had ruptured and leaked about 50 tons of fuel before it was secured. *RYAN* lay astern of us and was beginning to burn. The admiral made an observation, which had escaped me, about the special weapons she carried. I had not thought of this, but he had a point. Following his orders, when I was sure we had sound props, I gave ahead full and hard right rudder. We came around and I personally conned the ship through the burning portion of the destroyer.

After this, since the F-4s were reporting dry tanks, we got up to speed again and recovered them on a westerly course. When they were aboard I scrambled our ready rescue choppers after survivors.

Q. Now, will you continue your narrative and describe the search-and-rescue operation?

A. There is one thing I would like to put in before I do. I have prepared here a chart on which I and my officers reconstructed the tracks of *RYAN* and *KENNEDY* from the point at which we came right from zero-one-zero to the point where the collision occurred. It includes the proper maneuver *RYAN* should have followed and the track she did in fact follow.

Counsel for the Court requested that the reporter mark the chart Exhibit E. There being no objection, it was no marked and entered.

Q. I note that you have included ranges at various points between the two ships. Is this an estimate?

A. No, those are radar ranges.

Q. How is that possible? I understood that all ships were ordered to maintain radar silence.

A. That is so, and our ship's radars were shut down. However, on my own initiative, I had used some discretionary

458

funds to install a small Raytheon piloting radar. These are common on merchants. They don't give you away as being a warship. It was a safety measure I liked to have.

The chart shows that *KENNEDY* was here at 0201 [indicating]. Then the turn signal was executed. Through the turn, we lost a certain amount of speed – three knots or so. There was a range of 3,100 yards to *RYAN* at that time, so she really was just about exactly on her assigned station. At this time here [indicating] the range was about 2,000 yards. After that it closed very rapidly.

The turn into danger seems to have occurred here, where *RYAN* made a sharp swerve to port. And this cross marks where the collision occurred.

Q. Captain, given that you were getting apparently minute-by-minute reports on where *RYAN* was, why did you not detect earlier that she was off course and headed across your bow?

A. That assumes I knew what her intentions were. In practice, we just assign stations. Each ship decides the best way to get there.

Q. But what I am asking is, at what point should you have realized she was not making a normal maneuver?

Counsel representing Commander Packer objected to this question on the grounds that it assumed facts not in evidence, viz. the captain of *RYAN*'s intentions.

The counsel for the Court withdrew the question.

Q. Please go on then, if you have completed that portion of your testimony, and describe the search-and-rescue operation.

A. Well, as I said, I also had my birds to worry about. We had ten men up there and some millions of dollars' worth of planes that we had to get aboard or they'd be out of fuel and have to ditch. So the task group commander ordered the screen units to see to the survivors while we recovered aircraft. When they were safely aboard, we launched helos and steamed back to the site. By then both sections of *RYAN* had gone under.

I should also note that I ordered, when we were passing over *RYAN*, I ordered that all available lifesaving gear be tossed over from the fantail. Inventory shows we got over eleven life rafts and an undetermined number of life jackets, probably upwards of fifty.

Q. Went over from *KENNEDY*?

A. Yes.

Q. Please continue.

A. When we returned to the scene, about half an hour or forty minutes later, *TALBOT*, *GARCIA*, and *DEWEY* had boats in the water and searchlights going. I lowered two boats but did it standing off, as the destroyers with their lower freeboard were better for picking men up. There was so much stuff in the water, and we couldn't tell till the boats were right up on it whether it was men or not, that there was no attempt to organize the search in a square or such. They just went in and picked up everyone they could find. I lowered the deckedge elevator and the boats brought survivors; then they went back again. After about 0400 they came back empty. I sent them farther out. The helos got some, too.

Q. How long did you continue the search?

A. Till after dawn. Our boats got low on fuel then and I brought them back aboard.

Cross-examined by counsel for Commander Packer.

Q. Sir, did you have the conn at the time of collision?

A. I gave the order to back emergency. After that I maneuvered the ship. There was no explicit passing of the conn; as captain, I took it; it was understood.

Q. Who had it prior to that?

A. Lieutenant Commander Garner.

Q. And was Garner, in your opinion, a capable officer of the deck?

A. Yes, he's quite capable.

Q. How long before actual contact did you give that backing order?

A. That's hard to say. About a minute.

Q. Did it take effect?

A. I have to say I doubt it. Not in that space of time, on something the size of a carrier.

Q. Did you give any danger signal, or any whistle signal prior to the collision?

A. No.

Q. Why not?

A. I felt it would be confusing. We had so little time. If I got one blast out, it would have meant to *RYAN* that I was turning to starboard. If they had heard two, it would have meant I was turning to port. I judged it best to give no signal.

Q. When you realized collision was imminent, you said you gave the order to 'light ship.' That order means, I believe, to show all lights – deck-edge lights, landing lights, working lights, and so forth.

A. That is correct.

Q. Why did you not order only the navigation and running lights turned to full?

A. I preferred to light ship.

Q. Could that have confused the captain of *RYAN*? There are many lights aboard a carrier.

A. I can't speculate on that. I wanted to be as visible as possible.

Q. Captain, I now call your attention to Section 567 of the Allied Tactical Maneuvering Instructions. 'When ships are darkened, and any ship considers herself endangered by another, she is to switch on navigation lights.' Later it says, 'When it is necessary to change formation, formation axis, or course of a screened unit, navigation lights may be switched on if it is not certain that ships will clear each other.'

A. All I can say is, I didn't have time to refer to the instructions.

Q. Well, in the process, were your navigation lights turned on bright or not?

A. I can't say for certain at this point. I assume they were, along with everything else.

Cross-examined by counsel for Lieutenant Evlin.

Q. Captain, let us return to the signals exchanged just before the collision. As best you recall, what was the wording of the message that assigned *RYAN* plane guard?

A. As I said, Lieutenant Commander Garner had not included that in his original message. *RYAN* came back and asked whether they were to take it. His response was affirmative.

461

Q. Did you consider that answer as an order to take a different course from the formation course you ordered?

A. It was not a course order. It was permission to adjust her maneuvers so as to get into station.

Q. Was there any reference to how soon she was needed there?

A. No.

Q. In fact, how soon did you actually need her astern of you?

A. We would have had then twenty minutes or so to the first aircraft recovery.

Q. How often do aircraft go into the water, so that the guard ship is in fact needed?

A. Not every day, but it happens. Last year an A-4 had an engine failure on takeoff, went in off the bow, and we steamed right over her. She sank that fast. But the pilot came up from about forty feet, and the plane guard had him aboard in about three minutes. All he needed was a change of underwear.

Q. Let's go on to the last signal you sent. That is the signal changing your recovery course to two-five-zero.

A. Yes.

Q. I am not clear on your testimony as to whether *RYAN* receipted for that message.

A. I believe she did.

Q. Did you hear it?

A. No, I believe my officer of the deck did, though.

Q. We have heard testimony to the effect that Mr. Lenson, the officer remaining from *RYAN*'s bridge team, heard no such message.

A. Well, I am not prepared positively to state that we had a reply. As I said, we had trouble hearing *RYAN*'s transmissions. We had something from her at that point, but I can't say for certain –

Q. Let us leave it at that, then. The point is, you changed course toward the destroyer, without a certainty that she had heard your signal.

A. I suppose so, in a way. However, I must point out that we in fact had not come to two-five-zero when the collision occurred. We'd only come to about two-five-five. If I had

462

remained on two-six-zero, *RYAN* might have struck us amidships, instead of our striking her, but the collision would still have occurred. That course change made no difference.

Q. Let us look again at the light situation. You have said that you had lights burning other than running lights, presumably dimmed landing lights. Were there any other lights burning on your ship?

A. Yes, but they could not have been seen from a low platform like a destroyer.

Q. Would you describe the location and color of the aircraft landing lights on the *KENNEDY*?

A. They were all around red lights.

Q. How many, and where?'

A. Two, on the mast.

Q. How far apart?

A. About 6 feet, I think.

Q. The point I am getting at, Captain, is that as those lights are positioned, could *RYAN*'s captain have mistaken them for your port running lights? And since they were higher, might he not have thought *KENNEDY* was farther away than she in fact was?

A. I suppose that is possible.

Q. I submit to the court that in view of the multiplicity of lights on the carrier, their color, and their location, this combination of design flaws, along with the confused response of Captain Javits to the imminence of collision, in lighting ship instead of brightening only his navigation lights, as doctrine in fact specifies should be done, were contributing factors in the collision.

THE COURT: Mr. Barrett, you are not in a civilian court. We are capable of hearing testimony without the accompaniment of flamboyant rhetoric.

MR. BARRETT: Thank you, sir. I have no further questions of the witness.

The court then, at 1300, took a recess until 1415.

During the last part of Javits's testimony, Dan's arm had become a throbbing sizzle of steadily growing pain. He had to pay attention, he kept telling himself; but he needed medication more.

When the last admiral left the courtroom, he picked up the notebook in which he had been keeping track of the points each witness made, and headed, after the others, for the door. On the way his eyes met theirs: Bryce, glaring back; Lassard, sneering, whispering to Greenwald; Hauck, meeting his gaze expressionlessly before bending back to his papers. There was an old man beside him Dan didn't recognize, a geezer in a blue suit and string tie.

In the men's room, an Air Force major was shaving at one of the sinks. Dan pulled out the envelope and took a tablet. Then he gulped another, sucking water from the cup of his right hand.

He let himself into a stall and eased off his blouse. He rubbed his face, wishing he felt better. Well, a double dose, it should start working soon.

He sat there for some minutes, thinking. He couldn't tell how the trial was going. There didn't seem to be any point spread developing. But he was never sure he hadn't missed something. If he wasn't dopy, he hurt too much to concentrate. He worried about addiction, then smiled wryly to himself. A few months at sea would take care of that.

If they let him go to sea again.

The toilet flushed in the stall next to him. Thinking of his arm, he fingered the dressing. It was bulky gauze stained the color of sauterne where skin emerged. He'd seen the burn while the doctors were dressing it. An ugly slab of scorched meat, with blisters that broke and ran fluid. It extended from his back over his shoulder and down his arm. He must have hit the oil when his arm was up, swimming. Or jerked it up instinctively to protect his eyes. The gauze stank of ointment and rancid bodily fluids. He smoothed it down again and eased back into his uniform blouse.

If he got to sea again. As the testimony seesawed, first with Barrett gaining ground for Packer and, by definition, Evlin, then tipping against *Ryan*, his apprehension grew. He wanted the dead absolved. If the trial went against Javits and Hoelscher, then Packer and Evlin were innocent, and so was he.

But whether the blame came to rest on them or not, he wouldn't escape the stain. He'd lived again everything he'd done in the dying minutes of his ship, and judged himself wanting. As Johnstone had pointed out, he had not warned the captain. He hadn't replaced Lassard as lookout. He hadn't checked the running lights. He hadn't worked out the maneuver himself, as a backup.

At Annapolis they told stories of that worst thing that could happen in a career at sea; more terrible than death. They said that when the court-martial was over, you were called into a room where the judges waited around a green table. A sword lay on it. If its hilt was toward you, as you came in, it meant you could draw breath; you were free. If the point was toward you, all that remained was to hear sentence pronounced. . . .

He set his cap and reached for the door.

The cafeteria tables were littered with the leavings of Pentagon officials, civilian analysts, contractors. A few were still eating; one was an Army three-star, surrounded by a bevy of thickset men in suits wearing admission badges on chains. He picked up a tray and got in line for beef tips on noodles.

He bumped into Reed at the checkout. 'Hey, Aaron.'

'Hey.'

'How much longer, you think?'

'I get the feeling they'd like to wind up.'

He hesitated, wanting to sit with the ASW officer, but decided it wouldn't look right. Instead he found a dirty table off by himself. The food was cotton wool in his dry mouth. At last he gave up and just drew and quartered the Jell-O with his fork. Gradually the medication took effect. His pain faded. His anxiety sidled back into the shadows.

'Dan? Got a minute?'

He recognized the voice first. He raised his eyes and blinked slowly. Alan Evlin was sitting across from him, in the same khakis he'd worn on the bridge.

'What the hell – ?'

'Not so loud. Just whisper, okay?'

'But you can't be here. Are you really here?'

Evlin raised his eyebrows, his expression whenever Dan had uttered some absurd naïveté. The overhead lights glinted on the round lenses of his glasses. 'Of course not. How could I be? But we still had some things to discuss. If you don't want to – '

'No, I mean yes, go ahead, I'm listening. You been following the trial? Deanne's got you counsel – sharp, a civvie lawyer. Anything, uh, anything you want me to tell her?'

'Don't babble. No, nothing she doesn't already know. About my counsel and that, the trial – it's not important. Not to me. It's mainly for her peace of mind.'

'Well . . . then . . . why?' He felt stupid and, unaccountably, afraid.

'Remember our last talk?'

'Yes.'

'You're doing fine. I told you you would. You make mistakes but never the same one twice.'

'Thanks.' He had a sudden thought. 'You don't know – say, can you tell me what they're going to decide?'

'Who? The court?' Evlin seemed to find that amusing. 'Does that matter?'

'Maybe not to you. But it's not going right, Al.'

'Remember the waves?'

'Sure I remember.'

'Don't let the lies and insinuations scare you. Stick to the truth as you see it.'

'They don't believe me.'

'So what does that change? Just keep telling it. Till somebody's ready to listen. Remember, everything's for the best.'

'It is, huh?'

'Yes. That's all I really wanted to tell you. All you have a need to know. That everything will turn out all right at the wrap-up.'

'Okay,' said Dan, still not trusting it but unwilling to contradict Evlin. But then he thought, If this is really him, then I've got to believe it. And then: But is this really him? A lassitude was soaking him, making him blink and yawn. He looked down at shimmering green and moved his fork with an effort, dreamlike, everything slow like underwater. Damn, he thought, I shouldn't have taken two.

466

'Sir?'

When he looked up again, it was not to Evlin's face but that of a marine guard, one of the big ones. 'You one of them off the *Ryan?* Court's getting ready to reconvene.'

'Thank you,' he said, and cursed himself. Stupid. Stupid! Why hadn't he simply reached across, taken Evlin's hand? But he hadn't. Now he'd never know for sure. He got up, looking around, looking for him in the crowd. But he wasn't there.

The Court reconvened at 1423. Present: all members, counsel for the Court, the parties, and their counsel.

Captain Roland Javits, on the stand when recess was taken, resumed his seat. He was warned that the oath taken previously was still binding.

WITNESS: Before we begin, may I make a statement?

COUNSEL FOR THE COURT: Please go ahead, Captain.

WITNESS: I would like to have the record show paragraph 1506, from the manual for carrier air operations. It states, 'Carriers, right of way. Carriers have the right of way in launching and recovering aircraft. Other ships are to keep clear.' Also, paragraph 532: 'In addition to the International Regulations for Prevention of Collision at Sea, the following rules are applicable: A carrier has the right of way when showing a signal to indicate that she is launching or recovering aircraft.'

COUNSEL FOR THE COURT: Your point is made, sir.

WITNESS: May I also read from *Allied Tactical Publication 1:* 'A clear situation should not be changed to an awkward one by any ship either through lack of timely indication to others of her intent, or from an impatient haste in accomplishing this movement.'

COUNSEL FOR LT EVLIN: Apropos of doctrine, Captain Javits, are there any provisions in those publications that authorize a carrier to change course without ensuring ships in company are notified?

WITNESS: I don't – while conducting flight operations?

MR BARRETT: Yes.

WITNESS Not to the best of my knowledge.

COUNSEL FOR THE COURT: Let us return to normal examination. Captain, I would like you to try to reconstruct what happened from a different point of view. In your experience as a navigating officer, if you were on *RYAN* and a carrier was on your port bow, apparently closing fast, and you received a signal saying, 'My course two-five-zero – '

A. I don't believe you can ask me to guess at another man's responses.

Q. I am asking you to tell me what you would do in that situation, not guess what Commander Packer thought.

THE COURT: Question is correct. Witness will answer.

Q. As I was saying, if you were CO of *RYAN* and you received a signal saying. 'Mike corpen two-five-zero' from the carrier, assuming he did in fact receive it, what would you do?

A. I think you are misinterpreting the signal. It does not mean as you seem to be saying that 'My course is two-five-zero.' It is a signal of intention, meaning 'my course will be' or 'I am coming to two-five-zero.'

In the second place, if I was in a formation where I knew my ordered station, where I clearly saw where the carrier was and understood that other units had to remain clear of her, not pass close aboard or in front of or in any way embarrass her when she is engaged in flight operations, my answer is that I would have turned right and given sea room.

Q. You would have turned right?

A. To starboard, that's correct.

Cross-examined by counsel for Lieutenant Evlin.

Q. Captain, you have testified that a 'mike corpen' signal means that your intention is to come to a certain course. Are you quite sure of that, sir?

A. Yes, that's what it means.

Q. I show you, sir, a copy of the *Allied Tactical Signal Book*. Does the signal 'mike corpen' appear there, sir?

A. Yes.

Q. Will you read for us what the meaning of that signal is?

A. It says, 'My course is.'

Q. Thank you, sir. Would you like to modify your testimony in view of this?

A. My rudder was over and the bow was swinging. In another minute, we would have been on two-five-zero. So no, I still consider that a correct signal. As I pointed out, the collision would still have occurred.

Q. Perhaps.

A. I think certainly.

Q. I don't want to get too far away from the points I have already made, but I would like to ask you this: After *RYAN* had increased rudder on her last left turn, could you have avoided the collision?

A. I didn't know he had increased his rudder. All I knew was that his lights were getting too damn close.

Q. I am sorry, sir, I may have phrased that question badly. What I meant was: Knowing what you do now, do you feel that there was any way you could have averted the collision by any procedure or act other than what you actually did, which was essentially to do nothing?

A. I backed emergency and lighted ship. Carriers don't turn or stop on a dime. No, collision was inevitable then.

THE COURT: Captain, before you step down. As a result of this collision, do you have any recommendations for changes in tactical instructions or doctrine?

A. I will have to think about that one, sir. There may be something in what the various counsels have said about lighting aboard carriers being confusing.

I also think perhaps we need to deemphasize speed in maneuvering. Admiral Hoelscher is not at fault here. He was merely trying to execute current doctrine. Maybe we need to modify it in the direction of safety, at least in peacetime.

Neither the counsel for the Court, the Court, nor the parties desired further to question this witness. He was duly warned and withdrew.

The Court was cleared. When all witnesses other than the parties and their counsel had left, Lieutenant Reed was recalled and reminded that his previous oath was still binding. Cross-examined by counsel for the Court.

Q. Mr. Reed, were you in charge of the nuclear weapons aboard *RYAN*?

A. Yes.

Q. What was her loadout?

A. *RYAN* was carrying four Mark 5 nuclear warheads, with associated boosters, and sixteen conventional homing torpedoes. Two practice torpedoes, Mark 43s, had been expended in the Arctic.

Q. Did *RYAN*'s weapons doctrine call for flooding of the torpedo magazines upon collision or fire aft?

A. The answer is yes, but it wasn't in the weapons doctrine. That tells you how to use the weapons in battle. It was in the damage-control instructions.

Q. To your knowledge, were the magazines flooded after the collision?

A. To my knowledge, they were not.

Q. Whose responsibility was it to flood them?

A. Mine.

Q. Did you attempt to flood?

A. I was in my stateroom when the collision occurred. I endeavored to make my way aft to ascertain the condition of the magazine. Due to fire, I was unable to reach it.

Q. Did the guard on duty know he was expected to flood them?

A. Yes.

Q. But you do not know if he did?

A. No. He did not survive.

Cross-examined by counsel for Commander Packer.

Q. Mr. Reed, given the location of the warheads, do you think it likely that they could have gone off in the manner Admiral Hoelscher feared?

A. It's possible.

Q. Please elaborate.

A. There's nothing to elaborate on. They might have gone off.

Neither the counsel for the Court, the Court, nor the parties desired further to examine this witness. He resumed his seat.

A witness was then called by counsel representing Commander Packer. He entered, was duly sworn, and was informed of the subject matter of the inquiry.

Examined by the counsel for the Court.

Q. Please state your name, rank, branch of service, and present duty station.

A. I am Olen P. Piasecki, captain, U.S. Navy, retired. I am attached in a civilian capacity to the surface combatant branch of the Bureau of Ships.

Q. Captain Piasecki, please describe your experience with destroyers.

A. I have spent most of the last thirty-nine years in them. I was on *REUBEN JAMES* as a boatswain's mate and on *HICKOX* and *BENHAM* in the Pacific. After the war, I was on *FRANK EVANS*, fleeted up to her XO. I commanded an NROTC unit at University of Pennsylvania, then did another XO stint on *TURNER JOY*, then commanded USS *NORFOLK*. I taught at the Emergency Shiphandling School and after that commanded USS *ALBANY* and then *DESTRON TWENTY*. I am presently in charge of design workup for a new class of frigates.

COUNSEL FOR CDR PACKER: I would like to offer for Captain Piasecki's examination the diagrams drawn by Ensign Lenson and Admiral Hoelscher, previously offered in evidence.

Examination by Lieutenant Hauck continued.

Q. Captain, have you had experience operating with carriers?

A. Yes, considerable.

Q. In the light of your experience, is it your opinion that the angles on the bow of an aircrafat carrier can be accurately estimated at night?

A. That would depend on what angle was showing. For example, if it was bow-on, that would not be hard. For 10 or 20 degrees aspect, it could be tough.

Q. Are you aware that a collision took place between USS *KENNEDY* and USS *RYAN*?

A. Yes.

Q. I shall now ask you some questions wherein I will specify certain conditions. I ask you to indicate the action you would take in the light of your experience.

A. Very well, go ahead, sir.

Q. Assume that conditions are as follows. Sea calm to moderate; wind light from the west; dark, overcast night. An aircraft carrier and four escorts are maneuvering in night launch and recovery under battle conditions. They are darkened and radar silence is in effect. Formation course is zero-one-zero true at twenty knots.

One of the destroyers is on station 3,000 yards bearing two-four-five from the carrier. The commanding officer is sick and fatigued. The day before he received a message, which I now show you.

He then receives a signal that planes will be recovered on two-six-zero true at twenty-seven knots. He is simultaneously ordered to take plane guard station.

Now, Captain, in your opinion, would an initial course and speed to station of one-three-zero at twenty-seven knots be reasonable or unreasonable, considering the conditions given?

A. Reasonable.

Q. Tactically sound?

A. Yes.

Q. I show you now this maneuvering board. Assume the commanding officer proceeded on course one-three-zero till he reached a position where the guide bore zero-six-zero true, range a little over 3,000 yards, and the guide had nearly completed her right turn from zero-one-zero around to two-six-zero. If, under these circumstances, he ordered left rudder until the course was zero-nine-zero, and when he had reached that course continued down the port side of the carrier, intending to later put his rudder hard right, coming to the recovery course and reaching his station by a hard turn, in your opinion would this intention be reasonable or unreasonable considering the conditions existing?

RADM HOELSCHER: I had better object here. The lieutenant is injecting suppositions into his question that have not come out in evidence. Specifically, you say that there was an intention to turn left to zero-nine-zero when the bearing was zero-six-zero; but the statement on this point, from the ensign, was the commanding officer of *RYAN* intended to stay on one-three-zero and not modify course until he was past *KENNEDY*'s stern.

COUNSEL FOR CDR PACKER: In answer to that objection, the diagram you yourself gave the court, sir, shows that *RYAN* did in fact change course at this point [indicating] where the carrier was at zero-six-zero true. It seems to me that an intention can be proven by the act, even if it was not expressed aloud.

RADM HOELSCHER: I object to this process of feeding Captain Piasecki selected facts and then citing his conclusions, as I expect Mr. Hauck here will do, as proof Packer's decisions were right.

THE COURT: Is this an allowable procedure, Lieutenant Commander Johnstone?

COUNSEL FOR THE COURT: It is my understanding that an expert witness may be asked a hypothetical question provided it is based on the evidence or on reasonable inferences drawn therefrom.

THE COURT: The objection is not sustained. Proceed.

COUNSEL FOR CDR PACKER: Let the clerk read back the question.

The question was repeated.

WITNESS: It would be risky but acceptable.

Q. Would such a maneuver be good professional practice?

A. Yes. It's a fast, smart way to drive a ship.

Q. Which was what his orders required. Now, assuming that the commanding officer is carrying out the maneuver as described, passing the carrier at a minimum acceptable distance in order to reach station quickly, and then, at approximately this point [indicating] receives a message that tells him that she has altered course 10 degrees toward his intended track – as a 'mike corpen' signal actually means – would such a signal cause uncertainty in his mind?'

A. It would.

Q. Assuming him to be momentarily uncertain under these conditions – leaving aside any question of fatigue or sickness – and that he observed himself to be on the carrier's starboard bow at a short and closing range, and that the rudder was at that time at or close to rudder amidships and the ship steadied up; if, as I say, he saw himself on the carrier's starboard bow, would you consider such action reasonable?

A. Under those circumstances, eminently; that would be the only way to escape.

CAPT JAVITS, A PARTY: I object to this misstatement of the evidence. It is clear that *RYAN* was not on *KENNEDY*'s starboard bow when this left rudder order was given but, rather, to port. Only when the turn to launch course commenced was it on the starboard quarter, and then at a distance of 3,000 yards.

RADM HOELSCHER: I join in that objection.

THE COURT: Once again, a court of inquiry is not bound by strict evidential procedure. Counsel representing *RYAN* has been asking hypothetical questions. The Court does not sustain, but will expect counsel to show evidence.

COUNSEL for CDR PACKER: Thank you, sir, I will at this time. Now, Captain Piasecki, you will note from the diagram that when *RYAN* was approaching the position where she turned left *KENNEDY*'s track shows a waver to the left, as if she began to turn to two-five-zero. By your eye, what is the angle between her bow and *RYAN* at that moment?

A. In the neighborhood of 10 degrees, roughly.

Q. Captain, recall that shortly after you took the stand I asked you whether the angle on the bow of a carrier could be accurately estimated at night. You replied, and I quote, 'That would depend on what angle was showing. For example, if it was bow-on, that would not be hard. For 10 or 20 degrees aspect, it could be tough.' Based on his having been informed that *KENNEDY* was actually on two-five-zero, would it not be easy for the destroyer's commanding officer to conclude he was on the carrier's starboard bow, and that he had to turn left to avoid her?

A. I suppose so. But he was wrong.

Q. Surely; but why? Gratuitous error? Or because of poor lighting on the carrier and a misleading signal?

A. I would say the latter.

Q. Thank you, sir.

Cross-examined by counsel for the Court.

Q. Captain, don't you think that if the man described in Lieutenant Hauck's imaginary scenario was confused, he should have sounded whistle signals, or called the carrier to ask his intentions?

A. Assuming that he had time to do so, yes.

Cross-examined by Captain Javits, a party.

Q. Sir, you have agreed that there were things the captain of the destroyer could have done to let the carrier know he was uncertain or felt he was in danger. If he had not done any of these, would there have been anything in the actions of his ship that would have led the carrier to think anything was wrong?

A. Negative.

Cross-examined by Rear Admiral Hoelscher, a party.

Q. Captain, I must question your statement that it is impossible to determine a carrier's target angle at night within 20 degrees. That's hard to swallow.

A. I did not say it was impossible, but that it was difficult. It can be done with practice – observing the individual lights, the silhouette, over a period of days. In the daytime, it's possible to tell how a carrier is pointing and turning by her list. But for a captain who had just joined, it would definitely be difficult. I stand by that answer.

None of the counsels or parties had further questions of the witness.

Examined by the Court.

Q. Captain, as a result of what you have learned about this collision, as well as your extensive experience, do you have any suggestions or recommendations to read into this testimony?

A. Well, sir, this issue of taking plane guard during a course change has been around a while. Not only do people get confused, you have the possibility of a steering casualty or a loss of power. I have recommended in years past that at night and in fog or rain we should put plane guards on station before turning into the wind. Some commanders do that and some don't. I think it should be made mandatory. It may take a few minutes more, but we should eat those minutes in the interests of safety.

THE COURT: We will consider this recommendation in our final report.

The witness was duly warned and withdrew.

*

A witness called by counsel representing Commander Packer entered, was duly sworn, and was informed of the subject matter of the inquiry.

Examined by counsel for Commander Packer.

Q. State your name, occupation, and permanent address.

A. Burford Packer, retired projectionist, 1113 Preuss Avenue, Los Angeles.

Q. Mr. Packer, will you inform the court of the nautical experience of your son, other than that performed in the U.S. Navy?

A. Jimmy left home early, sir. Before he joined the Navy, he was a crewman on the *ORIENT HONOLULU* out of San Francisco, with the Bear Line. He made several cruises with her and ended up as third mate. He was studying for his master's ticket when he decided to try for the Navy. He was only twenty-one then.

Q. Do you know whether your son could swim?

A. They made him swim some at school back east. He wrote his ma he couldn't get the hang of it. Come to it too late, I guess.

Neither the counsel for the Court, the Court, nor the parties desired further to examine this witness.

The Court then, at 1647, adjourned until 0830 the next day, the fourth day of the inquiry.

26

When the Court sat the survivors settled with a collective sigh and rustle. The members slid tablets in front of them. One cleared his throat. Another leaned back, his expression inscrutable as a heron's. The court reporter turned a pencil in a hand sharpener.

The witness entered from the corridor, a guard flanking him. As they came up the aisle, the marine dropped back and he walked the last few feet to the stand alone, his gait rolling, a sailor home from the sea.

'You are called here to give material evidence in the matter of the recent collision between USS *Reynolds Ryan* and USS *Kennedy*. Raise your right hand. Do you swear to tell the truth, the whole truth, and nothing but the truth, so help you God?'

'I do.'

The man in the chair was familiar. Medium height. Heavy shoulders. Slow big hands working at a heat-darkened pipe.

'State your name, rank, branch of service, and present duty station.'

The witness turned to the onlookers, the pipe jutting above a hard, tanned jaw.

'My name is James Packer, U.S. Navy, captain of USS *Reynolds Ryan*.'

Lenson came awake suddenly in the darkened room. His sheets were damp with sweat. Beside him his wife slept, her breath soft on his shoulder. Warm air hissed through ventilators, a shiplike sound, comforting.

He lay motionless, retracing his dreams. They'd been more vivid, more real than this anonymously comfortable room.

He'd wandered across a wasteland with a party of pilgrims,

and bowed, hands together, before a shriveled elder with agate eyes and yellowing beard. The ancient face was familiar. With no sense of surprise, he recognized it as his own. Then they were together on the bridge of a ship, sliding outward over a sea hot and clear and flat as a melt of flint glass.

But somehow the voyage had ended in the wasteland again. Dark faces crowded round where he lay staked to the sand. Something he wasn't supposed to tell. Under him the desert burned, and a hand set live coals to smolder on his chest and arm.

'So. Who was this trusting lamb?'

'I can't tell you that, sir.'

'This here's the real world, boy. We all have to bend a little once in a while.'

Then suddenly the stuffy room where men sat like Osiris in judgment on the dead. He'd read that in one of Susan's books. From those dead, the captain had returned, and he'd laughed in relief –

He turned impatiently yet carefully, tossing back the sheets. The only thread stitching his dreams was heat. He thought of adjusting the thermostat, but Susan liked it warm. He had no idea what time it was. The sky beyond the window was black.

He frowned. Not completely black. Distant, but clear, several small lights glimmered white and red and green –

The towering silhouette of an aircraft carrier condensed silently and tremendously out of the dark. The creaming hiss of the bow wave stopped his heart. No, he thought. Not again! Sweat stung his face. He stared up helplessly as his fingers clamped on the steel splinter shield.

At last the dream, or vision, faded, leaving him rigid and trembling. The North Atlantic, the cries of burning men became grieving ghosts in the wind, then merged again with the seamless hiss. You're safe, he told vengeful memory. You're alive and Betts is here and the worst that can happen is prison. No, being honest with himself, that wasn't likely, either. They'd take his inexperience into account. He'd be assigned an office somewhere, issued a typewriter and

478

paper, and left alone till he got around to his letter of resignation.

He sweated like an iceberg in the sun, staring into the hissing dark. The Navy had been all he'd wanted for so long, he couldn't imagine himself outside it.

The inquiry couldn't last much longer. They'd gone through *Ryan*'s dying moments again and again; had seen it through his eyes, Silver's, Bryce's, Traven's, Reed's, Lassard's. Johnstone kept things moving. He broke each witness's pride and made him admit error. The counsel for the court had grilled Hoelscher and Javits as hard as anyone from *Ryan*. So far as Dan could tell, he had no partiality. But the scales were weighted against Packer.

Dan saw again the steady, passionless, attentive faces of admirals. Their judges said little. Only the senior member, Ausura, put an occasional question. Only at the end would they pronounce. First they listened.

Listened to Bryce, and Lassard, and the others who lied. . . .

But he couldn't prove they lied.

He was the only one left who was telling the truth. The only one Bryce had not somehow suborned or intimidated.

But he couldn't prove it.

Therefore . . . maybe he'd better just accept that. He was only an ensign. Dead men's reputations weren't his concern. Maybe he'd better *bend a little*. Or after the trial, Lassard and the others might come by one day.

On the far side of the bed, Susan muttered, rolled, tossed out an arm. Her curled fingers brushed his face. Against the wash of city lights, he studied her unconscious shadow.

Since his attempt at intimacy, she'd lost interest in the trial. She went out during the day, to museums or to the Library of Congress, she said. When the Court adjourned, she was waiting in the car. But there was no warmth. Always before when they'd disagreed, they'd smoothed it over; one would apologize and the other forgive. Now she received his attempts at making up with outward acquiescence but without a smile, without sign of love.

He let self-pity scorch his eyes. Didn't she know how hard

this was for him? Wasn't she supposed to understand? A tear trickled into his ear.

They should go away somewhere, after the trial. Maybe they could catch a hop to San Juan, there were flights out of Andrews, spend a few days in a hotel on the beach –

As he was thinking this, her arm flinched and the fingers closed. They moved upward, brushed his cheek again, then fell on his shoulder. Not hard enough to hurt, but unexpected enough to make him flinch.

'Dan?' A whisper.

'Yeah?'

'You awake?'

'Yeah.'

'Jesus. What time – wait – it's four. Can't you sleep?'

'I slept for a while. Just woke up.'

She was silent. He said, 'I was thinking . . . wouldn't you like to go somewhere after the trial, someplace down south? I was hoping – '

'Dan, I'm due in a few weeks. And even if I wasn't, I've got finals coming. I'm missing classes to be here.'

'Just three days. A weekend.'

'I don't think so. It's not a good idea.'

'Betts, what's wrong?'

'Nothing. I've just got some thinking to do.'

He felt the shadow creep over him, cover his heart, and darken. She lay turned from him, and he listened to the slow ticking of the clock.

The Court reconvened at 0920.

Present: Vice Admiral Ausura, USN, president; Rear Admiral Morehead, USN, member.

Lieutenant Commander Stanley Johnstone, counsel for the Court.

Lieutenant Robert Hauck, counsel representing Commander Packer.

Mr. Charles Barrett, counsel for Lieutenant Evlin.

No witnesses or personnel not otherwise connected with the inquiry were present.

Lieutenant Commander Benjamin Bryce was recalled as a

witness by the counsel for the Court. He was reminded that his previous oath was still binding.

Examined by the counsel for the Court.

Q. Commander, during your previous testimony you made allegations relating to the competence of Lieutenant Alan Evlin and Ensign Daniel Lenson. Will you refresh the court as to their gist?

A. Yes. Evlin and Lenson were lax in their duties. They permitted the use of illegal and dangerous substances among the crew. I also think it possible that one or both used such substances.

Q. You were aware of such matters before the collision?

A. I had suspected Evlin for a long time.

Q. Did you so inform the captain?

A. He knew we had dope aboard.

Q. Did you tell him your suspicions about Evlin?

A. Not in so many words.

Q. Have you in the intervening time been able to recall any concrete evidence of their dereliction of duty?

A. I regret that due to the sinking, the loss of evidence and key witnesses, I am unable to substantiate what I say. However, I stand by it.

You see, I have kind of an instinct about what goes on among the men. I myself enlisted at sixteen, right after Pearl Harbor. Fibbed about my age. I was a white hat for five years. I understand them in a way your direct commissioned officers never will. *RYAN*'s crew wasn't a bad bunch, but you can't let the animals run the zoo. As I said, the night before the collision we turned up a lot of the stuff. A little more time and I'd have traced it to the source.

Cross-examined by counsel for Lieutenant Evlin.

Q. We have been through this before, Commander, but since you're back, let's do it again. First, the connection between this and the collision escapes me. Commander Packer was unquestionably in charge during the maneuvers leading to it. Are you intimating he was involved in drug use?

A. Ridiculous. I never suggested anything like that.

Q. Then what's the connection?

A. As I've said, I think those two squirrels screwed up and Jimmy – and Commander Packer was trying to save the ship.

Q. But you were not on the bridge, and all this is empty conjecture. Let us go on. Were you not responsible as executive officer for the safety and well-being of the crew, and for the enforcement of discipline?

A. Of course.

Q. If discipline was poor and drug use rife, was it not your responsibility as much as or more than anyone else's?

A. I hear what you're saying. The difference is, I was fighting it, and they were going along.

Q. Commander Bryce, why did you hate Lieutenant Evlin?

A. I didn't hate him, just what he was doing to the ship.

Neither the counsel for the Court, the Court, nor the parties desired further to question this witness. He resumed his seat.

Ensign Daniel Lenson, a party, was recalled as a witness, advised of his rights, and was reminded that the oath previously taken was still binding. Examined by the counsel for the Court.

He eased himself down again, numb and light-headed, into the hard embrace of the chair. From the front row, eyes pinned him: Bryce. Lassard. Norden. Gonzales. Greenwald. He jerked his gaze from them to find Johnstone's horn-rims hovering between him and the light.

'Mr. Lenson, I have noticed you nodding from time to time – '

'I'm well enough to testify.'

'Then let's try to clear up several points of testimony that conflict with yours. First, you said, I believe, that you heard a whistle signal from *Kennedy* before the collision. Is that correct?'

He cleared his throat. 'Yes.'

'Captain Javits states he did not give any signal. Do you still say you heard one?'

'Yes; I heard a signal.'

'A long blast, or a short one?'

'I can't say how long it lasted.'

'Before *Kennedy* struck *Ryan*, did you notice additional lights come on?'

'Yes.'

'Were the navigation lights among them?'

He closed his eyes, trying to recapture that glimpse through the alidade cross hairs. It refused to come. Damn his mind; it gave what he didn't need when he didn't want it and lost what he had to have. 'I couldn't tell. There were too many to make them out clearly, if they were.'

'Counsel for Commander Packer has argued that it was possible he intended not a left but right turn to take his final station for plane guard. Do you have any recollection that might substantiate that?'

'No. All the plans I heard ended with a left turn into station.'

'There is also disagreement over whether the last signal sent by *Kennedy* to *Ryan*, that is, 'Mike corpen two-five-zero,' was heard on *Ryan*'s bridge.'

An easy one at last. He hitched himself up in the chair. 'I didn't hear it. I may have been on the wing when it came over. It's possible that the captain or Mr. Evlin heard it.'

'Were *Ryan*'s radios working properly, to your knowledge?'

'I was told by other watch members that we often had trouble with the radios. On that night, the speaker was barely audible. I don't know whether that was an equipment problem or whether it was just turned low to keep the noise level down.'

'You have heard the executive officer's testimony that Lieutenant Evlin was a substandard, undisciplined officer, and possibly involved with drugs. Do you have an opinion on these allegations?'

He forced himself erect again against a wave of dizziness. Through a blur like heat rising from flames, faces danced before him. Some of them were men he knew were dead. He coughed and coughed and they steadied, and he lifted his head a little and said into the gauntlet of eyes, 'I've heard his remarks. Commander Bryce is lying. Lieutenant Evlin was not involved in drug use. There were drugs on *Ryan*, but they were the property of Seaman Lassard, as I've said. Bryce's dislike of Evlin was a personal grudge, probably based on envy, and had no foundation in fact.'

He exhaled. Johnstone shifted a little, and he heard the creak of leather from the direction of the court table. Bryce and Lassard were staring him down. He looked away, back at Johnstone.

'Stating that an officer is "lying" in this context, Mr. Lenson, in this room, constitutes placing a charge of perjury into the official record. The executive officer also suggests you permitted drug dealing in your division. Please respond.'

'That's another lie. Commander Bryce says he wants things out in the open. All right, let's do that.' He licked his lips. 'It was widely known aboard that he took rake-offs and gave favors in exchange for money.'

Johnstone looked off into the distance. 'Disrespectful and false accusations under oath are prosecuted under the Uniform Code of Military Justice, Articles 89, 107, and 131, as well as the general article, 134. You may be called to account for such statements at subsequent trial by court-martial. Knowing this, do you desire to let these remarks stand?'

'I'm aware of that and I stand by them.'

'Have you ever used marijuana or other illegal substances?'

'No.'

'You stated that Bryce "envied" Evlin. Why should he envy an officer junior to him?'

'Lieutenant Evlin was a better man than Bryce. A decent, honest one. That was all.'

'Mr. Lenson.'

He twisted in the chair, catching his breath as his arm reminded him it was there. Ausura was tapping a pencil against the edge of the table. All three admirals were studying him. 'Sir?'

'Is there anything further you would like to place on the record? Anything that has not been brought out by previous questioning.'

He swallowed and looked away, searching his mind. After what seemed like too long, he said, 'What I've said is the truth. I have nothing to add to it.'

'Does anyone else wish to examine this witness?'

The rattle of the transcriber stopped, leaving silence hanging in the air like smoke.

'You may resume your seat, Ensign,' said Johnstone, gazing away through the walls. A cough, a rustle of papers, and he was hoisting himself to his feet; he was sliding past Lassard's flat stare, Bryce's hard triumphant smile, Rich Norden's dropped eyes. He was done.

And that was it, he thought bitterly, taking his seat again. He could see by their faces that the Court hadn't believe him. He'd spoken out, tried his best, and failed. *Ryan*'s executive officer had won all along the line. What would Evlin have said? That it was meant to be this way?

Bullshit. What about all the men in the water, the men whose screams woke him at night? Had it all turned out for the best for them?

He stared at the stern faces of admirals, and was filled with hate.

When he began listening again, Johnstone was talking in his level monotone to the back of the room. Apparently no one wanted to call any more witnesses. He glanced at his watch.

'Does any party desire to exercise his right under Section 0308h, *Manual for Courts-Martial*, and make a statement, oral or written?'

He looked around the room. Hauck shook his head. Barrett lowered his eyes.

'Do any of the witnesses desire to make any further statement?'

The audience stirred. A few reached for coats, briefcases, glancing toward the door.

'I do, sir, if I can do that now,' said a deep, slow voice behind Dan.

'Please come forward and state your name,' said Johnstone, and for the first time, he, too, sounded weary.

When the man who had spoken got to the front and turned around, Dan saw that it was Isaacs. 'Boatswain's Mate First Class Lemond Isaacs, USN.'

'Is this a substantive statement, Petty Officer Isaacs?' asked one of the admirals. Dennison, Dan recalled. He sounded annoyed.

'What is that, sir?'

'Is it important? he is asking you,' said Ausura.

'I believe it is, sir.'

'Recall the witness.'

Johnstone went through the procedure, reminding him about the oath he'd taken, as they all had, the first day of testimony. He didn't sound surprised. He sounded as if he'd been expecting Isaacs to stand up. The black first-class answered with his head lowered, avoiding their eyes.

Ikey looked scared, Dan thought. Makes sense. But why am I suddenly trembling, too?

'You are the same Boatswain's Mate First Class Lemond Isaacs who testified on the first day of this inquiry.'

'That is right, sir.'

'You indicated then, if I recall correctly, that you had no objection to the narrative submitted by the senior survivor, nor did you have any charges to lay. Do you now wish to modify that statement?'

'Yes, sir.'

'With new evidence, or something you knew then?'

'I knew it then, sir.'

'A little louder, please. Why was it not brought out when you first testified?'

'I was ordered not to give it.'

'*Ordered* not to? By whom?'

'Commander Bryce, sir.'

Bryce stood up. Ausura glanced up, studying him over his reading glasses. 'Please sit down, Commander. Isaacs, is it? If you have material knowledge that ought to be brought to the attention of this Court, those orders have no legal effect.'

'I can't get charged for it? Is that right, Admirals?'

The men in blue and gold nodded, murmured agreement. They pushed back their chairs and looked carefully at Isaacs.

'All right, then. The XO thought I was drunk during the underway replenishment. I take a drink, but I wasn't drunk then. So he lock me up in the supply storeroom. That's where

486

I was when all this happening. And when it did, they all forgot about me down there. The XO and all them others, the master-at-arms and them. Except Mr. Lenson. He come down after me and bust me out.

'I didn't stop to thank him then. Mr. Lenson, you back there, I see you. I do not like to hear the things the exec been saying about you. After thinking about it some, I decided I got to tell what really happened in the whaleboat.'

'Go on,' said Ausura. 'Take your time. We're very interested in what you have to say, Petty Officer.'

'Thank you, sir.' The boatswain cleared his throat, glanced up for a moment at Bryce, then dropped his eyes again. His voice gained a little volume.

'After the ensign let me out the brig, I went topside. I looked for my life raft. It wasn't there. So I went on aft, thinking to find one I could join up on the muster for.

'When I got to the boat deck, I seen the crew putting the boat in the water. Only they couldn't get the engine started. Weatherspoon, the engineman in charge, he wasn't anywhere around.

'Well, I knew I could get it started. They said if I could, I could come with them. So we got her in the water.'

'Who was in the whaleboat at this time?' Johnstone asked him.

'Lassard, Greenwald, Gonzales, Mr. Norden, Commander Bryce, and me.'

'Go on.'

The boatswain drew a square with big, scarred hands. 'There was a little shiny box under the thwart. It belong to Mr. Bryce. He keep shoving it back under there with his foot.'

'I object. This man is an alcoholic and a liar.'

'Please resume your seat, Commander. We will call you presently. Go on with your testimony, Isaacs.'

'I was keeping the engine going, it was not easy because it had got some kind of solids in the intake. But I did. So soon as we hit the water, Greenwald, he ask, "Where to, Commander? You want to pick up some of these guys?" '

'Mr. Bryce, he say, "They got plenty of rafts and things. So, let's head on over there, toward one of the other ships." '

Dan hauled himself upright in the chair. Around him he heard the soft rush of people breathing in. 'Then what happened?' asked Dennison gently.

'Greenwald, he kind of argued back over this, but Mr. Bryce, he shouted at him, ordered them to do what he say. The others didn't seem to care much one way or n'other.'

Johnstone looked away, through the walls. 'What was Mr. Norden's contribution to this discussion?'

'He didn't say nothing – didn't say a mumbling word. He just sit there in the bow holding his head. He looked sick, but he never said nothing.'

Everyone waited.

'We head away from the ship. After about fifteen minutes, the engine craps out and won't start again. We drift around some after that while I disassembles the intake. Finally, might be a hour or so, I get her started again. Then we heads for one of the ships.'

Isaacs glanced briefly up at Johnstone. 'Guess that's about all. Sir.'

'Have you anything now to lay to the charge of any officer or man with regard to the loss of USS *Ryan*, or their conduct after the collision?'

Isaacs inclined his head with great dignity. 'Yes sir, I believe I do. I believe Mr. Bryce, he did not act proper in not picking up them men in the water.'

'To clarify the sequence of events: The boat's engine was running at the time Commander Bryce gave the order to head away from the ship. It only stopped running some time later, when you were already distant from *Ryan*?'

Isaacs nodded soberly. Morehead opened his eyes and said, 'What happened to the box?'

'XO had it under his arm when he went aboard *TALBOT*. I never seen it after that.'

'Do you have anything to add?'

'I think that is about it, Admiral, sir.'

As soon as Isaacs unfolded from the witness chair Bryce stood again. 'I request the stand to answer this witness.'

'Please resume your seat, Petty Officer Isaacs. Mr. Bryce, come forward.'

'Commander, you have heard the testimony just given by Boatswain's Mate First Class Isaacs. It is evident that it casts doubt on your conduct after the colision and perhaps before it, as well. Do you have any – '

Bryce crossed his legs and said, coolly and a little sadly, 'It is a lie and a fabrication; that's all; and I will be happy to prove it.'

'Please elaborate.'

'This Isaacs, like Evlin, was in restriction – actually he was confined in the brig – because of incapacity and drunkenness on duty, infractions that had resulted in the death of the boatswain's mate chief the night before.

'Now, it gives me no pleasure to say this, but occasionally you see a case in the service where someone is promoted beyond their competence, so to speak. That – what do you call it? Peter's Law thing. This is as tragic for the man concerned as it is for anyone else. Isaacs here is one of these unfortunate cases. He was incompetent and, like I have said, an alcoholic. These are just malicious, wild accusations, or delusions; anyway, there's nothing to them. To prove this, I suggest you call any of the men in *Ryan*'s whaleboat with me. They'll all back me up, to the T.

'So, this nonsense about a box. There is a box, was a box, but it contained only personal papers, a will, photographs, personal letters, and so forth, which I didn't wish to lose.'

'You gave no order to leave the scene of the sinking, without picking up other survivors?'

'No. Never. The motor died immediately after we lowered and we were carried away by the wind.

'Now, do us all a favor. Since accusations against me are on the record now. Call the other men in the gig. Any or all of them.'

'With the court's permission,' said Johnstone distantly, 'I will do that. Please step down, Commander.

'I recall Lieutenant Richard N. Norden to the stand.'

Norden looked like a wan, sick child propped in the chair. His hands lay limp on his lap. For an infinitely brief moment, Dan felt pity for him.

'Mr. Norden, please give us your opinion of Boatswain's Mate First Class Isaacs.'

Dan didn't catch the muttered reply. Apparently Johnstone didn't either. The admirals leaned forward, Dennison cupping his ear.

'Please speak up.'

'I said, he was not a very effective petty officer.'

'Is he an alcoholic and liar, as Commander Bryce has stated?'

'I don't know.'

'I'll read back your testimony given on the first day of this inquiry: "Apparently I went aft, got into the whaleboat, and abandoned ship." Was the whaleboat your assigned "abandon ship" station?'

'It was not. I repeat, as I said, my recollection of this is not of the best, because I had a head injury – '

He stopped speaking. 'Please go on,' said Johnstone after a few seconds.

Dan rubbed his hand on his trousers. It left a damp smear. On the stand, Norden sat motionless, wilted, his chin in his left hand. He seemed to be looking at the flag. But when Dan followed his gaze, he saw a short, white-haired man in a dark gray suit. The old man, looking back, was ancient and grim as death itself. As Dan watched he nodded slightly, almost to himself.

Vice Admiral Ausura said, 'Please respond to the question, Lieutenant Norden.'

'I did not have a head injury,' Norden muttered.

'Please elaborate.'

'I said, I didn't have a head injury. I was struck in the head, but it didn't affect my memory. As I – as I said it did.'

'You have been warned that any testimony you may give may be used against you in the event of a trial by court-martial.'

'I understand that. I still wish to retract my previous testimony. I have – I've thought better of it.'

Bryce lumbered to his feet, lifting his hand like a child wanting to be called on in class. 'I wish to have a word with the witness in private. Or else he needs to be assigned counsel. He's injured and not responsible; he's not acting in his best interests.'

Johnstone was already speaking when Ausura broke in and overrode him. 'Your request is not granted. Please resume your seat, and make no further interruptions of testimony before this Court. Please proceed, Lieutenant.'

Norden said, 'Ikey's, I mean, Isaacs's testimony is correct. We manned the boat with the crew, Bryce, Isaacs, and myself. Seaman Vogelpohl was originally with us, too. He attempted to let others aboard and was clubbed down. We then lowered away without permitting any other people to board. I saw two other men struck with boat hooks and oars when they attempted to climb aboard during lowering. They fell into the water.

'We had a capacity of at least twenty-three in the whaleboat. We did not pick up any of the many . . . the many injured and dying men who surrounded us. Instead we proceeded through them away from the *Ryan*. They called to us. They screamed. Some of them cursed us. Shortly thereafter, the oil on that side of the ship ignited – '

'This witness is lying, too – '

Ausura said grimly, 'Sit down, Commander. You will be given a chance to explain yourself thoroughly at a later date.' He glared at Bryce till he sat, then returned his gaze to the shrunken figure in the witness chair.

'Please go on.'

'I asked him once to go back. He replied that I'd left my post to save myself. If I didn't want to be in the boat with them, I could get out of it.

'I did not make any further objections.'

Dennison said gently, 'Lieutenant Norden, you stated that "two other men were struck." Were you struck?'

'I was struck in the head with an oar by Seaman Lassard before Commander Bryce ordered him to let me aboard.'

Morehead raised a pencil. 'Why did he and the others

change their minds, and permit you in the boat after all, when they did not permit others to board it?'

'I believe he felt it would look better if he was not the only officer in the boat.'

'Did you observe the box Isaacs referred to?'

'Yes.'

'Do you know what was in it?'

'I assume it was Bryce's cash box.'

'His cash box?'

'The executive officer had a rake-off going of the poker games and such on board. He also made short-term loans to enlisted men. I asssume that this was what was in the box that he took with him from *Ryan* as she sank.'

'Did you hear the statement Boatswain's Mate First Class Isaacs alleges hearing, ordering the boat away from the men in the water?'

'His words as I remember them were: "Make for that ship over there, Slick, don't hang around here; she could go down sudden and pull us down, too."'

'Who was "Slick"?'

'Seaman Recruit Lassard.'

Johnstone was about to speak when Ausura cleared his throat. The vice admiral said, 'Mr. Norden, please advise the court why you did not bring this matter forward in your earlier testimony.'

Dan watched Norden's fingers twist, like mooring lines under terrific strain, then lie flat again. 'I was – I had been advised by Commander Bryce that if I did, my career would be over. I'd already made my decision that night on deck. My only chance was to back up their stories. If I did, they would back up mine, and all would be well.'

Again Norden raised his head, and again his eye locked with those of the old man in the back of the room. He said, 'Because of – matters concerning my family's service reputation – I at first thought it best to agree. However, I have – I have come to feel over the period of the trial – '

'Please speak up, Lieutenant.'

Rich Norden said in a firm, loud voice, 'I have come to feel over the course of the trial that my career was not worth the price I would have to pay for it.'

The civilian counsel, Barrett, stood. At Ausura's nod, he said, 'Do you now desire to withdraw your previous remarks relative to Lieutenant Evlin?'

'Yes, I withdraw them. Al was perfectly competent. Bryce hated him because Evlin opposed his abuse of his position. I supported those remarks of his for the reason I already gave: that we were all in the – in the same boat.' His grim chuckle echoed in the listening silence.

'Lieutenant Hauck, do you desire to cross-examine?' Ausura asked heavily.

Packer's counsel rose. 'Do you now have any additional testimony to volunteer relative to the collision itself?'

'I don't think so, sir, but I'll answer any questions you may have pertaining – pertaining to anything.'

'Was Seaman Recruit Lassard, in your opinion, under the influence of drugs at the time he was with you in the whaleboat?'

'He had marijuana with him, and he and Greenwald and Gonzales smoked it during the time that we drifted. They offered it to others, but none of us partook.'

When Hauck was done, the Court talked together in a low tone, then announced a break. Dan stood quickly, but not quickly enough to reach Norden. He and the man in gray were standing together. The old man was holding him, not close, just holding him and looking over his shaking shoulders with the expression of an ancient Roman condemning his own son to death.

He limped out into the corridor, guarding his arm, and stood in line for the bubbler. He was still too confused to feel much. He expected a buzz of speculation, but the witnesses and counsels stood about smoking silently. Bryce came out, lighting a Camel before he was out of the courtroom. The others glanced at him, glanced away. His eyes passed over Dan's, over those of the others. He bent a bland, mysterious smile toward the flame of his Zippo.

*

COUNSEL FOR THE COURT: Sir, it was my assignment as counsel for the Court to elicit evidence on every circumstance having to do with the *RYAN* incident. I feel that I have fully and impartially performed that duty. The Court is now in possession of all the facts that can be ascertained surrounding the collision and subsequent events of interest.

COURT: The Court is now ready to proceed with the closing arguments.

Captain Roland Javits, a party, made the following closing oral argument.

'In beginning my remarks, I want first to reemphasize the status of USS *Kennedy* during the maneuver in question.

'It is common knowledge in the fleet that the carrier, a much larger ship than the rest, is restricted in her maneuverability and is therefore to be regarded with caution and to some degree even suspicion. This is heightened by her frequent turns to seek the wind for launching and recovering aircraft.

'In addition, doctrine and maneuvering instructions explicitly direct that while engaged in flight operations, as *Kennedy* was, all ships are to stay clear and not embarrass her in any way. It is not too much to say that when so engaged, a carrier can do no wrong.

'None of my testimony on this point has been challenged by any of the counsels.

'I now refer to Exhibit E, the track of the two ships before collision. Subsequently testimony has not challenged its validity and it must be regarded as a true record of the courses followed.

'It is in evidence that shortly before my turn to flight course, *Ryan*'s OOD prepared a conservative solution to take her safely to station. However, her CO preferred a high-speed turn, a high-speed transit across my bow, and a second high-speed, split-second turn into station. Even if it was "good practice," any error in execution would result in his ending up out of position, if not in mortal danger.

'Perhaps what we are seeing here is an example of a man

being seduced by his own seamanship into a gamble that failed.

'The signals leading up to the maneuver were standard, easily understood, straight from the book. Also, there is no question but that they were received and understood.

'It has been brought out in testimony that the night, though overcast, was clear. Visibility was good. Though my lights were dimmed, *Ryan*'s JOD has testified they could be clearly seen. The course and station change could have been executed without haste, misunderstanding, or risk.

'The fact that my OOD had to be reminded to assign *Ryan* her plane guard station is minor. The fact that they called back to ask about it shows that they had anticipated that order and were prepared for it.

'Regarding my adjustment of course to two-five-zero, there seems to be some question that *Ryan* even heard it. Whether or not they did, I have shown it would have made little difference, as it was a matter only of a few degrees.

'On remarking the dangerous proximity of the destroyer, I immediately backed emergency and ordered "light ship." I did not sound whistle signals because they would have been confusing. To reconcile the ensign's testimony with that, it is possible that my boatswain gave a squeak on the horn in excitement, but if so it was not long enough to register with anyone on the bridge. It is also possible that one of the flight-deck crew, driving a plane-handling vehicle, saw *Ryan* ahead and sounded his horn as a warning to the bridge.

'In any event these are side issues. The single initiating and immediate cause of the accident was Commander Packer's fatal left-rudder order. This is true regardless of any extenuating circumstances. The collision was not caused by any action or lack of action by *Kennedy*, and there was no action anyone on her bridge could have taken to avert it.

'It has been theorized by Captain Piasecki that some momentary confusion in Packer's mind as to his relative position caused him to conclude that his only hope lay in a turn to the left. However, on cross-examination, he agreed that first, there were other actions Commander Packer could have taken to clear up the confusion, and second, that confused or not, he was still accountable. Confusion is not a forgivable attribute of men commanding U.S. Navy ships.

'However, in view of the sea experience of Commander Packer, and the uniformly excellent opinion of him brought out in this inquiry, it seems to me there is a more logical explanation than "confusion" for such a horrendous mistake.

'It has been clearly brought out that prior to going to his sea cabin, Packer described his intention to pass me close aboard and then turn left sharply to reach station.

'I believe that the argument in regard to his maneuver firmly fixed in his mind that fact of a final left turn. It fixed it there subconsciously rather than consciously.

'Once he had begun the maneuver, and realized he was standing into danger, his conscious mind was so occupied with that danger that at the critical moment he subconsciously reverted to his original plan, and said "left rudder" when at a cooler moment he would have said "right" – which was the proper order.

'After he came to zero-nine-zero, almost the reciprocal of my course, the closing speed of the ships was over sixty miles an hour. Warnings from his OOD and JOD led to a rapid realization that he was dead ahead of me at a short and rapidly closing range. If he had ordered right rudder then, he would have ended up roughly where he wanted to be – on my port quarter.

'Unfortunately, though he sensed the proper moment to turn, it must have been at that point that his intense concentration, blunted as it may have been, reverted to the original plan fixed in his mind by the argument. Instead of "right rudder," what came out of his mouth was "left rudder."

'The subconscious plays that trick on all of us occasionally. In this very hearing, experienced witnesses have said *Kennedy* when they meant *Ryan* or two-three-zero when they meant three-two-zero. The slip is easily corrected here.

'It was not so on *Ryan*. Even if after a second or two he realized his error, the die was cast. If he tried to shift his rudder back, he would meet me head-on. He had to bend on every bit of speed he had to get across my bow before I hit him.

'It may be that it is difficult to tell which way a carrier is heading. If that's so, it seems to me to be an additional reason to be cautious. However, it's hard to believe that any commanding officer could start out crossing a carrier's bow and not pay the most intense attention to it.

'No, Packer knew where he was. He might not have been able to tell the exact angle, but he knew he was in mortal danger and had to act instantly. I believe he simply said the wrong thing. He realized it only when he noticed his bow swinging toward me instead of away. He made the instant decision not to reverse his rudder and plow into me bow-on, but acted decisively in an attempt to tighten his turn and get by fast. The evidence? The moment he saw his bow swing in the wrong direction, he gave the proper orders in rapid succession – "left full, hard left, all ahead emergency flank." He did all he could to retrieve the slip of the tongue. I profoundly wish he had made it, and for a second there that night, I thought he had. But it was not enough.'

Rear Admiral Leonard A. Hoelscher, USN, then made the following oral argument.

'Admiral Ausura, Admiral Dennison, Admiral Morehead: counsels and parties, witnesses. The collision of *Kennedy* and *Ryan* while under my tactical command has been exhaustively examined. The points in contention are many, including some internal to *Ryan*, but as Captain Javits has just pointed out, the most important fact is not at issue: that her commander made an error that sank his ship and killed one hundred and seventy-eight of his crew and officers, including himself. The facts surrounding this are about as clear as they can be.

'I am a party to these investigations due to my position as CTG 21.1. Now, let us note that no allegations have been made by any person questioning my handling of the formation. The maneuvers ordered under my authority were clear, standard, and in accordance with regulations. Finally, there have been no criticisms of events subsequent to the collision: my action to extinguish the fire aboard *Ryan*, for reasons discussed in closed session, the hardest decision I have ever had to make; the entire process of search and rescue, which succeeded in saving over sixty men.

'Let us go on to the only issue of possible culpability that has been raised against me, first by Ensign Lenson, later by counsels for the deceased officers. That is the issue of my stationkeeping instruction.

'Prima facie, its import is rather innocuous. It's the kind of combination pat on the back and kick in the pants I imagine has been used since the first man commanded another. From time to time, even with subordinates who know their stuff, it's necessary to rake them over the coals a bit. In fact, that's one of the prime things a skipper, a commodore, or even the Chief of Naval Operations is there for.

'In the last few days, though, we've heard the entire blame for the collision traced, as though by magic, to that message. That it caused Commander Packer to throw his good sense and training overboard and stake his ship in a reckless gamble to save a few seconds.

'Now, I'm not worried that the civilian counsel, Mr. Barrett, and the counsel for Commander Packer, Lieutenant Hauck, are going to succeed in convincing men with years at sea that because of a message like that one man should be relieved of responsibility for an accident while his senior bears the blame. If that was so, if error or excess in a subordinate was to condemn the senior, no officer could escape the wrath of the law.

'I, too, like Captain Javits, believe that there may be some single clear explanation for Packer's mistake. But we may wander in the murk of supposition as long as we will, and never know for sure. Like him, I wish fervently that it hadn't happened, or that *Ryan*'s captain had been able to ramrod her past *Kennedy*'s bow.

'The question remains, how do we prevent this from happening again? At this moment in the Atlantic, the Pacific, the Indian Ocean, destroyers are maneuvering as the Navy guards the distant stations of the world. There have been suggestions made here as to how to prevent a duplication of this disaster. I will dedicate from now on in my career a portion of my time and influence toward getting them adopted. If we can learn from what I've already heard called "the *Ryan* Incident," her men will not have died in vain.'

The Court then, at 1215, took a recess until 1400, at which time it reconvened.

Counsel representing Commander Packer, a party, then made the following oral argument.

'The narrative of the collision that follows, and its attribution of the responsibility of that collision, hinges on three facts. One: The signal that the *Kennedy* was on course two-five-zero true was erroneous and misleading. Two: That it was received aboard *Ryan* in time for action by her commanding officer. Three: That it, and others errors and omissions by the captain of the *Kennedy*, exacerbated by mistakes in judgment by Rear Admiral Hoelscher, in charge of the task force, constitute the true causes of the collision, and not errors or omissions by the commanding officer of USS *Reynolds Ryan*.

'First, let's look at the fatal "mike corpen" signal, transmitted, as *Kennedy*'s signal book shows, approximately one minute and forty seconds before her bow split *Ryan* in two.

'The fact that it was entered in the signal book shows that aside from Captain Javits, who directed it, and Lieutenant Commander Garner, who transmitted it, others in *Kennedy*'s CIC heard it go out. I have made message inquiries of the other ships in formation and have received replies from *Talbot* and *Dewey* corroborating this.

'It has also been established in cross-examination by Mr. Barrett that confusion existed in Captain Javits's mind as to the proper meaning of the signal "mike corpen," and that this confusion persisted right up till he was confronted with the signal book on the stand.

'Conclusion: that an erroneous and misleading signal was sent less than two minutes before the collision.

'Second, we ask, was the signal received by *Ryan*? For if it was not, we face a different set of deductions, though also tending to show that the responsibility for the collision was not Commander Packer's.

'Captain Javits has told us he tested his comms at midnight, and that all ships answered the check, though *Ryan* came back weak. Apparently no one bothered to tell her this, so no action could be taken to correct it. However, it is proof that two hours before collision, the circuit was functioning.

'In addition, only minutes before the fatal signal, *Ryan* and *Kennedy* communicated about whether *Ryan* was to resume her plane guard station. Again, the circuit was functioning.

'Now, the JOD of *Ryan*, Lenson, has stated that the pritac speaker was either malfunctioning or turned down to reduce the noise on the bridge. The receiver was located on the starboard side of the pilothouse. The pilothouse on *Gearing*-class destroyers is only twenty feet wide. Let's look at the positions of the officers approximately two minutes before the collision, as given by Mr. Lenson.

'At this time, Captain Packer had given his first rudder order, left standard, with no indication of alarm or urgency. During this period, Lenson was on and off the port wing. The receiver was at least twenty feet from him, with a doorway intervening. Thus it is not surprising that he did not hear the transmission. Lieutenant Evlin, the OOD, apparently was on the port side, by the chart table, checking the solution that he had been ordered to work out by the captain.

'Where was Packer?

'The evidence shows that he was either on the centerline of the bridge, using the alidade, or more likely standing by his chair on the starboard side. In the first instance, he would be fifteen feet from the receiver; in the second, he would have been beside it. In either case, he was the closest man to it.

'Conclusion: The commanding officer was the most likely person to have heard *Kennedy*'s signal changing her course, and probably, considering the low volume and the locations of the other officers, he was the only one who did.

'Let's go on to something that I only learned this morning, with the receipt of a message from USS *Garcia*. Her captain informs me that from 0100 to 0330 on the 25th, his primary receiver was inoperative. He was operating with his secondary, which had lower sensitivity. *Garcia* states that although he received the formation turn signal, which went out with the carrier's antennas basically pointing at him, he did not receive or hear the "mike corpen" signal. Yet Captain Javits stated that he received an acknowledgment from *Garcia*.

'At the time, it seemed unimportant. *Garcia* wasn't involved in the collision. But now we see that the testimony on this point was inaccurate. The signal went out to five ships; it was acknowledged by four. We thought the missing ship was *Ryan*. It now appears that it was *Garcia*.

'Conclusion: It is probable that the "mike corpen" two-five-zero signal was not only received but acknowledged by *Ryan*'s captain.

'Now, at one minute and forty-five seconds before the collision, we see from Exhibit E that the bearing and range of *Kennedy* from *Ryan* was zero-six-zero true, two thousand yards. Yardner and Pettus testified that it was then Captain Packer abruptly ordered his helm left full and shortly thereafter left hard. What were his other choices? A centered rudder would have resulted in a head-on collision. He could have slowed; could have brightened his lights; he could have sounded his whistle. But all of these would have taken time, the one thing he did not have.

'In the evidence of any evidence to the contrary, Commander Packer must be presumed to have acted as a reasonable and prudent officer would have *in that circumstance*.

'And, in fact, it is likely that if *Kennedy* had really been on a course of two-five-zero – *as she had just told* Ryan *she was* – rather than five or ten degrees away, and swinging toward it, Packer's actions would have resulted in *Ryan* passing clear, this court would not be sitting, and one hundred and seventy-eight men would still be alive.

'Conclusion: It was the misleading signal that led to his last-minute increase in left rudder and the subsequent collision.

'With these facts in mind, it is easy to reconstruct the chain of events that led to the accident.

'My narrative begins with the conversation between Evlin and Commander Packer. The captain had formulated a maneuver he would make if *Kennedy* came to recovery course and he was instructed to take plane guard again. He indicated the intention to come right to one-three-zero until *Kennedy* bore about zero-one-zero true, then turn left and slide into position behind her.

'Mr. Evlin objected, but Packer overruled him in view of the hortatory but ill-advised message from Rear Admiral Hoelscher. This ended the discussion, and he left the bridge.

'No one will ever know what effect Evlin's recommendation had on him. It seems logical to conclude that it had some effect. In the time between this discussion and the commencement of the maneuver, while he was getting his pipe, it is reasonable to think that Commander Packer reexamined this decision in the privacy of his cabin. As he did, he probably realized that Evlin's suggestion had some merit, though not in the way the lieutenant meant it.

'That is, Packer must have belatedly realized that one-three-zero would take him wide of the carrier and that he would conclude the maneuver aft of her and somewhat wide of station. During the turn that would then be necessary to reach it, he would be falling astern every moment. If he did so, he would never regain position. Why? Because *Ryan* had boiler power available for only about 29 or 30 knots, and the recovery speed was twenty-seven. Losing speed in the turn, and accelerating only gradually, he would lag behind the carrier, and would take long minutes – perhaps as long as half an hour – to regain station, if indeed he ever did.

'This, if anything, would constitute "sluggish maneuvering" in Admiral Hoelscher's book.

'I believe he then formulated a different maneuver in his mind. When he felt *Ryan* heel, he went to the bridge and found Evlin on a course of one-three-zero, as directed. He took the conn from him and ordered a course change to zero-nine-zero. Then, waiting as *Kennedy* closed, watching her intently, he ordered a left rudder. What was in his mind?

'I believe that he intended to fulfill his orders to maneuver smartly by steaming down *Kennedy*'s port side at close range, then executing a Williamson turn. As the Court knows, this is a high-speed course reversal used to pick up men overboard.

Its effect is to bring the ship rapidly around in a loop so that she has swapped ends and is steaming back along her original wake.

'At the moment of maximum danger, however, Packer hears the carrier announce she is not on two-six-zero but on two five-zero. Taken aback, he acknowledges the signal, simultaneously considering how to react. Looking at *Kennedy*, he may very well have concluded that he was actually on her starboard bow, as he would have been if she had swung a little past two-five-zero in coming to it – certainly not unlikely. Remember, as Captain Javits has said, destroyermen are taught to regard a carrier with "caution and to some degree even suspicion." '

'Now Packer had to act. The range was closing rapidly. His rudder was already left. He did not have time to reverse it, and if he believed he was on her starboard bow, such an order would have been fatal, anyway. His decision was to increase his rudder to left full.

'A few seconds later, with horror, he must have noted that *Kennedy*'s bearing was nearly constant. He immediately increased rudder and ordered emergency flank speed. Unfortunately, as Lieutenant Talliaferro has testified, he was disappointed in this because of the slow response of the engines due to water remaining in the fuel tanks from ballasting in the Arctic – a decision he made reluctantly, and events bore him out.

'So, at hard left rudder and high speed, *Ryan* tried to shoot across the bow of an oncoming ship thirty-five times heavier than she was. If she had traveled another two hundred feet, she would have made it. If she had made another hundred feet, *Kennedy* would have hit her fantail, damaging her, but without much loss of life, since most of the crew were midships and forward.

'But the emergency speed was not forthcoming. There was a collision, and *Ryan* went down.

'Every fact in this narrative is in the record. The proximate cause of the collision was Admiral Hoelscher's ill-advised threat. The immediate cause was Captain Javits's mistaken course signal.

'It is true that Commander Packer did not inform *Kennedy* of his intentions, nor did he use his whistle. It can be said that his only thought at that point was to save his ship. No knowledge given to *Kennedy* could have done that. Signals could not have changed the momentum of thousands of tons of steel.

'We have now covered the major causes of the collision and found Commander Packer guiltless. Let us now go on to contributing causes.

'There is no reason why the plane guard could not have been stationed prior to turning the carrier to recovery course. Doubtless because it takes a few seconds more, it was not Hoelscher's policy.

'Next, Commander Packer was called on to perform like an expert on the first night he had been with the formation, after four months in the yard and two and a half weeks of independent steaming.

'Finally, there is the question of the adequacy of an old ship like *Ryan* to keep up with modern carriers. *Kennedy* can make upward of thirty or thirty-five knots. If we're honest, we must conclude that *Ryan* could actually manage no more than about twenty-eight or twenty-nine on the night in question. The task group commander and the commanding officer of *Kennedy* had no compunction about maneuvering at very high speeds, and there is no evidence they gave any thought to the demands this placed on their screening units.

'But we should not place the mantle of guilt solely on the shoulders of Captain Javits and Rear Admiral Hoelscher. The maneuver that ended this time in disaster has been performed many times before, and as Captain Javits has pointed out, is probably being performed at this moment somewhere on the oceans of the world. At least two ships to my knowledge have been lost to collisions with carriers since World War Two. One wonders how many near-misses there have been. Unfortunately, last Christmas Eve, all the links in the chain of circumstances were there for disaster.

'I submit that if *Ryan* had not been run down, it might have been *Bordelon*, *Belknap*, *Laffey*, or *Claude Ricketts*. If the carrier had not been *Kennedy*, it might have been *Coral Sea* or

Enterprise. By assigning blame to one man, we set the stage for recurrence of such disasters. I respectfully ask the Court to bear that in mind when they find where the responsibility for it lies.

'I know that in so doing, they will decide that the captain of USS *Reynolds Ryan*, Commander James J. Packer, USN, performed his final duties coolly, competently, and in the best traditions of the naval service.'

Counsel for Lieutenant Evlin then made the following oral argument.

'President and members of the Court: The able counsel for the Court, together with the other counsels, parties, and witnesses, have set forth in the course of this inquiry every detail concerning a maritime disaster that resulted in the loss of a fine ship and nearly two hundred men.

'It is unnecessary for me to recount again a narrative that has been reiterated until the final moments of *Ryan* had been engraved on our memories forever. It would be presumptuous for me, as a civilian, to attempt to tell you what your findings should be. You have far more experience than I at sea and can judge both with wisdom and compassion.

'That said, I would like to make a few remarks about Lieutenant Alan Evlin.

'During this hearing, Lieutenant Evlin has been the subject of the lowest sort of gossip and character assassination, such sly and loathsome chatter as I never heard during my time in service, though I have since – in divorce cases. Now we hear dismaying hints of the motives that may have lain behind those insinuations. No, sir, you need not object; I will say no more about Commander Bryce's testimony. Far too much has been heard about it already.

'We are concerned rather in this hearing with Lieutenant Evlin's performance in the half hour or so prior to his heroic death – for his last act, fighting the flames as *Ryan* was going down, can only be described as that of a hero. He gave his life for his shipmates. Is this the act of an incompetent coward? I think you will agree it is not.

'Instead, we see from all the testimony here given that in the last moments of his career, Lieutenant Evlin acted wisely and correctly. He recommended a safe maneuver to the captain and persisted to the point of argument when he was overruled. Once given his orders, however, he carried them out punctiliously, meanwhile setting his junior partner to a continuous surveillance of the prime source of danger.

'In the last moments before collision, yielding the conn to the captain as naval law requires, he nevertheless did not turn aside. He plotted the new course and advised Packer he was standing into danger. Our account of subsequent events is spotty, but it is clear he continued to assist the captain until all hope was gone. When *Ryan* drifted broken like a child's toy, to whom did James Packer turn for an opinion? To Evlin. It is evident that the commander of *Ryan*, whether or not he was ultimately responsible for the disaster, had the highest confidence in his senior watch officer.

'Finally, when "abandon ship" was passed, did Evlin follow the dictates of fear? No. He went in harm's way to save his shipmates, and paid for their lives with his own.

'Members of the Court, I believe that considering these facts, you will conclude that if you had been in charge on *Ryan*'s bridge in those terrible last moments, you could have wished for no better officer beside you than Alan Evlin. Quiet, deliberate, selfless, courageous, he was a man the Navy could ill afford to lose. I have been proud to represent him, and I thank you for that opportunity.'

There being no further arguments, the counsel for the Court closed as follows:

Although the widest latitude has been given to parties and counsel for argument, this Court will base its findings solely on evidence produced in Court and not on theory, conjecture, hearsay, or hypothesis.

I additionally wish to call the Court's attention to, and ask the Court to take judicial notice of in their deliberation, certain sections and articles in current U.S. Navy and NATO tactical publications. I mention specifically Articles 476, 477, 478, and 1273A of the General Tactical Instructions;

Articles 513, 532, 533, 576, 577, 581, 1506, 1508, and 1522, Allied Naval Maneuvering Instructions; Articles 923, 924, 951, 952, and 1191 of Carrier Task Force Maneuvering Instructions. I also mention the International Rules for Prevention of Collision at Sea and U.S. Navy Regulations. These materials have been placed in the room set aside for your deliberation.

I have no further remarks.

At 1638, the members retired to their deilberations.

6

THE AFTERIMAGE

Epilogue

The Pentagon, Washington, D.C.

In the silent room, the old clock ticked. The stir in the corridors as men and women deserted the great building had departed long ago. At the door the guard's back was motionless, still. Beyond it through the far window night had come, covering the graves with the cold shadow of everlasting winter.

Waiting, he had slipped from impatience to resignation, to doze and then waken. His thoughts had wearied of their endless round. He sat now in a calm different from anything he had ever felt before.

He no longer cared about the pain. He wasn't thinking about his wife or his career, or of the men he had left in the light of the flames, never to see again.

He waited, and did not glance up even at the murmured exchange outside his door.

'Sir. Sir?'

He started and came back. 'Yes.'

'The Court will see you now.'

Weariness lay like the foreshadow of age along the muscles of his legs. He stretched, hearing joints crack. He straightened his tie and buttoned his blouse as best he could over the sling, all by habit, without thought.

The corridor was brightly lighted and empty, reflecting, as he walked, his face, distorted and pale in the gray-green tile. The marine led, a few paces in front. He took a breath, searching for fear, and was a little surprised to find none. If they'd called him in the morning, his heart would have been hammering as he walked toward judgment. But now he was at peace. *Everything will turn out all right.* At last he suspected what those words might mean.

The guard stopped, faced about, and snapped back to

parade rest. A brass plaque read PRIVATE against walnut brightwork. Dan tucked his cap under his arm. The sling got in the way, but he got it wedged in. He knocked and entered and came to attention.

The room was larger then he'd expected. Someone's office, preempted for the court. The three admirals sat silent, awaiting him. He took a step forward, his sight narrowing, as if with tunnel vision, to the green baize surface of the table.

There was no sword on it.

'Please stand at ease, Ensign,' said the tall one, Dennison. 'We'll keep you only a moment. Admiral Ausura, will you read the decision or shall I?'

The short man cleared his throat and picked up a typed sheet. Gold gleamed dully on his sleeves. Some part of Dan's mind noted the heavy, lustrous circle of gold on his left hand.

'Mr. Lenson, this Court has found you absolved of responsibility in the collision between USS *Kennedy* and USS *Ryan*. You are free to go.'

The words were in no sense dramatic, but they hung in the air for what seemed to Dan like a long time. They played over the surface of his mind like a breeze over a still sea.

'Do you have anything further to say?' asked Ausura, raising his eyes first to Morehead, so far silent, then to Lenson.

'What did you decide about – the rest of us? Evlin, and Bryce, and the captain?' he said.

A trace of expression flitted across the president's eyes, then was gone, dissolved back into the still, bleak face. 'Lieutenant Evlin was also absolved in the matter. We have recommended that Commander Bryce's conduct after the collision be the subject of a separate court-martial.'

'And Captain Packer?'

'As a party, you will be sent a copy of the Findings and Recommendations. You can read our opinions and the grounds for them in full there. We found Commander Packer guilty of full responsibility for the collision. Captain Javits and Rear Admiral Hoelscher we found guilty of contributory negligence in that aspect of the matter. We have recommended they be issued letters of admonition. We are also recommending that Hoelscher's decision to extinguish the fire by ramming, though not necessarily unjustified, be looked into more closely than we can in this investigation.'

Guilty . . . *absolved* . . . *admonished*: The words echoed on and on in a mind as empty as deserted corridors. Godlike words, sounding of doom. *Guilty* . . . to bear that stain forever in the minds of men. *Absolved* . . . blameless in legal terms, but the name *Ryan* would follow the man marked with it to the end of his days. *Admonished* . . . it sounded innocuous, but it meant Javits's and Hoelscher's careers were finished. They'd serve out their tours, but they'd never hold another command.

'That's not right,' he said.

'I beg your pardon?' The eyes, which had dismissed him, came back up. Faces lined and leathered by age and weather lifted to study him.

'It isn't right that he gets – all the blame. Don't you know what he did in the Arctic, with that worn-out ship, that worthless crew?'

Ausura frowned. He glanced at the others, then cleared his throat and leaned back. 'Mr. Lenson, you've been through a lot. Your remark's out of line. But your loyalty to your captain is commendable. And – pardon me, but you're very young. Let me explain something to you.

'A ship is different from anyplace on earth. It's dangerous at sea, as you've surely grasped by now. Dangerous, and separate. A captain has absolute power out there, extending – and it still does – to death. To trust a man with the lives of others is a grave thing. Only three principles make it work. Authority; responsibility; accountability.

'Authority is the root of command. We delegate it only for a time, only in exercise of an office, only as defined by custom and law. Never as an individual, never for very long, never as if by right, never without bounds.

'Responsibility defines what a man is trusted with, with the ship, with the conn, whatever. So it's all clear, up front, and everybody understands his duty.

'To be accountable means to be subject to justice. To punishment, if you will. If you fail your trust – are derelict in your duty, misuse your power, make a professional error – you will pay a price.

'In our profession, this accountability is absolute. When a naval officer accepts authority, he knows he will answer for the actions of his ship, whether or not he is directly and personally responsible in the way a civilian court would understand. For it is his responsibility to know and govern all that goes on aboard her, her flaws, her limitations, as well as her strengths.

'If error occurs, no matter whose, the fault is rightfully and inevitably his. Each commander knows this and accepts it as part of the job. No previous service, however meritorious, can make up for it.

'No matter what the extenuating circumstances may be, Commander Packer was accountable, utterly and alone, for his ship's maneuvers. Perhaps you see our decision as vengefulness, or expedience. It is neither. I assure you, if he were here today, the verdict would be the same. *Ryan* and her men died under his charge. Therefore, he was to blame.'

Dan was silent for a moment. Then he said. 'That's wrong, sir.'

The three senior officers stiffened.

'By law and custom, you may be right. But I was responsible, too.'

'Mr. Lenson – '

'Wait. Lassard was responsible, too. Evlin was. Bryce. Commander Packer was sure, but not alone.'

Ausura half-rose, anger darkening his face. Dan plunged on, neither daring nor caring to think what he was saying. He had to say these things, now, to these men.

'Javits and Hoelscher made mistakes and you acknowledged that. But does it end there? Somebody should mention the others. I will.

'The ones who sent *Ryan* to the Arctic in winter, pulled from the yard, unready – they're responsible. Who got us into a war we couldn't win, and tore the country apart? Who neglected the Navy, made it keep on with worn-out ships and no parts? They're responsible.'

'Ensign – '

'I only have a little more, sir. We may not be accountable, but we're all guilty. The degree may vary, but the stain's on each of us.

'But I can't accept it for others. Only for myself. So I do. I'm responsible too. Punish me.'

'And if we refuse?' said Morehead in a dry voice.

'I will resign and carry my accusations to the press.'

The three men sat as if carved from dark blue stone. Morehead rolled a pencil slowly, his Academy ring gleaming. Ausura was breathing heavily. Dennison reached up to scratch his head. He sighed. 'Step outside, please,' he said.

The guard came to attention as he came out. 'Stand easy, Sergeant,' Dan said. 'They'll want me back in a little while.'

A few minutes later Dennison opened the door. 'Get in here,' he said.

He stood again in front of the table. 'Ensign,' said the president heavily, 'the Court of Inquiry has reconsidered. It now finds you and Alan Evlin, because he was senior to you on *Ryan*'s bridge, and thus cannot be absolved if you are guilty, culpable of contributory negligence in the matter of the collision between *Ryan* and *Kennedy*. We have recommended that you be issued a letter of caution, to form a permanent part of your service jacket.'

'Thank you, sir,' he said, and his voice, though calm, held a note of happiness.

Outside in the corridor, the guard muttered, 'How'd it go, sir?'

'Not as bad as I thought.' He took a deep breath and explored his shoulder with his fingers. 'No, not too bad.'

'Good. I was pulling for you. Need a cab?'

'Thanks, I should have a ride waiting.'

Outside, on the granite steps, he paused to flip up the collar of his bridge coat. The night wind pierced his cheeks, brushing his lashes with the vanishingly faint kiss of new snow. He took a deep breath, letting its clean cold wash through his blood. It smelled of the river, of the bay beyond, and he caught or imagined in it a trace of the dank salt scent of the sea. A great elm reached up beside the deserted bus stop, bare and spectral beneath its coating of ice. Beyond the empty lots the lights of the city glittered like a distant fleet at anchor.

A letter of caution. It wasn't as bad as an admonition or reprimand. It wouldn't be easy to make a career, with that in his record. But it wasn't impossible.

It was a fair judgment.

And Evlin? He smiled faintly. Somehow he felt that wherever he was, he'd understand. He'd have to explain to Deanne, though. And why he'd done it.

He stood under the granite loom, waiting. In the darkness the elm chattered faintly, the ice-encased branches trembling and rattling against one another for a moment in the cold wind before it died away. He shivered.

All at once, for an unimaginably brief and transient sliver of a moment, he felt as if he wasn't there, or that someone was, but not him; that he was nameless, manifold, myriad, as if he existed or had existed in as many selves as the multitude of carpeted lights. He wasn't alone. He was part of a great circle, which closed, which joined hands with itself.

'Al?' he muttered uncertainly. 'Captain?'

But there was no answer. Out of the darkness the wind came again, and the branches rattled, and he was alone again on the steps. The world ran by accident, by random chance. There was no answer in the stars. None on the hollow wind. They were meaningless and mute, barren of all message save the enormous and incomprehensible fact that they existed.

Below him, in the empty lot, headlights came on. They swept around toward him, then grew brighter, searching through the falling snow.

Now that it was over, he'd have some time with her. Time to talk it out, to search out and heal whatever had torn between them. And he would. He had to. She and the Navy, those were the two givens in his life. The two things he loved, and was part of, and always would be, no matter what.

Holding the bill of his cap to keep it from blowing away, he began limping down the steps, toward the waiting shadow of his wife.

Office of the Judge Advocate General
Washington Navy Yard
Washington, DC 20402

From: President, *Kennedy-Ryan* Court of Inquiry
To: Secretary of the Navy
Subject: Opinion and Recommendations

Sir:

This court having inquired into all facts and circumstances connected with the collision recently occurring between USS *KENNEDY* and USS *RYAN*, and having considered the evidence adduced in the attached transcript, finds as follows.

OPINION

1. That the maneuver into the wind carried out by USS *KENNEDY* was a normal maneuver, properly ordered, and could have been safely executed.

2. That the left turn of *RYAN* across *KENNEDY*'s bow was the direct cause of the collision.

3. That in making his final left turn, the Commanding Officer of *RYAN* made a grave error in judgment.

4. That the evolution originally planned by the Commanding Officer of *RYAN* to reach his new station involved unnecessary and considerable risk, and was in violation of the directive governing such maneuvers.

5. That the Commanding Officer of *RYAN* could have predicted the position of *KENNEDY* throughout her turn with a good degree of accuracy.

6. That the Commanding Officer of *KENNEDY* could not have predicted the course and speed of *RYAN* in proceeding to her assigned plane guard station.

7. That the message from CTG. 21.1 may have influenced the Commanding Officer of *RYAN* to expedite his evolution, but does not excuse courting danger in its execution.

8. That Commander James John Packer, Commanding Officer of *RYAN*, was derelict in his duties in that he failed to comply with U.S. Navy Regulations Articles 0701 and 0751, which assigned him responsibility for the safety of his ship and for the observance of every caution prescribed by law and regulation to prevent collision on the high sea, in the following respects:

(a) Violation of Article 27, International Rules of the Road (General Prudential Rule).

(b) Violation of Article 22: Did not keep out of the way of a privileged vessel, but crossed ahead.

(c) Violation of Article 23: *RYAN* did not slacken speed, stop, or reverse.

(d) Violation of *Allied Tactical Publication 1*, Article 533 and others: *RYAN*, a small ship, hampered the movements of *KENNEDY*; crossed the bow of the carrier when it was not safe; and changed a clear situation into an awkward one by lack of timely indication of her intent and through an impatient haste to accomplish her evolution.

9. That the above derelictions of duty by Commander Packer were due to poor judgment, due principally to:

(a) Fatigue and sickness.

(b) Lack of recent experience in maneuvering with carriers.

(c) Lack of allowance for restricted boiler power and slow engine response.

(d) His confusion at a critical time during a rapidly evolving situation, as a possible result of the following factors:

(1) Night and radar silence

(2) High closing rates

(3) Desire to effect a rapid maneuver

(4) Incorrect reading of *KENNEDY*'s position angle.

10. That the above derelictions of duty by Commander Packer were the direct cause of the collision.

11. That the reason for the final left turn of *RYAN* that led to the collision is ultimately irretrievable.

12. That Rear Admiral Hoelscher, commander of the task group, was negligent in his duties in that he failed to comply with U.S. Navy Regulations, Article 0611, which assign him responsibility as senior officer present for the safely of ships in company. This opinion as to negligence is based on the following factors, in that:

(a) As senior officer present, he was responsible for the planning and execution of maneuvers of the force, even though this duty had been delegated.

(b) He prescribed complex high speed maneuvers at night, darkened, by ships that had not first practiced such maneuvers during daylight.

(c) He might have been more prudent by setting a policy that ordered plane guard ships to station prior to executing turns to recovery courses; and might have prescribed the use of running lights during maneuvers, until such time as he was satisfied all units were capable of safely executing them while darkened; and thus.

(d) He failed to comply with the International Rules of the Road, Article 27, by not having due regard to all risks of collision.

13. That there exists a further question as to negligence or dereliction of duty in Rear Admiral Hoelscher's actions subsequent to the collision proper in regard to *RYAN*.

14. That Captain Javits, Commanding Officer of *KENNEDY*, was negligent in his duties in that he failed to comply with Article 0701, U.S. Navy Regulations, which assign him responsibility for the safety of his ship, in that he:

(a) Assumed *RYAN* had turned right initially at the execution of his turn signal, and therefore that everything was proceeding normally.

(b) Was not alert, as *KENNEDY* was turning, to the risk inherent in the positions of the two ships, which increased as they drew closer.

(c) Commenced executing a course adjustment toward *RYAN* without ascertaining her position and bearing drift, and without ascertaining properly whether she understood his intentions.

(d) Failed to comply with the International Rules of the Road, Article 27, by not having due regard to all risks of collision, and Article 21, by not keeping his course.

15. That there was no negligence or dereliction of duty in connections with Captain Javits's actions subsequent to the collision.

16. That there was no negligence or dereliction of duty on the part of Lieutenant Commander Arthur Garner, Officer of the Deck of *KENNEDY*.

17. That Lieutenant Evlin and Ensign Lenson, Officer of the Deck and Junior Officer of the Deck respectively on *RYAN*, were negligent in their duties, in that they failed to comply with U.S. Navy Regulations, Articles 1008 and 1010, which assign them responsibility for the safety of the ship. This opinion as to negligence is based on the factors that they failed to comply with the International Rules of the Road by not having due regard to all dangers of navigation and collision (Article 27).

18. That no persons other than Commander Packer,

Captain Javits, Rear Admiral Hoelscher, Lieutenant Evlin, and Ensign Lenson are in any way responsible for the collision.

19. That the deaths and injuries resulting from the collision and subsequent events were not due to the intent of any person in the naval service, except as may be subsequently found in the cases of Lieutenant Commander Bryce, Lieutenant Norden, BM1 Isaacs, SN Greenwald, SN Gonzales, SR Lassard, and Rear Admiral Hoelscher.

20. That all deaths and injuries suffered in the course of these events occurred in the line of duty.

21. That confusion exists as to the exact meaning of the signal 'mike corpen.'

22. That the combat readiness and material condition of *RYAN* at the time of collision was unsatisfactory due to no fault of the crew or commanding officer.

23. That a deficiency in design exists as to lighting aboard aircraft carriers, in that it is difficult to ascertain angle visually under dimmed lighting.

24. That a deficiency of design exists as to flooding of nuclear weapons magazines aboard destroyers.

RECOMMENDATIONS

1. That in view of the death of Commander James John Packer, whose dereliction of duty was the direct cause of the collision, no disciplinary action be taken in his case.

2. That Rear Admiral Hoelscher be addressed a letter of admonition for the negligent acts specified in the Court's opinion.

3. That Captain Javits be addressed a letter of admonition for the negligent acts specified in the Court's opinion.

4. That in view of the death of Lieutenant Alan Evlin, whose dereliction of duty contributed to the cause of the collision, no disciplinary action be taken in his case.

5. That Ensign Lenson be addressed a letter of caution for the acts specified in the Court's opinion.

6. That a court-martial be convoked to try Lieutenant Commander Benjamin Bryce, Lieutenant Richard Norden, Boatswain's Mate First Class Lemond Isaacs, Seaman Nathaniel Greenwald, Seaman Tulio Gonzales, and Seaman Recruit William Lassard for actions subsequent to the collision.

7. That a court-martial be convoked to try Rear Admiral Hoelscher for actions subsequent to the collision.

8. That no disciplinary action be taken against any other persons involved in the case.

9. That in future classes of nuclear-carrying ships, a remotely operated flood valve for the nuclear magazines be installed, such that flooding can be initiated from the bridge or damage-control central in case of fire.

10. That in order to reduce the possibility of a recurrence of this type of incident, the following action be taken:

(a) Revise tactical orders, publications, and doctrine to provide:

(1) An indication that operational commanders recognize that commanding officers and crew of ships are not automatically experienced in night carrier operations, and that therefore before such operations are undertaken, especially darkened and in radar silence, consideration be given to the actual experience of the commanding officers to be involved.

(2) That during night air operations, with ships darkened, the officer in charge shall station plane guards in advance of turning to the launch or recovery course, unless the tactical situation shall dictate otherwise.

(3) That a special signal be provided for use by carriers while operating aircraft, indicating 'I am ajusting my course to – ', and that acknowledgment for all screen units be received before execution.

(b) That a more distinctive lighting measure be developed to make aircraft carrier courses easier to judge for ships in company.

(c) That renewed emphasis be placed on thorough familiarity of officers with the International Rules of the Road, and that appropriate action be taken to impress on them the importance of constant alertness.

AUSURA

DENNISON

MOREHEAD

FIRST ENDORSEMENT

From: SECRETARY OF THE NAVY

To: CHIEF OF NAVAL OPERATIONS

1. Noted. Approved. Advise me of actions re Recommendations 9 and 10.

M.